Joseph Henry

A memorial of Joseph Henry

Joseph Henry

A memorial of Joseph Henry

ISBN/EAN: 9783742809650

Manufactured in Europe, USA, Canada, Australia, Japa

Cover: Foto ©Andreas Hilbeck / pixelio.de

Manufactured and distributed by brebook publishing software
(www.brebook.com)

Joseph Henry

A memorial of Joseph Henry

Prof. Joseph Henry.

CONTENTS.

INTRODUCTION.

PART I.

Obsequies of Joseph Henry.

PART II.

Memorial Exercises at the Capitol.

PART III.

Memorial Proceedings of Societies.

(iii)

iv CONTENTS.

INTRODUCTION.

On the death of JOSEPH HENRY, who for the third of a century had administered the operations of the Smithsonian Institution, as its first Secretary and executive officer,—with honor to himself and credit and distinction to the Institution,—the Board of Regents felt that in grateful appreciation of one whose services in the advancement of science, no less than in the promotion of the interests of the General Government, had been so conspicuous and so valuable, some formal and public memorial was pre-eminently fitting. Accordingly, at a meeting of the Regents held on the day following the funeral, the Executive Committee of the Board (consisting of Dr. Parker, Dr. Maclean and General Sherman) were requested to make arrangements for a public commemoration in honor of the late Secretary, "of such a character and at such time as they may determine."

In pursuance of this instruction, the said Committee, through the Hon. Hiester Clymer, a Regent, and a Member of the House of Representatives, presented the subject to the attention of Congress.

IN THE HOUSE OF REPRESENTATIVES.

Monday, December 9, 1878.

Mr. CLYMER. (Member from Pennsylvania.) "I ask unanimous consent to submit for adoption at this time a concurrent resolution, to which I think there will be no objection."

The concurrent resolution was read, as follows:

"*Resolved by the House of Representatives, (the Senate concurring,)* That the Congress of the United States will take part in the services to be observed on Thursday evening, January 16, 1879, in honor of the memory of JOSEPH HENRY, late Secretary of the Smithsonian Institution, under the auspices of the Regents thereof, and for that purpose the Senators and Representatives will assemble on that evening in the Hall of the House of Representatives, the Vice-President, supported by the Speaker of the House, to preside on that occasion."

There being no objection, the resolution was adopted.

IN THE SENATE.

Tuesday, December 10, 1878.

Mr. HAMLIN. (Senator from Maine.) "Mr. President, I ask the indulgence of the Senate to take from the table the resolution of the House making provision for the services in memory of the late Professor HENRY. I think it will occupy no time of the Senate, and it is desirable that it shall be passed, so that it may be known that the agreement is concluded."

The PRESIDING OFFICER. (Mr. HOAR, Senator from Massachusetts, in the chair.) "The Chair will lay before the Senate the concurrent resolution of the House of Representatives."

The resolution was read by the Clerk: [as before given.]

The resolution was agreed to.

IN THE HOUSE OF REPRESENTATIVES.

Thursday, January 16, 1879.—Evening Session.

At five minutes before eight o'clock the Senate of the United States, preceded by the Sergeant-at-Arms and the Chaplain, and headed by the Vice-President of the United States, with the Secretary, entered the Hall, and were properly announced, and the Vice-President took his seat on the right of the Speaker, and the Senators took the seats assigned them.

At eight o'clock the Chief-Justice and the Associate Justices of the Supreme Court and the President of the United States and the members of the Cabinet entered the Hall, were properly announced, and were conducted to the seats assigned them.

The SPEAKER of the House of Representatives (Hon. S. J. RANDALL.) then called the assembly to order, and, after announcing the occasion of the meeting, presented his official gavel to the VICE-PRESIDENT, who thereupon presided, supported by the SPEAKER.

The VICE-PRESIDENT. (Hon. W. A. WHEELER.) "The Senators and Members of the Congress of the United States, in pursuance of the resolutions of their respective bodies, have assembled for the purpose of taking part in the services to be observed in memory of JOSEPH HENRY, late Secretary of the Smithsonian Institution, under the auspices of the Regents of that Institution."

The VICE-PRESIDENT then announced that the exercises would be commenced by prayer from Rev. Dr. McCOSH, the president of the College of New Jersey, at Princeton.

The Memorial Services were then proceeded with; the VICE-PRESIDENT announcing each of the speakers by name, in accordance with the order of exercise arranged and adopted by the Executive Committee of the Board of Regents.

The VICE-PRESIDENT, after the concluding prayer by the Chaplain of the Senate, (at eleven o'clock P. M.) announced that the exercises of the evening were closed; whereupon the President of the United States with his Cabinet, the Chief-Justice and Associate Justices of the Supreme Court, and the Senate of the United States with the Vice-President, retired from the Hall.

The SPEAKER then said: "The object of this evening's session, as provided for by the order of both Houses of Congress, having been fittingly realized, the duty remains to me to declare this House adjourned until to-morrow at twelve o'clock."

IN THE HOUSE OF REPRESENTATIVES.

Wednesday, January 22, 1879.

Mr. STEPHENS. (Member from Georgia.) "I submit a resolution upon which I ask immediate action."

The Clerk read as follows:

"*Resolved by the House of Representatives, (the Senate concurring,)* That the memorial exercises in honor of Professor HENRY, held in the Hall of the House of Representatives on the 16th of January, 1879, be printed in the CONGRESSIONAL RECORD, and that fifteen thousand extra copies of the same be printed in a MEMORIAL VOLUME, together with such articles as may be furnished by the Board of Regents of the Smithsonian Institution; seven thousand copies of which shall be for the use of the House of Representatives, three thousand copies for the use of the Senate, and five thousand copies for the use of the Smithsonian Institution."

The SPEAKER. "The Chair is not advised whether these fifteen thousand extra copies to be published in book-form would cost five hundred dollars. If they would, then under the requirement of the law the resolution must be referred to the Committee on Printing.

"The Chair is advised that the book would cost over five hundred dollars, and therefore it had better go to the Committee on Printing, under the law. The committee has a right to report at any time."

Mr. STEPHENS. "Let it take that reference."

The resolution was accordingly referred to the Committee on Printing.

Saturday, January 25, 1879.

Mr. SINGLETON, (Member from Mississippi,) Chairman of the Committee on Printing, reported back with a favorable recommendation the following resolution of the House: [the resolution to print, as above given.] The resolution was adopted.

In the Senate.

Tuesday, January 28, 1879.

The VICE-PRESIDENT laid before the Senate the following concurrent resolution from the House of Representatives; which was read and referred to the Committee on Printing: [the resolution to print, as before given.]

Thursday, February 6, 1879.

Mr. ANTHONY. (Senator from Rhode Island.) "I am instructed by the Committee on Printing, to whom was referred a concurrent resolution of the House of Representatives to print the Memorial Exercises in honor of the late Professor Henry, to report it without amendment, and to recommend its passage. I ask for its present consideration."

The resolution was considered by unanimous consent and agreed to, as follows:

"*Resolved by the House of Representatives, (the Senate concurring,)* That the memorial exercises in honor of Professor HENRY, held in the Hall of the House of Representatives on the 16th of January, 1879, be printed in the CONGRESSIONAL RECORD, and that fifteen thousand extra copies of the same be printed in a MEMORIAL VOLUME, together with such articles as may be furnished by the Board of Regents of the Smithsonian Institution; seven thousand copies of which shall be for the use of the House of Representatives, three thousand copies for the use of the Senate, and five thousand copies for the use of the Smithsonian Institution."

In the SENATE, April 7, 1879.— Mr. ANTHONY, by unanimous consent, introduced a joint resolution authorizing the engraving and printing of a portrait of the late JOSEPH HENRY, to accompany the Memorial Volume heretofore ordered, and appropriating five hundred dollars for that purpose.

The joint resolution was reported to the Senate April 9, 1879, ordered to be engrossed for a third reading, read the third time, and passed.

In the HOUSE OF REPRESENTATIVES, April 11, 1879.— Mr. CLYMER moved to take from the table the joint resolution received from the Senate; which was accordingly read three times and passed.

The joint resolution authorizing the engraving and printing of the portrait for the Memorial Volume, as passed by Congress, was approved by the PRESIDENT April 18, 1879.

PART I.

OBSEQUIES OF JOSEPH HENRY.

Smithsonian Institution,

Washington, D. C., May 14, 1878.

On behalf of the Regents of the Smithsonian Institution, it becomes my mournful duty to announce the death of the Secretary and Director of the Institution,

JOSEPH HENRY, LL. D.,

which occurred in this city on Monday, May 13th, at 12.10 o'clock p. m.

Professor Henry was born in Albany, in the State of New York, December 17th, 1799. He became Professor of Mathematics in the Albany Academy in 1826; Professor of Natural Philosophy in the College of New Jersey, at Princeton, in 1832; and was elected the first Secretary and Director of the Smithsonian Institution in 1846.

He received the honorary degree of Doctor of Laws from Union College in 1829; and from Harvard University in 1851.

He was President of the American Association for the Advancement of Science in 1849; was chosen President of the United States National Academy of Sciences in 1868; President of the Philosophical Society of Washington in 1871; and Chairman of the Light-House Board of the United States in the same year; the last three positions he continued to fill until his death.

Professor Henry made contributions to science in electricity, electro-magnetism, meteorology, capillarity, acoustics, and in other branches of physics; he published valuable memoirs in the transactions of various learned societies of which he was a member; and devoted thirty-two years of his life to making the Smithsonian Institution what its founder intended it to be, an efficient instrument for the "increase and diffusion of knowledge among men."

M. R. WAITE,
Chancellor of the Smithsonian Institution.

PROCEEDINGS

BOARD OF REGENTS OF THE SMITHSONIAN INSTITUTION.

———

WASHINGTON, D. C., MAY 13, 1878.

A meeting of the Board of Regents of the Smithsonian Institution was held this day at the Institution, at eight o'clock P. M., under the call of the Chancellor, for the purpose of making suitable arrangements for the obsequies of Professor JOSEPH HENRY.

Present: The Chancellor, Chief Justice WAITE, Hon. HANNIBAL HAMLIN, Hon. AARON A. SARGENT, Hon. ROBERT E. WITHERS, Hon. HIESTER CLYMER, Hon. JAMES A. GARFIELD, Hon. PETER PARKER, and General WILLIAM T. SHERMAN.

The Chancellor made the following remarks:

MY BRETHREN OF THE BOARD OF REGENTS: I have asked you to come together this evening not to take action upon the great loss our Institution has sustained, but to consult as to what may best be done to pay honor to all that is mortal of the great and good man who, conceiving what SMITHSON willed, has devoted his life to making the bequest of our benefactor what he wished it to be, an instrument "for the increase and diffusion of knowledge among men."

(9)

The Chancellor stated that he understood that the family of Professor HENRY had expressed the wish that the Board of Regents should make all the arrangements for the funeral.

The following resolutions were adopted:

Resolved, That the Chancellor be directed to notify the President of the United States and his Cabinet, the Supreme Court of the United States, the Supreme Court of the District of Columbia, the two houses of Congress, the General of the Army, the Admiral of the Navy, the Diplomatic Corps, the Light-House Board, the National Academy of Sciences, the Washington Philosophical Society, and other organizations with which he was connected, of the death of Professor JOSEPH HENRY, and to invite them to attend his funeral.

Resolved, That the funeral take place on Thursday, the 16th of May, at the New York Avenue Presbyterian Church, at half past four o'clock P. M.

Resolved, That the Regents meet at the Institution on Thursday next, at four o'clock P. M., to attend the funeral in a body.

Resolved, That a committee, consisting of General SHERMAN, Hon. PETER PARKER, and Professor S. F. BAIRD, Assistant Secretary of the Institution, be appointed to make arrangements for the funeral ceremonies.

Resolved, That a meeting of the Board of Regents be held on Friday next, 17th of May, at ten o'clock A. M., for the purpose of transacting such business as may come before it.

The Board then adjourned.

THE OBSEQUIES.

The funeral of Professor JOSEPH HENRY, late Secretary of the Smithsonian Institution, took place at half-past four o'clock, Thursday, May 16, 1878. The services were in the New York Avenue Presbyterian Church. The interment was in Oak Hill Cemetery, Georgetown.

The arrangements for the funeral were made by General WILLIAM T. SHERMAN, Dr. PETER PARKER, and Professor SPENCER F. BAIRD, a special committee appointed by the Regents of the Smithsonian Institution. The supervision of the arrangements at the church was intrusted to General ALEXANDER McCOOK, U. S. Army. The pall-bearers were—

Mr. Justice STRONG, of the Supreme Court of the United States.
WILLIAM W. CORCORAN, of Washington.
Admiral JOHN RODGERS, Superintendent National Observatory.
General ANDREW A. HUMPHREYS, Chief Engineer U. S. Army.
JOSEPH PATTERSON, of Philadelphia.
GEORGE W. CHILDS, of Philadelphia.
General JOSEPH K. BARNES, Surgeon-General U. S. Army.
Captain CARLILE P. PATTERSON, Sup't of U. S. Coast Survey.
General ORLANDO M. POE, member of U. S. Light-House Board.
Professor SIMON NEWCOMB, Sup't U. S. Nautical Almanac.
Professor ARNOLD GUYOT, of the College of New Jersey.
Dr. JAMES C. WELLING, President of Columbian University.

A few intimate friends of the family, the Board of Regents and the officers and attendants of the Smithsonian Institution met at the residence, where brief services were held at four o'clock, com-

(11)

sisting of selections of Scripture, by the Rev. Dr. JAMES H. CUTHBERT, of the First Baptist Church, and prayer by the Rev. Dr. BYRON SUNDERLAND, of the First Presbyterian Church.

The leading officials in every branch of the Government, men eminent in science, in literature, in diplomacy, and in professional and business life, assembled at the church. Among them were the President of the United States; the Vice-President of the United States; the Secretary of State; the Secretary of the Treasury; the Secretary of War; the Secretary of the Navy; the Secretary of the Interior; the Postmaster General; the Chief Justice and Associate Justices of the Supreme Court of the United States; the General of the Army; the Admiral of the Navy; the Senate and the House of Representatives of the United States; the Regents of the Smithsonian Institution; Officers of the Army and Navy; the Clergy of the District; the National Academy of Sciences represented by its officers and others; the Philosophical Society of Washington; the Alumni of the College of New Jersey; the Trustees of the Corcoran Art Gallery; the Washington National Monument Society; the Examining Corps of the Patent Office; the Superintendent and Trustees of Public Schools; and the Telegraphic Operators' Association of Washington.

Only a small portion of the vast concourse of citizens and strangers could gain access to the church.

The services in the church were begun with Mendelssohn's anthem *Beati Mortui*, which was impressively sung by the choir of St. John's Episcopal Church.

The fifteenth chapter of first Corinthians was read by Rev. Dr. SUNDERLAND; prayer was offered by the venerable CHARLES HODGE, D. D., of Princeton, N. J.; and the address was delivered by the Rev. SAMUEL S. MITCHELL, D. D., pastor of the church of which Professor HENRY became a member when he removed to Washington, thirty years ago.

PRAYER

BY

REV. CHARLES HODGE, D. D.

———

ALMIGHTY GOD, we adore Thee as infinite in thy being and perfections, as the creator of heaven and earth, and as the Father of the spirits of all men. We adore Thee as the rightful and absolute sovereign of the universe, governing all thy creatures and all their actions.

We confess our absolute dependence on Thee for our existence, our faculties, for all we have, all we hope. We acknowledge our responsibility to Thee for our character and conduct—for all we think, or do, or say. We humbly confess that we have sinned against Thee, that we have broken thy holy law times and ways without number, and have forfeited all claim to thy favor.

We call upon all that is within us to bless Thee, that Thou hast not left our apostate race to perish in their state of sin and misery, but didst give thy only begotten Son that whosoever believes on Him should not perish but have everlasting life. We thank Thee, O Lord, that Thou hast given us thy testimony concerning thy Son Jesus Christ, that He is God manifest in the flesh, God in fashion as a man — the wonderful — the central object of adoration to the intelligent universe, to whom every knee of things in heaven, things on earth, and things under the earth must bow. We thank Thee that Thou hast made Him the light of the world, our infallible teacher as to the things unseen and eternal; that He is the High Priest of our profession, who offered Himself unto God as a sacrifice for the sins of the world; that He died the just for the

(13)

unjust, and redeemed us from the curse of the law by being made
a curse for us. We thank Thee for the promise that whosoever,
renouncing every other dependence, trusts simply to what Christ
is and what Christ has done, and who devotes himself to his
service, shall share his kingdom and glory. We thank Thee for
the mission of the Holy Ghost to apply to men the redemption
purchased by Christ, without which all else had been in vain.

And now, O God, in this solemn hour, standing as we now do
around the remains of our illustrious friend, from our hearts we
bless Thee that this is the faith in which he was nurtured, the
faith which molded his character, controlled his life, and now
illumines his tomb, banishing the gloom of uncertainty and fear,
and making the grave to him the gate of heaven.

We thank Thee, O God, that JOSEPH HENRY was born; that
Thou didst endow him with such rare gifts—intellectual, moral,
and spiritual; that Thou didst spare him to a good old age, and
enable him to accomplish so much for the increase of human knowledge and for the good of his fellow men; and above all, that Thou
didst hold him up before this whole nation as such a conspicuous
illustration of the truth that "moral excellence is the highest dignity
of man."

We would remember before Thee his widow and daughters.
He gave them to Thee. They are safe within thy arms. Thou
canst give the peace which passes all understanding. May their
father's name illumine his children's path through life, and their
father's faith sustain their souls in death.

To the Father, Son, and Holy Ghost, be glory in the highest,
world without end. Amen.

FUNERAL ADDRESS

BY
REV. SAMUEL S. MITCHELL, D. D.

"KNOW YE NOT THAT THERE IS A PRINCE AND A GREAT MAN FALLEN THIS DAY IN ISRAEL?"

These words, coming down through the centuries from the mouth of Israel's King, I take up as the fittest ones with which to open my mouth in the presence of all that is not already immortal of JOSEPH HENRY.

Know ye not that there is a prince and a great man fallen this day? And yet why do I ask the question? This day, this hour, this assemblage, this pageant, so unusual and so illustrious even in this world of death — these are my answer before that I utter a word of the sublime interrogatory.

Yes! the nation's capital knows that a prince and a great man has fallen. So does our whole country; so does the civilized world. That quick-footed servant which years ago was yoked to the car of human progress by the hands which have now forgotten their cunning,' — the swift messenger which he himself lured from duty in the skies unto the service of man, — this messenger, slower-winged, it seems to me, than usual, as if loath to tell the story, has already run earth's circuits with the sad news; and at this hour, wherever science is known, or learning respected, or goodness revered, there are those who clasp hands with us in the consciousness of a great loss and in the communion of a heartfelt sorrow.

You will not, therefore, blame me, I am sure, my hearers, if, in a world where great men are ever scarce, and in a capital city which better perhaps than any other illustrates the truth that even

(15)

a nation's production of this class of men, its noblest wealth, is ever
very small, — you will not blame me if, under these circumstances,
I ask you, within this inner circle of family and church relation-
ships, to pause and meditate upon the thought that in the great man
who has fallen a pure and noble spirit has passed from the commn-
nion of the Christian Church on earth to the communion of the
church triumphant in the heavens.

While human learning and science are pressing forward to do
honor to one who was known and loved as a leader, I come in the
name of the Christian Church, and in the name of my Saviour, to
place upon this casket a simple wreath of immortelles, forming,
weaving the words — JOSEPH HENRY, THE CHRISTIAN.

He was such in his disposition, in the spirit and temper of his
mind. " Let this mind be in you, which was also in Christ Jesus,"
is the injunction of the apostle, in which he sets forth the essence of
Christianity and points the path to individual discipleship.

And Professor HENRY walked this path. He came unto the
possession of this essence. Look back, I pray you, through the
centuries. Scrutinize that Life which is the life of the world.
Analyze that Mind which molds the ages, which is world-regnant
through the sceptre of the Cross, which is the leaven working unto
the regeneration of earth and man. What is it? What were its
leading qualities? How is it differentiated? Purity, simplicity,
benevolence — these were its characteristics; these formed the Christ
mind; these were the forces by which it impressed itself upon the
world eighteen centuries ago, and through which it makes itself felt
upon the world of to-day.

Purity, simplicity, benevolence! A purity without a spot, a
simplicity which is transparency itself, a benevolence wide as the
sphere of human want and as limitless as the love of Heaven — this
is God taking shape in human life; this is the mind of Christ trans-
forming the mind of the world; this is the new creation, the redeemed

life, the ideal man, unto which, through the mighty power of the
Cross, the whole creation moves. Upon whatever land the sun of
the Gospel rises, there these moral qualities spring up; and whatever and wherever the human heart which is touched by the love
of Christ, that heart becomes Heaven's soil for the growth of this,
which is Heaven's life.

Now, Professor HENRY possessed these constituent qualities of
the Christian mind, and possessed them in a degree at once beautiful
and rare. You who knew him, and who knew him well, will bear
cheerful witness to my words. He was simple as a child — without
folds, without dissimulation, without guile. He was not smart, as
some men count smartness. Neither was his Saviour. Neither
have been many of the great spirits of time. His mind was the
crystal depths of our Northern lakes, — not the noisy course of the
shallow and frothy river.

And he was *pure*. Pure! — we lay him to rest to-day without a
spot. The product of four-score years in this rough world, we lift
up his character to-day and say, "Behold it! — the freshness, the
purity, the stainlessness of childhood are yet upon it." Grand, is
it not, and comforting, is it not, my hearers, that God now and then
builds up a man before us of whom we can say, "Look upon him;
walk round about him; you will find no ugly scar, — you will discover no running sore." Grand, is it not, and comforting, is it not,
that now and then, in this world of smirched reputations and dis-
eased lives, God gives us a whole man — a man whom, without a
blush, we can lift up to the Great Maker, saying, "Take him again;
he is unharmed, and he is worthy of Thee."

But Professor HENRY was not only Christian in the spirit and
temper of his mind, but also in the unselfish aims and purposes of
his life. Christianity is not a quality simply. It is also a force, —
a force which, under the law of love, works unto external results,
unto a reproduction of itself in the world. Here again the Christ

2

is perfection. "I came not to be served, but to serve." So He
announced His life-philosophy. "Went about doing good." So
history stereotyped that life itself. A manger here, and a cross
there; and between these two, and binding them together, a span
of service—this was the Incarnation of the Divine principle in
human history;—this was the Christ-life giving itself for the life
of the world.

And here again was the life which we reverence,—the life of a
disciple. Never was more unselfish service rendered by man than
was given by Professor HENRY. Through long years, and under
temptations which would have been too strong for the ordinary
man, he served his Institution on a half-salary, and the Government,
saving it tens of thousands, on no salary at all. And the lack
here, he made up in no other way. Paying for not a half of it, the
Smithsonian and the Government had all his time,—all his service.
He used not his high position as a watch-tower for the discovery of
personal opportunities. He grew not rich on a small salary. And
having given all of himself to the service of his country in the
cause of science, he also, as freely and as unselfishly, gave all the
results of his labor. His was the greater part, the nobler work, to
discover principles. He lifted up this force of nature only to say
to the inventor: "Use this while I look for another." And then
he went on searching.

So he lived; so he labored. He served others; himself he did
not serve. With AGASSIZ, he could have said: "I have not time
to make money." Neither had he. God does not give time to
such men for such a purpose. The vision of the true life and the
endless glory breaking upon such minds forbids the debasement.
The eyes which are to look into the universe for the generations
must not have the death-weight of the dollar upon their lids.

But once more. Professor HENRY was a Christian, in that he
held as his pronounced creed the truth contained in the Scriptures

of the Old and New Testaments,—is that he regarded them as a
revelation from God.

These moral qualities to which I have alluded were not in him
so much natural amiability, nor were they the product of so much
culture. They were the inspiration of a Christian faith. They
were moral ends aimed at, principles chosen for life's guidance,
by one who believed in God, and in Jesus Christ whom He has
sent. But Sunday last, with mind as clear as ever, his conversation
hindered only by his rapidly-shortening breath, he said to me: "I
have not given much attention to the minutiæ of theology; possibly
not so much as I ought; but as to the Christian scheme in its main
outlines—that there is one God, an infinite Spirit; that man is
made up of body and soul; that there is an immortal life for man
reaching out beyond the present world; that the power and love
of God are brought into relation with the weakness and sinfulness
of man in the Lord Jesus Christ—of these great truths, I have no
doubt. I regard the system which teaches them as rational beyond
any of the opposing theories which have come under my view.
Upon Jesus Christ—[and here his eyes filled with tears and his
voice broke as he repeated the words]—upon Jesus Christ, as the
One who, for God, affiliates himself with man—upon Him I rest
my faith and my hope." This was all the strength of the dying
man allowed him to utter; but that it was not a casual or spasmodic
utterance, but the drift of his life-long thought and the faith of his
calmest moments, is beautifully shown in the last formal letter he
ever wrote, and which is now, happily, given to the world.*

So our friend and brother lived and thought; so he reasoned
upon the mystery of the universe; and so he came to rest his hope
of a blessed immortality upon the heaven-sent One, who came to
seek and to save the lost of earth. And this faith, which was the
product of his ripest thought and calmest days, was his support

---

* See page 33.

and consolation in the supreme hour. It was a rock beneath him
when the cold waves of the dark river dashed upon his feet; it
was a pillow of rest beneath his head when flesh and heart failed
him. Faith in Jesus Christ, as the revealer of God and Saviour
of man—this anchor he had cast within the veil, and his spirit held
firm and steady, while its earthly moorings were being sundered and
its fleshly tabernacle dissolved.

But once more. Professor HENRY was a Christian, in that he
lived and died in the communion of the Christian Church. He
emphasized no church-ism. It was impossible that he should.
Only narrow minds, only little souls, do this. But he found his
chosen spiritual home in the Presbyterian Church, and while he laid
no stress upon any one of her peculiarities, yet in all loyalty, and in
all comfort, he abode in her communion until the day of his death.
So, again, the great man witnessed to the world that he was a
follower of the Saviour. He heard the voice of the Christ calling
him unto confession; and he obeyed. His heart listened to the
tender accents of the Crucified One, saying, "Do this in remembrance of Me," and in glad and grateful loyalty he reached forth
for the consecrated emblems of the broken body and the shed blood.

The Church was not too narrow for JOSEPH HENRY, as it has
not been too narrow for many of the profoundest minds and noblest
souls of the ages. And his example teaches, with emphasis, what
many of us knew before—that in the Church, as in the State, it is
not always the largest man who requires the most room.

But I must not detain you. These—that he possessed the mind
of Christ; that in the aims and purposes of his life he was like
unto the Master; that his faith of immortality was the faith of the
Son of God, and that he lived and died in the communion of the
Christian Church—these are my reasons, and these my justification,
for pressing through the illustrious throng which surrounds it, to
place upon this casket this simple wreath—JOSEPH HENRY, THE

CHRISTIAN. And while I do this, I must believe that there is a world wider, grander, crystalline above this one, in the eyes of which my offering will not be counted the meanest or the smallest of those which crowd and crown this bier to-day. Methinks, even as human hands, after the funeral, select from all the floral offerings some few choice ones which they may embalm and preserve, so will angel hands, after that the world has paid its honors to-day, culling over all the offerings which have been laid upon this princely bier, select the simple token that I now place upon it, and hang high up upon Heaven's walls, this fragrant and imperishable symbol—"JOSEPH HENRY, THE CHRISTIAN." For, my hearers, whether there be prophecies, they shall fail; and whether there be knowledge, it shall vanish away; but Faith, Hope, Charity,—these endure; and *character* is the man forever and forever.

Two voices sound out from this occasion, as its highest inspiration and noblest lesson. First, a pure heart, a good life—a heart touched by the love of Christ, and a life bowing in loyalty to him,—these easily unite the profoundest thought and the simplest faith. We hear much about the conflict between science and religion, chiefly, we must believe, from those who are young in science or ignorant of religion; but, in reality, there is no necessary clashing. Obedience, character,—this is the amalgam which easily and forever unites the two.

Secondly, how beautifully the truth and fact of human immortality supplements and crowns the human life! The career of earth, imperfect as it must always be, demands the hypothesis of a future existence, and from this hypothesis receives completeness and symmetry—

> "Even as the arches of the bridge
> Are rounded in the stream."

That great mind, clear, strong, vigorous on Sunday noon, is it at an end now? Is it nothing, now? Is it dispersed through the universal all, now? Then are man's works greater than man himself! Then are the Pyramids grander than their builders! Then it were better to be a Yosemite pine than a JOSEPH HENRY! But the truth of human immortality forbids this supposition of debasement, and speaks the truth which our hearts crave, and which our minds demand, as the necessary supplement of the interrupted human career.

Yes! we shall see him again. In a land that is fairer than day!—In the full possession and active exercise of those mental powers which have been the admiration and gratitude of earth, shall we see him;—see him as along the pathway of an unending progress, and amid the ever-rising, ever-thickening glories of the universe, he makes his way upward and onto the infinite goal, "lost in wonder, love, and praise." The sublime creation of God which we have known as JOSEPH HENRY is endowed with the power of an endless life.

> "Eternal form shall still divide
> The eternal soul from all beside;
> And we shall know him when we meet."

Till then, reverent philosopher, humble Christian, noble man,—farewell and farewell!

LETTER OF
PROFESSOR HENRY,

REFERRED TO IN THE FOREGOING ADDRESS.

SMITHSONIAN INSTITUTION, APRIL 12, 1878.

MY DEAR MR. PATTERSON: We have been expecting to see you, from day to day, for two weeks past, thinking that you would be called to Washington to give some information as to the future of our finances and the possibility of resuming specie payment.

I commenced, on two occasions, to write to you, but found so much difficulty in the use of my hand, in the way of holding a pen, that I gave up the attempt.

The doctors say that I am gradually getting better. Dr. MITCHELL gave me a visit on his going South and on his return. His report was favorable, but I still suffer a good deal from oppression in breathing.

I have learned with pleasure that —— and yourself intend to go to Europe this summer. Travel is the most agreeable way of obtaining cosmopolitan knowledge, and it is probable that events of great importance will transpire in the East within a few months. You will have subjects of interest to occupy your attention.

I have also learned that —— is to be married next month; and we shall be happy to receive a visit from him and his bride, when they go upon their wedding tour.

We live in a universe of change: nothing remains the same from one moment to another, and each moment of recorded time has its separate history. We are carried on by the ever-changing events in the line of our destiny, and at the end of the year we are always at a considerable distance from the point of its beginning. How short the space between the two cardinal points of an earthly career!—the point of birth and that of death; and yet what a universe of wonders is presented to us in our rapid flight through

(29)

this space! How small the wisdom obtained by a single life in its passage, and how small the known, when compared with the unknown, by the accumulation of the millions of lives, through the art of printing, in hundreds of years! How many questions press themselves upon us in the contemplations whence come we, whither are we going, what is our final destiny, the object of our creation?

What mysteries of unfathomable depths environ us on every side! But, after all our speculations, and an attempt to grapple with the problem of the universe, the simplest conception which explains and connects the phenomena is that of the existence of one Spiritual Being—infinite in wisdom, in power, and all divine perfections, which exists always and everywhere—which has created us with intellectual faculties sufficient, in some degree, to comprehend His operations as they are developed in Nature by what is called "Science."

This Being is unchangeable, and, therefore, His operations are always in accordance with the same laws, the conditions being the same. Events that happened a thousand years ago will happen again a thousand years to come, provided the condition of existence is the same. Indeed, a universe not governed by law would be a universe without the evidence of an intellectual director.

In the scientific explanation of physical phenomena, we assume the existence of a principle having properties sufficient to produce the effects which we observe; and when the principle so assumed explains, by logical deductions from it, all the phenomena, we call it a theory. Thus, we have the theory of light, the theory of electricity, &c. There is no proof, however, of the truth of these theories, except the explanation of the phenomena which they are invented to account for.

This proof, however, is sufficient in any case in which every fact is fully explained, and can be predicted when the conditions are known. In accordance with this scientific view, on what evidence does the existence of a creator rest?

First. It is one of the truths best established by experience in my own mind, that I have a thinking, willing *principle* within me, capable of intellectual activity and of moral feeling.

Second. It is equally clear to me that you have a similar spiritual principle within yourself, since when I ask you an intelligent question you give me an intellectual answer.

Third. When I examine the operations of Nature, I find everywhere through them evidences of intellectual arrangements, of contrivances to reach definite ends, precisely as I find in the operations of man; and hence I infer that these two classes of operations are results of similar intelligence.

Again, in my own mind, I find ideas of right and wrong, of good and evil. These ideas, then, exist in the universe, and, therefore, form a basis of our ideas of a moral universe. Furthermore, the conceptions of good which are found among our ideas associated with evil, can be attributed only to a Being of infinite perfection, like that which we denominate "God." On the other hand, we are conscious of having such evil thoughts and tendencies that we cannot associate ourselves with a Divine Being, who is the Director and the Governor of all, or even call upon Him for mercy, without the intercession of One who may affiliate himself with us.

I find, my dear Mr. PATTERSON, that I have drifted into a line of theological speculation; and without stopping to inquire whether what I have written may be logical or orthodox, I have inflicted it upon you.

Please excuse the intrusion, and believe me, as ever,

Truly yours,

JOSEPH HENRY.

MR. JOSEPH PATTERSON,
Philadelphia.

OF THE BOARD OF REGENTS.

SMITHSONIAN INSTITUTION,
WASHINGTON, D. C., MAY 17, 1878.

A meeting of the Board of Regents of the Smithsonian Institution was held this day at ten o'clock A. M.

Present: The Chancellor, Chief Justice WAITE, Hon. HANNIBAL HAMLIN, Hon. AARON A. SARGENT, Hon. ROBERT E. WITHERS, Hon. HIESTER CLYMER, Hon. JAMES A. GARFIELD, Rev. Dr. JOHN MACLEAN, Hon. PETER PARKER, Dr. ASA GRAY, General WILLIAM T. SHERMAN, President NOAH PORTER.

General GARFIELD was requested to act as Secretary.

At the request of the Chancellor, a prayer was offered by Rev. Dr. MACLEAN for Divine guidance of the Regents in their present deliberations.

The following resolutions were then adopted:

1. *Resolved*, That the Regents of the Smithsonian Institution hereby express their profound sorrow at the death of Professor JOSEPH HENRY, late Secretary of this Institution, and tender to the family of the deceased their sympathy for their great and irreparable loss.

2. *Resolved*, That in consideration of the long-continued, faithful, and unselfish services of JOSEPH HENRY, our late Secretary, there be paid to his widow the same sum to which he would have been entitled, as salary, for the remainder of this year, and that the Secretary be directed to make payment to her for the amount thereof monthly.

(27)

3. *Resolved*, That Mrs. HENRY be informed of this action of the Board, and the desire of the Regents that she will continue the occupancy of the apartments now in her use for such period, during the remainder of this year, as may suit her convenience.

4. *Resolved*, That a committee be appointed who shall prepare and submit to this Board at its next annual meeting a sketch of the life, character, and public services of the late lamented Secretary, which shall be entered upon the records.

5. *Resolved*, That the Executive Committee of the Board be requested to make arrangements for a public commemoration in honor of the late Secretary of the Institution, of such a character and at such a time as they may determine.

The Chancellor appointed as the special committee under the fourth resolution, President PORTER, Dr. GRAY, and Dr. MACLEAN.

*   *   *   *   *

On motion, it was

Resolved, That the Chancellor prepare a suitable notice of the death of Professor HENRY, to be sent to foreign establishments in correspondence with the Institution. - - -

The Board then adjourned *sine die*.

SMITHSONIAN INSTITUTION,
WASHINGTON, D. C., JANUARY 15, 1879.

A meeting of the Board of Regents of the Smithsonian Institution was held this day in the Regents' room, at ten o'clock A. M.

Present: The Chancellor, Chief Justice WAITE, Hon. WILLIAM A. WHEELER, Vice-President of the United States, Hon. AARON A. SARGENT, Hon. ROBERT E. WITHERS, Hon. JAMES A. GARFIELD, Hon. HIESTER CLYMER, Dr. JOHN MACLEAN, Dr. ASA GRAY, Dr. HENRY COPPÉE, Hon. PETER PARKER, President NOAH PORTER, General WILLIAM T. SHERMAN, and the Secretary, Professor SPENCER F. BAIRD.

Dr. PARKER, in behalf of the Executive Committee, presented a report in relation to the duty imposed on them by the fifth resolution of the Board of Regents, adopted at the meeting of May 17, 1878, "to make arrangements for a public commemoration in honor of the late Secretary of the Institution." The Committee had held numerous meetings, the minutes of which were read, and the arrangements had finally been made as follows:

The exercises will be held in the Hall of the House of Representatives on Thursday evening, 16th of January, 1879.

The Vice-President of the United States, supported by the Speaker of the House, will preside on this occasion, and the Senate and House will take part in the exercises.

1. Opening prayer by Rev. Dr. JAMES McCOSH, President of Princeton College.

2. Address by Hon. HANNIBAL HAMLIN, of the United States Senate, and one of the Regents.

3. Address by Hon. ROBERT E. WITHERS, of the United States Senate, and one of the Regents.

4. Address by Professor ASA GRAY, of Harvard University, and one of the Regents.

5. Address by Professor WILLIAM B. ROGERS, of Boston.

6. Address by Hon. JAMES A. GARFIELD, of the House of Representatives, and one of the Regents.

7. Address by Hon. SAMUEL S. COX, of the House of Representatives.

8. Address by General WILLIAM T. SHERMAN, one of the Regents.

9. Concluding prayer by Rev. Dr. SUNDERLAND, Chaplain of the Senate.

By authority of the Speaker of the House, reserved seats will be provided on the floor of the House for the following bodies with which Professor HENRY was associated:

1. The Regents of the Smithsonian Institution and the orators of the evening, who will meet in the room of the Speaker of the House.

2. The National Academy of Sciences.

3. The Washington Philosophical Society.

4. The Light-House Board, who will meet in the room of the Committee of Ways and Means.

5. The Alumni Association of Princeton College.

6. The trustees of the Corcoran Gallery of Art.

7. The Washington Monument Association, who will meet in the room of the Committee on Appropriations.

On motion of Mr. SARGENT, the action of the committee was approved.

On motion of General GARFIELD, it was

Resolved, That the Board of Regents assemble on Thursday evening next at half-past seven o'clock, in the Speaker's room at the Capitol, to proceed in a body to attend the exercises in the Hall of the House of Representatives in honor of the memory of Professor HENRY.

On motion of General GARFIELD, it was

Resolved, That the Chancellor be empowered to act for the Board of Regents in making the final arrangements for the memorial exercises.

President PORTER, from the special committee appointed at the last meeting, under the fourth resolution adopted by the Board, to "prepare a sketch of the life, character, and public services of Professor HENRY," made a report that Dr. GRAY had been selected by the committee to prepare the eulogy on behalf of the Board of Regents, and that it would form part of the exercises at the public commemoration at the Capitol.

WASHINGTON, D.C., JANUARY 16, 1879.

A meeting of the Board of Regents was held this day at half past seven o'clock P. M., in the room of the Speaker of the House of Representatives, and at eight o'clock the Regents proceeded in a body to the Hall of the House of Representatives, to attend the public exercises in honor of Professor JOSEPH HENRY, late Secretary of the Smithsonian Institution.

On the day after that on which the Memorial Services were held in the Capitol, the following action was taken by the Board of Regents, with reference to the preparation of a Memorial Volume, in commemoration of Professor JOSEPH HENRY.

WASHINGTON, D.C., JANUARY 17, 1879.

A meeting of the Board of Regents was held this day in the Regent's room at half past nine o'clock A. M.

Present: The Chancellor, Chief Justice WAITE, Hon. AARON A. SARGENT, Hon. ROBERT E. WITHERS, Hon. JAMES A. GARFIELD, Hon. HIESTER CLYMER, Hon. PETER PARKER, Rev. Dr. JOHN MACLEAN, Prof. ASA GRAY, Professor HENRY COPPÉE, President NOAH PORTER, General WILLIAM T. SHERMAN, and the Secretary, Professor SPENCER F. BAIRD.

The subject of the publication of the eulogies on Professor HENRY, together with an account of his scientific writings, &c., was discussed, and on motion of Dr. MACLEAN, it was

Resolved, That a special committee of three be appointed, of which the Secretary of the Institution shall be one, to prepare a memorial of Professor HENRY, to include in a separate volume of the Smithsonian series such biographies and notices of the late Secretary of the Institution as may be considered by them worthy of preservation and publication.

The Chancellor appointed Messrs. GRAY, PARKER, and BAIRD as the committee.

The Chancellor then stated that any remarks the Regents desired to make in relation to Professor HENRY were in order.

Dr. PARKER addressed the Board as follows:

Mr. CHANCELLOR AND FELLOW-REGENTS: We are making history, and I wish to say a few words that shall remain upon its page, in memory of JOSEPH HENRY, our beloved and lamented friend and Secretary, when we, like him, shall have passed from earth. Many have already pronounced his eulogy and set forth his rare talents and influence upon the world, and I need not, and could not, were I to attempt it, add to your appreciation of Professor HENRY, his life and character, as a friend, scientist, and christian, the highest type of man.

For twenty years I have been intimately acquainted with Professor HENRY, and happily associated with him in many ways; for ten years as a Regent of the Smithsonian Institution, and as a member of the Executive Committee, during all that period our intercourse has been frequent and intimate. *I have never known a more excellent man.*

His memory has been much on my mind since he left us, and I often find myself inquiring how he and others like him are occupied now. His connection with time is severed, but his existence continues. When I recall the names of Professors FRANKLIN BACHE, CHARLES G. PAGE, LOUIS AGASSIZ, and JOSEPH HENRY, and others of similar intellect and virtue, I find myself asking the question, Are to them all consciousness and thought suspended by separation from the body? I am reluctant to come to such conclusion. But this I know, *the Infinite Father's ways are right.*

It seems most providential that Professor HENRY had the opportunity and the strength to give in person his last words, a priceless legacy, to the National Academy at its annual meeting in Washington, in April, and through that association to the civilized and scientific worlds; I refer to his sentiment "*that moral excellence is the highest dignity of man.*" The loftiest talents and highest attainments without this are deficient in that, which, in the judgment of wise men and of Infinite Wisdom, is of greatest worth. Was there ever a man from whom the sentiment could come with better grace?

The opinion has been expressed, and I do not regard it extravagant, that the letter addressed by Professor HENRY to his friend JOSEPH PATTERSON, emanating from such a mind, *such a man,* at the close of a protracted life of singular distinction, was worth a man's lifetime to produce. It has probably been read by millions, in various languages, and will be by future generations.

Professor HENRY was not only a man of science, a discoverer of nature's laws and forces, but a sincere believer in God their Author and in his atoning Son. To quote his language: "We are conscious of having evil thoughts and tendencies that we cannot associate ourselves with a Divine Being, who is the Director and Governor of all, or even call upon him for mercy, without the intervention of One who may affiliate himself with us."

Let me quote from the prayer offered at his obsequies, and to which we repeat our sincere *Amen;* the lips that uttered it, in less than one short month were silent in death, and the two remarkable men, Professors JOSEPH HENRY and CHARLES HODGE, closely united in life were not long divided by death: "We thank Thee, O God, that JOSEPH HENRY was born; that Thou didst endow him with such rare gifts, intellectual, moral, and spiritual; that Thou didst spare him to a good old age, and enable him to accomplish so much for the increase of human knowledge and for the good of his fellow-men; and above all that Thou didst hold him up before this whole nation as such a conspicuous illustration of the truth that moral excellence is the highest dignity of man."

3

On motion of Dr. MACLEAN, it was—

Resolved, That the thanks of the Board of Regents be presented to the gentlemen who took part in the memorial services held in the United States Capitol on the 16th of January, in honor of the late Professor HENRY, and that they be requested to furnish copies of their remarks on that occasion.

PART II.

MEMORIAL EXERCISES AT THE CAPITOL

MEMORIAL EXERCISES

IN HONOR OF

JOSEPH HENRY.

HELD IN THE HALL OF THE HOUSE OF REPRESENTATIVES

On Thursday Evening, January 16, 1879.

ANNOUNCEMENT.

PUBLIC COMMEMORATION IN HONOR OF THE LATE JOSEPH HENRY.

The Board of Regents of the Smithsonian Institution, on the 17th of May, 1878, passed a resolution requesting the executive committee to make arrangements for a public commemoration in honor of the late Secretary of the Institution, of such character and at such time and place as they might determine.

The committee has now the satisfaction of announcing that in conformity with the above action the following concurrent resolution was unanimously adopted by both Houses of Congress on the 8th and 10th of December, 1878:

Resolved, That the Congress of the United States will take part in the services to be observed on Thursday evening, January 16, 1879, in honor of the memory of JOSEPH HENRY, late secretary of the Smithsonian Institution, under the auspices of the Regents thereof, and for that purpose the Senators and Members will assemble on that evening in the Hall of the House of Representatives, the Vice-President of the United States, supported by the Speaker of the House, to preside on that occasion.

(21)

In accordance with the foregoing resolution, the services will be held in the Hall of the House of Representatives on Thursday, the 16th of January, 1879, at eight p. m., which the public are invited to attend.

PETER PARKER,
JOHN MACLEAN,
WILLIAM T. SHERMAN,
Executive Committee of the Board of Regents.

WASHINGTON, January 6, 1879.

PROCEEDINGS.

HALL OF THE HOUSE OF REPRESENTATIVES, OF THE UNITED STATES,

THURSDAY EVENING, *January 16, 1879.*

In accordance with the arrangements made by order of Congress, the Senate and House of Representatives of the United States assembled in the Hall of the House, and were called to order at eight o'clock by the Hon. SAMUEL J. RANDALL, the Speaker of the House, the President with members of the Cabinet occupying front seats on the right and the Chief-Justice with associate justices of the Supreme Court corresponding seats on the left. The Speaker announced briefly the object of the meeting, and then handed the gavel to the Hon. WILLIAM A. WHEELER, the Vice-President of the United States, who thereupon presided on the occasion, supported by the Speaker of the House.

PRAYER

REV. JAMES McCOSH, D. D.

O God, we look up and by faith we behold Thee as the Infinite
and the Perfect One; almighty in power, unerring in wisdom,
inflexible in justice, spotless in holiness, and with thy tender mer-
cies over all thy works; our Maker, our Preserver, our Redeemer,
our Sanctifier, our Judge, our exceeding great reward.

We adore Thee as a Spirit; and we would worship Thee in spirit
and in truth. We adore Thee as light, and we would walk in that
light. We adore Thee as love, and we would dwell and rejoice in
that love. We bless and praise Thee as the creator of all things;
and we would see and acknowledge Thee in all thy works. All
the powers of nature are thine; light and heat and attraction are
thine; they obey thy will, and fulfill thy pleasure, and accomplish
thy end. Thou sayest unto them go, and they go; come, and they
come; do this, and they do it.

O Lord, how manifold are thy works; in wisdom hast Thou
made them all. The earth is full of thy riches. We bless Thee,
because Thou didst make man after thine image, taught him more
than the beasts of the earth, and made him wiser than the fowls of
heaven, and capable of so far knowing Thee, and believing Thee,
and loving Thee. We cannot indeed with our finite minds comprehend Thee in thy amplitude. Who can by searching find out
God? Who can find out the Almighty unto perfection? But
being in thy likeness we can know Thee in part, and sufficiently
to call forth our admiration and our affection; we feel the behold-
ing of thy glory to be the highest contemplation in which we can

(39)

engage; and the more we know, we adore Thee and love Thee
the more. No man indeed can find out the work which God doeth
from the beginning unto the end; yet thy intelligent creatures can
behold thy working, and understand the invisible things of God
from the things that are made.

We thank Thee, Lord, for the high gifts with which Thou didst
so plentifully endow thy servant, whose services in the cause of
science and humanity we meet this evening to commemorate. We
praise Thee because Thou didst put wisdom into his inward parts,
and give understanding to his heart, so that he applied himself to
seek out and to reach knowledge and the reasons of things. We
bless Thee because he was enabled to throw light on that which
God doeth, on those things which are forever, and those things to
which no man can add and from which no one can take away.

We exalt Thee because mankind have been able to take advantage of the discoveries of the departed in order to make knowledge
to pass to and fro all over the earth, and to add to the intelligence,
the wealth, and the comfort of thy creatures. We pray Thee to
raise up other great and good men who, in like spirit, will carry on
the work in which he was so honorably engaged.

We pray for his widow and for his family, whom he so loved;
that the prayers he offered for them when on earth may return in
the richest blessings from heaven and from earth upon their heads
and upon their hearts.

We thank Thee, Lord, because Thou didst bestow on him not
only gifts, but graces, faith, and humility, and integrity and love.
We rejoice that we can this day contemplate so pleasantly his character; that we can cherish the remembrance of him as of a man
of high aims and lofty purpose, devoting his life to the cause of
science and to the glory of God and the good of mankind.

We bless Thee for that faith in Christ which supported him in
life, and for that hope that cheered him in death, and that we can

believe that he is still occupied in thy service, and that now, in a clearer light, he is doing nobler work than he performed on earth.

We rejoice this day because by his profession and by his consistent walk and conversation he gave such evidence that he was truly a follower of Christ and led by the sanctifying Spirit. May we all be enabled to follow his good example, trusting like him in Thee, and giving praise to Father, Son, and Holy Ghost: Amen.

ADDRESSES.

The VICE-PRESIDENT. The first address in the order of exercises was to have been delivered by Hon. HANNIBAL HAMLIN, a Senator from Maine, and a Regent of the Smithsonian Institution. Mr. HAMLIN having been appointed one of the committee on the part of the Senate to attend the remains of the late GUSTAVE SCHLEICHER, late a member of the House of Representatives, before leaving requested that I should read the remarks which he would have submitted in person if present; which the Chair will now proceed to do.

ADDRESS
OF
HON. HANNIBAL HAMLIN.

HISTORY teaches us that in every age and country of the civilized world homage has been paid by the living to the illustrious dead. In all time art has been invoked to preserve the form and features of the great and the good. Monuments of bronze, of marble, and of granite have been erected and dedicated to their memory. In the wisdom of this the judgment of mankind has concurred. It is a custom honored in the observance.

The learned and incorruptible judge, with a mind stored with legal knowledge, who dispenses justice with an even balance, alike to the elevated and the lowly, the rich and the poor; the heroic and able commander of armies, who has contributed largely in founding or preserving the institutions of his country; and the statesman and the executive officer who respectively frame and execute the

(43)

laws of the nation, so that "the greatest good to the greatest number" shall be promoted and the individual rights of every citizen, however humble, shall be fully protected, are all, whether living or dead, entitled to the homage of their countrymen. But he who like Professor HENRY, through a long life of unwearying labor and research, has drawn from science her hidden treasures; has enlarged the dominion of mind over matter, and made the forces of nature contribute to the welfare and comfort of man—whose genius originated the great idea that in its perfection has put a girdle of communication around the earth, which acts with the speed of thought and brings distant parts of the world into instant intercourse; who, by "the diffusion of knowledge among men," has assisted in raising the world to a higher plane and given a broader value to thought, knowledge, and action; who has made it wiser and better that he lived, is entitled to the honor and undissembled homage of mankind.

The usefulness and distinguished achievements of Professor HENRY are limited by no national boundaries, but are co-extensive with civilization itself; and his name will be perpetuated and remembered wherever science is cultivated or knowledge is cherished. We pause then, as we are borne along by the tide and onward current of human life, to pay a just and fitting tribute to the eminent life, character, and services of Professor HENRY; and we can but be reminded of the marked parallel which he furnishes in many respects to the distinguished philosophers of the early republics.

But of his triumphs and distinction in science, specifically, it is not within my province to speak: that duty will be most successfully discharged by the learned gentlemen who are to follow me.

It was my fortune to have been officially connected with others in framing and enacting the organic law which created the Smithsonian Institution. Thus I became early acquainted with Professor HENRY, and in a long intercourse of years from then until the time of his decease, it is indeed a pleasant memory that no word, or thought, or deed ever marred the harmony of that association. To Professor HENRY must be awarded the credit for what has been done by the Smithsonian Institution in science and the "diffusion of knowledge among men." It was his mind that conceived the plan best calculated to accomplish the object designed by Mr. SMITHSON, and steadily, with a zeal that never faltered, with persistent toil that hardly knew a limit, he pressed on in his noble work until the Institution under his inspirations stands to-day recognized and acknowledged as among the first of a like character in the world. There were times when a change was sought and earnestly urged in the scope, mode, and manner in which the Institution should be conducted. But the wiser plans and wiser counsels of Professor HENRY prevailed, and it is safe to say that now no ruthless hand would substantially change them. The test of time has fully established and vindicated his wisdom.

Professor HENRY was distinguished in an eminent degree for his dignity of character and rare modesty. To those who knew him well and intimately he was always unassuming, speaking never of himself or his great achievements. He appeared in his possession and dissemination of knowledge, as NEWTON said of himself, like a child upon the sea-shore, picking here and there a grain of sand, while a vast and unexplored ocean was before him.

Though gifted with knowledge vast, varied, and profound, he exemplified and illustrated the maxim of the poet—"Of their own merits modest men are dumb." His dignity and modesty were unerring marks of his intellectual greatness, and adorned his wealth of science and learning.

Eminent and distinguished as was Professor HENRY to those familiar with and who knew the administration of the Smithsonian Institution in all its parts, he was no less great for the rare ability with which he cared for and managed its finances. Here, too, as in

all else, he was modest and without pretension, but firm and un-
flinching in the policy which he pursued, and which was crowned
with such prominent success. He was learned in the science of
finance, and his knowledge and opinions on important occasions
were sought and adopted by others. But in the administration of
the funds of the Institution his financial theory, in practice, was
reduced to two simple rules from which volumes of useful instruction may be drawn, and if wisely followed, how much of what
are called the misfortunes of the world would be averted. Indeed,
an approximate adherence to his rules, and the financial world
would hardly have been darkened by the floods of such light as has
been deluged upon it. PAY AS YOU GO.—SPEND LESS THAN YOUR
INCOME. These were the two rules that he laid down for his course
of action, and he followed them without a single departure. There
were times of pressing necessity and great desirability of extending
the fields already occupied and of seeking new ones by the Institution. But Professor HENRY still held to his rules with an iron hand
and a Spartan will. The end again illustrates his wisdom.

A condensed statement of the Smithsonian fund at the end
of Professor HENRY's administration as its Secretary shows as
follows:

The amount originally received as the bequest of
   JAMES SMITHSON, of England, deposited in
   the Treasury of the United States in accordance
   with the act of Congress of August 10, 1846,
   was ----------------------------------- $515,169 00

The residuary legacy of Smithson, received in
   1865, deposited in the Treasury of the United
   States in accordance with the act of Congress of
   February 8, 1867----------------------- 26,210 63

      Total bequest of Smithson----------- 541,379 63

Amount brought forward----------------	$541,379 63
Amount deposited in the Treasury of the United States as authorized by act of Congress of February 8, 1867, derived from savings of income and increase in value of investments ---------	108,620 37
Amount received as the bequest of JAMES HAMILTON, of Carlisle, Pennsylvania, February 24, 1874 ---------------------------------	1,000 00
Total permanent Smithson fund in the Treasury of the United States bearing interest at 6 per cent., payable semi-annually in gold----------	651,000 00
To that sum should be added as the present value of State stocks held by the Institution --------	35,000 00
Making a total fund of----- ---------	686,000 00
In addition to the above the Institution has—	
Cash on hand for current operations----------	25,000 00
Value of building and furniture, cost---------	500,000 00
Value of library ----- ---------------------	200,000 00
Value of stock on hand of its own publications, including twenty-one quartos and fifteen octavos, wood-cuts, and plates-------------	50,000 00
Value of philosophical apparatus-----------	5,000 00
Value of works of art---------------------	2,000 00
Total------------------------------	1,468,000 00

The foregoing statement shows a fund and property of the Institution of nearly one and a half millions of dollars in gold, or, to analyse a little, a fund of six hundred and fifty-one thousand dollars at an interest of six per cent. per annum for the yearly operations of the Institution. This is noticeable particularly in the fact that the fund has been increased nearly one hundred and

fifty thousand dollars over and above the sum bequeathed by Mr.
SMITHSON. The other property of the Institution in value, as has
been stated, is over seven hundred thousand dollars. Such is the
correct statement of the fund and financial condition of the Smithsonian Institution at the decease of Professor HENRY. For him
how proud the record, and for the future usefulness of the Institution how grand the prospect! With this flattering condition of its
finances, the Institution may widen its present and enter new fields
to seek for additional knowledge to be diffused among men, while
Professor HENRY, its world-distinguished secretary, shall be remembered away in the stillness of ages as one of the most learned men
of his time and a benefactor of mankind.

ADDRESS

OF

HON. ROBERT E. WITHERS.

This thronging hall, this august assemblage, this imposing pageant are suggestive and significant to a degree that anticipates and almost consummates the duty of the hour.

The death of the soldier, the patriot, or the statesman who has won glory, honor, or distinction in the public service, has usually been made the occasion of impressive memorial ceremonial; for as different as nations are in many other respects, they all agree in this, — gratitude for distinguished services, and reverence for the mighty dead. This is a feeling peculiar to no era or country; it is common to all mankind — whether civilized or savage, barbarous or refined. The rude tumuli of the savage, the magnificent mausolea of the East, and the marble monuments of the West, alike point to where sleep the ashes of the warrior, the patriot, and the sage whose services have endeared them to their countrymen and whose deeds have rendered their nation illustrious.

I see around me, congregated in this, the capitol of a great nation, its highest functionaries in the executive, legislative, and judicial departments of government, distinguished diplomatic representatives of almost every civilized people, the chiefest dignitaries of church and state, men most renowned in peace and in war, those most honored in the world of science, of literature, and of art, convened to do homage to the memory of one whose brow was decked neither with the laurel wreath of the conqueror nor yet with the civic crown of the statesman. He chose rather to dedicate his powers to the pursuits of science, to the investigation of

4   (49)

those abstruse and occult problems which baffle the efforts of
scientists, hoping thus perchance to add to the stores of human
knowledge and the happiness of human life. Surely, mankind are
not mere followers of fame nor blind worshipers of Mammon, but
are prompt to recognize true greatness wherever found.

When JAMES SMITHSON'S munificent donation to the cause of
knowledge was heralded to the world, scientists and *literati* differed
widely in their views of the proper method of carrying into effect
the wishes of the donor, and of utilizing the bequest. Many were
the suggestions and varied the projects which were successively proposed, considered, and rejected. Steadily adhering to his own far-
seeing convictions, Professor HENRY finally secured such legislation
as was necessary to consummate with literal exactitude the wishes of
the generous donor, and from that hour the Smithsonian Institution has been dedicated to its great work, "the increase and diffusion of knowledge among men."

Himself arranging all the details whereby these results could be
most surely attained, the work of original investigation has under
his guidance gone steadily forward, until to-day the name and fame
of the Smithsonian Institution and its late secretary are known and
appreciated among the nations of the earth, wherever knowledge
has found a votary or science an abiding place. The system is
unique, for neither in the Old World nor the New is its counter-
part to be found, and I may safely say that its achievements are
as widely known and as highly valued in other continents as in
this. Time will not suffice to enumerate the varied and useful
results which have been thus attained; but we know, and the world
knows, that to the sagacity, industry, and administrative ability of
JOSEPH HENRY is alone due the credit of this great success.
Unwilling to lessen the interest or mar the beauty of the biographical sketch to which you will soon listen, the preparation of which
has been delegated to the able hands of one who knew him long

and intimately, I forbear to do more than briefly glance at some of the salient points of Professor HENRY's character and services.

To speak of him as he was is to praise him; to describe his daily walk and conversation as he lived, moved, and had his being is his highest eulogy. He was not a genius. The characteristics of his mind are typified rather by the steady illumination of the well-trimmed lamp, than by the scintillations of those brilliant pyrotechnics which for a while dazzle, startle, and amaze, but suddenly expire in the blackness of darkness forever. Simplicity, purity, and earnestness were his chief attributes; guileless and unaffected as a child he was wise with more than worldly wisdom. Genius may be admired as the mountain torrent or the lightning's flash for its force and brilliancy, but a higher homage is due to morality and virtue, which should guide the strength of the one and the splendor of the other to beneficent results.

That "knowledge is power" has been accepted as an axiom, but it is a power for good or for evil; it becomes a blessing or a curse as it is well or illy used. It is a treasure above all price when consecrated to the cause of morality and virtue, but an inexhaustible fountain of woe when wedded to immorality and vice.

If these things be true, then may we confidently point to him as an example calculated to inspire a deeper reverence for the majesty of virtue in public and in private life, and as furnishing a higher incentive to virtuous deeds of emulation in his countrymen.

He acted on the principle that no success in life, whether measured by wealth or fame, could compensate for the loss of that calm sunshine of conscious integrity, and that deserved praise so surely awarded a life of usefulness and beneficence.

Viewing the mere acquisition of wealth with philosophic indifference, he was, nevertheless, as a financier a model of sagacity. The full and satisfactory detail to which you have just listened of the principles which guided, and the success which attended his administration of the funds intrusted to his management will abundantly verify this assertion.

In his own affairs, however, he exhibited an indifference to gain which was by many regarded as almost inexcusable. Consecrated to the cause of science, he freely and unselfishly gave to mankind the results of all his discoveries. When with untiring assiduity he had traced to its matrix the germ of a useful idea, and became satisfied that he had brought to light a principle destined to benefit his fellow-man, he left to others the task of applying this principle and reaping the pecuniary recompense, while he, again returning to the domain of original research, boldly invaded the very penetralia of nature's laboratory in quest of further knowledge. This trait of his character is strikingly illustrated in the history of the electric telegraph, for to him is the world indebted for the discovery of the principle from which has been developed by the labors of others such wondrous results. In these results, with their accompanying emoluments, he had no share, nor ever seemed to regard them as of the slightest moment.

Though thus devoted to scientific pursuits and standing second to none in the expansive breadth of his inquiries or the acuteness of his analytical investigations, Professor HENRY belonged not to the class of ultra-scientists, whose sharpened faculties forbid the recognition of a first great cause, and whose boasted reason scorns to accept the simple story of the Cross. The uniform tenor of a long life, the unsullied purity of his character, the uniform practice of all the Christian virtues, the regular attendance upon the Christian ministry, and the testimony he left us in his dying hour, all attest that for him faith had bridged the dark gulf which separates the seen from the unseen, and led him safely through the gates into the eternal city whose builder and maker is God.

BIOGRAPHICAL MEMORIAL,

BY

PROFESSOR ASA GRAY,

IN BEHALF OF THE BOARD OF REGENTS.

THE Regents of the Smithsonian Institution, on the day following the obsequies of their late Secretary, resolved to place upon record, by the hands of their committee, a memorial of their lamented associate. The time has arrived when this should be done, now that the Institution enters upon another official year, and its bereavement is brought freshly to mind.

Although time may have assuaged our sorrow, as time will do, and although the recollection that a well-spent life was well appreciated and not prematurely closed, should temper regret, yet they have not dulled our sense of loss, nor lessened our estimate of the signal service to science, to this Institution, and to the general good which remarkable gifts and a devoted spirit enabled this man to render.

If we would fit this memorial to the subject of it, we must keep in mind Professor HENRY's complete and transparent, but dignified simplicity and modesty of character, in which a delicate sense of justice went along with extreme dislike of exaggeration, and aversion to all that savored of laudation.

Yet it is not for ourselves, his associates—some of few, some of many years—that this record is made; nor need we speak for that larger circle of his associates, the men of science in our land, who will, in their several organizations, recount the scientific achievements of their late leader and Nestor. And nothing that we can say will enhance the sentiments of respect, veneration, and trust with which he was regarded here, in Washington, by all who knew him, whether of high or humble station. Even those, here or elsewhere, who came only into occasional intercourse with him, will remember that thoughtful and benignant face;—certainly it will be remembered by those who, in that recourse to him which it was always easy to gain, have seen the mild seriousness of a somewhat abstracted and grave mien change into a winning smile, sure precursor of pleasant words, cheerful attention, and, if need were, wise counsel and cordial help. But we are all passing, as he has passed, and the tribute to his memory which it is our privilege to pay, is a duty to those who are to come after us.

JOSEPH HENRY was of Scotch descent. His grandparents, paternal and maternal, landed at New York from the same vessel on the day before the battle of Bunker Hill. The HENRYS settled in Delaware County, the ALEXANDERS in Saratoga County, New York. Of his father, WILLIAM HENRY, little is known. He died when his oldest son, JOSEPH, was eight or nine years old. His mother lived to a good age.[*] He was born at Albany very near the close of the last century.[†] His boyhood was mostly passed with his maternal grandmother in the country at Galway. His early education was such as a country common school would furnish to a lad of inquisitive mind but no aptness for study. The fondness for reading came early, but in a surreptitious way.

One day, in the pursuit of a pet rabbit, he penetrated through an opening in the foundation-wall of the village meeting-house. A glimmer of light enticed him through the broken floor into a room above, in which an open bookcase contained the village library. He took down a book — Brooke's Fool of Quality — was soon absorbed in the perusal, returned again and again to this, which he

[*] She is remembered as a lady of winning refinement of mien and character, of small size, with delicate Grecian features, fair complexion, and when young she is said to have been very beautiful.

[†] The date, December 17, 1797, given in the American Cyclopædia, appears to be wrong; was perhaps misprinted. There is little doubt that he was born on the 17th of December, 1799.

said was the first book he ever opened voluntarily, and to all the works of fiction which the library contained. Access in the regular way was soon granted to him.

The lad at this time was a clerk, or office-boy, in the store of a Mr. Broderick. He returned to Albany at the age of fourteen or fifteen. We may count it as a part of his education that he there served a brief apprenticeship to a silversmith, in which he acquired the manual dexterity afterward so useful to him. Opportunely perhaps, the silversmith soon failed in business, and young Henry was thrown out of employment. His powers were now developing, but not in the line they were soon to take. To romance reading was now joined a fondness for the theater. Not content with seeing all the plays he could, he found his way behind the scenes, and learned the methods of producing stage effects. He joined a juvenile forensic and theatrical society, called the Rostrum, and soon distinguished himself in it by his ingenuity in stage arrangements. He was made president, and having nothing else to do at the time, he gave his whole attention to the Rostrum. He dramatized a tale, wrote a comedy, and took a part in its representation. Unusually comely in form and features, and of prepossessing address, our future philosopher was in a fair way to become an actor, perhaps a distinguished one.

But now a slight illness confined him for a few days to his mother's house. To while away the hours he took up a small book which a Scotchman, who then occupied a room in the house, had left upon his mother's table. It was "Lectures on Experimental Philosophy, Astronomy, and Chemistry, intended chiefly for the use of young persons, by G. Gregory," an English clergyman. It is an unpretending volume, but a sensible one. It begins by asking three or four questions, such as these:

"You throw a stone, or shoot an arrow into the air; why does it not go forward in the line or direction that you give it? Why does

it stop at a certain distance, and then return to you? - - - On
the contrary, why does flame or smoke always mount upward,
though no force is used to send them in that direction? And why
should not the flame of a candle drop toward the floor when you
reverse it, or hold it downward, instead of turning up and ascending
into the air? - - - Again, you look into a clear well of water
and see your own face and figure, as if painted there. Why is this?
You are told that it is done by reflection of light. But what is
reflection of light?"

Young HENRY's mind was aroused by these apt questions, and
allured by the explanations; he now took in a sense of what
knowledge was. The door to knowledge opened to him, that door
which it thence became the passion of his life to open wider.
Thenceforth truth charmed him more than fiction. At the next
meeting of his dramatic association he resigned the office of president
and took his leave in a valedictory address, in which he assured his
comrades that he should now prepare to play his part on another
stage, with nobler and more impressive scenes. The volume itself
is preserved in Professor HENRY's library. On a fly-leaf is the
following entry:

"This book, although by no means a profound work, has, under
Providence, exerted a remarkable influence upon my life. It accidentally fell into my hands when I was about sixteen years old, and
was the first work I ever read with attention. It opened to me a
new world of thought and enjoyment; invested things before almost
unnoticed with the highest interest; fixed my mind on the study of
nature, and caused me to resolve at the time of reading it that I
would immediately commence to devote my life to the acquisition
of knowledge."

The pursuit of elementary knowledge under difficulties and pri-
vations now commenced. At first he attended a night-school, where
he soon learned all the master could teach. At length he entered

Albany Academy, earning the means at one time by teaching a country district school, later by serving as tutor to the sons of General STEPHEN VAN RENSSELAER the patroon. Then he took the direction of a road-survey across the southern portion of the State, from West Point to Lake Erie, earning a little money and much credit. He returned to Albany Academy as an assistant teacher, but was very soon, in 1828, appointed professor of mathematics. He had already chosen his field, and began to make physical investigations.

It is worth noticing that just when HENRY's youthful resolution to devote his life to the acquisition of knowledge was ready to bear fruit, another resolve was made, in England, by another scientific investigator, JAMES SMITHSON, in his will, executed in October, 1826, wherein he devoted his patrimony "TO FOUND AT WASHINGTON AN ESTABLISHMENT FOR THE INCREASE AND DIFFUSION OF KNOWLEDGE AMONG MEN." Who could have thought that the poor lad, who resolved to seek for knowledge as for hid treasure, and the rich man of noble lineage, who resolved that his treasure should increase and diffuse knowledge, would ever stand in this interesting relation; that the one would direct and shape the establishment which the other willed to be founded!

The young professor's position was an honorable but most laborious one. Although Albany Academy was said by the distinguished president of Union College in those days to be "a college in disguise," it began its work low down. Its new professor of mathematics had to teach seven hours of every day, and for half of this time to drudge with a large class of boys in the elements of arithmetic. But he somehow found time to carry on systematically the electro-magnetic researches which he had already begun. In the very year of his appointment, 1828, he described in the Transactions of the Albany Institute a new application of the galvanic multiplier, and throughout that year and the two next he carried on those investigations which, when published at the beginning of the ensuing year, January, 1831, in that notable first paper in the American Journal of Science and the Arts, at once brought HENRY's name to the front line among the discoverers in electromagnetism.

STURGEON may be said to have first made an electro-magnet; HENRY undoubtedly made the electro-magnet what it is. Just after BARLOW, in England, had declared that there could be no electric telegraph to a long distance, HENRY discovered that there could be, how and why it could be; he declared publicly its practicability, and illustrated it experimentally by setting up a telegraph with such length of wire as he could conveniently command, delivering signals at a distance by the sounding of a bell.

Previously to his investigations the means of developing magnetism in soft iron were imperfectly understood (even though the law from which they are now seen to flow had been mathematically worked out by OHM), and the electro-magnet which then existed was inapplicable to the transmission of power to a distance. HENRY first rendered it applicable to the transmission of mechanical power to a distance; was the first actually to magnetize a piece of iron at a distance, and by it to deliver telegraphic signals. He also showed what kind of battery must be employed to project the current through a great length of wire, and what kind of coil should surround the magnet used to receive this current and to do the work. *

---

* The following appear to be the main points in the order of discovery which led to the electro-magnetic telegraph. They are here condensed from Professor HENRY's "Statement," in the "Proceedings of the Regents," published in the Smithsonian Report for the year 1857, and from a note appended by Mr. William B. Taylor to his "Memoir of Joseph Henry and his Scientific Work," read before the Philosophical Society of Washington:

1819–1820. OERSTED showed that a magnetic needle is deflected by the action of a current of galvanic electricity passing near it. It recently appears that this discovery had already been made as early as the year 1802, by ROMAGNESI, and published in 1802.

1825. ARAGO discovered that while a galvanic current is passing through a copper wire it is capable of developing magnetism in soft iron.

For the telegraph, and for electro-magnetic machines, what was now wanted was not discovery, but invention, not the ascertainment of principles, but the devising of methods. These, the proper subjects of patent, have been supplied in various ways and, as to the telegraph, with wonderful efficiency; — in Europe, by the transmission of signs through the motion of a magnetic needle; in America, by the production of sounds or records by the electromagnet. MORSE was among the first to undertake the enterprise, and, when directed to the right way through Professor GALE's acquaintance with HENRY's published researches, he carried the

---

1820. AMPÈRE discovered that two wires through which currents are passing in the same direction attract, and in opposite directions repel, each other; and thence he inferred that magnetism consists in the attraction of electrical currents revolving at right angles to the line joining the two poles of the magnet, and is produced in a bar of steel or iron by induction from a series of electrical currents revolving in the same direction at right angles to the axis of the bar.

1820. SCHWEIGGER in the same year produced the galvanometer.

1825. STURGEON made the electro-magnet by bending the bar, or rather a piece of iron wire, into the form of a horse-shoe, covering it with varnish to insulate it, and surrounding it with a helix of wire the turns of which were at a distance.

1828–1831. HENRY, in accordance with the theory of AMPÈRE, produced the intensity or spool-wound magnet, insulating the wire instead of the rod or bar, and covering the whole surface of the iron with a series of coils in close contact. He extended the principle to the full by winding successive strata of insulated wire over each other, thus producing a compound helix formed of a long wire of many coils. At the same time he developed the relation of the intensity magnet to the intensity battery, and their relations to the magnet of quantity. He thus made the electro-magnet capable of transmitting power to a long distance, demonstrated the principle and perfected the magnet applicable to the purpose, was the first actually to magnetize a piece of iron at a distance, and to demonstrate and devise the applicability of the electro-magnet to telegraphy at a distance. Using the terminal short-circuit magnet of quantity, and the armature as the signaling device, he was the first to make by it audible signals, sounding a bell at a distance by means of the electro-magnet.

1832. WHEATSTONE discovered that the conducting-wires of an electric telegraph could be left without insulation except at the points of support.

1833. GAUSS ingeniously arranged the application of a dual sign in such manner as to produce a true alphabet for telegraphy.

1836. DANIELL invented and brought into use a constant galvanic battery.

1837. STEINHEIL discovered that the earth may form the returning half of the circuit, so that a single conducting wire suffices for telegraphy.

1837. MORSE adopted, through the agency of Dr. LEONARD GALE, the principle of the HENRY electro-magnet, and made of the armature a recording instrument.

1838. MORSE devised his "dot and dash" alphabet, a great improvement upon the GAUSS and STEINHEIL alphabets.

1841. MORSE suggested and brought into use the system of relay-magnets, and relay-circuits, to reinforce the current.

latter mode into practical and most successful execution. If HENRY
had patented his discovery, which he was urged, but declined to do,
MORSE could have patented only his alphabetical mode of signaling,
and perhaps the use of relay-batteries, the latter indispensable for
long lines upon that system.

The scientific as well as popular effect of Professor HENRY'S
first paper in Silliman's Journal was immediate and great. With the
same battery that STURGEON used he developed at least a hundred
times more magnetism. The instantaneous production of magnets
lifting four hundred and twenty times their own weight, of those
which with less than a pint of dilute acid acting on two hands'
breadth of zinc would lift seven hundred and fifty pounds, and
this afterward carried up to a magnet lifting thirty-three hundred
pounds, was simply astonishing. Yet it was not these extraordinary
results, nor their mechanical applications which engaged Professor
HENRY'S attention so much as the prospect they opened of a way
by which to ascend to higher discovery of the laws of nature. In
other hands, his discoveries furnished the means by which diamag-
netism, magnetic effects on polarized light, and magneto-electricity —
now playing so conspicuous a part — soon came to be known. In
his own hands, the immediate discovery of the induction of a current in a long wire on itself* led the way to his next fertile field
of inquiry, the following up of which caused unwise tardiness in
the announcement of what he had already done. For it is within
our knowledge that the publication of the paper which initiated his
fame had been urged for months by scientific friends, and at length
was hastened by the announcement of some partly similar results
reached in a different way by MOLL, of Utrecht. In a letter not
long afterward written to one of us, Professor HENRY had occasion
to declare: "My whole ambition is to establish for myself *and to
deserve* the reputation of a man of science." Yet throughout his

* Announced in American Journal of Science and the Arts in 1832.

life ardor for discovery and pure love of knowledge were unattended by corresponding eagerness for publication. At the close of that very year, 1832, however, he did announce the drawing of a spark from a magnet, that first fact in magneto-electricity, and, as he supposed, a new one. But he had been anticipated.

In May, 1830, Professor HENRY married HARRIET L. ALEXANDER, of Schenectady, New York, who, with three daughters, survives. Two earlier children died in infancy, and a son in early manhood.

Pleasant in most respects as his situation at Albany was, it was not an unwelcome invitation which, in the summer of 1832, it became the duty and the privilege of the most venerable of our number, then vice-president of the College of New Jersey, to give to Professor HENRY, offering him the chair of Natural Philosophy at Princeton. By this early call that college secured him for her own during the years most prolific for science. It was on a later occasion that Sir DAVID BREWSTER wrote: "The mantle of FRANKLIN has fallen upon the shoulders of HENRY." But the aureole was already visible to his fellow-workers in science; and SILLIMAN, RENWICK, and TORREY urged his acceptance of the new position, and congratulated Princeton upon the acquisition.

The professorship came to him unsought. In his last address to one of the learned societies over which he presided, Professor HENRY mentions that the various offices of honor and responsibility which he then held, nine in number, had all been pressed upon him; that he never occupied a position for which he had of his own will and action been made a candidate. It did not occur to him at that moment to make one exception. When a pupil in Albany Academy he once offered himself as a teacher of a country district school. The school trustees thought him too young, but took him on trial at eight dollars a month. At the beginning of the second month they raised his pay to fifteen.

At Princeton Professor HENRY found congenial companions and duties well suited to his powers. Here he taught and investigated for fourteen fruitful and happy years; here he professed the faith that was in him, entering into the communion of the Presbyterian Church, in which he and his ancestors were nurtured; and here he developed — what might not have been expected — a genius for education. One could count on his being a clear expositor, and his gifts for experimental illustration and for devising apparatus had been already shown. But now, as a college professor, the question how to educate came before him in a broader way. He appreciated, and he made his associates and pupils appreciate, the excellence of natural philosophy for mental discipline, for training at once both the observing and the reasoning faculties. A science which rises from the observation of the most familiar facts, and the questioning of these by experiment, to the consideration of causes, the ascertaining of laws, and to the most recondite conceptions respecting the constitution of matter and the interplay of forces, offers discipline to all the intellectual powers, and tasks the highest of them. Professor HENRY taught not only the elementary facts and general principles from a fresh survey of both, but also the methods of philosophical investigation, and the steps by which the widest generalizations and the seemingly intangible conceptions of the higher physics have been securely reached. He exercised his pupils in deducing particular results from admitted laws, and in then ascertaining whether what was thus deduced actually occurred in nature; and if not, why not. Though very few of a college class might ever afterward undertake a physical or chemical investigation, all would or should be concerned in the acquisition of truth and its relations; and by knowing how truth was won and knowledge advanced in one field of inquiry, they would gain the aptitude which any real investigation may give, and the confidence that springs from a clear view and a sure grasp of any one subject.

He understood, as few do, the importance of analogy and hypothesis in science. Premising that hypothesis should always be founded on real analogies and used interrogatively, he commended it as the prerequisite to experiment, and the instrument by which, in the hands of sound philosophers, most discoveries have been made. This free use of hypothesis as the servant and avant-courier of research — as means rather than end — is a notable characteristic of HENRY. His ideas on the subject are somewhat fully and characteristically expounded by himself in his last presidential address to the Philosophical Society of Washington, — one which he evidently felt would be the last.

How HENRY was valued, honored, revered at Princeton, the memorial published by his former associates there feelingly declares. What he did there for science in those fourteen years would be long to tell and difficult to make clear without entering into details, here out of place. Happily the work has been done to our hand by the Professor himself, in a communication which is printed in the index volume of the Princeton Review, and reprinted in the Princeton Memorial.

One of these, of the Princeton period, ought to be mentioned. It is upon the origin of mechanical power and its relations to vital force. It is a characteristic example of Professor HENRY's happy mode of treating a scientific topic in an untechnical way. It also illustrates his habit of simply announcing original ideas without putting them prominently forward in publication, as any one who was thinking of himself and of his own fame would be sure to do. The doctrine he announced was communicated to the American Philosophical Society in 1844 in brief outlines. He developed it further in an article published in the Patent Office Report for 1856, twelve years later; a medium of publication which was naturally overlooked. Only at a friend's desire was the paper reproduced, in 1860, in the American Journal of Science, where it would be noticed. The attention of Professor HENRY was turned to the topic (as we happen to know) by an abstract which was given to him of DUMAS' celebrated lecture, in 1841, on the Chemical Statics of Organized Beings. If he had published in 1844, with some fullness, as he then wrought them out, his conception and his attractive illustrations of the sources, transformation, and equivalence of mechanical power, and given them fitting publicity, HENRY's name would have been prominent among the pioneers and founders of the modern doctrine of the conservation of energy.

In the year 1837 Professor HENRY first visited Europe, and came into personal communication with the principal men of science of England, Scotland, and France. One of us had the pleasure, a few years afterward, of hearing FARADAY speak of HENRY in terms of hearty regard and admiration. The two men were in some respects alike, wholly alike in genuine simplicity of character and in disinterested devotion to scientific discovery. They were then rival investigators in the same line; and the race for a time was not unequal, considering how HENRY was weighted with onerous professional work. For FARADAY, while that most acute mind retained its powers, there was the congenial life of pure research, undistracted by cares of administration or of instruction, beyond a few popular lectures; supplied with every means of investigation; stimulated by the presence or proximity of many fellow-workers; rewarded by discovery after discovery, and not unconscious of the world's applause—such was the enviable life of the natural philosopher favorably placed. But in this country, where fit laborers are few, duty rather than inclination must determine their work. Midway in his course Professor HENRY was called to exchange a position which allowed the giving of considerable time to original researches, for one of greater prominence, in which these had practically to be abandoned. Not, indeed, that this was assuredly expected, but it was contemplated as probable.

And the event justified the apprehension, while it opened other fields of not inferior usefulness.

In August, 1846, the act of Congress establishing the Smithsonian Institution was passed and approved. On the 7th of September ensuing, the Regents held their first meeting. On the 3d of December following they resolved:

"That it is essential for the advancement of the proper interests of the trust that the Secretary of the Smithsonian Institution be a man possessing weight of character and a high grade of talent; and that it is further desirable that he possess eminent scientific and general acquirements; that he be a man capable of advancing science and promoting letters by original research and effort, well qualified to act as a respected channel of communication between the Institution and scientific and literary individuals and societies in this and foreign countries; and, in a word, a man worthy to represent before the world of science and letters the Institution over which this Board presides."

Immediately following the adoption of this resolution, Professor JOSEPH HENRY, of Princeton, was elected Secretary. On the 14th of December a letter was read from him accepting the appointment. At the meeting a week later, he appeared and entered upon the duties of his office. From this time the biography of Professor HENRY is the history of the Institution. That history is set forth in the Secretary's annual reports, presented by the Board of Regents to Congress, and it need not be recapitulated. A few words may give some idea of the deep impression he made upon the Institution while it was yet plastic.

Some time before his appointment he had been requested by members of the Board of Regents to examine the will of SMITHSON, and to suggest a plan of organisation by which the object of the bequest might, in his opinion, best be realised. He did so, and the plan he drew was in their hands when he was chosen Secretary.

5

As he himself summed it up, the plan was based on the conviction "that the intention of the donor was to advance science by original research and publication; that the establishment was for the benefit of mankind generally, and that all unnecessary expenditures on local objects would be violations of the trust." The plan proposed was, in the leading feature, "to assist men of science in making original researches, to publish them in a series of volumes, and to give a copy of these to every first-class library on the face of the earth."

His "Programme of Organization," filled out in its details and adjusted to the conditions prescribed by the law and by the action of the Regents, was submitted to the Board in the following year, was adopted as its "governing policy," and it has been reprinted, in full or in part, in almost every annual report. All would understand, therefore, that Professor HENRY's views were approved, and that they would be carried into effect as far and as fast as they commended themselves to the judgment of the Regents, and as opportunity made them practicable.

If the Institution is now known and praised throughout the world of science and letters, if it is fulfilling the will of its founder and the reasonable expectations of the nation which accepted and established the trust, the credit is mainly due to the practical wisdom, the catholic spirit, and the indomitable perseverance of its first Secretary, to whom the establishing act gave much power of shaping ends which, as rough-hewn by Congress, were susceptible of various diversion. For Congress, in launching, did not shape the course of the Institution, except in a general way. And in intrusting its guidance to the Regents, the law created only one salaried and permanent officer, the Secretary, on whom, by its terms and by the conditions of the case, it devolved great responsibility and commensurate influence. Some of us are old enough to remember the extreme diversity of opinion in Congress over the use to be made of SMITHSON's legacy. One party, headed by an eminent statesman and ex-President, endeavored to found with it an astronomical observatory, for which surely the country need not be indebted to a foreigner. A larger party strove to secure it for a library; not, probably, because they deemed that use most relevant to the founder's intention, but because rival schemes might fritter away the noble bequest. In popular lecturing, itinerant or stationary, of which the supply and the quality are in this country equal to the demand; or in the dissemination of elementary knowledge by the printing-press, as if that were beyond the reach of private enterprise; or in setting up one more college, university, or other educational establishment on half an endowment; or in duplicating museums and cabinets, which, when supported by a fixed capital, necessarily soon reach the statical condition in which all the income is absorbed in simply taking care of what has been accumulated.

Congress rejected, one after the other, the schemes for making of the Institution an observatory, a library, a normal school, and a lecturing establishment with professors at Washington. It created a Board of Regents, charged it with the care of the collections and museums belonging to the United States; authorized the expenditure, if the Regents saw fit, of a sum not exceeding twenty-five thousand dollars annually for the formation of a library; and in all else it directed them to make such disposal of the income "as they shall deem best suited for the promotion of the purpose of the testator."

Under this charter, and with the course of the Institution still to be marked out, it is not surprising that the official adviser and executive of the Board should look to the will of SMITHSON for the controlling interpretation of the law. He knew moreover that in an earlier will, SMITHSON had bequeathed his fortune to the Royal Society of London, an institution expressly for the furtherance of

scientific research; and that he changed, as we may say, the trustee-
ship for a purely personal reason. HENRY took his stand on the
broad and simple terms of the bequest, "for the increase and diffusion of knowledge among men." And he never —

> Narrowed his mind,
> And to loyalty gave what was meant for mankind.

He proposed only one restriction, of obvious wisdom and necessity, that, in view of the limited means of the Institution, it ought
not to undertake anything which could be done, and well done, by
other existing instrumentalities. So, as occasion arose, he lightened
its load and saved its energies by giving over to other agencies some
of its cherished work — meteorology, for instance, in which a most
popular bureau now usefully expends many times more than the
whole Smithsonian income.

He has in these last years signified his desire to go still further
in this direction, and to have the institution relieved from the charge
of the National Museum, now of imperial dimensions and importance. His reasons were summed up in a few words in his last
report, along with his synopsis of the appropriate functions of the
Institution, which he prays may not be merged in or overshadowed
by any establishment of the Government, but may stand "free to
the unobstructed observation of the whole world, keeping in perpetual remembrance the will of its founder." Its true functions
he declares are —

"First. To enlarge the bounds of human thought by assisting
men of science to make original investigations in all branches of
knowledge; to publish these, and to present copies to all the principal libraries of the world. Second. To institute investigations
in various branches of science, and explorations for the collection
of specimens in natural history and ethnology, to be distributed to
museums and other establishments. Third. To diffuse knowledge
by carrying on an extended international series of exchanges by

which the accounts of all the original researches in science, the
educational progress, and the general advance of civilization in the
New World are exchanged for similar works of the Old World."

The plan which our late Secretary originated has commended
itself to the judgment of successive Boards of Regents, and, we
may be permitted to add, is now approved wherever it is known
and understood.

Professor HENRY took his full share of the various honorable
duties to which such men are called. He was in turn President
of the American Association for the Advancement of Science, in
the year 1849; of the Society for the Advancement of Education,
in 1855; a Trustee of Princeton College, and of Columbian University, also of the Corcoran Gallery of Art, in which the Smithsonian Institution deposits its art collections; Visitor of the Government Hospital for the Insane; President of the Philosophical
Society of Washington; President of the National Academy of
Sciences at Washington. For many years a member of the Light-
House Board, to which he gave gratuitous and invaluable services
as Chairman of its committee on experiments, he added for the
last seven years the chairmanship of the board itself, in his administration no sinecure. Advice and investigation were sought from
him, from time to time, by every department of Government. All
were sure that his advice was never biased by personal interest;
and his sound judgment, supported by spotless character, was
greatly deferred to.

We have said that in coming to Washington a career of investigation was exchanged for a life of administration. It should rather
be said that his investigations thereafter took a directly practical
turn, as his mind was brought to bear upon difficult questions of
immediate importance which were referred to him by Government
or came in the course of official duty. In the light-house service
alone his timely experiments upon lard-oil lighting, and the firmness

with which he pressed his conclusions into practice when sperm-oil
became dear, has already saved more than a million of dollars; the
adaptation of mineral oil to the lesser lights made another great
saving; and the results reached by his recent investigations of the
conditions which influence the transmission of sound and their application to acoustical signaling are not to be valued by the saving
of money only.

It was in the prosecution of these last investigations, over a year
ago, and probably in consequence of exposure in them, at the light-
house station on Staten Island, that an intimation of the approaching end of those labors was received. Yet a few months more
of useful life were vouchsafed to him, not free from suffering,
but blessed with an unclouded mind and borne with a serene
spirit; and then, at midday on the 13th of May last, the scene
was closed.

At the sepulture of his remains (on the 16th) and afterward, it
was generally remarked at Washington that never before had the
funeral of a private citizen called forth such sense of loss, such
profound demonstrations of respect and affection.

It is not for us to assign Professor HENRY's place among the men
of science of our time. Those who do this will probably note that
his American predecessors were FRANKLIN and RUMFORD; that all
three were what we call self-made men; that all three, after having
proved their talents for original investigation in physics, were called
in their mature years to duties of administration and the conduct
of affairs. There are interesting parallels to be drawn from their
scientific work, if one had time to trace them.

Not often is a great man of science a good man of business.
HENRY's friends at Princeton, who besought him not to abandon
the peaceful academic life which he was enjoying and the quiet
pursuits which had given him fame, were surprised when in another
sphere he developed equal talents for organization and administra-

tion. We have seen how he always developed the talent to do wisely and well whatever he undertook. His well-poised spirit, at once patient and masterful, asserted itself in the trials he encountered in the early years of the Institution, and gave assurance that he could deal with men as well as with the forces of nature.

Again, not often is a man of science free from the overmastering influence of his special pursuit. More or less his "nature is subdued to what it works in, like the dyer's hand." Now, HENRY's mind was uncolored by the studies of his predilection. His catholic spirit comes out in his definition of science: "Science is the knowledge of the laws of phenomena, whether they relate to mind or matter." It appears in his choice of the investigations to be furthered and memoirs to be published by the Institution. These nowhere show the bias of a specialist.

Then, he was a careful, painstaking man, very solicitous — perhaps unduly anxious — about the particulars of everything for which he felt responsible. Therefore he was sometimes slow in making up his mind on a practical question. May we here condescend to a trivial anecdote of his early boyhood, which he amusingly related to one of us many years ago and pleasantly recalled at one of our latest interviews. It goes back to the time when he was first allowed to have a pair of boots, and to choose for himself the style of them. He was living with his grandmother in the country, and the village Crispin could offer no great choice of patterns; indeed, it was narrowed down to the alternative of round toes or square. Daily the boy visited the shop and pondered the alternatives, even while the manufacture was going on, until at length the shoemaker, who could brook no more delay, took the dilemma by both horns and produced the most remarkable pair of boots the wearer ever had; one boot round-toed, the other square-toed.

Deliberate as HENRY was in after years, taught by this early lesson he probably never again postponed decision till it was too late to choose. One result of due deliberation was that he rarely had to change his mind. When he had taken his course, he held to it. His patience and kindness under demands upon his time were something wonderful. Some men are thus patient from easy good-nature; HENRY was so from principle. A noticeable part of the Secretary's correspondence was with a class of men—more numerous than would be supposed—who thought they had discovered new laws of nature or new applications of them, and who appealed to him to make their discoveries known. The Secretary never returned a curt answer to such appeals or inquiries, whether made personally or by letter. Many are the hours which he would conscientiously devote to such paradoxical schemes—sometimes of wonderful ingenuity—and to the dictation of elaborate replies to them. Detecting far down in the man's mind the germs of the fallacy which had misled him, he would spare no pains to present it and its consequences so plainly to his bewildered correspondent that he could find his own way out of it; while at the same time he awarded credit and encouragement for whatever was true, probable, or ingenious.

Although of sensitive spirit and with a just sense of what was due to himself, Professor HENRY kept free from controversy. Once he took up the pen, not because his discoveries were set at naught, but because his veracity was implicitly assailed. His dignified recital of undeniable facts (in his Annual Report for 1857) was all that was necessary, and not even a word of indignant comment was added.

He left his scientific work to form its part of the history of science and to be judged by scientific men. The empiric he once sententiously defined to be "one who appeals his cause to an incompetent tribunal." He never courted publicity; not from fastidious dislike, still less from disdain of well-earned popular applause, but simply because he never thought of it.

His disinterested devotion to this Institution was shown in many ways; among others in successive refusals to accept increase of salary lest it should be thought that the office he held was lucrative. Twice or thrice, moreover, while cumbered with anxieties, he promptly declined calls to positions of greater emolument, less care, and abundant leisure for the pursuits he loved.

We cannot here continue these delineations, and it may be that the character of the man has portrayed itself in general outlines as the narrative proceeded. But one trait may not be wholly omitted from the biography of one who has well been called "the model of a Christian gentleman," and who is also our best example of a physical philosopher. His life was the practical harmony of the two characters. His entire freedom from the doubts which disturb some minds is shown in that last letter which he dictated, in which he touches the grounds of faith both in natural and revealed religion; also in his sententious declaration upon some earlier occasion, that the person who thought there could be any real conflict between science and religion must be either very young in science or ignorant of religion.

The man for whom this memorial is placed was a veteran in both; was one of that noble line of natural philosophers for whom we may in all sincerity render to Almighty God hearty thanks, not only for the good example and fruit of their lives, but also that, having finished their course in faith, they do now rest from their labors.

READING OF TELEGRAMS

BY

HON. HIESTER CLYMER.

This evening from across the sea there have come to us, by means which his genius and immortal discovery have made possible, messages, telling of the estimation in which the name and fame of HENRY are held in the Motherland. By the request of the Regents I will read them, so that they may become a part of the record which this nation to-night is making in honor of our greatest son of science since the days of FRANKLIN.

The first I shall read is from the University of Glasgow:

LONDON, January 16, 1879.

"Sir WILLIAM THOMSON, of University of Glasgow, congratulates your nation on a perennial possession. HENRY's name and works are yours forever, though you now mourn the loss of his life among you."

The next is from the Anglo-American Telegraph Company:

LONDON, January 16, 1879.

"The board of directors of this company and myself desire to express our sympathy with the memorial services in honor of the late Professor HENRY, which are to take place in your House of Representatives. We sincerely unite in the grief at this irreparable loss with the relatives and friends of this great man, who has rendered such signal service to the science of electricity and to the world in general, by his important discoveries. This company has to mourn the loss of a staunch friend.

"The Right Hon. Viscount Monck,
"*Chairman of the Anglo-American Company — London.*"

The next dispatch is from the Eastern Telegraph Company and the direct United States Cable Company:

LONDON, January 16, 1879.

"Kindly express in the name of my company, directors, and myself our association in spirit with the memorial services in honor of the late Professor HENRY, whose services have been so great, not only to those interested in electrical science, but to the world at large. The work of such a man as he, helps human progress; and Professor HENRY has left a distinct mark on our times. We sympathize with his family in their sad bereavement, and feel while they have lost a warm friend the world has lost a great benefactor."

"JOHN PENDER,
*Chairman of the Eastern Telegraph Company,
and of the Direct United States Cable Company.*"

"To CYRUS W. FIELD,
Care of MR. Justice FIELD,
Capitol Hill, Washington, D. C."

ADDRESS

OF

PROF. WILLIAM B. ROGERS.

In the opening years of the present century a learned Italian philosopher and experimenter devised and brought to the notice of the scientific world a new engine of electric force, a contrivance for accumulating the peculiar form of electric energy, which since the observations of GALVANI had engaged the attention of scientific men. So general and profound was the interest created by this discovery that the great First Consul of France invited VOLTA to Paris, witnessed his experiments with the newly invented instrument in the august presence of the National Institute, and soon after conferred upon him the highest scientific honors and the most distinguished decorations in his gift.

Striking as was this tribute to the worth and dignity of science, to my mind the present occasion constitutes a far grander recognition than could be accorded by a First Consul of France, though he were NAPOLEON BONAPARTE himself. For here the high functionaries and chosen representatives of a great people are assembled in its Capitol almost as if by a spontaneous impulse to testify to the worth of science and to do honor to one who has been among the foremost in its advancement, making this, perhaps beyond any former occasion in the world's history, a national testimonial to achievements wrought in the peaceful domain of scientific Investigation.

I am unwilling to interpret this noble memorial meeting as inspired simply by a regard for the valuable official services of the philosopher who wisely, discreetly, and firmly carried out the

trust committed to him by the Government of the country. Surely
it is largely due to the services which JOSEPH HENRY rendered
to mankind by his scientific discoveries and researches. Let the
philosopher be ever so great in the administration of affairs, even
though these connect themselves directly with the increase and
spread of knowledge among men, yet the merit and the glory of
the discovery of great scientific truths transcend the honors of any
merely administrative success. This occasion then rises to the
height of a national recognition of science for its own sake in
enlarging the sphere of human intelligence, as well as for its promotion of the material welfare of mankind, and I do not doubt
that the knowledge of what we are this night doing will everywhere give to men of science a new incentive to labor, and will
win for our country an added claim to the honors of an advancing
civilization.

That first year of the century which brought to view the electric
properties of the voltaic apparatus opened an active campaign in
this department of research among the physicists and chemists of
Europe. Within a few months of the announcement of the electric
polarity and the physiological effects of the voltaic pile, NICHOL-
SON and CARLISLE, of England, discovered that its polar wires
had the property, in transmitting the current, of decomposing
water, and gathering its elements at opposite extremities; and soon
with improved forms of the apparatus its marvelous analytic power
was brought to bear on other liquids and solutions, until, through
the labors mainly of BERZELIUS and of DAVY, the great generalization of electro-positive and electro-negative substances was established, and with it the fruitful theory of the electro-chemical composition of compound bodies.

Greatest among the active investigators of this period was DAVY,
who, but a few years before an apothecary's apprentice, was now
seen, inspired by the enthusiasm of an ardent genius, applying the

new instrument of research to yet untried purposes of chemical
analysis. DAVY was a poet as well as a philosopher, and we can
imagine the glow of poetic enthusiasm which warmed his soul when
he saw for the first time the fiery globules of potassium gathering and exploding around the electric pole. And well might his
prescient thought exult, for from this and his immediately succeeding discoveries it became established that the fixed alkalies and the
earths, till then supposed to be elementary bodies, out of which the
solid crust of our globe is constituted, are nothing more than the
rust or cinders; that is, the oxides of metals and metalloidal bodies.

Passing from the years 1807–'08, when these splendid discoveries were made, we mark for several years no further brilliant
achievement in electrical science, but follow the ingenious labors of
distinguished experimenters in improving the efficiency of the
voltaic apparatus, multiplying its applications and giving a broader
basis to the laws of electro-chemistry.

In a little more than a decade after the era illustrated by DAVY's
experimental genius, the progress of our science was signalized
by another momentous event, the discovery or more properly re-
discovery by the Danish philosopher, OERSTED, of the directive
influence of the voltaic current on the magnetic needle, a fact which,
first noticed by ROMAGNOSI at the beginning of the century, * had
been practically overlooked, but which as discovered anew and
more fully investigated by OERSTED, gave him a celebrity such as
a life-long devotion to science has often failed to secure.

A relation between electricity and magnetism had long been
suspected, but as yet no demonstration of the nature of their connection had been attained. The electric pile of VOLTA and the
various forms of galvanic battery, exhibiting opposite electrical

* In the address as delivered, no reference was made to this anticipation of
OERSTED's discovery; and I am indebted for the correction of the generally
accepted history, to Mr. WILLIAM B. TAYLOR's able Historical Sketch, in the Smithsonian Report for 1873.—W. B. R.

polarities at their extremities, suggested a strong analogy to magnetic action, and led in many minds to the thought amounting almost to to a conviction that there existed an inherent connection between electricity and magnetism.

The attempts to discover this connection had been made with galvanic piles or batteries whose poles were not connected by conductors, under the expectation that these would show magnetical relations, although in such cases the electricity, accumulated at the extremities, was evidently stagnant. It was reserved for OERSTED first to bring into prominent view the fact that it was not while the electricity was thus at rest, but while it was flowing through the wire connecting the two poles, that it exhibited magnetic action, and that a wire thus carrying a current — while it had the power of affecting a magnetic needle, was in turn susceptible of being acted on by a magnet; and this was the initial step in the science of electro-magnetism.

The announcement of this discovery in 1820 at once brought into the field a host of experimenters, repeating and extending the observations of OERSTED, and by various methods of research multiplying the proofs of the magnetic relations of the voltaic currents. Soon ARAGO and DAVY discovered the magnetizing power of the voltaic conductor on iron filings, and the former found that when a soft iron wire was placed in a conducting helix it became a temporary magnet as long as the current was maintained. Now came forward to take part in these investigations one who was at the same time a distinguished mathematician and a great experimenter, a combination which is to be regarded as the consummation of power in the investigation and discovery of natural laws.

The French philosopher AMPÈRE, here referred to, made the momentous discovery that when two wires are conveying currents in the same direction they mutually attract, but that when these currents flow in opposite directions the conducting wires repel.

His quick imagination led him at once to what may be called the electrical construction of the magnet. To his thought each linear current is but a magnetic element, and every magnet is but a congeries of such currents revolving around its axis; and he said to himself, "I will construct a magnet with copper wires, and without the metal hitherto supposed to be essential to this result, for I will make the current revolve in a copper helix." He did so; suspended the conducting helix, and found, as he had expected, that its ends were attracted and repelled by the poles of the ordinary magnet, and that when free to move it pointed like the compass needle in obedience to the earth's directive power, and that in fact this copper wire had the distinctive properties of a magnet. AMPÈRE has been styled the NEWTON of electricity, and his electro-dynamic theory of the action of currents and of magnets has been thought worthy, so far as the logic of its demonstration is concerned, of a place near the Principia of NEWTON.

Electro-dynamic experiments were now rapidly multiplying and numerous ingenious forms of apparatus were contrived to illustrate the actions of currents on each other and of currents on magnets, a class of phenomena which, from their novelty at the time, as well as their intrinsic interest, some of my hearers will recall as having been among the most surprising and fascinating of lecture-room exhibitions.

It was at this stage of discovery that another scientific genius, FARADAY, who was destined to be the successor and perhaps more than the equal of his great instructor, DAVY, leaving the chemical labors in which he had already attained distinction, entered the field of electrical research. After aiding DAVY in 1820 in repeating and extending OERSTED'S experiments soon after they had been announced, he succeeded in producing, for the first time, the continuous rotation of a magnet around an electric conductor and the converse rotation of the conductor around the magnet, and a few years later entered upon that series of investigations which, continued for many years, gave to science, as embodied in his well-known "Researches in electricity," those varied and brilliant discoveries which have placed him in the first rank of the philosophers of modern times.

About the same period our countryman, Dr. ROBERT HARE, gave a new interest to the study of electric currents in another aspect, that of their heating energy, by his invention of the calorimotor and deflagrator, the early products of his untiring ingenuity, which in the laboratories of former years so dazzled us by their exhibition of transformed electric power.

Allusion has already been made to the observation of ARAGO in 1820, that an iron wire, surrounded by a helix conducting a voltaic current, became a temporary magnet. In the same year SCHWEIGGER, of Halle, conceived the idea of greatly augmenting the deviating effect of an electric current on a magnetic needle by causing it to traverse successive parallel closely adjacent coils of the conducting wire, in which the needle was suspended, and in this way constructed the well-known galvanometer; an instrument which, as improved by NOBILI, became indispensable in the measurement of current electricity, and which through the recent refined improvements given to it by Sir WILLIAM THOMSON, the first of living electricians, has been made one of the most perfect and delicate of all known means of measuring force.

At length, in 1825, an English electrician, STURGEON, who had done much in the contrivance of electro-dynamic apparatus, improved upon ARAGO's experiment by using an iron wire bent in horse-shoe form covered with non-conducting varnish, around which was wound in an open helix the conducting wire. As long as the voltaic current was allowed to pass through the conductor the inclosed iron wire was made magnetic with poles like those of a horse-shoe magnet. When the current ceased, the magnetic force disappeared. This was STURGEON's electro-magnet; and although its lifting-power was small — limited at the utmost to a few pounds — it had the merit of being in a practical sense the first electro-magnet.

After making many experiments with this instrument and with currents variously applied, Professor BARLOW, an English mathematician and engineer, announced as his conclusion that the current of electricity, under these circumstances, is so greatly retarded in its progress through the wire that in a short distance it is rendered incapable of accomplishing any decided mechanical effect. This discouraging result was made public in the year 1825, when in many quarters schemes began to be proposed for telegraphing through the medium of electric force, and it seems for a time to have satisfied the minds of practical and scientific men generally that an electro-magnetic telegraph was impossible.

During all this time America was comparatively silent. It is true that COKE had suggested a chemical telegraph, and HARE had made numerous improvements in galvanic apparatus, but as yet no representative of FRANKLIN had entered the field of electrical research. Soon, however, there appeared on the scene, first as a country schoolmaster and a student in the Albany Academy, then as a professor in this Academy, the man whose worth and scientific labors we are assembled to commemorate, and who, in virtue of his various discoveries in electrical science, may well be held entitled to the honor of such a representation.

Beginning his career of original experiment in 1827, JOSEPH HENRY early directed his thoughts to the improvement of electro-magnetic apparatus, and especially to the development of increased force in the soft-iron electro-magnet. He took up the rude instrument of STURGEON, experimented with it, studied the means by which its efficiency could be varied and augmented, and at length succeeded in so modifying its construction and its relation to the exciting current as to convert it into an instrument which, instead of being able to bear a few ounces, or at most a few pounds, was capable of sustaining a load of hundreds of pounds, and which by still later improvements, perfected soon after his removal to Princeton, exhibited, under the impulse of but a moderate battery power, the enormous sustaining force of more than three thousand pounds.

I can well remember the astonishment which was created by the announcement of this result and the delight of those who first witnessed it. As might well be imagined, this striking achievement at once drew the attention of the scientific world to the rising American electrician.

It was not that there was extraordinary merit simply in constructing an apparatus which would support one thousand pounds instead of ten, in making a colossal magnet, but the result claimed admiration because of the series of thoughtful experiments leading to it and to yet wider applications; experiments involving an investigation of the laws which regulated the relation between the bar of iron, the wire or wires which encircled it, the prolonged conductor, and the battery which furnished the power.

Availing himself of the principle already applied in SCHWEIGGER's galvanometer, HENRY succeeded in multiplying the effect of the current by causing it to revolve in an insulated wire closely wound about the iron core in coils of many thicknesses; and with this arrangement he compared the forces developed by currents derived from different galvanic elements and through different lengths of conducting wire, and he soon established the fact that such currents were not of necessity quickly spent, as had been maintained by BARLOW, but that, under proper conditions, they retained an available magnetizing force after having traversed wires of considerable length. He showed that for securing this persistence over great distances an intensity-battery was required, while for producing great magnetic power near to the source of the current a large surface with but few elements, that is, a quantity-battery, should be used; and that in the latter case the effect was greatly increased by using many separate short coils to inclose the magnet, each connected with the galvanic source, or in place of these a single thicker wire, forming thus what he termed a "quantity-magnet."

It was in this stage of his researches that, in 1831–'32, HENRY produced a machine moved by electro-magnetism, and exhibited in the Albany Academy the memorable experiment of transmitting signals by means of his electro-magnet through more than a mile of wire, and soon after pointed out the application of the principles shown to the transmission of intelligence to a distance. This was undeniably the first example of what was virtually an electro-magnetic telegraph, and furnished a scientific foundation for those multiplied inventions which in later years have made the electro-magnetic telegraph co-extensive with the civilized world.

We may not here consider the various claims of the ingenious inventors who in later years originated the numerous details of practical telegraphy. It was a period in which discovery and invention were, as it has been said, "in the air;" and it would be impossible to assign to any, even the most illustrious contributor to the result, his own precise share in the general progress.

Not pausing to make further applications of the discoveries referred to, so suggestive of great practical use, and not for a moment considering the profitable return which might be secured from them, HENRY, in the spirit of a true lover of science, continued his investigations in the same general field, and after his removal to Princeton made other and larger additions to the store of electrical knowledge. Here, repeating an earlier experiment, he made the important discovery of the reaction of the current upon itself, causing what is called the extra-current, and carried on the very original investigations which revealed the existence and the laws of induced currents of successive orders, which, for their novelty, ingenuity,

and conclusiveness in the development of an entirely new class of
phenomena, may, I think, be regarded as the most remarkable and
classical of his electrical researches.

From this time forward, until his active scientific career was
interrupted, and in a measure terminated, by his removal to Washington to assume the great responsibility of the Smithsonian trust,
HENRY continued his zealous investigations. Passing in succession
into new departments of physical inquiry, including questions in
atmospheric electricity, in heat and light, and in molecular physics,
and embracing theoretical generalizations on the origin of mechanical power and the nature of vital force, he never failed to enrich
with new facts and new suggestions every subject to which his
philosophical genius was directed. Indeed, it may well be said of
him in connection with science, as once it was said of a literary
genius whom the world admires: "*Nihil tetigit quod non ornavit.*"

Into the details of these researches and discoveries, so full of
interest to science and so replete with practical suggestions, I am
forbidden here to enter, and must leave them to other and abler
hands, and to a less popular occasion. Neither can I more than
passingly allude to those later labors of HENRY, by which he initiated a system of meteorological research on a uniform method and
of rational comprehensiveness, nor to the great improvement which
he introduced in our light-house illumination and our fog-signals,
or in connection with the last, to the admirable series of observations undertaken to elucidate the acoustic phenomena due to variations of atmospheric movement and density, observations in which,
as we all know, he was zealously engaged until but a few months
before the time when the veteran philosopher was compelled by
failing health to retire from the field of his beneficent activity.

On reviewing the long and fruitful career of Professor HENRY
we are impressed by his ingenuity and accuracy as an experimentalist
and by his clearness and breadth as a scientific thinker. Of the

former of these qualifications we have proof in the readiness with which he could devise means, at once simple and efficient, for his investigations, such as are seen in the construction of his first electro-magnetic machine, in the conversion of the electro-magnet into a means of signaling at a distance, in the thermal telescope by which he noted the heat reflected from clouds or distant objects on the land, in his device for measuring the velocity of projectiles, and in that by which he measured the tenacity of liquid films of differing curvature, anticipating PLATEAU's later and fuller researches, and in numerous other instances which we may not here recount.

Of his clearness and comprehensiveness in the discussion of scientific questions perhaps no better example can be cited than the remarkable paper on the "Origin of mechanical power and the nature of vital force," which, following at a very short interval the publications of GROVE, MAYER, and JOULE on the conservation of force, for the first time clearly expounded and illustrated the application of this the grandest of the generalizations of modern science to the organic world.

Ingenious, zealous, and patient in experiment, HENRY was most conscientious in reporting his results, allowing no preconceived theories to modify the record or to warp the conclusions to which it pointed. He loved scientific truth supremely, and the discovery of it was a source of unalloyed delight, for he had early been a greedy seeker of knowledge, and had learned, as Lord BACON has said, that "while in all other pleasures there is satiety, of knowledge there is no satiety, but satisfaction and appetite are perpetually interchangeable."

As in the case of most men who have attained eminence in science, HENRY used his imagination as a stimulus and even as a guide to his investigations; but while in the course of his work he could not but frame hypotheses, he treated them as but the scaffolding to aid in building the solid structure of physical truth, to be thrown to the ground as soon as the walls were completed.

Professor HENRY was strongly imbued with the spirit of inductive philosophy, and knew how, in searching for a true generalization, to carry out the process of successive exclusion, to try this and then the other experiment in order to discover which of his theories corresponded with the facts, believing, doubtless, with the wittiest of Frenchmen that a theory is like a mouse, which, after passing through nine holes, may be caught in the tenth.

Although accustomed to distinguish strongly between the merit of the discovery of a scientific principle and that of invention through which the principle was to be applied to the world's use, he well knew how inseparable are the two, and how greatly even inventions not directly inspired by science have quickened its march and extended the field of its activity. The large humanity which was a marked feature in his character led him to welcome heartily every instance of inventive application, as well when simply conducive to the welfare of society as when giving to science a new implement for investigation. Indeed, the genius of HENRY was eminently practical, if we extend this term to embrace the highest, widest, and most enduring forms of utility. Valuing highly a legitimate hypothesis, he had, I think, no relish for those flights of the imagination in which men of science sometimes indulge themselves amid regions of pure conjecture or of vague and indeterminate data, in the hope, by the spell of a profound mathematics, to convert shadowy suggestions into substantial truth.

Large and accurate as were his attainments in physical science, HENRY was too modest and too just to dogmatize on questions in regard to which opinions are divided. Whatever were his convictions in matters transcending scientific inquiry and proof, he did not allow them to be the standard by which other consciences were to be judged, and he felt, as I cannot but believe, that dogmatism, where there are grounds for doubt, in any province of thought, is injurious to the cause of truth and incompatible with that genuine philosophy which recognizes how small is the segment of our actual knowledge as compared to the infinite sphere of possible discovery.

In closing this imperfect notice of the labors and the character as a philosopher which have given to JOSEPH HENRY so high a place among the men of science of our day, and have won for him the crowning honor of this national memorial meeting, I am led to allude to the illustration which he has furnished of the peculiar genius and temperament of the American people. In his example we see that combination of the practical and the philosophical which we may claim as characteristic of our nation, and which refutes the charge, sometimes made, that, although fertile beyond other nations in invention, we do not rise to the higher level of scientific thought. Nor can I refrain, in this connection, from appropriating to our country the words in which MILTON so nobly characterized the capacities of the great nation of which, in his time, we were a part: "A nation not slow and dull, but of a quick, ingenious, and piercing spirit, acute to invent, subtle and sinewy to discourse, and not beneath the reach of any point the highest that human capacity can soar to."

ADDRESS

OF

HON. JAMES A. GARFIELD.

In the presence of these fathers of science who have honored this occasion with their wisdom and eloquence, I can do but little more than express my gratitude for the noble contribution they have made to this national expression of love and reverence. So completely have they covered the ground, so fully have they sketched the great life which we celebrate, that nothing is left but to linger a moment over the tributes they have offered and select here and there a special excellence to carry away as a lasting memorial.

No page of human history is so instructive and significant as the record of those early influences which develop the character and direct the lives of eminent men. To every man of great original power there comes, in early youth, a moment of sudden discovery — of self recognition — when his own nature is revealed to himself, when he catches, for the first time, a strain of that immortal song to which his own spirit answers, and which becomes thenceforth and forever the inspiration of his life —

"Like noble music unto noble words."

More than a hundred years ago, in Strasburg on the Rhine, in obedience to the commands of his father, a German lad was reluctantly studying the mysteries of the civil law, but feeding his spirit as best he could upon the formal and artificial poetry of his native land, when a page of WILLIAM SHAKESPEARE met his eye and changed the whole current of his life. Abandoning the law, he created and crowned with an immortal name the grandest epoch of German literature.

Recording his own experience, he says: "At the first touch of
SHAKESPEARE's genius I made the glad confession that something
inspiring hovered above me. - - - The first page of his that
I read made me his for life; and when I had finished a single play,
I stood like one born blind on whom a miraculous hand bestows
sight in a moment. I saw, I felt, in the most vivid manner that
my existence was infinitely expanded."

This Old World experience of GOETHE's was strikingly reproduced, though under different conditions and with different results,
in the early life of JOSEPH HENRY. You have just heard the
incident worthily recounted; but let us linger over it a moment.
An orphan boy of sixteen, of tough Scotch fibre, laboring for his
own support at the handicraft of the jeweler, unconscious of his
great powers, delighted with romance and the drama, dreaming of
a possible career on the stage, his attention was suddenly arrested
by a single page of an humble book of science which chanced to
fall into his hands. It was not the flash of a poetic vision which
aroused him. It was the voice of great Nature calling her child.
With quick recognition and glad reverence his spirit responded;
and from that moment to the end of his long and honored life,
JOSEPH HENRY was the devoted student of science, the faithful
interpreter of nature.

To those who knew his gentle spirit, it is not surprising that
ever afterward he kept the little volume near him and cherished it
as the source of his first inspiration. In the maturity of his fame,
he recorded on its fly-leaf his gratitude. Note his words: "This
book under Providence has exerted a remarkable influence on my
life. - - - It opened to me a new world of thought and
enjoyment, invested things before almost unnoticed with the highest
interest, fixed my mind on the study of nature, and caused me to
resolve at the time of reading it that I would devote my life to the
acquisition of knowledge."

We have heard from his venerable associates with what resolute perseverance he trained his mind and marshaled his powers for the higher realms of science. He was the first American, after FRANK-LIN, who made a series of successful original experiments in electricity and magnetism. He entered the mighty line of VOLTA, GALVANI, OERSTED, DAVY, and AMPÈRE, the great exploring philosophers of the world, and added to their work a final great discovery which made the electro-magnetic telegraph possible.*

---

* As a fuller statement of the steps by which the telegraph was achieved I append a passage from an address which I delivered at the Morse memorial meeting, in the Hall of the House of Representatives, April 16, 1872:

"The electro-magnetic telegraph is the embodiment, I might say the incarnation, of many centuries of thought, of many generations of effort to effect these natures one of her deepest mysteries. No one man, no one century could have achieved it. It is the child of the human race, 'the heir of all the ages.' How wonderful were the steps which led to its creation! The very name of this telegraphic instrument bears record of its history—'electric, magnetic.' The first, extinct from the bit of yellow amber whose qualities of attraction and repulsion were discovered by a Grecian philosopher twenty-four centuries ago; and the second, from Magnesia, the village of Asia Minor, where first was found the loadstone, whose touch turned the needle toward the North. These were the earliest forces in which the infinite, all-pervading force revealed itself to men. In the childhood of the race men stood dumb in the presence of its more terrific manifestations. When it gleamed in the purple aurora, or shot dusky-red from the clouds, it was the overflow of an angry God, before whom trembled quailed in helpless fear. When the electric light flamed blue in the spear-points of the Roman legions it was to them and their leaders a portent from the gods beckoning them to victory. When the phosphorescent light, which the sailors still call Saint Elmo's fire, hovered in the masts and spars of the Roman ship, it was Castor and Pollux, twin gods of the sea, guiding the mariner to port, or the beacon of an avenging God luring him to death.

"When we consider the standing forms in which this element presents itself, it is not surprising that so many centuries elapsed before men dared to confront and question its fitful mystery. And it was fitting that here, in this new, free world, the first answer came revealing to one FRANKLIN the great truth that the lightning of the sky and the electricity of the laboratory were one; that in the simple electric toy were embodied all the mysteries of the thunderstorm. Until near the beginning of the present century the only known method of producing electricity was by friction. But the discoveries of GALVANI in 1790, and of VOLTA in 1800, resulted in the production of electricity by the chemical action of acids upon metals, and gave to the world the galvanic battery and the voltaic pile, and the electric current. This was the first step in that path of modern discovery which led to the telegraph. But further discoveries were necessary to make the telegraph possible. The next great step was taken by OERSTED, the Swedish professor, who, in 1819–'20, made the discovery that the needle when placed near the galvanic battery was deflected at right angles with the electric current. In the four modest pages in which OERSTED announced this discovery to the world the science of electro-magnetism was found. As FRANKLIN had exhibited the relation between lightning and the electric fluid, so OERSTED exhibited the relation between magnetism and electricity. From 1820 to 1825 his discovery was further developed by DAVY and STURGEON, of England, and ARAGO and AMPÈRE, of France. They found that by sending a current of electricity through

It remained only for the inventor to construct an instrument and an alphabet. Professor HENRY refused to reap any pecuniary rewards from his great discovery, but gave freely to mankind what nature and science had given to him.

I observe that these venerable gentlemen who have spoken, express some regret that Professor HENRY left their higher circle to come down to us; and to some extent I share in their regret. Doubtless it was a great loss to science. I remember that AGASSIZ once said that he had made it the rule of his life to abandon any scientific investigation as soon as it became useful. I fancied I saw him and his brethren going beyond the region of perpetual frost, up among the wild elements of nature and the hidden mysteries of science, and when they had made a discovery and brought it down to the fire of commercial value, leaving it there, knowing that the world would make it useful and profitable, while they went back to resume their original search. I do not wonder that those men regretted the loss of such a comrade as JOSEPH HENRY.

But something is due to the millions of Americans outside the circle of science; and the Republic has the right to call on all her children for service. It was needful that the Government should have, here at its capital, a great, luminous-minded, pure-hearted man, to serve as its counselor and friend in matters of science.

a wire coiled around a piece of soft iron, the iron became a magnet while the current was passing, and ceased to be a magnet when the current was broken. This gave an intermittent power, a power to grapple and to let go at the will of the electrician. AMPÈRE suggested that a telegraph was possible by applying this power to a needle. In 1825, BARLOW, of England, made experiments to verify this suggestion of the telegraph, and pronounced it impracticable on the ground that the batteries then used would not send the fluid through even two hundred feet of wire without a sensible diminution of its force. In 1831, JOSEPH HENRY, now Secretary of the Smithsonian Institution, then a professor at Albany, New York, as the result of numerous experiments, discovered a method by which he produced a battery of such intensity as to overcome the difficulty spoken of by BARLOW in 1825. By means of this, his discovery, he magnetized soft iron at a great distance from the battery, pointed out the fact that a telegraph was possible, and actually rang a bell by means of the electro-magnet acting on a long wire. This was the last step in the series of great discoveries which preceded the invention of the telegraph."

Such an adviser was never more needed than at the date of Professor HENRY's arrival at the capital.

The distinguished scientific gentlemen who have addressed us so eloquently, have portrayed the difficulties which beset the Government in its attempt to determine how it should wisely and worthily execute the trust of SMITHSON. It was a perilous moment for the credit of America when that bequest was made. In his large catholicity of mind, SMITHSON did not trammel the bequest with conditions. In nine words he set forth its object—"for the increase and diffusion of knowledge among men." He asked and believed that America would interpret his wish aright and with the liberal wisdom of science.

A town meeting is not a good place to determine scientific truths. And the yeas and nays that are called from this desk from day to day are not the supreme test of science, as the country finds when we attempt to settle any scientific question, whether it relates to the polariscope or to finance.

For ten years Congress wrestled with those nine words of SMITHSON and could not handle them. Some political philosophers of that period held that we had no constitutional authority to accept the gift at all, and proposed to send it back to England. Every conceivable proposition was made. The colleges clutched at it; the libraries wanted it; the publication societies desired to scatter it. The fortunate settlement of the question was this: after ten years of wrangling, Congress was wise enough to acknowledge its own ignorance, and authorized a body of men to find some one who knew how to settle it. And these men were wise enough to choose your great comrade to undertake the task. Sacrificing his brilliant prospects as a discoverer, he undertook the difficult work. He drafted a paper, in which he offered an interpretation of the will of SMITHSON, mapped out a plan which would meet the demands of science, and submitted it to the suffrage of the republic of scientific scholars. After due deliberation it received the almost unanimous approval of the scientific world. With faith and sturdy perseverance, he adhered to the plan and steadily resisted all attempts to overthrow it.

In the thirty-two years during which he administered the great trust, he never swerved from his first purpose; and he succeeded at last in realizing the ideas with which he set out. But it has taken all that time to get rid of the incumbrances with which Congress had overloaded the Institution. In this work Professor HENRY taught the valuable lesson to all founders and supporters of colleges, that they should pay less for brick and mortar and more for brains. Under the first orders imposed upon him by Congress, he was required to expend $25,000 a year in purchasing books. By wise resistance he managed to lengthen out the period for that expenditure ten years; and a few years ago he had the satisfaction of seeing Congress remove from the Institution the heavy load by transferring the Smithsonian library to the Library of Congress. The fifty-eight thousand volumes and forty thousand pamphlets of rare scientific value which are now upon our shelves, have added greatly to the value of the national library; but their care and preservation would soon have absorbed the resources of the Smithsonian. When Congress shall have taken the other incumbrance, the national museum, off the hands of the Institution by making fit provision for the care of the great collection, they will have done still more to realize the ideas of Professor HENRY.

He has stood by our side in all these years, meeting every great question of science with that calm spirit which knew no haste and no rest. At the call of his Government he discovered new truths and mustered them into its service. The twelve hundred lighthouses that shine on our shores, the three thousand buoys along our rivers and coasts, testify to his faithfulness and efficiency.

When it became evident that we could no longer depend upon the

whale fisheries to supply our beacon-lights, he began to search for a
substitute for sperm oil; and after a thousand patient experiments
he made the discovery that of all the oils of the world, the common,
cheap lard oil of America, when heated to 250° Fahrenheit, became
the best illuminant. That discovery gave us at once an unfailing
supply, and for many years saved the Treasury a hundred thousand
dollars a year.

He had no such pride of discovery as to cling to his own methods
when a better could be found. He has recently tested the qualities
of petroleum as an illuminant, and recommended its use for the
smaller lights. In instances far too numerous to be recounted we
have long had this man as our counselor, our guide, and our friend.

During all the years of his sojourn among us, there has been one
spot in this city across which the shadow of partisan politics has
never fallen; and that was the ground of the Smithsonian Institution. We have seen in this city at least one great, high trust so
faithfully discharged for a third of a century that no breath of
suspicion has ever dimmed its record. The Board of Regents have
seen Professor HENRY's accounts all closed; and, after the most
rigid examination, the unanimous declaration is made that, to the
last cent, during the whole of that period his financial administration
was as faultless and complete as his discoveries in science. The
blessing of such an example in this city ought at least to do something to reconcile these men of science to the loss they suffered when
their friend was called to serve the Government at its Capital.

Remembering his great career as a man of science, as a man who
served his Government with singular ability and faithfulness, who
was loved and venerated by every circle, who blessed with the light
of his friendship the worthliest and the best, whose life added new
luster to the glory of the human race, we shall be most fortunate,
if ever in the future, we see his like again.

7

ADDRESS

OF

HON. SAMUEL S. COX.

We have found by recent and experience in this Hall that death is no respecter of persons. Neither is he a respecter of seasons. He may choose the merriest month for the saddest bereavement. In May last, when the sun was warm, the sky blue, the flowers in bloom, and the trees luxuriant in leaf, he entered yonder quaint structure secluded amid its greenery and bore away one of our rarest minds and purest men. By one fatal wrench of his skeleton hand a splendid career of eighty years was closed; in a twinkling the one hard problem of a long and studious life was solved; the wonder-world beyond had become a "discovered country" to JOSEPH HENRY. Its season, we trust, is perpetual May to him. Its new life removed from him, if not from his bereaved family and friends, the sting of death, and from the grave its victory.

The lightning, which had been evoked by him to transmit its instantaneous message to the remotest parts of the earth, sped on its quick errand to tell the learned of all lands that an intellectual magnate had been translated. The magnetic cord whose first duty, as arranged by him, was to send the tidings of a new star over land and under ocean to every seat of science, heralded to all that "God had unloosed his weary star," and that he was a lost luminary in the galaxy of intellect,

> Wail! for the glorious Pleiad fled!
> Wail! for the ne'er returning star!
> Whose mighty music ever led
> The spheres in their high heaven afar,

Associated with our Government through the Smithsonian Institution, and with the world through the amenities of science which it created, the loss of JOSEPH HENRY is not merely national; it is cosmopolitan, universal. It is fitting that the head of an institution which welcomes all countries and all worlds should have a tribute here worthy of such extended and shining fame.

In our federal way, we order condemned cannon to make bronzes for our soldiers. Our land is full of the effigies of military heroes. I have no criticism upon such a patriotic custom. Indeed, I see that the gallant soldier (General SHERMAN) is to follow me; and I am more than reluctant to suggest a word of dissent from such an honored observance. Our parks display also the forms of literary celebrities — SHAKESPEARE, GOETHE, SCOTT, and BURNS, and the grand bead-roll, favored of the muses, with only now and then a HUMBOLDT, and a dim memory of GOETHE as a devotee of science. The WASHINGTONS and TELLS, soldiers and patriots, arouse the enthusiasm of the masses of mankind. This too may be well; for the Princes of Science, like ARCHIMEDES, GALILEO, KEPLER, NEWTON, GIOIA, TORRICELLI, BOYLE, LEIBNITZ, LAPLACE, DAVY, HERSCHEL, ARAGO, LYELL, FARADAY, and HENRY, have their niche in a more exalted and enduring Pantheon.

BACON, the father of experimental science! What are divines, jurists, statesmen, soldiers, princes, to this great and audacious leader of human investigation for truth against mere speculation? NEWTON, of whom MACAULAY says that "in no other mind have the demonstrative faculty and the inductive faculty coexisted in such supreme excellence and perfect harmony?"—what are the mere temporary favorites of the mass of men compared with him? History gives its muse unbounded license to sing the glories of the NAPOLEONS of our world. They were indeed guiding intellects; they were wonderful for civic organization and still more wonderful in their genius for destruction. But to the thoughtful mind their heroism is not comparable with that of humble EDMUND HALLEY, who investigated the properties of the atmosphere, the tides, magnetism, and the comets, and who periled his life in seeking the distant Island of Saint Helena, there to map out in sublime isolation the southern constellations. He was no prisoner, no exile, no modern defiant Prometheus chained to a rock. He was the peaceful observer and serene conqueror of worlds which ALEXANDER never sighed to conquer and which NAPOLEON never looked upon save in selfish moroseness from that historic rock.

Lord BACON has been referred to most pertinently by the learned gentleman, Professor ROGERS. May I make another reference to the father of induction? He gave us written wisdom beyond that of the ancients. He has said that — " Whereas founders of States, law-givers, extirpers of tyrants, fathers of the people were honored but with titles of worthies or demi-gods — inventors were ever consecrated with the gods themselves."

These are golden words. They properly interpret a philosophic mind. In BACON'S meaning of the word inventor, he comprehended those who both discover and apply, originate and use, the secrets of nature for the increase and diffusion of knowledge and the benefaction of mankind.

States come and go; a king to-day is a subject to-morrow; the discrowned suzerain of the Orient last year, this year is the vassal of a newly crowned empress. Lawgivers who pursue their tortuous and tangled paths, what can they do among the atoms or the spaces? They appropriate money, fix taxes, raise armies, declare war; but to change one little chemical relation, how powerless! Not all the statutes ever inscribed on parchment can stop soft iron from becoming a magnet by a certain process of galvanic polarization; yet he who discovered so simple a relation with such magnificent results would have been deified by the Greeks along with that god of beauty who drove the chariot of the sun or that god of strength who colonized men, conquered nature, and achieved civilization along the shores of the classic azure sea.

In this age of physical progress and grandeur, when experiments show that the "constant elements" are coquetting with us by their inconstancy; when the tough old gases are being tortured, liquefied, and solidified; when oxygen no longer holds out and hydrogen begins to succumb; when microphones, telephones, phonographs, and electric lights and Menlo Park wizards, astound us by their miracles; when cables are duplexed and spectroscopes are bringing down almost to our crucibles those remote stars fixed and "pinnacled dim in the intense inane;" when LOCKYER is said to be proving by the bands of the spectrum the unity of nature, by showing that all the elements are in some modification, our familiar hydrogen; when the many are made one, or all elements are unified, it is no light honor to be the hero or even one of the heroes of such an age,—an age not merely of iron and steam and gold, but emphatically the age of light and lightning!

What ARCHIMEDES was to the lever, NEWTON to gravitation, the HERSCHELS to astronomy, DAVY to the mining lamp, TORICELLI to the barometer, GIOIA to the compass, RUMFORD to heat, FARADAY to electro-chemical affinity, BOYLE to pneumatics, GUTENBERG to printing, WATT to steam, FRAUNHOFER to the spectrum, DRAPER to photography, and what LOCKYER is becoming to spectroscopic analysis, that was HENRY to electro-magnetic force. No quest for the holy grail was ever made with more chivalric, vigilant, and reverent pursuit than he made for the subtile and secret forces of the magnet.

Yet this man moved in our midst for thirty years, little known to the throng who visit and vanish here with our political vicissitudes. With them he had little or no fame. He pursued no devious path to fleeting honors. But there was nothing wanting to give him present delectation and lasting renown. His old-time courtesy, his charming simplicity, his loving domestic relations, his singleness of purpose, his freedom from sordid, jealous, harsh, and bitter qualities, his chaste, subdued, and genial humor, his pure, poetic, and aesthetic susceptibility, his benignant and dignified manner, his delight in acquiring, what he imparted with so much suavity, and his earnest and unobtrusive pursuit of lofty ends through noble means, gave him felicity, ay, even genuine fame, in this life.

Called to administer the Smithsonian trust, his conscientious devotion gave it from the first the direction designed by the testator. His aim was to originate and disseminate. He scattered the seed broadcast, not through whim or favoritism, but on a matured plan. His place required a love of science, along with a talent for organization. He brought these to bear upon the origination of knowledge, and by his scientific sympathy and ready recognition of others of his guild he commanded honest homage and became the director, helper, and umpire in scientific disputation. Did the War Department require his aid in meteorology? He gave the plan of weather signals. Did the Census Bureau ask his help? He planned the remarkable atlas as to rain-falls and temperature. Did the Coast Survey require scientific suggestion, or the Centennial Commissioners his judgment, or the new library and the "School of Art" a friend and adviser, or the Light-House Board laws of sound for fogs, and cheaper and better illumination? He freely gave what was gladly welcomed. His Institution gave AGASSIZ opportunity to study fishes, BAIRD birds, and all students encouragement to investigate our American archaeology and ethnology, as well as our fauna and flora.

The fund which was under his control was scrupulously used. At our annual meetings as regents I cannot fail to recall the blackboard where his figure was chalked with all the exactness of an old accountant and explained with all the nervous solicitude of a schoolboy doing his first sum.

Never was trustee so free from suspicion of personal enrichment. He died as he had lived, with little incumbrance from the dross of the world. Those learned men who have spoken will recall some of his experiments which showed how the metals could penetrate each other; he cared more for this than to fill his own coffers with them, however precious.* He was content with the golden key to the enchanted chambers of science. In all his discoveries and with a name whose emphasis was worth millions in speculation, there was not in his heart a commercial inclination. He was too proud to patent his thoughts. They were the property of mankind, made sacred by the seal of Omniscience! He had his own exceeding great reward in their meditation and diffusion. His modest salary, limited by his own choice, supplied his modest wants; and his services in the Light-House Board from first to last were gratuitously rendered. He planted the vineyard and others had the fruit and drank the wine thereof. MORSE, GRAHAM, BELL, EDISON, and others gave to the mysteries which he unshadowed, definite, practical, paying results; but, to use his own words, he never thus compromised his independence. He was hungry and thirsty for knowledge, but not for ease and luxury. To prostitute his knowledge for gain was incxpressible profanation. Not all the bonanzas from the Sierras could tempt him from his rectitude. Without money and without price, he gave what he acquired. To make merchandise in his grand temple and out of his sacred calling was to touch with sacrilegious hands the ark of the covenant he had made as a high priest of nature. His good name was better than

* Another investigation had its origin in the accidental observation of the following fact: A quantity of mercury had been left undisturbed in a shallow saucer with one end of a piece of lead wire, about the diameter of a goose-quill, and six inches long plunged into it, the other end resting on the shelf. In this condition it was found after a few days that the mercury had passed through the solid lead, as if it were a siphon, and was lying on the shelf still in a liquid condition. The saucer contained a series of minute crystals of an amalgam of lead and mercury.—*Letter of Professor Henry, concerning researches at Princeton, December 4, 1876.*

riches, and all money which did not contribute to his lofty aims,
like the money of the fairy, was as ashes in his sight.

With this idea of his trust need we wonder at his measureless
contempt for the mercenaries and jobbers who filled this city and
even dishonored the halls of legislation? His life was a living
protest against this age of thrift and greed. He drew his rules of
duty not from the silly codes of ostentatious modern society. The
wisdom and humanity, embodied in that ancient code of freedom
which the mailed barons and the great primate of England coerced
from an unwilling king, he applied to his function as a finder and
teacher of truth: "We will sell to no man; we will not deny or
delay to any man right or justice!" JOSEPH HENRY had, as his
organic law from the Magna Charta engraved on the tablet of his
being, this affirmation: "*I will sell to no man, nor will I deny or
delay to any man the precious knowledge drawn under the providence
of God from the arcana of nature.*"

But it is not by his personal virtues or official trustworthiness
that he will be best remembered; not even by his varied accomplishments in the sciences, nor because he was a successful specialist
in many fields. Yet how multiplied and diverse were his gifts and
services? Did Japan try the experiment of progress, or KANE and
HAYES struggle to reach the North Pole and its open sea for
discovery — his sympathy was cordial and ready. Was it as an
engineer, geologist, mechanician, ethnologist, meteorologist, or archæ-
ologist, he was equally at home in each and all. Was it in the
practical application of science? As master of acoustics, he applied
his researches to buildings for human comfort, and to fog-signals
for the saving of values and life. Was it in optics? The greatest
star and the least atom were in harmony before his telescope and
microscope. Would Government know projectiles to use in war;
would the farmer know how his potatoes and wheat grew, or whence
the egg, and how it matured out of the elements into life — would

be know when to sow and when to harvest; would the mariner
have signals of danger and the merchant, warrior, and diplomat
messages as fleet as thought; the knowledge of this philosophic
mind rallied to its work, with a zeal which never flagged, and a
practical success beyond all expectations and praise. And thus in
various branches of physics he was the companion of HARE, SILLI-
MAN, DRAPER, TORREY, AGASSIZ, GUYOT, GRAY, PEIRCE,
BACHE, and BAIRD; the student of NEWTON, CUVIER, ARAGO,
WOLLASTON, and others of perpetual fame; and the correspondent
of FARADAY, TYNDALL, PROCTOR, and others of another hemisphere who are engaged in active, daily, arduous duty to science.

In a treatise which he wrote in December, 1876, concerning his
researches while at Princeton, he gives a most interesting account of
his contribution with reference to the origin of mechanical power
and the nature of vital force. How plainly he defined and how
richly he colored this recondite subject! He takes the crust of the
earth in a state of equilibrium and describes the substances which
constitute that crust, such as acids and bases. He pursues them
into a state of permanent combination, inert and changeless. True,
he finds what he calls an infinite thin pellicle of vegetable and
animal matter on the surface—men and mollusks, Caucasians, con-
gressmen, and coniferæ, elephants, and forests; but all the changes
on that surface he refers to a beautiful law of light radiating from
celestial space! How comprehensively he generalizes all the prime
movers which produce molecular changes in matter!

These he refers to two classes: the first, that of water, tide, and
wind power; the second, steam and other powers developed by
combustion, and animal power. Gravity, cohesion, electricity, and
chemical attraction, while they tend to produce a state of equilibrium
or repose on our planet, are only secondary agents in producing
mechanical effects. Must not the water have its level on the surface
of the ocean? In seeking it, is it not a force for the welfare of

man? Yes; but its primary cause of motion is the force which
elevated it in vapor under the radiance of the sunbeam.   Combustion, too, is but the passage from an unstable into a stable combination of the carbon and hydrogen of the fuel, with oxygen of the
atmosphere. These he resolves into the force which causes the
separation of these elements from their previous combination in the
state of carbonic acid, to the radiant heat of the sunbeam!   What
is the mechanical power exerted by animals?   It is but the passage
of organized matter taken into the stomach, from an unstable to a
stable equilibrium.   It is the combustion of food.   Animal power,
like the combustion of fuel, is potential again in the sunbeam!
Arriving thus at the very threshold of the mystery of vitality, he
asks: What is its office?   Only that of the engineer who directs the
power of the engine.

But these exploits and associations, inventives and accomplishments, do not furnish the substantial pediment of HENRY's fame.
Did he spend his vacation as Princeton professor in blowing soap-bubbles for a fortnight?   It was not the bubble reputation which he
sought.   He was seeking something less fragile and prismatic; he
was then investigating the law of liquid films and molecular energy.
What is he doing with the thermal telescope, so exquisitely constructed, referred to this evening by Professor ROGERS, with such
loving and delicate analysis, and so recently used in our country
under the auspices of EDISON?   Finding out not merely that the
moon has no heat, but measuring the heat of some animate object
in a distant field.   He is making the type of a mechanism beyond
all expression refined.

In all these branches he was a central light.   EDMUND SPENSER
has been called the poets' poet.   JOSEPH HENRY may be called the
savant of the physicists.   He loved to show what science was in its
essence, lifting in living harmony all speculations and experiments
into a higher plane; Scientia scientiarum!   For half a century he

never ceased to investigate the uses and the correlation of forces, and the modification and conservation of energy. Here his faith was paramount to his knowledge. Whether the energy possessed by any set of bodies were potential, stored up and unseen, or whether it were visibly performing its work; yet in all its phases be believed it never altered. Wherever it might go, and howsoever it might elude human vigilance, it was not lost. It was conserved. It could not but by "annihilation die," and God permitted no annihilation of his forces. These studies led him to the grand discovery by which he will be ever remembered.

Above all, he was an electrician. COLUMBUS had no better title to the discovery of the new world than HENRY has to the discovery of the principle of the magnetic telegraph. Make a catalogue of his score and more of general and special services in science; digest his thirty years of Smithsonian reports, and at last his simple magnet — the horseshoe — is the emblem and evidence of his power over the wizardry of nature in her most marvelous manifestations.

His experiences from youth fitted him for his work. His Scotch Presbyterianism did not unfit him for a combat with the diablerie of the storm. His engineering from the Hudson to Erie strengthened him for the *labor lime* of closet and laboratory. His experience as a jeweler-journeyman gave him a knowledge of mechanism and tools not to be despised in experiment and in an age which CARLYLE sings as that of "Tools and the man." His profession of mathematics gave precision to his thoughts and calculations. Only one anomaly appears in his early days, before the magnetic current attracted him by its spell. He loved fiction, poetry, and play-acting. Like AMPÈRE and other scientists, he, too, had his romantic mood and his tender age. Perhaps this tendency quickened his imagination and gave hope and success to his experiments by its *a priori* allurements. Why should it not? Hypothesis may be delusive; so was alchemy, but it was the pro-

genitor of chemistry. Was not astrology a theory, a poem, a dream?
Yet it led up a ladder of stars to the sublimest of sciences. It was
said by one of my predecessors, (the Hon. Mr. WITHERS,) who
spoke this evening, that Professor HENRY was not a genius. In
the sense of a poetaster of a small coterie and of little fancy, he
was no genius. It was said his illumination came slowly and
through labor. Ah! so it did, perhaps, until he found the volume
that awoke and started his peculiar tendency and talent. He had
genius; but he had the masterly genius to curb and control it, to
direct and glorify it.

It has been said that at one time he was enamored of the drama
and was almost persuaded to make it his permanent occupation.
He had a friendship for Damon, and a morbid desire after the melancholy Dane. But he was disenchanted of this illusory ambition by
friends who knew his sedate and studious mind, to which an
academic course and the little volume on physics, which provoked
his curiosity, gave a useful and permanent bent. Then came, all
roseate and radiant, the blossom of that magnificent fruitage which
was the promise of a life rounded and full of cautious experiments
and philosophic deduction.

What of fancy he had, he restrained by patience in details and
thoroughness in work. Glittering generalization he avoided, as he
did controversy. His plan of education for others was that which
he applied to himself. He began with the concrete. If indeed
LOCKYER has found Nature's inner secret, it is by his two thousand
photographs and one hundred thousand observations. If DRAPER
successfully controverts, it will be done by like patience and labor
in details. If HENRY succeeded in his grand inquisition, it was
by similar detailed labors. While measuring and weighing the
forces of nature he cautiously deduced his theory. He gathered
the efforts of others—OERSTED, ARAGO, DAVY, and STURGEON—
in his favorite domain of electro-magnetism, and made a sheaf

which stood above them all. He forged the viewless vinculum in the chain of causes, which bound the universe of matter and mind in intelligent unity and linked the soul close to the great white throne!

Yet he was in his most special sphere a pioneer who blazed his way through the forest. He was more than the Baptist of a new dispensation of science. He was both herald and hero of our age of electro-magnetic wonders.

In speaking of Professor MORSE in 1872 in this Hall, I undertook to distinguish between those who found principles and those who adapt them to practical ends. I said: "Your NEWTONS and LAPLACES in the celestial mechanism, and your ARAGOS, AMPÈRES, and HENRYS in electro-magnetism, are not the temporary but the eternal heroes; but the lower intellect carries off the chaplet and sometimes the lucre." I then gave a history of the electric magnet from its beginning down to Professor HENRY's discovery; and I asserted what I was proud to say during his life, and what all now confess — that MORSE was but the inventor of a machine, HENRY the philosophic discoverer of the principle! Others had discovered the relations between magnetism and electricity; and others had made divers limited applications of the magnet, but the inventor of only one form of application carried off the reward.

It may seem to some a little thing to ring a bell at one end of a mile-wire by a current incited at the other end. It may seem to some a little thing to discover the induction of currents, as HENRY did; or to call in a relay magnet at a distance to help the halting power; or to produce the spark by means of purely magnetic induction. It seemed doubtless to many a foolish thing to talk to members of his family across the Princeton campus by an electric wire, or by a pole from basement to attic in the college have his negro boy play a real fiddle in the cellar whose tune was repeated in a mock fiddle in the garret. But these experiments were the gradations to a higher plane, where the genius of his science was consummate.

Before he began his researches something was known of the electro-magnet. But it was as feeble in its energy as the child who toyed with it. It was little besides soft iron. HENRY energized it so as to make its results stupendous and far-reaching. Instead of the insulated bar surrounded by an uninsulated coil, he insulated the wire. He employed many coils and begot the ton-lifting magnet; and lo! there follows in time the telegraph and telephone. This is accomplished simply by the arrangement of the acid and zinc in one way, in his way. He adds to the cells of the battery; and there is literally no limit in distance for the effect. When he found that the power of the battery must be as the length of the conductor, he so intensifies the iron at such a distance that it gives enchantment to this modern Merlin's magic wand of wire. It was not mere by-play when he made a mechanical motor out of his big magnet, nor in overcoming resistance hitherto insurmountable, for distance is resistance. It was not a sportive thing to lift a ton by his magnet; nor was it an inconsequential freak when he severed a current and thus dropped heavy weights at a distance. Such experiments made the lightning his familiar, his demon, his servitor. He lured it into his lecture-room from out of its clouded home in the thunder-storm. He tamed it so that he could bridle, mount, ride, curb, and spur it at will. Thus he planted the germ of a system which now numbers 492,913 miles of intelligent wire, and traverses all climates and dips under all seas.

He stood upon his vantage-ground not only to signal the world by lightning, but to measure time, calculate longitudes, follow the flight of the cannon-ball, and record the stellar motions and transits. It is a remarkable fact that only one improvement in the magnetic system of telegraph has been made since Professor HENRY gave it to us. It now transmits more than one message at a time. But when Professor HENRY made it phonetic, it so remained. The alphabetic symbols are obsolete. The distant magnet when excited makes its dots and clicks its audible language, just as HENRY designed. Blot out MORSE and his machine, and Professor HENRY'S instrument, the telegraph, would go on. Like STEPHENSON'S multi-tubular boiler, it remains amid all change; for it is perfect because it has a principle. Discard Professor HENRY'S plan, and no message is possible with sound. All the signals, alarms, and devices for distant intelligence have their fountain in Professor HENRY'S brain. Given his brain, and you have MORSE, BELL, EDISON, and the entire circle of electric inventors.

What a grand occasion was that at the Centennial, when Sir WILLIAM THOMPSON and Professor HENRY met about the telephone! What fruition of hope! How jocund the exuberant heart leaped up to see fresh evidences of the truth of his early experiments under the rigid laws of science!

These laws however never shadowed his devotion to the beautiful, good, and true. His modest methods of research, while they extended his knowledge and enlarged his reason, never disturbed his faith. While like the magnetic needle it ever pointed in one direction, it was never tremulous with skepticism. He who knew so much of earth, and believed so much of Heaven, had a faith which was larger than his reason. When he said to his students: "We explain a fact, when we refer it to a law"—did he stop there? He bowed reverently, as he added—"When we explain a law, we refer it to the will of God." He never allowed sense to obscure spirit or secondary causes to be primal! He spoke no spell and taught no creed for evil or chance. He had the eye of reason to guide his radiant path and the ear of faith to inspire and exalt his reason. The impetuosity of the one was tempered by the docility of the other. The dilettante, the mystic, the pantheist, and the transcendentalist were to him less than flippancy and vanity; for he knew the limits of all human philosophy, physical, mental, and ethical, and never leaped the flaming bounds to raise issues on insoluble problems or dispute the divine mission of Him who spake as never man spake. "That which we know is little, but that which we know not, is immense," exclaimed LAPLACE; and the humility of Professor HENRY found in his highest aspiration reason for the lowliest modesty. He took shelter in the healing balm of evening from the dazzling radiance of speculation, and in its sweet and inviting undertones found whisperings of infinite love.

During his long life and its closing hours he clung to the Rock of Ages as the foundation of all his knowledge and the source of all his comfort. For him there was no gauge of prayer; for prayer, as he said, was above and beyond science. There was for him no greater light to shine on the daily path of life than that Sun of Righteousness whose reflection was but the faint illumination in our finite mind.

We have written testimony but a few weeks before his death to his exalted faith in our religion. Amidst a universe of change, where nothing remained the same from one moment to another, and where each moment of recorded time had its separate history, and while a universe of wonders is presented to us in our rapid flight through space, he held to the steadfast truth that after all our attempts to grapple with the problem of the universe, the simplest conception which expands and connects the phenomena of nature is that of the existence of one spiritual Being, infinite in wisdom, in power, and all divine perfections, which exists always and everywhere, which has created us with intellectual faculties in some degree to comprehend his operations as they are developed in nature. This was his divine creed of creeds! It was reconciled with science. He believed that this Infinite Being was unchangeable and that therefore his operations were in accordance with

H

the uniform laws. Finding everywhere evidences of intellectual
arrangements as he found them in the operations of man, he inferred
that these two classes of phenomena were the results of similar
intelligence. He found within himself ideas of right and wrong,
and deduced and believed that they formed the basis of our ideas
of the moral universe. In other words, he believed in a Divine
Being as the director and governor of all, and lived as he died,
hoping and praying for his infinite mercy.

Aloof from the lights and shadows of hope and fear, what unimagined and "wondrous glory beyond all glory ever seen" is his
to-day! Flowers and fishes, ruins and rivers, skeletons and scoriæ,
all the forms of things and forces of nature; the motions of wind,
tide, and water; the elasticity of steam and the explosions of
electricity, which were here in unrest, seeking immobility by laws
of their own—all these mobile elements, which he demonstrated
were seeking repose even in slag or cinders and seeking it by celestial motions and forces—these are all one to him now! The correlation of forces and the conservation of energy are solved. The
principle of chemistry and vitality, of the moving atom and the
immortal mind, no longer vex him with their mystery. His soul,
which was never tried on earth by the crucible, and his religion,
which was never limited to the laboratory—whose relict radiance
it is ours to recall—has that rest which he observed to be the final
law of all animate nature here.

He believed with OERSTED that the practice of science was
religious worship; and like that Danish physicist—like FARADAY
and BOYLE—"sweetness and light were blended in his pure
nature." With unblemished eye, like the eagle, his scientific ken
gazed into the sun itself for its revelation; and yet he nestled,
dove-like, amidst his human domestic affections. His processes of
thought were chastened by his Christ-like life and heavenly faith;
and he has his reward in eternal bliss.

When the first telegraph message went from this capital on the 24th of May, 1844, "What hath God wrought," it but echoed the thought of this reverent thinker, who had discovered its mission, and who thus recognized the infinite intelligence whose processes were beyond human ken. This belief chastened his intellectual dignity, and while it gave him added courage to explore the secrets of time and space, made his science not that of the carping critic, but of the loving handmaiden of divinity.

If "we are of a nobler substance than the stars;" if "we have faculties while they have none," it is impossible, in thinking of JOSEPH HENRY and his life here, to unduly magnify that intellectual orb which, when it left our limited horizon, arose upon another world to glorify anew the God of all the graces and the fountain of all the forces!

ADDRESS

OF

GENERAL WILLIAM T. SHERMAN.

From the beginning the living have paid homage to the virtues of the dead; for immortality is the dream of man. From Agra to Washington scarce a city, town, or village but contains some monument designed to perpetuate the memory of one who has passed from earth. Mountains have been excavated; pyramids built; temples have been erected, and granite, marble, and bronze shaped into every conceivable form, to give expression to honor, respect, affection, and love for some dead hero, warrior, statesman, or philosopher. These earthly tributes can be of no service to the dead, but they form lasting records of deeds held honorable among men; are strong incentives to noble acts in the present, and mark a steady progress toward that better condition which is the ultimate destiny of the human race.

We are not assembled to-night to shape in marble, or granite, or bronze, the human form of our countryman and friend, Professor Joseph Henry, but in order that those who knew him best may, by simple tributes of thought and feeling, bear public testimony to the merits of one who in our day stood forth a most resplendent type of moral and intellectual manhood, and who with little thought of self rendered eminent service in the cause of mankind. He needs no monument: for wherever man goes, or human thought travels, the poles and continuous wires will remind him that to Professor Henry of all men we are most indebted for the inestimable blessings of the telegraph.

JOSEPH HENRY was pre-eminently a philosopher, but none the less a hero. His conquest was not over cities razed, homes desolated, or the forms of men crushed and lacerated, but over the obstacles of nature, in mastering her laws and harnessing them to the uses of his fellow-men. No widows or orphans are left to mourn over his victories, but millions who have reason to rejoice in the increased knowledge and stimulated industry which followed in the wake of his intellectual triumphs. By these all men are brought nearer to each other, and the mysterious wires which now connect all parts of the habitable earth have done more to harmonize the prejudices and passions of man than the conquests of XERXES, ALEXANDER, and NAPOLEON. No one knew better than Professor HENRY that all of nature's laws had not yet been revealed, and that there remained an infinite field for further exploration and study.

It was a scientific Englishman, a skillful analytical chemist of London, who conceived the thought and provided the means whereby Professor HENRY was enabled to accomplish so much further good. Arts may have been lost or forgotten, because no longer needed, and the world's libraries and universities already possessed in abundance the vast accumulations of knowledge which had for ages been garnered and stored away in these valuable repositories of learning, yet nature remained so bountiful that there could be no danger that her fountains would become exhausted, and Mr. SMITHSON provided for an institution which accepts all the past, and provides only for the future. He endowed munificently the Institution (which bears his name here in Washington) for collecting new knowledge, and for distributing it to all parts of the earth. Great was the conception, generous the endowment, and fortunate that the execution fell to the lot of Professor HENRY! Though he loved his country as he loved his family, still, in the matter of science he knew no bounds. The heavens above and the earth beneath were his studio, and his thoughts and his feelings were as boundless as the orbit of the most distant star. Whatever the mind of man could compass — yea, whatever the most oriental imagination could fancy — were to him as precious as the germination of a seed or the blooming of a flower in his own door-yard. The student in Australia or the Fiji Islands knew that any inquiry of him on scientific subjects would receive the same patient, kindly notice as if it came from the most learned professor of Berlin or Stockholm.

In like manner, how patient was he with the young inquirer after truth, and still more with that large class of mechanics who, in their hours of leisure, were working on some long-exploded theory or error. He did not upbraid or ridicule honest labor or study, but with simple, kindly language would explain to the comprehension of the most unlearned the immutable laws of nature, and guide his mind and steps back to the right path which would lead him to perfect success.

Professor HENRY always seemed to me to take especial pleasure in every development of science which added to the beautiful in life, or which contributed to the general happiness of mankind. Though great progress had been made in his day, he had an absolute faith that more remained to reward the toil and labor of other students long after he had passed from earth.

For this reason the memory of his life and fame should be treasured by all as an example to the youth of our land, to show that honor and fame may be earned in the school of philosophy as well as in the more tempting and active scenes of public life; and therefore I rejoice that this occasion has been honored by the presence of so marked and distinguished an audience in this the Hall of Representatives of the Capitol of our nation.

Many students, who at this moment are hard at work on their studies for the advantage of mankind, will feel themselves personally encouraged and honored by the tokens of respect and affection thus paid their prototype, Professor HENRY; and their stimulated labors in the cause of that science he loved so well will erect to him a monument more lasting than of brass or marble.

PRAYER

BY

REV. BYRON SUNDERLAND, D. D.

Our Father and our God, Thou who dwellest in supernal light, and yet with him who is of an humble and contrite heart — Thou who hast been so often dishonored in the anarchic thoughts of men and yet dost bear the same with ineffable patience, behold us! Fain would we with all our hearts bow before Thee in wonder and adoration.

We give Thee hearty thanks for that creation when the morning stars sang together and for that redemption heralded by a multitude of the heavenly hosts — "Glory to God in the Highest and on earth peace, good-will to men!"

We thank Thee for the mighty train of human generations. We thank Thee for the capacities of the human race opening out toward the future for evermore. We thank Thee for the great nations that have run their course and for the great nations that are still enacting their parts in this wondrous field of time. We thank Thee for the vigor of intelligence and the grandeur of enterprise that have discovered so many great things for man. We thank Thee for the many toilers on every side who are unravelling the secrets of nature and building up a possibility for the still more noble triumphs of the immortal soul.

And we thank Thee for him whose memory, so fragrant, has been made to bloom so freshly in this winter night. God be praised for the name of him in whom knowledge and faith blended their glorious light. God be praised for the evolution and exaltation to which a higher than material philosophy will surely sum-

mon all the ignorant and erring families of men.   By the brink
of the grave, over the end of all that perishes on earth, we read,
O God, our Father, that mighty apothegm, " The things that are
seen are temporal, the things that are not seen are eternal."

Be very nigh to the hearts that knew him best, and bless them
with the blessing he in life invoked.   Be very nigh to our rulers
and our chiefs, and to all our people in the state and in the church
and to all those in our schools and seminaries and laboratories, and
in our Congresses and Legislatures who are molding the thoughts
of the nations and the civilization of our times.   Grant free scope
to the awakened faculties of men.   Protect the mighty march of
the coming millions, and crown their toil with an unfading crown,
through Jesus Christ.   Amen.

PART III.

MEMORIAL PROCEEDINGS OF SOCIETIES.

PROCEEDINGS

OF THE

PHILOSOPHICAL SOCIETY OF WASHINGTON.

SPECIAL MEETING.   MAY 14, 1878.

Vice-President HILGARD in some preliminary remarks on the death of Professor JOSEPH HENRY, President of the Society, stated that he had called a special meeting of the members, for the purpose of taking some appropriate action on this solemn and mournful occasion.

The Secretary read a communication from Chief-Justice M. R. WAITE, Chancellor of the Smithsonian Institution, announcing the death of Professor JOSEPH HENRY, the Secretary and Director of the Institution, in this city, on Monday, May 13, at ten minutes past noon, and inviting the Philosophical Society of Washington to attend his funeral on Thursday next, May 16, at half-past four o'clock P. M.

On motion, a committee of three (Messrs. WELLING, W. B. TAYLOR, and GILL) was appointed to prepare suitable resolutions.

Remarks on the character and labors of the deceased were made by Messrs. HILGARD, JOHNSON, TONER, ALVORD, ABBE, MASON, PARKER, GALLAUDET, and GEORGE TAYLOR.

The special committee reported the following resolutions, which were unanimously adopted:

Resolved, That in the death of Professor JOSEPH HENRY the Philosophical Society of Washington is called to deplore the loss of its venerable and beloved President, who from its first institution, and subsequently from year to year, has been unanimously chosen to the position he filled among us, in deference not only to the exalted fame which made him the chief ornament of our association, but in grateful tribute as well to the varied philosophical learning, the calm even-balanced judgment, and the serene wisdom which so admirably qualified him to be the moderator of opinions in a body composed of zealous and independent workers in nearly every department of scientific research.

Resolved, That while we are called to sit in the shadow of a great bereavement, which naturally casts its deepest gloom on those who, like ourselves, were daily admitted to the privilege of his personal friendship and to the precious opportunities afforded by his sagacious and logical suggestions and wide erudition, as well as by his ready co-operation in every enterprise which had for its object the extension of knowledge or the promotion of human welfare, we at the same time feel that we should be culpably insensible to the surviving radiance of the bright example he has set us, if even here, in the presence of his unfilled grave, we did not testify and record our solemn thanksgiving for the length of days accorded to our revered friend and illustrious exemplar, permitted as he was to extend his useful life beyond the period usually allotted to man, and not only filling that life with abundant labors which have reflected the highest honor on science, but also adorning it with the moral virtues and Christian graces which made him so lovely for the beauty and simplicity of his nature as he was remarkable for the strength and dignity of his high and noble character.

Resolved, That when we transfer our thoughts from the precincts of this Society, within which he has shed so long and so graciously the mild light of his high and varied intelligence, to that wider arena in which he moved as minister and interpreter of nature, plucking out the heart of her hidden mysteries,—as teacher of ingenuous youth, quickening in their minds an ardent love of knowledge,—as apostle of science, deeply imbued with reverence for his holy calling,—as unselfish worker for the Government, serving it even unto death in so many fields of useful and unrewarded activity,—and above all, when we refer to his long and beneficent career as Director of the great institution to which SMITHSON gave his name, but to which HENRY has given the distinctive direction and specific character which compose the chief element of its glory in the past and constitute the highest pledge of its usefulness in the future, we are filled with admiration not only for the variety and depth of his lore, and for the amplitude of the intellectual sympathies which enabled our honored head to take "all knowledge for his province," but also for the rare executive talent which in the sphere of administration fitted him successfully to touch the springs of original inquiry at almost every point in the wide domains of modern science.

Resolved, That as we survey the long and splendid career of the great philosopher, who has just fallen at his post of duty, on the high places of the land, and to whose finished life the seal of death has now been set, amid the universal regrets of his countrymen, shared by the civilized world wherever science has a votary, we shall best prove our love and veneration for his memory, not by indulging in fruitless repinings, but by borrowing inspiration and incentive from the sublime example left us in the purity of his life, and in the beneficence of the works which still follow him though he has rested from his labors.

Resolved, That cherishing for his memory a profound admiration and affection, we proffer to his bereaved family our sincerest sympathy and condolence, and that we will attend his funeral as co-mourners, in a body.

On motion, it was further *Resolved*, That the Secretary transmit copies of these resolutions to the family of Professor HENRY, and to the Regents of the Smithsonian Institution.

———————

At a meeting of the General (executive) Committee of the Society held May 25, 1878, it was

Resolved, That Saturday evening, October 26, (being the time of the regular meeting of the Society next preceding the annual meeting for the election of officers,) be specially set apart and exclusively devoted to a commemoration of the life, character, and services of the first President of this Society—JOSEPH HENRY ; and that Vice-Presidents JAMES C. WELLING and WILLIAM B. TAYLOR be requested to prepare, for that occasion, addresses illustrative of the personal and scientific character of the deceased.

PROCEEDINGS

OF THE

ALBANY INSTITUTE.

ALBANY, MAY 14, 1878.

On taking the chair the President, Professor HALL, announced with much emotion the recent death of Professor JOSEPH HENRY, many years ago an active member of the Institute, and long recognized as one of the most prominent and useful scientific men of this generation.

On motion of Mr. HOGAN, a committee of three in addition to the President was appointed to prepare a minute relative to the death of the late Professor JOSEPH HENRY, LL.D. Vice-President ORLANDO MEADS, Professor GATES, and the Recording Secretary were named as the additional members of the committee, and President HALL was appointed to represent the Institute at the funeral of Professor HENRY.

On motion of Mr. COLVIN, out of respect to Professor HENRY, the Institute then adjourned.

MAY 28, 1878.

Vice-President MEADS, in behalf of the committee appointed at the last meeting, submitted the draft of a Memorial Minute relative to the late Professor JOSEPH HENRY, LL.D., one of the original members of the Institute, which he read, and the same was unanimously adopted by the Institute and ordered to be entered on the minutes, and a copy to be sent to the family of Professor HENRY; also, to be furnished to the daily newspapers of the city.

Mr. MEADS also read a communication from President HALL, excusing his absence, on account of illness, from the meeting of the committee of which he was a member, and paying a worthy tribute of personal regard to the memory of the late Professor HENRY, which communication was ordered to be entered on the minutes.

The following is a copy of Professor HALL'S letter:

PORT HENRY, May 27, 1878.

ORLANDO MEADS, Esq.

Dear Sir: I am very sorry not to meet with the members of the Albany Institute to-morrow evening, but I am quite unable to do so.

For some weeks before the last meeting of the Institute I had been too feeble to go out at night, and I went on that occasion only from respect to the memory of Professor HENRY and that I might say a few words in eulogy of his character. I now find that I had kept up and about my work quite too long. Since I came here I have not been able to sit up more than half the time, and I have scarcely the energy to write a letter. I am suffering from extreme nervous prostration.

I write to explain the cause of my absence, and I am very sorry not to be present with the committee on this occasion. I believe you know very well my esteem and veneration for Professor HENRY, and I wish not to fail in joining in any expression of regard for his memory, or of sympathy and condolence with his most excellent and amiable family in their great affliction.

Professor HENRY was the realization of my ideal of a scientific man. During a long life he has kept apart from all those influences which serve to destroy the independence of so many men of science. His simple and unassuming life, and his quiet and unpretending manner, while confessedly at the head of all scientific men of his country, has presented a grand example to the younger men, while it has secured for him their love, esteem, and veneration. I believe there has been no scientific man of the generation in which he lived who has so endeared himself and his memory to men of all professions and departments of scientific inquiry, and we cannot too strongly express our sentiments of appreciation of such a character.

I am, very sincerely and respectfully yours, etc.,

JAMES HALL.

9

MEMORIAL MINUTE:

BY

ORLANDO MEADS.

Professor JOSEPH HENRY, LL.D., who for more than half a
century has stood at the head of American scientific men, and who
for more than thirty years has held, with equal honor to himself
and advantage to the great interests committed to him, the eminent
position of Secretary of the Smithsonian Institution, died at his
post of duty in the city of Washington, on the 13th day of May,
1878, in the eighty-first year of his age. The death of one so
venerable in years, and whose long life has been devoted so assiduously and successfully to the advancement of science in some of its
highest departments, makes it especially fitting that the members of
this Institute, of which he was one of the founders, should place
upon its records some suitable expression of their estimate of his
character and services.

It is with just pride that we call to mind that he was a native
of this city; that it was here in the Albany Academy, and in the
very building in which we are now assembled, that he received
much of his early education, and especially in those branches which
contributed most to prepare him for his subsequent scientific career;
that after ceasing to be a pupil in the academy, much of his leisure
time, for several years, was spent in the laboratory, then in this very
room, in experimental investigations in chemistry, electricity, in the
application of steam, and in other branches of physical science, in
which he was destined afterwards to attain so great distinction.
While thus engaged, he took an active part in the organization of
the Albany Lyceum, and afterward of the Albany Institute. In
1826, he was appointed professor of mathematics and natural
philosophy in the academy. The place was not unworthy of the
high qualifications he brought to it; for in that day few of the
colleges of this country afforded such a large and thorough course

(131)

of instruction, both in the classics and in mathematics and natural philosophy, as did the academy. Soon after his appointment to this professorship, he entered upon the course of original and experimental researches in electro-magnetism that were rewarded with results so brilliant and valuable as to attract the attention of the scientific world and place him at once in the front rank of original investigators. Here be made those great discoveries which in their practical application, have given us the electric telegraph.

He not only showed how a greater magnetic power than had ever before been supposed possible, could be obtained, but he showed also how by means of a battery of a greater number of plates, known as an intensity battery, the power thus obtained might be transmitted through a circuit so as to produce its effect at a great distance from the operator, and he also distinctly pointed out the application of this to the transmission of telegraphic signals. It is within the recollection of some now here present, that while he was yet connected with this academy, and long before the Morse telegraph was invented, there might be seen, strung circuit upon circuit, around the walls of the large room in the upper part of the building, thousands of feet of copper wire, through the whole length of which he sent a galvanic current so as to excite a magnet and move a lever at the farther end, which was thus made to strike its signal on a bell. Here, in a scientific point of view, was all that was essential to the magnetic telegraph. That he did not attempt to apply these discoveries to their practical use, was not that he did not see their application, or that he had not inventive genius, but that he had formed for himself a high ideal of a life devoted to science for its own sake, from which he would not be diverted by any inferior claims upon his attention. The stand taken by him thus early was inflexibly adhered to through his whole subsequent life.

In 1832, he was called to the professorship of natural philosophy in the college of New Jersey, at Princeton, where he not only continued to prosecute with great success and growing fame his favorite investigations in electricity and magnetism, but he also greatly enlarged the range of his acquirements by studies in acoustics, optics, astronomy, geology, mineralogy, and architecture, in some

of which departments his lectures excited great interest and admiration. He had rare power as a lecturer. With always a full
knowledge of his subject, his language was well chosen and exact,
his elocution dignified and impressive, and he had in a rare degree,
both in conversation and in his public discourses, the faculty characteristic of the highest order of minds — of presenting the deepest
truths with a clearness and simplicity that brought them within the
grasp of ordinary minds. In 1837 he for the first time visited
Europe, where his valuable contributions to physical science had
made him well known to such men as FARADAY, WHEATSTONE,
AIRY, and others, who received him with the most flattering
attentions.

By the noble bequest of JAMES SMITHSON, the United States
were made the recipients of a fund "to found at Washington, under
the name of the Smithsonian Institution, an establishment for the
increase and diffusion of knowledge among men." On the establishment of this institution under an act of Congress in 1846, the
eyes of the leading scientific men in this country and abroad were
at once turned to Professor HENRY as the man most eminently
qualified to carry out the great objects of this trust in accordance
with the spirit of the founder. The trust itself, as prescribed in
the will of the founder, was of the grandest and most comprehensive
character. It was intended for both the increase and the diffusion
of knowledge. It was limited to no particular branch of knowledge, and it was for the benefit of all mankind. It was with great
hesitation and reluctance that Professor HENRY was induced to
give up the line of original research to which he had been devoted,
and undertake a work so different from any in which he had been
engaged, and involving so great responsibility. But having yielded
to the wishes of his friends, he gave himself to the work earnestly
and conscientiously, still hoping that after the organization was
completed he might be enabled again to resume his former pursuits.
Fortunate it was for the honor of the country and for the permanent interests of the institution that such a man was brought to
preside over its original organization, and afterward to direct and
control its administration for nearly a third of a century. How
broadly and wisely he laid the foundations of the institution —

with what a large view and just appreciation of the claims of all the various departments of liberal knowledge; how skillfully he guarded it through the manifold perils of its earlier years; with what vigilance and stern integrity he protected and secured the trust funds, not only from loss, but from perversion to improper purposes, or to the promotion of local and selfish interests; how scrupulously he held himself aloof from all entanglements with gainful enterprises and from everything that could withdraw his thoughts from the high duties to which he had devoted himself; and how strongly he thus entrenched himself in the respect and confidence not only of those immediately associated with him, but of the whole American people—is well known to us, and is witnessed to by the voice that now comes to us from every part of the country.

In commemorating his public services we should not omit to notice the valuable gratuitous services he has rendered to the country for so many years as president of the Light-House Board, nor should we fail also to record the not less important relation in which, as the head of the Smithsonian Institution, he has stood to the Government as its trusted adviser in all matters involving scientific inquiry. Every successive administration for the last thirty years has had the benefit of his wise and disinterested counsels, and has ever given to him its fullest confidence. But above all should we bear witness to the great moral worth and dignity of the example he has furnished in our own country and in our times of a man of the highest intellectual endowments and with more than ordinary aptitude for success in the practical walks of life giving himself, from the very outset of his career, with stern inflexibility of purpose, exclusively to the pursuit of science for its own sake, esteeming its path one of all-sufficient honor and distinction, and its satisfactions and rewards higher and better than all other worldly success, content to live simply and virtuously, so be it only that it might be "in the pure and serene air of liberal studies."

He was a man of warm affections and of a most sincere, generous, and noble nature. His sympathies with all earnest seekers after truth, and especially with the young, were ever quick and ready. He loved truth for its own sake, and had an utter detestation of

sham, and charlatanism, and all devices for cheap popularity,
whether in science or in other things.   He was, moreover, a man
of calm, well considered and decided Christian faith.   No seeming
conflict between the truths of science and those of religion ever
disturbed his well assured faith in both,—for he had a mind large
enough, and honest enough, to grasp the relation between them.
No one knew better than he whose life had been spent in seeking
to penetrate the secrets of the natural world, what were the powers,
and what were also the limitations of the human intellect; but
believing as he did, that truth in all its forms proceeded from its
one Great Author, he doubted not, that when faith is exchanged
for sight, it will be found in all its varied manifestations to be at
perfect unity with itself.

PROCEEDINGS

OF THE

UNITED STATES LIGHT-HOUSE BOARD.

OFFICE OF THE LIGHT-HOUSE BOARD,
Washington, May 16, 1878.

[Extract from the minutes of the meeting of the Light-House Board, held May 15, 1878.]

The Naval Secretary read a letter from Chief Justice M. R. WAITE, Chancellor of the Smithsonian Institution, announcing the death of Professor JOSEPH HENRY, and inviting the Light-House Board to attend his funeral on Thursday afternoon at half-past four o'clock.

On motion, it was ordered that the Light-House Board accept the invitation to attend the funeral, and that the Naval Secretary be charged with making the necessary arrangements.

The following resolutions submitted by the Naval Secretary were adopted:

Resolved, That in the death of Professor JOSEPH HENRY we have lost an impartial Chairman, who has done so much to obtain the harmonious co-operation of the several workers composing the Board.

Resolved, That we have lost in his death the head of our Committee on Experiments, in which position for more than a quarter of a century be has by his patient, able, and successful investigations into the laws of light and sound, and by his fertile suggestions as to their application, put the Light-House Service into the front ranks of practical science.

Resolved, That we sincerely deplore his death; as thus we have each one of us lost a personal friend who by his kindness of heart, his honest frankness, his genial bearing, and his genuine sympathy, has commanded our respect and won our affection.

(135)

Resolved, That as a token of our appreciation of our loss, the Board attend his funeral in a body; that the colors of the vessels in the Light-House Service be set at half-mast on the day of the funeral; that the offices of the Light-House Establishment throughout the country be closed on that day; and that the members of the Board, and the officers of the Light-House Service, wear the usual badge of mourning for thirty days.

Resolved, That we tender to the family of the deceased our deepest sympathy in their great bereavement.

Resolved, That these resolutions be spread on the Journal of the Board; and that a properly engrossed copy of them be sent to the family of the deceased.

The Board then adjourned.

C. P. PATTERSON,
Chairman pro tem.

GEORGE DEWEY,
PETER C. HAINS,
        Secretaries.

•   OFFICE OF THE LIGHT-HOUSE BOARD,
                        Washington, July 9, 1878.

SIR: I transmit herewith a copy of a letter dated London, June 25, 1878, from Mr. ROBIN ALLEN, Secretary to the Light-House Establishment of Great Britain, (Trinity House,) condoling with the Board upon the death of its late Chairman, Professor HENRY, and expressing the high appreciation of his distinguished services in Pharology, entertained by the "Elder Brethren" of the first named body.

In transmitting this letter, allow me to express the hope that its reception will be as agreeable to you, as it has been to the Light-House Board.

Very respectfully, your obedient servant,

GEORGE DEWEY,
Naval Secretary.

To the Secretary
        of the Smithsonian Institution.

[COPY TRANSMITTED.]

TRINITY HOUSE, LONDON, E. C.,
25th June, 1878.

SIR: I have it in command to request that you will be good
enough to convey to the members of the Light-House Board of
the United States the high sense which the Elder Brethren of
this corporation entertain of the many good services rendered to
the science of Pharology by Professor HENRY, your lamented
predecessor.

It was the good fortune of two of the members of this Board to
make your late Chairman's acquaintance when on a tour of inquiry
and observation in the United States, and the survivor of that
deputation, Captain SYDNEY WEBB, has a very cordial recollection
of the manner in which Professor HENRY placed the experience
of the Department unreservedly at their disposal, and of the extremely courteous way in which he assisted their researches, and
indicated the directions in which those researches were likely to
bear fruit.

It is at all times a matter of satisfaction to the Trinity House to
remember that its main function is one of such general interest, that
its members may count upon fellow-workers wherever maritime
civilization exists; but they trust it may be taken as an evidence of
their especial hope that through you, Sir, this friendly intercourse
with the Light-House authorities of the United States may be
continued; that they thus desire to record their grateful appreciation of the important contributions to the applied sciences both of
Light and of Sound, for maritime purposes, with which the name
of Professor JOSEPH HENRY will always be so honorably associated.

I have the honor to be, sir, your obedient servant,

ROBIN ALLEN,
Secretary.

To the Chairman
of the Light-House Board of the United States.

DISCOURSE MEMORIAL:*

REV. SAMUEL BAYARD DOD.

"I have written unto you, young men, because ye are strong, and the word of God abideth in you."—1 John ii. 14.

THE beloved Apostle, in giving unto each class of his readers a word in season, uses the language of our text in addressing the young men, pointing them to the abiding of the word of God in their hearts as furnishing the necessary elements for the formation of a strong character. I shall try to point out to you how the word of God meets the necessities of human character in the period of youth, and what special value it has for the young, in correcting the errors incident to that period of life, and in supplying the elements needed for the formation and fixing of character.

Perhaps no one thing contributes more to retard the growth and permanent progress of our character than the changes and fluctuations of feeling through which we are continually passing.

The mere progress of life, by enlarging our views and bringing us into new associations, works a great change in our feelings. The mountains of our youth are but hills in the eye of manhood; its palaces are transformed into plain houses; its suns dwindle into stars; its visions splendid "fade into the light of common day;" its ardent and generous impulses are tamed into a cool worldly wisdom.

Beside this more general and permanent change, there are fleeting clouds of feeling, quick changes of sunshine and shadow continually passing over us. What alternations of hope, fear, anxiety, joy, melancholy we pass through in a single week! How, with each aspect of the mind, the outer world seems changed, according to the medium through which we view it!

---

*This Sermon, delivered in the College Chapel, PRINCETON, N. J., on the 16th of May, 1878, (the Sunday following Professor HENRY's death,) was published in the "Princeton Memorial."

How then amid all this change, shall the heart be kept in one steady, consistent course of progress, and not be at the mercy of transient states of feeling? Are there not passages of your own experience that verify this description? I do not speak of that ordinary experience exposed to the view of the world in your actions, but of that inner life, which you keep hidden from the world's gaze.

Of what does that testify? Of struggles between opposing desires; of broken vows and resolutions; of calm views suddenly overcast with dark clouds; of elevated aims dragged down to the mire and dust; of fitful seasons of repentance and self-humiliation. Our own inner experience reveals purposes formed far higher than we have ever evaluated in action—an ideal life which has little influence on our real life, which consists mainly in unhappy grasping after a higher life, but which is only realized in the dreams of our imagination.

To counteract this tendency we must learn to act on some fixed principle. We must choose some great purpose for which we will live, great enough to be a controlling influence over all our life, which we can set as our pole-star in the heavens. Such a purpose, and influence, is furnished by the word of God.

*   *   *   *   *   *   *

But we rest the argument for this truth not only upon what we may infer the influence of the abiding of the word of God in the heart to be, but also upon the experience of our fellow-men who have made that word the guide of their lives.

There passed away from among us, on Monday last, one whose life and labors beautifully illustrate this truth. It is meet that within the precincts of this college, special mention should be made, in terms of reverent affection, of Professor JOSEPH HENRY.

We claim him as one of us—not a son of Princeton, it is true, for in a far humbler academy his early studies were prosecuted; but we claim him as a brother, beloved and loving, for he loved Princeton sincerely. From her he received his title of Professor; in her old Hall of Natural Philosophy he prosecuted his researches, begun in Albany; among her professors he found kindred spirits whom he honored and loved; to her students he delighted to impart the fruits of his study, and kindle in them some of the earnest enthusiasm which marked his pursuit of knowledge. And, when a call which he regarded as imperative, carried him away from here, he retained his place still among her professors, and often revisited Princeton; and those who knew him well, remember his constant expression of regret and of longing for this peaceful academic life, with its opportunity for research.

As we look at the appliances of a physical laboratory in these days, and remember the meagre apparatus of forty years ago, we wonder at the genius and patience of this great discoverer, who with limited means, devised and in great measure constructed the apparatus with which many of his wonderful discoveries were made.

I presume that you are familiar with the few incidents of his life. With no advantages in the way of early education, with limited means, with no patronage of friends to aid him, by his own labor he earned his livelihood, by his own efforts he obtained recognition and position. First called at his graduation, to the chair of Mathematics in the Albany Academy, from there he was called, in 1832, to the professorship in Princeton, and from there, in 1846, to the Smithsonian Institution at Washington.

This is not the time nor the place to enter into a detailed account of those discoveries, begun in Albany and carried on here, which have given him not only a national, but a world-wide fame. I shall only attempt to point out some of those characteristics which distinguished Professor HENRY as a philosopher and as a man.

As a student of science he was ardent and enthusiastic in his love for the chosen pursuit of his life. He did not dally with it as a pastime, nor prosecute it with the greed of gain, nor pursue it with the ambition of making himself famous among men. He desired knowledge, and searched out wisdom in the love of it. One of his students says, speaking of his construction of his second and largest magnet: "We shall always remember the intense eagerness with which he superintended and watched his preparations, and how he fairly leaped from the floor in excitement when he saw his instrument suspending and holding a weight of more than a ton and a half." Another writer, speaking of his examination of the telephone at Philadelphia, says: "It was a most lovely sight, at the Grand Exhibition at Philadelphia, when Professor HENRY, the father of the system" of electro-magnetic communication, "and Sir WILLIAM THOMPSON, the greatest living electrician in Europe, met and experimented with that mysterious telephone. Their pleasure reminded me more than anything else of the exuberant joy of childhood, when some beautiful revelation of nature has been for the first time brought to its brain, and when the innocent child expresses happiness in every feature of its face and every movement of its person."

He was characterized by great reverence in the pursuit of truth. Singularly modest as to his own powers and attainments, he never suffered the advancement of his own opinions to warp his judgment or govern his investigations; he held the progress of truth dearer than the success of a theory. And nothing moved his gentle nature to greater indignation than the pretensions of the charlatan or bigot in science.

In all his researches he was actuated principally by the desire to make the results of his study of benefit to his fellow-men. His own noble words sum up the ruling principles of his life as a scientific man. He says, when put on trial for his character as a man of science and a man of honor, "My life has been principally devoted to science and my investigations in different branches of physics have given me some reputation in the line of original discovery. I have sought however no patent for inventions and solicited no remuneration for my labors, but have freely given their results to the world; expecting only in return to enjoy the consciousness of having added by my investigations to the sum of human knowledge. The only reward I ever expected was the consciousness of advancing science, the pleasure of discovering new truths, and the scientific reputation to which these labors would entitle me." And verily I say unto you, he hath his reward.

As an investigator, Professor HENRY was characterized by great patience and thoroughness in his work of observation, and by broad, well-considered, and far-reaching generalizations. He distrusted the so-called "brilliant generalizations" with which those favor us who love speculation rather than study. He never took anything for granted, never despised the details of his work, but carefully established, step by step, those data on which he based his conclusions. In 1849 he says, "Since my removal to Princeton I have made several thousand original investigations on electricity, magnetism, and electro-magnetism, bearing on practical applications of electricity, brief minutes of which fill several hundred folio pages. They have cost me years of labor and much expense."

Combined with this thoroughness, there was great fertility of mind. He was distinguished not in one branch of physics, but in all. In the catalogue of his published papers (and these represent but a small part of his work, for he worked much and published comparatively little) there is evidence of the varied fields in which he wrought. While a large part of them are devoted to his favorite and most famous line of research, yet there are numbers of them on problems in acoustics, on acoustics applied to building, on building materials, on the sun spots, on natural history, on the prediction of the changes in the weather, on various problems in meteorology, on capillarity, on light and heat, on the velocity of projectiles, on the correlation of forces, and the conservation of energy.

He was possessed of great foresight. The various forms of electro-motors which have since been attempted are all on the basis of Professor HENRY's made thirty years ago; nor has all the ingenuity and money expended since that time advanced us one step beyond the conclusion which he reached then. "I never regarded it as practical in the arts because of its great expense of power, except in particular cases where expense of power is of little consequence."

The results of his labors I can only briefly sum up.

As president of the American Association for the Advancement of Science, and of the National Academy of Sciences, he gave the weight of his influence and the benefit of his experience to the successful conduct of these societies.

He was Chairman of the Light-House Board, and during the rebellion, a member of the commission to examine inventions for facilitating military and naval operations.

In these varied capacities he has served the Government with zeal and fidelity, and has made his scientific knowledge of avail in protecting commerce and saving human life; giving to all the arduous duties of these positions his thorough personal supervision. In conjunction with Professor GUYOT, through the agency of the Smithsonian Institution, he first inaugurated the systematic observation and study of the law of storms that has given us our present signal-service observations.

But the greatest triumph of his genius and reward of his patient labor was the discovery of the telegraph. In 1825 Mr. BARLOW, of the Royal Military Academy, published a pamphlet which was accepted as the demonstration that the telegraph was impossible. In 1830 Professor HENRY had a telegraph in successful operation of over a mile and a half in length; and a little later, in Princeton, one of several miles in length. A writer, (Mr. E. N. DICKERSON,) who, as counsel in a patent case, had occasion to examine this matter thoroughly, says: "The thing was perfect as it came from its author, and has never been improved from that day to this as a sounding telegraph." And he further calls attention to the fact that the subsequent invention of an alphabet impressed on paper strips has been abandoned, and, to-day, men read the telegraph phonetically, as Professor HENRY did at the first.

How can we estimate the influence on the world's history, on the progress of nations, on the individual lives of men, of the man who gave to the world, without money and without price, the discovery that made the telegraph possible?

As over the land and under the sea, the voiceless viewless message goes, freighted with its burden of joy or woe, of life or death, of war or peace, it speaks his praise.

This wonderful discovery, beginning a century ago, is the fruit of the combined efforts of great men. OERSTED, ARAGO, AMPERE, DAVY, BARLOW, STURGEON, FARADAY—each contributed his share of discovery to the result; but it was reserved for HENRY to apply the discoveries already made, and to add the missing factor that solved the problem and created the electro-magnetic telegraph.

In the later years of his life his arduous and varied duties as head of the Smithsonian Institution hindered in great measure his prosecution of original research. This position he accepted as a sacred trust from its founder, whose simple declaration, that it was to be for the increase and diffusion of knowledge among men, he kept steadily in view. His purity and simplicity of character foiled, as no other armor could have done, the artifice of politicians who sought to wield its influence for political ends. Professor HENRY kept it pure from any such taint, and thus saved it to the nation and the world.

In all his investigations Professor HENRY allowed himself perfect freedom. He followed with simplicity of heart and firmness of mind, whither the revelations of nature led him. He belonged to no scientific clique, was no bigot nor partisan, but calm and unbiased in his conclusions.

But the chief significance of his life to us as Princetonians, as students, and as men, is that he was an humble, sincere, consistent Christian.

The following extract from a letter written April 12, 1878, contains a clear exposition of Professor HENRY'S views. I invite your thoughtful attention to them; they are the well-weighed, mature convictions uttered at the close of a long life of earnest study of nature; and, written but a month before his death, we may regard them as his last testament on this great theme:

"We live in a universe of change; nothing remains the same from one moment till another, and each moment of recorded time has its separate history. We are carried on by the ever-changing events in the line of our destiny, and at the end of the year we are always at a considerable distance from the point of its beginning. How short the space between the two cardinal points of an earthly career, the point of birth and that of death; and yet what a universe of wonders are presented to us in our rapid flight through this space. How small the wisdom obtained by a single life in its passage; and how small the known when compared with the unknown by the accumulation of the millions of lives through the art of printing in hundreds of years.

"How many questions press themselves upon us in these contemplations. Whence come we? Whither are we going? What is our final destiny? The object of our creation? What mysteries of unfathomable depth environ us on every side; but after all our

10

speculations and an attempt to grapple with the problem of the universe, the simplest conception which explains and connects the phenomena is that of the existence of one spiritual Being, infinite in wisdom, in power, and all divine perfections; who exists always and everywhere; who has created us with intellectual faculties sufficient in some degree to comprehend His operations as they are developed in nature by what is called 'science.' - - -

"In accordance with this scientific view, on what evidence does the existence of a Creator rest? First, it is one of the truths best established by experience in my own mind that I have a thinking, willing principle within me, capable of intellectual activity and of moral feeling. Second, it is equally clear to me that you have a similar spiritual principle within yourself, since, when I ask you an intelligent question, you give me an intellectual answer. Third, when I examine operations of nature, I find everywhere through them evidences of intellectual arrangements, of contrivances to reach definite ends precisely as I find in the operations of man; and hence I infer that those two classes of operations are results of similar intelligence. Again, in my own mind I find ideas of right and wrong, of good and evil. These ideas then exist in the universe, and therefore form a basis of our ideas of a moral universe. Furthermore, the conceptions of good which are found among our ideas associated with evil, can be attributed only to a being of infinite perfections like that which we denominate 'God.' On the other hand, we are conscious of having such evil thoughts and tendencies that we can not associate ourselves with a Divine being, who is the director and the governor of all, or even call upon Him for mercy without the intercession of one who may affiliate himself with us."[*]

Into the kingdom of nature he entered as a little child, and she laid bare her secrets before him; she opened the leaves of her wonderful book, and he read therein, and told us some of her most marvelous secrets, which others had but dimly guessed.

So also into the kingdom of heaven he entered as a little child, and in the same simplicity and sincerity of faith with which he had accepted the truths of nature, he received the word of God.

* This letter of Professor HENRY will be found entire on pages 25-26 of this volume.

There are some who, in these days, tell us that if a man believe in God as his maker, in Christ as his redeemer, in the Holy Spirit as his sanctifier, and in the word of God as the guide of his life, he is no more to be ranked among scientific men, nor fit to be trusted as a student of nature. Where then shall we place this father of American science? Who that vaunts his skeptical conjectures before the world to-day, as the badge of his scientific acumen and liberty of thought, can show so wide, and free, and fair a record of high scientific and beneficent work for his day and generation, as this avowed Christian philosopher?

To those who knew Professor HENRY personally, there was the charm of a singularly gentle and unaffected sincerity of heart and manner, that made him approachable to all. His attachments were warm and lasting. He remembered always with undiminished affection his associates in his professorship at Princeton, and now their children rise up and call him blessed. "None knew him but to love him."

Modest, unassuming, gentle in his deportment, he bore the fruit of Christian faith in his life. Following the example and precepts of his Master, "When he was reviled, he reviled not again; when he was persecuted, he threatened not." He was the model of a Christian gentleman.

And now he has passed from this school, where, by patient labor and with docile heart, he had learned, from the two great books of God, such wondrous lessons of the Divine wisdom and power and love. To-day that noble intellect and simple heart stands, stripped of the clogs of sense, before the unveiled presence of his God, and looks not at the things seen and temporal, but at the things unseen and eternal. With what rapture and amazement there has opened to his view wonders, surpassing immeasurably all that he had guessed on earth, we cannot tell; "for eye hath not seen, nor ear heard, neither have entered into the heart of man the things that God hath prepared for them that love Him."

But who of us, if called to make the choice, would hesitate as to which were the higher honor and which the happier destiny — the place which JOSEPH HENRY, the philosopher, holds, and will ever hold among the great of this world, by virtue of his scientific

achievements, or the place which is his at the right hand of God,
by virtue of his simple Christian faith? We who love this college,
and cherish the memory of the great and good men who have made
her name illustrious and sacred, from her foundation to the present
hour, feel a thrill of gratification that our illustrious brother was
borne to the grave followed by the chief men of the nation, as one
whom the people delight to honor. But a higher and tenderer joy
fills the heart, when we picture to ourselves his reception at the
court of the King of kings, his welcome into the great company of
those who are "washed and made white in the blood of the Lamb,"
and the honor, above all earthly plaudits, when the Master graciously said unto him, "Well done, thou good and faithful servant;
enter thou into the joy of thy Lord."

God grant that Princeton College may ever maintain, for American science, the noble succession of such Christian princes in the
realms of thought as JOSEPH HENRY.

NOTE.

I have appended a letter, which I received from Professor HENRY,
in reply to one soliciting from him some account of his work while
connected with the College of New Jersey. While I wish that one
better fitted to portray that noble life and enforce its lessons had
stood in my place, yet it was a labor of love to pay what tribute I
was able to the memory of one who, whenever I met him, spoke in
terms of warm affection of my father, who was one of his colleagues.

I now publish it in the hope that it may commend, especially to
the students of the college of New Jersey, the noble example of
this life, passed in the service of men and the fear of God.

                                                    S. B. DOD.

MAY, 1878.

WASHINGTON, D. C., *December 4, 1876.*

MY DEAR SIR: In compliance with your request that I would give an account of my scientific researches during my connection with the College of New Jersey, I furnish the following brief statement of my labors within the period mentioned:

1. Previous to my call from the Albany Academy to a professorship in the College of New Jersey, I had made a series of researches on electro-magnetism, in which I developed the principles of the electro-magnet and the means of accumulating the magnetic power to a great extent, and had also applied this power in the invention of the first electro-magnetic machine; that is, a mechanical contrivance by which electro-magnetism was applied as a motive power.

I soon saw, however, that the application of this power was but an indirect method of employing the energy derived from the combustion of coal, and, therefore, could never compete, on the score of expense, with that agent as a means of propelling machinery, but that it might be used in some cases in which expense of power was not a consideration to be weighed against the value of certain objects to be attained. A great amount of labor has since been devoted to this invention, especially at the expense of the Government of the United States, by the late Dr. CHARLES G. PAGE, but it still remains in nearly the same condition it was left in by myself in 1831.

I also applied, while in Albany, the results of my experiments to the invention of the first electro-magnetic telegraph, in which signals were transmitted by exciting an electro-magnet at a distance, by which means dots might be made on paper, and bells were struck in succession, indicating letters of the alphabet.

In the midst of these investigations I was called to Princeton, through the nomination of Dr. JACOB GREEN, then of Philadelphia, and Dr. JOHN TORREY, of New York.

I arrived in Princeton in November, 1832, and as soon as I became fully settled in the chair which I occupied, I recommenced my investigations, constructed a still more powerful electro-magnet than I had made before—one which would sustain over three thousand pounds,—and with it illustrated to my class the manner in which a large amount of power might, by means of a relay magnet, be called into operation at the distance of many miles.

I also made several modifications in the electro-magnetic machine before mentioned, and just previous to my leaving for England, in 1837, again turned my attention to the telegraph. I think the first actual line of telegraph using the earth as a conductor was made in the beginning of 1836. A wire was extended across the front campus of the college grounds, from the upper story of the library building to the philosophical hall on the opposite side, the ends terminating in two wells. Through this wire, signals were sent, from time to time, from my house to my laboratory. The electro-magnetic telegraph was first invented by me, in Albany, in 1830. Professor MORSE, according to his statements, conceived the idea of an electro-magnetic telegraph in his voyage across the ocean in 1832, but did not until several years afterward—1837—attempt to carry his ideas into practice; and when he did so, he found himself so little acquainted with the subject of electricity that he could not make his simple machine operate through the distance of a few yards. In this dilemma he called in the aid of Dr. LEONARD D. GALE, who was well acquainted with what I had done in Albany and Princeton, having visited me at the latter place. He informed Professor MORSE that he had not the right kind of a battery nor the right kind of magnets, whereupon the professor turned the matter over to him, and, with the knowledge he had obtained from my researches, he was enabled to make the instrument work through a distance of several miles. For this service Professor MORSE gave him a share of his patent, which he afterward purchased from him for $15,000. At the time of making my original experiments on electro-magnetism in Albany, I was urged by a friend to take out a patent, both for its application to machinery and to the telegraph, but this I declined, on the ground that I did not then consider it compatible with the dignity of science to confine the benefits which might be derived from it to the exclusive use of any individual. In this perhaps I was too fastidious. In briefly stating my claims to the invention of the electro-magnetic telegraph, I may say I was the first to bring the electro-magnet into the condition necessary to its use in telegraphy, and also to point out its application to the telegraph, and to illustrate this by constructing a working telegraph, and had I taken out a patent for my labors at that time, Mr. MORSE could have had no ground on which to found his claim for a patent for his invention. To Mr. MORSE however great credit is due for his alphabet, and for his perseverance in bringing the telegraph into practical use.

II. My next investigation, after being settled at Princeton, was in relation to electro-dynamic induction. Mr. FARADAY had discovered that when a current of galvanic electricity was passed through a wire from a battery, a current in an opposite direction was induced in a wire arranged parallel to this conductor. I discovered that an induction of a similar kind took place in the primary conducting wire itself, so that a current which, in its passage through a short wire conductor, would neither produce sparks nor shocks, would, if the wire were sufficiently long, produce both those phenomena. The effect was most strikingly exhibited when the conductor was a flat ribbon, covered with silk, rolled into the form of a helix. With this, brilliant deflagrations and other electrical effects of high intensity were produced by means of a current from a battery of low intensity, such as that of a single element.

III. A series of investigations was afterwards made, which resulted in producing inductive currents of different orders, having different directions, made up of waves alternately in opposite directions. It was also discovered that a plate of metal of any kind, introduced between two conductors, neutralized this induction, and this effect was afterward found to result from a current in the plate itself. It was afterward shown that a current of quantity was capable of producing a current of intensity, and vice versa, a current of intensity would produce one of quantity.

IV. Another series of investigations, of a parallel character, was made in regard to ordinary or frictional electricity. In the course of these it was shown that electro-dynamic inductive action of ordinary electricity was of a peculiar character, and that effects could be produced by it at a remarkable distance. For example, if a shock were sent through a wire on the outside of a building, electrical effects could be exhibited in a parallel wire within the building. As another illustration of this, it may be mentioned that when a discharge of a battery of several Leyden jars was sent through the wire before mentioned, stretched across the campus in front of Nassau Hall, an inductive effect was produced in a parallel wire, the ends of which terminated in the plates of metal in the ground in the back campus, at a distance of several hundred feet from the primary current, the building of Nassau Hall intervening. The effect produced consisted in the magnetization of steel needles.

In this series of investigations, the fact was discovered that the induced current, as indicated by the needles, appeared to change its direction with the distance of the two wires, and other conditions of the experiment, the cause of which for a long time baffled inquiry, but was finally satisfactorily explained by the discovery that the discharge of electricity from a Leyden jar is of an oscillatory character, a principal discharge taking place in one direction, and immediately afterward a rebound in the opposite, and so on forward and backward, until the equilibrium is obtained.

V. The next series of investigations related to atmospheric induction. The first of these consisted of experiments with two large kites, the lower end of the string of one being attached to the upper surface of a second kite, the string of each consisting of a fine wire, the terminal end of the whole being coiled around an insulated drum. I was assisted in these experiments by Mr. Brown, of Philadelphia, who furnished the kites. When they were elevated, at a time when the sky was perfectly clear, sparks were drawn of surprising intensity and pungency, the electricity being supplied from the air, and the intensity being attributed to the induction of the long wire on itself.

VI. The next series of experiments pertaining to the same class, was on the induction from thunder clouds. For this purpose the tin covering of the roof of the house in which I resided was used as an inductive plate. A wire was soldered to the edge of the roof near the gutter, was passed into my study and out again through holes in the window-sash, and terminated in connection with a plate of metal in a deep well immediately in front of the house. By breaking the continuity of that part of the wire which was in the study, and introducing into the opening a magnetizing spiral, needles placed in this could be magnetized by a flash of lightning so distant that the thunder could scarcely be heard. The electrical disturbance produced in this case was also found to be of an oscillatory character, a discharge first passing through the wire from the roof to the well, then another in the opposite direction, and so on until equilibrium was restored. This result was arrived at in this case, as well as in that of the Leyden jar, before mentioned, by placing the same, or a similar needle, in succession, in spirals of greater and greater number of turns; for example, in a spiral of a single turn the needle would be magnetized *plus*, or in the direction due to the first and more powerful wave. By increasing the number of coils, the action of the second wave became dominant, so that it would more than neutralize the magnetism produced by the first wave, and leave the needle *minus*. By further increasing the number of turns, the third wave would be so exalted as to neutralize the effects of the preceding two, and so on. In the case of induction by lightning, the same result was obtained by placing a number of magnetizing spirals, of different magnetizing intensities, in the opening of the primary conductor, the result of which was to produce the magnetization of an equal number of needles, plus and minus, indicating alternate currents in opposite directions.

VII. In connection with this class of investigations a series of experiments was made in regard to lightning-rods. It was found that when a quantity of electricity was thrown upon a rod, the lower end of which was connected with a plate of metal sunk in the water of a deep well, that the electricity did not descend silently into water, but that sparks could be drawn from every part of the rod sufficiently intense to explode an electrical pistol and to set fire to delicate inflammable substances. The spark thus given off was found to be of a peculiar character, for while it produced combustion and gave a slight shock, and fired the electrical pistol, it scarcely at all affected a gold leaf electroscope. Indeed, it consisted of two sparks, one from the conductor and the other to it, in such quick succession that the rupture of the air by the first served for the path of the second. The conclusion arrived at was, that during the passage of the electricity down the rod each point in succession received a charge analogous to the statical charge of a prime conductor, and that this charge, in its passage down the rod, was immediately preceded by a negative charge; the two in their passage past the point at which the spark was drawn giving rise to its duplex character. It was also shown by a series of experiments in transmitting a powerful discharge through a portion of air, that the latter, along the path of discharge, was endowed for a moment with an intense repulsive energy. So great is this that in one instance, when an electrical discharge from the clouds passed between two chimneys through the cockloft of a house, the whole roof was lifted from the walls. It is to this repulsive energy, or tendency in air to expand at right angles to the path of a stroke of lightning, that the mechanical effects which accompany the latter are generally to be attributed.

In connection with this series of investigations an experiment was devised for exhibiting the screening effect, within a space inclosed with a metallic envelope, of an exterior discharge of electricity. It consisted in coating the outside of a hollow glass globe with tinfoil, and afterward inserting, through a small hole in the side, a delicate gold leaf electrometer. The latter, being observed through a small opening in the tinfoil, was found to be unaffected by a discharge of electricity passed over the outside coating.

VIII. Another series of investigations was on the phosphorogenic emanation from the sun. It had long been known that when the diamond is exposed to the direct rays of the sun, and then removed to a dark place, it emits a pale blue light, which has received the name of phosphorescence. This effect is not peculiar to the diamond, but is possessed by a number of substances, of which the sulphuret of lime is the most prominent. It is also well known that phosphorescence is produced by exposing the substance to the electric discharge. Another fact was discovered by BECQUEREL, of the French Institute, that the agent exciting phosphorescence traverses with difficulty a plate of glass or mica, while it is transmitted apparently without impediment through plates of black quartz impervious to light.

My experiments consisted, in the first place, in the reproduction of these results, and afterward in the extension of the list of substances which possess the capability of exhibiting phosphorescence, as well as the effects of different interposed media. It was found that, among a large number of transparent solids, some were permeable to the phosphorescing agent, and others impermeable or imperfectly permeable. Among the former were ice, quartz, common salt, alum. Among the latter glass, mica, tourmaline, camphor, etc. Among liquid permeable substances were water, solutions of alum, ammonia; while among the impermeable liquids were most of the acids, sulphate of zinc, sulphate of lead, alcohol, etc.

It was found that the emanation took place from every point of the line of the electric discharge, but with more intensity from the two extremities; and also that the emanation producing phosphorescence, whatever be its nature, when reflected from a mirror obeys the laws of the reflection of light, but no reflection was obtained from a surface of polished glass. It is likewise refracted by a prism of rock salt, in accordance with the laws of the refraction of light. By transmitting the rays from an electrical spark through a series of very thin plates of mica, it was shown that the emanation was capable of polarization, and, consequently, of double refraction.

IX. The next series of investigations was on a method of determining the velocity of projectiles. The plan proposed for this purpose consisted in the application of the instantaneous transmission of the electrical action to determine the time of the passage of the ball between two screens, placed at a short distance from each other in the path of the projectile. For this purpose the observer is provided with a revolving cylinder moving by clock-work at a uniform rate, and of which the convex surface is divided into equal parts indicating a fractional part of a second. The passage of the ball through the screen breaks a galvanic circuit, the time of which is indicated on the revolving cylinder by the terminal spark produced in a wire surrounding a bundle of iron wires. Since the publication of this invention various other plans founded on the same principle have been introduced into practice.

X. Another series of experiments was in regard to the relative heat of different parts of the sun's disk, and especially to that of the spots on the surface. These were made in connection with Professor S. ALEXANDER, and consisted in throwing an image of the sun on a screen in a dark room by drawing out the eye-piece of a telescope.

Through a hole in the screen the end of a sensitive thermo-pile was projected, the wires of which were connected with a galvanometer. By slightly moving the smaller end of the telescope, different parts of the image of the sun could be thrown on the end of the thermo-pile, and by the deviation of the needle of the galvanometer, the variation of the heat was indicated. In this way it was proved that the spots radiated less heat than the adjacent parts, and that all parts of the sun's surface did not give off an equal amount of heat.

XI. Another series of experiments was made with what was called a thermal telescope. This instrument consisted of a long hollow cone of pasteboard, lined with silver leaf and painted out-side with lampblack. The angle at the apex of this cone was such as to cause all the parallel rays from a distant object entering the larger end of the cone to be reflected on to the end of a thermo-pile, the poles of which were connected with a delicate galvan-ometer. When the axis of this conical reflector was directed toward a distant object of greater or less temperature than the surrounding bodies, the difference was immediately indicated by the deviation of the needle of the galvanometer. For example, when the object was a horse in a distant field, the radiant heat from the animal was distinctly perceptible at a distance of at least several hundred yards. When this instrument was turned toward the celestial vault, the radiant heat was observed to increase from the zenith downward; when directed, however, to different clouds, it was found to indi-cate in some cases a greater, and in others a less, degree of radiation than the surrounding space. When the same instrument was directed to the moon, a slight increase of temperature was observed over that of the adjacent sky, but this increase of heat was attrib-uted to the reflection of the heat of the sun from the surface of the moon, and not to the heat of the moon itself. To show that this hypothesis is not inconsistent with the theory that the moon has cooled down to the temperature of celestial space, a concave mirror was made of ice and a thermo-pile placed in the more distant focus; when a flame of hydrogen, rendered luminous by a spiral platinum wire, was placed in the other focus, the needle of the galvanometer attached to the pile indicated a reflection of heat, care being taken to shade the pile by a screen with a small opening introduced between it and the flame.

XII. Another series of experiments connected with the preceding may be mentioned here. It is well known that the light from a flame of hydrogen is of very feeble intensity; the same is the case with that of the compound blowpipe, while the temperature of the latter is exceedingly high, sufficiently so to melt fine platinum wire. It is also well known that by introducing lime or other solid substance into this flame its radiant light is very much increased. I found that the radiant heat was increased in a similar ratio, or in other words, that in such cases the radiant heat was commensurate with the radiant light, and that the flame of the compound blowpipe, though of exceedingly high temperature, is a comparatively cool substance in regard to radiant heat. To study the relation of the temperature of a flame to the amount of heat given off, four ounces of water were placed in a platinum crucible and supported on a ring stand over a flame of hydrogen; the minutes and seconds of time were then accurately noted which were required for the raising of the water from the temperature of 60° to the boiling point. The same experiment was repeated with an equal quantity of water, with the same flame, into which a piece of mica was inserted by a handle made of a narrow slip of the same substance. With this arrangement the light of the flame was much increased, while the time of bringing the water to the boiling point was also commensurately increased, thus conclusively showing that the increase of light was at the expense of the diminution of the temperature. These experiments were instituted in order to examine the nature of the fact mentioned by Count RUMFORD, that balls of clay introduced into a fire under some conditions increase the heat given off into an apartment. From the results just mentioned it follows that the increase in the radiant heat, which would facilitate the roasting of an article before the fire, would be at the expense of the boiling of a liquid in a vessel suspended directly over the point of combustion.

XIII. Another investigation had its origin in the accidental observation of the following fact: A quantity of mercury had been left undisturbed in a shallow saucer, with one end of a piece of lead wire, about the diameter of a goose-quill, and six inches long,

plunged into it, the other end resting on the shelf. In this condition it was found, after a few days, that the mercury had passed
through the solid lead, as if it were a siphon, and was lying on the
shelf still in a liquid condition. The saucer contained a series of
minute crystals of an amalgam of lead and mercury. A similar
result was produced when a piece of the same lead wire was coated
with varnish, the mercury being transmitted without disturbing the
outer surface.

When a length of wire of five feet was supported vertically, with
its lower end immersed in a vessel of mercury, the liquid metal
was found to ascend, in the course of a few days, to a height of
three feet. These results led me to think that the same property
might be possessed by other metals in relation to each other. The
first attempt to verify this conjecture was made by placing a small
globule of gold on a plate of sheet-iron and submitting it to the
heat of an assaying furnace; but the experiment was unsuccessful,
for although the gold was heated much beyond its melting point, it
showed no signs of sinking into the pores of the iron. The idea
afterward suggested itself that a different result would have been
obtained had the two metals been made to adhere to each other, so
that no oxide could form between the two surfaces. To verify
this a piece of copper, thickly plated with silver, was heated to near
the melting point of the metals, when the silver disappeared, and,
after the surface was cleaned with diluted sulphuric acid, it presented a uniform surface of copper. This plate was next immersed
for a few minutes in a solution of muriate of zinc, by which the
surface of copper was removed and the surface of silver again
exposed. The fact had long been observed by workmen in silver-
plating, that in soldering the parts of plated metal, if care be not
taken not to heat them unduly, the silver will disappear. This
effect was supposed to be produced by evaporation, or the burning
off, as it was called, of the plating. It is not improbable that a
slow diffusion of one metal into the other takes place in the case of
an alloy. Silver coins slightly alloyed with copper, after having
lain long in the earth, are found covered with a salt of copper.
This may be explained by supposing that the alloy of copper at
the surface of the coin enters into combination with the carbonic

acid of the soil, and being thus removed, its place is supplied by a diffusion from within, and so on; it is not improbable that a large portion of the alloy may be removed in progress of time, and the purity of the coin be considerably increased. It is known to the jeweler that articles of copper plated with gold lose their brilliancy after awhile, and that this can be restored by boiling them in ammonia. This effect is probably produced by the ammonia acting on the copper and dissolving off its surface so as to expose the gold, which by diffusion had penetrated into the body of the metal.

The slow diffusion of one metal into another at ordinary temperatures would naturally require a long time to produce a perceptible effect, since it is probably only produced by the minute vibrations of the particles due to variations of temperature.

The same principle is applied to the explanation of the phenomenon called segregation—such as the formation of nodules of flint in masses of carbonate of lime, or in other words, to the explanation of the manner in which the molecular action, which is insensible at perceptible distances, may produce results which would appear, at first sight, to be the effect of attraction acting at a distance.

XIV. Another series of experiments had reference to the constitution of matter in regard to its state of liquidity and solidity, and they had their origin in the examination of the condition of the metal of the large gun constructed under the direction of Captain STOCKTON, by the explosion of which several prominent members of the United States Government were killed at Washington. It was observed in testing the bars of iron made from this gun that they varied much in tensile strength in different parts, and that in breaking these bars the solution of the continuity took place first in the interior. This phenomenon was attributed to the more ready mobility of the outer molecules of the bars, the inner ones being surrounded by matter incapable of slipping, and hence the rupture. A similar effect is produced in a piece of thick copper wire, each end when broken exhibiting at the point of rupture a cup-shaped surface, showing that the exterior of the metal sustained its connection longer than the interior.

From these observations the conclusion was drawn, that rigidity differs from liquidity more in a polarity which prevents slipping of the molecules, than in a difference of the attractive force with which the molecules are held together; or that it is more in accordance with the phenomena of cohesion, to suppose that in the case of a liquid, instead of the attraction of the molecules being neutralized by heat, the effect of this agent is merely to neutralize the polarity of the molecules, so as to give them perfect freedom of motion around any imaginable axis. In illustration of this subject the comparative tenacity of pure water in which soap had been dissolved, was measured by the usual method of ascertaining the weight required to detach from the surface of each the same plate of wood, suspended from the beam of a balance, under the same condition of temperature and pressure. It was found by this experiment that the tenacity of pure water was greater than that of soap and water. This novel result is in accordance with the supposition that the mingling of the soap and the water interferes with the perfect mobility of the molecules, while at the same time it diminishes the attraction.

XV. A series of experiments was also made on the tenacity of soap-water in films. For this purpose sheets of soap-water films were stretched upon rings, and the attempt made to obtain the tenacity of these by placing on them pellets of cotton until they were ruptured. The thickness of these films was roughly estimated by Newton's scale of the colors of thin plates, and from the results the conclusion was arrived at that the attractive force of the molecules of water, for those of water, is approximately equal to those of ice for those of ice, and that the difference in this case, of the solidity and liquidity, is due to the want of mobility in the latter, which prevented the slipping of the molecules on each other. It is this extreme mobility of the molecules of water that prevents the formation of permanent bubbles of it, and not a want of attraction.

The roundness of drops of water is not due to the attraction of the whole mass, but merely to the action of the surface, which in all cases of curvature is endowed with an intense contractile power.

This class of investigation also included the study of soap bubbles, and the establishment of the fact of the contractile power of these films. The curvature of the surface of a bubble tends to urge each particle toward the center with a force inversely as the diameter. Two bubbles being connected, the smaller will collapse by expelling its contents into the larger. By employing frames of wire, soap bubbles were also made to assume various forms, by which capillarity and other phenomena were illustrated. This subject was afterward taken up by PLATEAU, of Ghent. Another part of the same investigation was the study of the spreading of oil on water, the phenomenon being referred to the fact that the attraction of water for water is greater than that of oil for oil, while the attraction of the molecules of oil for each other is less than the attraction of the same molecules for water; hence the oil spreads over the water. This is shown from the fact that when a rupture is made in a liquid compound, consisting of a stratum of oil resting on water, the rupture takes place in the oil, and not between the oil and water. The very small distance at which the attraction takes place is exhibited by placing a single drop of oil on a surface of water of a considerable extent, when it will diffuse itself over the whole surface. If however a second drop be placed upon the same surface, it will retain its globular form.

XVI. Another contribution to science had reference to the origin of mechanical power and the nature of vital force. Mechanical power is defined to be that which is capable of overcoming resistance; or in the language of the engineer, that which is employed to do work.

If we examine attentively the condition of the crust of the earth, we find it, as a general rule, in a state of permanent equilibrium. All the substances which constitute the material of the crust, such as acids and bases, with the exception of the indefinitely thin pellicle of vegetable and animal matter which exists at its surface, have gone into a state of permanent combination, the whole being in the condition of the burnt slag of a furnace, entirely inert, and incapable in itself of no change. All the changes which we observe on the surface of the globe may be referred to action from without, from celestial space.

11

The following is a list which will be found to include all the prime movers used at the present day, either directly or indirectly, in producing molecular changes in matter:

Class I.	{	Water power. Tide power. Wind power.	}	Immediately referable to celestial disturbance.
Class II.	{	Steam and other powers developed by combustion, Animal power.	}	Immediately referable to what is called vital action.

The forces of gravity, cohesion, electricity, and chemical attraction tend to produce a state of permanent equilibrium on our planet; hence those principles in themselves are not primary, but secondary agents in producing mechanical effects. As an example, we may take the case of water-power, which is approximately due to the return of the water to a state of stable equilibrium on the surface of the ocean; but the primary cause of the motion is the force which produced the elevation of the liquid in the form of vapor—namely, the radiant heat of the sun. Also in the phenomena of combustion, the immediate source of the power evolved in the form of heat is the passage from an unstable state into one of stable combination of the carbon and hydrogen of the fuel with oxygen of the atmosphere. But this power may ultimately be resolved into the force which caused the separation of these elements from their previous combination in the state of carbonic acid—namely, the radiant light of the sun. But the mechanical power exerted by animals is due to the passage of organized matter in the stomach from an unstable to a stable equilibrium, or as it were from the combustion of the food. It therefore follows that animal power is referable to the same source as that from the combustion of fuel—namely, developed power of the sun's beams. But according to this view, what is vitality? It is that mysterious principle—not mechanical power—which determines the form and arranges the atoms of organized matter, employing for this purpose the power which is derived from the food.

These propositions were illustrated by different examples. Suppose a vegetable organism impregnated with a germ (a potato, for instance) is planted below the surface of the ground in a damp soil, under a temperature sufficient for vegetation. If we examine it from time to time, we find it sending down rootlets into the earth, and stems and leaves upward into the air. After the leaves have been fully expanded we shall find the tuber entirely exhausted, nothing but a skin remaining. The same effect will take place if the potato be placed in a warm cellar; it will continue to grow until all the starch and gluten are exhausted, when it will cease to increase. If however we now place it in the light, it will commence to grow again, and increase in size and weight. If we weigh the potato previous to the experiment, and the plant after it has ceased to grow in the dark, we shall find that the weight of the latter is a little more than half that of the original tuber. The question then is, what has become of the material which filled the sac of the potato? The answer is, one part has run down into carbonic acid and water, and in this running down has evolved the power to build up the other part into the new plant. After the leaves have been formed and the plant exposed to the light of the sun, the developed power of its rays decomposes the carbonic acid of the atmosphere, and thus furnishes the pabulum and the power necessary to the further development of the organization. The same is the case with wheat, and all other grains that are germinated in the earth. Besides the germ of the future plant, there is stored away, around the germ, the starch and gluten to furnish the power necessary to its development, and also the food to build it up until it reaches the surface of the earth and can draw the source of its future growth from the power of the sunbeam. In the case of fungi and other plants that grow in the dark, they derive the power and the pabulum from surrounding vegetable matter in process of decay, or in that of evolving power. A similar arrangement found is in regard to animal organization. It is well known that the egg continually diminishes in weight during the process of incubation, and the chick, when fully formed, weighs scarcely more than one-half the original weight of the egg. What is the interpretation of this phenomenon? Simply that one part of the contents of the shell has run down into carbonic acid and water, and thus evolved the power necessary to do the work of building up the future animal. In like manner when a tadpole is converted into a frog, the animal, for a while, loses weight; a portion of the organism of its tail has been expended developing the power necessary to the transformation, while another portion has served for the material of the legs.

What then is the office of vitality? We say that it is analogous to that of the engineer who directs the power of the steam-engine in the execution of its work. Without this, in the case of the egg, the materials, left to the undirected force of affinity, would end in simply producing chemical compounds — sulphureted hydrogen, carbonic acid, etc. There is no special analogy between the process of crystallization and that of vital action. In the one case definite mathematical forms are the necessary results, while in the other the results are precisely like those which are produced under the direction of will and intelligence, evincing a design and a purpose, making provision at one stage of the process for results to be attained at a later, and producing organs intended evidently for locomotion and perception. Not only is the result the same as that which is produced by human design, but in all cases the power with which this principle operates is the same as that with which the intelligent engineer produces his result.

This doctrine was first given in a communication to the American Philosophical Society, in December, 1844, and more fully developed in a paper published in the Patent Office Report in 1857.

The publication, in full, of three of the series of investigations herein described, was made in the "Transactions of the American Philosophical Society." Others were published in "Silliman's Journal," and both these are noticed in the "Royal Society's Catalogue of Scientific Papers;" but the remainder of them were published in the "Proceedings of the American Philosophical Society," and are not mentioned in the work just referred to.

In 1846, while still at Princeton, I was requested by members of the Board of Regents of the Smithsonian Institution, which was then just founded, to study the will of Smithson, and to give a plan of organization by which the object of the bequest might be realized. My conclusion was that the intention of the donor was to advance science by original research and publication, that the establishment was for the benefit of mankind generally, and that all unnecessary expenditures on local objects would be violations of the trust. The plan I proposed for the organization of the Institution was to assist men of science in making original researches, to publish these in a series of volumes, and to give a copy of these to every first-class library on the face of the earth.

I was afterward called to take charge of the Institution, and to carry out this plan, which has been the governing policy of the establishment from the beginning to the present time.

One of the first enterprises of the Smithsonian Institution was the establishment of a system of simultaneous meteorological observations over the whole United States, especially for the study of the phenomena of American storms. For this purpose the assistance of Professor ARNOLD GUYOT was obtained, who drew up a series of instructions for the observers, which was printed and distributed in all parts of the country. He also recommended the form of instruments best suited to be used by the observers, and finally calculated, with immense labor, a volume of meteorological and physical tables for reducing and discussing observations. These tables were published by the Institution, and are now in use in almost every part of the world in which the English language is spoken. The prosecution of the system finally led to the application of the principles established to the predictions of the weather by means of the telegraph.

JOSEPH HENRY.

Rev. SAMUEL B. DOD.

REMINISCENCES:*

BY

HENRY C. CAMERON, D.D,

PROFESSOR OF GREEK IN THE COLLEGE OF NEW JERSEY.

THE death of Professor HENRY may be justly termed a national loss, for probably no American since the days of Franklin has done so much for the cause of physical science as the late Secretary of the Smithsonian Institution and former Professor of Natural Philosophy in the College of New Jersey. His eminent attainments and great reputation reflected honor upon the institution with which he was connected from 1832 to 1848, and no graduate of Nassau Hall in that period went forth from its walls without a profound sense of the great benefit derived from the instructions of the professor, and warm attachment to the man.

The writer happened to be a member of the Senior Class at Princeton when Professor Henry was elected Secretary of the Smithsonian Institution, and for a short time held closer relations to him than students are wont to enjoy with a professor. When beginning his lectures to a new class, the Professor was accustomed to select some member of the preceding to assist him, and the writer had the good fortune to occupy this position during a portion of his "senior vacation," as the interval between the final examination and the commencement was styled. Hence these reminiscences, which were given in the College Chapel May 19th and June 2d, and which in response to requests from various quarters are now given to the public.

When Professor Henry was elected Secretary of the Smithsonian Institution, numerous biographies of him appeared in the public journals. While these were correct in the main facts, yet, as was to have been expected, they contained many errors. To correct these, and for the sake of truth, the Professor, overcoming his own

* "Reminiscences of Joseph Henry, LL. D."—Prepared in the College Chapel, at Princeton, on the afternoons of May 19th and June 2d, 1878.

(166)

modesty, upon one occasion gave the Senior Class a sketch of his life instead of the usual lecture. His lectures always received the most profound attention, and nothing that he said was unheeded; but upon that day his audience hung upon his lips and drank in every word that he uttered. In the simplest words he told the story of his life. Born in Albany, N. Y., December 17, 1700, he received a plain education and was destined to a mechanical pursuit, but, as he expressed it, "he was considered too dull to learn the trade." He read much, however, obtaining the books from a library which was kept in a room adjoining a church. The room had been closed for some years, but he and some of his companions gained access to the books in some way, and he thus enjoyed these hidden treasures. He subsequently attended the Albany Academy, then under the care of Dr. T. Romeyn Beck. After completing his studies he taught a district school, and was private tutor for a time in the family of Mr. S. Van Rensselaer, the patroon. He then devoted a year to the practice of civil engineering, and subsequently became Professor of Mathematics in the Academy, although at an earlier period he said he was "unable to learn geometry."

His attention was first turned to science in a singular manner. He had sustained an injury to his face and was compelled to remain at home for some days. At this time he happened to pick up a small book upon science intended for popular use. This was *Lectures on Experimental Philosophy, Astronomy and Chemistry; intended chiefly for the use of students and young persons, by G. Gregory, D. D.* The following sentences especially attracted his attention:

"Again: You throw a stone, or shoot an arrow upward into the air; why does it not go forward in the line or direction that you give it? Why does it stop at a certain distance, and then return to you? What force is it that pulls it down to the earth again, instead of its going onwards? On the contrary, Why does flame or smoke always mount upwards, though no force is used to send them in that direction? And why should not the flame of a candle drop toward the floor, when you reverse it or hold it downwards, instead of turning up and ascending into the air?"

Young Henry could not answer these questions, but proceeded to read the answer and the full explanation. He perused the volume with ever increasing interest. He asked some of his friends these and other questions, and found that they were no better acquainted with science than himself. He now determined to investigate the subject that had thus presented itself. This little book and these simple questions invited him to enter upon that scientific career and those investigations which have rendered his name immortal. A copy of this little book he was wont ever after to keep beside him. It bore the following lines from his own pen:

"This book, although by no means a profound work, has, under Providence, exerted a remarkable influence upon my life. It accidentally fell into my hands when I was about sixteen years old, and was the first book I ever read with attention. It opened to me a new world of thought and enjoyment; invested things, before almost unnoticed, with the highest interest; fixed my mind on the study of nature, and caused me to resolve at the time of reading it that I would immediately commence to devote my life to the acquisition of knowledge.   J. H."

Professor Henry's subsequent career as a teacher in Albany, Professor of Natural Philosophy in the College of New Jersey, Secretary of the Smithsonian Institution, President of the United States Light-house Board, and President of the National Academy; his discoveries in electricity, magnetism, and electro-magnetism; his interesting experiments in optics and acoustics;—are well known, not only to the scientific world, but to the general public. It is proper to state here that the venerable Dr. John Maclean, who was connected with the Faculty for fifty years, and was for fourteen years the President of the College of New Jersey, suggested and secured the appointment of Joseph Henry as a professor in this college in 1832. The friendship of these two men continued unbroken for nearly half a century. They are separated now, but it can be for only a short time. Dr. Maclean, in his History of the College, vol. ii, pp. 288–291, gives a most interesting account of the circumstances attending his appointment. Although known to scientific men, the public had heard so little of him that a trustee

of the college inquired, "Who is Henry?" Even at that time
Professor Silliman wrote: "Henry has no superior among the
scientific men of the country — at least among the young men;" and
Professor Renwick wrote, "he has no equal."

Professor Henry's great modesty prevented him from asserting
his own scientific claims; and it was only in connection with suits
pertaining to the electric telegraph that his own statements and the
testimony of others, judicially presented, irrefragably established
his just merits before the general public. From Henry's article
in Silliman's *Journal* in 1831, and from personal intercourse with
him in Princeton at a later period, Professor Morse obtained a
knowledge of those principles of electro-magnetism which rendered
his plan successful. Into this controversy the writer does not propose to enter. It is well known, however, that after eminent scientific men had pronounced an electric telegraph impossible, a vision
of Utopia, Henry, by his discoveries in Albany and at Princeton,
had accomplished the great result, and furnished ocular and *audible*
demonstration of the fact. And it is not a little remarkable that
the operator now writes his message from the sound of his instrument, upon Henry's original principle. He was never tempted
to disparage others in consequence of any attempt to detract from
his own merits. He once remarked that he "wished to be judged
simply by what he had done; it was no great compliment to be told
that he had done a great deal considering his few early advantages;
but if he was to be remembered, he desired to be remembered for
the real value of any discoveries he had made."

He was elected Secretary of the Smithsonian Institution without
any effort on his part. The scientific men of this country and of
Europe brought him to take the place. While others were seeking the appointment, the late Professor A. D. Bache, Superintendent of the Coast Survey, wrote to Europe and obtained the opinions
entertained by the most distinguished scientific men abroad in reference to Professor Henry. The letters of Sir David Brewster,
Faraday, Arago, and others, with those of Bache, Silliman, Hare,
and similarly distinguished men, were laid before the Board of
Regents, and Professor Henry was unanimously elected. It was
at that time that Sir David Brewster wrote, "The mantle of

Franklin has fallen upon the shoulders of Henry." It was no selfish motive that induced him to accept the appointment, but a sincere devotion to the cause of science. At that time various plans had been proposed for the employment of the Smithsonian fund, which had been lying in the United States Treasury for some years. A National University, a Public Library had been suggested; but Smithson's known devotion to science, and the wise choice of Professor Henry, made in deference to the most enlightened judgment and in view of his merits, determined the character of the Institution to be established. The first fair copy of the plan of the Smithsonian Institution was in the handwriting of the author of these reminiscences. He would give much now to recover that MS. In its plain, boyish chirography. He remembers that it was "*An Institution for the increase and diffusion of knowledge among men.*" "*To increase knowledge,* men were to be stimulated to original research ; *to diffuse knowledge,* the results of such research and reports on the progress of the various branches of knowledge were to be published." This general idea was then wrought out into details. This plan, in an enlarged form, was presented to the Board of Regents, and adopted December 13, 1817, and has been repeatedly published. In copying the plan a single word happened to be omitted, and the writer well recalls the nervous twitching of the Professor's lips when he discovered the mistake, and his own regret at the occurrence, and his sorrow that anything should mar the face of a MS. that was intended to be submitted either to the Board of Regents or to eminent scientific men at a distance. Professor Henry remarked to the writer that, except scientific terms, he was very reluctant to use any words not found in Johnson's Dictionary, which he kept upon his study table. His style was pure and simple, very terse and forcible; his manner of lecturing easy, graceful, and impressive. No one who was ever under his instruction can ever forget his definition of science, or his manner of enunciating it with his handsome face and magnificent physique. "SCIENCE, gentlemen, is the knowledge of the *laws* of phenomena, whether they relate to *mind* or *matter*." And what better definition can be given? So admirably were the principles of physical science expressed, so clearly were the facts presented, and so successfully were the experiments performed, that even the dullest members of the class had knowledge forced into them almost without an effort on their part, and the brightest were aroused to the utmost enthusiasm. The writer remembers the occasion when the Professor first formulated what may certainly be considered a very happy expression. He was accustomed to dictate a syllabus of each lecture to his assistant, who wrote it upon the blackboard for the use of the class. The students were required to "write up" the lectures from this syllabus, and from their notes taken during the delivery of the lectures. But few books in the writer's library are more highly prized than the two volumes containing these lectures, especially when the kind words of the Professor in commendation of them are recalled. But to return to the incident. He was walking to and fro, and had just dictated: "We explain a fact when we refer it to a *law;*" and then it occurred to him to express the corresponding idea in a similar form: "We explain a *law* when we refer it to *the will of God.*" He stopped, and exclaiming, "Yes! that is it!" he repeated the expression. In his notion of law he differed very much from the views of many scientific men of the present time. With him the material never obscured the spiritual, sense never gained the victory over faith. While accepting all the facts and established principles of science, his simple trust in Christ remained unshaken, and his confidence in the God who reveals Himself in His Word, as well as in His works, was undiminished. While, like Sir Thomas Brown, he could say, "There are two books from which I collect my divinity; besides that written one of God, another of His servant, Nature — that universal and public manuscript that lies expanded unto the eyes of all," he could also add, that "the person who thought that there could be any real conflict between science and religion, must be very young in science or very ignorant of religion."

Professor Henry was very successful in his experiments, and took the greatest delight in them. His apparatus was always in perfect order, and if failure ever occurred in his experiments it was a matter of surprise, and could not be attributed to any failure on his part. His lecture-room was in the upper story of the Philosophical Hall, which formerly occupied the site of the present library;

and it is a matter of the most profound regret that it was ever de-
molished. It corresponded in appearance with the building containing the Geological lecture-room and the Philadelphian rooms.
The main room was equal in size to the two rooms of the Philadelphian Society, and there was a smaller room in a projection in the
rear, which was subdivided into a room of moderate size, and two
small ones. The apparatus was placed in glass cases surrounding
the main room, the seats occupying the centre. Probably the most
interesting things in this room were the little horse-shoe electro-
magnet, with which he made some of his most important discoveries—the little machine which he invented, and which was the first
machine moved by electro-magnetism,—and the large electro-magnet,
which could support 3,300 pounds, and which was for many years
the largest in the world. It could be magnetized, demagnetized,
and remagnetized so rapidly that a weight of hundreds of pounds
could not detach itself from the grasp of the magnet in the interval
of reversing the currents. These things are still preserved in the
Scientific School, along with the small glass cylinders, covered with
sealing-wax, and the electrical machine prepared after the directions
of Franklin. As an illustration of character it may be mentioned that in the largest room of the projection hung a tradesman's
placard, upon which was depicted a folded whip, with the legend:
"A PLACE FOR EVERYTHING, AND EVERYTHING IN ITS PLACE."
From his lecture-room to the opposite building, and thence to his
house, which was the house now occupied by General Kargé, but
then standing on the site of Re-Union Hall, stretched a wire, through
which currents of electricity were sent that rang bells and thus conveyed messages. In his house he also had wire connected with the
lightning-rod, and needles inserted in the coils of it, that, like
Franklin, he might study the effects of electricity while the storms
were raging. The little machine mentioned was simply a small
beam of iron, surrounded by a conductor of insulated copper wire
and supported by a fulcrum, which was caused to oscillate by the
influence of two small stationary upright magnets near its ends. A
maker of philosophical apparatus once visited Princeton to sell
Professor Henry some of his machines. He showed the person
this little machine, and was threatened with a suit for "infringe-
ment of patent rights!"

In the discovery of the mode of magnetizing soft iron at a distance by means of currents of galvanism, and in his invention of this little machine, was not merely the possibility, but the fact of the electro-magnetic telegraph. Whatever may be the judgment of the general public, men of science and of education will never deny to Joseph Henry his just meed of praise in connection with this subject. It must ever be remembered that he always placed discovery above invention, and thought more highly of the principles of science than of their practical application.

Some of his discoveries came upon him suddenly, although he never pursued any other than the inductive method, questioning facts, and obtaining principles as results. Upon one occasion in Albany, he was seated in the room with his family, and engaged in profound thought. Suddenly he brought his hand down with force upon the table by which he was sitting, and — like Archimedes when he discovered the mode of ascertaining the specific gravity of bodies and cried out εὕρηκα, εὕρηκα, — he exclaimed, "I have it," "I have it." He had solved the problem on which he had been engaged, and discovered an important principle of science. In 1844 the College Commencement was changed from the Fall to the Summer, and the vacation lasted only two weeks. He spent these two weeks in scientific experiments. And in what do you suppose these experiments consisted? The answer will excite a smile. *In blowing soap-bubbles.* And yet from this childish amusement the philosopher, like the great Newton before him, was deriving important truths in physical science. All his old pupils will recall how careful he was in explaining, and how rigid he was in insisting upon the inductive method of scientific investigation. None of his pupils was ever likely to confound a mere *hypothesis* with a *theory*, as too many scientific men at present are prone to do.

In going to Washington he remarked that he "sacrificed reputation to fame." He felt that he should become known throughout the country simply as the Director of the Smithsonian Institution and to some extent of the science of the country, but that he should have little time for scientific investigation which would increase his reputation. This remark was, alas! too true. At that time he seemed to be upon the verge of most important discoveries; he had made many thousands of experiments, especially upon points in electro-magnetism, and his inductions were leading him to most interesting results. But his career was interrupted, and it was sad afterward to bear him say, "Ten, fifteen, or twenty years ago I made various experiments upon these points, but my duties in Washington have prevented me from pursuing my investigations further." And even the record of those experiments perished in the flames when a portion of the Smithsonian building was burned a few years since. Henceforth he incited others to work and guided them in their investigations. He was the representative of American science, and the contributions of the Smithsonian Institution, and his Annual Reports for thirty years, show how faithfully he carried out the purpose of the Institution. Into the management of its funds he carried the same economy and scrupulous delicacy that he exhibited in his private financial transactions. He would not employ for the use of his family funds which legally belonged to him, because he thought that morally they belonged to a single member of it. If any fault could be found with the financial affairs of the Institution over which he presided, it was that the compensation of the men of science who labored for it was entirely inadequate. Occasionally they were not even paid for their time, much less for their labor or with reference to their scientific reputation. He persistently declined to have his own modest salary increased, and even gave the net proceeds of any lectures he delivered to the Institution. A single incident will illustrate his high character and his delicate sense of honor. Shortly after he was elected Secretary of the Smithsonian Institution, Dr. Hare resigned his position as Professor of Chemistry in the Medical Department of the University of Pennsylvania, at that time probably the most desirable scientific chair in this country. Philadelphia was the headquarters of Medical education; this Medical School was the oldest and the largest in the land; the salary from fees amounted to $5,000 or $6,000; the duties occupied less than six months annually, leaving *the remainder of the year free for scientific investigation.* Professor Henry was sent for, and was asked if he would accept the appointment. The writer well recalls the day. The Professor, as he was returning from his interview with the Trustees of the University in

Philadelphia, met him in the college campus in Princeton. He had not yet reached his home, and standing with his carpet-bag in his hand, he gave the writer an account of the interview, and the reasons which induced him to decline a position so well suited to his taste, his wishes, his attainments. He said it would not be honorable for him to decline a position which his scientific brethren desired him to occupy, and where he could accomplish much for science if not for himself; but especially because, if he accepted the chair in Philadelphia, to which a larger salary was attached than he should receive in Washington, *it might be supposed that he was influenced by pecuniary reasons.* How different would have been the great philosopher's career had his decision been different!

He did not favor the erection of a large building for the Institution, remarking that he needed only two rooms as an office. When it was determined to erect the fine building which now adorns the public grounds at Washington, he employed only a portion of the interest that had accumulated, and built slowly, so that a portion of this was saved and was added to the original fund.

The first paper that was offered him for publication, according to the writer's recollection, was one by Dr. John Locke, upon the Ancient Mounds in Ohio. The writer well remembers the large bundle of MS., a portion of which, at least, was published in the first volume of the Smithsonian Contributions, if the entire paper was not accepted.[*]

How faithfully the Secretary discharged all his duties is well known. Amid all the corruption of public life at Washington, there was never a spot upon the fair fame of Joseph Henry; not a breath ever tarnished his reputation. In addition to his duties as Secretary of the Smithsonian Institution, as President of the Light-house Board, he annually inspected the light-houses, and devoted a considerable portion of his vacations for sixteen years to experiments on light and sound for the benefit of the General Government. His only compensation was his expenses. In the desk in the small room that had been fitted up for him near the

[*] [The paper of Dr. Locke was incorporated (with due acknowledgement) in the extended Memoir on "The Ancient Monuments of the Mississippi Valley," by Messrs. Squier and Davis; which work occupied the entire first volume of the Smithsonian Contributions.]

light-house on Staten Island will probably be found the record of his last summer's observations. As a member of the National Academy, he made many scientific investigations for the Government, and thus saved the country large sums of money.

He died, as he lived, a comparatively poor man; and except a policy of life insurance, the only money he ever laid aside was the few hundred dollars he gained in the year when he was a civil engineer engaged in locating a road for the State of New York. This small sum was taken by a wealthy capitalist, and the interest was annually added to the capital. This money has remained untouched for fifty years, and is now in the hands of the son of the friend of his youth, ready to be given to those to whom he has left a nobler legacy than money, even a good name that is better than precious ointment.

THE LIFE AND CHARACTER

OF

JOSEPH HENRY.*

BY

JAMES C. WELLING, LL. D.,

PRESIDENT OF COLUMBIAN UNIVERSITY.

JOSEPH HENRY was born in Albany, N. Y., on the 17th of December, 1799. His grandparents on both his father's and mother's side emigrated from Scotland, and landed in this country on the 16th of June, 1775, the day before the battle of Bunker's Hill. At the age of seven or earlier, for what reason is unknown, he went to live with his maternal grandmother, who resided at Galway, in the county of Saratoga, N. Y., and his father having died soon afterward, he continued to dwell for years under her roof. At Galway he attended the district school, of which one Israel Phelps was the master, and having there learned the rudiments of an English education, he was placed at the early age of ten in a store kept in the village by a Mr. Broderick. Receiving from his employer every token of kindness, and, indeed, of paternal interest in his welfare, the boy-clerk, already remarkable for his handsome visage, his slender figure, his delicate complexion, and his vivacious temper, became a great favorite with his comrades, who, according to the customs of the village store, were wont to saunter about the door in summer, and to gather round the stove in winter, for the interchange of such trivial gossip as pertains to village life. Though released at this time for the half of each day from the duty of waiting in the store that he might attend the sessions of the common school In the afternoon, it does not appear that he had as yet evinced any taste for books, notwithstanding the

---

* Read before the "Philosophical Society of Washington," October 28, 1878. (Bulletin of the Phil. Soc. W. vol. II. p. 202.)

(177)

fact, as he afterwards recalled, that his young brain was even then troubled at times with the "malady of thought," as he lost himself in the mazes of revery or speculation about God and creation — "those obstinate questionings of sense and outward things," which the philosophical poet of England has described as the natural misgivings of a "creature moving about in worlds not realized." "Delight and liberty," as was natural to a bright boy in the full flush of his animal spirits, still remained the simple creed of his childhood, until one day his pet rabbit escaped from its warren and ran into an opening in the foundation of the village church. Finding the hole sufficiently large to admit of pushing his person through it, he followed on all fours in eager pursuit of the fugitive, when his eyes were attracted in a certain direction by a glimmer of light, and groping his way toward it, beneath the church, he discovered that it proceeded from a crevice which led into the vestibule of the building, and which opened immediately behind a book-case that had been placed in the vestibule, as the depository of the village library. Working his way to the front of the book-case, he found himself in the presence of all the literature stored on its shelves, and on his taking down the first book which struck his eye, it proved to be Brooke's Fool of Quality, a work of fiction in which views of practical life and traits of mystical piety are artfully blended, insomuch that even John Wesley was inclined to except it from the *auto-da-fé* which, after the manner of the curate and barber in the story of Don Quixote, he would have gladly performed upon the less edifying products of the novel-writing imagination. Poring over the pages of this fascinating volume, young Henry forgot the rabbit in quest of which he had crept beneath the church. It was the first book he had ever read with zest, because it was the first book he had ever read at the impulse of his "own sweet will." Mrs. Browning has told us that we get no good from a book by being ungenerous with it, by calculating profits — "so much help by so much reading."

> ——"It is rather when
> We gloriously forget ourselves, and plunge
> Soul-forward, headlong, into a book's profound,
> Impassioned for its beauty and salt of truth—
> 'Tis then we get the right good from a book."

Such was the "soul-forward, headlong plunge" which the boyish Henry now first took in the waters of romance, rendered only the sweeter to him, it may be, because, without affront to innocence, they took the flavor of "stolen waters" from the stealth with which they were imbibed. From that time forth he made frequent visits to this library, by the same tortuous and underground passage, reading by preference only works of fiction, the contents of which he retailed to listening comrades around the stove by night, until, in the end, his patron, who shared in his taste for such "light reading," procured for him the right of access to the library in the regular way, and no longer by the narrow fissure in the rear of the book-case.

At the age of fifteen he left the store of Mr. Benderick in Galway, and, returning to the place of his birth, entered a watch-maker's establishment in Albany, but finding nothing congenial to his taste in the new pursuit, he soon abandoned it. At this time he had formed a strong predilection for the stage. Two or three years before, while living at Galway, he had seen a play for the first time, on the occasion of a casual visit to Albany, and the impression it made upon his mind was as vivid as that left by the perusal of his first novel. He described and re-enacted its scenes for the wonderment of the Galway youth, and now that he was living in Albany he could give full vent to his new inclination. His spare money was all spent in theatrical amusements, until at length he won his way behind the scenes, and procured admission to the green room, where he learned how to put a play on the boards and how to produce the illusion of stage effects. In the skill with which he learned thus early to handle the apparatus of the stage we may discern, perhaps, the first faint prelude of the skill to which he subsequently attained in handling the levers and screws with which, according to Goethe, the experimental philosopher seeks to extort from nature the revelation of her mysteries.

Invited at this period of his life to join a private theatrical association in Albany, known by the name of "The Rostrum," the young enthusiast soon distinguished himself among his fellow-members of riper years by the ingenuity of his dramatic combinations and the felicity of his scenic effects, insomuch that he was made

President of the Society. Meanwhile, the watchmaker had left Albany, and young Henry, no longer having the fear of the silversmith's file and crucible before his eyes, was left free to follow the lead of his dramatic tastes and aspirations. He dramatized a tale, and prepared a comedy; both of which were acted by the association. Indeed, so much was he absorbed in this new vocation that our amateur Roscius seemed, according to all outward appearance, in a fair way of making a place for himself among the "periwig-pated fellows who tear a passion to tatters" on the stage; or, at the best, of taking rank with the great dramatic artists who, standing in front of the garish foot-lights, "hold the mirror up to nature" in a sense far different from that of the experimental philosopher, standing in the clear beams of that *lumen siccum* which Bacon has praised as the light that is best of all for the eyes of the mind. But in the midst of these disguises, under which the unique and original genius of Henry has thus far seemed to be masquerading, we have now come to the time when his mind underwent a great transfiguration, which revealed its native brightness, and a transfiguration as sudden as it was great.

Minds richly endowed, if started at first in a wrong direction, may sometimes have, it would seem, an intellectual conversion as marked as that moral conversion which is often visible in the lives of great saints. It certainly was so in the case of Henry. Overtaken in the sixteenth year of his age by a slight accident, which detained him for a season within doors, he chanced, in search of mental diversion, to cast his eyes upon a book which a Scotch gentleman, boarding with his mother, had left upon the table in his chamber. It was Dr. Gregory's Lectures on Experimental Philosophy, Astronomy, and Chemistry. It commences with an address to the young reader, in which the author stimulates him to deeper inquiry concerning the familiar objects around him. "You throw a stone," he says, "or shoot an arrow upwards into the air; why does it not go forward in the air, and in the direction you give it? What force is it that presses it down to the earth? Why does flame or smoke always mount upward? You look into a clear well of water, and see your own face and figure, as if painted there; why is this? You are told it is done by reflection of light. But

what is reflection of light?" etc., etc. These queries certainly are
very far from representing the *prudens quæstio* of Bacon in even
its most elementary form, but they opened to the mind of young
Henry an entirely "new world of thought and enjoyment." His
attention was enchained by this book as it had not been enchained by
the fiction of Brooke or by the phantasmagoria of the drama.*
The book did for him what the spirits did for Faust when they
opened his eyes to see the sign of the macrocosm, and summoned
him "to unveil the powers of nature lying all around him." Not
more effectual was the call which came to St. Augustine, when, as
he lay beneath the shadow of the fig-tree, weeping in the bitterness
of a contrite soul, he seemed to hear a voice that said to him: "*Tolle,
lege; tolle, lege,*" and at the sound of which he turned away forever
from the Ten Predicaments of Aristotle, and all the books of the
rhetoricians, to follow what seemed to him the "lively oracles of
God." No sooner had Henry recovered from his sickness, than,
obedient to the new vision of life and duty which had dawned upon
him, he summoned his comrades of "the Rostrum" to meet him in
conference, formally resigned the office of President, and, in a valedictory address, announced to his associates that, subordinating the
pleasures of literature to the acquisition of serious knowledge, he
had determined henceforth to consecrate his life to arduous and
solid studies.

There are doubtless those who, in the retrospect of Professor
Henry's youth, as contrasted with the rich flower and fruitage of his
riper years, will please themselves with curious speculations on what
"might have been," if his rabbit had never slipped its inclosure, if
there had been no crack in the wall behind the book-case, or if
Gregory's Lectures had never fallen in his way at the critical

* He soon became so much interested in this book that its owner gave it to him,
and in token of the epoch it had marked in his life, Professor Henry ever afterwards preserved it among the choicest memorials of his boyhood. In the leaf
of this book the following memorandum is found, written in the year 1847: This
book, although by no means a profound work, has, under Providence, exerted a
remarkable influence on my life. It evidently fell into my hands when I was about
sixteen years old, and with the first book that I ever read with attention. It opened
to me a new world of thought and enjoyment; it rivited my mind on the study of nature, and
caused me to resolve at the time of reading it that I would immediately commence
to devote my life to the acquisition of knowledge.—J.H.

juncture of his life, much as the great mind of Pascal pleased itself with musing how the fate of Europe might have been changed if the Providential grain of sand in Cromwell's tissue had not sent him to a premature grave; or how the whole face of the earth would have been changed if the nose of Cleopatra had been a little shorter than it was, and so had marred the beauty of face which made her, like another Helen, the *teterrima causa belli* for a whole generation. Such fanciful speculations are well calculated to import into the philosophy of human life, and into the philosophy of human history, a theory of causation which is as superficial as it is false. As honest Horatio says to Hamlet in the play, when the latter proposes to trace the noble dust of Alexander the Great, in imagination, until perchance it may be found stopping a bung-hole, one feels like saying in the presence of such fine-spun speculations, "'Twere to consider too curiously to consider so." The strong intellectual forces which are organic in a great mind, as the strong moral and political forces which are organic in society, do not depend for their evolution, or for their grand cyclical movements, on the casual vicissitudes which ripple the surface of human life and affairs. To argue in this wise is to mistake occasion for cause, and by confounding what is transient and incidental with what is permanent and pervasive, is to make the noblest life, with its destined ends and ways, the mere creature of accident, and is to convert human history, with its great secular developments, into the fortuitous rattle and chance combinations of the kaleidoscope. We may be sure that Henry was too great a man to have lived and died without making his mark on the age in which his lot was cast, whatever should have been the time, place, or circumstance which was to disclose the color and complexion of his destiny. The strong, clear mind, like the crystal, takes its shape and pressure from the play of the constituent forces within it, and is not the sport of casual influences that come from without.

Armed, however, with his new enthusiasm, the nascent philosopher hastened to join a night school in Albany, but soon exhausted the lore of its master. Encountering next a peripatetic teacher of English grammar, he became, under the pedagogue's drill, so versed in the arts of orthography, etymology, syntax, and prosody, that be started out himself on a grammatical tour through the provincial districts of New York, and returning from this first field of his triumphs as a teacher, he entered the Albany Academy (then in charge of Dr. T. Romeyn Beck) as a pupil in its more advanced studies. Meanwhile, in order to "pay his way" in the academy, he sought employment as a teacher in a neighboring district school, this being, as he afterwards was wont to say, the only office he had ever sought in his life; and in this office he succeeded so well that his salary was raised from $8 for the first month to the monificent sum of $15 for the second month of his service. From pupil in the academy and teacher of the district school, he was soon promoted to the rank of assistant in the academy, and henceforward had ample means for the further prosecution of his studies. Leaving the academy, he next accepted the post of private tutor in the family of the patroon in Albany, Mr. S. Van Rensselaer; and, devoting his leisure hours to the study of the higher mathematics, in conjunction with chemistry, physiology, and anatomy, he at this time purposed to enter the medical profession, and had made some advances in this direction, when he was called, in the year 1826, to embark in a surveying expedition, set on foot under the auspices of the State government of New York, for the purpose of laying out a road through the southern tier of counties in that State. Starting with his men at West Point, and going through the woods to Lake Erie, he acquitted himself so well in this expedition that his friends endeavored to procure for him a permanent appointment as captain of an engineering corps, which it was proposed to create for the prosecution of other internal improvement schemes, but the bill projected for this purpose having fallen through, Mr. Henry again accepted, though with some reluctance, a vacant chair which was offered him in the Albany Academy.

In connection with the duties of this chair, he now commenced a series of original experiments in natural philosophy—the first connected series which had been prosecuted in this country. Dr. Hare, indeed, had already invented the compound blowpipe, as Franklin before him, by his brilliant but desultory labors, had given an immense impulse to the science of electricity; yet none the less is it true that regular and systematic investigations, designed

to push forward the boundaries of knowledge abreast with the
scientific workers of Europe, had hardly been attempted at that
time in the United States.

The achievements of Henry in this direction soon began to win
for him an increase of reputation as well as an increase of knowledge; but in the midst of the fervor which had come to quicken
his genius, he was visited by the fancy (or was it a fact?) that a
few of the friends who had hitherto supported him in his high
ambition were now beginning to look a little less warmly on his
aspirations. Suffering from this source the mental depression
which was natural to a sensitive spirit, no less remarkable for its
modesty than for its merit, he found solace in the friendly words
of good cheer and hopefulness addressed to him by Mr. William
Dunlap.[*] While one day making, with Mr. Henry, a trip down
the Hudson River on board the same steamboat, Mr. Dunlap
observed in the young teacher's face the marks of sadness, and, on
learning its cause, he laid his hand affectionately on Henry's
shoulder, and closed some reassuring advice with the prophetic
words, "Albany will one day be proud of her son." The presage
was destined to be abundantly confirmed. Soon afterward came
the call to Princeton College, and, because of the wider career it
opened to him, the call was as grateful to Henry as its acceptance
was gratifying to the friends of that Institution. And shortly
before this promotion a new happiness had come to crown his life
in his marriage to the excellent lady who still survives him.

He entered upon the duties of his new post in the month of
November, 1832, and bringing with him a budding reputation,
which soon blossomed into the highest scientific fame, he became
the pride and ornament of the Princeton Faculty. The prestige
of his magnets attracted students from all parts of the country;
but the magnetism of the man was better far than any work of
his cunning hand or fertile brain. It was in Princeton, as he
was afterward wont to say, that he spent the happiest days of
his life, and they were also among the most fruitful in scientific

---

[*] This Mr. Dunlap had been the manager of the Park Theatre in New York,
and combined with his dramatic vocation the pursuits of literature and the
painter's art. He wrote the "History of Arts and Designs in the United States," a
work which was esteemed a standard one at the date of its first publication in 1834.

discovery. Leaving the record of his particular achievements at
this epoch to be told by Mr. Taylor, who is so well qualified to
do them justice, I beg leave only to refer to this period in the
career of Professor Henry as that in which it was my good fortune to come, for the first time, under the personal influence of the
great philosophical scholar, who, after being my teacher in science
during the days of my college novitiate at Princeton, continued
during the whole of his subsequent life to honor me with a friendship which was as much my support in every emergency that called
for counsel and guidance as it was at all times my joy and the
crown of my rejoicing.

In the year 1847, when Professor Henry was in the forty-eighth
year of his age, he was unanimously elected by the Regents of the
Smithsonian Institution as its Secretary, or Director.   At that time
the institution existed only in name, under the organic act passed by
Congress for its incorporation, in order to give effect to the bequest
of James Smithson, Esq., of London, who by his last will and
testament had given the whole of his property to the United States
to found at Washington, under the name of the "Smithsonian Institution," an establishment for "the increase and diffusion of knowledge among men."   It does not need to be said that Professor
Henry did not seek this appointment.   It came to him unsolicited,
but it came to him from the Board of Regents not only by the free
choice of its members, but also at the suggestion and with the
approval of European men of science, like Sir David Brewster,
Faraday, and Arago, as also of American scientific men, like Bache
and Silliman and Hare.   I well remember to have heard the late
George M. Dallas (a member of the constituent Board of Regents
by virtue of his office as Vice-President of the United States)
make the remark on a public occasion, immediately after the election of Professor Henry as Director of the Smithsonian Institution,
that the Board had not had the slightest hesitation in tendering
the appointment to him "as being peerless among the recognized
heads of American science."

At the invitation of the Regents he drew up an outline plan of
the Institution, and the plan was adopted by them on the 13th of

December, 1847. The members of this Society, living, as they do, beneath the shadow of the great Institution to which Smithson worthily gave his name and his estate, but of which Henry was at once the organizing brain and the directing hand from the date of its inception down to the day of his death, do not need that I should sketch for them the theory on which it was projected by its first Secretary, or that I should rehearse in detail the long chronicle of the useful and multiform services which in pursuit of that theory it has rendered to the cause of science and of human progress. And, moreover, in doing so I should here again imprudently trench on the province assigned to my learned colleague. But I may be allowed to portray the method and spirit which he brought to the duties of this exacting post, at least so far as to say that he proved himself as great in administration as he was great in original research; as skilful in directing the scientific labors of others as he was skilful in the conduct of his own. Seizing, as with an intuitive eye, the peculiar genius of an Institution which was appointed to "*increase* knowledge" and to "*diffuse*" it "among men," he touched the springs of scientific inquiry at a thousand points in the wide domain of modern thought, and made the results of that inquiry accessible to all with a catholicity as broad as the civilized world. And the publications of the Smithsonian Institution, valuable as they are, and replete as they are with contributions to human knowledge, represent the least part of his manifold labors in connection with the Institution. His correspondence was immense, covering the whole field of existing knowledge, and ranging, in the persons addressed, from the genuine scientific scholar in all parts of the world to the last putative discoverer of perpetual motion, or the last embryo mathematician who supposed himself to have squared the circle.

In accepting a post where he was called by virtue of his office to promote the labors of other men rather than his own, Professor Henry distinctly saw that he was renouncing for himself the paths of scientific glory on which he had entered so auspiciously at Albany and Princeton. He once said to me, in one of the self-revealing moods in which he sometimes unbosomed himself to his intimate friends, that in accepting the office of Smithsonian Secretary he was conscious that he had "sacrificed future fame to present reputation."

He was in the habit of recalling that Newton had made no discoveries after he was appointed Warden of the Mint in 1695,* and the remark is historically accurate, unless we should incline with Biot, against the better opinion of Sir David Brewster, to place after that date the "discoveries" which Newton supposed himself to have made in the Scriptural chronology and in the interpretation of the Apocalypse—discoveries which, whenever made, provoked the theological scoff, as they perhaps deserved the theological criticism, of the polemical Bishop Warburton. Yet, having convinced himself that it was a duty he owed to the cause of science to sink his own personality in the impersonal institution he was called to conduct, Henry never paused for an instant to confer with flesh and blood, but moved "right onward" in the path of duty, with only the more of steadfastness because he felt that it was for him a path of sacrifice.

How sedulously he strove to maintain the Institution in the high vocation to which he believed it was appointed no less by a sacred regard for the will of its founder than by an intelligent zeal for the promotion of human welfare, is known to you all. And the success with which he resisted all schemes for the impoverishment of the exalted function it was fitted to perform in the service of abstract science, is a tribute at once to his rare executive skill and to the native force of character which made him a tower of strength against the clamors of popular ignorance and the assaults of charlatanism. Whatever might be the consequences to himself personally, he was determined to magnify its vocation and make it honorable. And hence I do not permit myself to doubt that during the long period of his administration as Secretary of the Smithsonian Institution, covering a period of thirty years, he has impressed upon its conduct a definite direction which his successors will be proud to maintain, not simply in reverence for the memory of their illustrious predecessor, but also in grateful recognition of the fruitful works which,

* The effect of the Wardenship on Newton's scientific labors may be seen in the warmth with which he rebuked Flamsteed for purposing to publish, in 1695, the fact that Newton was then engaged on a revision of the Horroxian theory of the moon. Newton wrote: "I do not love to be printed on every occasion, much less to be dunned and teased by foreigners about mathematical things, or to be thought by our own people to be trifling away my time when I should be about the King's business."

in the pursuit of his enlightened plans, will continue to follow him now that he has rested from his labors.

The rest into which he has entered came to him in a green old age, after a life as full of years as it was full of honors. He was not only blest with an old age which was

> ——— serene and bright,
> And lovely as a Lapland night,

but he also had that which, according to the great dramatist, should accompany old age — "As honor, love, obedience, troops of friends." And the manner of his death was in perfect keeping with the manner of his life. Assured for months before the inevitable hour came that his days on earth were numbered, he made no change in his daily official employments, no change in his social and literary diversions. None was needed. Surprise, I learn, has been expressed that in the full prospect of death he should have "talked" so little about it. But the surprise is quite unfounded. Professor Henry was little in the habit of talking about himself at any time. Yet to his intimate friends he spoke freely and calmly about his approaching end. Two weeks before he died he said to one such, a gentleman from New York, to whom he was strongly attached: "I may die at any moment. I would like to live long enough to complete some things I have undertaken, but I am content to go. I have had a happy life, and I hope I have been able to do some good." In an hour's conversation which I had with him six days before he died, he referred to the imminence of his death with the same philosophic and Christian composure. And perfectly aware as he was, on the day before he died, and on the day of his death, that he had already entered the Dark Valley, he feared no evil as he looked across it, but, poised in a sweet serenity, preserved his soul in patience, at an equal remove from rapture on the one hand or anything like dismay on the other. For his friends he had even then the same benignant smile, the same warm pressure of the hand, and the same affable words as of yore. With the astronomer, Newcomb, he pleasantly and intelligently discoursed about the then recent transit of Mercury — not unheedful of the great transit he was making, but giving heed none the less to every opportunity for the inquiry of truth. Toward the attendants watching around his couch he was as observant as ever of all the "small sweet courtesies" which marked consideration for others rather than for himself even in the supreme moment of his dissolution. The disciples of Socrates recalled, with a sort of pathetic wonder at the calm and intrepid spirit of their dying master, that as the chill of the fatal hemlock was stealing toward his heart, he uncovered his face to ask that Crito should acquit him of a small debt he owed to Æsculapius; and so in like manner I recall that our beloved chief did not forget in the hour of his last agony to make provision for the due dispatch of a letter of courtesy, which on the day before he had promised to a British stranger.

And so in the full possession of all his great mental powers—in his waking hours filled with high thoughts and with a peace which passed all understanding; in his sleep stealing away

"To dreamful wastes where footless fancies dwell,"

and talking even there of experiments in sound on board the steamer Mistletoe, or haply taking note of electric charges sent through imaginary wires at his bidding,* —the soul of Joseph Henry passed away from the earth which he had blessed and brightened by his presence.†

From these imperfect notes on the life of Professor Henry I pass to consider some of his traits and characteristics as a man.

He was endowed with a physical organization in which the elements were not only fine and finely mixed, but were cast in a mould remarkable for its symmetry and manly beauty. The perfection of his "outward man" was not unworthy of the "inward man" whom it enshrined, and if, as a church father has phrased it, "the human soul is the true Shechinah," it may none the less be said that the human body never appears to so much advantage as when, transfigured by this Shechinah, it offers to the informing spirit a temple which is as stately as it is pure. When Dr. Bentley was called to write the epitaph of Cotes, (that brilliant scholar of whom Newton

---

* Professor Henry took great delight in the acoustical researches which, during the closing years of his life, he made at sea on board the steamer Mistletoe, while it was in electricity that he won his first triumphs as a scientific man. That his first love and last passion in science still filled his thoughts in his dying moments was attested by the words which even then fell from his lips, in sleep.

† He died ten minutes after twelve o'clock, on the 13th of May, 1878.

said that "if he had lived we might have known something,") the accomplished master of words thought it not unmeet to record that the fallen Professor, who had been snatched away by a premature death, was only "the more attractive and lovely because the virtues and graces which he joined to the highest repute for learning were embellished by a handsome person." The same tribute of admiration might be paid with equal justice to the revered Professor whose "good gray head" has just vanished from our sight.

The fascination of Professor Henry's manner was felt by all who came within the range of its influence — by men with whom he daily consorted in business, in college halls, and in the scientific academy; by brilliant women of society who, in his gracious presence, owned the spell of a masculine mind which none the less was feminine in the delicacy of its perceptions and the purity of its sensibilities; by children, who saw in the simplicity of his unspoiled nature a geniality and a kindliness which were akin to their own. A French thinker has said that in proportion as one has more intellectuality he finds that there are more men who possess original qualities. It was the breadth and catholicity of Henry's intelligence which enabled him to find something unique and characteristic in persons who were flat, stale, and unprofitable to the average mind.

Gifted with a mental constitution which was "feelingly alive to each fine impulse," he possessed a high degree of æsthetic sensibility to the beautiful in nature and in art. It cannot be doubted that a too exclusive addiction to the analytic and microscopic study of nature, at the instance of science, has a tendency to blunt in some minds a delicate perception for the "large livingness" of Nature, considered as a source of poetic and moral inspiration, but no such tendency could be discovered in the intellectual habitudes of Professor Henry. To a mind long nurtured by arts of close and critical inquiry into the logic of natural law he none the less united a heart which was ever ready to leap with joy at "the wonder and bloom of the world." When on the occasion of his first visit to England, in the year 1837, he was travelling by night in a stage-coach through Salisbury Plain, he hired the driver to stop, while all his fellow-passengers were asleep, that he might have the privilege of inspecting the ruins of Stonehenge, as seen by moonlight,

and brought away a weird sense of mystery which followed him in
all his after life.   At a later day, in the year 1870, after visiting
the Aar Glacier, the scene of Professor Agassiz's well-known labors,
he crossed over the mountain to the Rhone Valley, until, at a sudden
turn of the road, he came full in the presence of the majestic Glacier
of the Rhone.   For minutes he stood silent and motionless; then,
turning to the daughter who stood by his side, he exclaimed, with
the tears running down his checks: "This is a place to die in.   We
should go no further."

And as he rejoiced in natural scenery so also was he charmed with
the beauties of art, and felt as much at home in the atelier of the
painter or sculptor as in the laboratory of the chemist or the apparatus room of the natural philosopher, and exulted as sincerely in
the Louvre or the Corcoran Gallery of Art as in the cabinet of the
mineralogist or the museum of the naturalist.

He was as remarkable for the simplicity of his nature as for the
breadth of his mind and the acumen of his intellect. Those who
analyze the nature and charm of simplicity in a great mind suppose
themselves to find the secret of both in the fact that simplicity,
allied with greatness, works its marvels with a sweet unconsciousness of its own superior excellence, and it works them with this
unconsciousness because it is greater than it knows. Talent does
what it can. Genius does what it must. And in this respect, as an
English writer has said, there is a great analogy between the highest
goodness and the highest genius; for under the influence of either,
the spirit of man may scatter light and splendor around it, without
admiring itself or seeking the admiration of others. And it was
in this sense that the simplicity of Henry's nature expressed itself
in acts of goodness and in acts of high intelligence with a spon-
taneity which hid from himself the transcendent virtue and dignity
of the work he was doing; and hence all his work was done without the slightest taint of vanity or tarnish of self-complacency.

As might be expected, he was a fervent lover of the best literature. His acquaintance with the English poets was not only wide
but intimate. His memory was stored with choice passages, di-
dactic, sentimental, witty, and humorous, which he reproduced at
will on occasions when they were apt to his purpose. His famil-

iarity with fiction dated, as we have seen, from early boyhood, and
in this fountain of the imagination he continued to find refreshment
for the "wear and tear" of the hard and continuous thought to
which he was addicted in the philosopher's study. His knowledge
of history was accurate, and it was not simply a knowledge of facts,
but a knowledge of facts as seen in the logical coherence and rational
explanation which make them the basis of historic generalization.
The genesis of the Greek civilization was a perpetual object of
interest to his speculative mind, as called to deal with the phenomena of Grecian literature, art, philosophy, and polity.

He was a terse and forcible writer. If, as some have said, it is
the perfection of style to be colorless, the style of Henry might
be likened to the purest amber, which, invisible itself, holds in clear
relief every object it envelops. Without having that fluent delivery which, according to the well-known comparison of Dean
Swift, is rarely characteristic of the fullest minds, he was none
the less a pleasing and effective speaker—the more effective because his words never outran his thought. We loved to think and
speak of him as "the Nestor of American Science," and if his
speech, like Nestor's, "flowed sweeter than honey," it was due to
the excellent quality of the matter rather than to any rhetorical
facility of manner.

He was blest with a happy temperament. He recorded in his
diary, as a matter of thanksgiving, that through the kindness of
Providence he was able to forget what had been painful in his past
experiences, and to remember only and enjoy that which had been
pleasurable. The same sentiment is expressed in one of his letters.
Radiant with this sunny temper, he was in his family circle a perpetual benediction. And, in turn, he was greatly dependent on his
family for the sympathy and watch-care due in a thousand small
things to one who never "lost the childlike in the larger mind." His
domestic affections were not dwarfed by the exacting nature of his
official duties, his public cares, or his scientific vigils. He had none
of that solitary grandeur affected by isolated spirits who cannot
descend to the tears and smiles of this common world. He was never
so happy as when in his home he was communing with wife and children around the family altar. He made them the confidants of all

his plans. He rehearsed to them his scientific experiments. He
reported to them the record of each day's adventures. He read
with them his favorite authors.* He entered with a gleeful spirit
into all their joys; with a sympathetic heart into all their sorrows.
And while thus faithful to the charities of home he was intensely
loyal to his friends, and found in their society the very cordial of
life. Gracious to all, he grappled some of them to his heart with
hooks of steel. The friendship, fed by a kindred love of elegant
letters, which still lends its mellow lustre to the names of Cicero
and Atticus, was not more beautiful than the friendship, fed by
kindred talents, kindred virtues, and kindred pursuits, which so
long united the late Dr. Bache and Professor Henry in the bonds
of a sacred brotherhood. And this was but one of the many similar
intimacies which came to embellish his long and useful career.

His sense of honor was delicate in the extreme. It was not only
that "chastity of honor which feels a stain like a wound," but at
the very suggestion of a stain it recoiled as instantly as the index
finger of Mr. Edison's tasimeter at the "suspicion" of heat. I
met him in 1847, when, soon after his election as Secretary of the
Smithsonian Institution, he had just been chosen to succeed Dr.
Hare as Professor of Chemistry in the Medical Department of the
University of Pennsylvania, at a salary double that which he was
to receive in Washington, and with half the year open to free
scientific investigation, because free from professional duties. It
was, he said, the post which, of all others, he could have desiderated
at that epoch in his scientific life, but his honor, he added, forbade
him to entertain, for a moment, the proposition of accepting it after

* The following extract from a diary, kept by one of his daughters, is descriptive
of his habits under this head: "Had father with us all the evening. I modelled his
profile in clay while he read Thomson's Seasons to us. In the earlier part of the
evening he seemed restless and depressed, but the influence of the poet drove away
the cloud, and then an expression of almost childlike sweetness rested on his lips,
singularly in contrast yet beautifully in harmony with the intellect of the brow
above."

Or take this extract from the same diary: "We were all up until a late hour,
reading partly with father and mother, father being the reader. He attempted Cow-
per's Grave, by Mrs. Browning, but was too tender-hearted to finish the reading of
it. We then laughed over the Address to the Mummy, soared to heaven with Shel-
ley's Skylark, roamed the forest with Bryant, culled flowers from other poetical
fields, and ended with Tam O'Shanter. I took for my task to recite a part of the
latter from memory, while father corrected, as if he were 'playing schoolmaster.'"

13

the obligations under which he had come to the interests represented by the Smithsonian Institution. At a later day, after he
had entered on his duties in Washington, and found the position
environed with many difficulties, Mr. Calhoun came to him, and
urged his acceptance of a lucrative chair in a Southern college,
using as a ground of appeal the infelicities of his present post, and
the prospect of failing at last to realize the high designs he had
projected for the management of the Smithsonian Institution.
Admitting that it might be greatly to his comfort and advantage
at that time to give up the Smithsonian, he declined at once to
consider the proposal that was made to him, on the ground that his
"honor was committed to the Institution." Whereupon Mr. Calhoun seized his hand and exclaimed, "Professor Henry, you are a
man after my own heart."

When in 1853, and again in 1867, he was entreated by friends to
allow the use of his name in connection with a call to the Presidency of Princeton College, the college of his love, and the scene of
his "happiest days," he instantly turned away from the lure, as feeling that he could not love the dear old college so much if he loved
not more the honor and duty which bound him to the establishment
in Washington, with which, for good or for evil, he had wedded his
name and fortune. And in all other concerns, from the greatest to
the least, he seemed like one

> Intent each lurking frailty to disclaim,
> And guard the way of life from all offence,
> Suffered or done.

The "Man of Ross," portrayed by the pencil of Pope, was not
more benevolent in heart or act than Professor Henry. His
bounty was large and free. The full soul mantled in his eyes at
every tale of woe, and the generous hand was quick to obey the
charitable impulses of his sympathetic nature. This benevolent
spirit ran like a silver cord through the tissue of his life, because it
was interwoven in the very warp and woof of his being, and
because it was kept in constant exercise. It appeared not only in
acts of kindness to the poor and afflicted, but interpenetrated his
whole demeanor, and informed all his conduct wherever he could
be helpful to a fellow-man. He did good to all as he had oppor-

tunity, from "the forlorn and shipwrecked brother," who had
already failed in the voyage of life, to the adventurous young
mariner who sought his counsel and guidance for the successful
launching of his ship from its ways. Many are the young men,
who, in all parts of the land, could rise up to-day and call him
blessed, for the blessing he brought to them by the kind word
spoken and the kind deed done, each in its season.

Unselfishness was a fundamental trait in the character of Professor Henry, and he made the same trait a fundamental one in
his conception of the philosopher's high calling. The work of scientific inquiry was with him a labor of love, not simply because he
loved the labor, but because he hoped by it to advance the cause
of truth and promote the welfare of man. He never dreamed of
profiting by any discovery he made. He would not even have his
salary increased, so tenaciously did he hold to the Christ-like privilege of living among men "as one that serveth." This was a
crown which he would let no man take from him. To the Government he freely gave, in many spheres of public usefulness, all the
time he could spare from his official duties. And it was in one of
these subsidiary public labors, as chairman of the Light-House
Board, that he contracted, as he believed, the disease which carried
him to the grave.

A sense of rectitude presided over all his thoughts and acts.
He had so trained his mind to right thinking, and his will to right
feeling and right doing, that this absolute rectitude became a part
of his intellectual as well as moral nature. Hence in his methods
of philosophizing he was incapable of sophistical reasoning. He
sat at the feet of nature with as much of candor as of humility,
never importing into his observations the pride of opinion, and
never yielding to the seductions of an overweening fancy. He
was sober in his judgments. He made no hasty generalizations.
His mind seemed to turn on "the poles of truth."

I could not dwell with enough of emphasis on this crowning
grace of our beloved friend if I should seek to do full justice to
my conception of the completeness it gave to his beautiful character.
But happily for me I need dwell upon it with only the less of
emphasis because it was the quality which, to use a French idiom,

"leaped into the eyes" of all who marked his walk and conversation. In the crystal depths of a nature like his, transparent in all directions, we discern as well the felicity as the beauty of that habit of mind which is begotten by the supreme love of Truth for her own sake—a habit which is as much the condition of intellectual earnestness, thoroughness, and veracity in penetrating to the reality of things, as of moral honesty, frankness, sincerity, and truthfulness in dealing with our fellow-men. The great expounder of the Nicomachean Ethics has taught us, and one of our own moralists has amplified the golden thesis,[*] that high moral virtue implies the habit of "just election" between right and wrong, and that to attain this habit we need at once an intelligence which is impassioned and an appetite which is reflective. And so in like manner all high intellectual virtue implies a habit of just election between truth and error—an election which men make, other things being equal, according to the degree in which their minds are enamored with the beauty of truth, as also in proportion to the degree in which their appetencies for knowledge have been trained to be reflective and cautious against the enticements of error. I never knew a man who strove more earnestly than Henry to make this just election between right and wrong, between truth and error, or who was better equipped with a native faculty for making the wise choice between them. He had brought his whole nature under the dominion of truthfulness.

But while thus eager and honest in the pursuit of truth he had nothing controversial in his temper. It was a favorite doctrine of his that error of opinion could be most successfully combated, not by the negative processes of direct attack, rousing the pride and provoking the contumacy of its adherents, but rather by the affirmative process of teaching, in meekness and love, the truth that is naturally antagonistic to it. The King of Sweden and Norway made him a Knight of St. Olaf, but St. Olaf's thunderous way of propagating Christianity—by battering down the idols of Norway with Thor's own hammer—is not the way that his American votary would have selected. There was nothing iconoclastic in Henry's zeal for truth. He believed that there is in all truth a

[*] Dr. James H. Thornwell: Discourses on Truth.

self-evidencing quality, and a redemptive power which makes it at once a potent and a remedial force in the world. Hence he never descended to any of those controversies which, in the annals of science, have sometimes made the *odium scientificum* a species of hatred quite as distinct, and quite as lively, too, as its more ancient congener, the *odium theologicum*. When once it was sought to force a controversy of this kind upon him, and when accusations were made which seemed to affect his personal honor, as well as the genuineness of his scientific claims, he referred the matter for adjudication to the Regents of the Smithsonian. Their investigation and their report disposed him from the necessity of self-defense. The simple truth was his sufficient buckler. And this equanimity was not simply the result of temperament. It sprang from the largeness of his mind, as well as from the serious view he took of life and duty. He was able to moderate his own opinions, because, in the amplitude of his intellectual powers, he was able to be a moderator of opinions in the scientific world. You all know with what felicity and intellectual sympathy he presided over the deliberations of this Society, composed as it is of independent scientific workers in almost every department of modern research. Alike in the judicial temper of his mind and in the wide range of his acquisitions he was fitted to be, as Dante has said of Aristotle, "the master of those who know."

And this power of his mind to assimilate knowledge of various kinds naturally leads me to speak of his skill in imparting it. He was a most successful educator. He had many other titles of honor or office, but the title of *Professor* seemed to rank them all, for everybody felt that he moved among men like one anointed with the spirit and power of a great teacher. And he had philosophical views of education, extending from its primary forms to its highest culminations—from the discipline of the "doing faculties" in childhood to the discipline of the "thinking faculties" in youth and manhood. No student of his left the Albany Academy, in the earlier period of his connection with that institution, without being thoroughly drilled in the useful art of handling figures, for then and there he taught the rudimental forms of arithmetic, not so much by theory as by practice. No student of his left Princeton

College without being thoroughly drilled in the art of thinking as applied to scientific problems, for then and there he was called to indoctrinate his pupils in the rationale as well as in the results of the inductive method. And I will venture to add that no intelligent student of his at Princeton ever failed, in after life, to recognize the useful place which hypothesis holds in labors directed to the extension of science, or failed to discriminate between a working hypothesis and a perfected theory.

Pausing for a moment at this stage in the analysis of Professor Henry's mental and moral traits, I cannot omit to portray the effect produced on the observer by the happy combination under which these traits were so grouped and confederated in his person as to be mutual complements of each other. Far more significant than any single quality of his mind, remarkable as some of his qualities were, was the admirable equipoise which kept the forces of his nature from all interference with the normal development of an integral manhood. He was courtly in his manners, but it was a courtliness which sprang from courtesy of heart, and had no trace of affectation or artificiality; he was fastidious in his literary and artistic tastes, but he had none of that dilettantism which is "fine by defect and delicately weak;" he was imbued with a simplicity of heart which left him absolutely without guile, yet he was shrewd to protect himself against the arts of the designing; he was severe in his sense of honor without being censorious; benevolent yet inflexibly just; quick in perception yet calm in judgment and patient of labor; tenacious of right without being controversial; benignant in his moral opinions yet never selling the truth; endowed with a strong imagination yet evermore making it the handmaid of his reason; a prince among men yet without the slightest alloy of arrogance in the fine gold of his imperial intellect; in a word, good in all his greatness, he was, at the same time, great in all his goodness. Such are the limitations of human excellence in most of its mortal exhibitions that transcendent powers of mind, or magnificent displays of virtue exerted in a single direction, are often found to owe their "splendid enormity" to what Isaac Taylor has called "the spoliation of some spurned and forgotten qualities," which are sacrificed in the pursuit of a predominant taste, or an overmastering ambition." The "infirmities of genius" often attest in their subjects the presence of a mental or moral atrophy, which has hindered the full-orbed development of one or more among their mental and moral powers. But in Professor Henry no one quality of mind or heart seemed to be in excess or deficiency as compared with the rest. All were fused together into a compactness of structure and homogeneity of parts which gave to each the strength and grace imparted by an organic union. And hence, while he was great as a philosopher he was greater as a man, for, laying on he did all the services of his scientific life on the altar of a pure, complete, and dignified manhood, we must hold that the altar which sanctified his gifts was greater than even the costliest offerings he laid upon it.

It will not be expected that I should close this paper without referring to the religious life and opinions of Professor Henry. If in moral height and beauty he stood like the palm tree, tall, erect, and symmetrical, it is because a deep religious faith was the tap-root of his character. He was, on what he conceived to be rational grounds, a thorough believer in theism. I do not think he would have said, with Bacon, that he "had rather believe all the fables in the Legend, the Talmud, and the Alcoran, than that this universal frame is without a mind," for he would have held that in questions of this kind we should ask not what we would "rather believe," but what seems to be true on the best evidence before us. He was in the habit of saying that, next to the belief in his own existence, was his belief in the existence of other minds like his own, and from these fixed, indisputable points, he reasoned, by analogy, to the conclusion that there is an Almighty Mind pervading the universe. But when from the likeness between this Infinite Mind and the finite minds made in His image, it was sought, by *a priori* logic, or by any preconceived notions of man, to *infer* the methods of the Divine working, or the final causes of things, he suspected at once the intrusive presence of a false, as well as presumptuous, philo-

* The phrase, as originally applied by Taylor, is descriptive of certain incomplete ethical systems, but it is equally applicable to certain typical exemplifications of human character, in which "the strength and the materials of six parts of morality have been brought together wherewith to construct a seventh part."

sophism, and declined to yield his mind an easy prey to its bland-
ishments. To his eyes much of the free and easy teleology, with
which an under-wise and not over-reverent sciolism is wont to
interpret the Divine counsels and judgments, seemed little better
than a Broken phantom—the grotesque and distorted image of
its own authors projected on mist and cloud, and hence very far
from being the inscrutable teleology of Him whose glory it is to
conceal a thing, and whose ways are often past finding out, because
His understanding is infinite.

As Professor Henry was a believer in theism, so also was he a
believer in revealed religion—in Christianity. He had not made
a study of systematic, or of dogmatic, theology as they are taught
in the schools, and still less was the interest he took in polemical
divinity, but he did have a theology which, for practical life, is
worth them all—the theology of a profound religious experience.
He was a fresh illustration of Neander's favorite saying: *Pectus
facit theologum.* The adaptation of the Christian scheme to the
moral wants of the human soul was the palmary proof on which
he rested his faith in the superhuman origin of that scheme. The
plan had to him the force of a theory which is scientific in its exact
conformity to the moral facts it explains, when these facts are properly known and fully understood.

Hence he was little troubled with the modern conflict between
science and religion. History, as well as reason and faith, was here
his teacher. He saw that the Christian church had already passed
through many epochs of transition, and that the friction incident to
such transition periods had only brushed away the incrustations of
theological error and heightened the brightness of theological truth.
In a world where the different branches and departments of human
knowledge are not pushed forward *pari passu*—where " knowledge
comes but wisdom lingers"—he held it nothing strange that the
scientific man should sometimes be unintelligible to the theologian,
and the theologian unintelligible to the scientific man. He believed,
with the old Puritan, that "the Lord has more truth yet to break
out of His holy word" than the systematic theologian is always
ready to admit; and as the humble minister and interpreter of
nature he was certain that the scientific man has much truth to

learn of which he is not yet aware. There must needs be fermentation in new thought as in new wine, but the vintage of the brain, like the vintage of the grape, is only the better for a process which brings impurities to the surface where they may be scummed off, and settles the lees at the bottom, where they ought to be. It is under the figure of a vintage that Bacon describes the crowning result of a successful inductive process. When this process has been completed in any direction, it remains for a wider critical and reconciling philosophy to bring the other departments of knowledge into logical relation and correspondence with the new outlook that has been gained on nature and its phenomena.

Erasmus tells us in his Praise of Folly, mingling satire with the truth of his criticism, that in order to understand the scholastic theology of his day, it was necessary to spend six-and-thirty years in the study of Aristotle's physics and of the doctrines of the Scotists. What a purification of method has been wrought in theology since the times of Erasmus! And for that purification the Church is largely indebted to the methodology of modern science, in clearing up the thoughts and rationalizing the intellectual processes of men. The gain for sound theology is here unspeakable, and amply repays her for the heavy baggage she has dropped by the way at the challenge of science—baggage which only impeded her march without reinforcing her artillery.

Hence, as a Christian philosopher, Professor Henry never found it necessary to lower the scientific flag in order to conciliate an obscurantist theology, and he never lowered the Christian flag in order to conciliate those who would erect the scientific standard over more territory than they have conquered. He had none of that spirit which would rather be wrong with Plato than right with anybody else. He wanted to follow wherever truth was in the van. But better than most men I think he knew how to discriminate between what a British scholar calls the duty of "following truth wherever it leads us, and the duty of yielding to the immediate pressure of an argument." He saw, as the same writer adds, that for whole generations "the victory of argument may sway backward and forward, like the fortune of single battles," but the victory of truth brings in peace, and a peace which comes to stay. He swept the scene of conflict with the field-glass of a commander-in-chief, and did not set up his trophies because of a brilliant skirmish on the picket lines of science. But he believed in the picket line, and rejoiced in every sharpshooter who fought with loyalty to truth in the forefront of the scientific army.

A man of faith, Professor Henry was a man of prayer. But his views of prayer were perhaps peculiar in their spirituality. There was nothing mechanical or formal in his theory of this religious exercise. He held that it was the duty and privilege of enlightened Christians to live in perpetual communion with the Almighty Spirit, and in this sense to pray without ceasing. Work was worship, if conducted in this temper. He accepted all the appointments of nature and Providence as the expressions of Infinite Wisdom, and so in everything gave thanks.* He believed that familiarity with the order of nature and scientific assurance of its uniformity need not and should not tend to extinguish the instinct, or abolish the motives of prayer by seeming to imply its futility, but should rather tend to purify and exalt the objects of prayer. The savage prays to his idol, that he may have success in killing his enemies. The Hottentot whips and worships his fetich in blind but eager quest of some sensual boon, that he may consume it upon his lusts. The prayers of the Vedic Books are the childish prayers of an unspiritual and childish people. "They pray," says Max Müller, "for the playthings of life, for houses and honors, for cows and horses, and they plainly tell the gods that if they will only be kind and gracious they will receive rich offerings in return." And do we, asks the critic of comparative religions, we Christians

---

* The "sacred remembrances" lists which he had attended; his temper was made to suffer by the great trial which befell him in the year 1865, when the Smithsonian building suffered from the ravages of a fire which destroyed all the letters written down to that date by Professor Henry, as Smithsonian Secretary, in reply to innumerable questions relating to almost every department of knowledge. Besides, the Annual Report of the Institution in manuscript, nearly ready for the press, a valuable collection of papers on meteorology, with written memoranda of his own to aid in their digest, and countless minutes of scientific researches which he purposed to make, all perished in the flames. Yet he was more concerned about the loss of Bishop Johns's library, which had been intrusted to his care, than about the loss of his own papers and records. Referring to the latter in a note written to his friend, Dr. Torrey, a few days after the fire, he held the following language: "A few years ago such a calamity would have paralyzed me for future efforts, but in my present view of life I take it as the dispensation of a kind and wise Providence, and trust that it will work to my spiritual advantage."

of this nineteenth century, "do we do much otherwise," if regard
be had to the quality of our petitions? Professor Henry held
that it was both the duty and privilege of enlightened Christians to
"do much otherwise," by praying pre-eminently, if not exclusively,
for spiritual blessings. And hence he held that the highest natural
philosophy combines with the highest Christian faith to transfer the
religious thoughts, feelings, and aspirations of man more and more
from things seen to things unseen, and from things temporal to
things eternal. This view of his had nothing of quietism or of
mysticism in it. Still less was it the expression of an apathetic
stoicism. It was only the philosopher's way of praying to the great
All-Father, in the spirit of St. Augustine, "Da quod jubes, et jube
quod vis."

I have made this reference to the opinions of Professor Henry
on the relations of science to religion, as also on the relations of
natural philosophy to prayer, not only for the light they shed on the
character of the man, but also for a reason which is peculiar to this
Society, and which it may be a matter of interest for you to know.
Immediately after his last unanimous election as the President of
our Society, he communicated to me his purpose to make the relations of science and religion, as also the true import of prayer, the
subject of his annual presidential address. He gave me an outline
of the views he intended to submit, and I have here given but a
brief résumé of them, according to my recollections of the colloquy,
which was only one of many similar conferences previously had on
the same high themes. He said that it would be, perhaps, the last time
he should ever be called to deliver a presidential address before the
Society he so much loved, and that he wished to speak as became
an humble patron of science, believing fully in her high mission,
and at the same time as an humble Christian, believing fully in the
fundamental truths of Revelation. That he was not able to fulfil
this purpose will be as much a source of regret to you as it is to me;
but when we compare the valediction which it was in his heart to
utter, with the peaceful end which came a few months later to crown
his days with the halo of a finished life, we may console ourselves
with the thought that no last words of his were needed to seal on
our hearts the lesson taught by his long and splendid career. Being
dead he yet speaketh.

It is, indeed, the shadow of a great affliction which his death has cast upon our Society, but the light of his life pierces through the darkness, and irradiates for us all the paths of duty and labor, of honor and purity, of truth and righteousness, in which he walked with an eye that never blenched, and a foot that never faltered. We shall not see his face any more, beaming with gladness and with the mild splendor of chastened intellect, but we shall feel his spiritual presence whenever we meet in this hall. We shall never hear his voice again, but its clear and gentle tones, as from yonder chair he expounded to us the mysteries of nature, will re-echo in the chambers of memory with only a deeper import, now that he has gone to join the "dead but accepted sovereigns who still rule our spirits from their urns."

THE SCIENTIFIC WORK

OF

JOSEPH HENRY.*

BY

WILLIAM B. TAYLOR.

To cherish with affectionate regard the memory of the venerated dead is not more grateful to the feelings, than to recall their excellences and to retrace the stages and occasions of their intellectual conquests is instructive to the reason. Few lives within the century are more worthy of admiration, more elevating in contemplation, or more entitled to commemoration, than that of our late most honored and beloved president—JOSEPH HENRY.

Distinguished by the extent of his varied and solid learning, possessing a wide range of mental activity, so great were his modesty and self-reserve, that only by the accidental call of occasion would even an intimate friend sometimes discover with surprise the fullness of his information and the soundness of his philosophy, in some quite unsuspected direction. Remarkable for his self-control, he was no less characterized by the absence of self-assertion. Ever warmly interested in the development and advancement of the young, he was a patient listener to the trials of the disappointed, and a faithful guide to the aspirations of the ambitious. Generous without ostentation, he was always ready to assist the deserving—by services, by counsel, by active exertions in their behalf.

In his own pursuits Truth was the supreme object of his regard,—the sole interest and incentive of his investigations; and in its quest he brought to bear in just allotment qualities of a high order;—quickness and correctness of perception, inventive ingenuity in

* Read before the "Philosophical Society of Washington," October 28th, 1878. (Bulletins of the Phil. Soc. W., vol. II, p. 224.) A large portion of the discourse (including nearly the whole of the section on the "Administration of the Smithsonian Institution") was necessarily omitted on the occasion of its delivery.

experimentation, logical precision in deduction, perseverance in exploration, sagacity in interpretation."

EARLY CAREER.

Of Henry's early struggles,—of the youthful traits which might afford us clue to his manhood's character and successes, we have but little preserved for the future biographer. Deprived of his father at an early age, he was the sole care and the sole comfort of his widowed mother. Carefully nurtured in the stringent principles of a devout religious faith, he adhered through life to the traditions and to the convictions derived from his honorable Scottish ancestry.

At the age of about seven years, (his mother having been induced to part with him for a time,) he was sent by his uncle to attend the district school at Galway, in Saratoga county, N. Y., at a distance of 36 miles from Albany, his native city. He remained under the care of his grandmother in this village for several years, until the death of his uncle; when he returned to his mother at Albany.

As a youth he was by no means precocious, as seldom have been those who have left a permanent influence on their kind. He seems to have felt no fondness for his early schools, and to have shown no special aptitude for the instructions they afforded. Like many another unpromising lad, he followed pretty much his own devices, unconcerned as to the development of his latent capabilities. The books he craved were not the books his school-teachers set before him. The novel and the play interested and absorbed the active fancy naturally so exuberant in youth; and the indications from his impulsive temperament and dreamy imaginative spirit were that he would probably become an actor—a dramatist—or a poet.

He was however from his childhood's years a close observer—both of nature and of the peculiarities of his fellows; and one char-

---

* Henry's tribute to Peltier, seems peculiarly applicable to himself. "He possessed in an eminent degree the mental characteristics necessary for a successful scientific discoverer; an imagination always active in suggesting hypotheses for the explanation of the phenomena under investigation, and a logical faculty never at fault in deducing consequences from the suggestions best calculated to bring them to the test of experience; an invention ever fertile in devising apparatus and other means by which the test could be applied; and finally a moral constitution which sought only the discovery of truth, and could alone be satisfied with its attainment." (Smithsonian Report for 1867, p. 156.)

acteristic early developed gave form and color to his mental disposition throughout later years.—an unflagging energy of purpose.

In 1810, or 1811, when about thirteen years of age, he was ap-
prenticed to Mr. John F. Doty, a watch-maker and silver-smith,
in Albany. He remained in this position about two years; when
he was released by his employer giving up the business.

About the year 1811, while a boy of still indefinite aims and of
almost as indefinite longings, having been confined to the house for
a few days in consequence of an accidental injury, he took up a small
volume on Natural Philosophy, casually left lying on a table by a
boarder in the house. Listlessly he opened it and read. Before he
reached the third page, he became profoundly interested in the statement of some of the enigmas of the great sphinx — Nature. A new
world seemed opening to his inquisitive eyes. Eagerly on he read,—
intent to find the hidden meanings of phenomena which hitherto
covered by the "veil of familiarity" had never excited a passing
wonder or a doubting question. Was it possible ever to discover
the real causes of things? Here was a new Ideal—if severer, yet
grander than that of art. He no longer read with the languid enjoyment of a passive recipient; he felt the new necessity of reaching
out with all the faculties of a thinker, with all the activity of a co-
worker.* For the first time he realized (though with no conscious
expression of the thought) that there is—so to speak,—an imagination of the intellect, as well as of the emotional soul;—that *Truth*
has its palaces no less gorgeous—no less wonderful than those reared
by fancy in homage to the *Beautiful.*

The new impulse was not a momentary fascination. Thenceforr-
ward the novel was thrown aside, and poesy neglected; though to
his latest day a sterling poem never failed to strongly impress him.
As it dawned upon his reason that the foundation of the coveted

* "There is a great difference between reading and study, or between the indolent
reception of knowledge without labor, and that effort of mind which is always necessary in order to secure an important truth and make it fully our own." J. Henry.
(*Agricultural Report* of the Patent Office for 1852, p. 411.) The book which so strongly
impressed him was entitled "Lectures on Experimental Philosophy, Astronomy,
and Chemistry: by G. Gregory, D. D., Vicar of West-ham." 12mo. London, 1808.
The owner of the book—a young Scotchman named Robert Doyle—observing the
clear application of the boy, very kindly presented the book to him. Many years
afterward Henry wrote in it: "It accidentally fell into my hands when I was about
sixteen years old, and was the first book I ever read with attention."

knowledge must be the studies he had thought so irksome, he at once determined to repair as far as possible his loss of time by taking evening lessons from two of the professors in the Albany Academy; applying himself diligently to geometry and mechanics. And here shone out that strength of will which enabled him to rise above the harassing obstacle of the *res angusta domi*. As soon as he felt able (although yet a mere boy), he managed to procure a position as teacher in a country school, where for seven months successfully instructing boys not much younger than himself, in what he had acquired, he was enabled by rigid economy to take a regular course of instruction at the Albany Academy. Again returning to his school-teaching, he furnished himself with the means of completing his studies at the Academy; where learning that the most important key to the accurate knowledge of nature's laws is a familiarity with the logical processes of the higher mathematics, he resolutely set himself to work to master the intricacies of the differential calculus.

Having finished his academic course and passed with honor through his examinations, he then through the warm recommendation of Dr. T. Romeyn Beck — the distinguished principal of the Academy, obtained a position as private tutor in the family of General Stephen Van Rensselaer.* As this duty did not exact more than about three hours a day of his attendance, he applied his ample leisure (having in view the medical profession) — partly to the assistance of Dr. Beck in his chemical experiments, and partly to the study of anatomy and physiology, under Doctors Tully and Marsh.

His devotion to natural philosophy which had only grown and strengthened with his own growth in knowledge, led him constantly to repeat any unusual experiment as soon as reported in the foreign scientific journals; and to devise new modifications of the experiment for testing more fully the range and operation of its fundamental principles.

Communications to the Albany Institute.—The "Albany Institute" was organized May 5th 1824, by the union of two older societies; with General Stephen Van Rensselaer as its President:[*] and young Henry became at once an active member; though with his modest estimate of his own attainments, he preferred the part of listener and acquirer, to that of seeming instructor, till urged by those who knew him best to add his contributions to the general career.

Henry's first communication to the Institute was read October 30th, 1824, (at the age of about twenty-six years,) and was "On the chemical and mechanical effects of steam: with experiments designed to illustrate the great reduction of temperature in steam of high elasticity when suddenly expanded."[†] From the stop-cock of a strongly made copper vessel in which steam could be safely generated under considerable pressure, he allowed an occasional escape; and he showed by holding the bulb of a thermometer in the jet of steam, at a fixed distance (say of four inches) from the orifice, that as the temperature and pressure increased within the boiler, the indications of the thermometer without grew lower; — the expansion and consequent cooling of the escaping steam under great pressure, increasing in a higher ratio than the increased temperature required for the pressure. And finally he exhibited the striking paradox, that the jet of saturated steam from a boiler will not scald the hand exposed to it, at a prescribed near distance from the try-cock, provided the steam be sufficiently hot.[‡]

Prolific and skillful in devising experiments, Henry delighted in making evident to the senses the principles he wished to impress upon the mind. Extending the law of cooling by expansion, from steam at high temperatures, to air at ordinary temperatures, his

---

[*] The Albany Institute resulted from the fusion of "The Society for the Promotion of Useful Arts in the State of New York," organized Feb. 1791, (incorporated April 2nd, 1804,) and the "Albany Lyceum of Natural History" formed and incorporated April 23rd, 1823; of which latter society, Henry had been a member. See "Supplement," Note A.

[†] Trans. Albany Institute, vol. i. part 2. p. 23.

[‡] While it requires a temperature of 250° F. to generate a steam-pressure of two atmospheres (i. e. one additional to the existing), 25° higher will produce a pressure of three atmospheres, and 100° higher, (or 350° F.) will produce a pressure of nine atmospheres: the curve (by rectangular co-ordinates of temperature and pressure) resembling a hyperbola. The increased velocity at high pressure produces a molecular momentum of expansion carrying the rarefaction beyond the limit of atmospheric pressure: and in the case of the exposed hand, the injected air current doubtless adds to the cooling impression.

14

next communication to the Institute (made March 2nd 1825,) was "On the Production of Cold by the Rarefaction of Air." As before, he accompanied his remarks by several characteristic exhibitions.

"One of these experiments most strikingly illustrated the great reduction of temperature which takes place on the sudden rarefaction of condensed air. Half a pint of water was poured into a strong copper vessel of a globular form, and having a capacity of five gallons; a tube of one-fourth of an inch caliber with a number of holes near the lower end, and a stop-cock attached to the other extremity, was firmly screwed into the neck of the vessel; the lower end of the tube dipped into the water, but a number of holes were above the surface of the liquid, so that a jet of air mingled with water might be thrown from the fountain. The apparatus was then charged with condensed air, by means of a powerful condensing pump, until the pressure was estimated at nine atmospheres. During the condensation the vessel became sensibly warm. After suffering the apparatus to cool down to the temperature of the room, the stop-cock was opened: the air rushed out with great violence, carrying with it a quantity of water, which was instantly converted into snow. After a few seconds, the tube became filled with ice, which almost entirely stopped the current of air. The neck of the vessel was then partially unscrewed, so as to allow the condensed air to rush out around the sides of the screw: in this state the temperature of the whole interior atmosphere was so much reduced as to freeze the remaining water in the vessel." *

Although the principle on which this striking result was based was not at that time new, it must be borne in mind that this particular application, thus publicly exhibited, was long before any of the numerous patents were obtained for ice-making, not a few of which adopted substantially the same process.

State Appointment as a Civil Engineer.—Through the friendship and confidence of an influential judge, Henry received about this time an unexpected offer of an appointment as engineer on the survey of a route for a road through the State of New York, from

----

* *Trans. Albany Institute.* vol. I, part I, p. 38.

the Hudson river on the east, to lake Erie on the west, a distance of about three hundred miles. The proposal was too tempting to his natural proclivities to be refused; and being appointed, he embarked upon his new and arduous duties with the zeal and energy which were so prominent a feature of his character. "His labors in this work were exceedingly arduous and responsible. They extended far into the winter, and the operations were carried on in some instances amid deep snows in primeval forests." In connection with Professor Amos Eaton, he completed the survey with credit to himself, and to the entire satisfaction of the Commissioners of the work.

So attractive appeared the profession of engineer to his enterprising disposition, that he was about to accept the directorship in the construction of a canal in Ohio, when he was informed that the Chair of Mathematics in the Albany Academy would soon become vacant, and that his own name had already been prominently brought forward in connection with the position. At the urgent solicitation of his old friend and former teacher Dr. T. Romeyn Beck, he consented with some hesitation to signify his willingness to accept the vacant chair if appointed thereto.

Election as Professor of Mathematics.—In the spring of 1826, Henry was duly elected by the Trustees of the Albany Academy to the Professorship of Mathematics and Natural Philosophy in that institution. As the duties of his office did not commence till September of that year, he was allowed a practical vacation of about five months; which was partly occupied with a geological exploration in the adjoining counties, as assistant to Professor Eaton, of the Rensselaer School, and partly devoted to a conscientious preparation for his new position.

In a worldly point of view, this variety of occupation and versatility of adaptation might perhaps be regarded as unfavorable to success. As a method of culture, it was of unquestionable advantage to his intellectual powers. A hard student, with great capacity for close application, he accumulated large stores of information; and in addition to the slaking of his constant thirst for acquirement in different directions, his leisure was occupied to a considerable extent with physical and chemical investigations. On the 21st of March 1827, he delivered before the Albany Institute a lecture on "Flame," accompanied with experiments.[*]

Meteorological Work.—The Regents of the University of the State of New York, endowed by the State Legislature with supervisory functions over the public educational institutions of the State,—in 1825 established a system of meteorological observation for the State, by supplying to each of the Academies incorporated by them, a thermometer and a rain-gauge, and requiring them to keep a daily register of prescribed form, to entitle them to their portion of the literature fund of the State. In 1827, the Hon. Simeon De Witt, Chancellor of the Board of Regents, associated with himself Dr. T. Romeyn Beck and Professor Henry of the Albany Academy, to prepare and tabulate the results of these observations. The first Abstract of these collections (for the year 1828) comprised tabulations of the monthly and yearly means of temperature, wind, rain, etc. at all the stations, an account of meteorological incidents generally, and a table of "Miscellaneous Observations" on the dates of notable phases of organic phenomena connected with climatic conditions. These annual Abstracts, to which Henry devoted a considerable share of his attention, were continued through a series of years and were published in the "Annual Reports of the Regents of the University to the Legislature of the State of New York.[†] The third Abstract (for 1830) includes an accurate tabulation by Henry of the latitudes, longitudes, and elevations of all the meteorological stations; over forty in number.

ELECTRICAL RESEARCHES AT ALBANY: FROM 1827 TO 1832.

Of Henry's distinguished success as a lecturer and teacher, in imparting to his pupils a portion of his own zeal and earnestness in the pursuit of scientific knowledge, as well as in winning their affection and in inspiring their esteem, it is not designed here to discourse; but rather of his solitary labors outside of his professional

---

[*] *Trans. Albany Institute*, vol. I, part 2, p. 49.
[†] *Reports of Regents, etc.* Albany, vol. I, 1828-1832.

occupation in communicating and diffusing knowledge. Very
shortly after his occupation of the academic chair of mathematics
and physics, he turned his attention to the experimental study of
that mysterious agency—electricity. Professor Schweigger of
Halle, had improved on Oersted's galvanic indicator (of a single
wire circuit) by giving the insulated wire a number of turns around
an elongated frame longitudinally enclosing the compass needle;
and by thus multiplying the effect of the galvanic circuits, had converted it into a real *measuring* instrument—a "galvanometer."[*]
Ampère and Arago of Paris, developing Oersted's announcement
of the torsional or equatorial reaction between a galvanic conductor
and a magnetic needle, had found that a circulating galvanic current was capable not only of deflecting a suspended magnet, but of
generating magnetism—permanently in sewing needles, and temporarily in pieces of iron wire, when placed within a glass tube
around which the conjunctive wire of the battery had been wound
in a loose helix; and had thus created the "electro-magnet."[†] The
scientific world was just aroused to the close interrogation of this
new marvel, each questioner eager to ascertain its most efficient
conditions, and to increase its manifestations. William Sturgeon
of Woolwich, England, had extended the discoveries of Ampère
and Arago, by dispensing with the glass tube, constructing a "horse-
shoe" bar of soft iron (after the form of the usual permanent
magnet) coated with a non-conducting substance, and winding the
copper conjunctive wire directly upon the horse-shoe; and had thus

---

[*] The name of GALVANI (as original discoverer of chemico-electricity) is usually
retained to designate both the current and its generator; although the chemico-
electric pile and battery were really first contrived by VOLTA in 1800. In the same
manner OERSTED is generally accounted the discoverer of electro-magnetism,
although he never devised an electro-magnet, and appears not to have been the first
even to discover the directive influence of a current on a magnetic needle. Eighteen
years before his announcement, GIAN DOMENICO ROMAGNOSI, a physicist of Trent,
published in an Italian newspaper of that city, the *Gazetta di Trento*, on the 3d of
August, 1802, his observation of the galvanic deflection of the needle. This important discovery was also published in Professor O. Aldini's "Essai théorique et
expérimental sur le Galvanisme." 4to, Paris, 1804, p. 151; and in Professor J. Izarn's
"Manuel du Galvanisme." 8vo, Paris, 1805, sect. ix. p. 139.

[†] *Annales de Chimie et de Physique*, 1820, vol. xv. pp. 93-100. VAN BECK of Utrecht,
in 1821 inverting Arago's experiment, had found that an iron or steel wire coiled
around a glass tube on a short helix, became magnetic on passing a charge from a
Leyden jar through a straight brass wire placed within the glass tube. Communicated by Professor G. Moll. (Brewster's *Edinburgh Journal of Science*, Jan. 1822, vol.
vi. p. 44.)

produced the first *efficient* electro-magnet;—capable of sustaining several pounds by its armature, when duly excited by the galvanic current. He had also greatly improved lecture-room apparatus for illustrating the electro-magnetic reactions of rotations, etc. (where a permanent magnet is employed), by introducing stronger magnets, and had thereby succeeded in exhibiting the phenomena on a larger scale, with a considerable reduction of the battery power. *

Faraday had not yet commenced the series of researches which in after years so illumined his name, when Henry published his first contribution to electrical science, in a communication read before the Albany Institute, October 10th, 1827, "On some Modifications of the Electro-Magnetic Apparatus." From his experimental investigations he was enabled to exhibit all the class illustrations attempted by Sturgeon, on even a still larger and more conspicuous scale, with the employment of very weak magnets (where required), and with a still further reduction of the battery power. These quite striking and unexpected results were obtained by the simple expedient of adopting in every case where single circuits had previously been used, the manifold coil of fine wire which Schweigger had employed to increase the sensibility of the galvanometer. He remarks:

"Mr. Sturgeon of Woolwich, who has been perhaps the most successful in these improvements, has shown that a strong galvanic power is not essentially necessary even to exhibit the experiments on the largest scale. - - - Mr. Sturgeon's suite of apparatus, though superior to any other as far as it goes, does not however form a complete set: as indeed it is plain that his principle of strong magnets cannot be introduced into every article required, and particularly into those intended to exhibit the action of the earth's magnetism on a galvanic current, or the operation of two conjunctive wires on each other. To form therefore a set of instruments on a large scale that will illustrate all the facts belonging to

* Trans. Soc. Encouragement Arts, etc. 1825, vol. xliii. pp. 38-42. His battery (of a single element) consisted "of two fixed hollow concentric cylinders of thin copper, having a movable cylinder of zinc placed between them. Its superficial area is only 120 square inches, and it weighs no more than 1 lb. 4 oz." Mr. Sturgeon was deservedly awarded the Silver Medal of the Society for the Encouragement of Arts, etc., "for his improved electro-magnetic apparatus." Described also in Annals of Philos. Nov. 1825, vol. xii. new series, pp. 357-361.

this science, with the least expense of galvanism, evidently requires some additional modification of apparatus, and particularly in those cases in which powerful magnets cannot be applied. And such a modification appears to me to be obviously pointed out in the construction of Professor Schweigger's Galvanic Multiplier: the principles of this instrument being directly applicable to all the experiments in which Mr. Sturgeon's improvement fails to be useful." [*]

The coils employed in the various articles of apparatus thus improved, comprised usually about twenty turns of fine copper wire wound with silk to prevent metallic contact, the whole being closely bound together. To exhibit for example Ampère's ingenious and delicate experiment showing the directive action of the earth as a magnet on a galvanic current when its conductor is free to move, (usually a small wire frame with its extremities dipping either into mercury cups, or into mercury channels,) or its simpler modification, the "ring" of De la Rive, (usually an inch or two in diameter and made to float freely with its galvanic element in its own bath,) the effect was strikingly enhanced by Henry's method of suspending by a silk thread a large circular coil twenty inches in diameter, of many wire circuits bound together with ribbon,—the extremities of the wire protruding at the lower part of the hoop, and soldered to a pair of small galvanic plates;—when by simply placing a tumbler of acidulated water beneath, he caused the hoop at once to assume (after a few oscillations) its equatorial position transverse to the magnetic meridian. By a similar arrangement of two circular coils of different diameters, one suspended within the other, Ampère's fine discovery of the mutual action of two electric currents on each other, was as strikingly displayed. Such was the character of demonstration by which the new Professor was accustomed to make visible to his classes the principles of electro-magnetism: and it is safe to say that in simplicity, distinctness, and efficiency, such apparatus for the lecture-room was far superior to any of the kind then existing.

Should any one be disposed to conclude that this simple extension of Schweigger's multiple coil was unimportant and unmeritorious, the ready answer occurs, that talented and skillful electri-

cians, laboring to attain the result, had for six years failed to make
such an extension. Nor was the result by any means antecedently
assured by Schweigger's success with the galvanometer. If Sturgeon's improvement of economizing the battery size and consumption, by increasing the magnet factor (in those few cases where
available), was well deserving of reward, surely Henry's improvement of a far greater economy, by increasing the circuit factor
(entirely neglected by Sturgeon) deserved a still higher applause.

In a subsequent communication to Silliman's Journal, Henry
remarks on the results announced in October, 1827:—"Shortly
after the publication mentioned, several other applications of the
coil, besides those described in that paper, were made in order to
increase the size of electro-magnetic apparatus, and to diminish
the necessary galvanic power. The most interesting of these was
its application to a development of magnetism in soft iron, much
more extensive than to my knowledge had been previously effected
by a small galvanic element." And in another later paper, he
repeated to the same effect: "After reading an account of the galvanometer of Schweigger, the idea occurred to me that a much
nearer approximation to the theory of Ampère could be attained
by insulating the conducting-wire itself, instead of the rod to be
magnetized; and by covering the whole surface of the iron with a
series of coils in close contact."

The electro-magnet figured and described by Sturgeon (in his
communication of November, 1825,) consisted of a small bar or
stout iron wire bent into a ∩ or horse-shoe form, having a copper
wire wound loosely around it in eighteen turns, with the ends of
the wire dipping into mercury-cups connected with the respective
poles of a battery having 130 square inches of active surface.
This was probably the only electro-magnet then in existence.

In June of 1828, Henry exhibited before the Albany Institute a
small-sized electro-magnet closely wound with silk-covered copper
wire about one-thirtieth of an inch in diameter. By thus insulating the conducting wire, instead of the magnetic bar or core, he
was enabled to employ a compact coil in close juxtaposition from
one end of the horse-shoe to the other, obtaining thereby a much
larger number of circuits, and with each circuit more nearly at

right angles with the magnetic axis. The lifting power of this magnet is not stated, though it must obviously have been much more powerful than the one described by Sturgeon.

In March of 1829, Henry exhibited before the Institute a somewhat larger magnet of the same character. "A round piece of iron about one-quarter of an inch in diameter was bent into the usual form of a horse-shoe, and instead of loosely coiling around it a few feet of wire, as is usually described, it was tightly wound with 35 feet of wire covered with silk, so as to form about 400 turns; a pair of small galvanic plates which could be dipped into a tumbler of diluted acid, was soldered to the ends of the wire, and the whole mounted on a stand. With these small plates the horse-shoe became much more powerfully magnetic than another of the same size and wound in the usual manner, by the application of a battery composed of 28 plates of copper and zinc each 8 inches square." In this case the coil was wound upon itself in successive layers.

To Henry, therefore, belongs the exclusive credit of having first constructed the magnetic "spool" or "bobbin," that form of coil since universally employed for every application of electro-magnetism, of induction, or of magneto-electrics. This was his first great contribution to the science and to the art of galvanic magnetization.

In the latter part of 1829, Henry still further increased the magnetic power derived from a single galvanic pair of small size, by a new arrangement of the coil. "It consisted in using several strands of wire each covered with silk, instead of one." Employing a horse-shoe formed from a cylindrical bar of iron half an inch in diameter and about 10 inches long, wound with 30 feet of tolerably fine copper wire, he found that with a current from only two and a half square inches of zinc, the magnet held 14 pounds. Winding upon its arms a second wire of the same length (30 feet) whose ends were similarly joined to the same galvanic pair, he found that the magnet lifted 28 pounds. "With a pair of plates 4 inches by 6, it lifted 39 pounds, or more than fifty times its own weight."[*]   On these results he remarks:

---

[*] It must not be forgotten that at the time when this experimental magnet was made, the strongest if not the only electro-magnet in Europe was that of Sturgeon, capable of supporting 9 pounds, with 130 square inches of zinc surface in the battery.

"These experiments conclusively proved that a great development of magnetism could be effected by a very small galvanic element, and also that the power of the coil was materially increased by multiplying the number of wires, without increasing the length of each. The multiplication of the wires increases the power in two ways: first, by conducting a greater quantity of galvanism, and secondly, by giving it a more proper direction; for since the action of a galvanic current is directly at right angles to the axis of a magnetic needle, by using several shorter wires we can wind one on each inch of the length of the bar to be magnetized, so that the magnetism of each inch will be developed by a separate wire. In this way the action of each particular coil becomes directed very nearly at right angles to the axis of the bar, and consequently the effect is the greatest possible. This principle is of much greater importance when large bars are used. The advantage of a greater conducting power from using several wires might in a less degree be obtained by substituting for them one large wire of equal sectional area; but in this case the obliquity of the spiral would be much greater, and consequently the magnetic action less." *

But in the following year, 1830, Henry pressed forward his researches to still higher results. Assisted by his friend Dr. Philip Ten-Eyck, he proceeded to test the power of electro-magnetic attraction on a larger scale. "A bar of soft iron 2 inches square and 20 inches long was bent into the form of a horse-shoe 9 inches high; (the sharp edges of the bar being first a little rounded by the hammer;) it weighed 21 pounds. A piece of iron from the same bar, weighing 7 pounds, was filed perfectly flat on one surface for an armature or lifter. The extremities of the legs of the horse-shoe were also truly ground to the surface of the armature. Around this horse-shoe 540 feet of copper bell-wire were wound in nine coils of 60 feet each; these coils were not continued around the whole length of the bar, but each strand of wire (according to the principle before mentioned) occupied about two inches, and was coiled several times backward and forward over itself. The several ends of the wires

* Silliman's Am. Journal of Science, Jan. 1831, vol. XIX. p. 42. The three names—ARAGO, RITCHIE, and HENRY,—may well typify the infancy, the youth, and the mature manhood, of the electro-magnet.

were left projecting, and all numbered, so that the first and the last end of each strand might be readily distinguished. In this manner we formed an experimental magnet on a large scale, with which several combinations of wire could be made by merely uniting the different projecting ends. Thus if the second end of the first wire be soldered to the first end of the second wire, and so on through all the series, the whole will form a continued coil of one long wire. By soldering different ends, the whole may be formed into a double coil of half the length, or into a triple coil of one-third the length, &c. The horse-shoe was suspended in a strong rectangular wooden frame 3 feet 9 inches high and 20 inches wide."

Two of the wires (one from each extremity of the legs) when joined together by soldering, so as to form a single circuit of 120 feet, with its extreme ends connected with the battery, produced a lifting-power of 80 pounds. The same two wires being separately connected with the same battery (forming a double circuit of 60 feet each), a lifting-power of 200 pounds was obtained, or more than three times the power of the former case with the same wire. Four wires (two from each extremity of the legs) being separately connected with the battery (forming four circuits) gave a lifting-power of 500 pounds. Six wires (three from each leg) united in three pairs (forming three circuits of 180 feet each) gave a lifting-power of 290 pounds. The same six wires being separately connected with the battery in six independent circuits, produced a lifting-power of 570 pounds, or very nearly double that of the same wires in double lengths. When all the nine wires were separately attached to the battery a lifting-power of 650 pounds was evoked. In all these experiments "a small single battery was used, consisting of two concentric copper cylinders, with zinc between them; the whole amount of zinc-surface exposed to the acid from both sides of the zinc was two-fifths of a square foot; the battery required only half a pint of dilute acid for its submersion."

"In order to ascertain the effect of a very small galvanic element on this large quantity of iron, a pair of plates exactly one inch square was attached to all the wires; the weight lifted was 85 pounds." For the purpose of obtaining the maximum attractive power of this magnet, with its nine independent coils, "a small battery formed with a plate of zinc 12 inches long and 6 wide, and surrounded by copper, was substituted for the galvanic element used in the former experiments; the weight lifted in this case was 750 pounds." [*] In illustration of the feeble power of the magnetic poles when exerted separately, it was found that with precisely the same arrangements giving a holding power of 750 pounds to the double contact armature, either pole alone was capable of sustaining only 5 or 6 pounds; "and in this case we never succeeded in making it lift the armature—weighing 7 pounds. We have never seen the circumstance noticed of so great a difference between a single pole and both."

Henry's "Quantity" Magnet compared with Moll's.—About the same time that Henry was developing this wonderful power in the electro-magnet, Dr. Gerard Moll, Professor of Natural Philosophy in the University of Utrecht, was engaged in a similar research. In a paper published in the latter part of 1830, he states that his attention was drawn to the electro-magnet of Sturgeon in 1828, during a visit to London.[†] "This apparatus I saw in 1828 at Mr. Watkins's, curator of philosophical apparatus to the London University; and the horse-shoe with which he performed the experiment, became capable all at once of supporting about nine pounds.[‡] I immediately determined to try the effect of a larger galvanic apparatus on a bent iron cylindrical wire, and I obtained results which appear astonishing, and are—as far as the intensity of magnetic force is concerned, altogether new. I have anxiously looked since that time into different scientific continental and English journals, without finding any further attempt to extend and improve Mr. Sturgeon's original experiment." Moll's first magnet, a horse-shoe formed of a round bar of iron about one inch thick, was about eight and one-half inches in height, and had a wrapped copper wire of about one-eighth inch diameter coiled eighty-three times around it. The weight of the horse-shoe and wire was about

*Silliman's Am. Journal of Science, Jan. 1831, vol. xix. pp. 404, 405.

†Bibliothèque Universelle des Sciences, etc. Sept. 1830, vol. xlv. pp. 19-33. Also Edinburgh Journal of Science, Oct. 1830.

‡(At the date referred to, Henry had already exhibited before the Albany Institute a much more powerful magnet.)

five pounds; of the armature, about one and one-fourth pound; and with a single galvanic pair whose acting zinc surface was about eleven square feet, the electro-magnet supported about 50 pounds. With cautious additions, the load could be increased to 75 pounds. An additional galvanic pair of about six square feet was applied without increasing the power of the magnet. Another horse-shoe about twelve and a half inches in height, formed of a rod two and one-fourth inches in diameter, was prepared by Professor Moll, with a brass wire, one-eighth of an inch thick, wound around it in forty-four coils; the weight of the whole being about twenty-six pounds. With the galvanic element of eleven square feet, this magnet lifted 135 pounds. The largest load this magnet was afterward made to support was 154 pounds. *

As soon as the account of Moll's magnet reached this country, (late in October, or early in November,) Henry—who had obtained and had publicly exhibited nearly two years previously, considerably higher results, and who realized that there was at least one very important difference of construction between his own magnet and that of the Dutch savant, felt it a duty at once to publish the details of his own researches, in a more public form. He accordingly proceeded in the latter part of November, 1830, to write out a description of his former experiments and results, which he forwarded to Silliman's American Journal of Science, (then published only quarterly,) in time for insertion in the forthcoming number of that journal, for January, 1831; causing a copy of Professor Moll's paper, taken from Brewster's Edinburgh Journal of Science for October 1830, to be inserted in the same number. At the conclusion of his own article he remarks: "The only effect Professor Moll's paper has had over these investigations, has been to hasten their publication: the principle on which they were instituted was known to us nearly two years since, and at that time exhibited to the Albany Institute."

Comparing now Moll's results with Henry's,—we find that Henry's magnet of November or December, 1829, (a half-inch bar

---

* Brewster's Edinburgh Jour. Art. (art. XIX, vol. III. n. s. pp. 209-211. An account of Moll's magnet is also given in the Annales de Chimie et de Physique, 1872, vol. L. pp. 334-338.

of iron covered with several strands of wire,) excited by a galvanic pair of one-sixth of a square foot of zinc surface, sustained 39 pounds, or more than fifty times its own weight; while Moll's magnet of about double the dimensions, employing eleven square feet of battery, lifted only 75 pounds, or fifteen times its own weight. That is, Henry's magnet while about only one-seventh of the weight of Moll's (without their wrappings) supported more than half the load of the latter. Or comparing their larger magnets, — while Moll's twelve and a half inch magnet (of two and a quarter inch iron) lifted as its greatest effort 154 pounds, (a result with which the author justly felt elated,) Henry's nine and a half inch magnet (of about the same sized iron) lifted 750 pounds; or about five times its maximum load. But the most surprising contrast between the two series of experiments, resulting from their different systems, was the enormous difference of battery-power respectively applied; — Moll pushing his up to seventeen square feet, — Henry reducing his in the first case to one-sixth of a square foot, and in the latter case obtaining his five-fold duty with one-eleventh of the quantity of galvanic current. The philosopher of Utrecht, though he evidently realized with him of Albany, the importance of close-winding, employed but a single layer of coil. The latter, by means of well-considered trials had ascertained the great increase of magnetic force resulting from a considerable number of coils. On the theoretical grounds assigned by Henry therefore, Moll's single conducting wire of one-eighth inch diameter, while *electrically* equivalent to some half a dozen of Henry's conducting wires (of the same length and collective weight) would be *magnetically* inferior thereto — for equal iron cores.

Notwithstanding that Henry's successes were thus both earlier and more brilliant than those of Moll, the two names are usually associated together by European writers in treating of the development of the magnet.*

* Faraday in subsequently investigating the conditions of galvanic induction, referred with approbation to the magnets of Moll and Henry as best calculated to produce the effects sought. In constructing his duples, before not observing the direction of the induced current, he however adopted Henry's method by winding twelve coils of copper wire each twenty-seven feet long — one upon the other. (*Phil. Trans. Roy. Soc.* Nov. 24, 1831, vol. cxxii. (for 1832), pp. 126, and 128. *Experimental Researches*, Sec. vol. 1, art. 6, p. 2; and art. 57, p. 18.)

Henry's "Intensity" Magnet.—But Henry's remarkable paper of January, 1831, contains still another original contribution to the theory and practice of electro-magnetics, no less important than his invention of the magnetic spool. While Moll had endeavored to induce strong magnetism by the use of a powerful "quantity" battery, Henry had labored to derive from a minimum galvanic power its maximum magnetizing effect: and in his varied experiments on these two factors, he discovered very curious and unsuspected relations between them. A great majority of investigators—after having definitely ascertained the striking fact of the great inferiority in magnetizing power, of a single long continuous coil, to a proportionally shortened circuit of multiple coils,—would naturally have been led to abandon all further investigation of the feebler system. Henry however recognized in this a field of instructive inquiry: and for the first time showed that the coil of short and numerous circuits, least affected by a battery of many pairs, was on the contrary most responsive to a single galvanic element; while the single extended coil, least influenced by a single pair, was most excited by a battery of numerous elements.

The illustrious Laplace had suggested to Ampère in 1820,—immediately upon the discovery of the galvanometer, that it would be desirable to test the deflection of the needle through a long circuit of conjunctive wire. The latter having made the experiment "through a very long conducting wire," (the length of which is not stated,) and having found the result "completely successful," had remarked in a paper presented to the "Royal Academy of Sciences," October 2nd, 1820, that by sending the galvanic current through long wires connecting two distant stations, the deflections of inclosed magnetic needles would constitute very simple and efficient signals for an instantaneous telegraph. *

Peter Barlow the eminent English mathematician and magnetician taking up the suggestion, had endeavored more fully to test its practicability. He has thus stated the result: "In a very early stage of electro-magnetic experiments it had been suggested that an instantaneous telegraph might be established by means of conducting wires and compasses. The details of this contrivance are so obvious, and

* Annales de Chimie et de Physique, 1820, vol. xv. pp. 72, 74.

the principle on which it is founded so well understood, that there
was only one question which could render the result doubtful; and
this was,—is there any diminution of effect by lengthening the conducting wire? It had been said that the electric fluid from a common
[tin-foil] electrical battery had been transmitted through a wire
four miles in length without any sensible diminution of effect, and
to every appearance instantaneously;* and if this should be found
to be the case with the galvanic circuit, then no question could be
entertained of the practicability and utility of the suggestion above
adverted to. I was therefore induced to make the trial; but I found
such a sensible diminution with only 200 feet of wire, as at once to
convince me of the impracticability of the scheme. It led me however to an inquiry as to the cause of this diminution, and the laws
by which it is governed."†

Henry in his researches just referred to, (assisted by his friend
Dr. Ten-Eyck,) employed a small electro-magnet of one-quarter
inch iron "wound with about 8 feet of copper wire." Excited
with a single pair "composed of a piece of zinc plate 4 inches by
7, surrounded with copper," (about 56 square inches of zinc surface,) the magnet sustained four pounds and a half. With about
800 feet of insulated copper wire (0.045 of an inch in diameter)
interposed between the battery and the magnet, its lifting power
was reduced to two ounces;—or about 36 times. With double
this length of wire, or a little over 1000 feet, interposed, the lifting
power of the magnet was only half an ounce: thus fully confirming the results obtained by Barlow with the galvanometer. With

*[SALVA in 1798, had successfully worked an electric telegraph from Madrid to
Aranjuez,—a distance of 26 miles. (Turnbull's Electro-Magnetic Telegraph, 2nd. ed. 1853,
pp. 21, 22.) Frictional or mechanical electricity does not observe Ohm's law of resistance. The only drawback to its application, is the greatly increased difficulty of
insulation.]

†"On the laws of Electro-magnetic Action." Edinburgh Philosophical Journal,
Jan. 1831, vol. xii. pp. 105-113. In explanation and justification of this discouraging
judgment from so high an authority in magnetics, it must be remembered that both
in the galvanometer and in the electro-magnet, the coil best calculated to produce
large effects, was that of least resistance; which unfortunately was not that best
adapted to a long circuit. On the other hand, the most efficient magnet or galvanometer was not found to be improved in result by increasing the number of galvanic elements. Barlow in his inquiry as to the "law of diminution" was led
(erroneously) to regard the resistance of the conducting wire as increasing in the
ratio of the square root of its length. (pp. 110, 111.)

a small galvanic pair 2 inches square, acting through the same length of wire (over 1000 feet,) "the magnetism was scarcely observable in the horse-shoe." Employing next a trough battery of 25 pairs, having the same zinc surface as previously, the magnet in direct connection, (which before had supported four and a half pounds,) now lifted but seven ounces;—not quite half a pound. But with the 1060 feet of copper wire (a little more than one-fifth of a mile) suspended several times across the large room of the Academy, and placed in the galvanic circuit, the same magnet sustained eight ounces: that is to say, the current from the galvanic trough produced greater magnetic effect after traversing this length of wire, than it did without it.

"From this experiment it appears that the current from a galvanic trough is capable of producing greater magnetic effect on soft iron after traversing more than one-fifth of a mile of intervening wire than when it passes only through the wire surrounding the magnet. It is possible that the different states of the trough with respect to dryness may have exerted some influence on this remarkable result; but that the effect of a current from a trough if not increased is but slightly diminished in passing through a long wire is certain." And after speculating on this new and at the time somewhat paradoxical result, suggesting that "a current from a trough possesses more 'projectile' force (to use Professor Hare's expression,) and approximates somewhat in 'intensity' to the electricity from the common machine," Henry concludes: "But be this as it may, the fact that the magnetic action of a current from a trough is at least not sensibly diminished by passing through a long wire, is directly applicable to Mr. Barlow's project of forming an electro-magnetic telegraph;* and it is also of material consequence in the construction of the galvanic coil. From these experiments it is evident that in forming the coil we may either use one very long wire, or several shorter ones, as the circumstances may require: in the first case, our galvanic combination must consist of a num-

---

*(Really Ampère's project, not Barlow's. In a subsequent paper Henry corrected this allusion by saying, "I called it 'Barlow's project,' when I ought to have stated that Mr. Barlow's investigation merely tended to disprove the possibility of a telegraph.")

ber of plates so as to give 'projectile' force; in the second, it must
be formed of a single pair." *

The importance of this discovery can hardly be overestimated.
The magnetic "spool" of fine wire, of a length — tens and even
hundreds of times that ever before employed for this purpose, —
was in itself a gift to science, which really forms an epoch in the
history of electro-magnetism.   It is not too much to say that
almost every advancement which has been made in this fruitful
branch of physics since the time of Sturgeon's happy improvement, from the earliest researches of Faraday downward, has
been directly indebted to Henry's magnets.   By means of the
Henry "spool" the magnet almost at a bound was developed from
a feeble childhood to a vigorous manhood.   And so rapidly and
generally was the new form introduced abroad among experimenters, few of whom had ever seen the papers of Henry, that probably very few indeed have been aware to whom they were really
indebted for this familiar and powerful instrumentality.   But the
historic fact remains, that prior to Henry's experiments in 1829,
no one on either hemisphere had ever thought of winding the limbs
of an electro-magnet on the principle of the "bobbin," and not till
after the publication of Henry's method in January of 1831, was
it ever employed by any European physicist. †

But in addition to this large gift to science, Henry (as we have
seen) has the pre-eminent claim to popular gratitude of having
first practically worked out the differing functions of two entirely
different kinds of electro-magnet: the one surrounded with numerous coils of no great length, designated by him the "quantity"
magnet, the other surrounded with a continuous coil of very great
length, designated by him the "intensity" magnet. ‡   The latter

_____

* Silliman's Am. Jour., Art. Jan. 1831, vol. xix, pp. 88, 401.

† Henry's "spool" magnet appears to have been introduced into France by
Pouillet in 1832.   Nouveau Bulletin des Sciences, publié par la Société Philoma-
tique de Paris, Séance of 2d June, 1832, p. 127.   In Pouillet's Éléments de Physique Expérimentale, third edition, published in 1837, (vol. I. p. 572,) the date of this
magnet is inadvertently given as 1831; an inaccuracy which though unimportant,
is perpetuated in every subsequent edition of that popular text-book.   In the
second edition, published in 1832, no allusion to the magnet occurs.

‡ "In describing the results of my experiments the terms 'intensity' and
'quantity' magnets were introduced to avoid circumlocution, and were intended
to be used merely in a technical sense.   By the intensity magnet I designated a

and feebler system (requiring for its action a battery of numerous elements,) was shown to have the singular capability (never before suspected nor imagined) of subtile excitation from a distant source. Here for the first time is experimentally established the important principle that there must be a proportion between the aggregate internal resistance of the battery and the whole external resistance of the conjunctive wire or conducting circuit; with the very important practical consequence, that by combining with an "intensity" magnet of a single extended fine coil an "intensity" battery of many small pairs, its electro-motive force enables a very long conductor to be employed without sensible diminution of the effect.* This was a very important though unconscious experimental confirmation of the mathematical theory of Ohm, embodied in his formula expressing the relation between electric flow and electric resistance, which though propounded two or three years previously, failed for a long time to attract any attention from the scientific world. †

Never should it be forgotten that he who first exalted the "quantity" magnet of Sturgeon from a power of twenty pounds to a power of twenty hundred pounds, was the absolute CREATOR of the "intensity" magnet; and that the principles involved in this creation, constitute the indispensable basis of every form of the electro-

piece of soft iron so surrounded with wire that its magnetic power could be called into operation by an 'intensity' battery; and by a quantity magnet, a piece of iron so surrounded by a number of separate coils that its magnetism could be fully developed by a 'quantity' battery." (Smithsonian Report for 1857, p. 101.) These terms though somewhat antiquated and generally discarded by recent writers, are still very convenient designations of the two classes of action, both in the battery and in the magnet. See "Supplement," NOTE R.

* Beyond a certain maximum length there is of course, a decrease of power for each particular coil of the "intensity" magnet, proportioned to the increased resistance of a long conductor; but the magnetizing effect has not been found to be diminished in the ratio of its length. In a very long wire, the magnetizing influence (with a suitable "intensity" battery) appears to be inversely proportioned to the square of the length of the conductor.

† George Simon Ohm, professor in physics at Munich, published at Berlin, in 1827, his "Galvanische Kette, mathematisch bearbeitet;" and in the following year, he published a supplementary paper entitled "Nachtrage zu seiner mathematischen Bearbeitung der galvanischen Kette;" in Kastner's Archiv für gesammte Naturlehre (two Nürnberg:) 1829, vol. xiv. pp. 475-493. Fourteen years after the publication of the former memoir, this elaborate discussion was for the first time translated into English, by Mr. William Francis. ("The Galvanic Circuit investigated mathematically." Taylor's Scientific Memoirs, etc. London, 1841, vol. ii. pp. 401-506.)

magnetic telegraph since invented. They settled satisfactorily (in Barlow's phrase) the "only question which could render the result doubtful;" and though derived from the magnet, were obviously as applicable to the galvanometer needle.* Professor Moll, the foremost of Europeans in the electro-magnetic chase, and close upon the heels of Henry in one portion of his researches, produced a powerful "quantity" magnet, but one hopelessly and radically incapacitated from any such application.

It is idle to say in disparagement of those successes, that in the competitive race of numerous distinguished investigators in the field, diligently searching into the conditions of the new-found agency, the same results would sooner or later have been reached by others. For of what discovery or invention may not the same be said? Only those who have sought in the twilight of uncertainty, can appreciate the vast economy of effort by prompt direction to the path from one who has gained an advance. Not for what might be, but for the actual bestowal, does he who first grasps a valuable truth merit the return of at least a grateful recognition.

If these results apparently so simple when announced by Henry, have never been justly appreciated either at home or abroad, no such complaint ever escaped their author. No such thought seems ever to have occurred to his artless nature. For him the one sufficient incentive and recompense was the advancement of himself and others in the knowledge of nature's laws. With the telegraph consciously within his grasp, he was well content to leave to others the glory and the emoluments of its realization.

At the beginning of the year 1831, Henry had suspended around the walls of one of the upper rooms in the Albany Academy, a mile of copper bell-wire interposed in a circuit between a small Cruickshanks battery and an "intensity" magnet of continuous fine coil. A narrow steel rod (a permanent magnet) pivoted to swing horizontally like the compass needle, was arranged so that one end remained in

* "For circuits of small resistance, galvanometers of small resistance must be used. For circuits of large resistance, galvanometers of large resistance must also be used; not that their resistance is any advantage, but because we cannot have a galvanometer adapted to indicate very small currents without having a very large number of turns in the coil, and this involves necessarily a large resistance." Professor F. Jenkin, *Electricity and Magnetism*, 12mo. London, and New York, 1873, chap. IV. sect. 3, p. 98.

contact with a leg of the soft iron core, while near the opposite end of the compass rod, a small stationary office-bell was placed. At each excitation of the electro-magnet, the compass rod or needle was repelled from one leg (by its similar magnetism) and attracted by the other leg, so that its free end tapped the bell. On a reversal of the current, the compass rod moved back to the opposite leg of the electro-magnet. This simple device the Professor was accustomed to exhibit to his classes, during the years 1831 and 1832, in illustration of the facility of transmitting signals to a distance by the swift action of electro-magnetism.[*]

Henry regarded his "quantity" magnet as being *scientifically* more important than his "intensity" magnet; and his success in constructing such, of almost incredible power, caused numerous requisitions on his skill. In April, 1831, Professor Silliman published in his *Journal* "An Account of a large Electro-Magnet made for the Laboratory of Yale College," under his charge. The iron horseshoe about one foot high was made from a three-inch octagonal bar 30 inches long; and was wrapped with 26 strands of copper wire each about 28 feet long. When duly excited by a single galvanic element consisting of concentric cylinders of copper and zinc, presenting about five square feet of active surface, the magnet lifted 2,300 pounds, more than a ton weight. For reversing the polarity of the magnet, a duplicate battery was oppositely connected with extensions of the ends of the coils, so that either battery could be alternately dipped. With a load of 56 pounds suspended from the armature, the poles of the magnet could be so rapidly reversed, that the weight would not fall during the interval of inversion. Professor Silliman remarks of the maker: "He has the honor of having constructed by far the most powerful magnets that have ever been known; and his last, weighing (armature and all) but 82½ pounds, sustains over a ton;— which is eight times more powerful than any magnet hitherto known in Europe."[†] And Sturgeon

---

[*] For an account of Henry's relation to the electro-magnetic Telegraph, see "Supplement." Note C.

[†] Silliman's Am. Jour. Sci. April, 1831, vol. XX. p. 201. Relatively, some of Henry's smaller magnets were many times more powerful than this. A miniature one made by Dr. Ten-Eyck under his direction, sustained 20 times its own weight; and one still smaller, sustained more than 60 times its own weight (Sill. Am. Jour. Sci. vol. xix. p. 407.)

(the true foster-father of the magnet) thus heralds the Yale College triumph: "By dividing about 800 feet of conducting wire into 26 strands and forming it into as many separate coils around a bar of soft iron about 60 pounds in weight and properly bent into a horse-shoe form, Professor Henry has been enabled to produce a magnetic force which completely eclipses every other in the whole annals of magnetism; and no parallel is to be found since the miraculous suspension of the celebrated oriental impostor in his iron coffin." *

The first Electro-magnetic Engine.—Among his ingenious applications of the new power, Henry's invention of the Electro-magnetic Engine should here be noticed. In a letter to his friend Professor Silliman, he says: "I have lately succeeded in producing motion in a little machine, by a power which I believe has never before been applied in mechanics, — by magnetic attraction and repulsion." The device consisted of a horizontal soft iron bar, about seven inches long, pivoted at its middle to oscillate vertically, and closely wrapped with three strands of insulated copper wire, whose ends were made by suitable extensions to project and bend downward at either end of the beam in reversed pairs, so as conveniently to dip into mercury thimbles in connection with the plates of the battery. Two upright permanent magnets having the same polarity, were secured immediately under the two ends of the oscillating bar, but separated from them by about an inch. So soon as the circuit was completed by the depression of one end of the oscillating electro-magnetic bar, a repulsion at this end co-operating with an attraction at the opposite end, caused immediately a contrary dip of the bar, which by reversing the polarity of this magnetic beam, thus produced a constant reciprocating action and movement. The engine beam oscillated at the rate of 75 vibrations per minute for more than an hour, or as long as the battery current was maintained.†
This simple but original device comprised the first automatic pole-

---

* *Philosoph. Magazine; and Annals, March, 1832, vol. xl. p. 163.* Henry's "quantity" magnet was at once adopted by FARADAY in his researches, as well as by the continental electricians; and his device of multiple coils is still recognised as the system best adapted for powerful magnetization. See "Supplement," NOTE D.

† Silliman's Am. Jour. Art, July, 1831, vol. xx. pp. 340-343.

changer or commutator ever applied to the galvanic battery,—an essential element not merely in every variety of the electro-magnetic machine, but in every variety of magneto-electric apparatus, and in every variety of the highly useful induction apparatus.

In an interesting "Historical Sketch of the rise and progress of Electro-magnetic Engines for propelling machinery;" by the distinguished philosopher James P. Joule, he remarks: "Mr. Sturgeon's discovery of magnetizing bars of soft iron to a considerable power, and rapidly changing their polarity by miniature voltaic batteries, and the subsequent improved plan by Professor Henry of raising the magnetic action of soft iron,—developed new and inexhaustible sources of force which appeared easily and extensively available as a mechanical agent; and it is to the ingenious American philosopher above named, that we are indebted for the first form of a working model of an engine upon the principle of reciprocating polarity of soft iron by electro-dynamic agency." *

In Henry's deliberate contemplation of his own achievement, his remarkable sagacity and sobriety of judgment were conspicuously displayed. Unperturbed by the enthusiasm so natural to the successful inventor, he carefully scanned the capabilities of this new dynamic agent. Considering the source of the power, he arrived at the conclusion that the de-oxidation of metal necessary for the battery, would require the expenditure of at least as much power as its combustion in the battery could refund; and that the coal consumed in such de-oxidation could be much more economically employed directly in the work to be done.† As the battery consumption moreover was found to increase more rapidly than the magnetic power produced, he was at once convinced that it could

---

* Sturgeon's Annals of Electricity, etc. March, 1839, vol. III. p. 439. Sturgeon himself the first to devise a rotary electro-magnetic engine, deserves honorable mention for correcting the statement of an American writer, and declining his mistaken award by frankly recognizing Henry's right to priority. (Annals of Electricity, April, 1839, vol. III. p. 354.)

† These considerations have been more than justified by later comparative investigations. Rankine estimates that the consumption of one pound of zinc will not produce more than one-tenth the energy that one pound of coal will; and that though in the efficient utilization of this energy it is four times superior, its useful work is therefore less than half that of coal; while its cost is from forty to fifty times greater. (The Steam Engine and other Prime Movers. By W. J. M. Rankine. London and Glasgow, 1859, part IV. art. 384, p. 541.)

never supersede or compete with steam.* He believed however
that the engine had a useful future in many minor applications
where economy was not the most important consideration.

When sometime afterward, a friend urged him to secure patents
on his inventions,—the "intensity" electro-magnet with its combinations, and the magnetic engine with its automatic pole-changer,
earnestly assuring him that either one with proper management
would secure an ample fortune to its owner, he firmly resisted every
importunity; declaring that he would feel humiliated by any
attempt at monopolizing the fruits of science, which he thought
belonged to the world. And this aversion to self-aggrandizement
by researches undertaken for truth, was carried with him through
life. †

While such disinterestedness cannot fail to excite our admiration,
it may perhaps be questioned whether in these cases it did not from
a practical point of view, amount to an over-fastidiousness:—
whether such legal establishment of ownership, shielding the pos-
sessor from the occasional depreciations of the envious, and securing
by its more tangible remunerations the leisure and the means for
more extended researches, would not have been to science more
than a compensation for the supposed sacrifice of dignity by the
philosopher. ‡

Nor did this repugnance to patenting arise (as it sometimes does)
from any theoretical disapproval of the system. On the contrary,

*JAMES P. JOULE (himself an inventor of an electro-magnetic engine) in a
letter dated May 20, 1839, said: "I can scarcely doubt that electro-magnetism will
eventually be substituted for steam in propelling machinery." (Sturgeon's
Annals of Electricity, vol. iv, p. 131.) This was some years before he commenced his
investigations on the mechanical equivalent of heat and other motors. He subsequently estimated that the consumption of a grain of zinc though sixty times
more costly than a grain of coal, produces only about one-eighth of the same
mechanical effect.

† This trait calls to mind Faraday's avowal made nearly thirty years later,
when in a letter to Messrs. Smith & Bentley, dated January 3, 1849, (declining
their offer for the publication of his "Juvenile Lectures,") he said: "In fact I
have always loved science more than money; and because my occupation is
almost entirely personal, I cannot afford to get rich." (Bence Jones' *Life of
Faraday*, vol. II. p. 63.)

‡ Several hundred patents have since been granted in this country for ingenious modifications of—or improvements upon the electro-magnetic telegraph; and
probably a hundred for equally ingenious varieties of the electro-magnetic engine;
all of which would have been tributary to HENRY as an original patentee.

be frequently expressed his strong conviction that a judicious code
of patent laws—if faithfully administered—furnishes the most
equitable method of recompensing meritorious inventors. The
institution was a good one—for others.

The discovery of Magneto-electricity.—From the magnetizing
influence of the galvanic current, physicists were almost inevitably
led to expect the converse reaction; and this anticipation appears to
have been co-eval with electro-magnetism. As early as 1820, the
illustrious Augustin Fresnel remarked: "It is natural to try
whether a magnetic bar will not produce a galvanic current in a
helical wire surrounding it;" and he made various experiments to
determine a question which was supposed to involve the soundness
of Ampère's theory. In November, 1820, he announced that
though he at first supposed his attempt at the magneto-electric
decomposition of water was partially successful, he was finally
satisfied that no decisive result was obtained.[*]

Five years later, Faraday attempted the same experimental
inquiry; and among his earliest publications gave an account of his
unsuccessful trials. After describing his arrangements he says:
"The magnet was then put in various positions and to different
extents into the helix, and the needle of the galvanometer noticed:
no effect however upon it could be observed. The circuit was made
very long, very short, of wires of different metals and different
diameters, down to extreme fineness, but the results were always
the same. Magnets more and less powerful were used, some so strong
as to bend the wire in its endeavors to pass round it. Hence it
appears that however powerful the action of an electric current may
be upon a magnet, the latter has no tendency by re-action to diminish
or increase the intensity of the former; a fact which though of a
negative kind, appears to me to be of some importance."[†]

Nor were American physicists discouraged by the records of repeated failures: and when the great Henry magnet was received
at Yale College, Professor C. U. Shepard (chemical assistant to
Professor Silliman) at once attacked the problem with this new

* *Annales de Chimie et de Physique,* 1820, vol. xv. pp. 219-222.
† *Quarterly Journal of Science, etc,* of the Royal Institution of Great Britain, July,
1825, vol. xii. p. 338. This well shows the danger of generalizing too broadly from
negative results.

equipment. He remarks: "As its magnetic flow was so powerful, I had strong hopes of being able to accomplish the decomposition of water by its means. My experiment however proved unsuccessful. - - - I hope however to resume the research hereafter, under more favorable circumstances."[a]

Henry, unsatisfied with past efforts, determined to pursue the subject in an exhaustive series of experiments; and had reached some momentary indications of the galvanometer, when his experiments were temporarily interrupted. Meanwhile it was announced in May, 1832, that Faraday had secured the long sought prize; though the announcement was brief, and to those eager for particulars, somewhat disappointing. Henry was accordingly induced to publish in the following number of Silliman's Journal (that for July) a sketch of his own trials both before and after the announced discovery. With reference to Faraday's discovery he remarks: "No detail is given of the experiments, and it is somewhat surprising that results so interesting, and which certainly form a new era in the history of electricity and magnetism, should not have been more fully described before this time in some of the English publications. The only mention I have found of them is the following short account from the 'Annals of Philosophy' for April, under the head of Proceedings of the Royal Institution.—'Feb. 17. Mr. Faraday gave an account of the first two parts of his researches in electricity; namely volta-electric induction, and magneto-electric induction. - - - If a wire connected at both extremities with a galvanometer, be coiled in the form of a helix around a magnet, no current of electricity takes place in it. This is an experiment which has been made by various persons hundreds of times, in the hope of evolving electricity from magnetism. But if the magnet be withdrawn from or introduced into such a helix, a current of electricity is produced *while the magnet is in motion*, and is rendered evident by the deflection of the galvanometer. If a single wire be passed by a magnetic pole, a current of electricity is induced through it which can be rendered sensible.'†

---

* Silliman's Am. Jour. Art. April, 1832, vol. XII. p. 399, and note.

† Philosoph. Mag. and Annals of Phil. April, 1832, vol. XI. pp. 300, 301. [Although FARADAY'S first communication on galvanic induction, and on magneto-electricity, was read before the Royal Society November 24, 1831, the published Trans-

"Before having any knowledge of the method given in the above account, I had succeeded in producing electrical effects in the following manner, which differs from that employed by Mr. Faraday, and which appears to me to develop some new and interesting facts. A piece of copper wire about thirty feet long and covered with elastic varnish, was closely coiled around the middle of the soft iron armature of the galvanic magnet described in vol. six of the American Journal of Science, and which when excited will readily sustain between six hundred and seven hundred pounds. The wire was wound upon itself so as to occupy only about one inch of the length of the armature, which is seven inches in all. The armature thus furnished with the wire, was placed in its proper position across the ends of the galvanic magnet, and there fastened so that no motion could take place. The two projecting ends of the helix were dipped into two cups of mercury, and these connected with a distant galvanometer by means of two copper wires each about forty feet long. This arrangement being completed, I stationed myself near the galvanometer and directed an assistant at a given word to immerse suddenly in a vessel of dilute acid, the galvanic battery attached to the magnet. At the instant of immersion the north end of the needle was deflected 30° to the west, indicating a current of electricity from the helix surrounding the armature. The effect however, appeared only as a single impulse, for the needle after a few oscillations resumed its former undisturbed position in the magnetic meridian, although the galvanic action of the battery, and consequently the magnetic power still continued. I was however much surprised to see the needle suddenly deflected from a state of rest to about 20° to the east, or in a contrary direction, when the battery was withdrawn from the acid,—and again deflected to the west when it was re-immersed. This operation was repeated many times in succession, and uniformly with the same result, the armature the whole time remaining immovably attached to the poles of the magnet, no motion being required to produce the effect, as it appeared to take place only in consequence of the instantaneous devel-

actions for 1832, containing this memoir, did not reach this country till more than a year later; so that the meagre abstract of the Royal Institution Proceedings above given, was the only notice of this important discovery, here accessible for many months.]

opment of the magnetic action in one case and the sudden cessation
of it in the other. - - - From the foregoing facts it appears that
a current of electricity is produced for an instant in a helix of copper
wire surrounding a piece of soft iron whenever magnetism is induced in the iron; and a current in an opposite direction when the
magnetic action ceases; also that an instantaneous current in one or
the other direction accompanies every change in the magnetic intensity of the iron.

"Since reading the account before given of Mr. Faraday's
method of producing electrical currents, I have attempted to combine the effects of motion and induction." No increase of effect
was however observable. On comparing the two methods separately it was found that while the sudden introduction of the end
of a magnetized bar within the helix connected with the galvanometer, deflected the needle seven degrees, the sudden magnetization of the bar when within the helix deflected the needle thirty
degrees. A cylindrical iron bar was made to rotate rapidly on its
axis within a stationary helix, by means of a turning lathe, but no
result followed.

In the following month (June) by employing an armature of
horse-shoe form (admitting longer coils), Henry succeeded in obtaining vivid sparks from the magnet. "The poles of the magnet
were connected by a single rod of iron bent into the form of a
horse-shoe, and its extremities filed perfectly flat so as to come in
perfect contact with the faces of the poles; around the middle of
the arch of this horse-shoe, two strands of copper wire were tightly
coiled one over the other. A current from one of these helices
deflected the needle one hundred degrees, and when both were used,
the needle was deflected with such force as to make a complete
circuit. But the most surprising effect was produced when instead
of passing the current through the long wires to the galvanometer,
the opposite ends of the helices were held nearly in contact with
each other, and the magnet suddenly excited; in this case a small
but vivid spark was seen to pass between the ends of the wires, and
this effect was repeated as often as the state of intensity of the
magnet was changed. - - - It appears from the May number
of the 'Annals of Philosophy,' that I have been anticipated in this

experiment of drawing sparks from the magnet by Mr. James D. Forbes of Edinburgh, who obtained a spark on the 30th of March:[*] my experiments being made during the last two weeks of June. A simple notification of his result is given, without any account of the experiment, which is reserved for a communication to the Royal Society of Edinburgh. My result is therefore entirely independent of his, and was undoubtedly obtained by a different process."[†]

Henry's gratification at the acquisition of the new insight into natural law, quite absorbed all sentiment of personal pride in its independent attainment; and his appreciation and congratulation of Faraday as the first discoverer of magneto-electricity, were hearty and unreserved. He was also particular always to assign to Faraday the first observation of the curious phenomena of momentary galvanic induction; although himself an independent discoverer of the fact.

Discovery of the "Extra Current."—In the course of these experiments he made a very important original observation on a peculiar case of self-induction, whereby he was enabled to convert a galvanic current of "quantity" into one of "intensity." This entirely new result seemed to contradict all previous experience. He thus concludes his paper;

"I may however mention one fact which I have not seen noticed in any work, and which appears to me to belong to the same class of phenomena as those above described. It is this:—when a small battery is moderately excited by diluted acid and its poles (which should be terminated by cups of mercury) are connected by a copper wire not more than a foot in length, no spark is perceived when the connection is either formed or broken: but if a wire thirty or forty feet long be used (instead of the short wire), though no spark will be perceptible when the connection is made, yet when it is broken by drawing one end of the wire from its cup of mercury, a vivid spark is produced. - - - The effect appears somewhat increased by coiling the wire into a helix: it seems also to depend in some measure on the length and thickness of the wire. I can

* Philosoph. Mag. and Annals, May, 1832, vol. xI. pp. 90, 98.
† Silliman's Am. Jour. Art, July, 1832, vol. xxII. pp. 408-409.

account for these phenomena only by supposing the long wire to
become charged with electricity which by its reaction on itself projects a spark when the connection is broken."[*]   This is the earliest
notice of the curious phenomenon of self-induction in an electric
discharge.

Election as Professor at Princeton.—The Trustees of the College
of New Jersey at Princeton, were about this time in search of a Professor to fill the chair of Natural Philosophy in that College, made
vacant by the resignation of Professor Henry Vethake, who had
accepted a Professorship of Natural Philosophy in the recently
established University of the City of New York. Professor Henry
had already won considerable reputation as a lecturer and teacher,
no less than as an experimental physicist. Professor Benjamin
Silliman of Yale College, urging his appointment, wrote: " Henry
has no superior among the scientific men of the country." And
Professor James Renwick of Columbia College (New York) still
more emphatically added: "He has no equal."

Professor Henry was unanimously elected by the Trustees;[†]
and he accepted the appointment: although strongly attached to his
first Academy, endeared to him by early memories, by six years of
successful labors, and by the warm regard of all his associates. May
it not be added that his residence at the capital of the State of New
York was further endeared to him by life's romance,—a most congenial and happy marriage contracted in 1830.

ELECTRICAL RESEARCHES AT PRINCETON: FROM 1832 TO 1842.

In November, 1832, Henry left the scene of his early scientific
triumphs, the Albany Academy, and removed to Princeton with
his family. For a year or two he gave his whole attention and
exertions to the duties of exposition and instruction; and during Dr.
Torrey's visit to Europe in 1833, at the Doctor's request, Professor Henry filled *ad interim* his chair of Chemistry, Mineralogy,

*Silliman's Am. Jour. Sci. July, 1832, vol. xxii.p. 408.

†Dr. MACLEAN, connected with the Faculty of the College of New Jersey at Princeton for fifty years, and for fourteen years its venerable president, in his History of
the College (2 vols. 8vo. Philadelphia, 1877,) gives a very interesting account of the
appointment and election of JOSEPH HENRY as Professor of Natural Philosophy in
1832, vol. II. pp. 290-291.

and Geology. These occupations left him no leisure for the pursuit of original research. He subsequently gave lectures on Astronomy, and also on Architecture.

In 1834, Henry constructed for the Laboratory of his College an original form of galvanic battery; so arranged as to bring into action any desired number of elements, from a single pair to eighty-eight. Each zinc plate 9 inches wide and 12 inches deep was surrounded by a copper case open at top and bottom, and giving thus one and a half square feet of efficient surface. Eleven of these, in eleven separate cells, formed a sub-battery; and eight of these were grouped together by means of adjustable conductors, so as to form from the whole a single battery. By means of a crank and windlass shaft in proper connection, any one or more of the eight sub-batteries could be immersed or disengaged, and if desired, a single cell alone could be charged. By another arrangement of adjustable conductors, all the zinc plates could be directly connected together, and all the copper plates together, after the plan of Dr. Hare's "calori-motor" battery; thus giving the "quantity" effect due to a single element of 132 square feet of zinc surface, or of any smaller area desired. As the author remarks concerning its various arrangements, "they have been adopted in most cases after several experiments and much personal labor." A detailed account of this battery was given in a communication read January 16th, 1835, before the American Philosophical Society (of which he had recently been elected a member), and was published in its Transactions.[*]

Electrical Self-Induction.— Meanwhile he had been engaged in his brief intervals of relaxation from his exacting professional cares during the past year, in repeating and extending his interesting observations (commenced at Albany in 1832), on the remarkable intensi-fying influence of a long conductor, and especially of a spiral one, when interposed in a galvanic circuit of a single pair, or a battery of low "intensity." A verbal communication on this curious form of "induction," was made to the Society on the same occasion as the description of his battery, and was illustrated by experiments exhibited before the Society.

Faraday in his "eighth series of Researches" (read before the Royal Society June 5th, 1834), pointed out very fully the differing actions of a single galvanic element giving a "quantity" current, and of a series of elements giving an "intensity" current; [*] thus entirely confirming the results obtained by Henry more than three years previously.

In the Philosophical Magazine for November, 1834, appeared a paper by Faraday, "On a peculiar condition of electric and magneto-electric Induction:" In which he notices as a remarkable fact, that while a short circuit wire from a single galvanic element, gives little or no visible spark, a long conductor gives a very sensible spark. "If the connecting wire be much lengthened, then the spark is much increased."[†] In his interesting research, Faraday appears to have entirely overlooked Henry's earlier labors in the same field;—as contrary to his usual custom, he makes no allusion to the same results having been obtained, and published in Silliman's Journal two years and a half before.[‡]

These observations were made by Faraday the subject of his "ninth series of Researches," in a communication "On the influence by induction of an electric current on itself:" read before the Royal Society January 20th, 1835. In this paper he states: "The inquiry arose out of a fact communicated to me by Mr. Jenkin,—which is as follows: If an ordinary wire of short length be used as the medium of communication between two plates of an electro-motor consisting of a single pair of metals, no management will enable the experimenter to obtain an electric shock from this wire: but if the wire which surrounds an electro-magnet be used, a shock is felt each time the contact with the electro-motor is broken." Having varied the experiment, Faraday adds: "There was no sensible spark on making contact, but on breaking contact there was a very large and bright spark, with considerable combustion of the mercury." He found a similar result with the wire helix alone,—without its magnetic core. "The power of producing these phenomena exists therefore in the simple helix, as well as in the electro-magnet,

* Phil. Trans. Roy. Soc. June 5, 1834, vol. cxxiv. art. 1810-1814, pp. 655, 656. Experimental Researches in Electricity, vol. I, pp. 361, 362.

† L. & E. Philosoph. Mag. Nov. 1834, vol. v. pp. 351, 352.

‡ Silliman's Am. Jour. for July, 1832, vol. xxii. p. 408, above quoted.

although by no means in the same high degree." With continuous
straight wire of the same length, he obtained a similar effect,—"yet
not so bright as that from the helix." "When a short wire is used,
all these effects disappear;" although there is undoubtedly a greater
"quantity" of electric current in the shorter wire; thus giving "the
strange result of a diminished spark and shock from the strong
current, and increased effects from the weak one."[*]

While Henry derived only satisfaction from these extended
verifications of his own observations, by one whom he had accustomed himself to look up to with admiration and regard, Dr. A.
Dallas Bache, his attached friend, then Professor of Natural
Philosophy in the University of Pennsylvania,—more jealous than
himself of his scientific fame, strongly urged and insisted that he
should immediately publish an account of his later researches.
Henry accordingly sent to the American Philosophical Society a
memoir (comprising the details of his recent verbal communication)
"On the Influence of a Spiral Conductor in increasing the Intensity of Electricity from a galvanic arrangement of a Single pair,
etc.," which was read before the Society, February 6th, 1835.

After citing his former paper of July, 1832, the writer remarks
that he had been able during the past year to extend his experiments on the curious phenomenon. "These though not so complete
as I could wish, are now presented to the Society with the belief
that they will be interesting at this time on account of the recent
publication of Mr. Faraday on the same subject." He then
relates that employing a single pair of his battery (comprising one
and a half square feet of zinc surface), he found as in his earlier
experiment in 1832, that the poles being connected by a piece of
copper bell-wire five inches long, no spark was given on making or
breaking contact. Fifteen feet of interposed wire gave a very
feeble spark; and with successive additions of fifteen feet, the effect
increased until with 120 feet the maximum spark appeared to be
reached, and beyond this there was no perceptible increase; while
with double this length (or 240 feet) there seemed to be a diminu-

---

[*] Phil. Trans. Roy. Soc. Jan. 9, 1835, vol. cxxv. articles 1061-1097, and 1873, pp. 11-63.
Experimental Researches in Electricity, vol. I. pp. 324-371. This memoir did not reach
this country, of course, till a year later.

16

tion of intensity. From various trials the inference was drawn
that the length required for maximum effect varied with the size of
the galvanic element. Thicker wires of the same length produced
greater effect, depending in some degree on the size of the battery.
A wire of forty feet when coiled into a cylindrical helix "gave a
more intense spark than the same wire uncoiled." A ribbon of
sheet copper about an inch wide and twenty-eight feet long, being
covered with silk and coiled into a flat spiral—like a watch
spring—(after the plan of Dr. Ritchie) gave a vivid spark with a
loud snap. When uncoiled, it produced a much feebler spark.
With the insulated copper ribbon folded in its middle, and the
double thickness coiled into a flat spiral, there was no spark whatever, although the same ribbon unrolled gave a feeble spark: thus
showing that the induction of the current upon itself was neutralized by flowing equally in opposite directions in the double spiral.
With a larger copper ribbon one inch and a half wide, and 98 feet
long (weighing 15 pounds), spirally coiled, the snap of the spark
could be heard in an adjoining room with the door closed. Want
of material prevented the result being pushed further, so as to
ascertain the range of maximum effect with this form of conductor.
With increased battery surface, the effect was also increased; so that
with eight elements of his battery arranged as a single pair (of 12
square feet) the spark on breaking contact "resembled the discharge
of a small Leyden jar highly charged." With the flat spiral, no
increase of effort was observable on the introduction of a soft iron
core into the axis of the spiral, forming a magnet. With a helical
or cylindrical coil about nine inches long, enclosing an iron core,
"the spark appeared a little more intense than without the iron."
The inference is also drawn "from these experiments, that some of
the effects heretofore attributed to magneto-electric action are
chiefly due to the reaction on each other of the several spirals of
the coil which surround the magnet."

In these researches it was found that when the two plates of a
single pair were placed even fourteen inches apart in an open trough
of diluted acid, "although the electrical intensity in this case must
have been very low, yet there was but little reduction in the apparent intensity of the spark." It was also shown that "the spiral

conductor produces however, little or no increase of effect when introduced into a galvanic circuit of considerable intensity." When for example an "intensity" battery of two Cruickshanks troughs, each containing fifty-six elements was employed with the larger copper spiral, "no greater effect was perceived than with a short thick wire:" in either case, only a feeble spark being given.* An abstract of the results thus announced, (and which were obtained by Henry during the summer of 1834,) was communicated by Dr. A. D. Bache, as a Secretary of the American Philosophical Society, to the Franklin Journal, in order to give these interesting facts an earlier currency.† The date of original discovery was however so well established, that this friendly effort was scarcely necessary.‡

Combined Circuits.—In 1835, wires had been extended across the front campus of the college grounds at Princeton from the upper story of the library building to the Philosophical Hall on the opposite side, through which signals were occasionally sent, distinguished by the number of taps of the electro-magnetic bell, as first exhibited five years previously in the hall of the Albany Academy. It has already been noticed, that contrary to all the antecedent expectations of physicists, Henry had established the fact that the most powerful form of magnet (designated by him the "quantity" magnet) is not the form best adapted to distant action through an extended circuit. The ingenious idea occurred to him that notwithstanding this fundamental fact, it would be quite easy to combine the two systems so as to enable an operator to produce the most energetic mechanical effects, at almost any required distance. It is simply necessary to employ with the distant "intensity" magnet an oscillating armature with a suitable prolongation so arranged as to open and close the short circuit of an adjoining

* Trans. Am. Phil. Soc. vol. v. (n. s.) art. x. pg. 223-231.

† Journal of the Franklin Institute, March, 1835, vol. xv. pp. 169, 172. See "Supplement," Note E.

‡ M. Becquerel, in his elaborate Treatise on Electricity, in the chapter on "The influence of an electric current on itself by induction," says with regard to the increase of tension in a feeble current when passing through a long spiral conductor, "The effects observed in these circumstances appear to have been nothing for the first time by Professor Henry." (Traité expérimental de l'Électricité et du Magnétisme, 8vo. 7 vols. Paris, 1834-1840, vol. v. art. 1331, p. 23.)

"quantity" magnet of any practicable power:—a work which indeed could be accomplished by the mere swing of the most delicate galvanometer needle. Professor Henry had constructed for his own laboratory a large electro-magnet designed to surpass the celebrated magnet made for Yale College; and with it he was enabled to exhibit to his class, by employing a small portion of his "quantity" battery, an easy lifting power of more than three thousand pounds.* Such was the mechanical agency he called into action through his telegraphic circuit, by simply lifting its galvanic wire from a mercury thimble, or by again dipping it into the same. This combination has since found an important application; its principle underlying all the various forms and uses of the "relay" magnet, and of the "receiving" magnet and local battery, since employed.

Visit to Europe.—In order to give Professor Henry a much-needed rest from his diligent services and close application during the last four years, the Trustees of his College liberally allowed him a year's absence with full salary: thus affording him for the first time a long coveted opportunity of visiting Europe.

In February of 1837, in company with his valued and faithful friend, Professor Bache, he arrived in England; where the two American physicists formed ready and lasting intimacies with some of the most distinguished worthies of Great Britain. Everywhere received with courteous and cordial consideration, they both ever carried with them agreeable memories of their holiday sojourn abroad.

In London, many pleasant interviews with Faraday, formed a memorable circumstance. Wheatstone, then Professor of Experimental Philosophy in King's College, was engaged in developing his system of needle telegraph, and he unfolded freely to his visitors his numerous projects; and particularly his arrangement of supplementary local circuit from an additional battery, for sounding an electro-magnetic signal, by being brought into action by a movement from the main line circuit.† Henry had then the pleasure

---

* It is said that this magnet has been made to sustain 3,500 pounds. (Turnbull's *Electro-Magnetic Telegraph*, 2nd ed. 1853, p. 63.)

† This was early in April, 1837. (*Smithsonian Report* for 1857, p. 111.) Two months later, or June 12th, 1837, Wheatstone in conjunction with W. F. Cooke had secured a patent on his system of telegraph, including the combination of circuits.

of detailing to him his own similar combination of two electro-
magnetic circuits, experimentally tried more than a year previously.[*]

Nearly a year was employed in foreign travel, most pleasantly
and beneficially both for mind and body: the greater portion of the
time however being spent in London, in Paris, (where Henry
formed the acquaintance of Arago, Becquerel, De la Rive, Biot,
Gay-Lussac, and other celebrities,) and in Edinburgh, where he also
found a galaxy of eminent and congenial minds.

In September of the same year (1837) he attended the meeting
of the British Association at Liverpool; where being invited to
speak, he made a brief communication on some electrical researches
in regard to the phenomenon known as the "lateral discharge:" — a
study to which he had been led by some remarks of Dr. Roget on
the subject. "The result of the analysis was in accordance with an
opinion of Biot — that the lateral discharge is due only to the escape
of the small quantity of redundant electricity which always exists
on one side or the other of a jar, and not to the whole discharge."
Hence we could increase or diminish the lateral action by any means
which affect the quantity of free electricity: — as by "an increase
of the thickness of the glass, or by substituting for the small knob
of the jar, a large ball. But the arrangement which produces the
greatest effect is that of a long fine copper wire insulated, — parallel
to the horizon, and terminated at each end by a small ball. When
sparks are thrown on this from a globe of about a foot in diameter,
the wire at each discharge becomes beautifully luminous from one
end to the other, even if it be a hundred feet long; rays are given
off on all sides perpendicular to the axis of the wire:" — forming a
continuous electrical brush. It was also stated "that the same
quantity of electricity could be made to remain on the wire, if gradually communicated [by a point]; but when thrown on in the form
of a spark, it is dissipated as before described:" — as though possessing a kind of momentum. When two or more wires are arranged
in parallel lines (in electrical connection), only the outer sides of the

<hr/>

[*] "I informed him that I had devised another method of producing effects somewhat similar; this consisted in opening the circuit of my large quantity magnet at
Princeton, when loaded with many hundred pounds weight, by attracting upward
a small piece of movable wire with a small internally magnet connected with a long
wire circuit." (Henry's Deposition in the case of O'Rielly and Morse, September
7, 1849.)

exposed wires become luminous: and "when the wire is formed into
a flat spiral, the outer spiral alone exhibits the lateral discharge, but
the light in this case is very brilliant: the inner spirals appear to
increase the effect by induction." In like manner when a ball was
attached to the middle of a vertical lightning-rod having a good
earth-connection, "when sparks of about an inch and a half were
thrown on the ball, corresponding lateral sparks could be drawn
not only from the parts of the rod between the ground and the ball,
but from the part above, even to the top of the rod." [*]

At the same meeting, before the section on Mechanics and Engineering, Henry gave by request an account of the great extension
of the Railway and Canal systems in the United States : which was
listened to with great attention and interest. He also referred to
the inland or river navigation in our country, describing the improvements introduced into our large river steamboats, especially on
the Hudson river in New York State; where the usual speed was
fifteen miles per hour or more. [†]

In November, 1837, Henry returned from his foreign tour
greatly invigorated, — bringing with him some new apparatus; and
with increased zest he re-embarked upon the duties of his professorship. Continuing his studies of electrical action, he presented
verbally to the American Philosophical Society, February 16th,
1838, a notice of further observations on the "lateral discharge"
of electricity while passing along a wire, going to show that even
with good earth connection, free electricity is not conducted silently
to the ground. [‡]

In May, 1838, he announced to the Society the production of
currents by induction from ordinary or mechanical electricity,
analogous to that first obtained by Faraday from galvanism in
1831: and the further curious fact that on the discharge from a
Leyden jar through a good conductor, a secondary shock from a

---

* Report of Brit. Association, for 1837, pp. 23-24, of Abstracts.

† Same Report, Abstracts, p. 135. It was on this occasion that Dr. Lardner, generalizing probably from his observations on the Thames, ventured (not very cautiously) to doubt whether any such speed as fifteen miles per hour on water, could
ordinarily be effected. (Bill. Am. Jour. Sci. Jan. 1839, vol. xxxiii. p. 205.) The same
authority affirmed the futility of attempting oceanic steam navigation.

‡ Proceedings Am. Phil. Soc. Feb. 16, 1838, vol. I. p. 6.

perfectly insulated near conductor could be obtained — more intense
than the primary shock directly from the jar. *

These investigations having in view the discovery of "inductive
actions in common electricity analogous to those found in galvanism"
(commenced in the spring of 1836), led to renewed examination of
the secondary galvanic current, which since November 24th, 1831,
(or for seven years,) had received no special attention. Henry's
very interesting series of experiments were detailed in a somewhat
elaborate memoir read before the American Philosophical Society,
November 2nd, 1838. Employing five different sized annular spools
of fine wire (about one-fiftieth of an inch thick) varying from one-
fifth of a mile to nearly a mile in length (which might be called
"intensity" helices); and six flat spiral coils of copper ribbon varying from three-quarters of an inch to one inch and a half in width,
and from 60 to 90 feet in length (which might be called "quantity"
coils), he was able to combine them in various ways both in connection and in parallelism. A cylindrical battery of one and three-
quarters square feet of zinc surface was principally used; and the
galvanic circuit was interrupted by drawing one end of the copper
ribbon or wire over a rasp in good metallic contact with the other
pole of the battery.

From the energetic action of the flat ribbon coil in producing
the induction of a current on itself, it was inferred that the secondary current would also be best induced by it. With the single
larger ribbon coil in connection with the battery, and another ribbon
coil placed over it resting on an interposed glass plate, at every
interruption of the primary circuit an induction spark was obtained
at the rubbed ends of the second coil; though the shock was feeble.
With a double wire spool (one within the other) of 2650 yards,
placed above the primary coil (having about the same weight as the
copper ribbon) the magnetizing effects disappeared, the sparks were
much smaller, "but the shock was almost too intense to be received
with impunity." The secondary current in this case was one of
small "quantity" but of great "intensity." With a single break
of circuit in the primary, it was passed through a circle of 56 students of his senior class, with the effect of a moderate charge from

a Leyden jar. From various experiments, the limit of efficient length for a given galvanic power was ascertained; beyond which the induced current was diminished. Employing a Cruickshanks battery of 00 small elements (4 inches square) he found with the ribbon coil that the induced currents were exceedingly feeble, but with the long wire helix as the primary circuit that strong indications were produced. By the alternations of the ribbon and wire coils, the fact was established "that an intensity current can induce one of quantity, and by the preceding experiments the converse has also been shown that a quantity current can induce one of intensity;" a result which has had an important bearing on the subsequent development of the electro-magnetic "Induction-Coil." With a long ribbon coil receiving the galvanic current from 35 feet of zinc surface, sensible induction shocks could be felt from a large annular coil of four feet diameter (containing five miles of wire) when placed in parallelism at a distance of four feet from the primary coil; while at the distance of one foot the shock became too severe to be taken. With this arrangement an induction shock was given from one apartment to another, through the intervening partition.

Successive orders of Induction.—When it is considered that the primary current in such cases has a considerable duration, while the secondary current is but momentary, being developed only at the instant of change in the primary, it could certainly not have been expected that this single instantaneous electrical impulse of reaction would be capable of acting as a primary current, and of similarly inducing an action on a third independent circuit: and during the seven years in which galvanic induction had been known, no physicist ever thought of making the trial. Theoretically it might perhaps have been inferred, if such tertiary induction had any existence, as it would be coincident not with the instantaneous secondary induction, but with the initiation and termination of such momentary current, and hence in opposite signs—separated by an inappreciable interval of time, that the whole phenomenon would probably be entirely masked by a practical neutralization.

The experiments of Henry fully established however the new and remarkable result—of a very appreciable tertiary current. By con-

necting the secondary coil with another at some distance from the
primary so as not to be influenced by it directly, but forming with
the secondary a single closed circuit, not only was the distant coil
capable of producing in an insulated wire helix placed over it, a
distinct current of induction at the interruption of the primary,
but sensible shocks were obtained from it. The experiment was
pushed still further; and inductive currents of a fourth degree
were obtained. "By a similar but more extended arrangement,
shocks were received from currents of a fourth and a fifth order:
and with a more powerful primary current, and additional coils, a
still greater number of successive inductions might be obtained.
- - - It was found that with the small battery a shock could
be given from the current of the third order to twenty-five persons
joining hands; also shocks perceptible in the arms were obtained
from a current of the fifth order." As Henry simply remarks:
"The induction of currents of different orders, of sufficient intensity to give shocks, could scarcely have been anticipated from our
previous knowledge of the subject." By means of the small
magnetizing helix introduced into each circuit, the direction of
these successive currents was found to be alternating or reversed to
each other. These remarkable results were obtained in the summer
of 1838. "

The concluding section of this important memoir is occupied
with an account of "The production of induced currents of the
different orders, from ordinary electricity." An open glass cylinder
about six inches in diameter was provided with two long narrow
strips of tin foil pasted around it in corresponding helical courses,
the one on the outside and the other on the inside, directly opposite
to each other. The inner coiled strip had its extremities connected
with insulated wires which formed a circuit outside the cylinder,
and included a small magnetizing helix. The outer tin foil strip
was also connected with wires so that an electrical discharge from a
half-gallon Leyden jar could be passed through it. The magnetization of a small needle indicated an induced current through the
inner tin-foil ribbon corresponding in direction with the outer cur-

rent from the jar.[*] By means of a second glass cylinder similarly provided with helical tin-foil ribbons in suitable connection, a tertiary current of induction was obtained, analogous to that derived from galvanism. "Also by the addition in the same way of a third cylinder, a current of the fourth order was developed."

Similar as these successive inductions from an electrical discharge were to those previously observed in the case of the galvanic current, they presented one puzzling difference in the direction of the currents of the different orders. "These in the experiments with the glass cylinders, instead of exhibiting the alternations of the galvanic currents, were all in the same direction as the discharge from the jar, or in other words they were all *plus*. On substituting for the tinned glass cylinders, well insulated copper coils, "alternations were found the same as in the case of galvanism." The only difference apparently between the two arrangements, was that the tin-foil ribbons were separated only by the thin glass of the cylinders, while the copper spiral coils were placed an inch and a half apart. By varied experiments, the direction of the induced currents was found to depend notably on the distance between the conductors;—the induction ceasing at a certain distance, (according to the amount of the charge and the characters of the conductors,) and the direction of the induced current beyond this critical distance being contrary to that of the primary current." "With a battery of eight half-gallon jars, and parallel wires about ten feet long, the change in the direction did not take place at a less distance than from twelve to

[*] About a year later, the distinguished German electrician Peter Riess, apparently unaware of Henry's researches, discovered the secondary currents induced from galvanized electricity, by a very similar experiment. (Poggendorff's *Annalen der Physik und Chemie*, 1848, No. 3, vol. xlvii. pp. 65-68.)

[†] The variation in the direction of polarization (without reference to induction extension) appears to have been first noticed by Felix Savary, some dozen years before, in an important memoir communicated to the Paris Academy of Sciences July 31, 1826. M. Savary announced that "The direction of the magnetic polarity of small needles exposed in an electric current directed along a wire stretched longitudinally, varies with the distance of the wire."—the action being found to be periodical with the distance. M. Savary observed three periods, and also that that the distances of maxima and of the nodal areas "vary with the length and diameter of the wire, and with the intensity of the discharge." He also found that "when a needle is used for magnetizing, the distance at which the needle placed within it is from the conducting wire, is indifferent but the direction and the degree of magnetization depends on the intensity of the discharge, and on the ratio between the length and size of the wire." (Brewster's *Edinburgh Jour. Sci. Oct.* 1826, vol. v. p. 369.)

fifteen inches, and with a still larger battery and longer conductors, no change was found although the induction was produced at the distance of several feet." With Dr. Hare's battery of 32 one-gallon jars, and a copper wire about one-tenth of an inch thick and 80 feet long stretched across the lecture-room and back on either side toward the battery, a second wire stretched parallel with the former for about 36 feet and extended to form an independent circuit, (its ends being connected with a small magnetizing helix,) was tested at varying distances beginning with a few inches until they were twelve feet apart: at which distance of the parallel wire, its induction though enfeebled, still indicated by its magnetizing power, a direction corresponding with the primary current. The form of the room did not permit a convenient separation of the two circuits to a greater distance.*

The eminent French electrician Antoine C. Becquerel, in a chapter on Induction in his large work, remarks: "Very recently M. Henry, Professor of Natural Philosophy in New Jersey, has extended the domain of this branch of physics: the results obtained by him are of such importance, particularly in regard to the intensity of the effects produced, that it is proper to expound them here with some detail." Twenty pages are then devoted to three researches.†

A memoir was read before the Society, June 19th, 1840, giving an account of observations on the two forms of induction occurring on the making and on the breaking of the primary galvanic circuit, the two differing in character as well as in direction. In these experiments he employed a Daniell's constant battery of 30 elements; the battery being "sometimes used as a single series with all its elements placed consecutively, and at others in two or three series, arranged collaterally, so as to vary the quantity and intensity of the electricity as the occasion might require." As the initial induction had always been found so feeble as to be scarcely perceptible, (although in quantity sufficient to affect the ordinary galvanometer

* Trans. Am. Phil. Soc., vol. vi. (n. s.) art. ii. pp. 303-337. In the Proceedings of the Society for November 2d, 1838, when this memoir was read, it is recorded "Professor Henry made a verbal communication during the course of which he illustrated experimentally the phenomena developed in his paper." (Proceed. Am. Phil. Soc. Nov. 2, 1838, vol. i. pp. 54-56.)

† Traité expérimental de l'Électricité et du Magnétisme, vol. v. pp. 67-187.

as much as the terminal induction,) most of the results previously
obtained (such as the detection of successive orders of currents) were
derived from the strong inductions at the moment of breaking the
circuit. It became therefore important to endeavor to intensify the
initial induction for its more especial examination; and this it was
found could be effected in two ways,—by increasing the "intensity"
of the battery, and by diminishing within certain limits the length
of the primary coil.

"With the current from one element, the shock at breaking the
circuit was quite severe, but at making the same it was very feeble,
and could be perceived in the fingers only or through the tongue.
With two elements in the circuit the shock at the beginning was
slightly increased: with three elements the increase was more decided,
while the shock at breaking the circuit remained nearly of the same
intensity as at first, or was comparatively but little increased.
When the number of elements was increased to ten, the shock at
making contact was found fully equal to that at breaking, and by
employing a still greater number, the former was decidedly greater
than the latter, the difference continually increasing until all the
thirty elements were introduced into the circuit. - - - Experiments were next made to determine the influence of a variation in
the length of the coil, the intensity of the battery remaining the
same." For this purpose the battery consisting of a single element
"was employed; and the length of the copper ribbon coil was successively reduced from 60 feet, by measures of 15 feet. With 45
feet, the initial induction was stronger than with 60 feet: with the
next shorter length it was more perceptible, and increased in
intensity with each diminution of the coil, until a length of about
fifteen feet appeared to give a maximum result." At the same time
it was found that "the intensity of the shock at the *ending* of the
battery current diminishes with each diminution of the length of
the coil. - - - By the foregoing results we are evidently furnished with two methods of increasing at pleasure the intensity of
the induction at the beginning of a battery current, the one consisting in increasing the intensity of the source of the electricity,
and the other in diminishing the resistance to conduction of the
circuit while its intensity remains the same."

Having thus succeeded in exalting the initial induction, Henry proceeded in his investigation. Distinct currents of the third, fourth, and fifth orders were readily obtained from it; and as was anticipated, with their signs (or directions) the reverse of the corresponding orders derived from the terminal induction. In other respects "the series of induced currents produced at the beginning of the primary current appeared to possess all the properties belonging to those of the induction at the ending of the same current."

In the course of these investigations the idea having occurred to him "that the intense shocks given by the electric fish may possibly be from a secondary current," as it appeared to him that "this is the only way in which we can conceive of such intense electricity being produced in organs imperfectly insulated and immersed in a conducting medium," he endeavored to simulate the effect by arranging a secondary wire coil furnished with terminal handles, over a primary copper ribbon coil, the two being insulated as usual. "By immersing the apparatus in a shallow vessel of water, the handles being placed at the two extremities of the diameter of the helix, and the hands plunged into the water parallel to a line joining the two poles, a shock is felt through the arms."

The former experiment of obtaining an induction shock from one room to another through a partition, was repeated on a still larger scale. All the coils of copper ribbon having been united in a single continuous conductor of about 400 feet in length, "this was rolled into a ring of five and a half feet in diameter, and suspended vertically against the inside of the large folding doors which separate the laboratory from the lecture-room. Beyond the doors, in the lecture-room and directly opposite the coil, was placed a helix formed of upwards of a mile of copper wire, one-sixteenth of an inch in thickness, and wound into a hoop of four feet in diameter. With this arrangement, and a battery of 147 square feet of zinc surface divided into eight elements, shocks were perceptible in the tongue when the two conductors were separated to the distance of nearly seven feet. At the distance of between three and four feet, the shocks were quite severe. The exhibition was rendered more interesting by causing the induction to take place through a number of persons standing in a row between the two conductors."

The second section of the memoir is mainly occupied with details of experiments on the screening effect of conducting plates (of non-magnetic metals) when interposed between the primary and secondary coils: showing remarkable contrasts in the "quantity" and "intensity" classes of galvanic effects. When the annular spool or helix (of nearly one mile of copper wire) was employed with the large spiral coil of copper ribbon, "the coil being connected with a battery of ten elements, the shocks both at making and breaking the circuit were very severe; and these as usual were almost entirely neutralized by the interposition of the zinc plate. But when the galvanometer instead of the body, was introduced into the circuit, its indications were the same whether the plate was interposed or not: or in other words the galvanometer Indicated no screening, while under the same circumstances the shocks were neutralized. A similar effect was observed when the galvanometer and the magnetizing helix were together introduced into the circuit. The interposition of the plate entirely neutralized the magnetizing power of the helix (in reference to tempered steel) while the deflections of the galvanometer were unaffected." The induction currents of the third, fourth, and fifth orders, were found to be of considerable "intensity;"—magnetizing steel needles, giving shocks, not being interrupted by a drop of water placed in the circuit between the ends of the severed wire,—and yet being screened or neutralized by a metallic plate interposed between the coils.[*]

A continuation of the memoir was read before the Philosophical Society November 20th, 1840, discussing further the theoretical differences between an initial or an increasing galvanic current, and a decreasing or an arrested current, in producing the phenomena of induction. On the same occasion Henry described "an apparatus for producing a reciprocating motion by the repulsion in the consecutive parts of a conductor through which a galvanic current is passing." About ten years before, he had devised the first electro-magnetic engine (operating by intermittent magnetic attractions and repulsions); and now he had contrived the first galvanic engine, operating by the analogous intermittent attractions and repulsions of the electric current.[†]

* Trans. Am. Phil. Soc. June 1840, vol. viii. (n. s.) art. i. pp. 1-16.
† Proceedings Am. Phil. Soc. Nov. 20, 1840, vol. i. p. 281.

Oscillation of Electrical Discharge.—In June, 1842, he presented a communication to the Society recounting an investigation of some anomalies in ordinary electrical induction. While with the larger needles ("No. 3 and No. 4") subjected to the magnetizing helix, the polarity was always conformable to the direction of the discharge, he found that when very fine needles were employed, an increase in the force of the electricity produced changes of polarity. About a thousand needles were magnetized in the testing helices in these researches.

This puzzling phenomenon was finally cleared up by the important discovery that an electrical equilibrium was not instantaneously effected by the spark, but that it was attained only after several oscillations of the flow. "The discharge—whatever may be its nature, is not correctly represented by the single transfer from one side of the jar to the other: the phenomena require us to admit the existence of a principal discharge in one direction, and then several reflex actions backward and forward, each more feeble than the preceding, until the equilibrium is obtained."[*] In every case therefore of the electrostatic discharge, the testing needles were really subjected to an oscillating alternation of currents, and consequently to successive partial de-magnetizations and re-magnetizations. The complications produced by this residual action, satisfactorily explained for the first time, the discordant results obtained by different investigators. This singular reflux of current was ingeniously applied by Henry to explain the apparent change of inductive current with differing distances. Should the primitive discharge wave be in excess of the magnetic capacity of the needle at a given position, the return wave might be just sufficient to completely reverse its polarity, and the diminished succeeding wave insufficient to restore it to its former condition; while at a greater distance, the primitive wave might be so far reduced as to just magnetize the needle fully,

* *Proceedings Am. Phil. Soc.* June 17, 1842, vol. II. pp. 193–196.—Prof. Hermann L. F. Helmholtz some five years later (in 1847), but quite independently, suggested "a backward and forward motion between the coatings" when the Leyden jar is discharged. (*Scientific Memoirs*, edited by Dr. J. Tyndall, 1853, vol. I. p. 131.) And still five years later (in 1853) Sir William Thomson made the same independent conjectures. (*L. E. D. Phil. Mag.* June, 1853, vol. v. pp. 393, 401.) To Felix Savary however is due the credit of having first advanced the hypothesis of electrical oscillations, as early as 1827. See "Supplement," Note F.

and the second wave, being still more enfeebled, would only partially de-magnetize it, leaving still a portion of the original polarity; and so for the following diminished oscillations.

In the course of these extended researches the presence of inductive action was traced to most surprising and unimagined distances. "A single spark from the prime conductor of the machine, of about an inch long, thrown on the end of a circuit of wire in an upper room, produced an induction sufficiently powerful to magnetize needles in a parallel circuit of wire placed in the cellar beneath, at a perpendicular distance of thirty feet, with two floors and ceilings—each fourteen inches thick intervening."

"The last part of the series of experiments relates to induced currents from atmospheric electricity. By a very simple arrangement, needles are strongly magnetized in the author's study, even when the flash is at the distance of seven or eight miles, and when the thunder is scarcely audible. On this principle he proposes a simple self-registering electrometer, connected with an elevated exploring rod." For obtaining the results above alluded to, a thick wire was soldered to the edge of the tin roof of his dwelling and passed into his study through a hole in the window frame; while a similar wire passing out to the ground, terminated in connection with a metal plate in a deep well close by. Between the wire ends within his study, various apparatus, including magnetising helices of different sizes and characters, could be attached, so as to be within the line of conduction from the roof to the ground. The inductions from atmospheric discharges were found to have the oscillatory character observed with the Leyden jar; and by interposing several magnetizing helices with few and with many convolutions, Henry was able to get from a needle in the former the polarity due to the direct current, and in the latter, that due to the return current; thus catching the lightning (as it were) upon the rebound.

In examining the "lateral discharge" from a lightning-rod in good connection with the earth, he had often observed that while a spark could be obtained sufficiently strong to be distinctly felt, it scarcely affected in the slightest degree a delicate gold-leaf electroscope. How explain so incongruous a phenomenon? Henry discovered the very simple solution, by a reference to the self-induction of the rod,—a negative wave passing, succeeded immediately by a positive wave so rapidly as to completely neutralize the effect upon the electroscope before the inertia of the gold-leaf could be overcome, while actually producing a double spark (sensibly co-incident) to and from the recipient.

A few months later, "he had succeeded in magnetizing needles by the secondary current, in a wire more than two hundred and twenty feet distant from the wire through which the primary current was passing, excited by a single spark from an electrical machine."[*] In this case the primary wire was his telegraph line stretched seven years before across the campus of the college grounds in front of Nassau Hall; the secondary or induction wire being suspended in a parallel direction across the grounds at the rear of Nassau Hall, with its ends terminating in buried metallic plates;—the large building intervening between the two wires.

This brilliant series of contributions to our knowledge of a most recondite and mysterious agent, placed Henry, by the concurrent judgment of all competent physicists, in the very front rank of original investigators. His persevering researches in the electrical paradoxes of induction, perhaps more than any similar ones, tended to strengthen the hypothesis of an ætherial dynamic agency; although he himself had for a long time been inclined to favor the material hypothesis.[†]

INVESTIGATIONS IN GENERAL PHYSICS; FROM 1830 TO 1846.

In order to give a proper connection to the experimental inquiries undertaken by Henry in various fields, it is necessary to pause here, and to recur to some of his earlier scientific labors,—beginning again at Albany.

_____

[*] *Proceedings Am. Phil. Soc.* Oct. 21, 1842, vol. II. p. 259. It is barely possible that the primary current might have returned through the second wire.

[†] In a paper "On the Theory of the so-called Imponderables" published some years later, in referring to the phenomena of electrical oscillation in discharge, and of the series of inductions taking place and "extending to a surprising distance on all sides," he remarks: "As these are the results of currents in alternate directions, they must produce in surrounding space a series of plus and minus motions, analogous to—if not identical with oscilulations." (*Proceed. Amer. Association*, Albany, Aug. 1851, p. 99.)

17

Meteorology.—From an early date Henry took a deep interest in the study of meteorology: not only on account of its practical importance, but from its relation to chemical physics, and because from the very complexity and irregularity of its conditions, it challenged further investigation and stood in need of larger generalizations. His early association with Dr. T. Romeyn Beck in the first development of the system of meteorological observations established in the State of New York, has already been referred to in the sketch of his "Early Career." (Page 212.) This active and zealous co-operation continued from 1827 to 1832; or as long as he resided in Albany.

In September of 1830, he commenced a series of observations for Professor Renwick of Columbia College, to determine the magnetic intensity at Albany. With the assistance of his brother-in-law, Professor Stephen Alexander, these observations were continued daily for two months. [*] In April, 1831, a second series of observations was commenced; in the course of which his attention was attracted by a great disturbance of the needle during the time of a conspicuous "aurora" on the 19th of April, 1831. At noon of the 19th the oscillations were found to be perfectly accordant with previous ones, but at 6 o'clock P. M. a remarkable increase of magnetic intensity was indicated. At 10 o'clock of the same evening, during the most active manifestation of the aurora, the oscillations of the needle were again examined. "Instead of still indicating as at 6 o'clock an uncommonly high degree of magnetic intensity, it now showed an intensity considerably lower than usual." Thus, designating the normal intensity at the place as unity, at 6 o'clock it had increased to 1.024, and at 10 o'clock had subsided to 0.993, which according to Hansteen's observations is the usual

---

[*] The needles employed in these observations were a couple received by Professor RENWICK from Capt. SABINE.—one of which had belonged to Professor HANSTEEN of Norway. "They were suspended according to the method of Hansteen in a small mahogany box, by a single fiber of raw silk. The box was furnished with a glass cover, and had a graduated arc of ivory on the bottom to mark the amplitude of the vibrations. In using this apparatus, the time of three hundred vibrations was noted by a quarter-second watch, well regulated to mean time; a register being made at the end of every tenth vibration, and a mean deduced from the whole, taken as the true time of the three hundred vibrations. Experiments carefully made with this apparatus were found susceptible of considerable accuracy;" the individual observations not differing from the mean number, ordinarily more than one-thousandth. (Silliman's Am. Jour. Sci. April, 1832, vol. xxii. p. 16.)

relation of magnetic disturbance by an aurora." An account of
these results was communicated by Henry to the Albany Institute,
January 26, 1832; and was also published in the Report of the
Regents of the New York University. A little more than a month
later (to wit on March 6, 1832,) he had been able to collate the
various published accounts of this aurora; and he learned "the fact
of a disturbance of terrestrial magnetism being observed by Mr.
Christie in England on the same evening, and at nearly the same
time the disturbance was witnessed in Albany, and that too in connection with the appearance of an aurora." This circumstance led
him to make a careful comparison of the notices of auroral displays
given in the meteorological reports in the Annals of Philosophy for
1830 and 1831, with those of the Reports of the New York
Regents for the same period. "By inspecting these two publications it was seen that from April, 1830, to April, 1831, inclusive,
the aurora was remarkably frequent and brilliant both in Europe
and in this country; and that most of the auroras described in the
Annals for this time, particularly the brilliant ones, were seen on
the same evening in England and in the State of New York."
From which he argues that " these simultaneous appearances of the
meteor in Europe and America would therefore seem to warrant the
conclusion that the aurora borealis cannot be classed among the
ordinary local meteorological phenomena, but that it must be referred
to some cause connected with the general physical principles of the
globe; and that the more energetic action of this cause (whatever
it may be) affects simultaneously a greater portion of the northern
hemisphere." †

In attempting to classify and digest the meteorological data
within his reach, Henry became strongly impressed with the
necessity of much more extensive, continuous, and systematic observations than any as yet undertaken: and he neglected no opportunities of directing influence upon the minds of our national

---

* Professor HANSTEEN has remarked that "A short time before the aurora
borealis appears, the intensity of the magnetism of the earth is apt in rise to an uncommon height; but so soon as the aurora borealis begins, in proportion as its force
increases, the intensity of the magnetism of the earth decreases, recovering its
former strength by degrees, often not till the end of twenty-four hours." (Edinburgh
Philosoph. Jour. Jan. 1825, vol. xii, p. 91.)

† Silliman's Am. Jour. Sci. April, 1832, vol. xxii. pp. 150-155.

legislators, to impress them with the great need — as well as the
practical policy of prosecuting the subject by governmental
resources. No one at that day seemed so fully awake both to the
importance and to the methods of prosecuting such inquiry: and
no one more effectually advanced both by direct and by indirect
exertions the wide-spread interest in this study, than he.

In 1839, while at Princeton, he in conjunction with his friend
Professor Bache, induced the American Philosophical Society
officially to memorialize the National Government to establish
stations for magnetic and meteorological observations: a movement
which was partly successful, though not to the extent desired.   On
the subject of international systems of observation and register, he
justly remarks at a later date: "In order that the science of
meteorology may be founded on reliable data, and attain that rank
which its importance demands, it is necessary that extended systems
of co-operation should be established.   In regard to climate, no
part of the world is isolated: that of the smallest island in the
Pacific, is governed by the general currents of the air and the
waters of the ocean.   To fully understand therefore the causes
which influence the climate of any one country, or any our place,
it will be necessary to study the conditions, as to heat, moisture, and
the movements of the air, of all others.   It is evident also that as
far as possible, one method should be adopted, and that instruments
affording the same indications under the same conditions should be
employed. - - - A general plan of this kind, for observing
the meteorological and magnetical changes, more extensively than
had ever before been projected, was digested by the British Association in 1838, in which the principal Governments of Europe
were induced to take an active part; and had that of the United
States, and those of South America, joined in the enterprise, a series
of watch-towers of nature would have been distributed over every
part of the earth. - - - Though the Government of the
United States took no part with the other nations of the earth, in
the great system before described, yet it has established and supported for a number of years a partial system of observation at the
different military posts of the army." *

---

* Agricultural Report of Commissioner of Patents, for 1855, pp. 357, 358.

A large collection of original notes of various meteorological observations,—on magnetic variations, on auroræ with attempts at ascertaining their extreme height, on violent whirlwinds, on hailstones, on thunder-storms, and the deportment of lightning-rods,— unfortunately never published nor transcribed, were lost (with much other precious scientific material) by fire in 1865. The phenomena of thunder-storms were always studied by Henry with great interest and attention. A very severe one which visited Princeton on the evening of July 14, 1841, was minutely described in a communication to the American Philosophical Society, November 5th, 1841. [*]

On November 3d, 1843, he made a communication to the Society "in regard to the application of Melloni's thermo-electric apparatus to meteorological purposes, and explained a modification of the parts connected with the pile, to which he had been led in the course of his researches. He had found the vapors near the horizon, powerful reflectors of heat; but in the case of a distant thunder-storm, he had found that the cloud was colder than the adjacent blue space." [†]

On June 20, 1845, he read a paper before the Society on "a simple method of protecting from lightning, buildings covered with metallic roofs;" urging the importance in such cases of having the vertical rain pipes always in good electrical connection with the earth, since "on the principle of electrical induction, houses thus covered are evidently more liable to be struck than those furnished either with shingle or tile. It is of course necessary to have the metallic roof in good metallic connection with the gutters and pipes; and the latter may conveniently have soldered to the lower end a ribbon of sheet copper two or three inches wide, continuing into the ground surrounded with charcoal and extending out from the house till it terminates in moist ground. [‡]

---

[*] *Proceed. Am. Phil. Soc. vol. ii. pp. 111-114.*

[†] *Proceed. Am. Phil. Soc. vol. iv. p. 22.*

[‡] *Proceed. Am. Phil. Soc. vol. iv. p. 171. Henry appears to have been much impressed with the conducting value of the tinned sheet-iron pipes commonly used as rain spouts, from observing that amid the strange vagaries of the circuitous path pursued by the lightning (in cases of houses struck by this destructive agent), the rain pipe was not unfrequently selected as part of the route;—marks of explosive violence being exhibited at its lower end, and sometimes at its top as well,—while the pipe itself was found to be uninjured.*

In this paper he incidentally meets the much debated question whether a lightning-rod is efficient as a conductor by its solidity, or by its surface only. While he had been able to magnetise small needles placed transversely to the *edges* of broad strips of copper, through which electrical discharges were passed, he could obtain no signs of magnetism in needles when placed transversely near the *sides* of such strips about mid-way from the edges. In like manner he failed to discover any action in a small magnetizing helix placed within a section of gas-pipe and connected with it at either end, when transmitting through the system an electrical spark; while he easily obtained magnetic effects with a galvanic current passed through the same arrangement.[*] From these and other experiments he was led to believe that mechanical electricity tends to pass mainly along the exterior surface of a conductor, and accordingly that Ohm's law of conduction is not applicable to lightning or mechanical electricity.[†]

Some popular uneasiness having been excited in 1846, in consequence of telegraph poles being occasionally struck by lightning, and of the supposed danger to travellers along highways likely to result therefrom, a communication on the subject addressed to Dr. Patterson, one of the Vice-Presidents of the American Philosophical Society, was read before the Society, and referred to Professor Henry for report. This was in the very infancy of the electro-magnetic telegraph; as it had not then been in existence more than a couple of years. Henry responded in a communication read June 19th, 1846, to the effect that while telegraph wires as long conductors were eminently liable to receive discharges of atmospheric electricity both from charged clouds and from the varying electrical condition of the air at distant points along the line (as for

---

[*] In passing a galvanic current through an iron tube, he obtained the evidence of an induction from both the inside and the outside of the tube, but in opposite directions.

[†] This very important question cannot be regarded as even yet decisively settled;—eminent authorities maintaining that electricity in flow—of whatever origin—obeys equally the ratio of proportionality to area of cross section in the conductor. Probably the law of conductivity varies with circumstances. BITTHIE remarks that "if a metallic rod be raised to a red heat, its power of conducting common electricity is increased, whilst its conducting power for voltaic electricity is considerably diminished." (*Journal of the Royal Institution of Great Britain*, Oct. 1830, vol. i. (n. s., p. 2).)

example even by a fog or precipitation of vapor at one station) as
also from induction at a distance, the danger to travellers along a
telegraph road would be very slight, unless a person should be
standing or passing quite close to a pole at the moment of its being
struck. He however recommended that for the protection of the
poles, they should be provided with conductors. "The efforts of
powerful discharges from the clouds may be prevented in a great
degree by erecting at intervals along the line and beside the supporting poles a metallic wire connected with the earth at the lower end,
and terminating above at the distance of about half an inch from the
wire of the telegraph. By this arrangement, the insulation of the
conductor will not be interfered with, while the greater portion of
the charge will be drawn off. I think this precaution of great
importance at places where the line crosses a river and is supported
on high poles. Also in the vicinity of the office of the telegraph,
where a discharge falling on the wire near the station might send a
current into the house of sufficient quantity to produce serious accidents."[a] This precaution has now been largely adopted, especially
on the telegraph lines of the central portion of the United States,
which are more liable to the efforts of lightning.[b]

Molecular Physics. — Among other inquiries many original examinations were made by Henry in the domain of molecular physics.
While Professor in the College of New Jersey in 1839, his attention
was attracted to a curious case of metallic capillarity. A small lead
tube about eight inches long happening to be left with a bent end
lying in a shallow dish of mercury, he noticed a few days afterward
that the mercury had disappeared from the dish, and was spread
on the shelf about the other end of the tube. On a careful examination of the tube by incision, it appeared that the mercury had not
passed along the open canal of the tube, but had percolated through
its solid substance. To test this, a solid rod of lead about one-
fourth of an inch thick and seven inches long was bent into a siphon
form, and the shorter end immersed in a small shallow vessel of
mercury; a similar empty vessel being placed under the longer end.

[a] Proceed. Am. Phil. Soc. vol. iv. p. 28.
[b] Prescott. Electricity and the Electric Telegraph. 8vo. N. York, 1877, chap. xliii. pp. 88 and 411.

In the course of 24 hours a globule of mercury was found at the lower end of the lead rod; and in five or six days it had all passed over excepting what appeared in the form of crystals of a lead amalgam in the upper vessel. [*] A long piece of thick lead wire was afterward suspended in a vertical position, with its lower end dipping into a cup of mercury. In the course of a few days, traces of the mercury were found in the rod at the height of three feet above the cup: thus showing that a metal impervious to water or oil (excepting under very great pressure) was easily penetrated to great distances by a liquid metal.

Some years later on a visit to Philadelphia he endeavored with the assistance of his friend Dr. Patterson (then Director of the United States Mint), by melting a small globule of gold on a plate of clean sheet-iron, to obtain its capillary absorption; but without effect; probably owing to the interposition of a thin film of oxide. Applying to another personal friend, Mr. Cornelius of Philadelphia, a very intelligent and ingenious manufacturer of bronzes, and plated ornaments for chandeliers, etc. to try whether a piece of silver-plated copper heated to the melting point of silver would show any absorption of that metal, he learned that it was a common experience under such circumstances to find the silver disappear; but that this had always been attributed to a volatilization of the silver, or in the workman's phrase,—to its being "burnt off." At Henry's request the experiment was tried: the heated end of a silver-plated piece of copper exhibited on cooling and cleaning, a copper surface; the other end remaining unchanged. Henry next had the copper surface slightly dissolved off by immersion for a few minutes in a solution of muriate of zinc, when as he had anticipated, the silver was again exposed, having penetrated to but a very short and tolerably uniform distance below the original surface. [†]

In 1844, he made some important observations on the cohesion of liquids. Notwithstanding that Dr. Young early in the century maintained that "the immediate cause of solidity as distinguished from liquidity is the *lateral adhesion* of the particles to each other," and had shown that "the resistance of ice to extension or com-

* *Proceed. Am. Phil. Soc.* vol. I. p. 62.
† *Proceed. Am. Phil. Soc.* June 20, 1845, vol. iv. p. 377.

pression is found by experiment to differ very little from that of water contained in a vessel,"* all the most popular text-books on physics continued to teach that the cohesion of the liquid state is intermediate between that of the solid and the gaseous states. † It seemed therefore desirable to test the question by some more direct means than the resistance of liquids contained in closed vessels; and for this purpose Henry employed the classical soap-bubble. "The effort of dissolving the soap in the water is not as might at first appear, to increase the molecular attraction, but to diminish the mobility of the molecules." In fact the actual *tenacity* of pure water is greater than that of soap-water.

The first set of experiments was directed to determine "the quantity of water which adhered to a bubble just before it burst." The second set of experiments was devised to measure the contractile force of a soap-bubble blown on the wider end of a U-shaped glass tube half filled with water, by the barometric column sustained in the narrower stem of the tube; the difference of level being carefully observed by means of a microscope. The thickness of the soap-bubble film at its top was estimated by the last of the Newton rings shown previous to bursting. The result arrived at from both sets of experiments was that water instead of having a cohesion of 53 grains to the square inch (as was very commonly stated), has a cohesive force of several hundred pounds to the inch; or that the inter-molecular cohesion of a liquid is fully equal to that of the substance in the solid state. ‡

* Young's Lectures on Nat. Philos. Lect. 16, vol. I. p. 627.

† "If we attempt to draw up from the surface of water a circular disk of metal may of an inch in diameter, we shall see that the water will adhere and be supported several times above the general surface. This experiment which is frequently given in elementary books as a measure of the feeble attraction of water for itself, is improperly interpreted. It merely indicates the force of attraction of a single film of atoms around the perpendicular surface, and not of the whole column elevated." (Agricultural Report for 1857. p. 67.— Henry's paper on Meteorology.)

‡ Proceed. Am. Phil. Soc. April 5 and May 17, 1844, vol. iv. pp. 56, 57, and 81, 85. The original notes of these interesting experiments containing the numerical results obtained under a great variety of conditions, laid aside for further reductions and comparisons, were destroyed by fire in 1865. Since the density of most solid substances differs very slightly from that of their liquid state, being indeed less in many,—unless at considerably lower temperatures, (as in the case of ice, and most of the metals,) it appears quite improbable that the difference between solidity and liquidity could depend in any case on the degree of cohesion. On the contrary, the cohesion of water should be sensibly greater than that of ice, since its constituent

In 1846, he presented to the Philosophical Society an epitome of his views on the molecular constitution of matter; giving the reasons for accepting the atomic hypothesis of Newton. He pointed out that the discovery and establishment of a general scientific principle "is in almost all cases the result of deductions from a rational antecedent hypothesis, the product of the imagination; founded it is true on a clear analogy with modes of physical action, the truth of which has been established by previous investigation:" and he urged that the hope of further advancement lies in the assumption "that the same laws of force and motion which govern the phenomena of the action of matter in masses, pertains to the minutest atoms of these masses." He therefore felt "obliged to assume the existence of an ætherial medium formed of atoms which are endowed with precisely the same properties as those we have assigned to common matter."

"According to the foregoing rules we may assume with Newton, the existence of *one kind of matter* diffused throughout all space, and existing in four states, namely the ætherial, the aeriform, the liquid, and the solid." [*] [In referring to this postulated *fourfold state of matter,* Henry was accustomed to point out the remarkable analogy between this conception, and that of the four elements of the ancients, — fire, air, water, and earth.]

" In conclusion, it should be remembered that the legitimate use of speculations of this kind, is not to furnish plausible explanations of known phenomena, or to present old knowledge in a new and more imposing dress, but to serve the higher purpose of suggesting new experiments and new phenomena, and thus to assist in enlarging the bounds of science, and extending the power of mind over matter; and unless the hypothesis can be employed in this way, however much ingenuity may have been expended in its construction, it can only be considered as a scientific romance worse than

---

molecules are closer together. Of the nature of that "lateral adhesion" which resists the flow of solids (excepting under the conditions of great strain — long continued), and whose absence is marked in liquids by their almost perfect and frictionless mobility, our present science affords us no intimation.

[*] Two hundred years ago, NEWTON speculating on the unity of matter, ventured the suggestion, "Thus perhaps may all things be originated from æther."—Letter to the Secretary of the Royal Society — Henry Oldenburg, January, 1676. (*History of the Royal Society;* by Thomas Birch, vol. III. p. 250.)

useless, since it tends to satisfy the mind with the semblance of truth, and thus to render truth itself less an object of desire." *

Light and Heat. — Henry also made important investigations on some peculiar phenomena connected with light and heat. For the purpose of experimenting on sun-light he devised in 1840, a very simple form of heliostat, based on the suggestion of Dr. Young, whereby the solar ray was received into an upper room in a direction parallel to the earth's axis, by means of a simple equatorial movement of the reflector ;[†] which was effected by the aid of a common cheap pocket watch placed on a small hinged board set by a screw to the angle of latitude. The mirror mounted on a swivel and properly balanced, presented no sensible resistance to the running of the watch, which was arranged for the 24-hour rotation by a watchmaker of Princeton. The whole cost of the completed instrument (including the time-movement) was but sixteen dollars. If any particular direction of the ray was required, it was only necessary to place a stationary mirror in the fixed path of the ray, adjusted to the desired angle. [‡]

In 1841, on repeating experiments of Becquerel and Biot on "Phosphorescence," he discovered some new characteristics in the emanation (particularly when excited by electrical light) which had not before been observed.[§] These were more fully detailed in a communication made to the American Philosophical Society, in 1843, "On Phosphorogenic Emanation." This phenomenon had been first observed in the diamond, when taken into a dark room immediately after exposure to direct sunlight, or to a vivid electric spark; and was afterward observed in several other substances,— notably in the chloride of calcium — "Homberg's phosphorus."[‖] It had also been shown by Becquerel that while this phosphores-

* Proceed. Am. Phil. Soc. Nov. 6, 1846, vol. iv. pp. 287-290.

† Dr. Young's Lectures on Nat. Phil. lect. xxxvi, vol. i, p. 438. The equatorial heliostat appears to have been first suggested by FAHRENHEIT.

‡ Proceed. Am. Phil. Soc. Sept. 27, 1841, vol. ii, p. 97.

§ Proceed. Am. Phil. Soc. April 16, 1841, vol. ii, p. 46.

‖ Homberg's phosphorus is a calcium chloride prepared by melting one part of sal ammoniac (ammonic chloride) with two parts of slaked lime. Canton's phosphorus is a calcium sulphide formed by a mixture of three parts of sifted and calcined oyster shells, and one part of flowers of sulphur, exposed for an hour to a strong heat.

cence may be fully excited in the sensitive body by rays which
have passed through transparent sulphate of lime, or through
quartz, the effect is entirely arrested by a plate of transparent mica,
or glass.* Henry by a long series of experiments greatly extended these lists, including in them a large number of liquids.
He also subjected both the exciting rays (especially that of the electric spark), and the luminous emanation, to various treatment, by
reflection, refraction, polarization, etc. The Nicol prism was found
to obstruct this peculiar exciting ray so much as to permit scarcely
any impression; but what was remarkable and unexpected, a pile
of thin mica plates which seemed to cut off entirely the phosphorogenic impression, was found when placed obliquely at the best
polarizing angle, to distinctly excite a surviving luminous spot.
On examination of the phosphorescence excited by polarised light,
no effect was perceived by a rotation of the analyzer: "when the
beam was transmitted through crystals in different directions with
reference to their optical axis, no difference could be observed."
The phosphorescence was completely depolarized, as if taking an
entirely new origin in the sensitive substance: a fact re-discovered
by Professor George G. Stokes some ten years later, with regard to
fluorescent emanations.

That the phosphorogenic effect does not depend on a heating of
the substance, appeared to be shown by the fact that "the lime
becomes as luminous under a plate of alum as under a plate of
rock-salt." The emanation was examined by a prism of rock-
crystal, and by one of rock-salt:—science had not then the spectro-
scope. While the impression could be readily made by a reflected
beam from a metallic mirror, it failed entirely when directed from
a looking-glass. The luminous effect on the phosphorescent substance was found to be defined in location by the form of the opening made in sheet-metal screens. Different portions of the electric
spark being tested by means of a narrow slit in the screen, the
two terminals of the spark were found to be much more active (as
measured by the subsequent duration of the phosphorescence) than
the middle portion. By a suitable arrangement of double screens

_____

* That there should be such a difference between quartz and glass or mica, is certainly a remarkable circumstance.

with three slits each, he was able to make simultaneous star-like "photographs" on the substance, of the two extreme portions of the spark and of a middle point: and while the latter point "exhibited a feeble, phosphorescence for two or three seconds" only, the two former "continued to glow for more than a minute:" and yet the middle of the spark appeared to the eye quite as vivid as its extremities. It was also observed that while a sensitive daguerreotype plate received no impression from the electric spark, inversely another similar plate exposed for several minutes to the direct light of the full moon received a photographic impression, while the lime similarly exposed, exhibited no phosphorescence.*

As a striking illustration of the closely allied phenomenon of fluorescence, Henry was afterward accustomed on the occurrence of a bright aurora, to expose a sheet of paper written or figured with a solution of bisulphate of quinia to the auroral light, when the characters (quite invisible by lamp-light or even by day-light) would distinctly glow with a pale blue light; — indicating the electrical nature of the meteor.

In January, 1845, in conjunction with Professor Stephen Alexander, he instituted a series of experimental observations on the relative heat-radiating power of the solar spots. On the 4th of January a large spot through which our terrestrial globe could have been freely dropped, (having been estimated at more than 10,000 miles in diameter,) favorably situated near the middle of the disk, was examined with a telescope of four inches aperture. A screen having been arranged in a dark room, with a thermo-electric apparatus behind it and having its terminal or pile just projecting through a hole in the screen, the image of the spot was received upon it, giving a clearly defined outline about two inches long and one inch and a half wide. By a slight motion of the telescope the spot could readily be thrown on or off the end of the pile as desired. A considerable number of observations indicated very clearly by the

* Proceed. Am. Phil. Soc. May 28, 1845, vol. III. pp. 86-91. This interesting but obscure subject, although apparently connected with the phenomenon of "fluorescence" has yet an entirely distinct phase in its abnormal continuance of luminosity;—similar to the familiar effect of a thermal impression. It is possible however that the conversion of wave-periodicity (wave-length), shown by Stokes to be the characteristic of fluorescence, may require time for its full development.

differing deflections of the galvanometer needle "that the spot emitted less heat than the surrounding parts of the luminous disk."[*] A brief account of the results obtained by these researches given in a letter to his friend Sir David Brewster, was read by the latter at the Cambridge Meeting of the British Association in June, 1845.[†] The determinations arrived at have been fully confirmed by the later observations of Secchi and others.[‡]

In 1845, he contributed a paper to the Princeton Review, on "Color Blindness;" which although in the modest form of a literary review of two Memoirs then recently published, (that of Sir David Brewster in the Philosophical Magazine; and that of Professor Elie Wartman, of Lausanne, in the Scientific Memoirs,) supplied original observations on this interesting department of the physiology of vision.

Miscellaneous Contributions.—Henry's miscellaneous contributions to physical science are so numerous and varied, that only a brief allusion to some of them can be afforded. In 1829, he published quite an elaborate "Topographical sketch of the State of New York, designed chiefly to show the general elevations and depressions of its surface."[§] And in later years he devoted much attention to physical geography. He also made some geological explorations and observations in the State of New York. He performed at various times a good deal of chemical work (chiefly of an analytical character),—first as Dr. T. Romeyn Beck's assistant,[‖]

* *Proceed. Am. Phil. Soc., June 20, 1845, vol. IV, pp. 173-174.*

† *Report Brit. Assoc. 1845, part II, p. 8.*

‡ P. Angelo Secchi—during the years 1848 and 1849, (then a young man of thirty,) was Professor of Mathematics at the College of Georgetown, D. C. and in the preparation of his "Researches on Electrical Rheometry," published in the third volume of the Smithsonian Contributions, (art. II, 58 pp.) he received from Henry the friendly assistance of apparatus and suggestions. It is interesting to note to Henry's introduction of Professor Secchi's first researches to the attention of the Regents of the Smithsonian Institution, when the name was as yet wholly unknown in the scientific world. "Annexed article is by Professor Secchi, a young Italian of much ingenuity and learning, a member of Georgetown College. It consists of a new mathematical investigation of the reciprocal action of two galvanic currents on each other, and of the action of a current on the pole of a magnet." (Smithsonian Report for 1849, p. 172, 8. ed. and p. 184, H. R. ed.) Professor Secchi was appointed Director of the Observatory at Rome, in 1850.

§ *Trans. Albany Institute, vol. I, pp. 87-112.*

‖ "Henry was then Dr. Beck's chemical assistant, and already an admirable experimentalist." Address before the Albany Institute, by Dr. O. Meads, May 26, 1879. (Trans. Albany Institute, vol. VII, p. 26.)

and afterward independently, as well as mediately in directing his own pupils and assistants. In 1833, he devised an improvement on Wollaston's mechanical scale of the chemical equivalents, for the benefit of his pupils in chemistry:—a contrivance which was much used and highly appreciated at the time.

The suggestion had been thrown out by more than one astronomer, that carefully timed observations on characteristic meteors or "shooting-stars" might be made available for determining differences of longitude between the stations of observation. * For many years however the proposition had been generally regarded as offering rather a speculative than a practical method of solving a problem of so great nicety. Henry in concert with his brother-in-law, Professor Alexander, and with his friend Professor Bache, determined to ascertain by actual trial the availability and value of the system. On the 25th of November, 1835, Professor Bache observing at his residence in Philadelphia (assisted by Professor J. P. Espy,)—simultaneously with Professor Henry and Professor Alexander, at the Philosophical Hall at Princeton, they obtained seven co-incidences:—the instant of disappearance of the meteor being in each case selected as the most accurately attainable epoch. These seven observations (whose greatest discrepancies amounted to but a trifle over 3 seconds) gave a mean result of 2 minutes 0.61 second (time longitude), differing only one second and two-tenths from the mean estimate of relative longitude arrived at by other methods. †

In 1840, Henry gave an account of "electricity obtained from a small ball partly filled with water, and heated by a lamp." ‡

---

* "The merit of first suggesting the use of shooting-stars and fire-balls as signals for the determination of longitudes is claimed by Dr. Olbers and the German astronomers for Brandenberg, who published a work on the subject in 1821. Mr. Baily however has pointed out a paper published by Dr. Maskelyne twenty years previously, in which that illustrious astronomer calls attention to the subject, and distinctly points out this application of the phenomenon." This was dated Greenwich, November 8th, 1783. (*L. E. D. Phil. Mag.* 1841, vol. xix p. 651.)

† *Proceed. Am. Phil. Soc.* Dec. 20, 1835, vol. i. pp. 162, 163. "This appears to have been the first actual determination of a difference of longitude by meteoric observations." (*L. E. D. Phil. Mag.* 1841, vol. xix. p. 553.) Several years later (in 1848) similar meteoric observations were made between Altona and Bremen; and also between Rome and Naples.

‡ *Proceed. Am. Phil. Soc.* Dec. 18, 1840, vol. i. p. 322.

In 1843, he read a communication to the Society, "On a new method of determining the velocity of Projectiles;" for this purpose employing two screens of fine insulated wire each in circuit with a galvanometer, and at determined near distances in the path of the projectile;—whereby the galvanic currents would be successively interrupted at the instants of penetration. To record the interval, each galvanometer needle is provided at one end with a marking pen touching a horizontally revolving cylinder, which is divided by longitudinal lines into 100 equal parts, and is driven by clock-work at the rate of ten revolutions per second, giving therefore to the interval of passage between two consecutive lines, the thousandth part of a second.[*]   Another still more ingenious method is suggested, whereby the galvanometer may be dispensed with: each circuit including an induction coil, one end of whose secondary circuit is connected with the axis, and the other end placed very nearly in contact with the surface of the graduated paper on the revolving cylinder, so as to give the induction spark through the paper at the instant of the interruption of the primary circuits by the projectile passing through the wire screens. This is really a much neater and more direct application of the electric interruption than the employment of a galvanometer needle for making the record, as it involves no material inertia. If desirable, the cylinder may be made to have a very slow longitudinal movement by a screw, so as to give a helical direction to the tracings; and different pairs of screens similarly arranged at distant points in the path of the projectile may be employed to determine the variations of velocity in its flight.[†]

Henry was always a watchful student of psychological and subjective phenomena. Witnessing on one occasion the performance of an athlete before a large assembly, he noticed with a curious interest the "inductive" sympathy manifested by nearly every spectator (himself included) in being swayed by a movement as of

[*] It appears that WHEATSTONE devised his ingenious electro-magnetic "chronoscope" in 1840; though he unfortunately published no account of it till 1845; or two years after the publication by HENRY. And this was called out as a reclamation, on the publication of a similar invention by L. BREGUET, of Paris, in January of the same year. See "Supplement," NOTE G.

[†] Proceed. Am. Phil. Soc. May 20, 1843, vol. III. pp. 145-147.

assistance to the performer. In remarking the impression of being moved, while steadily watching a series of passing canal boats, he referred the impression (amounting almost to a sensation of movement on each boat reaching a certain point,) to the relative angle of vision formed by the moving body.

He made a number of experiments on the flow of water jets under varying conditions: also observations on sonorous flames when passing into a stove-pipe of eight inches diameter and about ten feet in length: on the comparative rates of evaporation from fresh and from salt water: on the slow evaporation of water from the open end of a U-shaped tube, and the much greater rapidity of evaporation when the tube is open at both ends: extended notes of which, with a great number of other researches, perished in the flames.

In 1844, he published a Syllabus of his Lectures at Princeton. In December of that year he presented to the Philosophical Society a communication of a somewhat more theoretical character than usual,—on the derivation and classification of mechanical motors. He refers these to two classes;—the first, those derived from celestial disturbance (as water, tide, and wind powers),—and the second, those derived from organic bodies or forces (as steam and other heat powers, and animal powers). The forces of gravity, cohesion, and chemical affinity are not included, since these tend speedily to stable equilibrium; and they become sources of mechanical power only as they are disturbed by some of those before mentioned. It is not the running down of the water-fall, or the clock-weight, which is the true origin of their useful work, but the lifting of them up. The same is true of the power derived from combustion. He then adds that his second class (the forces derived from the organic world) might perhaps by a similar process of reasoning be derived from the first class; (that of celestial disturbance;)—regarding "animal power as referable to the same sources as that from the combustion of fuel," and the action of the vegetative power as "a force derived from the divellent power of the sunbeam," being simply a case of solar de-oxidation. Organism—vegetable and animal, he considers as built up under the direction of a vital principle, which is not itself a mechanical force. Volcanic power is neglected as compara-

18

lively feeble and limited, and not practically utilized.* This interesting digest presents one of the earliest and clearest theoretical
statements we have, of the correlation and transformation of the
physical forces; including with these the so-called organic forces.

ADMINISTRATION OF THE SMITHSONIAN INSTITUTION.

By an Act of Congress approved August 10, 1846, the liberal
bequest to the United States, for the promotion of Science, by James
Smithson of London, England, was appropriated to the foundation
of the Institution bearing his name; the establishment being made
to comprise the chief dignitaries of the Government as the super-
vising body, and a Board of Regents being created for conducting
the business of the Institution after completing its organization.
As the testator had bequeathed his fortune,† in simple terms "for
the increase and diffusion of knowledge among men," there arose
not unnaturally a great diversity of opinion both among Congress-
men, and among the Regents, as to the most desirable method of
executing the purpose of the Will: and the organizing Act was
itself a sort of compromise, after many years of discussion and
disagreement in both branches of Congress. To literary men, no
instrument of knowledge could be so important as an extensive
Library: — to the professional, a seat of education or public instruction — general or special — supplemented by elaborate courses of
public lectures, appeared the obvious and necessary means of diffusing useful learning, — to the "practical," a large agricultural
and polytechnic institute — supplemented perhaps by a museum,
was the only fitting plan of developing the resources of our country; — to the artistic, extensive galleries of art were the most worthy
and instructive objects of patronage. The Regents sought counsel
from the distinguished and the learned: and several of them applied
to Professor Henry for his opinion. He gave the subject a careful

---

* *Proceed. Am. Phil. Soc. Dec. 21, 1841, vol. IV. pp. 127 139. This appears to be the
first — as it is probably the best — analysis of physical energy, which has been
proposed. Twenty years later, a similar analysis (with certainly no improvement
in the classification) was adopted by Professor Tait, in an essay on "Energy;"
(North British Review, 1864, vol. XL. art. III. p. 191, of Am. edition;) and by Dr. Balfour
Stewart, in his Elementary Treatise on Heat, Oxford, 1866: [book III. chap. v. art. 30,
p. 251.]

† The whole amount of the bequest was a trifle over 100,000 pounds, or about
500,000 dollars.

consideration; and announced very decided views. As Smithson was a man of scientific culture, a Fellow of the Royal Society, an expert analytical chemist, and devoted to original research, Henry held that the language of his Will must receive its most accurate and scientific and at the same time most comprehensive interpretation; that the words "increase and diffusion of knowledge among men" were deliberately and intelligently employed; and that no local or even national interests were as broad as its terms,—that no merely educational projects of whatever character, no schemes of material and practical advancement however useful, could justly be regarded as fulfilling the obvious intent—expressed by a scientific thinker and writer—first of all the increase of knowledge by the promotion of original research,—the addition of new truths to the existing stock of knowledge, and secondly—its widest possible diffusion among mankind.*

These wise and far-reaching views exerted a marked influence; and though hardly then in accord with the opinion of the majority, yet led to his election December 3d, 1846, as the "Secretary" and actual Director of the infant institution.† A second time was Henry called upon to sever dearly prized associations,—the prosperous and congenial pursuits of fourteen years within the classic halls of Princeton. One motive turned the wavering scale. Here was a rare occasion offered by the enlightened provision of James Smithson, to secure for abstract science and unpromising original research, a much needed encouragement and support; and an obligation imposed upon the scientific few to resist and if possible prevent the perversion of the trust to the merely popular uses of the short-sighted many. That years would be required for shaping the character and conduct of the institution as he desired, was certain;—that this could not be effected without much opposition and various obstacle, he very clearly foresaw. That during these years of active supervision and direction, he must abandon all hope of personal opportunity for original research, he as freely accepted in the expressive remark made to a trusted friend in consultation on

* "Programme of Organization," Smithsonian Report for 1847. See "Supplement," NOTE II.
† See "Supplement," NOTE J.

the occasion: "If I go, I shall probably exchange permanent fame for transient reputation."

With the assurance of the Trustees of the College of New Jersey, that should he fail to realize his programme, or should he satisfactorily accomplish his apostolic purpose, his chair should always be at his command, with a hearty welcome back, Henry, neither spurred by over-confidence, nor depressed with undue timidity, though filled with anxious solicitude for the future, accepted the appointment tendered to him. He removed with his family to Washington, December 14, 1846, and at once commenced his administration of the duties assigned to him by the Regents of the Institution.

Summoned thus to the occupancy of a new and untried field, and to the discharge of essentially executive functions, he from the first displayed a clearness and promptness of judgment, a singleness and steadiness of aim, a firmness and consistency of decision, combined with a practical sagacity and moderation in adapting his course to the exigencies of adverse conditions, which stamped him as a most able and successful administrator. Without concealment and without diplomacy, his distinctly avowed principle of action was steadily and patiently pursued. * With honest submission to the controlling Act of Congress, he made an honest avowal of his desire and of his endeavor to have that legislation modified. Hampered by provisions he deemed unwise and injurious, he yet skillfully managed to reconcile contestant interests, and to secure the entire confidence and concurrence of the Regents. Henceforth his purpose and his effort were to be directed to the unique object of encouraging and fostering the development of what has so flippantly been designated "useless knowledge;" and merging self in the community of physical inquirers and collaborators, to become the high-priest of abstract investigation; — prepared to lend all practicable assistance to that small but earnest band of nature-students, who inspired by no aims of material utility, seek from their mistress as the only reward of their devotion, a closer intimacy, a higher knowledge of truth.†

---

* See "Supplement," Note J.

† Henry has finely said: "Let censure or ridicule fall elsewhere,— on those whose lives are passed without labor and without object: but let praise and honor be bestowed on him who seeks with unwearied patience to develop the order, harmony, and beauty of even the smallest part of God's creation. A life devoted

Of the two distinct objects of endowment specified by Smithson's Will, — "the *increase* — and the *diffusion* — of knowledge," Henry forcibly remarked: "These though frequently confounded, are very different processes, and each may exist independent of the other. While we rejoice that in our country above all others, so much attention is paid to the *diffusion* of knowledge, truth compels us to say that comparatively little encouragement is given to its *increase*." There is another division with regard to knowledge which Smithson does not embrace in his design; viz. the application of knowledge to useful purposes in the arts. And it was not necessary he should found an institution for this purpose. There are already in every civilized country, establishments and patent laws for the encouragement of this department of mental industry. As soon as any branch of science can be brought to bear on the necessities, conveniences, or luxuries of life, it meets with encouragement and reward. Not so with the discovery of the incipient principles of science. The investigations which lead to these, receive no fostering care from Government, and are considered by the superficial observer as trifles unworthy the attention of those who place the supreme good in that which immediately administers to the physical needs or luxuries of life. If physical well-being were alone the object of existence, every avenue of enjoyment should be explored to its utmost extent. But he who loves truth for its own sake, feels that its highest claims are lowered and its moral influence marred by being continually summoned to the bar of immediate and palpable utility. Smithson himself had no such narrow views.† The promi-

---

exclusively to the study of a single insect, is not spent in vain. No animal however insignificant is isolated; it forms a part of the great system of nature, and is governed by the same general laws which control the most prominent beings of the organic world." (*Smithsonian Report for* 1855, p. 20.)

*[SWAINSON the Naturalist, the countryman and friend of Smithson, has very pointedly marked this recognized distinction. "The constitution of the Zoological Society is of a very inferior nature, admirably adapted indeed to the reigning taste. It is more calculated however to diffuse than to borrow the actual stock of scientific knowledge." (*Discourse on the Study of Natural History*, Cabinet Cyclopædia, 12mo. London, 1834, part iv. chap. i. sec. 23, p. 331.) And again: "It is very essential when we speak of the diffusion or extension of science, that we do not confound these stages of development with discovery or advancement; since the latter may be as different from the former as depth is from shallowness." (Same work, part iv. chap. ii. sec. 28, p. 345.)]

†[In regard to the value of scientific truth, Smithson in a communication dated June 10th, 1824, has forcibly expressed his strong "conviction that it is in his

nent design of his bequest is the promotion of abstract science. In this respect the Institution holds an otherwise unoccupied place in this country; and it adopts two fundamental maxims in its policy; — first to do nothing with its funds which can be equally well done by other means; and second to produce results which as far as possible will benefit mankind in general." [*]

Congress — naturally with a prevailing tendency to the literary, the showy, and the popular, had (after eight years of dilatory controversy) directed in its organizing Act (sec. 5,) the erection of a building "of sufficient size, and with suitable rooms or halls for the reception and arrangement upon a liberal scale, of objects of natural history, including a geological and mineralogical cabinet, also a chemical laboratory, a library, a gallery of art, and the necessary lecture-rooms." By the 9th section of the Act, the Board of Regents were authorized to expend the remaining income of the endowment "as they shall deem best suited for the promotion of the purpose of the testator." Out of an annual income of some 40,000 dollars, the Regents in full accord with their Secretary (whose carefully elaborated programme they officially adopted December 13, 1847,) succeeded in creditably inaugurating all the objects specified in the charter; and at the same time in establishing the system of publication of original Memoirs, to which Henry justly attached the first importance.

An incident in itself too slight to produce a visible ripple on the current of Henry's life, is yet too characteristic to be here omitted. Dr. Robert Hare having in 1847 decided upon resigning his Professorship of Chemistry in the Medical Department of the University of Pennsylvania, (the largest and best patronized in the country,) the vacant chair was tendered by the Board of Trustees to Professor Henry. His friend Dr. Hare himself used his influence to induce Henry to become his successor; particularly dwelling on the large amount of leisure afforded for independent investigations.

knowledge that man has found his greatness and his happiness, the high superiority which he holds over the other animals who inhabit the earth with him; and consequently that no ignorance is probably without loss to him, no error without evil." (Thomson's *Annals of Philosophy*, 1831, vol. xxiv. or new series, vol. viii. p. 55.)]

[*] *Smithsonian Report for 1853, p. 3.

The income of this professorship was more than double the salary of the Smithsonian Secretaryship. The position, tempting as it might have been under different circumstances, was however declined. Henry felt that to leave his present post before his cherished policy was fairly settled and established, would be most probably to abandon nearly all the results of the experiment; and having set before himself the one great object of directing the resources of the Smithsonian Institution as far as possible to the advancement of science, in conformity with the undoubted intention of its founder, (and as the execution therefore of a sacred trust,) he resolutely put aside every inducement that might divert him from the fulfillment of his task. *

Of the half a dozen objects of attention specified in the 5th section of the organizing Act, (the various inspiration of different partisans,) not one directly tended to further the primary requirements of the Will; — even the Laboratory being avowedly introduced simply as a utilitarian workshop for mining and agricultural analyses. Regarded as methods of *diffusing* existing knowledge they were obviously local and limited in their range; and as compared with the instrumentality of the Press, were certainly very inefficient for spreading the benefits of the endowment among men. †

Henry with a rare courage dared maintain against most powerful influence, that the interests specifically designated must all be subordinated to the fundamental requirement, the promotion of

* Some six years later, a somewhat similar temptation was presented. In 1853, on the resignation of President Carnahan of the College of New Jersey at Princeton, an effort was made to induce the return of Professor Henry to his academic seat, by a movement to obtain for him the Presidency of the College. Such a token of affectionate remembrance could not but be grateful and touching to his feelings; but a sense of obligation was upon him, not to be laid aside. He had undertaken a work and a responsibility which must not be left to the hazard of failure. He declined the proffered honor — with thanks; and warmly recommended Dr. Maclean to the vacant position; who thereupon was duly elected. (Maclean's *Hist. of College of New Jersey*, vol. II. p. 356.)

† "The objects specified in the Act of Congress evidently do not come up to the idea of the testator as deduced from a critical examination of his will. A library, a museum, a gallery of arts, though important in themselves, are local in their influence. I have from the beginning advocated this opinion on all occasions, and shall continue to advocate it whenever a suitable opportunity occurs." (Smithsonian Report for 1853, p. 122 (of Senate edit.)—p. 117 (of H. Rep. edit.) The superficial critics was not wanting on the part of some, that the words "increase and diffusion" were not to be taken too literally, but to be considered as the tautology of legal equivalents, applicable to the development of the individual mind; since school-boys (if not the pundits) were evidently capable of no "increase" of knowledge.

original research for increasing knowledge; and that this was
amply sustained by the residuary grant of authority to the Regents
(under the 9th section of the Act) "to make such disposal as they
shall deem best suited *for the promotion of the purposes of the testator,*
anything herein contained to the contrary notwithstanding," of any
income of the Smithsonian fund "not herein appropriated, or not
required for the purposes herein provided." Henry's carefully
studied programme comprised two sections: the first, embracing
the details of the plan for carrying out the explicit purpose of
Smithson; the second, indicating the proper steps for carrying out
the provisions of the Act of Congress. The first and principal
section proposed as methods of promoting research, — the stimula-
tion of particular investigations by special premiums, — the publication of such original memoirs furnishing positive additions to
knowledge by experiment and observation as should be approved
by a commission of experts in each case, — the active direction of
certain investigations by the provision of instruments as well as of
the necessary means, the appropriations being judiciously varied in
distribution from year to year, — the prosecution of experimental
determinations and the solution of physical problems, — the extension of ethnology (especially American), and in general the conduct
of such varied explorations as should ultimately result in a complete
physical atlas of the United States. As methods of promoting the
diffusion of knowledge, it was proposed to give a wide circulation
to the published original memoirs or Smithsonian "Contributions
to Knowledge" among domestic and foreign libraries, institutions,
and scientific correspondents, to have prepared by qualified collaborators, series of careful reports on the latest progress of science in
different departments, and to provide facilities for the distribution
and exchange of scientific memoirs generally.

It is unnecessary here to follow closely the slow steps by which —
through all the obstructions of narrow prejudice and ignorant misconstruction, of selfish interest and pretended philanthropy, of
friendly remonstrance and hostile denunciation, — the policy originally marked out by the Secretary was with unwavering resolution
and imperturbable equanimity steadily pursued, until it gained its

assured success; the vindication and the unpretentious triumph of "the just man tenacious of purpose."

The most formidable of the specialist schemes both in Congress and elsewhere, was that of the Library faction, which prosecuted with remarkable zeal and energy, threatened by the acknowledged ability of its leading advocates to control the action of the Regents, even to the neglect and abandonment of all the other interests indicated by the statute. * In Henry's judgment the Institution should possess simply a working library, an auxiliary for those engaged in scientific research, a repertory well supplied with the published Proceedings and Transactions of learned Societies, but which so far from aiming at an encyclopædic or a literary character, should be mainly supplementary to the large National Library already established at the Capital. † "The idea ought never to be entertained that the portion of the limited income of the Smithsonian fund which can be devoted to the purchase of books will ever be sufficient to meet the wants of the American scholar. On the contrary it is the duty of this Institution to increase those wants by pointing out new fields for exploration, and by stimulating other researches than those which are now cultivated. It is a part of that duty to make the value of libraries more generally known, and their want in this country more generally felt." ‡

Progress of Divestment.—Henry's declaration that the moderate means at command were insufficient to support worthily either a Library, or a Museum, alone, was early justified. The Library though slowly formed of only really valuable scientific works, and this largely by exchanges with the Smithsonian publications, § in

---

* See "Supplement," Note K.

† "To carry on the operations of the first section a working library will be required, consisting of the past volumes of the transactions and proceedings of all the learned societies in every language. These are the original sources from which the most important principles of the positive knowledge of our day have been drawn." (Smithsonian Report for 1847, p. 19 of Sen. ed.—p. 13 of H. Rep. ed.)

‡ Smithsonian Report for 1851, p. 24 (of Sen. ed.)—p. 24 (of H. Rep. ed.)

§ "It is the intention of the Regents to render the Smithsonian library the most extensive and perfect collection of Transactions and scientific works in this country, and this it will be enabled to accomplish by means of its exchanges, which will furnish it with all the current journals and publications of societies, while the separate series may be completed in due time as opportunity and means may offer. The Institution has already more complete sets of Transactions of learned societies than are to be found in the oldest libraries in the United States." (Smithsonian Report for 1855, p. 29.)

the course of a dozen years amounted to about 40,000 volumes: and the annual cost of binding, superintendence, and the constant enlargement of room and of cases, was becoming a serious tax upon the resources of the Institution. The propriety of transferring the custody of this valuable and rapidly increasing collection to the National Library established by Congress, was repeatedly urged upon the attention of that body; and by an Act approved April 5th, 1866, such transfer was at last effected.

"Congress had presented to the Institution a portion of the public reservation on which the building is situated. In the planting of this with trees, nearly 10,000 dollars of the Smithson income were expended." Ultimately however opportunity was taken to have the Smithsonian park included in the general appropriation by the Government for improving the public grounds.

The courses of Lectures which were continued from their establishment in 1849, to 1863, were then abandoned. In conformity with the judicious policy entertained from the beginning not to consume unprofitably the limited means of the Institution by attempting to do what could be as well or better accomplished by other organizations, its herbarium comprising 30,000 botanical specimens and other allied objects, was transferred to the custody of the Agricultural Department. Its collection of anatomical and osteological specimens was transferred to the Army Medical Museum. And its Fine-Art collections were transferred to the custody of the "Art-Gallery" established at Washington (with a larger endowment than the whole Smithsonian fund) by the enlightened liberality of Mr. W. W. Corcoran.

Such were the successive processes by which much of the early and injudicious legislative work of organization, intended for popularizing the activities of the Institution, was gradually undone; greatly to the dissatisfaction and foreboding of many of its well-meaning friends. "It should be recollected" said Henry, "that the Institution is not a popular establishment."[*]

---

[*] Smithsonian Report for 1870, p. 12. A distinguished politician, now many years deceased, (an influential Member of Congress—and possible statesman,) in the confidence of friendship pointed out with emphasis, how by a few judicious expedients—involving only a moderate reduction of the income of the Institution, golden opinions might be won from the press, and the Smithsonian really be made quite

The National Museum.—The last heritage of misdirected legislation—the National Museum, still remains in nominal connection with the Institution; although Congress has recognized the justice of making special provision for its custody by an annual appropriation ever since its establishment in 1842,—four years before the organization of the Smithsonian Institution. The Government collection of curiosities had accumulated from the contributions of the various exploring expeditions; and Henry from the first, had objected to receiving it as a donation, foreseeing that it would prove more than "the gift of an elephant."[a] In his *first Report*, he ventured to say: "It is hoped that in due time other means may be found of establishing and supporting a general collection of objects of nature and art at the seat of the general Government, with funds not derived from the Smithsonian bequest."[b] In his third annual Report he remarked: "The formation of a Museum of objects of nature and of art requires much caution. With a given income to be appropriated to the purpose, a time must come when the cost of keeping the objects will just equal the amount of the appropriation: after this no further increase can take place. Also, the tendency of an institution of this kind unless guarded against, will be to expend its funds on a heterogeneous collection of objects of mere curiosity." Justly jealous of any dependence of the Institution, designed as a monument to its founder, upon the varying favors or caprices of a political government, or of any confusion between the National Museum, and its own special collections for scientific study rather than for popular display, he added: "If the Regents accept this Museum, it must be merged in the Smithsonian collections. It could not be the intention of Congress

---

[a] "popular" establishment. Unswerved by three friendly suggestions of worldly wisdom, Henry astonished his adviser by the smiling assurance that his self-imposed mission and deliberate purpose was to prevent, as far as in him lay, precisely that consummation. Had the philosopher repudiated the "breath of his nostrils" he could not have been looked upon by the politician, as more hopelessly demented.

[b] His friend Professor Silliman in a letter dated December 4th 1847, wrote: "If it is within the views of the Government to bestow the National Museum upon the Smithsonian Institution, the very largest would seem to draw after it an obligation to furnish the requisite accommodations without taxing the Smithsonian funds; otherwise the gift might be detrimental instead of beneficial."

Smithsonian Report for 1847, p. 139 (Sen. ed.)—p. 187 (H. Rep. ed.)

that an Institution founded by the liberality of a foreigner, and to which he has affixed his own name, should be charged with the keeping of a separate Museum, the property of the United States. - - - The small portion of our funds which can be devoted to a museum may be better employed in collecting new objects, such as have not yet been studied, than in preserving those from which the harvest of discovery has already been fully gathered." Nor was he reconciled to the gift by the suggestion that a suitable appropriation would be granted by the National Government, for the expense of its custody. "This would be equally objectionable; since it would annually bring the Institution before Congress as a supplicant for government patronage."[*]

In his Report for 1851, he forcibly stated in regard to the requirements of a general Museum, that "the whole income devoted to this object would be entirely inadequate:" and he strongly urged a National establishment of the Museum on a basis and a scale which should be an honor and a benefit to the people and their Capital city. "Though the formation of a general collection is neither within the means nor the province of the Institution, it is an object which ought to engage the attention of Congress. A general Museum appears to be a necessary establishment at the seat of government of every civilized nation. - - - An establishment of this kind can only be supported by Government; and the proposition ought never to be encouraged of putting this duty on the limited though liberal bequest of a foreigner."[†] This policy was urged in almost every subsequent Report. "There can be but little doubt that in due time ample provision will be made for a Library and Museum at the Capital of this Union, worthy of a Government whose perpetuity depends upon the virtue and intelligence of the people. It is therefore unwise to hamper the more important objects of this Institution by attempting to anticipate results which will be eventually produced without the expenditure of its means."[‡] "The importance of a collection at the seat of government, to illustrate the physical geography, natural history,

* Smithsonian Report for 1849, pp. 161, 162 (of Rep. ed.)—pp. 173, 174 (of H. Rep. ed.)

† Smithsonian Report for 1851, p. 227 (of Rep. ed.)—p. 229 (of H. Rep. ed.)

‡ Smithsonian Report for 1852, p. 253 (of Rep. ed.)—p. 245 (of H. Rep. ed.)

and ethnology, of the United States, cannot be too highly estimated; but the support of such a collection ought not to be a burden upon the Smithsonian fund." *

The popular mind did not however appear to be prepared to accept these earnest precautations; and in 1858, the National Museum was transferred by law to the custody of the Smithsonian Institution, with the same annual appropriation (4,000 dollars) which had been granted to the United States Patent Office when in charge of it.

So rapidly were the treasures of the Museum increased by the gathered fruits of various government explorations and surveys, as well as by the voluntary contributions of the numerous and wide-spread tributaries of the Institution, that the policy was early adopted of freely distributing duplicate specimens to other institutions where they would be most appreciated and most usefully applied. And in this way the Smithsonian became a valuable center of diffusion of the means of investigation in geology, mineralogy, botany, zoology, and archæology.† The clear foresight which announced that the Museum must very soon outgrow the entire capacity of the Smithsonian resources, has been most amply vindicated:‡ and to-day a large Government building is stored from basement to attic, with boxed up rarities of art and nature, sufficient more than twice to fill the Smithsonian halls and galleries, in addition to their present overflowing display.§ The strong desire of Henry to see established in Washington a National Museum on a scale worthy of our resources, and in which the existing overgrown collections might be so beneficially exhibited, he did not live

---

* Smithsonian Report for 1853, p. 11 (of first. ed.)—p. 9 of H. Rep. ed.)

† See "Supplement," Note I.

‡ From the rapid growth of the national collection after it was transferred to the custody of the Smithsonian Institution, the annual appropriation of 4,000 dollars by Congress very soon became wholly insufficient to defray even one-half its necessary expenses. A memorial signed by the Chancellor and the Secretary, was presented to Congress May 1, 1868, in which the memorialists "beg leave to represent on behalf of the Board of Regents, that the usual annual appropriation of 4,000 dollars is wholly inadequate to the cost of preparing, preserving, and exhibiting the specimens;—the actual expenditure for that purpose, in 1867, having been over 12,000 dollars." (Smithsonian Report for 1867, p. 115.) It was not however till 1871 that the appropriation was raised to 10,000 dollars. In 1872, it was increased to 15,000 dollars, and in 1873, to 20,000 dollars.

§ See "Supplement," Note M.

to see gratified. That the realization of this beneficent project is
only a question of time, is little doubtful; for it cannot be supposed
that collections so valuable, and so manifestly beyond the capacities
of the Institution, will be suffered to waste in uselessness. And
when established, its being and its benefits will in no small degree
be due to him who first realizing its necessity, and most appreciating
its importance, with unwearying perseverance for twenty-
five years omitted no opportunity of urging upon members of
Congress its importunate claims.

Meteorological Work.—In the conduct of what were appropriately
called the "active operations" of the Institution—under the
first section of the programme (in contradistinction to the local and
statical objects of the second section), a rare energy and promptness
was exhibited. The very first Report of the Secretary announced
not only the acceptance and preparation for publication of an elaborate
work by Messrs. Squier and Davis, on explorations of "Ancient
Monuments of the Mississippi Valley," but the commencement of
official preparations "for instituting various lines of physical
research. Among the subjects mentioned by way of example in
the programme, for the application of the funds of the Institution,
is terrestrial magnetism. - - - Another subject of research
mentioned in the programme, and which has been urged upon the
immediate attention of the Institution, is that of an extensive system
of meteorological observations, particularly with reference to
the phenomena of American storms. Of late years in our country
more additions have been made to meteorology than to any other
branch of physical science. Several important generalizations have
been arrived at, and definite theories proposed, which now enable
us to direct our attention with scientific precision to such points
of observation as cannot fail to reward us with new and interesting
results. It is proposed to organize a system of observations
which shall extend as far as possible over the North American
continent. - - - The present time appears to be peculiarly
auspicious for commencing an enterprise of the proposed kind.
The citizens of the United States are now scattered over every
part of the southern and western portion of Northern America,
and the extended lines of telegraph will furnish a ready means of

warning the more northern and eastern observers to be on the watch for the first appearance of an advancing storm." *

An appropriation for the purpose having been made by the Regents, a large number of observers scattered over the United States and the Territories became voluntary correspondents of the Institution. Advantage was taken of the stations already established under the direction of the War, and of the Navy Departments, as well as of those provided for by a few of the States. The annual reports of the Secretary chronicled the extension and success of the system adopted; and in a few years between five and six hundred regular observers were engaged in its meteorological service. The favorite project of employing the telegraph for obtaining simultaneous results over a large area was at once organized; and in 1849, a system of telegraphic despatches was established, by which (a few years later) the information received in Washington at the Smithsonian Institution was daily plotted upon a large map of the United States by means of adjustable symbols. Espy's generalization that the principal storms and other atmospheric changes have an eastward movement,† was fully established by this rapidly gathered experience of the Institution; so that "it was often enabled to predict (sometimes a day or two in advance) the approach of any of the larger disturbances of the atmosphere."‡

Eminently efficient as the enterprise approved itself, increasing experience served to demonstrate the expanding requirements of the

* Smithsonian Report for 1847, pp. 145, 147 (of Sen. ed.)—pp. 159, 161 (of H. Rep. ed.) Professor Loomis (to whom among others "distinguished for their attainments in meteorology" letters inviting suggestions, had been addressed,) recommended that there should be at least one observing station within every hundred square miles of the United States; and he sagaciously pointed out that "When the magnetic telegraph [then an infant three years old] is extended from New York to New Orleans and St. Louis, it may be made subservient to the protection of our commerce." This interesting letter was published in full as "Appendix No. 2," to the Report. In 1848, a paper was read before the British Association by Mr. John Ball, "On rendering the Electric Telegraph subservient to Meteorological Research: in which the author suggested that simultaneous observations so collected, might reveal the direction and probable time of arrival of storms. (Report Brit. Assoc. Transactions, Aug. 1848. Abstracts, pp. 12, 13.)

† FRANKLIN is said to have been the first who stated the general law, that the storms of our Southern States move off to the northeastward over the Middle and Eastern States.

‡ Smithsonian Report for 1851, p. 14. An interesting and instructive résumé of results accomplished within fifteen years was given in this Report, pp. 42–65; and continued in the succeeding Report for 1865, pp. 54–59.

service; and it was seen that to prosecute the subject of meteorology over so large a territory, with the fullness necessary, would require a still larger force of observers, and a greater drain upon the resources of the Institution, than could well be spared from other objects; and as the great value of the system was fully recognized by the intelligent, the propriety of maintaining a meteorological bureau by the national support was early presented to the attention of Congress. This most important department of observation had been advanced by Henry to that position, in which a larger annual outlay than the entire income of the Institution was really required to give just efficiency to the system. In his Report for 1865, he remarked: "The present would appear to be a favorable time to urge upon Congress the importance of making provision for the reorganizing all the meteorological observations of the United States under one combined plan, in which the records should be sent to a central depot for reduction, discussion, and final publication. An appropriation of 50,000 dollars annually for this purpose would tend not only to advance the material interests of the country, but also to increase its reputation. - - - It is scarcely necessary at this day to dwell on the advantages which result from such systems of combined observations as those which the principal governments of Europe have established, and are now constantly extending." *

Five years later, in support of the proposition that the subject from its magnitude now appealed to the liberality of the nation, he briefly recapitulated the work accomplished by the limited means of the Institution. "The Smithsonian meteorological system was commenced in 1849, and has continued in operation until the present time. - - - It has done good service to the cause of meteorology; 1st, in inaugurating the system which has been in operation upward of twenty years: 2nd, in the introduction of improved instruments after discussion and experiments: 3rd, in preparing and publishing at its expense an extensive series of meteorological tables: 4th, in reducing and discussing the meteorological material which could be obtained from all the records from the first settlement of the country till within a few years: 5th, in being the first to show

* Smithsonian Report for 1865, p. 37.

the practicability of telegraphic weather signals; 6th, in publishing records and discussions made at its own expense, of the Arctic expeditions of Kane, Hayes, and McClintock; 7th, in discussing and publishing a number of series of special records embracing periods of from twenty to fifty years in different sections of the United States,—of great interest in determining secular changes of the climate; 8th, in the publication of a series of memoirs on various meteorological phenomena, embracing observations and discussions of storms, tornadoes, meteors, auroras, etc.; 9th, in a diffusion of a knowledge of meteorology through its extensive unpublished correspondence and its printed circulars. It has done all in this line which its limited means would permit; and has urged upon Congress the establishment with adequate appropriation of funds, of a meteorological department under one comprehensive plan, 'in which the records should be sent to a central depot for reduction, discussion, and final publication.'"*

In 1870, a meteorological department was established by the Government under the Signal Office of the War Department, with enlarged facilities for systematic observations: and agreeably to the settled policy of the Institution, this important field of research was in 1872, abandoned in favor of the new organization.† Of the voluminous results of nearly a quarter of a century of systematic records over a wide geographical area which have been slowly digested and laboriously discussed, only a small portion has yet been published. The publication of the series when practicable, will yet prove an inestimable boon to meteorological theory.

Although our country can boast of many able meteorologists, who have greatly promoted our knowledge of the laws of atmospheric phenomena, it is safe to say that to no single worker in the field is our nation more indebted for the advancement of this branch of science to its present standing, than to Joseph Henry. Quite as much by his incitement and encouragement of others in such researches, as by his own exertions, does he merit this award. To

---

* Smithsonian Report for 1870, p. 63.

† As an illustration of the popular favor in which this Signal service is held, it may be stated that the annual appropriation by Government for its support now exceeds not merely the entire Smithsonian income, but sixteen times that amount; or in fact its whole endowment.

him is undoubtedly due the most important step in the modern system of observation,—the installation of the telegraph in the service of meteorological signals and predictions.[*] While giving however his active supervision to the extensive system he had himself inaugurated, publishing many important reductions of particular features, as well as various circulars of detailed instructions to observers, of the desiderata to be obtained by those having the opportunities of arctic, oceanic, and southern explorations, and directing the constant observations recorded at the Institution as an independent station, he made many personal investigations of allied subjects;—as of the aurora, of atmospheric electricity and thunder-storms, of the supposed influence of the moon on the weather,—and contributed a valuable series of memoirs on meteorology, embracing a wide range of physical exposition, to the successive Agricultural Reports of the Commissioner of Patents, during the years 1855, '56, '57, '58, and 1859. Instructive articles on Magnetism and Meteorology were prepared in 1861 for the American Cyclopædia. And one of his latest published papers comprises a minute account of the effects of lightning in two thunder-storms; one occurring in the spring of last year (1877) at a Light-house in Key West, Florida, and the other occurring in the summer of last year at New London, Connecticut.[†]

Archæological Work.—One of the earliest subjects taken up for investigation by the Institution, was that of American Archæology; the attempt by extended explorations of the existing pre-historic relics, mounds, and monuments, of the aborigines of our country, to ascertain as far as possible their primitive industrial, social and intellectual character, and any evidences of their antiquity, or of

---

[*] "However frequently the idea may have been suggested of utilizing our knowledge by the employment of the electric telegraph, it is to Professor Henry and his assistants in the Smithsonian Institution that the credit is due of having first actually realized this suggestion. . . . It will thus be seen that without material aid from the Government, but through the enlightened policy of the telegraph companies, the Smithsonian Institution *first in the world organized* a comprehensive system of telegraphic meteorology, and has thus given — first to Europe and Asia, and now to the United States, that most beneficent national application of modern science—the Storm Warnings." Article on "Weather Telegraphy" by Professor Cleveland Abbe, (Am. Jour. Sci., Aug. 1871, vol. II. pp. 81, 82.)

[†] *Journal of the American Electrical Society,* 1878, vol. II. pp. 37–44. The communication is dated Oct. 15, 1877; though not published till during the author's last illness.

their stages of development. The first publication of "Smithsonian Contributions" comprised in a good sized quarto volume an account of extensive examinations of the mounds and earthworks found over the broad valley of the Mississippi, with elaborate illustrations of the relics and results obtained: and this volume extensively circulated by gift and by sale, attracted a wide-spread attention and interest, and gave a remarkable stimulus to the further prosecution of such researches. "Whatever relates to the nature of man is interesting to the students of every branch of knowledge; and hence ethnology affords a common ground on which the cultivators of physical science, of natural history, of archæology, of language, of history, and of literature, can all harmoniously labor. Consequently no part of the operations of this Institution has been more generally popular than that which relates to this subject."[*]

Special explorations inaugurated by the Institution, have supplied it with important contributions to archæological information, and with the rich spoils of collected relics; which together with much material gathered from Arctic and from Southern regions, from Europe, from Asia, and from Africa, fill now a large museum hall 200 feet long and 50 feet wide, exclusively devoted to comparative Anthropology and Ethnology. In 1868, the Secretary reported that "during the past year greater effort had been made than ever before to collect specimens to illustrate the ethnology and archæology of the North American continent:" and he dwelt upon the importance of the subject as a study connecting all portions of the habitable earth, pointing out that "it embraces not only the natural history and peculiarities of the different races of men as they now exist upon the globe, but also their affiliations, their changes in mental and moral development, and also the question of the geological epoch of the appearance of man upon the earth. - - - The ethnological specimens we have mentioned are not considered as mere curiosities collected to excite the wonder of the illiterate, but as contributions to the materials from which it will be practicable to reconstruct by analogy and strict deduction, the history of the past in its relation to the present."[†]

* Smithsonian Report for 1869, p. 38.
† Smithsonian Report for 1868, pp. 21 and 22.

Two years later he reported: "The collection of objects to illustrate anthropology now in possession of the Institution is almost unsurpassed, especially in those which relate to the present Indians and the more ancient inhabitants of the American continent." Deprecating the frequent dissipation of small private collections of such objects at the death of their owners, he forcibly urges that "the only way in which they can become of real importance, is by making them part of a general collection, carefully preserved in some public institution, where in the course of the increasing light of science, they may be made to reveal truths beyond present anticipation." *

In his last Report — for 1877, (just published, and which he did not live to see in print,) he says: "Anthropology, or what may be considered the natural history of man, is at present the most popular branch of science. It absorbs a large share of public attention, and many original investigators are assiduously devoted to it. Its object is to reconstruct as it were the past history of man, to determine his specific peculiarities and general tendencies. It has already established the fact that a remarkable similarity exists in the archæological instruments found in all parts of the world, with those in use among tribes still in a savage or barbarous condition. The conclusion is supported by evidence which can scarcely be doubted, that by thoroughly studying the manners and customs of savages and the instruments employed by them, we obtain a knowledge of the earliest history of nations which have attained the highest civilization. It is remarkable in how many cases, customs existing among highly civilized peoples are found to be survivals of ancient habits." He then argues from the significance thus developed of many trivial practices and unmeaning ceremonies handed down from immemorial time, the importance to a full comprehension of the customs of modern society, of a scientific study of the myths and usages of ancient peoples. "American anthropology" he remarks, "early occupied the attention of the Smithsonian Institution;" and alluding to its first published work, he says, "from the time of the publication of this volume until the present, contributions of value have been made annually by the

---

* Smithsonian Report for 1870, pp. 33, 34.

Institution to this branch of knowledge. - - - The collection of the archæology and ethnology of America, in the National Museum, is the most extensive in the world; and in order to connect it permanently with the name of Smithson, it has been thought advisable to prepare and publish at the expense of the Smithsonian fund, an exhaustive work on American anthropology, in which the various classes of specimens shall be figured and described." [*] This great work still remains to be perfected.

Publications.—To attempt the recapitulation of the various branches of original research initiated or directly fostered by the Institution, would be to write its history. The range and variety of its active operations, and the value of their fruits, are in view of the limited income, and the collateral drains of less important objects exacted from it, something quite surprising. Scarcely a department of investigation has not received either directly or indirectly liberal and efficient assistance: and a host of physicists in the successful prosecution of their diverse labors, have attested their gratitude to the Institution, and no less to the ever sympathetic encouragement of its Director.

Of the various works submitted to the Institution,—differing widely as they necessarily must in the comprehensiveness as well as in the originality of treatment of their diversified topics,—only those were accepted for publication, which had received the approval of a commission of distinguished experts in each particular field of inquiry. But even after such formal approval and acceptance, Henry ever maintained a sense of responsibility which entailed upon him a vast amount of unrecognized and little appreciated labor, in his desire to make each publication a credit to the Institution as well as to its author. In the editing of this multitudinous material, he gave a critical attention to each memoir; and there are probably few of the series which do not bear the marks of his watchful care, in the elimination of obscurities, of redundancies, or of personalities, and in the pruning of questionable metaphors, of

* Smithsonian Report for 1877, pp. 41, 42. Circulars broadly distributed by the Institution, have served to give desired direction to popular attention and activity in this field of research; and the extent of co-operation is such as probably only the "Smithsonian" could have secured, unless by a vastly greater outlay.

imperfect or hasty generalizations, or of incidental inaccuracies of statement or inference.

Over one hundred important original Memoirs, generally too elaborate to be published at length by any existing scientific society, issued in editions many times larger than the most liberal of any such society's issue, most of them now universally recognized as classical and original authorities on their respective topics, forming twenty-one large quarto volumes of "SMITHSONIAN CONTRIBUTIONS TO KNOWLEDGE," distributed over every portion of the civilized or colonized world, constitute a monument to the memory of the founder, James Smithson, such as never before was builded on the foundation of one hundred thousand pounds: and before which the popular Lyceums of our leading cities, with endowments averaging double this amount, are dwarfed into insignificance.

Such as these Lyceums with their local culture, admirable and invaluable in their way, but exerting no influence upon the progress of science, or outside of their own communities, and scarcely known beyond their cities' walls,—such was the type of institute which early legislators could alone imagine. Such as the "Smithsonian Institution" stands to-day,—such is the monument mainly constructed by the foresight, the wisdom, and the resolution of Henry.[*] All honor to the Regents, who with an enlightenment so far in advance of the ruling intelligence of former days, and against the pressures of overwhelming preponderance of even educated popular sentiment, courageously adopted the programme of the Secretary and Director they had appointed; and who throughout his career, so wisely, nobly, and steadfastly upheld his policy and his purpose.

Fifteen octavo volumes of "Smithsonian Miscellaneous Collections" of a more technical character than the "Contributions,"

---

[*] "It is not by its castellated building, nor the exhibition of the museum of the Government, that the Institution has achieved its present reputation; nor by the collection and display of material objects of any kind, that it has vindicated the intelligence and good faith of the Government in the administration of the trust. It is by its explorations, its researches, its publications, its distribution of specimens, and its exchanges, constituting it an active living organization, that it has rendered itself favorably known in every part of the civilized world; has made contributions to almost every branch of science; and brought, more than ever before, into intimate and friendly relations, the Old and the New Worlds." (Memorial to Congress, by Chancellor M. P. CHASE, and Secretary JOSEPH HENRY. Smithsonian Report for 1869, p. 114.)

(including systematic and statistical compilations, scientific summaries, and valuable accessions of tabular "constants,") form in themselves an additional series; and represent a work of which any learned Society or Institution might well be proud. And thirty octavo volumes of annual Reports, rich with the scattered thoughts and hopes and wishes of the Director, form the official journal of his administration.

The Bibliography of Science.—Among the needful preparations for conducting original inquiry, none is more important than ready access and direction to the existing state of research in the particular field, or its allied districts. This information is scattered in the thousands of volumes which form the transactions of learned Societies; and its acquisition involves therefore in most cases a very laborious preliminary bibliographical research. To make this vast store of observation available to scientific students, by the directory of well arranged digests, would appear to fall peculiarly within the province of an Institution specially established for promoting the increase and diffusion of knowledge among men: and was early an object of particular interest to Henry. In his Report for 1851, he remarked: "One of the most important means of facilitating the use of libraries (particularly with reference to science,) is well-digested indexes of subjects, not merely referring to volumes or books, but to memoirs, papers, and parts of scientific transactions and systematic works. As an example of this, I would refer to the admirably arranged and valuable catalogue of books relating to Natural Philosophy and the Mechanic Arts, by Dr. Young. This work comes down to 1807; and I know of no richer gift which could be bestowed upon the science of our own day, than the continuation of this catalogue to the present time. Every one who is desirous of enlarging the bounds of human knowledge, should in justice to himself as well as to the public, be acquainted with what has previously been done in the same line; and this he will only be enabled to accomplish by the use of indexes of the kind above mentioned."[*]

* *Smithsonian Report* for 1851, p. 225 (of Rep., ed.)—p. 217 (of H. Rep. ed.) The valuable *Repertorium commentationum a societatibus litterariis editarum*, edited by Prof. Jeremias D. Reuss, and published in 16 quarto volumes at Göttingen, (1801-1821,) to a large extent supplied this desideratum, down to the end of the last century.

At the time, and for years afterward, one-half of the Smithsonian income was diverted by the requirements of Congress to the
local objects of the Lyceum: and the hopelessness of attempting a
work —additional to that already mapped out, which would require
the united labors of a large corps of well-trained and educated
assistants for many years, and the subsequent devotion of the whole
available income for many years following, to complete its publication, was fully realized.   The project however was not abandoned:
and in 1854, Henry conceived the plan of taking up the more
limited department of American Scientific Bibliography; and by
the persevering application of a fixed portion of the income annually
for a succession of years, of finally producing a thorough subject-
matter index, as well as an index of authors, for the entire range of
American contributions to science from their earliest date.   Inspired
with this ambition, he sought to enlist the co-operation of the
British Association for the Advancement of Science, in procuring
with its large resources, a similar classified index for British and
European scientific literature.

The favorable reception of this project, was officially announced
to Henry by the Secretary of the Association, in the transmission
of the following extract from the proceedings of that body for 1855.
"A communication from Professor Henry of Washington having
been read, containing a proposal for the publication of a catalogue
of philosophical memoirs scattered throughout the Transactions of
Societies in Europe and America, with the offer of co-operation on
the part of the Smithsonian Institution, to the extent of preparing
and publishing in accordance with the general plan which might be
adopted by the British Association, a catalogue of all the American
memoirs on physical science, — the Committee approve of the suggestion, and recommend that Mr. Cayley, Mr. Grant, and Professor
Stokes be appointed a committee to consider the best system of
arrangement, and to report thereon to the council."*   The report of
this committee dated 13th June, 1856, was presented to the succeeding Meeting of the British Association; in which they take occasion
to say: "The Committee are desirous of expressing their sense of
the great importance and increasing need of such a catalogue. - -

---

* Report Brit. Assoc. Glasgow, Sept. 1855, p. lxvi.

The catalogue should not be restricted to memoirs in Transactions of Societies, but should comprise also memoirs in the Proceedings of Societies, in mathematical and scientific journals:" etc. - - - "The catalogue should begin from the year 1800. There should be a catalogue according to the names of authors, and also a catalogue according to subjects." * The committee comprising Fellows of the Royal Society of London finally succeeded in interesting that grave body in the undertaking; and the result was that greatly to Henry's satisfaction, the entire work was ultimately assumed by the Royal Society itself.

In the course of ten years that liberal Society aided by a large grant from the British Government gave to the world its half instalment of the great work, in its admirable "Catalogue of Scientific Papers" alphabetically classified by authors, in seven or eight large quarto volumes. In the Preface to this splendid monument of industry and liberality, stands the following history of its inception. "The present undertaking may be said to have originated in a communication from Dr. Joseph Henry, Secretary of the Smithsonian Institution, to the Meeting of the British Association at Glasgow in 1855, suggesting the formation of a catalogue of Philosophical memoirs. This suggestion was favorably reported on by a Committee of the Association in the following year. - - - In March, 1857, General Sabine, the Treasurer and Vice President of the Royal Society, brought the matter before the President and Council of that body, and requested on the part of the British Association, the co-operation of the Royal Society in the project: whereupon a committee was appointed to take into further consideration the formation of such a catalogue. - - - No further step was taken by the British Association or by the Royal Society in co-operation with that body: but the President and Council of the Royal Society acting on the recommendations contained in a Report of the Library Committee dated 7th January, 1858, resolved that the preparation of a Catalogue of scientific memoirs should be undertaken by the Royal Society independently, and at the Society's own charge."†

———

* Report Brit. Assn. Cheltenham, Aug. 1856, pp. 161, 161.
† Preface to Catalogue of Scientific Papers, (1800-1863) vol. I, 1867, pp. III, iv. The second and most important division of this great and invaluable work,—the classified index to Subjects,—still remains to be accomplished.

System of Exchanges.—For the diffusion of knowledge among men, one of the methods adopted by Henry from the very commencement of his administration was the organization of a system by which the scientific memoirs of Societies or of individuals from any portion of the United States, might be transmitted to foreign countries without expense to the senders: and by which in like manner the similar publications of scientific work abroad might be received at the Smithsonian Institution, for distribution in this country. * This privilege however is properly restricted to *bona fide* donations and exchanges of scientific memoirs; all purchased publications being carefully excluded and left to find their legitimate channels of trade. By an international courtesy —creditable to the wisdom and intelligence of the civilized Powers,—such packages to and from the Institution are permitted to pass through all custom-houses, free of duty; an invoice of authentication being forwarded in advance. When it is considered that this large work of collection and distribution (including the constant supply of the Institution's own publications, and the extensive returns therefor of journals, proceedings, and transactions, for its own library) requires the systematic records and accounts in suitable ledgers, with the accurate parcelling and labelling of packages, large and small, to every corner of the globe, it may well be conceived that no small amount of labor and expense is involved in these forwarding operations. † A recognition of the benefits conferred by this

* "The promotion of knowledge is much retarded by the difficulties experienced in the way of a free intercourse between scientific and literary societies in different parts of the world. In carrying on the exchange of the Smithsonian volumes, it was necessary to appoint a number of agents. These agencies being established other exchanges could be carried on through them and our means of conveyance, at the slight additional expense owing to the small increase of weight. - - - The result cannot fail to prove highly beneficial, by promoting a more ready communication between the literature and science of this country and the world abroad." (*Smithsonian Report for 1851, p. 126, Senate ed.*)

† It may be stated that the number of foreign institutions and correspondents receiving the Smithsonian publications exceeds two thousand; whose localities embrace not only the principal cities of Europe (from Iceland to Turkey), of British America, Mexico, the West Indies, Central and South America, and of Australia, but also those of New Zealand, Honolulu in the Sandwich Islands, twelve cities in India, Shanghai in China, Tokio and Yokohama in Japan, Batavia in Java, Manila in the Philippine Islands, Alexandria and Cairo in Egypt, Algiers in northern Africa, Monrovia in Liberia, and Cape Town in southern Africa. The correspondents and recipients in the United States, are probably nearly as numerous.

generous enterprise, is practically indicated by the rapid enlargement of the operations.   The weight of matter sent abroad by the
Institution at the end of the first decade was 14,000 pounds for the
year 1857; the weight sent at the end of the second decade was
22,000 pounds for the year 1867; and the weight sent at the end
of the third decade was 99,000 pounds for the last year 1877.
This admirable system has been greatly encouraged and facilitated
by the most praiseworthy liberality of the great lines of ocean
steamers, and of the leading railway companies, in carrying the
Smithsonian freight in many cases free of charge, or in other cases at
greatly reduced rates: an appreciative tribute alike to the beneficent
services and reputation of the Institution, and to the personal
character and influence of its Director. *

"This part of the system of Smithsonian operations has everywhere received the commendation of those who have given it their
attention or have participated in its benefits.   The Institution is
now the principal agent of scientific and literary communication
between the old world and the new. - . - -   The importance of
such a system with reference to the scientific character of our country, could scarcely be appreciated by those who are not familiar
with the results which flow from an easy and certain intercommu-
nication of this kind.   Many of the most important contributions
to science made in America have been unheard of in Europe, or
have been so little known, or received so little attention, that they
have been republished as new discoveries or claimed as the product
of European research."†   It would indeed be difficult to estimate
rightly the benefit to science in the encouragement of its cultivators,
afforded by this fostering service.   Few Societies are able to incur
much expense in the distribution of their publications; and hence

* "The cost of this system would far exceed the means of the Institution, were
it not for important aid received from various parties interested in facilitating
international intercourse and the promotion of friendly relations between distant
parts of the civilized world. The liberal aid extended by the steamship and
other lines, mentioned in previous reports, in carrying the boxes of the Smithson exchanges free of charge, has been continued, and several other lines have
been added to the number in the course of the year." (Smithsonian Report for
1857, p. 56.) Notwithstanding this unprecedented generosity, the exchange system
has reached such proportions as to require for its maintenance one-fourth of the
entire income from the Smithsonian fund.

† Smithsonian Report for 1852, p. 25 (of 8vo ed.)

their circulation is necessarily very limited. The fructifying interchange of labors and results, dependent on their own resources,
would be obstructed by the recurring expenses and delays of customs interventions, and by unconscionable exactions: and indeed
without the Smithsonian mechanism, nine-tenths of the present
scientific exchanges would be at once suppressed. Let it be hoped
that so beneficent a system will not break down from the weight of
its own inevitable growth.

Astronomical Telegraphy.—Analogous in principle to the system
of exchange, is that adopted for the instantaneous trans-Atlantic
communication of discoveries of a special order. In the year 1873,
in the interests of astronomy (to which Henry was ever warmly
devoted) he concluded " a very important arrangement between the
Smithsonian Institution and the Atlantic Cable Companies, by which
is guaranteed the free transmission by telegraph between Europe
and America of accounts of astronomical discoveries which for the
purpose of co-operative observation require immediate announcement."* This admirable service to science, so creditable to the
intelligence and the liberality of the Atlantic Telegraph Companies,
embraces direct reciprocal communication between the Smithsonian
Institution and the foreign Observatories of Greenwich, Paris,
Berlin, Vienna, and Pulkova. During the first year of its operation, four new planetoids were telegraphed from America, and seven
telescopic comets from Europe to this country.

" Although the discovery of planets and comets will probably
be the principal subject of the cable telegrams, yet it is not intended
to restrict the transmission of intelligence solely to that class of
observation. Any remarkable solar phenomenon presenting itself
suddenly in Europe, observations of which may be practicable in
America several hours after the sun has set to the European observer,—the sudden outburst of some variable star similar to that
which appeared in *Corona borealis* in 1866,—unexpected showers
of shooting stars, etc. would be proper subjects for transmission by
cable.

" The announcement of this arrangement has called forth the
approbation of the astronomers of the world : and in regard to it

we may quote the following passage from the fifty-fourth annual
report of the Royal Astronomical Society of England: 'The great
value of this concession on the part of the Atlantic telegraph and
other Companies, cannot be too highly prized, and our science must
certainly be the gainer by this disinterested act of liberality.
Already planets discovered in America have been observed in
Europe on the evening following the receipt of the telegram, or
within two or three days of their discovery.' "*

Official Correspondence.—A vast amount of individual work
having in view the diffusion of knowledge, has been performed by
the correspondence of the Institution; which may be best described
in the language of an extract from one of the early reports: "There
is one part of the Smithsonian operations that attracts no public
attention, though it is producing important results in the way of
diffusing knowledge, and is attended perhaps with more labor than
any other part. I allude to the scientific correspondence of the
Institution. Scarcely a day passes in which communications are
not received from persons in different parts of the country, containing accounts of discoveries, which are referred to the Institution,
or asking questions relative to some branch of knowledge. The
rule was early adopted to give respectful attention to every letter
received, and this has been faithfully adhered to from the beginning
up to the present time. - - - Requests are frequently made
for lists of apparatus, for information as to the best books for the
study of special subjects, for suggestions on the organization of
local societies, etc. Applications are also made for information by
persons abroad, relative to particular subjects respecting this country. When an immediate reply cannot be given to a question, the
subject is referred by letter to some one of the Smithsonian co-labor-
ers to whose line of duty it pertains, and the answer is transmitted
to the inquirer, either under the name of the person who gives the

---

* Smithsonian Report for 1873, p. 32. In 1876, a stellar outburst in the "Swan"
observed by Dr. Schmidt of Athens, on the 24th of November, was announced.
Less brilliant than the stellar outburst which occurred in the northern "Crown"
in May, 1866, it continued to decline through the month of December, and at the
close of the year, had dwindled from the third to the eighth magnitude. (This
may possibly be the same "temporary star"—seen in Cygnus in 1600, and again
in 1670; and having therefore a period of variability of about 60 years.)

information, or under that of the Institution, according to the circumstances of the case. - - - Many of those communications are of such a character, that at first sight it might seem best to treat them with silent neglect; but the rule has been adopted to state candidly and respectfully the objections to such propositions, and to endeavor to convince their authors that their ground is untenable. Though this course is in many cases attended with no beneficial results, still it is the only one which can be adopted with any hope of even partial good."[*]

The information given to scientific inquirers has been of an exceedingly varied and highly valuable character, not unfrequently involving a large amount of research from special experts; who have been accustomed cheerfully to bestow a degree of attention on difficult questions thus presented, which would have been accorded perhaps less ungrudgingly to others than to the universally honored Smithsonian Director. As to the pretensions and importunities of the unscientific,—such is the judgment pronounced after a quarter of a century of laborious experience with them:

"The most troublesome correspondents are persons of extensive reading, and in some cases of considerable literary acquirements, who in earlier life were not imbued with scientific methods, but who not without a certain degree of mental power, imagine that they have made great discoveries in the way of high generalizations. Their claims not being allowed, they rank themselves among the martyrs of science, against whom the scientific schools and the envy of the world have arrayed themselves. Indeed to such intensity does this feeling arise in certain persons, that on their special subjects they are really monomaniacs, although on others they may be not only entirely sane, but even evince abilities of a high order. - - - Two persons of this class have recently made a special journey to Washington, from distant parts of the country, to demand justice from the Institution in the way of recognition of their claims to discoveries in science of great importance to humanity; and each of them has made an appeal to his representative in Congress to aid him in compelling the Institution to acknowledge the merits of his speculations. Providence vindicates in such cases the equality of its justice in giving to such persons an undue share of self-esteem and an exaltation of confidence in themselves, which in a great degree compensate for what they conceive to be the want of a just appreciation by the public. Unless however they are men of great benevolence of disposition, who can look with pity on what they deem the ignorance and prejudice of leaders of science, they are apt to indulge in a bitterness of denunciation which might be injurious to the reputation of the Institution, were their effects not neutralized by the extravagance of the assertions themselves." [*]

To the projectors and propellers of Paine electric engines, and Keely motors, eager for a marketable certificate from such an authority, Henry would calmly reply: "We may say that science has established the great fact — without the possibility of doubt, that what is called power, or that which produces changes in matter, cannot be created by man, but exists in nature in a state of activity or in a condition of neutralization; and furthermore that all the original forces connected with our globe, as a general rule have assumed a state of permanent equilibrium, and that the crust of the earth as a whole (with the exception of the comparatively exceedingly small proportion, consisting of organic matter such as coal, wood, etc.) is as it were a burnt slag, incapable of yielding power; and that all the motions and changes on its surface are due to actions from celestial space, principally from the sun. - - - All attempts to substitute electricity or magnetism for coal power must be unsuccessful, since these powers tend to an equilibrium from which they can only be disturbed by the application of another power, which is the equivalent of that which they can subsequently exhibit. They are however, with chemical attraction, etc. of great importance as intermediate agents in the application of the power of heat as derived from combustion. Science does not indicate in the slightest degree, the possibility of the discovery of a new primary power comparable with that of combustion as exhibited in the burning of coal. Whatever unknown powers may exist in nature capable of doing work, must be in a state of neutralization, otherwise they would manifest themselves spontaneously; and from this state of neutralization or equilibrium, they can be released only by the action

* Smithsonian Report for 1873, pp. 87, 38.

of an extraneous power of equivalent energy; and we therefore do
not hesitate to say that all declarations of the discovery of a new
power which is to supersede the use of coal as a motive-power, have
their origin in ignorance or deception, and frequently in both. A
man of some ingenuity in combining mechanical elements, and having some indefinite scientific knowledge, imagines it possible to obtain a certain result by a given combination of principles, and by
long brooding over this subject previous to experiment, at length
convinces himself of the certainty of the anticipated result. Having thus deceived himself by his sophisms, he calls upon his neigh-
bors to accept his conclusions as verified truths; and soon acquires
the notoriety of having made a discovery which is to change the
civilization of the world. The shadowy reputation which he has
thus acquired, is too gratifying to his vanity to be at once relinquished by the announcement of his self-deception; and in preference he applies his ingenuity in devising means by which to continue
the deception of his friends and supporters, long after he himself
has been convinced of the fallacy of his first assumptions. In this
way what was commenced in folly, generally ends in fraud." [*]

In looking back upon the struggles, conflicts, and obstructions of
the past, it really seems quite marvelous that so much should have
been accomplished, with so limited expenditure. These large results are partly due to the admirable method of the Secretary, his
clear presage of effects, and his high power of systematic distribution and appliance; partly to the intelligent zeal and sympathetic
energy of the able assistants whom he had associated with him
almost from the organization of the institution; and partly to the
personal magic of the man,—to the surprising amount of voluntary
co-operation he was able to call forth in almost every direction, by
the sheer force of his own earnest industry, and the contagious influence of his own devotion to the cause of scientific advancement.

Scientific Observatories.—One of the objects very dear to Henry's
heart, was the establishment of a physical observatory (with a physical laboratory in connection) for the systematic observation and
record of important points in celestial and terrestrial physics. For

* Smithsonian Report for 1871, pp. 39, 40.

the proper maintenance of such an establishment, he thought an income as large as that of the Smithson fund, would not be too much: and on two different occasions he endeavored to enlist the interest of wealthy and public-spirited citizens in such an enterprise. One of these was Mr. McCormick of Illinois; and a letter on the subject was afterward printed (without its address) in the Report for 1870. * The other was Mr. Lick of California; who after some hesitation, decided in favor of an astronomical observatory. Another allied object of great interest to Henry, and one requiring as large an endowment, was a well-equipped chemical laboratory, in which —under judicious restrictions—those really engaged in original researches, should have liberal facilities of appliances and needed materials, furnished them. He considered that an important part of the work to be accomplished by a physical and chemical laboratory, would be the determination and tabulation of "The Constants of Nature and Art" with a much wider range of subjects, and on a scale of much greater completeness and accuracy, than had heretofore been attempted: and thus might be realized the great work or works of reference, suggested by Charles Babbage as a scientific *desideratum*. † Had the Smithsonian fund been twice as large as it is, both these great enterprises for the increase of knowledge, would undoubtedly have been successfully inaugurated by Henry.

Loss by Fire.—Early in the year 1865, (on the 24th day of January,) the central portion of the Smithsonian Building suffered from a disastrous fire, the effects of which were aggravated by the extreme severity of the winter cold, which greatly obstructed the efficiency of the engines brought into action. ‡ "The progress of the fire was so rapid, that but few of the contents of the upper rooms could be removed before the roof fell in. The conflagration was only stayed by the incombustible materials of the main building:" the flooring of the upper story, forming an iron and brick

* Smithsonian Report for 1870, pp. 141-144.
† Brewster's Edinburgh Jour. Art. April, 1832, vol. vi. pp. 334-342.—Smithsonian Report for 1856, pp. 289-302.
‡ This accident resulted from the carelessness of some workmen in the upper picture gallery, who in temporarily setting up a stove, inserted the pipe through a wall-lining into a furring space (supposing it a flue), but which conducted directly under the rafters of the roof.

vaulting over the lower or principal story. Neither wing of the building was reached by the fire; and the valuable Library (not then transferred to the Capitol), and the Museum, fortunately escaped without injury. The Stanley collection of Indian portraits, comprising about 200 paintings, and estimated as worth 20,000 dollars, was entirely destroyed. A fine full-sized copy in Carrara marble, by John Gott, of the antique statue known as "The Dying Gladiator," was crumbled into a formless mass of stone.

The Secretary's office unfortunately fell within the range of the flames. "The most irreparable loss was that of the records, consisting of the official, scientific, and miscellaneous correspondence; embracing 35,000 pages of copied letters which had been sent, (at least 30,000 of which were the composition of the Secretary,) and 50,000 pages of letters received by the Institution; the receipts for publications and specimens; reports on various subjects which have been referred to the Institution; the records of experiments instituted by the Secretary for the Government; four manuscripts of original investigations, [memoirs by collaborators,] which had been adopted by the Institution for publication; a large number of papers and scientific notes of the Secretary; a series of diaries, memorandum and account books." [*] This truly "irreparable loss" of the original notes of many series of experiments by Henry, of varied character, running back for thirty years, kept for the purpose of reduction and discussion, or further extension (as leisure might permit), and of which but few had been published even by results, — was borne by their author with his characteristic equanimity; and was very rarely alluded to by him, unless when in answer to inquiries respecting particular points of his researches, he was compelled to excuse the absence of precise data.

The Lecture Room —a model of its class — entirely burned out by the fire, was not reconstructed: but the space it occupied on the upper floor, was with the adjacent rooms (used as the apparatus room, and the art gallery) thrown into one large hall, 200 feet long, —at present occupied as the ethnological museum. Advantage was taken of the hazard demonstrated by the fire, to induce Congress in the following year to transfer the custody of the Smith-

---

[*] Smithsonian Report for 1865, p. 15.

sonian collection of scientific works to the National Library; and the propriety of this change was thus defended. "The east wing of the Smithsonian building, in which the books were deposited is not fire-proof, and is liable to destruction by accident or the torch of the incendiary, while the rooms of the Capitol are of incombustible materials. This wing was moreover filled to overflowing; and a more extended and secure depository could not be obtained, except by another large draught on the accumulated funds intended to form part of the permanent capital."[*]

Second Visit to Europe.—At a meeting of the Board of Regents, held February 3rd, 1870, "General Delafield in behalf of the Executive Committee, stated that they deemed it highly important for the interests of the Institution in the promotion of science, and due to the Secretary for his long and devoted services, that he should visit Europe to consult with the savans and societies of Great Britain and the continent; and he therefore hoped that a leave of absence would be granted to Professor Henry for several months, and an allowance be made for his expenses. On motion of Dr. Maclean it was unanimously *Resolved*, That Professor Henry, Secretary of the Institution, be authorized to visit Europe in behalf of the interests of the Smithsonian Institution, and that he be granted from three to six months leave of absence, and two thousand dollars for travelling expenses for this purpose."[†]

It is not necessary here to recount the particulars of this second visit of Henry to Europe, more fully than in the brief account given by him in his annual Report. "Before closing this report, it is proper that I should refer to a resolution adopted by your honorable board at its last session, granting me leave of absence to visit Europe to confer with savans and societies relative to the Institution, and making provision for the payment of my expenses. The presentation of this proposition was entirely without my knowledge, but I need scarcely say that its unanimous adoption was highly gratifying to my feelings; and that I availed myself of the privilege it offered with a grateful appreciation of the kindness

* Smithsonian Report for 1868, p. 14.
† Smithsonian Report for 1869, p. 40.

intended. I sailed from New York on the 1st of June, returning
after an absence of four and a half months, much improved in
health, and with impressions as to science and education in the Old
World, which may be of value in directing the affairs of the Institution. Although limited as to time, and my plans interfered with
somewhat by the war, I visited England, Ireland, Scotland, Bel-
gium, parts of Germany and France. But deferring for the present
an account of my travels, and the observations connected with
them, I will merely state that as your representative, I was everywhere kindly received, and was highly gratified with the commen-
dations bestowed on the character and operations of the Institution
intrusted to your care." *

Service on the Light-House Board.—While the whole high bent
of Henry's mind was rather toward abstract than utilitarian
research, there was no well devised system of practical benefit for
man, that did not command his earnest sympathy or enlist his
active co-operation,—no labor in such co-operation from which he
shrank, if he felt that without the sacrifice of other duties, he
could make such labor useful. On the establishment of the Light-
House Board, in 1852, Henry was appointed one of its members;
and although his valuable time was already fully occupied, he consented to serve on the Board, in the hope of aiding to benefit the
interests of navigation. To the requirements of his new position,
he brought his accustomed energy, skill, and eminently practical
judgment; and soon made his influence felt throughout the light-
house service.†

---

* *Smithsonian Report* for 1870, p. 45.

† In less than ten years from the organization of the Light-House Board, the
lenticular system of Augustin Jean Fresnel had been introduced into all the
light-houses of the United States. Leonor Fresnel, Secretary of the Light-House
Board of France, (the brother of that distinguished physicist,) in a letter addressed
to the Secretary of the United States Light-House Board, dated May 7th, 1861, says:
"The prodigious development of this service within so short a time under the
Light-House Board, has truly astonished me. My old experience in fact enables
me the better to appreciate how much energy and activity were necessary to
bring to this degree of perfection, the light-house service of such a vast expanse
of coast, as well on the Pacific as on the Atlantic, without mentioning the task
of succeeding in establishing against hostile prejudices the adoption of a new
system." (*Report to Secretary of the Treasury*, Feb. 4, 1862. Mis. Doc. No. 6, 37th
Cong. 2nd Sess. Senate, p. 14.)

When the steadily advancing cost of whale oil made it necessary to seek for some more economical illuminant, he attacked the problem with his habit of scientific method. Colza oil or rape-seed oil had been used in France with some success; and efforts were made to introduce its culture and production in this country. Lard oil had been tested by Professor J. H. Alexander of Baltimore, and pronounced by him of very inferior value as an illuminant. For accuracy of determination, Henry caused to be prepared at the Light-house Depot on Staten Island, a long dark fire-proof chamber, and had it painted black on all its interior surfaces for the purpose of photometric observations. In ordinary lamps, the colza oil was found to be about equal to whale oil in illuminating power, and lard oil inferior to it. Petroleum or mineral oil was also tried; but its quality was at that time too variable, and its use was found to be too dangerous. Experiment showed that lard oil had a greater specific gravity than sperm oil, a less capillarity or ascensional attraction in a wick, and a less perfect fluidity. The conditions were varied; and it was found that with elevation of temperature, the fluidity, and the capillarity, of the lard oil increased more rapidly than those of the sperm oil, until at about 250° F. the former surpassed the latter in these qualities. With these results, it became important to compare the oils in large lamps, such as were actually required for the lanterns of light-houses. The heat evolved by the large-sized Argand burners, would seem peculiarly to favor the lard oil: a few trials, with a proper adaptation of the lamps, established its supremacy; and conclusively demonstrated — contrary to all the laboratory trials of former experimenters, that for the purpose desired, this contemned article was for equal quantities a more brilliant illuminant than mineral kerosene oil, or vegetable colza oil, or animal sperm oil, while its market price was only about one-fourth that of the latter.[*] Against all the opposition of interested dealers, and prejudiced keepers, the lard oil was at once introduced into actual use in the years 1865 and 1866, in all the light-houses of the United States; with a saving of at least one dollar on every gallon of the hundred thousand in annual use; that is of 100,000 dollars per annum.

During the progress of these useful labors, no less important investigations were commenced, on the most efficient forms of apparatus for acoustic signalling, as the substitutes for light signals during the prevalence of sea-board fogs. "Among the impediments to navigation, none perhaps are more to be dreaded than those which arise from fogs. - - - The only means at present known for obviating the difficulty, is that of employing powerful sounding instruments which may be heard at a sufficient distance through the fog, to give timely warning of impending danger."[*]

Gun signals were early abandoned, as inefficient, dangerous, and expensive: inefficient, because of both "the length of the intervals between the successive explosions, and the brief duration of the sound, which renders it difficult to determine with accuracy its direction." Innumerable projects eagerly pressed upon the Board by visionary inventors (some of them being rattles, gongs, or organ pipes operated by manual cranks, many of them being varieties of automatic horn or whistle operated by the winds or the waves) were impartially tested, and uniformly rejected as wholly insufficient: very few of their projectors having the slightest practical idea of the requirements of the service. Experiments on steam-whistles of large size and on horns with vibrating steel tongues or reeds, sounded by steam-power, or by hot-air engines, varied and continued for several years under wide changes of conditions, finally determined their most efficient size and character.[†]

In 1867, comparative trials were made at Sandy Hook (on the Jersey shore, at the entrance to Raritan Bay, and to New York Bay,) with three powerful instruments; a large steam-whistle whose cup is 8 inches in diameter, and made adjustable in pitch; a large reed trumpet 17 feet long and 38 inches in diameter at its flaring mouth, whose steel tongue was 10 inches long, 2½ inches

---

* Report of Light-House Board for 1871, p. 18.

† An enterprising inventor had secured a patent for a metallic compound or alloy for steam-whistles, especially adapted to increase greatly their power as fog-signals. In vain was he assured that his "improvement" was a fallacy; that the cylindrical cup of the whistle was not a bell, but only a resonant chamber; and that its material was comparatively unimportant. He was only with difficulty convinced, when Henry had his whistle formally tested, with a stout cord wound tightly around its cylindrical surface; when its tone under steam escape was proved to be as full, as loud, and as penetrating, as with the cord removed.

wide, and half an inch thick at its smaller vibrating end, and was blown by a hot-air engine; and lastly a large siren horn operated by steam at different pressures, the aerial vibration being produced by the intermittence of a revolving grating disk or valve in the small end of the horn, driven at high velocities by the steam engine, and its pitch regulated by the adjustable speed of the revolving disk. The trumpet or fog-horn was provided with a series of replaceable steel tongues of different sizes, and the siren was driven at five-different pitches of from 250 to 700 impulses per second, and at steam pressures varying from 20 pounds to 100 pounds per square inch. For the purpose of accurate estimation, within short distances, a phonometer or "artificial ear" was employed, having at its smaller upturned end a horizontal drum of stretched membrane, sprinkled with sand, after the plan devised by Sondhauss. Trumpets of the same size, were made of different materials, as of brass, iron, and wood; but these differences were found to exercise little or no influence on the intensity or penetration of the sound. Trumpets were also made of different shapes, straight and curved, and square as well as round, with equal lengths and equal areas of cross section; from whose trials it appeared that the conical form gave nearly double the distance of action on the sand of the "artificial ear," that was given by the pyramidal form. Such investigations — varied and long-continued, serve to show the conscientious earnestness with which Henry sought to give the highest efficiency to the expedients available for the protection of life and property along our extended sea coast.

The steam-whistle was found to be less powerful than the trumpet, with the same expenditures of fuel. Steam-whistles were afterwards tried of 10 inches, 12 inches, and 18 inches in diameter. The largest size was not found to give results proportioned to its increased consumption; and the 10 or 12 inch size was regarded as practically the most efficient. The siren was found to be the most powerful and penetrating of the instruments tested, as it admitted more advantageously the application of a higher steam expenditure. The best result with this instrument was attained with a pressure of from 60 to 80 pounds, and at a pitch between 350 and 400 vibrations per second. Under favorable conditions,

this instrument frequently made itself heard at a distance of fifteen,
and twenty miles. Henry's large experience with the occasional
aerial impediments to sound propagation,* and his strong sense of
the vital importance of having fog-signals recognized at a distance,
under the most adverse conditions, led him to favor the introduction of the most powerful sounders attainable, without absolutely
limiting the decision to their relative economy. Hence he was the
first to devise improvements in the siren, and to press its adoption
at important or dangerous stations, notwithstanding its higher consumption of steam or heat power. †

Partly under the stimulus given to the sale of lard oil by the
striking proofs of its excellence as an illuminant under favorable
conditions, furnished by Henry, this article slowly advanced in
price; though probably not to an extent of more than a fourth part
additional cost. Henry's energies again were called into requisition
to devise a remedy. Neither gas, nor electricity, the favorite means
of numerous projectors and advisers, appeared justified, on the
score of economy. ‡ A new series of elaborate experiments was
undertaken to determine whether mineral oil (so abundant as to be
easily procurable at one-third the cost of lard oil) could not be
made available. The great improvements introduced into its prep-

---

* An abstract of Henry's elaborate and invaluable researches on some abnormal
phenomena of Sound — the crowning labor of his life, must be reserved for a concluding section.

† Major G. H. Elliott, commissioned by the U. S. Light-House Board to make a
tour of inspection of European Light-house establishments in 1873, in his Report
published by the Senate in 1874, says of the British and French systems, "I saw
many details of construction and administration which we can adopt to advantage, while there are many in which we excel. Our shore fog-signals particularly,
are vastly superior both in number and power." (Report on European Light-houses,
p. 12.) "To the careful and laborious investigations and experiments of the distinguished Chairman of the Light-House Board, prolonged through a series of
years, and prosecuted under a great variety of conditions, is largely to be attributed the acknowledged superiority of our fog-signal service." (Journal of
Franklin Institute, Jan. 1875, vol. lxxi. p. 53.)

‡ Report of L. H. Board for 1874, p. 11. No agency (for whatever purpose) has
proved so enticing to the half-informed as electricity. For years past scarcely a
month has elapsed without some new form of patent electric-light, or some
marvelous application of electric-lights, being pertinaciously urged by sanguine
"reformers" upon the Light-House Board for adoption; some of these ideal
schemes being the mounting of electric-lights on buoys, or on the masts of light-
ships, or their suspension from moored balloons. Many eminently original
minds have earnestly desired to obtain contracts for supplying all the light-
houses with oxy-hydrogen lime lights. In a fog, the most powerful electric-light
is as useless as the cheapest kerosene lamp.

aration in later years by high distillation, seemed to justify the attempt. Not only was a laborious inquiry into the best conditions of combustion, by precise photometric measurement required, but for the security of the service, equally laborious examinations into the best practicable methods of testing, of handling, and of storing this material.[*] To secure a proper oxygenation in burning, a modification of the lamp was required. "It was soon apparent that the use of mineral oil would necessitate a change of lamps, and attention is now directed to the perfection of one which will produce the best results from this illuminant. It is thought that the lamps now used with lard oil can be converted at no great expense and successfully used with mineral oil. Our experiments have shown that this oil can be more readily used in the smaller lamps; and it is proposed, as soon as suitable ones can be prepared, to put it into use at such stations of the fifth and sixth order, as may be thought expedient; when if it be found satisfactory, an attempt will be made to substitute it for lard oil in lamps of the higher orders."[†] "This change is proposed entirely with reference to economy; for it has been found by repeated experiment, that while a somewhat superior light may be obtained from a small lamp charged with kerosene, a larger lamp charged with lard oil affords the greater illuminating power. So great is this difference in lamps of the first order with five wicks, that the rates of light from kerosene and lard, are as three to four respectively. Since the safety of the keeper and the continuity of the light are essential elements in the choice of an illuminant, a thorough acquaintance with the nature of the substance is essentially necessary. With a view therefore to the introduction of kerosene, a series of experiments have been made during the last two years on the different varieties of this material found in the market."[‡]

---

[*] "It has been established that the ordinary fire-test is insufficient as usually applied, and that an explosive mixture may be formed by confining the vapors given off at a temperature in some cases twenty degrees lower than that credited to by the public inspector. That this inquiry is of great practical importance to the Light-house system, must be evident when we reflect that means must be devised for testing the oil offered for acceptance in accordance with contracts; for storing it; for transporting it to light-house stations; for preserving it in bulk at the stations; and for the instruction of the keepers in its daily use." (Report of L. H. Board, 1877, p. 5.)

[†] Report of L. H. Board, 1875, p. 4.

[‡] Report of L. H. Board, 1877, p. 4.

In 1871, on the resignation of Admiral Shubrick, Henry was chosen as the Chairman of the Light-House Board; and his energetic labors in behalf of the service, fully vindicated the wisdom of the choice. Punctual in his attendance on the weekly meetings of the Board, he inspired others with a portion of his own zealous devotion. Nor did he fail to urge upon the Government, the constant need and responsibility of maintaining an efficient establishment. He emphatically declared that "The character of the aids which any nation furnishes the mariner in approaching and leaving its shores, marks in a conspicuous degree its advancement in civilization. Whatever tends to facilitate navigation or to lessen its dangers, serves to increase commerce; and hence is of importance not only to the dweller on the seaboard, but to the inhabitants of every part of the country. - - - Therefore it is of the first importance that the signals, whether of light or sound, which indicate the direction of the course, and the beacons which mark the channel, shall be of the most improved character, and that they be under the charge of intelligent, efficient, and trustworthy attendants." * And rising to a higher argument, he pointed out that "It is not alone in its economical aspect that a light-house system is to be regarded: it is a life-preserving establishment founded on the principles of Christian benevolence, of which none can so well appreciate the importance as he who after having been exposed to the perils of the ocean—it may be for months—finds himself approaching in the darkness of night a lee shore. But it is not enough to erect towers, and establish other signals; they must be maintained in an efficient state with uninterrupted constancy." † Unfailing continuity was the watch-word of his administration.

---

* Report of L. H. Board, 1871, pp. 8, 9. The coast line of the United States is far more extended than that of any other nation on the globe. "The magnitude of the Light-house system of the United States may be inferred from the following facts: from the St. Croix River on the boundary of Maine, to the mouth of the Rio Grande in the Gulf of Mexico, includes a distance of over 5,000 miles; on the Pacific coast, a length of about 1,500 miles; on the great northern Lakes, about 3,000 miles; and on inland rivers about 500 miles; making a total of more than 10,000 miles. Nearly every square foot of the margin of the sea throughout the whole extent of 5,000 miles along the Atlantic and Gulf coast is more or less illuminated by light-house rays; the mariner rarely losing sight of one light until he has gained another." (p. 1, of same Report.)

† Report of L. H. Board, 1871, p. 5.

A formal report made to the Honorable Secretary of the Treasury by the Naval Secretary of the Light-House Board, dated May 21st, 1878, (very shortly after Henry's death,) simply detailing for information, the character of his gratuitous services to the light-house establishment during a quarter of a century, (and not intended for the public,) takes the inevitable form of eulogy. A portion of it is here quoted:

"As Chairman of this committee, Professor Henry acted as the scientific adviser of the Board. But in addition it was his duty to conduct the experiments made by the Board, not only in the matter of original investigation, and testing of the material used, but in examining and reporting on the models, plans, and theories, presented by others to the Board. The value of the services he rendered in this position is simply inestimable. He prepared the formula for testing our oils; he conducted the series of experiments resulting in the substitution of lard oil for sperm oil, which effected an immense saving in cost; and he also conducted the experiments which have resulted in making it possible to substitute mineral oil for lard oil, when another economy will be made. His original investigation into the laws of sound have resulted in giving us a fog-signal service conceded to be the best in the world. His examinations into the action of electricity, have enabled the Board to almost completely protect its stations from the effect of lightning. The result of his patient, continuous, practical experimentation is visible everywhere in the service. No subject was too vast for him to undertake; none too small for him to overlook. And while he has brought into the establishment so many practical applications of science, he has done almost as much service by keeping out what presented by others seemed plausible, but which on examination proved impracticable.

"Every theory, plan, or machine, which was pressed on the Board, as for the interests of commerce and navigation, was referred to the committee on experiments, when it was examined by its Chairman, and was formally reported upon. If it had no practical value, the report on record simply stated the inexpediency of its adoption: but the Professor often verbally pointed out to the presenter, its fallacy; and sent him away—if not satisfied—at least feeling that he had been well treated. He thus prevented not only the adoption of impracticable plans, but avoided the enmity of their inventors.

"Professor Henry made many valuable reports, containing the results of his elaborate experiments into matters which were formally referred to him, which are spread on the records of the Board; and the reports were drawn in such form that his suggestions were capable of and received practical application. But in addition to this, he was constantly extending his scientific researches for the benefit of the service in all directions. His summer vacations were as a rule passed in experimentation at the laboratory of the Establishment at Staten Island, on its steamers, or at its light-stations, pushing his inquiries to their last results. To experimentation in the interests of this service, Professor Henry seemed to give his whole heart. It appeared as if he never lost sight of the needs of the Establishment, and as if he never neglected an opportunity to advance its interests. In addition to his other duties, Professor Henry presided as Chairman of the Light-House Board for the last seven years at its weekly meetings, when he did much to infuse into the different members of the Board, his own spirit of labor for, and devotion to its interests." [*]

Services to the National Government.—The value of Henry's services to the various Executive Departments of our Government, faithfully and unostentatiously performed through a long series of years and a succession of Presidential Administrations, cannot be estimated, as its history can never be written. Whatever material for it existed in the form of abstracts of inquiries, trials, and reports, prior to 1865, unfortunately perished in the fire of that year. Whenever in any important case a scientific adviser could be useful to the proper conduct of a Bureau, Henry's reputation generally pointed him out as the most suitable expert and arbiter. On the outbreak of the great civil war, the number of such refer-

---

[*] *Executive Documents*, No. 94, Forty-fifth Congress, 2d Session, Senate, pp. 2, 3. It is gratifying to know that on the presentation of his report and recommendation to Congress, by the high-minded Secretary of the Treasury, a moderate appropriation for the benefit of his bereaved family was at once passed, in slight recognition of Henry's "inestimable" services.

ences was naturally very considerably increased. The Departments of War, of the Navy, and of the Treasury, were besieged by projectors with every imaginable and impossible scheme for saving the country, and demolishing the enemy. Torpedo balloons, electric-light balloons, wonderful compounds destined to supersede gunpowder and revolutionize the art of war; cheap methods for the manufacture of Government bonds and paper-money; multitudinous expedients for the prevention of counterfeiting, by devices in the engraving, by secret markings, by anti-photographic inks, by peculiar textures of paper, (applicable to coupons, to circulating notes, to revenue stamps,)—each warranted to be infallible; such were among the agencies by which patriotic patentees and adroit adventurers were willing to serve their country and to reap their reward by the moderate royalty or percentage due to the magnificence of the public benefit. Such were among the unenviable tasks of examination and adjudication accepted by Henry, only from an intrepid sense of duty.

"The course which has been pursued of rendering the Government in its late trials, every aid which could be supplied by scientific research, has been warmly approved. As most persons are probably entirely ignorant of the services really rendered to the Government by the Institution, I may here state the fact that a large share of my time, (all indeed which could be spared from official duties,) has been devoted for the last four years to investigations required by the public exigencies. Within this period, several hundred reports, requiring many experiments, and pertaining either to proposals purporting to be of high national importance, or relating to the quality of the multifarious articles offered in fulfillment of legal contracts, have been rendered. The opinions advanced in many of these reports, not only cost much valuable time, but also involved grave responsibilities. While on the one hand the rejection of a proposition would be in contravention to the high importance claimed for it by its author, on the other the approval of it would perhaps incur the risk of the fruitless expenditures of a large amount of public money. It is not necessary, I trust, to say that the labor thus rendered was entirely gratuitous, or that in the judgment pronounced in any case, no regard was paid to the inter-

ested solicitations or personal influence of the parties concerned: on
the contrary it has in some instances resulted from the examination
of materials sold to the Government, that attempted fraud has been
exposed, and the baffled speculator received his due reward in con-
demnation and punishment. These facts it is thought will be
deemed a sufficient answer to those who have seemed disposed to
reproach the Institution with the want of a more popular demonstration — but of a really far less useful or efficient aid in the
support of the Government." *

In the performance of these troublesome and often disagreeable
labors, conducted with the single aim necessitated by all his scientific habits and instincts, it of course resulted that a great majority
of his judgments and recommendations were decidedly adverse to
the hopes and wishes of the aspirants to fame and fortune. Having
once satisfied himself of the frivolity or the chicanery of an article
or project, his decision was inflexible; and although importunate
appeals to the Department Secretary, abetted by a prostituted
political or other influence, in one or two instances succeeded in
fastening for a time upon the public Treasury a worthless or a
noxious leech, the vast number of such, excluded from experimental imbibitions by Henry's critical supervision, must have been
a protection to the public interests quite beyond the reach of estimation: while on the other hand, the supplies of honest contractors
awarded their just commendation, and the rare proposals of real
merit favorably reported upon, which from a hasty survey might
have been confounded and overlaid with the mass of untried
puerilities, no less served to strengthen and assist the Government
during its years of greatest trial, need, and exhaustion.

From the outset of the unnatural sectional revolt, fully appreciating the vastness of the interests, the sacrifices, and the dangers
involved, Henry contemplated the crisis — not with despondency,
but with a profound sorrow and solicitude. While his sympathies
and his hopes were all for the preservation of the national integrity
of jurisdiction, he was little given to public exhibitions of his feelings. Undemonstrative — less from temperament than from the
deliberate and habitual subjection of emotional expression to reason,

---

* *Smithsonian Report* for 1864, p. 15.

during those times of feverish excitement apprehension and circumspection necessarily attendant on the prevalence of a gigantic rebellion, (unparalleled in incentive, in temper, and in magnitude,) many
of whose leaders had been among his personal friends, he was not
unnaturally looked upon by many as lukewarm in his patriotism,
if not disloyal in his citizenship. To the occasional innuendoes of
the press, he deigned no answer: he was the last man to accord
compliance with the urgency of a popular clamor. And yet during
the entire period of the Southern Insurrection, he was the personal
and trusted friend of President Lincoln. *

CONTRIBUTIONS TO SCIENCE AT WASHINGTON.

In addition to what may be called the public labors of Henry so
diligently performed in various fields after his advent to the Smithsonian Institution, it is well briefly to contemplate the special scientific work he was able to accomplish in the intervals of his exacting
occupations, that some estimate may be formed of the independent
value of his later contributions, as well as of his wonderful industry. While still engaged in his difficult task of organizing and
shaping the policy of the Institution, in 1850, on taking occasion
to present before the American Association at New Haven, Conn.

* Early in the war (in the autumn of 1861,) a caller at the Presidential Mansion
very anxious to see the Chief Magistrate of the nation, was informed that he
could not then be seen, being engaged in an important private consultation.
The caller not to be repulsed, wrote on a piece of paper that he must see Mr.
Lincoln personally, on a matter of vital and pressing importance to the public
welfare. This of course secured his admission to the presence of Mr. Lincoln,
who was sitting with a middle-aged gentleman. Observing the hesitancy of his
visitor, the President told him he might speak freely, as only a friend was
present. Whereupon the visitor announced that for several evenings past he
had observed a light exhibited on the highest of the Smithsonian towers, for a
few minutes about nine o'clock, with mysterious movements, which he felt
satisfied were designed as signals to the rebels encamped on Munson's hill in
Virginia. Having gravely listened to this information with raised eyebrows, but
a subdued twinkle of the eye, the President turned to his companion, saying
" What do you think of that? Professor Henry." Rising with a smile, the person
addressed replied, that from the time mentioned, he prepared the mysterious
light shone from the lantern of an attendant who was required at nine o'clock
each evening to observe and record the indications of the meteorological instruments placed on the tower. The painful confusion of the officious informant, at
once appealed to Henry's sensibility; and quite unmindful of the President, he
approached the visitor, offering his hand, and with a courteous regard committed
him never to be abashed at the issue of a conscientious discharge of duty, and
never to let the fear of ridicule interfere with its faithful execution.

a résumé of the electrical phenomena exhibited by the Leyden jar, and their true interpretation, he remarked that "for the last three and a half years, all his time and all his thoughts had been given to the details of the business of the Smithsonian Institution. He had been obliged to withdraw himself entirely from scientific research; but he hoped that now the Institution had got under way, and the Regents had allowed him some able assistants, that he would be enabled in part at least to return to his first love—the investigation of the phenomena of nature." [*]

Thermal Telescope.—Shortly after his establishment at Washington, he continued a series of former experiments with the "thermo-galvanic multiplicator" devised by Nobili and Melloni in 1831; and by some slight but significant modifications of the apparatus, he succeeded in imparting to it a most surprising delicacy of action. With the thermo-electric pile carefully adjusted at the focus of a suitable reflector, his "thermal telescope" when directed to the celestial vault, indicated that the heat radiated inward by our atmosphere when clear, is least at the zenith, and increases downward to the horizon; as was to have been inferred from its increasing mass: when directed to clouds, they were found to differ very widely accordingly as they were condensing or being dissipated; some even indicating a less amount of radiation than the surrounding atmosphere. When directed to a horse in a distant field, its animal heat concentrated on the pile, was distinctly made manifest on the galvanometer needle. Even the heat from a man's face at the distance of a mile could be detected; and that from the side of a house at several miles distance.[†] These and many similar observations demonstrated to sense the inductions of reason, that there is a constant and universal exchange by radiation in straight lines from every object in nature, following the same laws as the palpable emanation from incandescent bodies; and that even when the amplitude of the thermal vibrations (equivalent to the square root of their dynamic energy) is reduced a million fold, its existence may still be distinctly traced.

---

[*] *Proceed. Am. Assoc.* 4th Meeting, New Haven, Aug. 1850, p. 87.
[†] *Silliman's Am. Jour. Sci.* Jan. 1848, vol. v. pp. 113, 114.

Henry showed by experiment, that ice could be employed both as a convex lens for converging heat to a focus, and also as a concave mirror for the same purpose: a considerable portion of the incident rays being transmitted, a large portion reflected, and the remainder (a much smaller quantity) absorbed by the ice.

In 1849, for the purpose of estimating the effects of certain meteorological conditions of the atmosphere, he made some experiments on the lateral radiation from a current of ascending heated air at different distances above the flame; the latter being thoroughly eclipsed.

He also experimented on the radiation of heat from a hydrogen flame, which was shown to be quite small, notwithstanding the high temperature of the flame. By placing an infusible and incombustible solid in the flame, while the temperature is much reduced, the radiant light and heat are greatly increased:[*]—results closely analogous to those obtained by him in the differences between the audibility of vibrating tuning-forks when suspended by a soft thread, or when rigidly attached to a sounding-board. These results have also an undoubted significance with regard to celestial radiations; not only as to the differences between gaseous nebulæ and stars or clusters, but as to the differences between stars in a probably different state of condensation or of specific gravity.

A few years later, he continued his investigation of this subject of radiation, more especially with reference to Rumford's "Observations relative to the means of increasing the quantities of Heat obtained in the Combustion of Fuel:" published in Great Britain in 1802.[†] He found that Rumford's recommendation of the introduction of balls of clay or of fire brick (about two and a half inches in diameter) into a coal fire, was fully justified as an economic measure: more heat being thereby radiated from the fire into the room, and less being carried up the flue. He also showed however that for culinary purposes, while the incandescent or heated clay increases the *radiation*, and thereby improves the quality of the fire for *roasting*, it correspondingly expends the *temperature*, and thereby diminishes its power for *boiling*. "That a

* *Proceed. Am. Phil. Soc.* Oct. 19, 1849, vol. v. p. 108.
† *Journal Royal Institution*, 1802, vol. I. p. 39.

21

solid substance increases the radiation of the heat of a flame, is an
interesting fact in connection with the nature of heat itself.   It
would seem to show that the vibrations of gross matter are necessary to give sufficient intensity of impulse to produce the phenomena of ordinary radiant heat." [a]

In 1851, he read before the American Association at Albany, a
paper "On the Theory of the so-called Imponderables;" (mainly a
development of his earlier discussion in 1846,) of the molecular
constitution of matter,) in which he forcibly criticised a frequent
tendency to assume or multiply unknown and unrealizable modes
of action: holding that with regard to the most subtle agencies of
nature, we have no warrant by the strict scientific method, for
resorting to other than the observed and established laws of matter
and force, until it has been exhaustively demonstrated that these
are insufficient.   The fundamental laws of mechanical philosophy
"are five in number; viz. the two laws of force—attraction, and
repulsion, varying with some function of the distance; and secondly,
the three laws of motion—the law of inertia, of the co-existence
of motions, and of action and re-action.   Of these laws we can
give no explanation: they are at present considered as ultimate
facts; to which all mechanical phenomena are referred, or from
which they are deduced by logical inference.   The existence of
these laws as has been said, is deduced from the phenomena of the
operations of matter in masses; but we apply them by analogy to
the minute and invisible portions of matter which constitute the
atoms or molecules of gases, and we find that the inferences from
this assumption are borne out by the results of experience."   He
regarded the modern kinetic or dynamic theory of gases, by its
predictions and verifications, as furnishing almost a complete establishment of the atomic and molecular theory of matter.   Referring
to the ingenious hypothesis of Boscovich, he thought that though
well adapted to embrace the two static laws above mentioned, it did
not appear equally well adapted to satisfy in any intelligible sense
the three kinetic laws.   He contended that any attempt at conform-
ing our conception of the ultimate constitution of matter to the

* Proceed. Am. Assoc. Providence, Aug. 1855, pp. 112-118. "On the Effect of placing Radiating substances with Combustible Materials."

inductions of experience, would seem to conduct us directly to the
atomic hypothesis of Newton. A careful study of the dynamics
of the so-called "imponderables" certainly tended to their unifica-
tion. Admitting the difficulty of framing an entirely satisfactory
theory of the resultant transverse action of electricity, he suggested
that a tangential force was not accordant with any inductions from
actual experience; and was incapable of direct mechanical realization. Extending the atomic conception of matter to the ætherial
medium of space, he concluded by urging "the importance in the
adoption of mechanical hypotheses, of conditioning them in strict
accordance with the operations of matter under the known laws of
force and motion, as exhibited in time and space." *

Among the various public Addresses delivered by Henry on
special occasions, reference may be here made to his excellent exposition of the nature of power, and the functions of machinery
as its vehicle,—concluding with a sketch of the progress of art,
pronounced at the close of the Exhibition of the Metropolitan
Mechanics' Institute, in Washington, on the evening of March 19th,
1853. After representing to his hearers the close physical analogy
between the human body as a moving machine, and the steam locomotive under an intelligent engineer, he remarked: "In both, the
direction of power is under the influence of an immaterial, thinking, willing principle, called the soul. But this must not be confounded as it frequently is with the motive power. The soul of a
man no more moves his body, than the soul of the engineer moves
the locomotive and its attendant train of cars. In both cases the
soul is the directing, controlling principle; not the impelling
power." †

Views of Education.—Another address deserving of special notice
(delivered the following year,) is his introductory discourse before
the "Association for the Advancement of Education," as its retiring
President. In this, he maintained that inasmuch as "the several
faculties of the human mind are not simultaneously developed, in
educating an individual we ought to follow the order of nature, and
to adapt the instruction to the age and mental stature of the pupil.

* Proceed. Am. Assoc. Albany, Aug. 1851, pp. 81-91.
† Closing Address Metr. Mech. Inst. Washington, 1853, p. 19.

Memory, imitation, imagination, and the faculty of forming mental habits, exist in early life, while the judgment and the reasoning powers are of slower growth." Hence less attention should be given to the development of the reasoning faculties, than to those of observation: the juvenile memory should be stored rather with facts, than with principles: and he condemned as mischievous "the proposition frequently advanced, that the child should be taught nothing but what he can fully comprehend, and the endeavor in accordance with this, to invert the order of nature, and attempt to impart those things which cannot be taught at an early age, and to neglect those which at this period of life the mind is well adapted to receive. By this mode we may indeed produce remarkably intelligent children, who will become remarkably feeble men. The order of nature is that of art before science; the entire concrete first, and the entire abstract last. These two extremes should run gradually into each other, the course of instruction becoming more and more logical as the pupil advances in years."—"The cultivation of the imagination should also be considered an essential part of a liberal education: and this may be spread over the whole course of instruction, for like the reasoning faculties the imagination may continue to be improved until late in life."

Applying this same reasoning to the moral training of youth, he considered that (as in the intellectual culture) the object should be "not only to teach the pupil how to *think*, but how to *act* and to *do*; placing great stress upon the early education of the habits. - - - We are frequently required to act from the impulse of the moment, and have no time to deduce our course from the moral principles of the act. An individual can be educated to a strict regard for truth, to deeds of courage in rescuing others from danger, to acts of benevolence, generosity, and justice. - - - The future character of a child and that of the man also, is in most cases formed probably before the age of seven years. Previously to this time impressions have been made which shall survive amid the vicissitudes of life, amid all the influences to which the individual may be subjected, and which will outcrop as it were, in the last stage of his earthly existence, when the additions to his character made in later years, have been entirely swept away." Childhood (he intl-mated) is less the parent of manhood, than of age: the special vices of the individual child though long subdued, sometimes surviving and re-appearing in his "second childhood."

Affirming that culture is constraint,—education and direction an expenditure of force, and extending his generalization from the individual to the race, he controverted the idea so popular with some benevolent enthusiasts, that there is a spontaneous tendency in man to civilization and advancement. The origins of past civilizations — taking a comprehensive glance at far distant human populations — have been sporadic as it were, and their prevalence comparatively transitory. "It appears therefore that civilization itself may be considered as a condition of unstable equilibrium, which requires constant effort to be sustained, and a still greater effort to be advanced. It is not in my view the 'manifest destiny' of humanity to improve by the operation of an inevitable necessary law of progress: but while I believe that it is the design of Providence that man should be improved, this improvement must be the result of individual effort, or of the combined effort of many individuals animated by the same feeling and co-operating for the attainment of the same end. - - - If we sow judiciously in the present, the world will assuredly reap a beneficent harvest in the future: and he has not lived in vain, who leaves behind him as his successor, a child better educated—morally, intellectually, and physically, than himself. From this point of view, the responsibilities of life are immense. Every individual by his example and precept, whether intentionally or otherwise, does aid or oppose this important work, and leaves an impress of character upon the succeeding age, which is to mould its destiny for weal or woe, in all coming time. - - - The world however is not to be advanced by the mere application of truths already known: but we look forward (particularly in physical science) to the effort of the development of new principles. We have scarcely as yet read more than the title-page and preface of the great volume of nature, and what we do know is as nothing in comparison with that which may be yet unfolded and applied." *

* Prescott, Amer. Adv. Education, 4th Session, Washington, Dec. 28, 1854, pp. 17-31. The prevalent thought that human civilization is an artificial and coerced condition, would seem to have a suggestive bearing on the two great theories of

Experiments on Building-Stone.—In 1854, a series of experiments
on the strength of different kinds of building-stone, was undertaken
by Henry as one of a commission appointed by the President,
having reference to the marbles offered for the extension of the
United States Capitol. Specimens of the different samples — accurately cut to cubical blocks one inch and a half in height, were first
tried by interposing a thin sheet of lead above and below, between
the block and the steel plates of the crushing dynamometer. "This
was in accordance with a plan adopted by Rennie, and that which
appears to have been used by most if not all of the subsequent
experimenters in researches of this kind. Some doubt however
was expressed as to the action of interposed lead, which induced a
series of experiments to settle this question; when the remarkable
fact was discovered that the yielding and approximately equable
pressure of the lead caused the stone to give way at about half the
pressure it would sustain without such an interposition. For
example, one of the cubes precisely similar to another which with-
stood a pressure of upwards of 60,000 pounds when placed in
immediate contact with the steel plates, gave way at about 30,000
pounds with lead interposed. This interesting fact was verified in
a series of experiments embracing samples of nearly all the marbles under trial, and in no case did a single exception occur to vary
the result.

"The explanation of this striking phenomenon (now that the
fact is known) is not difficult. The stone tends to give way by
bulging out in the centre of each of its four perpendicular faces,
and to form two pyramidal figures with their apices opposed to
each other at the centre of the cube, and their bases against the
steel plates. In the case where rigid equable pressure is employed,
as in that of the thick steel plate, all parts must give way together.
But in that of a *yielding* equable pressure as in the case of inter-

development, and evolution, as generally contrasted by the superficial. What may
be called the radical difference between these two views of organic extension, is
that the former ascribes no inherent mysterious tendency to progression, whose
motto is ever "excelsior;" while the latter assumes a general tendency to variation within moderate limits in indefinite directions; so that elevation is no
more normal than degradation, and indeed may be regarded as rarer and more
exceptional, since at every upward stage attained by the few, there are probably
more further digressions downward than upward, the motto being ever "aspice."

posed lead, the stone first gives way along the outer lines or those of least resistance, and the remaining pressure must be sustained by the central portions around the vertical axis of the cube. After this important fact was clearly determined, lead and all other interposed substances were discarded, and a method devised by which the upper and lower surfaces of the cube could be ground into perfect parallelism. - - - All the specimens tested were subjected to this process, and on their exposure to pressure were found to give concordant results. The crushing force sustained was therefore much greater than that heretofore given for the same material." *

In the same communication, interesting remarks are made on the *tensile* strength of materials, particularly the metals. "According to the views presented, the difference in the tenacity in steel and lead does not consist in the attractive cohesion of the atoms, but in their capability of slipping upon each other;" that is on the difference of lateral *adhesion* of the molecules, as exemplified in ice and water. A bar of soft metal — as lead — subjected to tensile strain, by reason of the greater freedom of the exterior layers of molecules, exhibits a stretching and thinning; while the interior molecules being more confined by the surrounding pressure, are less mobile, permit less elongation of the mass, and are therefore the first to commence breaking apart. Accordingly on ultimate separation, each fragment exhibits a hollow or cup-like surface of fracture, where the interior portion of the material has first parted: the depth of the concavity being somewhat proportioned to the malleability or ductility of the substance. "With substances of greater rigidity, this effect is less apparent, but it exists even in iron, and the interior fibres of a rod of this metal may be entirely separated, while the outer surface presents no appearance of change. From this it would appear that metals should never be elongated by mere stretching, but in all cases by a process of wire-drawing, or rolling. A wire or bar must always be weakened by a force which permanently increases its length without at the same time compressing it." †

---

* Proceed. Am. Assoc. Providence, Aug. 1855, pp. 80-82.

† This conclusion is not at all in opposition to the ascertained fact of the increased strength imparted to soft iron rod by "thermotension," discovered by Professor WALTER R. JOHNSON, in 1836. (Journal of Franklin Institute, Oct. 1839, vol. xxiv. o. s. pp. 219-229.)

Hydrometric Experiment.—A novel project for the rectification of spirits by the simple process of static separation of the alcohol and water by the stress of their specific gravities when exposed in long columns, produced in 1854 a considerable sensation. It was alleged in various publications by those interested in the new enterprise, that the coercitive compression exerted by the water in a long hydrostatic column greatly accelerated the displacement and separation induced by gravitation, and that only a few hours were necessary to complete the process, if the depth of the liquid were sufficiently great.*

A patent was obtained: affidavits and samples fully attested the wonderful efficiency of the process; and only the co-operation of confiding capitalists was required, to realize fabulous profits, and effect a manufacturing and commercial revolution.

Simply in the interests of truth, Henry undertook the careful investigation of this surprising pretension. One of the towers of the Smithsonian Building supplied a convenient well for the experiment, easily accessible throughout its height. "A series of stout iron tubes of about an inch and a half internal diameter formed the column; the total length of which was one hundred and six feet. Four stop-cocks were provided; one at the bottom, one about four feet from the top, and the other two to the intermediate space equally divided or nearly so." Very careful hydrometer and thermometer registers were made at increasing intervals of time, the last being that of nearly half a year: a portion of the reserved liquor being simultaneously tested. The result stated, is: "There is not the slightest indication of any difference of density between the original liquor and that from the top or bottom of the column, after the lapse of hours, days, weeks, or months. The fluid at the bottom of the tube it must be remembered was for five months exposed to the pressure of a column of fluid at least one hundred feet high."†

---

* An incidental remark in Gmelin's "Handbook of Chemistry" seemed to give some color of plausibility to the scheme. "Brandy kept in casks is said to contain a greater proportion of spirit in the upper, and of water in the lower part." Gmelin's *Handbook*, Translated by Henry Watts, London, 1841, part I. sect. 4,—vol. I. p. 112.

† *Proceed. Am. Assoc.* Providence, Aug. 1855, pp. 162, 163.

Sulphuric-acid Barometer.—In 1858, Henry had constructed for the Smithsonian Institution, at the suggestion of Professor George C. Schaeffer, a large sulphuric-acid barometer, whose column being more than seven times the height of the mercurial column (almost 18½ feet) gave correspondingly enlarged and sensitive indications. Water barometers with cisterns protected by oil, (as that constructed by Daniell for the Royal Society,) have always proved instable. With reference to sulphuric acid, "The advantages of this liquid are: 1st that it gives off no appreciable vapor at any atmospheric temperature; and 2nd that it does not absorb or transmit air. The objections to its use are: 1st the liability to accident from the corrosive nature of the liquid, either in the filling of the tube or in its subsequent breakage; and 2nd its affinity for moisture, which tends to produce a change in specific gravity." The latter defect was obviated by a drying apparatus consisting of a tubulated bottle containing chloride of calcium, and connected by a tube with the glass bottle forming the reservoir, which excluded all moisture from the transmitted air. "The glass tube [of the barometer] is two hundred and forty inches long, and three-fourths of an inch in diameter; and is inclosed in a cylindrical brass case of the same length, and two and a half inches in diameter. The glass tube is secured in the axis of the brass case by a number of cork collars, placed at intervals." * This barometer continued in successful and satisfactory use for many years; and had its readings constantly recorded.

Of several of Henry's courses of experiments, no details have been published; and his original notes appear to have perished. In 1861, he made a number of experiments on the effects of burning gunpowder in a vacuum, as well as in different gases.

"A series of researches was also commenced, to determine more accurately than has yet been done, the expansion produced in a bar of iron at the moment of magnetization of the metal by means of a galvanic current. The opportunity was taken with the consent of Professor Bache, of making these experiments with the delicate instruments which had previously been employed in determining

---

* *Proceed. Am. Assoc. Albany, Aug. 1856, pp. 125-134.*

the varying length, under different temperatures, of the measuring apparatus of the base lines of the United States Coast Survey." [*] This wonderfully microscopic measuring apparatus—devised by Mr. Joseph Saxton, was capable of distinguishing (by means of the light-ray index of its contact reflector,) a dimension equal to a half wave-length of average light, or the 100,000th part of an inch. The long under-ground vaults of the Smithsonian building having been selected as a suitable place for the precise verification of the residual co-efficient of compensated temperature expansion of the base rods of the Survey, the opportunity was seized by Henry, at the termination of the investigation, to apply the same delicate apparatus to the determination of the polarized or magnetic expansion. The results of these delicate and interesting investigations are lost to the world.

In less than six years from the time of these researches, he was called on to mourn the death of his life-long intimate and honored friend, who had always exhibited so brotherly a sympathy and co-operation with his own varied labors. In consequence of this event—the death of his friend Professor A. Dallas Bache in 1867, Henry was chosen in 1868, to be his successor as President of the National Academy of Sciences. At the request of that body, he prepared a eulogy of his friend the late President, which was read before the Academy April 16th, 1869. In grateful acknowledgment of the wise counsels and valuable services of Dr. Bache as one of the Smithsonian Regents, he observed: "In 1846 he had been named in the act of incorporation as one of the Regents of the Smithsonian Institution, and by successive re-election was continued by Congress in this office until his death, a period of nearly twenty years. To say that he assisted in shaping the policy of the establishment would not be enough. It was almost exclusively through his predominating influence that the policy which has given the Institution its present celebrity, was after much opposition finally adopted. - - - Professor Bache with persistent firmness tempered by his usual moderation, advocated the appropriation of the proceeds of the funds principally to the plan set forth in the first

* Smithsonian Report for 1861, p. 36.

report of the Secretary, namely of encouraging and supporting
original research in the different branches of science. - - - It
would be difficult for the Secretary — however unwilling to intrude
anything personal on this occasion, to forbear mentioning that it
was entirely due to the persuasive influence of Professor Bache, that
he was induced — almost against his own better judgment, to leave
the quiet pursuit of science and the congenial employment of college instruction, to assume the laborious and responsible duties of
the office to which through the partiality of friendship he had been
called. Nor would it be possible for him to abstain from acknowl-
edging with heart-felt emotion, that he was from first to last supported and sustained in his difficult position by the fraternal
sympathy, the prudent counsel, and the unwavering friendship of
the lamented deceased." *

Many minor contributions in various fields of scientific observation, must here be omitted; but it would be inexcusable, in this
place and on this occasion, to neglect a reference to the active part
he took in the organization and advancement of this Society; † and
the unflagging interest ever exhibited in its proceedings, from the
date of its convocation, March 13th, 1871, to that of his last illness.
All here, remember with what punctuality he attended the meetings — whether of the executive committee or of the society,
undeterred by inclemencies of the weather which often kept away
many much younger members. All here, recall with what unpretentious readiness he communicated from his rich stores of well-
digested facts, observations — whether initiatory or supplementary,
on almost every topic presented to our notice; how apt his illustrations and suggestions in our spontaneous discussions; and with what
unfailing interest we ever listened to his words of exposition, of
knowledge, and of wisdom: utterances which we shall never hear
again; and which unwritten and unrecorded, have not been even
reported in an abstract.

---

* *Biographical Memoirs, Nat. Acad. Sci. vol. i. pp. 181-212. Republished in the Smithsonian Report for 1870, pp. 91-116. The father of Professor Bache—Richard Bache, was a son of the only daughter of the illustrious BENJAMIN FRANKLIN.*

† The Philosophical Society of Washington.

Range of information. — It was not alone in those physical branches of knowledge to which he had made direct original contributions, that the mental activities of Henry were familiarly exercised and conspicuously exhibited. There was scarcely a department of intellectual pursuit in which he did not feel and manifest a sympathetic interest, and in which he did not follow with appreciative grasp its leading generalizations. Holding ever to the unity of Nature as the expression and most direct illustration of the Unity of its Author, he believed that every new fact discovered in any of nature's fields, would ultimately be found to be in intimate correlation with the laws prevailing in other fields — seemingly the most distant. * To his large comprehension, nothing was insignificant, or unworthy of consideration. He ever sought however to look beyond the ascertained and isolated or classified fact, to its antecedent cause; and in opposition to the dogma of Comte, he averred that the knowledge of facts is not *science*, — that these are merely the materials from which its temple is constructed by the generalizations of sagacious and attested speculation.

Among his earlier studies, Chemistry occupied a prominent place. The youthful assistant in the laboratory of his former Instructor and ever honored friend, Dr. T. Romeyn Beck, and later, himself a teacher of the art and knowledge to others, a skillful manipulator, an acute analyst and investigator of re-actions, he seemed at first destined to become a leader in chemical research. Like Newton, he endeavored to bring the atomic combinations under the conception of physical laws; believing this essential to the development of chemistry as a true science. He always kept himself well-informed on the progress of the more recent doctrines of quantivalence, and the newer system of nomenclature.

He had also paid considerable attention to geology; with its relations to palæontology on the one side, and to physical geography on the other.

* "A proper view of the relation of science and art will enable him (the reader) to see that the one is dependent on the other; and that each branch of the study of nature is intimately connected with every other." (*Agricultural Report* for 1852, p. 419.) "The statement cannot be too often repeated, that each branch of knowledge is connected with every other, and that no light can be gained in regard to one, which is not reflected upon all." (*Smithsonian Report* for 1858, p. 13.)

As intimated in touching upon the stimulus given to "archæological work" by the Smithsonian publications, (*ante*, p. 200,) Henry ever displayed a warm sympathy with researches in Anthropology; and he would pleasantly justify this partiality by repeating the familiar "*homo sum*" of Terence." A student of the "comparative anatomy" of ethnology,—of the obscure but cumulative traces of a remote human ancestry,—and of the curious relics of social, civil, and religious customs, apparently derived from distant or from vanished races, he amassed a fond of well-digested information in these alluring fields, to be appreciated only by the specialist in such pursuits.

Familiar with the details—as well of astronomical observation as of the mathematical processes of reduction, he would have done honor to any Observatory placed under his charge. He was lenient in his judgment of the ancient star-worshippers; and was always greatly attracted by astronomical discoveries. As already mentioned (*ante*, p. 239,) he delivered in 1834, a course of Lectures on Astronomy.

Well read in the science of Political Economy, he had by observation and analysis of human nature, made its inductive principles his own, and had satisfied himself that its deductions were fully confirmed by an intelligent appreciation of the teachings of financial history. He attributed the lamentable disregard of its fundamental doctrines, by many of our so-called legislators, to a want of scientific training, and consequent want of perception and of faith in the dominion and autonomy of natural law.

A good linguist, he watched with appreciative interest the progress of comparative philology, and the ethnologic significance of its generalizations, in tracing out the affiliations of European nations. By no means neglectful of lighter literature, he enjoyed at leisure evenings, in the bosom of his cultivated family, the readings of modern writers, and the suggestive interchange of sentiment and criticism. Striking passages of poetry made a strong impression on his retentive memory; and it was not unusual to hear him embellish some graver fact, in conversation, with an unexpected but most apt quotation. With a fine æsthetic feeling, his appreciation and judgment of works of art, were delicate and discriminating.

Among the subjects to which he had given a close and critical attention, was the attractive field of Architecture, both in its historical development as a Fine-art—symbolizing devotional sentiment, and in its later manifestations as the application of antique and eclectic forms of ornamentation to utilitarian structures. His very admiration of ancient classic and gothic art, made him intolerant of the servile reproduction of Temple and Cathedral styles for purposes and uses to which they were wholly unsuited.* And he was severe in his criticisms on the too frequent practice of wasting a large portion of the funds bequeathed to scientific, educational, or charitable purposes, on showy and pretentious piles, (the inspiration and the monument of an ambitious architect,) to the permanent spoliation and restriction of the endowment intended for intellectual and moral ends.

The Reign of Law.—Henry held very broad and decided views as to the reign of order in the Cosmos. Defining science as the "knowledge of natural law," and law, as the "will of God," he was always accustomed to regard that orderly sequence called the "law," as being fixed and immutable as the omniscient providence of its Divine Author: admitting in no case caprice or variableness: and he would quote with expressive emphasis, Halley's classic lines,

> ——"Quæ dum primordia rerum
> Pangeret Omnipatens leges violare Creator
> Noluit, æternaque operis fundamina dedit."

* "The Greek architect was untrammelled by any condition of utility. Architecture was with him in reality a *flower*. The temple was formed to gratify the tutelar deity. Its minutest parts were exquisitely finished, since nothing but perfection on all sides and in the smallest particulars, could satisfy an observing and critical eye. It was intended for external worship, and not for internal use. . . . The uses therefore to which in modern times, buildings of this kind can be applied, are exceedingly few. . . . Modern architecture is not like painting or sculpture, a 'fine-art' *par excellence*; the object of these latter is to produce a moral emotion, to awaken the feelings of the sublime and the beautiful; and we egregiously err when we apply these productions to a merely utilitarian purpose. To make a fire-screen of Rubens' Madonna, or a candelabrum of the statue of the Apollo Belvidere, would be to debase these exquisite productions of genius, and do violence to the feelings of the cultivated lover of art. Modern buildings are made for other purposes than artistic effect, and in them the æsthetical must be subordinate to the useful; though the two may coexist, and an intellectual pleasure be derived from a sense of adaptation and fitness, combined with a perception of harmony of parts, and the beauty of detail. The buildings of a country and an age should be an ethnological expression of the wants, habits, arts, and sentiments of the time in which they were erected." (*Proceed. Am. Assoc.* at Albany, Aug. 1856, part i. pp. 129, 130, and *Smithsonian Report* for 1856, p. 224.)

The doctrine of the absolute dominion of law—so oppressive and alarming to many excellent minds, was to him accordingly but a necessary deduction from his theologic and religious faith.

The series of meteorological essays already referred to as contributed to the Agricultural Reports of the Commissioner of Patents, (ante, p. 290,) commences with this striking passage: "All the changes on the surface of the earth and all the movements of the heavenly bodies, are the immediate results of natural forces acting in accordance with established and invariable laws; and it is only by that precise knowledge of those laws, which is properly denominated science, that man is enabled to defend himself against the adverse operations of Nature, or to direct her innate powers in accordance with his will. At first sight, it might appear that meteorology was an exception to this general proposition, and that the changes of the weather and the peculiarities of climate in different portions of the earth's surface, were of all things the most uncertain and farthest removed from the dominion of law: but scientific investigation establishes the fact that no phenomenon is the result of accident, or even of fitful volition. The modern science of statistics has revealed a permanency and an order in the occurrence of events depending on conditions in which nothing of this kind could have been supposed. Even those occurrences which seem to be left to the free will, the passion, or the greater or less intelligence of men, are under the control of laws—fixed, immutable, and eternal." And after dwelling on the developments and significance of moral statistics, he adds: "The astonishing facts of this class lead us inevitably to the conclusion that all events are governed by a Supreme Intelligence who knows no change; and that under the same conditions, the same results are invariably produced." *

Organic Dynamics.—The contemplation of these uniformities leads naturally to the great modern generalization of the correlation of all the working energies of nature: and this to the subject of organic dynamics. "Modern science has established by a wide and careful induction, the fact that plants and animals consist princi-

* Agricultural Report Com. Pat. for 1855, pp. 207, 208.

pally of solidified air; the only portions of an earthy character which enter into their composition, being the ashes that remain after combustion." Some ten years before this, or in 1844, (as already noticed in an earlier part of this memoir,—ante, p. 273,) Henry had very clearly indicated the correlation between the forces exhibited by inorganic and organic bodies: arguing that from the chemical researches of Liebig, Dumas, and Boussingault, "it would appear to follow that animal power is referable to the same sources as that from the combustion of fuel:" * probably the earliest explicit announcement of the now accepted view. In the series of agricultural essays above referred to, he endeavored to frame more definitely a chemico-physical theory by which the elevation of matter to an organic combination in a higher state of power than its source, might be accounted for. Regarding "vitality" not as a mechanical force, but as an inscrutable *directing* principle resident in the minute germ — supposed to be vegetative, and inclosed in a sac of starch or other organic nutriment, he considered the case of such provisioned germ (a bean or a potato for instance) embedded in the soil, supplied with a suitable amount of warmth and moisture to give the necessary molecular mobility, soon sending a rootlet downward into the earth, and raising a stem toward the surface, furnished with incipient leaves. Supposing the planted germ to be a potato, on examination we should find its large supply of starch exhausted, and beyond the young plant, nothing remaining but the skin, containing probably a little water. What has become of the starch? "If we examine the soil which surrounded the potato, we do not find that the starch has been absorbed by it; and the answer which will therefore naturally be suggested, is that it has been transformed into the material of the new plant, and it was for this purpose originally stored away. But this though in part correct, is not the whole truth: for if we weigh a potato prior to germination, and weigh the young plant afterward, we shall find that the amount

* Proceed. Am. Phil. Soc. Dec. 1844, vol. iv. p. 128. The admirable treatise of Dr. Julius R. Mayer of Heilbronn, on "Organic Movement in its relation to material changes," in which for the first time he maintained the thesis that all the energies developed by animal or vegetable organisms, result from internal changes having their dynamic source in external forces, was published the following year, or in 1845. Grove nearly half a century earlier, had a partial grasp of the same truth. (Phil. Trans. R. S. Jan. 25, 1798, vol. lxxxviii. pp. 30-132.)

of organic matter contained in the latter, is but a fraction of that
which was originally contained in the former. We can account in
this way for the disappearance of a *part* of the contents of the sac,
which has evidently formed the pabulum of the young plant. But
here we may stop to ask another question: By what power was the
young plant built up of the molecules of starch? The answer
would probably be, by the exertion of the vital force: but we have
endeavored to show that vitality is a *directing principle*, and not a
mechanical power, the expenditure of which does work. The conclusion to which we would arrive will probably now be anticipated.
The portion of the organic molecules of the starch, &c. of the
tuber, as yet unaccounted for, has run down into inorganic matter,
or has entered again into combination with the oxygen of the air,
and in this running down and union with oxygen, has evolved the
power necessary to the organisation of the new plant. - - - We
see from this view that the starch and nitrogenous materials in
which the germs of plants are imbedded, have two functions to
fulfill, the one to supply the pabulum of the new plant, and the
other to furnish the power by which the transformation is effected,
the latter being as essential as the former. In the erection of a
house, the application of mechanical power is required as much as
a supply of ponderable materials."

The less difficult problem of the building up of the plant after
the consumption of the seed, under the direct action of the solar
rays, is then considered; the leaves of the young plant absorbing
by their moisture carbonic acid from the atmosphere, which being
decomposed by solar actinism, yields the de-oxidised carbon to enter

* *Agricultural Report*, for 1857, pp. 68-84. In May, 1842, Dr. Julius R. Mayer
published in Liebig's *Annalen der Chemie* etc. his first remarkable paper on
"The Forces of Inorganic Nature," constituting the earliest scientific enunciation
of the correlation of the physical forces; and (if we except the work of Séguin in
1839,) of the mechanical equivalent of heat. (*Annalen* s.a.w. vol. xlii. pp. 233-240.)
In September, 1858, Dr. R. Fowler read a short paper before the British Association at Birmingham, on "Vitality as a Force correlated with the Physical
Forces." (*Report Brit. Assoc.* 1858, part ii. pp. 77, 78.) In June, 1859, Dr. W. R. Carpenter presented to the Royal Society a much fuller memoir "On the Mutual
Relations of the Vital and Physical Forces." (*Phil. Trans. R. S.* vol. cxl. pp.
727-757.) Neither of these essays accounts for the amount of building energy displayed in the development of the seed, under conditions of low and diffused
heat: and the expression "Vital Force" used both by Fowler and Carpenter,
was studiously avoided by Henry.

29

into the structure of the organism. "All the material of which a
tree is built up, (with the exception of that comparatively small
portion which remains after it has been burnt, and constitutes the
ash,) is derived from the atmosphere. In the decomposition of the
carbonic acid by the chemical ray, a definite amount of power is
expended, and this remains as it were locked up in the plant so long
as it continues to grow." And thus under the expenditure of an
external force, the plant (whether the annual cellular herb or the
perennial fibrous tree) was shown to be built up from the simpler
stable binary compounds of the inorganic world to the more complex and unstable ternary compounds of the vegetable world. "In
the *germination* of the plant, a part of the organized molecules
runs down into carbonic acid to furnish power for the new arrangement of the other portion. In this process no extraneous force is
required: the seed contains within itself the power, and the
material, for the growth of the new plant up to a certain stage
of its development. Germination can therefore be carried on
in the dark, and indeed the chemical ray which accompanies light
retards rather than accelerates the process." This important
organic principle appears to receive in these passages its earliest
enunciation.

It was also pointed out that on the completion of the cycle of
growth (however brief or however extended), the decay of the
plant not only returns the elevated matter to its original lower
plane, but equally returns the entire amount of heat energy
absorbed in its elevation: an amount precisely the same, whether
the slow oxidation be continued through a series of years, or a
rapid combustion be completed in as many minutes. "The power
which is given out in the whole descent is according to the dynamic
theory, just equivalent to the power expended by the impulse from
the sun in elevating the atoms to the unstable condition of the
organic molecules. If this power is given out in the form of
vibrations of the etherial medium constituting heat, it will not be
appreciable in the ordinary decay say of a tree, extending as it may
through several years: but if the process be rapid, as in case of
combustion of wood, then the same amount of power will be given
out in the energetic form of heat of high-intensity."

The elevation of inorganic matter (carbonic acid, water, and ammonia,) to the vegetable plane of power, introduces naturally the consideration of the still higher elevation of vegetable organic matter to the animal plane of power. "As in the case of the seed of the plant, we presume that the germ of the future animal pre-exists in the egg; and that by subjecting the mass to a degree of temperature sufficient perhaps to give greater mobility to the molecules, a process similar in its general effect to that of the germination of the seeds commences. - - - During this process, power is evolved within the shell, we cannot say in the present state of science under what particular form; but we are irresistibly constrained to believe that it is expended under the direction again of the vital principle, in re-arranging the organic molecules, in building up the complex machinery of the future animal, or developing a still higher organization, connected with which are the mysterious manifestations of thought and volition. In this case as in that of the potato, the young animal as it escapes from the shell, weighs less than the material of the egg previous to the process of incubation. The lost material in this case as in the other, has run down into an inorganic condition by combining with oxygen, and in its descent has developed the power to effect the transformation we have just described." The consumption of internal power does not however stop with the development of the young animal, as it does in the case of the young plant. "The young animal is in an entirely different condition; exposure to the light of the sun is not necessary to its growth or its existence: the chemical ray by impinging on the surface of its body does not decompose the carbonic acid which may surround it, the conditions necessary for this decomposition, not being present. It has no means by itself to elaborate organic molecules; and is indebted for these entirely to its food. It is necessary therefore that it should be supplied with food consisting of organized materials; that is of complex molecules in a state of power. - - - The power of the living animal is immediately derived from the running down of the complex organized molecules of which the body is formed, into their ultimate combination with oxygen, in the form of carbonic acid and water, and into ammonia. Hence oxygen is constantly drawn into the lungs, and carbon is constantly evolved. - - - The animal is a curiously contrived arrangement for burning carbon and hydrogen, and for the evolution and application of power. A machine is an instrument for the application of power, and not for its creation. The animal body is a structure of this character. - - - A comparison has been made between the work which can be done by burning a given amount of carbon in the machine—man, and an equal amount in the machine—steam-engine. The result derived from an analysis of the food in one case, and the weight of the fuel in the other, and these compared with the quantity of water raised by each to a known elevation, gives the relative working value of the two machines. From this comparison, made from experiments on soldiers in Germany and France, it is found that the human machine in consuming the same amount of carbon, does four and a half times the amount of work of the best Cornish engine. - - -

"There is however one striking difference between the animal body and the locomotive machine, which deserves our special attention; namely the power in the body is constantly evolved by burning (as it were,) parts of the materials of the machine itself; as if the frame and other portions of the wood-work of the locomotive were burnt to produce the power, and then immediately renewed. The voluntary motion of our organs of speech, of our hands, of our feet, and of every muscle in the body, is produced not at the expense of the soul but at that of the material of the body itself. Every motion manifesting life in the individual, is the result of power derived from the death as it were of a part of his body. We are thus constantly renewed and constantly consumed; and in this consumption and renewal consists animal life." *

Seven years after the publication of this highly original and suggestive exposition, (whose topics and line of discussion had been

* Agricultural Report for 1857, pp. 115-440. This important essay it will be observed, antedates Prof. JOSEPH LE CONTE's paper "On the Correlation of Physical, Chemical, and Vital Force," read before the American Association at Springfield, Aug. 1859, (Proceed. Am. Assoc. pp. 187-204; and Sill. Am. Jour. Sci. Nov. 1859, vol. xxviii, pp. 305-319,) as well as Dr. CARPENTER's second and more mature paper "On the application of the Principle of Conservation of Force to Physiology," published in Crooke's Quarterly Journal of Science, for Jan. and April, 1864, (vol. I, pp. 78-97; and pp. 229-307.)

distinctly formulated and sketched out more than two years before, at the commencement of the series (in 1855,) the eminent physiologist Dr. Carpenter produced his valuable memoir on the Conservation of Force in Physiology; in which for the first time he distinctly affirms the development of vegetative reproductive energy, by the partial running down of matter to its stabler compounds,— "by the retrograde metamorphosis of a portion of the organic compounds prepared by the previous nutritive operations;" and also the ultimate return by decay, of the whole amount of force as well as of matter, temporarily borrowed from nature's store. Likewise with animal powers, "these forces are developed by the retrograde metamorphosis of the organic compounds generated by the instrumentality of the plant, whereby they ultimately return to the simple binary forms (water, carbonic acid, and ammonia,) which serve as the essential food of vegetables. - - - Whilst the vegetable is constantly engaged (so to speak) in raising its component materials from a lower plane to the higher, by means of the power which it draws from the solar rays,—the animal whilst raising one portion of these to a still higher level by the descent of another portion to a lower, ultimately lets down the whole of what the plant had raised." * So little was Henry's earlier paper known abroad, that his name does not occur in Dr. Carpenter's dissertation.

Derivation of Species.—With regard to the great biologic question of the past fifteen years—the affiliation of specific forms, it was impossible that Henry should remain an unconcerned observer. Brought up (as it may be said) in the school of Cuvier, but slightly impressed with the brilliant previsions of his competitor, Geoffroy Saint Hilaire, accustomed to look upon the recurrent hypotheses of automatic development as barren speculations, and beside all this, ever the warmly attached personal friend of Agassiz, he approached the consideration of this controverted subject, certainly with no antecedent affirmative pre-possessions. His general acquaintance with the ascertained facts of the metamorphic development of the individual organism from its origin, as well as with the remarkable analogies and homologies disclosed by the sciences of comparative

---

* Quart. Jour. Sci. 1861, vol. I. pp. 47 and 257.

physiology and embryology, served however in some measure to
prepare his mind to apprehend the significance of the indications
which had been so industriously collected, and so intelligently
collated: and from the very first, he accepted the problem as a
purely philosophical one; employing that much abused term in no
restricted sense. With no more reserve in the expression of his
views, than the avoidance of unprofitable controversies, (though no
one more than he—enjoyed the calm and purely intellectual discussion of an unsettled question by its real experts,) he yet found
no occasion to write upon the subject. The unpublished opinions
however, of one so wise and eminent, cannot be a matter of indifference to the student of nature; and their exposition cannot but assist
to enlighten our estimate of the mental stature of the man, and of
his breadth of apprehension and toleration.

Whatever may be the ultimate fate of the theory of natural
selection, (he remarked in the freedom of oral intercourse with
several naturalists,) it at least marks an epoch, —the first elevation
of natural history (so-called) to the really scientific stage: it is
based on induction, and correlates a large range of apparently dis-
connected observations, gathered from the regions of palæontology
or geological successions of organisms, their geographical distribution, climatic adaptations and remarkable re-adjustments, their
comparative anatomy, and even the occurrence of abnormal variations, and of rudimentary structures—seemingly so uselessly displayed as mere simulations of a "type." It forms a grand "working
hypothesis" for directing the investigations of the botanist and
zoologist. [*]   Natural selection indeed—no less than artificial, (he
was accustomed to say,) is to a limited extent a fact of observation;
and the practical question is to determine approximately its reach
of application, and its sufficiency as an actual agency, to embrace
larger series of organic changes lying beyond the scope of direct
human experience. It is for the rising generation of conscientious
zoologists and botanists to attack this problem, and to ascertain if
practicable its limitations or modifications.

[*] "In the investigation of nature, we provisionally adopt hypotheses as antecedent probabilities, which we seek to prove or disprove by subsequent observation and experiment: and it is in this way that science is most rapidly and
securely advanced." (Agricult. Report, 1858, p. 458.)

These broad and fearless views, entertained and expressed as early as 1860, or 1861, exhibiting neither the zealous confidence of the votary, nor the jealous anxiety of the antagonist, received scarcely any modification during his subsequent years. Nor did it ever seem to occur to him that any reconstruction of his religious faith was involved in the solution of the problem. So much religious faith indeed was exercised by him in every scientific judgment, that he regarded the teachings of science but as revelations of the Divine mode of government in the natural world: to be diligently sought for and submissively accepted; with the constant recognition however of our human limitations, and the relativity of human knowledge. * Not inappropriately may be here recalled a characteristic statement of the office of hypothesis, made by him some ten years earlier: presenting a consideration well calculated to restrain dogmatism — whether in science or in theology. " It is not necessary that an hypothesis be absolutely true, in order that it may be adopted as an expression of a generalization for the purpose of explaining and predicting phenomena: it is only necessary that it should be well conditioned in accordance with known mechanical principles. - - - Man with his finite faculties cannot hope in this life to arrive at a knowledge of absolute truth: and were the true theory of the universe, or in other words the precise mode in which Divine Wisdom operates in producing the phenomena of the material world revealed to him, his mind would be unfitted for its reception. It would be too simple in its expression, and too general in its application, to be understood and applied by intellects like ours." †

INVESTIGATIONS IN ACOUSTICS.

During the last quarter of a century, among the many interests which demanded and engaged his attention, Henry studied with

---

* With reference to the intimations of the comparative antiquity of man, Henry quoted with sympathetic approbation the sentiment so well expressed by the Bishop of London in a Lecture at Edinburgh, that "The man of science should go on honestly, patiently, diffidently, observing and storing up his observations, and carrying his reasonings unflinchingly to their legitimate conclusions, convinced that it would be treason to the majesty at once of science and of religion, if he sought to help either by swerving ever so little from the straight line of truth." (Smithsonian Report for 1868, p. 43.)

† Proceed. Am. Assoc. Albany, Aug. 1851, pp. 85, 86, and 87.

much care various phenomena of acoustics, and added much to our practical as well as theoretical knowledge of that important agency —sound. In 1851, he read a communication before the American Association, "On the Limit of Perceptibility of a direct and reflected Sound," in which he gave as the result of experimental observations, the subjective fact that a wall or other reflecting surface if beyond the distance of about 35 feet from the ear, or from the origin of the sound, gives a distinguishable echo from the sound; but that if the ear or the sounding agent be placed within this distance, the reflected sound appears to blend completely with the original one. From a number of experiments, he found that under the same circumstances, this limit of perceptibility did not vary more than a single foot; but that under differing conditions the limit of distance ranged from 30 to 40 feet, (equivalent to a difference of from 60 to 80 feet of sound travel,) depending partly on the sharpness or clearness of the sound, and partly on the pitch or the length of the soniferous wave, which affected the amount of overlapping of the two series. These results imply a duration of acoustic impression on the ear of about one-sixteenth of a second; serving to show that 10 vibrations to the second must be about the lower limit of a recognizable musical tone. * As applied to Lecture-rooms, he pointed out that the ceiling should not be more than about thirty feet high, within which elevation, a smooth ceiling would tend to re-inforce the sound of a speaker's voice. †

Many experiments were afterward made on the resonance of different materials, by means of tuning forks. While a tuning fork suspended by a fine thread continued to vibrate for upward of four minutes with scarcely any appreciable sound, if placed in contact with the top of a pine table, the same vibration continued but ten seconds, but gave a loud full tone. On a marble topped table the sound was much more feeble, and the vibration continued nearly two minutes. While the tuning fork against a brick wall gave a

* FELIX SAVART some twenty years previously, concluded from observations with the siren, "that sounds are distinctly perceptible, and even strong, when composed of no more than eight vibrations in a second." (See Savart, July, 1830. Quoted in Silliman's Am. Jour. Sci. for 1832, vol. XXII. p. 371.) This does not seem to agree with ordinary observations, as it is certain that intervals of one-eighth of a second would give a very appreciable rattle to almost every ear.

† Proceed. Am. Assoc. (Cincinnati, May, 1851, pp. 62, 63.

feeble tone continuing for 88 seconds, against a lath and plaster partition it gave a sound considerably louder but continuing only 18 seconds. On a large block of soft india-rubber resting on the marble slab, the vibration was very rapidly extinguished, but without giving any sensible sound. This anomaly required an explanation. By means of a compound wire of copper and iron inserted into the piece of rubber, and having the extremities connected with a thermo-galvanometer, it was found that in this case the acoustic vibrations were converted into heat. Sheets of india-rubber therefore are among the best absorbers and destroyers of sound. A series of experiments was also made on the reflection of sound, to determine the materials least adapted, and those best adapted to this purpose. A résumé of these researches, having reference to the acoustic properties of public halls, was read before the American Association in August, 1856.[*]

In 1865, as Chairman of the Committee of Experiments of the U. S. Light-House Board, Henry commenced an extended series of observations on the conduct and intensity of sound at a distance, under varying meteorological conditions. Well aware that for the practical purposes of giving increased security to navigation, the experiments of the laboratory were of little value, he undertook a number of experimental trips on board sailing vessels, and on steamers, in order to make his observations under the actual conditions of the required service. As many of his investigations demanded intelligent co-operation, and sometimes at the distances of many miles, he associated with him at different times, among members of the Light-House Establishment, Commodore Powell, Commodore Case, Admiral Trenchard, Commander Walker, Captain Upshur, General Poe, General Barnard, General Woodruff, Mr. Lederle, and other engineers of different Light-House Districts, and outside of the establishment, Dr. Welling and others.

At the outset of his experiments, he found that sound reflectors, which play so interesting a part in lecture-room exhibitions, were practically worthless (of whatever available dimensions) for the purpose of directing or concentrating powerful sounds to any con-

* Proceed. Am. Assoc. Albany, Aug. 1856, pp. 129-131.

siderable distance.   At the distance of a mile or two a large steam
whistle placed in the focus of a concave reflector 10 feet in diameter
could be heard very nearly as well directly behind the reflector, as
directly in front of it.   In like manner the direction of bell-
mouths and of trumpet-mouths, was found to be of comparatively
little importance at a distance; showing the remarkable tendency
to diffusion, especially with very loud sounds.   Most of the observations made on ship-board were afterward repeated on land; and
several weeks were occupied with these important researches.

"During this series of investigations an interesting fact was discovered, namely, a sound moving against the wind, inaudible to the
ear on the deck of the schooner, was heard by ascending to the
mast-head.   This remarkable fact at first suggested the idea that
sound was more readily conveyed by the upper current of air than
the lower."   After citing observations by others apparently confirming the suggestion of some dominant influence in the upper
wind, Henry adds: "The full significance however of this idea did
not reveal itself to me until in searching the bibliography of
sound, I found an account of the hypothesis of Professor Stokes in
the Proceedings of the British Association for 1857,* in which the
effort of an upper current in deflecting the wave of sound so as to
throw it down upon the ear of the auditor, or directing it upward
far above his head, is fully explained." †   A rough attempt was
made in the course of these observations (which were undertaken
at the Light-house near New Haven, Connecticut) to compare the
velocity of the wind in the upper regions with that near the surface
of the earth.   "The only important result however was the fact
that the velocity of the shadow of a cloud passing over the ground
was much greater than that of the air at the surface, the velocity
of the latter being determined approximately by running a given
distance with such speed that a small flag was at rest along the side
of its pole.   While this velocity was not perhaps greater than six
miles per hour, that of the shadow of the cloud was apparently
equal to that of a horse at full speed." ‡

---

* Report Brit. Assoc. Dublin, 1857, vol. xxvii. 2d part, pp. 22, 23.
† Report of Light-House Board for 1874, p. 82.
‡ This difference has since been established by a number of independent
observations.   Mr. Glaisher from his balloon ascents in 1862-1866, ascertained that

In October, 1867, a series of observations was made at Sandy
Hook (New Jersey) with various instruments. A sound reflector
being employed, the distance at which the sand on the phonometer
drum — carried in front, ceased to move was 51 yards, as compared
with a distance of 40 yards, without the reflector. At a greater
distance, with a more sensitive instrument, the ratio was very much
diminished. Experiments were also made on the relative distances
at which the trumpet affected sensibly the drum of the phonometer
in different directions, giving as their result a limiting spheroid
whose reach in the forward axis of the trumpet was about double
that in the rear axis, and at right angles to the axis, was about a
mean proportional between the two. With greater distances, these
differences were evidently very much reduced, the radii becoming
more equalized. In the summer of 1871, Henry made investigations at different Light-stations, on our western coast of California.

'.The very important observation that a sound could best be heard
at an elevation when the wind is adverse (that is when it blows
from the observer towards the acoustic signal,) and that after it had
even been entirely lost to the ear in such case, it might be regained
in full force by simply ascending to a suitable elevation,— admitted
apparently but one explanation, namely that the line of successive
impulse constituting a sound-beam was deflected or bent upwards
by the action of the opposing wind. If—as had already been
shown to be the case sometimes, and as might therefore be expected
generally,—the adverse wind were assumed to be a little stronger
at the elevation than at the surface, such a result would at once
follow. "The explanation of this phenomenon as suggested by the
hypothesis of Professor Stokes is founded on the fact that in the
case of a deep current of air the lower stratum or that next the
earth is more retarded by friction than the one immediately above,

the upper currents of air are frequently five or six times more rapid than the
surface currents. (Travels in the Air, p. 8.) Prof. Cleveland Abbe remarks: "From
seven balloon ascensions made on July 4th, 1871, at different points in the United
States, I have deduced the velocity of the upper currents as about four times that
of the surface wind prevailing." (Bulletin Philosoph. Soc. Washington, Dec. 16, 1871,
vol. I, p. 39.) And M. Prado states in general terms: "It is certain according to
all observations made both in mountains and in balloons, that the force of the
wind increases considerably as we ascend in the atmosphere." (Bulletin International de l'Observ. de Paris et de l'Observ. Phys. Prof. Montsouris, July 7, 1872.)

and this again than the one above it, and so on. The effect of this diminution of velocity as we descend toward the earth is in the case of sound moving with the current, to carry the upper part of the sound waves more rapidly forward than the lower parts, thus causing them to incline toward the earth, or in other words, to be thrown down upon the ear of the observer. When the sound is in a contrary direction to the current, an opposite effect is produced, the upper portion of the sound-waves is more retarded than the lower, which advancing more rapidly in consequence, inclines the waves upward and directs them above the head of the observer." *

From several observed and reported cases where the sound of a fog-signal was exceptionally heard to a greater distance against the wind than toward the direction of the wind, Professor Henry for a while hesitated to give the hypothesis of Professor Stokes an unqualified acceptance; but forced as he was constantly to recur to it as the only plausible explanation of the ordinary influence of wind on the transmission of sound, he finally was able to satisfy himself that even the apparent exceptions to the rule were really in accord with it. Having more than once observed that when the upper current of air, as indicated by the course of the clouds, is in an opposite or different direction from the lower or sensible wind, the range of audibility is more affected and favored by the upper current, it was a natural induction to extend such a condition in imagination to other cases of abnormal behavior of sound. A large amount of subsequent labor and attention was devoted to the determination of this important question.

In 1872 it was observed from on board a steamer approaching Portland Head station in the harbor of Portland (Maine) that the fog-signal which had been distinctly heard through many miles, was lost to the ear when within two or three miles of the point, that it continued inaudible throughout the nearer distance of a mile or so, and that it was again heard as the station was neared. At Whitehead light station on a small rocky island about a mile and a half from the coast, (being some 65 miles northeast of Portland Head,) it was observed on board a steamer approaching the station during a thick fog, that the signal (a 10-inch steam whistle) though

* Report of Light-House Board for 1874, p. 98.

distinctly heard at the distance of six miles or more, and with
increasing distinctness as the steamer advanced, was suddenly lost
at about three miles, and was not recovered until within a quarter
of a mile from the station; the wind at the time being approximately adverse to the sound. A six-inch steam whistle on board
the steamer was meanwhile distinctly heard at the station during
the whole time of inaudibility of the larger ten-inch whistle, which
had also been sounded without any interruption. This remarkable
phenomenon implied a compound flexure of the sound-beams, and
accorded with previous observations made at the same points by
General Doane the engineer in charge of the first and second Light-
House Districts.

In 1873 observations were again made at Whitehead station, and
at Cape Elizabeth light station, both on the coast of Massachusetts.
At Whitehead the steam whistle was heard through a distance of
15 miles, with a light adverse wind. At Cape Elizabeth, with a
stronger adverse wind, the siren was heard only about nine miles.

In 1874, observations were made at Little Gull island, (off the
coast of Connecticut;) at Block island, (off the coast of Rhode
Island;) and at Sandy Hook, (New Jersey.) At Little Gull island
the sound of a siren was heard against a moderate wind, only three
and a half miles. At Block island the siren was reported to have
been heard under favoring conditions of wind through a distance
of more than 25 miles. While it was frequently heard at Point
Judith station, and the siren at the latter point was as frequently
heard at Block Island, (the distance between the two points being
17 miles,) it was shown on comparison of records, that the two
instruments had not been heard simultaneously; the wind when
favorable to the one being unfavorable to the other.

At Sandy Hook, for the purpose of making simultaneous observations in different directions, three steamers (the tenders of different light-houses) were employed, with steam whistles specially
adjusted to the same tone and power. The latter quality having
been carefully tested by the phonometer, the three vessels steamed
out abreast on trial; and their whistles sounding in regular succession "became inaudible all very nearly at the same moment." One
of the vessels being then anchored at a distance from land, the two

others were directed in opposite courses, one with the wind, or eastward, the other against it, or westward. In 15 minutes the whistle of the former ceased to be heard, while that of the latter was very distinctly heard; the anemometer showing a wind of about six miles per hour. About noon the vessels changed positions, but the sound from the west continued audible for about three times the distance of that from the east, though the wind had declined to nearly a calm or to about half a mile per hour. In an hour and a half the wind had changed to "within two points of an exactly opposite direction, blowing from the indications of the anemometer at the rate of ten and a half miles per hour." The vessels once more departing, one with the wind, the other against it, the sound of the whistle coming against the wind was this time heard for the greater distance, contrary to expectation. On the following day a number of small balloons having been provided, a similar series of experiments to that of the preceding day was made; a station being selected at a greater distance from land. On the first trial, with a light wind from the west of about one and a quarter miles per hour as indicated by the anemometer, a balloon was set off which continued rising and moving eastward till lost to sight. Two of the vessels taking opposite courses as before, gave the sound in the direction of the wind about double the duration of that coming against the slight wind. The vessels then changed places in their opposite courses; the wind having subsided to a calm. "A balloon let off ascended vertically until it attained an elevation of about 1,000 feet, when turning east it followed the direction of the previous one. In this case the sound of the whistle coming from the east was heard somewhat longer than the opposite one. At the third trial made after noon, the wind had changed nearly one-third of the circle, its force being about five miles per hour. The vessels once more taking their courses with the wind and against it, "several balloons set off at this time were carried by the surface wind westwardly until nearly lost to sight, when they were observed to turn east, following the direction of the wind traced in the earlier observations." In this case the sound was heard with the wind very slightly farther than against it. It was thus shown that the upper current of wind had remained constant throughout the day, while

the changing surface wind was apparently a land and sea breeze
"due to the heating of the land as the day advanced;" and the
varying behavior of the sound-beams was easily explained by the
varying differences of velocity in their wave fronts at different
heights.

In 1875 Henry continued his observations at Block island, (R. I.)
and at Little Gull island: (Conn.) The southern light-house on
Block island standing on the edge of a perpendicular cliff 152 feet
above the sea level, and being itself 82 feet high (to its focal plane)
this point was selected for making investigations on the effect of
altitude in modifying unfavorable conditions of audibility. Observers were accordingly stationed on the beach at the foot of the cliff,
and also on the tower 200 feet above, to record simultaneously the
duration of the whistle signals of two steamers proceeding in opposite directions toward the right and the left. The sound coming
against the wind (of about seven miles per hour) continued audible
at the upper station four times longer, (i. e. for four times greater
distance) than at the lower station. The sound coming with the
wind, was unexpectedly heard at the lower station for a longer
period than at the upper one. Another observation (with the wind
about five miles per hour) gave for the sound against the wind,
rather more than twice the distance of audibility at the upper
station; and for the sound favored by the wind, a slightly greater
distance at the top than at the bottom station. The next observation gave as before, with the adverse wind, the advantage of more
than double the distance of audibility to the upper station; meanwhile one of the observers at the foot of the cliff, after the sound
was entirely lost, managed by climbing to a ledge about 30 feet
above the beach, to recover the signal quite distinctly, and to hear
it for some time. The sound coming with the wind continued to
be heard at both the higher and the lower stations for precisely the
same time, giving on this occasion no advantage to either. Observations made on board the two steamers while moving in opposite
directions, gave for the sound travelling with the wind, a duration
and distance more than five times that for the sound which came
against the wind. Five similar experiments gave very similar
results. The two vessels moving in opposite courses, each at right

angles to the direction of the wind, gave a very close equality for
the reciprocal durations of the sound. In the following month,
similar observations were made at Little Gull island, which were
very accordant with those made at the former station. As a result
of plotting the ranges of audibility in different directions from a
given point, producing a series of circular figures (more or less
distorted) of very different sizes, Henry was inclined to believe
that the whole area of audition is less in high winds than in gentle
winds. These investigations as their author well remarks,—
"though simple in their conception, have been difficult and laborious
in their execution. To be of the greatest practical value they
were required to be made on the ocean under the conditions in
which the results are to be applied to the use of the mariner, and
therefore they could only be conducted by means of steam vessels
of sufficient power to withstand the force of rough seas, and at
times when these vessels could be spared from other duty. They
also required a number of intelligent assistants skilled in observation and faithful in recording results."[*]

In the summer of last year, 1877, with undiminished ardor, he
continued his observations on sound; selecting this time Portland
harbor, Moohegan island, and Whitehead light station, on the coast
of Maine. At the latter station, the abnormal phenomenon of a
region of inaudibility near the fog-signal, and extending outward
for two or three miles, (beyond which distance the signal is again
very distinctly heard,) had for several years been frequently
observed. This singular effect is noticed only in the case of a
southerly wind when the vessel is approaching the signal from
the same quarter, and consequently with the wind adverse to the
direction of the sound-beams, a condition of the wind which is
the usual accompaniment of a fog. The observation showed this
intermediate "belt of silence" to be well marked on board the
steamer both on approaching the station and on receding from it
by retracing the same line of travel. Meanwhile the intermittent
signal whistle from the steamer was distinctly heard at the station
on both the outward and homeward trips of the vessel, throughout
its course. The next set of observations was made on the opposite

---

* Report of the Light-House Board for 1875, p. 107.

side of the small island, by directing the course of the steamer northward; and in this case the shore signal was distinctly heard throughout the trip, while the signal from the vessel passed through the "belt of silence" to the observers at the station. The hypothesis of a local sound shadow of definite extent, is excluded by the simple fact that the regions traversed were entirely unobstructed, the two points of observation — movable and stationary — being constantly in view from each other when not obscured by fog. The hypothesis of a stationary belt of acoustic opacity is equally excluded by the uninterrupted transmission of sound through the critical region in one direction; and this too whichever order of observation be selected. So that in one of the cases the powerful whistle ten inches in diameter blown by a steam pressure of 80 pounds, failed utterly to make itself heard, while the sound from a much feebler whistle only six inches in diameter and blown by a steam pressure of 25 pounds, traversed with ease and fulness the very same space. The only hypothesis left therefore is that of diacoustic refraction; by which the sound-beam from one origin is bent and lifted over the observer, while from an opposite origin the refraction is in a reversed direction; and such a quality in the moving air is referable to no other observed condition but that of its motion, that is to the influence of the wind. Observations were afterward made at Monhegan island, on some of the more normal effects of the refraction of sound by differences of wave velocity, all fully confirming the supposition which had been so variously and critically subjected to examination.

The principal conclusions summed up in the last Report for 1877, are: 1st. The audibility of sound at a distance depends primarily upon the pitch, the intensity, and the quantity of the sound: the most efficient pitch being neither a very high nor a very low one, — the intensity or loudness of sound resulting from the amplitude of the vibration, and the quantity of sound resulting from the mass of air simultaneously vibrating. 2nd. The external condition of widest transmission of sound through the air is that of stillness and perfect uniformity of density and temperature throughout. 3rd. The most serious disturbance of the audibility

23

of sound at a distance, results from its refraction by the wind, which as a general rule moving more freely and rapidly above than near the earth, tends by this difference to lift the sound-beams upward when moving against the wind, and in a downward curve when moving with it. 4th. When the upper current of air is adverse to the lower or sensible wind, or whenever from any cause the wind below has a higher velocity than that above—in the same direction, the reverse phenomenon is observed of sound being heard to greater distances in opposition to the sensible wind than it is when in the direction of the surface wind. 5th. While suitable reflectors and trumpet cones are serviceable in giving prominent direction to sounds within moderate or ordinary distances, yet from the rapid diffusibility of the sound-beams, such appliances are worthless for distances beyond a mile or two. 6th. The siren has been frequently found to have its clearest penetration through a widely extended fog, and also through a thick snow-storm of large area. 7th. Intervening obstructions produce sound shadows of greater or less extent, which however at a distance but slightly enfeeble the sound, owing to the lateral diffusion and closing in of the sound-waves. 8th. The singular phenomenon of distinct audibility of sound to a distance with a limited intermediate region of inaudibility where no optical obstruction exists, is due sometimes to a diffusion of upper sound-beams which have not suffered the upward refraction; sometimes to the lateral refraction of sound-beams or to the lateral spread of sound from directions not affected by the upward refraction; and very frequently to a double curvature of the refracted sound-beams under an adverse lower wind, by reason of the wave fronts being less retarded by the lower or surface stratum of wind than by that a short distance above, and at still greater heights being again less retarded, and finally accelerated by the superior favoring wind.

These remarkable series of acoustic investigations undertaken after the observer had considerably exceeded his three-score years,—perseveringly continued weeks at a time, and sometimes for more than a month,—extending through a period of twelve years, and pursued over a wide and extremely irregular range of sea-coast, and under great variety of both topographical and meteorological conditions, untiringly prosecuted by numberless sea trips of 10, 15, and even 20 miles in single stretches, in calm, in sunshine, in storm, with every variety of disregarded exposure,—form altogether a labor and a research, quite unequalled and unapproached by any similar ones on record. As a result of so great earnestness and thoroughness in the conduct of an enterprise of so great difficulty, Henry has advanced and enriched our knowledge by contributions to the science of acoustics, unquestionably the most important and valuable of the century. By persistent cross-examination of the bewildering anomalies of sound propagation under wide diversities of locality and condition, he has succeeded in evolving order out of apparent chaos, in reclaiming a new district, now subjected to the orderly reign of recognized law, and in raising the plausible but long neglected hypothesis of Stokes into the domain of a verified and fully established theory. Only on the subject of the aerial echo had he failed to reach a solution which entirely satisfied his judgment;[*] and at the ripe age of four-score years he had mapped out a further extension of his laborious search after truth, when his untiring and beneficent purposes were cut short by death.

With these great labors—(a full demand upon the energies of youthful vigor) fittingly closed the life of one whose long career had been dedicated to the service of his race,—no less by the unrecorded incitations and encouragements of others to the prosecution of original research, than by his own direct and earnest efforts on all occasions to extend the boundaries of our knowledge. Nor is it permitted us to indulge in vain regrets that thirty years of such a life were seemingly so much withdrawn from his own chosen

[*] "This question, therefore, remains to be answered: What is the cause of the aerial echo? As I have stated, it must in some way be connected with the motion. The only explanation which suggests itself to me at present is, that the spread of the sound which fills the whole atmosphere from the zenith to the horizon with sound-waves, may continue their rectilinear direction until they strike the surface of the water at such an angle and direction as to be reflected back to the ear of the observer; in this case the echo would be heard from a perfectly flat surface of water, and as different sound-rays would reach the water at different distances and from different azimuths, they would produce the prolonged character of the echo, and its angular extent along the horizon. While we do not present this hypothesis as a final solution of the question, we shall provisionally adopt it as a means of suggesting further experiments in regard to this perplexing question at another season." (Report of L. H. Board, 1877, p. 79.)

ministry at the altar of science, to be occupied so largely with the drudgery and the routine of merely administrative duties. True though it be, that talents adapted to such functions are very much more common and available than those which form the successful interrogator of Nature, who that knows by what exertions Smithson's wise endowment was rescued from the wasteful dissipation of heterogeneous local agencies and objects — by what heroic constancy, and through what ordeals of remonstrance and misconception, of contumely and denunciation, the modest income of the fund (husbanded and increased by prudent management) was yearly more and more withdrawn from merely popular uses and interests, and more and more applied to its truest and highest purpose, the fostering of abstract research, the founding of a pharos for the future,— the "increasing and diffusing of knowledge among men,"— who that knows all this, can say that Henry was mistaken in his devotion, or that his ripest years were wasted in an unprofitable mission?[*] But in addition to this vast work,— accomplished as probably no one of his scientific compeers would have had the fortitude and the indomitable persistence to carry through, his personal contributions to modern science (as has been shown) have throughout been neither few nor unimportant.

One remarkable circumstance relating to Henry's directorship of the Smithsonian publications (which have had so wide a distribution and influence)[†] must not be here passed over. Having himself,

[*] "But it is not alone the material advantages which the world enjoys from the study of abstract science on which its claims are founded. Were all further applications of its principles to practical purposes to cease, it would still be entitled to commendation and support on account of its more important effects upon the general mind. It offers unbounded fields of pleasurable, healthful, and ennobling exercise to the restless intellect of man, expanding his powers and enlarging his conceptions of the wisdom, the energy, and the beneficence of the great Ruler of the universe. From these considerations then, and others of a like kind, I am fully justified in the assertion that this Institution has done good service in placing prominently before the country the importance of original research, and that its directors are entitled to commendation for having so uniformly and persistently kept in view the fact that it was not intended for educational or immediately practical purposes, but for the encouragement of the study of theoretical principles and the advancement of abstract knowledge." (Smithsonian Report for 1859, p. 17.)

[†] "The number of copies of the Smithsonian Contributions distributed, is greater than that of the Transactions of any scientific or literary society; and therefore the Institution offers the best medium to be found for diffusing a knowledge of scientific discoveries." Smithsonian Report for 1851, p. 32.]

amidst the absorbing occupations of his position, conducted so valuable original investigations—on the strength of building materials,—on the best illuminants and their proper conditions,—and especially in his last great labor on the philosophy of sound, we should naturally expect to find them displayed in the "Smithsonian Contributions;" where in interest and importance second to none contained in that extensive and admirable series, these memoirs would have found their fitting place, and have given honor to the collection. But as if to avoid all semblance of a personal motive in his resolute policy of administration, he published nothing for himself at the expense of the Smithsonian fund; his numerous original productions being given to the public through the channel of various official reports. And thus it has occurred that his writings scattered in the different directions which seemed to him at the time most suitable, with little thought of any special publicity or perpetuity, have largely failed to reach the audience which would most appreciate them. And many of his most valuable papers—never by himself collected—must be searched for in unsuggestive volumes of Agricultural, or Light-House Board Reports. [*]

For him it seemed enough that what was once established, would not be willingly let die; that the medium or the occasion of communication was of comparatively little consequence, if but a new fact or principle were thrown into proper currency, and duly accepted as part of the world's wealth: and beyond all ordinary men he seemed to feel the insignificance of personal fame as compared with the infinite value of truth. The most appropriate monument of such a man would be a full collection of his writings, produced in a worthy and appropriate style of publication.

Less than a year ago, (on the evening of November 24th, 1877,) he delivered in this place before this Society his annual address, shortly after his re-election as its President;—an address which as we beheld the remarkable fulness and freshness of the speaker's

---

[*] Many valuable communications made to the American Association, to the National Academy of Sciences, to the Washington Philosophical Society, and to other bodies, from rough notes, which their author was prevented from writing fairly out, by the unceasing pressure of his multitudinous official and public duties, have unfortunately been published only by title.

mental and bodily powers,—we little thought was in reality his
valedictory. In it he concisely yet lucidly portrayed for the stimu-
lation of more youthful physicists, the processes and the qualities
necessary for success in original research;—the awakened attention
to "the seeds of great discoveries constantly floating around us,"—
the careful observation, the clear perception of the actual facts
uncolored as much as possible by a priori conceptions or expectations,—the faculty of persevering watchfulness, and the judgment
to eliminate (with all due caution) the conditions which are accidental,—the importance of a provisional hypothesis,—the conscientious and impartial testing of such by every expedient that
ingenuity may suggest,—the lessons taught by failure,—the firm
holding of the additional facts thus gleaned, though adverse and
disappointing,—the diligent pondering, and the logical application
of deductive consequences, to be again examined, until as the reward
of patient solicitation, the answer of nature is at least revealed.

"The investigator now feels amply rewarded for all his toil, and
is conscious of the pleasure of the self-appreciation which flows
from having been initiated into the secrets of nature, and allowed
the place not merely of an humble worshipper in the vestibule of
the temple of science, but an officiating priest at the altar. In this
sketch which I have given of a successful investigation, it will be
observed that several faculties of the mind are called into operation.
First, the imagination, which calls forth the forms of things unseen
and gives them a local habitation, must be active in presenting to
the mind's eye a definite conception of the modes of operation of
the forces in nature sufficient to produce the phenomena in question.
Second, the logical power must be trained in order to deduce from
the assumed premises the conclusions necessary to test the truth of
the assumption in the form of an experiment; and again the ingenuity must be taxed to invent the experiment or to bring about the
arrangement of apparatus adapted to test the conclusions. These
faculties of mind may all be much improved and strengthened by
practice. The most important requisite however to scientific
investigations of this character, is a mind well stored with clear
conceptions of scientific generalizations, and possessed of sagacity
in tracing analogies and devising hypotheses. Without the use of

hypotheses or antecedent probabilities, as a general rule no extended series of investigations can be made as to the approximate cause of casual phenomena. They require to be used however with great care, lest they become false guides which lead to error rather than to truth." * Who that listened could fail to perceive that the speaker was unconsciously giving us precious glimpses into his own experience ?

In less than two weeks after this, his last appearance among us, he suffered at New York a temporary numbness in his hands, which he feared might threaten a paralysis; but a subsequent swelling of his feet and hands revealed to his physician the nature of his inward disease as a nephritis, which had insidiously assailed him before it was suspected, and had doubtless been aggravated by his unremitting scientific labors continued as usual through his last summer vacation. Only a month before he died, he thus described the commencement of his malady : "After an almost uninterrupted period of excellent health for fifty years, I awoke on the 5th of December at my office in the Light-House Depot in Staten Island, finding my right hand in a paralytic condition. This was at first referred by the medical adviser, to an affection of the brain, but as the paralysis subsided in a considerable degree in the course of two days, this conclusion was doubted, and on a thorough examination through the eye, and by means of auscultation, and chemical analysis, Dr. S. Weir Mitchell and Dr. J. J. Woodward pronounced the disease an affection of the kidneys." †

---

* Bulletin Phil. Soc. Washington, Nov. 24, 1877, vol. II, pp. 68, 100.

† Opening Address, written for the meeting of the National Academy of Sciences, April 16th, 1878. (Proceed. Nat. Acad. Sci., vol. I, part 2, pp. 137, 138.) In the same address read to the Academy by the Secretary, he remarked: "I am worried that I must divide my energies with caution, and expend no more power—physical or mental, than is commensurate with my present condition, and in consideration of this I think it advisable to curtail as much as possible, the various offices which have been pressed upon me in consideration of my residence in the city of Washington, and my association with the Smithsonian Institution, . . . I therefore beg leave to renew my request to be allowed to resign the presidency of the Academy, the resignation to take effect at the next meeting. I retain the office six months longer, in the hope that I may be restored by such a condition of health as to be able to prepare some suggestions which may be of importance for the future of the Academy." And in his closing Address at the end of the session, three days later (April 18th), in earnest words having now the solemnity of a valedictory charge, he urged that moral integrity of character is essential to meritorious facility in scientific research; and that

Aware that his illness was fatal, he yet felt lulled by that strange flattery of disease when unattended with a painful wasting, into the thought that he might probably survive the approaching warmer weather; and fully prepared for death, with the sense of life still strong within him, he planned what might yet be accomplished.

But with occasional alternations of more favorable symptoms, with the uræmia steadily increasing, his strength slowly declined; and as he lay at noon of the 13th of last May, [1878,] with growing difficulty of breathing—surrounded by loving and anguished hearts—his last feeble utterance was an inquiry which way the wind came. With intellect clear and unimpaired, calmly that pure and all unselfish spirit passed away; leaving a void all the more real, all the more felt, that the deceased had reached a good old age, and had worthily accomplished his allotted work.

PERSONALITY AND CHARACTER.

Of Henry's personal appearance, it is sufficient to say, that his figure, above the medium height, was finely proportioned; that his mien and movement were dignified and imposing; and that on whatever occasion called upon to address an assembly,

> " With grave aspect he rose, and in his rising seemed
> A pillar of state; deep on his front engraven
> Deliberation sat, and public care."

His head and features were of massive mould; though from the perfect proportion of his form, not too conspicuously so. His expansive brow was crowned with an abundant flow of whitened hair; his lower face always smoothly shaven, expressed a mingled gentleness and firmness; and his countenance of manly symmetry was in all its varying moods, a pleasant study of the mellowing, moulding impress of long years of generous feeling, and a worthy exponent of the fine and thoughtful spirit within: wearing in

It should therefore be an indispensable test of membership in an Academy strenuous in maintaining its exalted function. "It is not social position, popularity, extended authorship, or success as an instructor in science which entitles to membership, but actual new discoveries; nor are these sufficient if the reputation of the candidate is in the slightest degree tainted with injustice or want of truth, indeed I think that immorality and great mental power exercised in the discovery of scientific truths, are incompatible with each other; and that more error is introduced from defect in moral sense than from want of intellectual capacity." (Same Proceedings, p. 128.)

repose a certain pensive but benignant majesty, in the abstraction
of study a semblance of constrained severity, in the relaxation of
friendly intercourse a genial frank and winning grace of expression.
The varying shades of such expression, with the changing current
of his thought, combined with a certain reserve, — or (perhaps more
properly) freedom from effusiveness, — imparted to his aspect and
his intercourse a singular charm.* His whole physique was in admirable harmony with his power of intellect; — the fitting venture of
the *mens sana in corpore sano*. Like his intimate personal friend
Agassiz, he seemed to stand and to move among men as the very
embodiment of unfailing vigorous health and physical strength; and
only a year ago, he walked with an erect and elastic a carriage,
with as firm and sprightly a step, as any one here present.

It is difficult to attempt even a sketch of Henry's intellectual
character, without allusion to his moral attributes; so constantly
did the latter dominate the former. It may be said that the most
characteristic feature of his varied activities was earnestness, and
this as usual, was the offspring as much of a moral as of a mental
purpose.

His mind was eminently logical; and this rational power was
exhibited in every department of his theoretical or his practical
pursuits. He never showed or felt uneasiness at necessary deductive consequences, if the premises were well considered or appeared
to be well founded; confident that all truth must ultimately be
found consistent. If presented with the problem of an untried
case, while avowing the necessity of reserve in predicting results,
he seemed to have an almost intuitive apprehension of the operation of natural law. If confronted with an unfamiliar phenomenon,
whether in the experience of others, or in his own observations,
his imagination was fertile in the suggestion of test conditions for
eliminating variable influences. While few have ever held the
function of hypothesis in higher estimation as an instrument of
research, no one ever held hypothesis in more complete subjection.

* Of the numerous photographic portraits of Henry taken within the past ten
or twenty years, it has been often remarked that no two appear to have the same
character, or to bear a very close resemblance to each other. Three or four portraits portraits in all (of these) perpetuate his likeness, with the same characteristic differences.

As a lecturer and instructor, he was always most successful.
Free from all self-consciousness, thinking only of his subject, and
its fittest mode of presentation, he spoke from the fullness of a
ripened knowledge,—intent on communicating to others the intellectual pleasures of insight he had made his own; and without
attempt at oratorical display, his expositions—in simple, direct, and
conversational language, were so lucid, satisfying, and convincing,
that they enlisted from the beginning and secured to the close,
the attentive interest of his auditors.

His sympathy with the pursuits of the rising generation of physicists was ever manifested in a disposition to frequent consultation and interchange of views with them; as if (aware of the usual
tendency to mental ossification with advancing years,) he thus
sought by familiar association to drink at the fountain of perennial
youth. And surely no one was ever more successful in retaining
life's coveted greenness in age;—not more in the child-like simplicity of his disposition, in the geniality of his affections, and in
his undimmed faith, hope, and charity, for mankind, than in his
intellectual freedom from undue prejudices, and in his readiness
calmly to discuss or adopt new theories.

And this leads to the reflection that in the seeming contrasts of
his nature were combined qualities which formed in him a resultant
of character and of temperament as rare as admirable. With this
great mobility of aptitude and of circumspection, this adaptability
of mental attitude, he yet possessed an unusual firmness of resolution. With a manly manliness of conviction he presented an
unvarying equability of temper and of toleration; and with perfect candor as perfect a courtesy. With a characteristic dignity of
figure of presence and of deportment, he preserved an entire freedom from any shade of arrogance. With a warm and active
charity, he still displayed a shrewd perception of character; and
while ever responsive to the appeals of real distress, his insight
into human nature protected him from being often deceived by the
wiles of the designing. Intolerant of charlatanry and imposture,
he was capable of exhibiting a wonderful patience with the tedium
of honest ignorance. Possessing in earlier life a natural quickness of temper, and always a high degree of native sensibility, his

perfect self-control led the casual acquaintance to regard him as
reserved and unimpressible. Of him it may be truly said in
simple and oft-quoted words:

> "His life was gentle: and the elements
> So mixed in him, that Nature might stand up
> And say to all the world—This was a MAN!"

With all his broad humanity, he possessed but little of what is
known as "humor." He could enjoy the ludicrous more heartily
when drolly narrated by its appreciative victims, than when sarcas-
tically recited at the expense of another. The sparkle of wit be
fully appreciated, provided it were free from coarseness and from
personal satire. From the subordination of his sense of humor to
his native instinct of sincerity, he had no approbation—or indeed
tolerance of "practical jokes," holding that the shock to the feelings or to the confidence of the dupe, is far too high a price for the
momentary hilarity enjoyed by the thoughtless at a farcical situation. Newspaper hoaxes—literary or scientific, in like manner
received his stern reprobation, as uncompensated injuries to popular
trust and to the cause of popular enlightenment.

Strong in his unerring sense of justice and of right, he allowed
no prospects of personal advantage to influence his judgment in
action, in decision, or in opinion: he never availed himself of
the opportunities offered by his position, of reaping gain from
profitable suggestions or favorable awards: and he never willingly
inflicted an injury even on the feelings of the humblest. This was
characteristically shown in the pains taken to convince the judgment of those against whose visionary projects he was so often called
upon to report in the public interests of the Smithsonian Institution,
of the Light-House service, and of the General Government:—
often expending an amount of valuable time and of patience which
few so situated would have accorded, or could well have afforded.
And yet on the other hand when himself the subject of injustice,
misconstruction, or abuse, he never suffered himself to be provoked
into a controversy;—as if holding life too serious, time too precious, to be wasted in mere disputation. Least of all did he ever
think of resorting to retaliatory conduct or to the expression of
opprobrious sentiments. He calmly put aside disturbing elements,

and seemed endowed with the power of excluding from his mental
vision all irritating incidents. In that benignant breast there
harbored no resentments.

Great as is the loss we have sustained of "guide, philosopher,
and friend," we have yet the mournful satisfaction of reflecting
that his influence, powerful as it always has been for good, still
survives—in his works, his high example, and his unclouded
memory;—that our community, our country, the world itself,
has been benefitted by his existence here; and that as time rolls
on, its course will be marked by increasing circles of appreciation, reverence, and gratitude, for the teachings of his high and
noble life.

LIST OF THE

SCIENTIFIC PAPERS OF JOSEPH HENRY.

1825. On the production of cold by the rarefaction of Air: accompanied with Experiments. (Presented Mar. 2.) Abstract, *Trans. Albany Institute*, vol. I. part II. p. 38.

1827. On some Modifications of the Electro-magnetic Apparatus. (Read Oct. 10.) *Trans. Albany Inst.* vol. I. pp. 22-24.

1829. Topographical Sketch of the State of New York; designed chiefly to show the General Elevations and Depressions of its Surface. (Read Oct. 28.) *Trans. Albany Inst.* vol. I. pp. 87-112.

1829. First Abstract of Meteorological Records of the State of New York, for 1826. (In conjunction with Dr. T. Romeyn Beck.) *Annual Report of Regents of University*, to the Legislature of New York.—Albany, 1829.

1830. On the Mean Temperature of Twenty-seven different Places in the State of New York, for 1826. (In conjunction with Dr. T. Romeyn Beck.) Brewster's *Edinburgh Jour. Science*, Oct. 1829, vol. I. n. s. pp. 349-359.

1830. Second Abstract of Meteorological Records of the State of New York for 1829. (In conjunction with Dr. T. Romeyn Beck.) *Annual Report of Regents of University*, to the Legislature of New York.—Albany, 1830.

1831. On the Application of the Principle of the Galvanic Multiplier to Electro-magnetic Apparatus, and also to the development of great Magnetic power in soft Iron, with small Galvanic Elements. Silliman's *American Jour. Science*, Jan. 1831, vol. xix. pp. 400-408. *Jour. of Roy. Institution of Gr. Brit.* May, 1831, vol. I. pp. 609, 610.

1831. Tabular Statement of the Latitudes, Longitudes, and Elevations, of 49 Meteorological Stations in New York. *Annual Report Regents of University* to Legislature N. Y. 1831.

1831. Third Abstract of Meteorological Records of State of New York for 1830. (In conjunction with Dr. T. Romeyn Beck.) *Annual Report of Regents of University*, to the Legislature of New York.—Albany, 1831.

1831. An Account of a large Electro-magnet, made for the Laboratory of Yale College. (In conjunction with Dr. Ten Eyck.) Silliman's *Am. Jour. Sci.* April, 1831, vol. xx. pp. 201-203. *Jour. of Roy. Institution of Gr. Brit.* Aug. 1831, vol. II. p. 192.

1831. On a Reciprocating Motion produced by Magnetic attraction and repulsion. Silliman's *Am. Jour. Sci.* July, 1831, vol. xx. pp. 340-343. Sturgeon's *Annals of Electricity*, etc. vol. III. pp. 430-432.

1832. On a Disturbance of the Earth's Magnetism in connection with the appearance of an Aurora as observed at Albany on the 19th of April, 1831. (Communicated to the Albany Institute, Jan. 26, 1832.) *Report of Regents of University, to the Legislature of New York.*—Albany, 1832. Silliman's *Am. Jour. Sci.* July, 1832, vol. xxii. pp. 143-155.

1832. Fourth Abstract of Meteorological Records of the State of New York for 1831. (In conjunction with Dr. T. Romeyn Beck.) *Annual Report of Regents of University, to the Legislature of New York.*—Albany, 1831.

1832. On the Production of Currents and Sparks of Electricity from Magnetism. Silliman's *Am. Jour. Sci.* July, 1832, vol. xxii. pp. 403-408.

1832. On the effect of a long and helical wire in increasing the intensity of a galvanic current from a single element. (Conclusion of preceding paper.) Silliman's *Am. Jour. Sci.* July, 1832, vol. xxii. p. 408. Becquerel's *Traité expérimental de l'Electricité,* etc. 1847, vol. v. pp. 231, 232.

1833. Fifth Abstract of Meteorological Records of the State of New York for 1832. (In conjunction with Dr. T. Romeyn Beck.) *Annual Report of Regents of University, to the Legislature of New York.*—Albany, 1833.

1835. Contributions to Electricity and Magnetism. No. I. Description of a Galvanic Battery for producing Electricity of different intensities. (Read Jan. 14.) *Transactions Am. Philosoph. Society,* vol. v. n. s. pp. 217-222. Sturgeon's *Annals of Electricity,* etc. vol. I. pp. 277-291.

1835. Contributions to Electricity and Magnetism. No. II. On the influence of a Spiral Conductor in increasing the intensity of Electricity from a Galvanic arrangement of a single Pair, etc. (Read Feb. 6.) *Trans. Amer. Phil. Soc.* vol. v. n. s. pp. 223-232. Sturgeon's *Annals of Electricity,* etc. vol. I. pp. 323-330. Taylor's *Scientific Memoirs,* vol. I. pp. 540-547.

1835. Facts in reference to the Spark, etc. from a long Conductor uniting the poles of a Galvanic Battery. *Journal of Franklin Institute,* Mar. 1835, vol. xv. pp. 169, 170. Silliman's *Am. Jour. Sci.* July, 1835, vol. xxviii. pp. 327-331.

1837. A Notice of Electrical Researches, particularly in regard to the "lateral discharge." (Read before the British Association at Liverpool, Sept. 1837.) *Report Brit. Assoc.* 1837. Part II. pp. 22-24. Silliman's *Am. Jour. Sci.* April, 1838, vol. xxxiv. pp. 16-19.

1838. A Letter on the production directly from ordinary Electricity of Currents by Induction, analogous to those obtained from Galvanism. (Read to Philosoph. Society, May 4.) *Proceedings Am. Phil. Soc.* vol. I. p. 14.

1838. Contributions to Electricity and Magnetism. No. III. On Electro-dynamic Induction. (Read Nov. 2.) *Trans. Am. Phil. Soc.* vol. vi. n. s. pp. 303-337. Silliman's *Am. Jour. Sci.* Jan. 1840, vol. xxxviii. pp. 209-243. Sturgeon's *Annals of Electricity,* etc. vol. iv. pp. 281-310. *L. E. D. Phil. Mag.* Mar. 1840, vol. xvi. pp. 200-210; pp. 254-265. pp. 551-562. Becquerel's *Traité expérimental de l'Electricité,* etc. vol. v. pp. 87-107. *Annales de Chimie et de Physique,* Dec. 1841, 3d série: vol. iii. pp. 394-407. Poggendorff's *Annalen der Physik und Chemie.* Supplemental vol. I. (Noch Band I.) 1842, pp. 294-319.

1839. A novel phenomenon of Capillary action: the transmission of Mercury through Lead. (Read Mar. 15.) Proceedings Am. Phil. Soc. vol. i. pp. 82, 83. Silliman's Am. Jour. Sci. Dec. 1839, vol. xxxviii. pp. 190, 191. Bibliotch. Universelle, vol. xxix. pp. 175, 176. Liebig's Annalen der Chemie, etc. vol. xi. pp. 168, 169.

1839. A Letter on two distinct kinds of dynamic induction by a Galvanic current. (Read to Phil. Soc. Oct. 18.) Proceedings Am. Phil. Soc. vol. i. pp. 131–132.

1839. Observations of Meteors made Nov. 25, 1835, simultaneously at Princeton and at Philadelphia, for determining their difference of Longitude. (In conjunction with Professors A. D. Bache, S. Alexander, and J. P. Espy.) Proceedings Am. Phil. Soc. Dec. 21, vol. i. pp. 162, 163. Silliman's Am. Jour. Sci. Oct. 1840, vol. xxxix. pp. 372, 373.

1840. Contributions to Electricity and Magnetism. No. IV. On Electro-dynamic Induction. (Read June 19.) Trans. Am. Phil. Soc. vol. viii. n. s. pp. 1–18. Silliman's Am. Jour. Sci. April, 1841, vol. xli. pp. 117–158. Sturgeon's Annals Electricity, etc. vol. vii. pp. 91–68. L. E. D. Phil. Mag. Jun. 1841, vol. xviii. pp. 463–514. Annales de Chim. et de Phys. Dec. 1841, 3d ser. vol. iii. pp. 407–431. Poggendorff's Annal. der Phys. und Chem. 1841, vol. liv. pp. 84–94.

1840. Contributions to Electricity and Magnetism. No. IV.—continued. Theoretical Considerations relating to Electro-dynamic Induction. (Read Nov. 20.) Trans. Am. Phil. Soc. vol. viii. n. s. pp. 14–35.

1840. On the production of a reciprocating motion by the repulsion in the consecutive parts of a conductor through which a galvanic current is passing. (Read Nov. 20.) Proceedings Am. Phil. Soc. vol. i. p. 201.

1840. Electricity from heated Water. (Read Dec. 16.) Proceedings Am. Phil. Soc. vol. i. pp. 213–214.

1841. Report of the Tenth Meeting of the British Association, etc. Princeton Review, Jan. 1841, vol. xiii. pp. 132–149.

1841. Description of a simple and inexpensive form of Hollstein. (Read Sept. 17.) Proceedings Am. Phil. Soc. vol. ii. pp. 97, 98.

1841. Observations on the effects of a Thunderstorm which visited Princeton on the evening of the 14th of July, 1841. (Read Nov. 5.) Proceedings Am. Phil. Soc. vol. ii. pp. 113–116.

1842. Edmond des Recherches faite sur les Courants d'Induction. Archives de l'Électricité, 1842, vol. ii. pp. 344–392.

1842. Contributions to Electricity and Magnetism. No. V. On Electro-dynamic Induction; and on the oscillatory discharge. (Read June 17.) Proceedings Am. Phil. Soc. vol. ii. pp. 193–196.

1843. On Phosphorogenic Emanation. (Read May 26.) Proceedings Am. Phil. Soc. vol. iii. pp. 34–44. Walker's Electrical Magazine, 1845, vol. i. pp. 444–450.

1843. On a new Method of determining the Velocity of Projectiles. (Read May 20.) Proceedings Am. Phil. Soc. vol. iii. pp. 165–167. Walker's Electrical Magazine, 1845, vol. i. pp. 250–252.

1843. Nouvelles Expériences sur l'Induction développée par l'Electricité ordinaire. (Translated.) *Archives de l'Electricité*, 1843, vol. III, pp. 514–520.

1843. On the application of Melloni's thermo-electric apparatus to Meteorological purposes. (Presented orally Nov. 3.) *Proceedings Am. Phil. Soc.*, vol. iv. p. 22.

1843. Theory of the discharge of the Leyden jar. (Presented Nov. 3.) *Proceedings Am. Phil. Soc.* vol. iv. pp. 22, 23.

1844. On the Cohesion of Liquids. (Read April 5.) *Proceedings Am. Phil. Soc.* vol. iv. pp. 56, 57. Silliman's *Am. Jour. Sci.* Oct. 1844, vol. xlvii. pp. 915, 916.

1844. On the Cohesion of Liquids,—continued. (Read May 17.) *Proceedings Am. Phil. Soc.* vol. iv. pp. 84, 85. Silliman's *Am. Jour. Sci.* Oct. 1844, vol. xlvii. pp. 916, 917. *L. E. D. Phil. Mag.* June, 1845, vol. xxvi. pp. 541–543.

1844. Syllabus of Lectures on Physics. Princeton, 8vo. 1844. Republished in part in *Smithsonian Report*, 1856, pp. 187–230.

1844. Classification and Sources of Mechanical Power. (Read Dec. 20.) *Proceedings Am. Phil. Soc.* vol. iv. pp. 127–132.

1845. On the Coast Survey. *Princeton Review*, April, 1845, vol. xvii. pp. 321–344.

1845. On the relative Radiation of Heat by the Solar Spots. (Read June 20.) *Proceedings Am. Phil. Soc.* vol. iv. pp. 173–176. Brief Abstract in *Report Brit. Assoc.* 1845, Part II. p. 6. Walker's *Electrical Magazine*, 1846, vol. II. pp. 321–391. Froriep's *Neue Notizen*, etc. No. 826, 1846, vol. xxxviii. col. 179–182. Poggendorff's *Annalen der Physik und Chemie*, 1846, vol. lxvii. pp. 100–104.

1846. On the Capillarity of Metals. (Read June 20.) *Proceedings Am. Phil. Soc.* vol. iv. pp. 175–176. Froriep's *Neue Notizen*, etc. No. 835, 1846, vol. xxxviii. col. 167–169. Poggendorff's *Annalen der Physik und Chemie*, 6tel supplemental vol. (Nach Band I xii.) 1848, pp. 384–391.

1846. On the Protection of Buildings from Lightning. (Read June 20.) *Proceedings Am. Phil. Soc.* vol. iv. p. 172. Silliman's *Am. Jour. Sci.* 1846, vol. II. pp. 400, 401. Walker's *Electrical Magazine*, 1846, vol. II. pp. 384–388. Froriep's *Neue Notizen*, etc. No. 823, 1846, vol. xxxviii. col. 133, 134.

1845. An account of peculiar effects on a house struck by Lightning. (Read June 20.) *Proceedings Am. Phil. Soc.* vol. iv. p. 180.

1845. On Color Blindness. *Princeton Review*, July, 1845, vol. xvii. pp. 453–469. *Smithsonian Report*, 1877, pp. 196–200.

1845. On the discharge of Electricity through a long wire, etc. (Read Nov. 7.) *Proceedings Am. Phil. Soc.* vol. iv. pp. 204, 219.

1846. Repetition of Faraday's Experiment on the Polarization of Liquids under the influence of a galvanic current. (Read Jan. 16.) *Proceedings Am. Phil. Soc.* vol. iv. pp. 229, 230.

1846. Extrait d'une Lettre à M. de la Rive, sur les Télégraphes Electriques dans les Etats-Unis de l'Amérique. *Bibliothèque Universelle. Archives*, 1846, vol. II. p. 178.

1846. Report on the action of Electricity on the Telegraph Wires; and Telegraph-poles struck by Lightning. (Read June 19.) *Proceedings Am. Phil. Soc.* vol. iv. pp. 300-305. Silliman's *Am. Jour. Sci.* 1847, vol. iii. pp. 25-33. *L. E. D. Phil. Mag.* May, 1847, vol. xxx. pp. 188-194. *Agricultural Report, Commr. Pats.* 1850, pp. 509-511.

1846. On the ball supported by a water jet; also experiments in regard to the "interference" of heat. (Read Oct. 16.) *Proceedings Am. Phil. Soc.* vol. iv. p. 265.

1846. On the corpuscular hypothesis of the constitution of Matter. (Read Nov. 6.) *Proceedings Am. Phil. Soc.* vol. iv. pp. 287-290.

1846. On the Height of Auroras. (Read Dec. 3.) *Proceedings Am. Phil. Soc.* vol. iv. p. 370.

1847. Programme of Organization of the Smithsonian Institution. (Presented to the Board of Regents, Dec. 8, 1847.) *Smithsonian Report,* 1847, pp. 120-134.

1847. Article on "Magnetism" for the Encyclopedia Americana. *Encycl. Amer.* 1847, vol. xiv. pp. 412-420.

1848. On Heat.—A Thermal Telescope. Silliman's *Am. Jour. Sci.* Jan. 1848, vol. v. pp. 113, 114.

1848. Explanations and Illustrations of the Plan of the Smithsonian Institution. Silliman's *Am. Jour. Sci.* Nov. 1848, vol. vi. pp. 316-317.

1849. On the Radiation of Heat. (Read Oct. 19.) *Proceedings Am. Phil. Soc.* vol. v. p. 102.

1850. Analysis of the dynamic phenomena of the Leyden jar. *Proceedings Amer. Association,* Aug. 1850, pp. 377, 378.

1851. On the Limit of Perceptibility of a direct and reflected Sound. *Proceedings Amer. Association,* May, 1851, pp. 42, 43.

1851. On the Theory of the so-called Imponderables. *Proceedings Amer. Association,* Aug. 1851, pp. 84-91.

1852. Address before the Metropolitan Mechanics' Institute, Washington. (Delivered March 19.) 8vo, Washington, 1852, 19 pp.

1854. Meteorological Tables of mean diurnal variations, etc.—Prepared as an Appendix to Mr. Russell's Lectures on Meteorology. *Smithsonian Report* for 1854, pp. 215-223.

1854. Thoughts on Education; an Introductory Discourse before the Association for the Advancement of Education. (Delivered Dec. 24.) *Proceedings Assoc. Adv. Education,* 4th Session, 1854, pp. 17-31. *Amer. Jour. of Education,* Aug. 1855, vol. i. pp. 17-31.

1855. On the mode of Testing Building Materials, etc. *Proceedings Am. Assoc.* Aug. 1855, pp. 102-112. Silliman's *Am. Jour. Sci.* July, 1856, vol. xxii. pp. 30-34; *Smithsonian Report,* 1856, pp. 305-310.

1855. On the effect of mingling Radiating Substances with Combustible Materials; (or incombustible bodies with fuel.) *Proceedings Am. Assoc.* Aug. 1855, pp. 112-116.

1855. Account of Experiments on the alleged spontaneous separation of Alcohol and Water. *Proceed. Am. Assoc.* Aug. 1855, pp. 140–144.

1855. On the Induction of Electrical Currents. (Read Sept. 21.) *Proceedings Am. Academy of Arts,* etc. vol. III. p. 194.

1855. Note on the Gyroscope. Appendix to Lecture by Professor E. S. Snell. *Smithsonian Report,* 1855, p. 190.

1855. Remarks on Rain-fall at varying elevations. *Smithsonian Report,* 1855, pp. 213, 214.

1855. Directions for Meteorological Observations. (In conjunction with Professor A. Guyot.) *Smithsonian Report,* 1855, pp. 215–244.

1855. Circular of Inquiries relative to Earthquakes. *Smithsonian Report,* 1855, p. 245.

1855. Instructions for Observations of the Aurora. *Smithsonian Report,* 1855, pp. 217–240.

1855. On Green's Standard Barometer for the Smithsonian Institution. *Smithsonian Report,* 1855, pp. 251–254.

1855. Circular of Instructions on Registering the periodical phenomena of animal and vegetable life. *Smithsonian Report,* 1855, pp. 259–263.

1855. Meteorology in its connection with Agriculture, Part I. *Agricultural Report of Commr. Pats.* 1855, pp. 357–394.

1856. On Acoustics applied to Public Buildings. *Proceedings Am. Assoc.* Aug. 1856, pp. 119–135. *Smithsonian Report,* 1856, pp. 221–234. *Canadian Journal,* etc. Mar. 1857, vol. II. n. s. pp. 120–140.

1856. Account of a large Sulphuric-acid Barometer in the Hall of the Smithsonian Institution Building. *Proceedings Am. Assoc.* Aug. 1856, pp. 155–159.

1856. Meteorology in its connection with Agriculture, Part II. General Atmospheric Conditions. *Agricultural Report of Commr. Pats.* 1856, pp. 455–492.

1857. Communication to the Board of Regents of the Smithsonian Institution, relative to a publication by Professor Morse. *Smithsonian Report,* 1857, pp. 95–106.

1857. Statement in relation to the history of the Electro-magnetic Telegraph. *Smithsonian Report,* 1857, pp. 99–106.

1857. Meteorology in its connection with Agriculture, Part III. Terrestrial Physics, and Temperature. *Agricultural Report of Commr. Pats.* 1857, pp. 419–506.

1858. Meteorology in its connection with Agriculture, Part IV. Atmospheric Vapor, and Currents. *Agricultural Report of Commr. Pats.* 1858, pp. 429–493.

1859. On Meteorology. *Canadian Naturalist and Geologist,* Aug. 1859, vol. iv. pp. 270–291.

1859. Application of the Telegraph to the Prediction of Changes of the Weather. (Read Aug. 9.) *Proceedings Am. Academy of Arts,* etc. vol. iv. pp. 271–275.

1859. Meteorology in its connection with Agriculture, Part V. Atmospheric Electricity. *Agricultural Report of Commr. Pats.* 1859, pp. 461–508.

1859. On the Protection of Buildings from the effects of Lightning. *Agricult. Report*, Com. Pat. 1859, pp. 511-524.

1859. On the Conservation of Force. Silliman's *Am. Jour. Sci.* July, 1859, vol. xxx. pp. 39-41.

1860. Circular to Officers of Hudson's Bay Company (April 20.) *Smithsonian Miscell. Collections*, No. 137, vol. viii. pp. 1-4.

1860. Description of Smithsonian Anemometer. *Smithsonian Report*, 1860, pp. 414-416.

1861. Letter on Aeronautics to Mr. T. S. C. Lowe. (March 11.) *Smithsonian Report*, 1860, pp. 118, 119.

1861. Article on "Magnetism" for the American Cyclopedia. Edited by Ripley and Dana. *Am. Cycl.* 1861, vol. xi. pp. 51-53.

1861. Article on "Meteorology" for the American Cyclopedia. Edited by Ripley and Dana. *Am. Cycl.* 1861, vol. xi. pp. 414-420.

1862. Report of the Light-House Board on the proposed Transfer of the Lights to the Navy Department. Exec. Docts. 37th Cong. 2d Sess. Senate, Mis. Doc. No. 61, pp. 9-16.

1862. Letter to Orlando Meads, Chairman of Committee of Trustees, etc. on the semi-centennial celebration of the Albany Academy. (Dated June 21.) *Proceedings on Semi-Centennial Anniversary*, etc. pp. 66, 67.

1862. Introduction to Memoir by Professor J. Plateau. On the Figure of Equilibrium of a Liquid Mass, etc. *Smithsonian Report*, 1863, pp. 207, 208.

1864. On Materials for Combustion in Lamps of Light-Houses. (Read Jan. 12, before the National Academy of Sciences.) [Not published in Proceedings.]

1865. Report relative to the Fire at the Smithsonian Institution, occurring Jan. 24th, 1865. (In conjunction with Mayor Richard Wallach.) Presented to the Regents February, 1865. *Smithsonian Report*, 1864, pp. 117-120.

1865. Queries relative to Tornadoes: directions to observers. *Smithsonian Miscell. Collections*, No. 190, vol. x. pp. 1-4.

1865. Remarks on the Meteorology of the United States. *Smithsonian Report*, 1865, pp. 50-59.

1865. Remarks on Ventilation: especially with reference to the U. S. Capitol. *Smithsonian Report*, 1865, pp. 67, 68.

1866. Report on the Warming and Ventilating of the U. S. Capitol. (May 4.) Exec. Doc. No. 100. H. of Rep. 39th Cong. 1st Sess. pp. 4-6.

1866. Report of Building Committee on Repairs to Sm. Inst. building from Fire. (In conjunction with Genl. Richard Delafield, and Mayor Richard Wallach.) Presented to Regents April 26. *Smithsonian Report*, 1865, pp. 111-114.

1866. On the aboriginal Migration of the American race. Appendix to paper by F. Von Hellwald. *Smithsonian Report*, 1866, pp. 344, 345.

1869. Remarks on Vitality. *Smithsonian Report*, 1869, pp. 387-388.

1869. Meteorological Notes. To Correspondents. *Smithsonian Report*, 1869, pp. 409-412.

1866. Investigations in regard to Sound. (Read Aug. 10, before the National Academy of Sciences.) [Not published in Proceedings.]

1867. Circular relating to Collections in Archæology and Ethnology. (Jan. 15.) Smithsonian Miscell. Collections, No. 205, vol. viii. pp. 1, 2.

1867. Circular relative to Exchanges. (May 16.) Smithsonian Report, 1867, p. 71.

1867. Suggestions relative to Objects of Scientific Investigation in Russian America. (May 27.) Smithsonian Miscell. Collections, No. 207, vol. viii. pp. 1–7.

1867. Notice of Pettler. Smithsonian Report, 1867, p. 156.

1867. Notes on Atmospheric Electricity. To Correspondents. Smithsonian Report, 1867, pp. 320–323.

1867. On the Penetration of Sound. (Read Jan. 24, before the National Academy of Sciences. [Not published in Proceedings.]

1868. Appendix to a Notice of Schoenbein. Smithsonian Report, 1868, pp. 189–191.

1868. On the Rain-fall of the United States. (Read Aug. 25, before the National Academy of Sciences.) [Not published in Proceedings.]

1869. Memoir of Alexander Dallas Bache. (Read April 16.) Biographical Memoirs of Nat. Acad. Sci, vol. 1. pp. 181–212. Smithsonian Report, 1870, pp. 91–116.

1870. Letter. On a Physical Observatory. (Dec. 20.) Smithsonian Report, 1870, pp. 141–144.

1871. Observations on the Rain-fall of the United States. Proceedings California Academy of Sciences, vol. iv. p. 152.

1871. Instructions for Observations of Thunder Storms. Smithsonian Miscell. Collections, No. 235, vol. x. p. 1.

1871. Circular relative to Heights. For a topographic chart of N. America. Smithsonian Miscell. Collections, No. 236, vol. x. p. 1.

1871. Directions for constructing Lightning-Rods. Smithsonian Miscell. Collections, No. 237, vol. x. pp. 1–3. Silliman's Am. Jour, Sci. Nov. 1871, vol. II. pp. 344–348.

1871. Letter to Capt. C. F. Hall, in regard to the Scientific Operations of the Expedition toward the North Pole. (June 9.) Smithsonian Report, 1871, pp. 364–366.

1871. Suggestions as to Meteorological Observations; during the Expedition toward the North Pole. Smithsonian Report, 1871, pp. 376–379.

1871. Meteorological Notes and Remarks. Smithsonian Report, 1871, pp. 458, 465, 450, 460, 461.

1871. Effect of the Moon on the Weather. Smithsonian Report, 1871, pp. 460, 461.

1871. Anniversary Address as President of the Philosophical Society of Washington. (Delivered Nov. 1st.) Bulletin Phil. Soc. Washington, vol. I. pp. 5–14.

1872. Remarks on Comical Theories of Electricity and Magnetism: an Appendix to a Memoir by Professor O. B. Donati. Smithsonian Report, 1872, pp. 307–309.

1871. On certain Abnormal Phenomena of Sound, in connection with Fog-signals. (Read Dec. 11.) *Bulletin Phil. Soc. Washington*, vol. I. p. 65, and Appendix in. 8 pp.

1872. Letter to John C. Green, Esq. of New York, on his establishment of the "Henry Chair of Physics" in the College of New Jersey. *Washington Daily Chronicle*, Mar. 21, 1873.

1873. On Telegraphic Announcements of Astronomical Discoveries. (May.) *Smithsonian Miscell. Collections*, No. 273, vol. xii. pp. 1–4.

1873. Remarks on the Light-House Service. *Report of Light-House Board*, 1873, pp. 3–7.

1874. Report of Investigations relative to Fog-Signals, and certain abnormal phenomena of Sound. *Report of Light-House Board*, 1874. Appendix, pp. 63–117.

1874. Memoir of Joseph Saxton. (Read Oct. 4.) *Biographical Memoirs of Nat. Acad. Sci.* vol I. pp. 287–316.

1874. Remarks on Recent Earthquakes in North Carolina. *Smithsonian Report*, 1874, pp. 259, 260.

1875. Remarks on the Light-House Service. *Report of Light-House Board*, 1875, pp. 5–8.

1875. An account of investigations relative to Illuminating Materials. *Report of Light-House Board*, 1875. Appendix, pp. 86–103.

1875. Investigations relative to Sound. *Report of Light-House Board*, 1875. Appendix, pp. 104–131.

1875. On the Organization of Local Scientific Societies. *Smithsonian Report*, 1875, pp. 217–219.

1876. Article on "Fog," for Johnson's Universal Cyclopædia. Edited by Dr. Barnard. *J. Univ. Cycl.* vol. ii. pp. 187, 188.

1876. Article on "Fog-Signals" for Johnson's Universal Cyclopædia. Edited by Dr. Barnard. *J. Univ. Cycl.* vol. ii. pp. 188–190.

1876. Article on "Hygrometry" for Johnson's Universal Cyclopædia. Edited by Dr. Barnard. *J. Univ. Cycl.* vol. ii. pp. 1073–1074.

1876. Letter to Rev. S. B. Dod; on researches made at Princeton. (Dated Dec. 4.) *Princeton Memorial*, May 19, 1876, 8vo. N. Y. pp. 61–70.

1877. Article on "Lightning" for Johnson's Universal Cyclopædia. Edited by Dr. Barnard. *J. Univ. Cycl.* vol. iii. pp. 29–30.

1877. Article on "Lightning-Rods" for Johnson's Universal Cyclopædia. Edited by Dr. Barnard. *J. Univ. Cycl.* vol. iii. pp. 36, 37.

1877. Remarks on the Light-House Service. *Report of Light-House Board*, 1877, pp. 3–7.

1877. Report of Operations relative to Fog-Signals. *Report of Light-House Board*, 1877. Appendix, pp. 61–72.

1877. Address before the Philosophical Society of Washington. *Bulletin Phil. Soc. Washington*, vol. II. pp. 162–174.

1878. On Thunder Storms. (Letter Oct. 13.) *Journal Am. Electrical Society*, 1878, vol. II. pp. 37-44.

1878. Letter to Joseph Patterson, Esq. of Philadelphia, on the "Joseph Henry Fund." (Dated Jan. 10.) *Public Ledger and Transcript*, May 14, 1878. *The Press* of Philadelphia, May 16. 1878.

1878. Report on the Ventilation of the Hall of the House of Representatives. (Jan. 28.) 45th Cong. 2nd Sess. H. R. Report, No. 119, pp. 1-6.

1878. Report on the Use of the Polariscope in Saccharimetry. (Feb. 5.) Mis. Doc. 45th Cong. 2nd Sess. H. R.

1878. Opening Address before the National Academy of Sciences. (Read April 16.) *Proceedings Nat. Acad. Sci.* vol. I. part 2, pp. 127, 128.

1878. Closing Address before the National Academy of Sciences. (Read April 19.) *Proceedings Nat. Acad. Sci.* vol. I. part 2, pp. 129, 130.

SUPPLEMENTARY NOTES.

Note A. (*From p. 209.*)

HENRY'S FIRST EXPERIMENTS.

From the time of leaving the Albany Academy young Henry exhibited a great fondness for chemical experimentation. The wonderful transformations of familiar substances under the magic spell of decomposing re-actions and combining affinities, seemed to his ardent imagination to offer a possible clue to the mystery of matter and of force. His mental activity sought an outlet in assisting to establish the "Albany Lyceum."

Orlando Meads, LL.D. in the "Annual Address" read before the Albany Institute, May 25, 1871, thus records his early reminiscences:

"When a boy in the Albany Academy in 1823 and 1824, it was my pleasure and privilege, when released from recitations, to resort to the chemical laboratory and lecture room. There might be found from day to day through the winter, earnestly engaged in experiments upon steam and upon a small steam-engine, and in chemical and other scientific investigations, two young men — both active members of the 'Lyceum,' then very different in their external circumstances and prospects in life, but of kindred tastes and sympathies; the one was Richard Varick DeWitt, the other was Joseph Henry, as yet unknown to fame, but already giving promise of those rare qualities of mind and character which have since raised him to the very first rank among the experimental philosophers of his time. Chemistry at that time was exciting great interest, and Dr. Beck's courses of chemical lectures, conducted every winter in the lecture room of the Academy, were attended not only by the students, but by all that was most intelligent and fashionable in the city. Henry, who had been formerly a pupil in the Academy, was then Dr. Beck's chemical assistant, and already an admirable experimentalist, and he availed himself to the utmost of the advantages thus afforded, of prosecuting his investigations in chemistry, electricity, and galvanism." [*]

---

[*] *Transactions of Albany Institute*, 1872, vol. vii pp. 2, 3.

Note B. (*From p. 227.*)

"INTENSITY" AND "QUANTITY" CURRENTS.

Early in the century, the eminent chemist Dr. Thomas Thomson endeavored to express the difference between mechanical electricity and chemical electricity, by characterizing the former as possessing "intensity," and the latter as possessing "quantity." From the increase of electrical effects with the multiplication of galvanic pairs in a pile or battery, Volta a short time before had designated such action as "electromotor" force. Dr. Robert Hare in 1816 devising a galvanic battery in which all the positive elements were directly connected together, as were all the negative elements, (thus constituting it virtually a battery of a single pair,) from the heating effects obtained, designated the action as "calorimotor" force. It appeared quite natural afterward to distinguish these classes of effects by the old terms—"intensity" for electromotive force, and "quantity" for calorimotive force. There is obviously a close analogy between these differences of condition or resultant, and the more strongly contrasted conditions of mechanical and chemical electricity: and indeed the whole may be said to lie in a continuous series, from the highest "intensity" with minimum quantity, to the greatest "quantity" with minimum intensity.

Peltier in 1850 published a paper entitled "Definition of the terms electric *Quantity* and *Intensity*, derived from direct experiment:" in which he showed that "if we form a voltaic pair of two fine wires, zinc and copper, immersed in pure water, and connected by a circuit of copper wire 300 metres (328 yards) long, although there is as we know a continuous current in this closed circuit, the copper wire if placed immediately over a magnetic needle, will not deflect it from the magnetic meridian. But if the needle be surrounded by a "multiplicator" formed of 100 or 200 coils of the long wire, there will be at once a notable deviation; and if the number of coils be increased to 2,000 the deviation may extend to 60 degrees." In this experiment, as the primitive current has not been changed, but a "fictitious quantity" only has been produced by conducting it 2,000 times around the magnetic needle, Peltier inferred that it is by the *quantity* (and by no other modification) that the action has been thus enhanced; and that it is therefore through its *quantity* that a current acts on the magnetic needle.

"Taking now a thermo-electric pair, zinc and copper, of five square millimetres, (the 120th part of a square inch,) and heating one of the solderings to 40 degrees, (104° F.) we find that with the same closed circuit and multiplicator of 2,000 coils, the needle will not be deflected; the electricity will not pass. But if we retrench

1,500 coils, (shortening the conductor to this extent,) the galvanometer now of 200 coils will begin to give notable deviations. If we reduce it to 10 coils, the deflection will be considerably augmented. Finally, if we reduce it to a single coil formed of a strip of copper containing as much substance as the 200 coils, the deflection of the needle may amount to even 60 degrees. The quantity of electricity produced in this experiment by the thermo-electric pair is therefore evidently 2,000 times greater than that of the above hydro-electric pair, since we obtain the same deviation with a single coil as with the factitious quantity given by the reduplication of the coils. On the other hand, in the first experiment the length of the conducting wire was easily traversed by the hydro-electric current; the inertia of the matter was overcome without difficulty and without appreciable loss of the current: in the second experiment this inertia could not be overcome; the power of action was insufficient and it was necessary to reduce the circuit to a very small length for the electricity to be able to traverse it." From these phenomena, Peltier argued that two very distinct conditions were presented, which should not be confounded; an action of *quantity* without resistance, and an action of *intensity* independent of quantity, capable of overcoming considerable resistance.[*]

In the same memoir however, Peltier took occasion to say that he considered "dynamic intensity" an inappropriate expression for electricity in movement; and that the term if retained should be used to designate not a modification of the electric current, but a particular disposition of the electro-motor. He discarded the idea that intensity represents a peculiar quality in the current itself; but considered the action as only the consequence of increased resistance offered by the pile to a backward movement or return of the electric flow: or in other words that intensity regarded as the power of overcoming obstacles in the external path, results from the greater obstacles presented by the battery to a neutralization by retrogradation.[†]

The designations under discussion have been largely superseded in modern authorities by the mathematical treatment of the subject, which takes cognizance alone of the ratio between electromotive force and resistance differences in the circuits. Thus Professor Jenkin, speaking of the two classes of batteries, remarks: "With a short circuit of small external resistance, we can increase the current by increasing the size of cells, or what is equivalent to this, by joining several cells in multiple arc. With a long circuit of great external resistance, large cells (or many of them joined in multiple

[*] *Annales de Chimie et de Physique*, 1838, vol. lxvii. pp. 265, 246.
[†] Same work, p. 263.

arc) will fail to give us strong currents, but we may increase the
current by joining the same cells in series. - - - Cells joined
in series are sometimes described as joined for 'intensity'; and cells
joined in multiple arc, as joined for 'quantity.' These terms are
remnants of an erroneous theory." *

Again, in speaking of galvanometers of long and fine coils, as
distinguished from those of short and thick wire coils, he says: "In
some writings these two classes of instruments are spoken of as
adapted to two different classes of 'currents' instead of to two
different classes of circuits. The instrument with numerous turns
of fine wire is said to indicate 'intensity' currents, the other class
to indicate 'quantity' currents. These two old names survive,
although the fallacious theory which assumed that there were two
kinds of currents is extinct: the term 'intensity galvanometer' is
used to signify an instrument with thousands of turns of thin wire
in its coil, and 'quantity galvanometer'—an instrument with few
turns of thick wire. I shall name the two varieties 'long coil'
and 'short coil' galvanometers." †

Admirable as the mathematical theory of galvanic circuits has
proved itself in its fullness and precision, it does not supply us with
any satisfactory physical conception of the palpable dynamic difference in the resultant galvanic currents. The old terms, whether
accurate or not, are still convenient designations of the acknowledged differences when reference is had to effects rather than to
arrangements. ‡

No one has more clearly pointed out the almost constant an-
tithesis between the actions of "static" and "dynamic" electricity,
than Peltier himself. "Static electricity is duplex; each of its
forms is collected, controlled, and maintained separately; being
manifested only in the state of isolation and separation: these forms
are only preserved thus separate by non-conducting substances, and
their action endures as long as their insulation. Dynamic electricity
is not double; it cannot be separately either collected, controlled,
or maintained; being manifested only at the instant of its transmission through conductors insulated or not; for continuous effect
it is necessary that the producing cause be continuous. The former
collects only at the surface, being equally or unequally distributed
thereon according to the form of the surface. The latter is propa-

* Electricity and Magnetism. By Fleeming Jenkin. 8vo. London and New
York, 8°3, chap. IV, sect. 7, p. 86.

† Same work, chap. XIII, sect. 8, p. 189.

‡ Peltier from experiments (the results of which he has detailed) controverted
the universality of the law of Ohm and times, that galvanic resistance is directly
proportioned to the length of the conducting wire, and inversely proportional to
the area of its cross-section. (Chemistry Review, vol. 12, 1855, vol. 1, pp. 28, 284.)

gated equally through the interior of conducting bodies, and in proportion to their mass quite irrespective of the form of their surfaces. Two bodies charged with the same kind of static electricity, exhibit mutual repulsion; while if charged with contrary kinds they exhibit mutual attraction: and by contact establish a complete neutralization. Two currents of dynamic electricity, in the same direction attract each other; in opposite directions repel each other: the contact of their conductors produces neither division nor neutralization; nor does any external communication disturb the current in a closed circuit. A body charged with either kind of static electricity exerts no action but attraction on a neutral body; it induces the opposite electrical state on the portion of a body approached, repelling its own kind to the further extremity. A current of dynamic electricity produces various inductive effects on neighboring bodies, as transverse magnetization, instantaneous impulses at the moment of any change, chemical actions, etc. The former finds an equilibrium of its two forms in very unequal degrees in different metals.* The latter finds only conducting differences between the metals; and is not affected by other currents. The former is feeble or intense according to the extent of surface on which it is accumulated; and manifests its *tension* by a greater or less attraction or repulsion. The latter exhibits the states of quantity — measured by the deflection of the galvanometer, and of intensity — measured by the power of overcoming resistance or of traversing poor conductors." †

Characteristically different as are the phenomena thus exhibited by mechanical and chemical electricities, (to distinguish which we have unfortunately no satisfactory expressions,) almost as marked — though in a much smaller degree, are the peculiarities of galvanism itself, in what must be called its varying states of tension. And for these striking differences, Ohm's celebrated law that "the strength of the current is proportional to the electro-motive force divided by the conducting resistance," affords no more intelligible explanation than it does for the peculiar department of so-called "static" electricity. Indeed Ohm's formula represents but a close

<hr/>

* Peltier first demonstrated that the electric capacity of the metals for the same kind from a constant source, is very unequal; thus zinc takes and retains more positive than negative electricity, while the contrary takes place with copper; so gold is more apt than silver or platina to become charged with positive electricity. (Comptes Rendus, 1855, vol. i. pp. 360 and 676.)

† Annales de Chimie et de Physique, 1838, vol. lxvii. pp. 425–429. The title of this memoir is "Experimental researches on the quantities of static and dynamic action produced by the oxidation of a milligramme of zinc;" and the author arrives at the conclusion that the static effects are as the squares of the dynamic effects; or conversely, the dynamic as the square roots of the static. (p. 46.)

approximation to the actual facts of electrical transmission; and gives us no account of the remarkable fact discovered by Henry that the magnetizing power of a current actually increases with the length of the conductor, up to a certain point: nor of his other discovery, the "extra current" or the induction of a current upon itself. Indeed it takes no cognizance of any of the numerous perturbations dependent on the mysterious re-actions of electrical "induction."

Note C. (*From p. 229.*)

THE ELECTRO-MAGNETIC TELEGRAPH.

From among living eye-witnesses of Henry's early telegraphic experiments in the years 1831 and 1832, the following may be cited:

Dr. Orlando Meads, a former student of the Albany Academy, in an anniversary discourse commemorating the fiftieth year of its existence, thus referred to the scenes he witnessed a third of a century before: "The older students of the Academy in the years 1830, 1831, and 1832, and others who witnessed his experiments which at that time excited so much interest in this city, will remember the long coils of wire which ran circuit upon circuit for more than a mile in length around one of the upper rooms in the Academy, for the purpose of illustrating the fact that a galvanic current could be transmitted through its whole length so as to excite a magnet at the farther end of the line, and thus move a steel bar which struck a bell. This in a scientific point of view, was the demonstration and accomplishment of all that was required for the magnetic telegraph. - - - Let us not forget that the click of the telegraph which is heard from every joint of those mystic wires which now link together every city, and village, and post, and camp, and station, all over this continent, is but the echo of that little bell which first sounded in that upper room of the Academy." [*]

On the same occasion, the Hon. Alexander W. Bradford, also a former pupil of the Academy, (who finished his course at the Institution and left it in 1832,) recalled the suspended lines of insulated copper wire through which his teacher had demonstrated "the magnetic power of the galvanic battery; and years before the invention of the telegraph, proclaimed to America and to Europe the means of communication by the electric fluid. I was an eye-

---

[*] "Historical Discourse" on the Celebration of the Semi-Centennial Anniversary of the Albany Academy, June 21, 1863. Proceedings, etc. pp. 35, 36.

witness to those experiments, and to their eventual demonstration and triumph." *

Professor James Hall, (in the same year in which he was President of the American Association at its Albany meeting,) in a letter addressed to Professor Henry, January 10, 1856, relates the circumstances of a visit to the Albany Academy in August, 1832, on which occasion he was shown a long circuit of wire about the walls of a larger upper room, "and at one termination of this, in the recess of a window, a bell was fixed, while the other extremity was connected with a galvanic apparatus. You showed us the manner in which the bell could be made to ring by a current of electricity transmitted through this wire; and you remarked that this method might be adopted for giving signals by the ringing of a bell at the distance of many miles from the point of its connection with the galvanic apparatus. All the circumstances attending this visit to Albany are fresh in my recollection; and during the past years while so much has been said respecting the invention of electric telegraphs, I have often had occasion to mention the exhibition of your electric telegraph in the Albany Academy, in 1832." †

Professor Morse, who states that the idea of an electric telegraph first occurred to him in October, 1832, commenced experimenting on this conception in the latter part of 1835. The following is his own account of his first experiments:

"In the year 1835, I was appointed a professor in the New York City University, and about the month of November of that year, I occupied rooms in the University buildings. There I immediately commenced with very limited means to experiment upon my invention. My first instrument was made up of an old picture or canvas frame fastened to a table, the wheels of an old wooden clock moved by a weight to carry the paper forward, three wooden drums upon one of which the paper was wound and passed over the other two, a wooden pendulum suspended to the top piece of the picture or stretching frame and vibrating across the paper as it passed over the center wooden drum, a pencil at the lower end of the pendulum in contact with the paper, an electro-magnet fastened to a shelf across the picture or stretching frame opposite to an armature made fast to the pendulum, a type-rule and type for breaking the circuit on an endless band (composed of carpet-binding) which passed over two wooden rollers moved by a wooden crank and carried forward by points projecting from the bottom of the rule downward into the carpet-binding, a lever with a small weight on the upper side and a

---

* "Commemorative Address"; at Semi-Centennial Anniversary of Albany Academy, June 23, 1883. Proceedings, etc. p. 16.

† Published in the Smithsonian Report for 1857, p. 96.

tooth projecting downward at one end operated on by the type, and a metallic fork also projecting downward over two mercury-cups and a short circuit of wire embracing the helices of the electromagnet, connected with the positive and negative poles of the battery and terminating in the mercury-cups. - - - Early in 1836, I procured forty feet of wire, and putting it in the circuit I found that my battery of one cup was not sufficient to work my instrument." [*]

The last statement exhibits a singular unconsciousness of the real defect of his receiving apparatus, and of the fact that no number of galvanic cups would have sufficed "to work the instrument" as then constructed. It is true (as first shown by Henry) that an "intensity" battery of many elements is required to operate a magnetic telegraph line; but (as also shown by him) a no less essential constituent, is an "intensity" magnet, if any use is to be made of the armature. And on this point Professor Morse seems never to have understood the vital importance of Henry's discoveries to the success of his own invention. Had he employed the most powerful of then existing magnets, (Henry's Yale College magnet of 1831, lifting 2,300 pounds, or Henry's Princeton College magnet of 1834, lifting 3,500 pounds,) he would still have found neither one cup nor one thousand cups "sufficient to work the instrument" through a circuit of fine wire, at the distance of a single mile.[†] Although Professor Morse was enabled therefore to operate the armature of his Sturgeon magnet through a few yards of wire, it is certain that his experiments in 1836 were, for any telegraphic purpose, an absolute failure:—a failure as complete as were those undertaken by Barlow in 1825. The relevancy of his incidental remark as in extenuation—"one cup was not sufficient to work my instrument," may therefore be appreciated.

As an artist of repute, Mr. Morse had been appointed professor of the "Arts of Design," in the newly established New York City University, in the autumn of 1835; but with any literature of science, he was remarkably unfamiliar. He therefore very naturally had recourse to his colleague Professor Leonard D. Gale (of the chair of chemistry) for needed scientific assistance. The following is Dr. Gale's account of Morse's original invention:

"In the winter of 1836–'37, Samuel F. B. Morse, who as well as myself was a professor in the New York University, city of

* Professor Morse's deposition in the "Bain case," 1849.

† "Electro-magnets of the greatest power, even when the most energetic batteries are employed, utterly cease to act when they are connected by considerable lengths of wire with the battery." (J. F. Daniell's *Introduction to the Study of Chemical Philosophy*. 2nd ed. 8vo. London, 1843, chap. xvi. sect. 469, p. 576.)

New York, came to my lecture room, and said he had a machine in his lecture room or studio which he wished to show me. I accompanied him to his room and there saw resting on a table a single-pair galvanic battery, an electro-magnet, an arrangement of pencil, a paper-covered roller, pinion wheels, levers, etc. for making letters and figures to be used for sending and receiving words and sentences through long distances. - - - It was evident to me that the one large cup-battery of Morse should be made into ten or fifteen smaller ones to make it a battery of intensity. - - - Accordingly I substituted the battery of many cups for the battery of one cup. The remaining defect in the Morse machine as first seen by me was that the coil of wire around the poles of the electro-magnet consisted of but a few turns only, while to give the greatest projectile power, the number of turns should be increased from tens to hundreds, as shown by Professor Henry in his paper published in the *American Journal of Science*, 1831. - - - After substituting the battery of twenty cups for that of a single cup, we added some hundred or more turns to the coil of wire around the poles of the magnet, and sent a message through 200 feet of conductors; then through 1,000 feet." [*]

After many trials at recording numbers by zig-zag markings counted in groups separated by a space, a continuous dispatch was for the first time effected on the 2d and 4th of September, 1837, in the form of V-shaped lines inscribed on the paper fillet, to the following effect: "215—30—2—58—112—04—01837:" which message as interpreted by a numbered vocabulary from which it was compiled, expressed the phrase "successful experiment with telegraph, September 4, 1837." [†]

About a month later, Professor Morse filed in the United States Patent Office a "Caveat," signed October 3d, 1837, comprising: "1st, a system of signs by which numbers and consequently words and sentences are signified; 2d, a set of type adapted to regulate and communicate the signs, with cases for convenient keeping of the type, and rules in which to set up the type; 3d, an apparatus called a port-rule for regulating the movement of the type-rules, which rules by means of the type in their turn regulate the times and intervals of the passage of electricity; 4th, a register which records the signs permanently; 5th, a dictionary or vocabulary of

---

* *Memorial of S. F. B. Morse.* 8vo. Washington, 1875, pp. 15-17.

† A facsimile of this first "successful experiment" was published in the New York *Journal of Commerce*, for Thursday, Sept. 7th, 1837; and was reproduced in Vail's *American Electro-Magnetic Telegraph.* 8vo. Philadelphia, 1845, p. 73. The date, September, 1837, is accordingly that of the reduction of Morse's telegraph to a practical operation.

words numbered and adapted to this system of telegraph; 6th, modes of laying the conductors to preserve them from injury."

A new and improved transmitting and recording apparatus was completed for Professor Morse, by his partner, Mr. Alfred Vail, of the Speedwell Iron-works, near Morristown, N. J. at the close of the year 1837; and early in January, 1838, Professor Morse first discarded the numeral signs for words, and employed a true *alphabet* of "dots and dashes." The first exhibition of an alphabetic record of words and sentences took place in the New York City University, January 24th, 1838, through ten miles of wire wound on reels. The New York *Journal of Commerce*, in a notice of this performance, remarked: "Professor Morse has recently improved on his mode of marking, by which he can dispense altogether with the telegraphic dictionary, using letters instead of numbers." * The biographer of Morse designates the dispatch transmitted through the wires on this occasion, "the first *sentence* that was ever recorded by the telegraph." †

An application for a patent (signed by Professor Morse, April 7th, 1838,) was filed in the Patent Office; and in addition to the several parts described in the earlier Caveat, this application included the new system of alphabetic symbols, and the "relay" of successive electro-magnetic circuits. At his own request, the grant of the patent was suspended until he should have made a visit to Europe: and it was not issued till June 20th, 1840. On his return from his European tour, Professor Morse, in May, 1839, sought an interview with Henry at Princeton, from which he received much encouragement: having the differences between the "quantity" and "intensity" magnets fully explained to him, and learning from that cautious investigator that he was aware of no obstacle to the magnetization of soft iron "at the distance of a hundred miles or more" from the battery. ‡

During the long and weary interval in which Professor Morse — with hope deferred — was unavailingly prosecuting his memorial to Congress for assistance, he received from Henry the following friendly and inspiriting letter:

"PRINCETON COLLEGE, Feb. 24, 1842.

"MY DEAR SIR: I am pleased to learn that you have again petitioned Congress in reference to your telegraph; and I most sincerely hope you will succeed in convincing our Representatives of the importance of the invention. - - - Science is now fully ripe

* New York *Journal of Commerce* of January 29th, 1838.
* Prime's *Life of Morse*, 8vo. New York, 1875, p. 331.
‡ Prime's *Life of Morse*, chap. x. pp. 121, 122.

for this application, and I have not the least doubt, if proper means
be afforded, of the perfect success of the invention. The idea of
transmitting intelligence to a distance by means of electrical action
has been suggested by various persons, from the time of Franklin
to the present; but until within the last few years, or since the
principal discoveries in electro-magnetism, all attempts to reduce it
to practice were *necessarily unsuccessful*. The mere suggestion
however of a scheme of this kind, is a matter for which little
credit can be claimed, since it is one which would naturally arise in
the mind of almost any person familiar with the phenomena of
electricity: but the bringing it forward at the proper moment when
the developments of science are able to furnish the means of certain
success, and the devising a plan for carrying it into practical operation, are the grounds of a just claim to scientific reputation as well
as to public patronage. About the same time with yourself, Professor Wheatstone of London, and Dr. Steinheil of Germany, proposed plans of the electro-magnetic telegraph; but these differ as
much from yours as the nature of the common principle would well
permit; and unless some essential improvements have lately been
made in these European plans, I should prefer the one invented by
yourself.

"With my best wishes for your success, I remain with much
esteem,

                 "Yours, truly,

                            "JOSEPH HENRY."

"This" says Morse's biographer, "was the most encouraging
communication Professor Morse received during the dark ages
between 1839 and 1843." [*] And appended to his memorial, it was
undoubtedly influential in enlisting a more favorable attention to
the unfamiliar project of an electro-magnetic telegraph. In December of the same year a bill appropriating thirty thousand dollars
for testing the system invented by S. F. B. Morse, was reported
in the House of Representatives by the Hon. C. G. Ferris of
New York; passing that body February 23rd, and the Senate
about a week later — March 3d, 1843, on the eve of the close of its
session.

Under the appropriation thus secured, a line of four wires was
extended from Washington to Baltimore, a distance of 40 miles;
and on the 24th of May, 1844, the first message was satisfactorily
transmitted between the two cities. The rapid success of the telegraph soon stimulated competition; and before many years elapsed,
a series of resisting litigations was the natural consequence.

---

* Prime's *Life of Morse*, chap. x, p. CII.

25

Henry summoned to testify as to the condition of telegraphic science, as well as to his own experimental researches, previous to Morse's invention, was compelled to give evidence which did not sustain entirely the theory of the complainants, and therefore did not satisfy their very broad pretensions; though it did tend to establish Professor Morse's just claims to originality. This account can best be given in Henry's own statement:

"A series of controversies and lawsuits having arisen between rival claimants for telegraphic patents, I was repeatedly appealed to, to act as expert and witness in such cases. This I uniformly declined to do, not wishing to be in any manner involved in these litigations, but was finally compelled, under legal process, to return to Boston from Maine, whither I had gone on a visit, and to give evidence on the subject. My testimony was given with the statement that I was not a willing witness, and that I labored under the disadvantage of not having access to my notes and papers, which were in Washington. That testimony however I now reaffirm to be true in every essential particular. It was unimpeached before the court, and exercised an influence on the final decision of the question at issue. I was called upon on that occasion to state, not only what I had published, but what I had done, and what I had shown to others in regard to the telegraph. It was my wish, in every statement, to render Mr. Morse full and scrupulous justice. While I was constrained therefore to state that he had made no discoveries in science, I distinctly declared that he was entitled to the merit of combining and applying the discoveries of others, in the invention of the best practical form of the magnetic telegraph. My testimony tended to establish the fact that though not entitled to the exclusive use of the electro-magnet for telegraphic purposes, he was entitled to his particular machine, register, alphabet, &c. As this however did not meet the full requirements of Mr. Morse's comprehensive claim, I could not but be aware that, while aiming to depose nothing but truth and the whole truth, - - - I might expose myself to the possible, and as it has proved, the actual, danger of having my motives misconstrued and my testimony misrepresented. But I can truly aver that I had no desire to arrogate to myself undue merit, or to detract from the just claims of Mr. Morse." *

From this time, Professor Morse seemed to regard Henry with the jealous eye of a rival, as if holding him disposed for purposes of self-aggrandizement to detract from his own merit as projector of the telegraph. After years of preparation, he had completed

* Smithsonian Report for 1857, pp. 97, 98.

and signed in December, 1853, and in January of 1855, under the ill-advised promptings of interested supporters, caused to be published in a pamphlet of 96 pages, an elaborate and artfully contrived attack upon Henry's character as a scientific explorer, and as a trustworthy man; undertaking the hazardous task of exposing "the utter *non-reliability* of Henry's testimony." In this assault—so unfortunate for his own reputation, (if not for candor, at least for intelligence,) he announced:

"1st. I certainly shall show that I have not only manifested every disposition to give due credit to Professor Henry, but under the hasty impression that he deserved credit for discoveries in science bearing upon the telegraph, I did actually give him a degree of credit not only beyond what he had received at that time from the scientific world, but a degree of credit to which subsequent research has proved him not to be entitled. 2d. I shall show that I am not indebted to him for any discovery in science bearing on the telegraph, and that all discoveries of principles having this bearing were made not by Professor Henry, but by others and prior to any experiments of Professor Henry in the science of electro-magnetism. 3d. I shall further show that the claim set up for Professor Henry to the invention of an important part of my telegraph system, has no validity in fact." *

Neglecting entirely the first allegation,— as a sufficient answer to the second, Henry simply appealed to the unimpeachable testimony of Dr. Gale, who certainly had a much more precise knowledge of Professor Morse's early experiments and apparatus than the inventor himself. And in reply to the third allegation, driven in self-defence to the unusual step of self-assertion, Henry presented to the Regents for their adjudication, the evidences of his discoveries and of their respective dates of application and promulgation. †

Professor Gale, who still preserved a faithful friendship for his former colleague, yet in the interests of truth did not hesitate to renew his former testimony to the vital bearing of Henry's researches

---

* *A Defence against the injurious deductions drawn from the Deposition of Professor Henry.* New York, 1855, p. 8.

† A select committee appointed by the Board of Regents to investigate the imputations made by this remarkable assault—against the truthfulness of their Secretary, after a careful examination of all the evidences presented or accessible, submitted through its chairman, President Felton of Harvard University, a very able and exhaustive report, in which the tenor of the pamphlet is characterized as "a disingenuous piece of sophistical argument," and the conclusion is announced, "that Mr. Morse has failed to substantiate any one of the charges he has made against Professor Henry, although the burden of proof lay upon him; and that all the evidence—including the unbiased admissions of Mr. Morse himself, is on the other side. Mr. Morse's charges not only remain unproved, but they are positively disproved." (*Smithsonian Report for 1857, pp. 94-98.*)

on the success of the telegraph; and he frankly responded to Henry's inquiry in the following letter:

"WASHINGTON, D. C., April 7, 1856.

"SIR: In reply to your note of the 3d instant, respecting the Morse telegraph, asking me to state definitely the condition of the invention when I first saw the apparatus in the winter of 1836, I answer: This apparatus was Morse's original instrument, usually known as the type apparatus, in which the types, set up in a composing stick, were run through a circuit breaker, and in which the battery was the cylinder battery, with a single pair of plates. This arrangement also had another peculiarity, namely, it was the electro-magnet used by Moll,* and shown in drawings of the older works on that subject, having only a few turns of wire in the coil which surrounded the poles or arms of the magnet. The sparseness of the wires in the magnet coils and the use of the single cup battery were to me, on the first look at the instrument, obvious marks of defect, and I accordingly suggested to the Professor, without giving my reasons for so doing, that a battery of many pairs should be substituted for that of a single pair, and that the coil on each arm of the magnet should be increased to many hundred turns each; which experiment, if I remember aright, was made on the same day with a battery and wire on hand, furnished I believe by myself, and it was found that while the original arrangement would only send the electric current through a few feet of wire, say 15 to 40, the modified arrangement would send it through as many hundred. Although I gave no reasons at the time to Professor Morse for the suggestions I had proposed in modifying the arrangement of the machine, I did so afterwards, and referred in my explanations to the paper of Professor Henry, in the 19th volume of the *American Journal of Science*, page 400 and onward.

"At the time I gave the suggestions above named, Professor Morse was not familiar with the then existing state of the science of electro-magnetism. Had he been so, or had he read and appreciated the paper of Henry, the suggestions made by me would naturally have occurred to his mind as they did to my own. But the principal part of Morse's great invention lay in the mechanical adaptation of a power to produce motion, and to increase or relax at will. It was only necessary for him to know that such a power existed for him to adapt mechanism to direct and control it. My suggestions were made to Professor Morse from inferences drawn by reading Professor Henry's paper above alluded to. Professor Morse

---

*[More correctly, the magnet of PIXII and MOLL.]

professed great surprise at the contents of the paper when I showed it to him, but especially at the remarks on Dr. Barlow's results respecting telegraphing, which were new to him, and he stated at the time that he was not aware that any one had even conceived the idea of using the magnet for such purposes.

"With sentiments of esteem, I remain, yours truly,

"L. D. GALE.

"Prof. JOS. HENRY, *Secretary of the Smithsonian Institution.*"

A simple reference to published documents, abundantly established the indisputable originality and priority of Henry's successful researches; and conclusively exposed the falsity of Professor Morse's remaining allegations. The following summary from the historic evidence, as stated by Henry himself, is certainly (in the language of the committee of the Regents) "within what he might fairly have claimed:"

."From a careful investigation of the history of electro-magnetism in its connection with the telegraph, the following facts may be established:

"1. Previous to my investigations the means of developing magnetism in soft iron were imperfectly understood, and the electro-magnet which then existed was inapplicable to the transmission of power to a distance.

"2. I was the first to prove by actual experiment that in order to develop magnetic power at a distance, a galvanic battery of intensity must be employed to project the current through the long conductor, and that a magnet surrounded by many turns of one long wire may be used to receive this current.

"3. I was the first actually to magnetize a piece of iron at a distance, and to call attention to the fact of the applicability of my experiments to the telegraph.

"4. I was the first to actually sound a bell at a distance by means of the electro-magnet.

"5. The principles I had developed were applied by Dr. Gale to render Morse's machine effective at a distance.

"The results here given were among my earliest experiments; in a scientific point of view I considered them of much less importance than what I subsequently accomplished; and had I not been called upon to give my testimony in regard to them, I would have suffered them to remain without calling public attention to them, a part of the history of science to be judged of by scientific men who are the best qualified to pronounce upon their merits." *

* Smithsonian Report for 1857, p. 105.

Note D. (*From p. 230.*)

HENRY'S MULTIPLE-COIL MAGNET.

Professor M. Faraday, in the first series of his "Experimental Researches in Electricity," commencing in the latter part of 1831, employed for the magnet by which he made his most important discovery—that of magneto-electricity,—the multiple coil of Henry. He thus describes it: "A welded ring was made of soft round bar-iron, the metal being seven-eighths of an inch in thickness, and the ring six inches in external diameter. Three helices were put around one part of this ring, each containing about twenty-four feet of copper wire one-twentieth of an inch thick; they were insulated from the iron and each other, and superposed in the manner before described.* They could be used separately or arranged together. On the other part of the ring about sixty feet of similar copper wire in two pieces were applied in the same manner. - - - There is no doubt that arrangements like the magnets of Professors Moll, Henry, Ten-Eyck, and others, in which as many as 2,000 pounds have been lifted, may be used for these experiments."†

Henry's warm friend—Dr. Robert Hare of Philadelphia, (Professor of Chemistry in the University of Pennsylvania,) who early repeated his magnetic experiments, says in a letter to Mr. Sturgeon, dated April 5, 1832: "As soon as I heard of the wonderful magnet of Professor Henry, I repeated his experiments with copper wire varnished as above described; and I have recently made a magnet by means of copper wire, shellac varnish, and paper surrounding the iron,—which in proportion to its weight, holds more than his. It weighs 17 pounds, and has held 783 pounds. It is furnished with fourteen coils, of sixty feet each."‡

Professor N. J. Callan, of the College of Maynooth, Ireland, in 1836, giving an account of his "new galvanic battery" remarks

---

* [In his preceding electrical induction coils, Professor Faraday employed "twelve helices superposed, each containing an average length of wire of 27 feet, and all in the same direction." Of these, six were connected by their extremities with the battery—for the primary current, and the alternate six were gathered by their extremities, for testing the secondary or induced current.]

† *Phil. Trans. Roy. Soc.* Nov. 24, 1831, vol. cxxii. sects. 27 and 57; pp. 130, 138.—Also *Experimental Researches, etc.* 8vo. London, 1839, vol. i. pp. 7, 11. At the time this was written, the only electro-magnet in existence—even approaching the lifting power stated, was the Yale College magnet of Henry. Nor had any other experiment approximated within a tenth of this magnetic attraction. And it is noteworthy that Professor Faraday adopted very precisely the character of coil originated and recommended by Henry, and did not adopt the single coil employed by Professor Moll.

‡ *Sturgeon's Annals of Electricity, etc.* Oct. 1836, vol. i. p. 18.

that "it rendered powerfully magnetic an electro-magnet on which were coiled 30 thick copper wires, each about 35 feet long." [*]

The only subsequent extension of Henry's results worthy of note, is that made by the ingenious English physicist Joule. It had been found that the maximum attractive force of the electro-magnet is exhibited near its surface, and that an enlargement of the iron does not correspondingly enhance its magnetic power.[†] If we adopt the conception of Coulomb and of Weber that the constituent molecules of the iron are each independent permanent magnets, this variation of magnetic force in a large iron bar, receives an easy explanation; since the middle portion of the bar is not only less coerced by the surrounding coil,[‡] but is powerfully impressed by the opposite induction of the outer belt of polarized molecules. While therefore we should a priori expect the aggregate attractive force to increase with the size of the bar, (i. e. the cross-section or end-surface of the poles,) we find that this very extension occasions a large amount of neutralization by the interior opposite magnetism; such depolarization being obviously the condition of least constraint.[§]

Acting on the theory that the power of the magnet would depend on the extent of efficient polar surface, and at the same time on the propinquity of the electric coil, Joule's highest magnetic triumph consisted in giving a greatly increased depth to the horse-shoe, (as though a vast number of small horse-shoes were laid side to side and cemented together,) without an increase of its width; the former dimension exceeding the latter many times; so that the two poles presented a pair of long narrow parallel surfaces close together, bounding a long trough or gutter. And the addition of the oblong armature gave the whole the general appearance of a tube. The author thus describes its construction: "A piece of cylindrical wrought-iron, eight inches long, had a hole one inch in diameter bored the whole length of its axis; one side was then planned until

---

[*] L. & E. Phil. Mag. Dec. 1838, vol. ix. p. 473.

[†] Barlow had shewn the conclusion from his own experiments, that the magnetic power of iron resides entirely at the surface, and is irrespective of mass.

[‡] The direct action of the electric circuit in the coil, would probably not be sensibly less on the interior than on the exterior of a large iron core; but its polarizing energy must necessarily be largely expended in coercing the homogeneous direction of the nearer outer layers of molecules, leaving the interior mass more under the immediate inductive influence of its state of magnets.

[§] Having this in view Joule (in imitation of Coulomb's figure of thin magnets employed with success in a bundle of wires, for the electro-magnetic core, (Sturgeon's Annals, etc. July, 1839, vol. iv. pp. 56-61.) It is evident also from the above, that the removal of the central portion of the inner core, in other words the employment of a tube of certain thickness, in place of the solid bar, would actually increase the resultant power of the magnet, with a diminished mass of iron.

the hole was exposed sufficiently to separate the 'poles' one-third of an inch.   Another piece of iron also eight inches long was then planed, and being secured with its face in contact with the other planed surface, the whole was turned into a cylinder eight inches long, three inches and three-quarters in exterior — and one inch interior diameter.   The larger piece was then covered with calico, and wound with four copper wires (covered with silk) each 23 feet long and one-eleventh of an inch in diameter; — a quantity which was just sufficient to hide the exterior surface, and entirely to fill the inside hole."[*]   This magnet weighing without wire but 13 pounds, lifted 2,090 pounds.

Joule subsequently made another magnet still deeper, or longer in its tubular extent; the grooved iron with its closed armature being not unlike a gun-barrel.   The length of this soft-iron cylinder was two feet; its external diameter about one inch and a half, and its internal diameter a half inch: the weight of the grooved magnet being 6 pounds 11 ounces, and that of its armature, 3 pounds 7 ounces.   A copper rod three-eighths of an inch thick was bent once around each side of the tube, or elongated pole.   With a battery of 8 cells of two square feet each (16 square feet) arranged as a single pair, a lifting power of 1,350 pounds was induced.   The single thick copper rod having then been replaced with a bundle of 60 copper wires, each one-twenty-fifth of an inch thick, the magnet lifted 1,656 pounds.   This remarkable success of the "multiple coil" led Joule to increase the number of coils in the former tube-like magnet. The four wires each one-eleventh of an inch thick were replaced by twenty-one wires of the same length, each one-twenty-fifth of an inch thick, the whole being bound together by cotton tape.   "Sixteen cast-iron cells of the same size as those previously described, [each of two square feet,] were then arranged in a series of four, and connected by sufficiently good conductors to the electro-magnet. The power which was then necessary to break it from its armature, was 2,775 pounds, or nearly a ton and a quarter.   An immense weight, when it is considered that the whole apparatus — magnet armature and coils — weighs less than 26 pounds."[†]

---

[*] Sturgeon's Annals of Electricity, etc. Sept. 1840, vol. v, pp. 190, 191. A second much smaller magnet of similar form, being 2.7 inches long, and half an inch in diameter, wrapped with 7 feet of insulated copper wire one-twentieth of an inch thick, and weighing 1,857 grains, (somewhat over two ounces,) lifted 40 pounds. A third magnet elliptical in form (0.37 inch broad and 0.15 inch thick) 0.7 inch long, covered with 18 inches of copper wire one-fortieth of an inch thick, and weighing 65.3 grains, lifted 12 pounds. And a fourth magnet one twenty-fifth of an inch thick and one-quarter of an inch long, with three turns of fine copper wire, weighing half a grain, lifted 1,417 grains.

[†] Sturgeon's Annals of Electricity, Dec. 1840, vol. v. pp. 671, 672.

Stimulated by Joule's successes, several attempts were made by others, embodying the same principle of narrow but greatly extended poles. Mr. Richard Roberts constructed what may be called a "disk" magnet, the square plate of iron being nearly two and a half inches thick, with a planed face six and five-eighths inches on the sides, and having a supporting eye formed on its back. Four equidistant parallel grooves each three-eighths of an inch wide and one inch and a quarter deep, divided the square face into five equal oblong "poles." A bundle of 36 copper wires (No. 18) was coiled in and out about these five poles, in three turns. The magnet with its coils weighed 35 pounds. The armature, a similar square plate one inch and a half thick, (without grooves,) weighed 23 pounds. With a battery of eight pairs, (each about 100 square inches, or five-sevenths of a square foot,) the magnet sustained 2,950 pounds; about one ton and a third.* This magnet is obviously equivalent to two or more of Joule's, placed side by side. Mr. Joseph Radford, about the same time, devised another form of "disk" magnet much more novel in construction. In this case a circular plate 9 inches in diameter and about an inch thick, (provided with a supporting eye at the middle of its back,) had a spiral groove cut in its planed face, one-quarter of an inch wide and three-eighths of an inch deep, making from the center about six turns, and leaving a spiral ridge of metal at the face about half an inch thick. Its weight (without wire) was 16 pounds 2 ounces, or with the wire coil 18 pounds 4 ounces. The armature, a similar smooth disk of about two-thirds the thickness of the magnet, weighed 14 pounds 14 ounces. The coil, a bundle of 23 small copper wires entering from the back through a hole at the center of the disk and following the spiral groove, (which it filled,) passed out at the edge of the disk. By this singular disposition of the coil, the single spiral "pole" or narrow ridge (half an inch in thickness) had a continuous north polarity on the one side and a continuous adjacent south polarity on its other side: being in the same condition as a long narrow bar of soft iron having a galvanic current passing longitudinally along its opposite sides in the same direction. With a battery of twelve pairs this spiral disk magnet sustained 2,500 pounds; about one ton and one-eighth.†

Another variety of the disk magnet devised by Joule, presented an annular face of about 12 inches exterior diameter and about 8 inches interior diameter, having 48 radial grooves separating 48 radial poles. A bundle of 18 copper wires bent alternately in and out about these 48 lateral ridges or face edges, produced a series of

* Sturgeon's Annals of Electricity, Feb. 1841, vol. vi pp. 187, 188.
† Sturgeon's Annals of Electricity, March, 1841, vol. vi. p. 222.

alternate poles. This was virtually an extension of the Roberts series of magnetic poles, equivalent to a series of 24 of Joule's narrow magnets placed side by side and arranged radially in a ring. This circular battery of magnets, excited by 10 cups arranged in a series of four, lifted 2,710 pounds.*

It will be noticed that in each of these interesting improvements on the simple horse-shoe "quantity" magnet, the highest efficiency was obtained by adopting Henry's system of "multiple coils."

This system has also been most successfully applied by Z. T. Gramme, of Paris, to the revolving annular inductor of his very ingenious and powerful form of magneto-electric machine.

Note E. (From p. 247.)

ABSTRACT OF PAPER ON SELF-INDUCTION.

Professor Bache, as a Secretary of the American Philosophical Society, (knowing that the "Transactions" of the Body, containing Henry's important Memoir, would not be formally published for a year or more,) with that energetic zeal of friendship so characteristic of the man, obtained permission to publish an abstract of the previous verbal communication; which he accordingly proceeded to have at once inserted in the forthcoming number of the Franklin Institute "Journal," with the following prefatory letter addressed "To the Committee of Publication" of that Journal:

GENTLEMEN:—The American Philosophical Society, at their last stated meeting, authorised the publication of the following abstract of a verbal communication made to the Society, by Professor Henry, on the 16th of January last. A memoir on this subject has been since submitted to the Society, containing an extension of the subject, the primary fact in relation to which was observed by Professor Henry as early as 1832, and announced by him in the American Journal of Science. Mr. Faraday having recently entered upon a similar train of observations, the immediate publication of the accompanying is important, that the prior claims of our fellow countryman may not be overlooked.

Very respectfully yours,

A. D. BACHE,
One of the Secretaries Am. Philos. Soc.

Philadelphia, Feb. 7th, 1835.

---

* Sturgeon's Annals of Electricity, June, 1841, vol. vi. p. 69.

" Extract from the proceedings of the stated meeting of the American
Philosophical Society, January 16, 1835.

"The following facts in reference to the spark, shock, &c. from
a galvanic battery, when the poles are united by a long conductor,
were communicated by Professor Joseph Henry, and those relating
to the spark were illustrated experimentally :

"1. A long wire gives a more intense spark than a short one.
There is, however, a length beyond which the effect is not increased;
a wire of 120 feet gave about the same intensity of spark as one of
240 feet.

"2. A thick wire gives a larger spark than a smaller one of **the**
same length.

"3. A wire coiled into a helix, gives a more vivid spark than
the same wire when uncoiled.

"4. A ribbon of copper, coiled into a flat spiral, gives a more
intense spark than any other arrangement yet tried.

"5. The effect is increased, by using a longer and wider ribbon,
to an extent not yet determined. The greatest effect has been produced by a coil 96 feet long, and weighing 15 pounds; a larger
conductor has not been received.

"6. A ribbon of copper, first doubled into two strands, and then
coiled into a flat spiral, gives no spark, or a very feeble one.

"7. Large copper handles, soldered to the ends of the coil of 96
feet, and these both grasped, one by each hand, a shock is felt at
the elbows, when the contact is broken in a battery with one and a
half feet of zinc surface.

"8. A shock is also felt when the copper of the battery is grasped
with one hand, and one of the handles with the other; the intensity however is not as great as in the last case. This method of
receiving the shock may be called the direct method, the other the
lateral one.

"9. The decomposition of a liquid is effected by the use of the
coil from a single pair, by intermitting the current, and introducing
a pair of decomposing wires.

"10. A mixture of oxygen and hydrogen is also exploded by
using the coil, and breaking the contact, in a bladder containing the
mixture.

"11. The property of producing an intense spark is induced, on
a short wire, by introducing, at any point of a compound galvanic
current, a large flat spiral.

"12. A spark is produced even when the plates of a single battery are separated by a foot or more of diluted acid.

"13. Little or no increase in the effect is produced by inserting a piece of soft iron into the center of a flat spiral.

"14. The effect produced by an electro-magnet, in giving the shock, is due principally to the coiling of the long wire which surrounds the soft iron." *

Note F. (From p. 255.)

OSCILLATION OF ELECTRICAL DISCHARGE.

Sir William Thomson, in 1853, indicated the probability of an oscillatory character in the electrical discharge; remarking: "It appears to me not improbable that double, triple, and quadruple flashes of lightning which I have frequently seen on the continent of Europe, and sometimes though not so frequently in this country, (lasting generally long enough to allow an observer after his attention is drawn by the first light of the flash, to turn his head around and see distinctly the course of the lightning in the sky,) result from the discharge possessing this oscillatory character. - - - The decomposition of water by electricity from an ordinary electrical machine, in which, as has been shown by Faraday, more than the electro-chemical equivalent of the whole electricity that passes, appears in oxygen and hydrogen rising mixed from each pole, is probably due to electrical oscillations in the discharges consequent on the successive sparks." †

In a foot-note at this point of the paper, the eminent physicist adds: "This explanation occurred to me about a year and a half ago, in consequence of the conclusions regarding the oscillatory nature of the discharge in certain circumstances, drawn from mathematical investigation. I afterward found that it had been suggested as a conjecture by Helmholtz in his *Erhaltung der Kraft*, (Berlin, 1847,) in the following terms: 'It is easy to explain this law, if we assume that the discharge of a battery is not a simple motion of the electricity in one direction, but a backward and forward motion between the coatings, in oscillations which become continually smaller until the entire *vis viva* is destroyed by the sum of the resistances. The notion that the current of discharge consists of alternately opposed currents is favored by the alternately opposed magnetic actions of the same; and secondly by the phenomena observed by Wollaston while attempting to decompose

* *Journal of the Franklin Institute*, March, 1855, vol. xv. pp. 149, 170.
† L. & D. *Phil. Mag.* June, 1853, vol. v. pp. 400, 401.

water by electric shocks, that both descriptions of gases are exhibited at both electrodes.'" [*]

Seventeen years after Henry's experimental determination, Mr. W. Feddersen, in 1859, observed the oscillatory nature of the electrical discharge, by employing the revolving mirror of Wheatstone, as first suggested by Sir William Thomson.[†]

It is remarkable however that very early in the century, the return discharge of electricity appears to have been distinctly noted. In Gilbert's *Annalen* for 1806, the phenomenon of a "back-stroke" is spoken of as being "not uncommon in thunder-storms."[‡] And twenty years before the conjecture by Helmholtz, or in 1827, the same suspicion or rather conviction of an oscillatory discharge was distinctly expressed by Felix Savary, who perplexed by the irregularity of magnetization in small needles, when effected by the Leyden jar, thus comments on the problem:

"An electrical discharge is a phenomenon of motion. In this motion a translation of matter — continuous — in a fixed direction? If so, the alternations of opposite magnetisms observed at various distances from a rectilinear conductor, or in a helix for gradually increasing discharges, would be due solely to the mutual re-actions of the magnetic particles in the steel needles. The manner in which the behavior of a wire changes with its length, appears to me to exclude this supposition. Does the electric flow during a discharge consist on the contrary of a series of oscillations transmitted from the wire to the surrounding medium, and speedily enfeebled by resistances which increase rapidly with the absolute velocity of the agitated particles? All the phenomena lead to this hypothesis; which assumes that not only the intensity, but the direction of the magnetism, depends on the laws according to which the minute motions die away in the wire, in the medium surrounding it, and in the substance which receives and preserves the magnetism. The oscillations in the wire would have an absolute velocity so much the less, and would subside so much the more rapidly, accordingly as the wire were longer, as it were finer, and as the resistance belonging to its constitution were greater. It may thus be explained how there is for a rectilinear conductor and a given discharge, a length of wire which will produce the strongest magnetization; if the

---

[*] Quoted from a memoir "On the Conservation of Force," by Dr. H. Helmholtz. Read before the Physical Society of Berlin, on the 23d of July, 1847. The memoir was translated by Dr. J. Tyndall, and published in his selection of "Scientific Memoirs," London, 1853, vol. i. p. 153. This interesting collection of foreign papers forms a continuation of Taylor's "Scientific Memoirs," in five volumes.

[†] Poggendorff's *Annalen der Physik*, 1859, vol. cviii. p. 69.

[‡] Gilbert's *Annalen der Physik*, 1806, vol. xxiv. p. 351.

length is less, the minute motions diminish too slowly; if greater, their intensity is too much enfeebled." [*]

Note G.   (From p. 272.)

WHEATSTONE'S CHRONOSCOPE.

For the purpose of measuring and registering extremely short intervals of time, Professor Charles Wheatstone, extending his earlier experiments of 1834, on the velocity of electricity by means of a revolving mirror, projected a "chronoscope" based on the automatic agency of electro-magnetism. Among the applications in view were the determination of the exact times of falling bodies, the duration of an explosion of gunpowder, etc. At what time this ingenious device was practically developed, it is difficult to say; but we learn that M. Konstantinoff, an accomplished Russian Artillery Officer, visiting England in 1842, had this project shown or explained to him by Professor Wheatstone. Looking at the possibilities of this suggestion from his professional stand-point, M. Konstantinoff at once directed his attention to the contrivance of a modification of the arrangement, adapted to measure the velocity of a projectile at various points of its flight. Invoking the well-known electrical knowledge and skill of his friend Mons. L. Breguet of Paris in 1843, the two commenced in June of this year the construction of a machine which should indicate and record 30 or 40 successive observations within the few seconds of a projectile's flight. The apparatus was successfully completed May 29, 1844; and an account of it was read before the French Academy, January 20th, 1845. [†] In this instrument, the various records were made on a timed revolving cylinder, by styles or pencils, actuated by electro-magnetic motions at the several moments of breaking successive circuits. Wheatstone's reclamation, and account of his own invention, were published four months later, through the same channel. [‡]

The two chronoscopes were undoubtedly the same in principle, although Wheatstone's gave but two records, — an initial one by the falling or projected ball breaking the galvanic circuit, and a terminal one by a re-establishment of the circuit on the ball striking a horizontal or a vertical spring plate and thus causing a metallic contact to be made. For measuring the interval, Wheatstone em-

---

[*] Annales de Chimie et de Physique, 1827, vol. xxxiv. pp. 51, 52.

[†] Comptes Rendus, Jan. 1845, vol. xx. pp. 157-161.

[‡] Comptes Rendus, May 26, 1845, vol. xx. pp. 1554-1561.

ployed a revolving time index on a dial, arrested by the armature of an electro-magnet. The arrangement adopted by Breguet and Konstantinoff in 1844, resembled much more closely that described and published by Henry in 1843, than that devised by Wheatstone and published in 1845; and both were really more complete for the specific purpose of measuring the velocity of projectiles, than the last-named, and first invented. Moreover, while the latter was a "chronoscope," the two former were really "chronographs."

Henry's second plan of registering by the induction spark, was far more delicate and exact than either; as it dispensed with the inertia of a moving galvanometer needle, or magnetic armature.

Note II. (From p. 275.)

HENRY'S "PROGRAMME OF ORGANIZATION."

The plan for the organization and conduct of the Smithsonian Institution, as more fully presented by the Secretary in his first annual report made December 8th, 1847, and adopted by the Board of Regents December 13th, 1847, is regarded as sufficiently interesting and important to be here given at length :

"INTRODUCTION.

General considerations which should serve as a guide in adopting a Plan of Organization.

1. Will of Smithson. The property is bequeathed to the United States of America, "to found at Washington, under the name of the SMITHSONIAN INSTITUTION, an establishment for the increase and diffusion of knowledge among men."

2. The bequest is for the benefit of mankind. The Government of the United States is merely a trustee to carry out the design of the testator.

3. The Institution is not a national establishment, as is frequently supposed, but the establishment of an individual, and is to bear and perpetuate his name.

4. The objects of the Institution are, 1st, to increase, and 2d, to diffuse knowledge among men.

5. These two objects should not be confounded with one another. The first is to enlarge the existing stock of knowledge by the addition of new truths; and the second, to disseminate knowledge, thus increased, among men.

6. The will makes no restriction in favor of any particular kind of knowledge; hence all branches are entitled to a share of attention.

7. Knowledge can be increased by different methods of facilitating and promoting the discovery of new truths; and can be most extensively diffused among men by means of the press.

8. To effect the greatest amount of good, the organization should be such as to enable the Institution to produce results, in the way of increasing and diffusing knowledge, which cannot be produced either at all or so efficiently by the existing institutions in our country.

9. The organization should also be such as can be adopted provisionally; can be easily reduced to practice, receive modifications, or be abandoned, in whole or in part, without a sacrifice of the funds.

10. In order to compensate, in some measure, for the loss of time occasioned by the delay of eight years in establishing the Institution, a considerable portion of the interest which has accrued should be added to the principal.

11. In proportion to the wide field of knowledge to be cultivated, the funds are small. Economy should therefore be consulted in the construction of the building; and not only the first cost of the edifice should be considered, but also the continual expense of keeping it in repair, and of the support of the establishment necessarily connected with it. There should also be but few individuals permanently supported by the Institution.

12. The plan and dimensions of the building should be determined by the plan of the organization, and not the converse.

13. It should be recollected that mankind in general are to be benefitted by the bequest, and that therefore all nonnecessary expenditure on local objects would be a perversion of the trust.

14. Besides the foregoing considerations, deduced immediately from the will of Smithson, regard must be had to certain requirements of the act of Congress establishing the Institution. These are, a library, a museum, and a gallery of art, with a building on a liberal scale to contain them.

SECTION I.

Plan of Organization of the Institution in accordance with the foregoing deductions from the Will of Smithson.

TO INCREASE KNOWLEDGE. It is proposed—1. To stimulate men of talent to make original researches, by offering suitable rewards for memoirs containing new truths; and, —2. To appropriate annually a portion of the income for particular researches, under the direction of suitable persons.

To DIFFUSE KNOWLEDGE. It is proposed — 1. To publish a series of periodical reports on the progress of the different branches of knowledge; and, — 2. To publish occasionally separate treatises on subjects of general interest.

DETAILS OF THE PLAN TO INCREASE KNOWLEDGE.

I. *By stimulating researches.* — 1. Facilities afforded for the production of original memoirs on all branches of knowledge. 2. The memoirs thus obtained to be published in a series of volumes, in a quarto form, and entitled Smithsonian Contributions to Knowledge. 3. No memoir on subjects of physical science to be accepted for publication which does not furnish a positive addition to human knowledge, resting on original research; and all unverified speculations to be rejected. * 4. Each memoir presented to the Institution to be submitted for examination to a commission of persons of reputation for learning in the branch to which the memoir pertains; and to be accepted for publication only in case the report of this commission is favorable. 5. The commission to be chosen by the officers of the Institution, and the name of the author (as far as practicable) concealed, unless a favorable decision be made. 6. The volumes of the memoirs to be exchanged for the Transactions of literary and scientific societies, and copies to be given to all the colleges and principal libraries in this country. One part of the remaining copies may be offered for sale; and the other carefully preserved, to form complete sets of the work, to supply the demand from new institutions. 7. An abstract or popular account of the contents of these memoirs to be given to the public through the annual report of the Regents to Congress.

II. *By appropriating a part of the income, annually, to special objects of research, under the direction of suitable persons.* — 1. The objects and the amount appropriated, to be recommended by counsellors of the Institution. 2. Appropriations in different years to different objects; so that in course of time each branch of knowledge may receive a share. 3. The results obtained from these appropriations to be published, with the memoirs before mentioned, in the volumes of the Smithsonian Contributions to Knowledge. 4. Examples of objects for which appropriations may be made:

* " It has been supposed from the adoption of this proposition, that we are disposed to undervalue abstract speculation: on the contrary, we know that all the advances in true science, (namely a knowledge of the laws of phenomena,) are made by provisionally adopting well-conditioned hypotheses, the product of the imagination, and subsequently verifying them by an appeal to experiment and observation." (Explanations of the programme.)

(a.) System of extended meteorological observations for solving
the problem of American storms. (b.) Explorations in descriptive
natural history, and geological, magnetical, and topographical surveys, to collect materials for the formation of a Physical Atlas of
the United States. (c.) Solution of experimental problems, such as
a new determination of the weight of the earth, of the velocity of
electricity, and of light; chemical analyses of soils and plants;
collection and publication of scientific facts, accumulated in the
offices of Government. (d.) Institution of statistical inquiries with
reference to physical, moral, and political subjects. (e.) Historical
researches, and accurate surveys of places celebrated in American
history. (f.) Ethnological researches, particularly with reference
to the different races of men in North America; also, explorations
and accurate surveys of the mounds and other remains of the
ancient people of our country.

DETAILS OF THE PLAN FOR DIFFUSING KNOWLEDGE.

I. *By the publication of a series of reports, giving an account of
the new discoveries in science, and of the changes made from year
to year in all branches of knowledge not strictly professional.*—
1. These reports will diffuse a kind of knowledge generally interesting, but which at present is inaccessible to the public. Some
of the reports may be published annually, others at longer intervals,
as the income of the Institution or the changes in the branches of
knowledge may indicate. 2. The reports are to be prepared by
collaborators eminent in the different branches of knowledge.
3. Each collaborator to be furnished with the journals and publications, domestic and foreign, necessary to the compilation of his
report; to be paid a certain sum for his labors, and to be named on
the title-page of the report. 4. The reports to be published in
separate parts, so that persons interested in a particular branch can
procure the parts relating to it without purchasing the whole.
5. These reports may be presented to Congress, for partial distribution, the remaining copies to be given to literary and scientific
institutions, and sold to individuals for a moderate price. †

---

* This part of the plan has been but partially carried out.

† The following are some of the subjects which may be embraced in the reports:
I. PHYSICAL CLASS.—1. Physics, including astronomy, natural philosophy, chemistry, and meteorology. 2. Natural history, including botany, zoology, geology, &c.
3. Agriculture. 4. Application of science to arts.
II. MORAL AND POLITICAL CLASS.—5. Ethnology, including particular history, comparative philology, antiquities, &c. 6. Statistics and political economy.
7. Mental and moral philosophy. 8. A survey of the political events of the world;
penal reform, &c.
III. LITERATURE AND THE FINE ARTS.—9. Modern literature. 10. The fine arts,
and their application to the useful arts. 11. Bibliography. 12. Obituary notices of
distinguished individuals.

II. *By the publication of separate treatises on subjects of general interest.*—1. These treatises may occasionally consist of valuable memoirs translated from foreign languages, or of articles prepared under the direction of the Institution, or procured by offering premiums for the best exposition of a given subject. 2. The treatises should in all cases be submitted to a commission of competent judges, previous to their publication. 3. As examples of these treatises, expositions may be obtained of the present state of the several branches of knowledge mentioned in the table of reports.

SECTION II.

Plan of Organization, in accordance with the terms of the resolutions of the Board of Regents providing for the two modes of increasing and diffusing knowledge.

1. The act of Congress establishing the Institution contemplated the formation of a library and a museum; and the Board of Regents, including these objects in the plan of organization, resolved to divide the income * into two equal parts.

2. One part to be appropriated to increase and diffuse knowledge by means of publications and researches, agreeably to the scheme before given. The other part to be appropriated to the formation of a library and a collection of objects of nature and of art.

3. These two plans are not incompatible with one another.

4. To carry out the plan before described, a library will be required, consisting, 1st, of a complete collection of the transactions and proceedings of all the learned societies in the world; 2d, of the more important current periodical publications, and other works necessary in preparing the periodical reports.

5. The Institution should make special collections, particularly of objects to illustrate and verify its own publications.

6. Also, a collection of instruments of research in all branches of experimental science.

7. With reference to the collection of books, other than those mentioned above, catalogues of all the different libraries in the United States should be procured, in order that the valuable books first purchased may be such as are not to be found in the United States.

8. Also, catalogues of memoirs, and of books and other materials, should be collected for rendering the Institution a centre of bibliographical knowledge, whence the student may be directed to any work which he may require.

9. It is believed that the collections in natural history will increase by donation as rapidly as the income of the Institution can make provision for their reception, and therefore it will seldom be necessary to purchase articles of this kind.

10. Attempts should be made to procure for the gallery of art casts of the most celebrated articles of ancient and modern sculpture.

11. The arts may be encouraged by providing a room, free of expense, for the exhibition of the objects of the Art-Union and other similar societies.

12. A small appropriation should annually be made for models of antiquities, such as those of the remains of ancient temples, &c.

13. For the present, or until the building is fully completed, besides the Secretary, no permanent assistant will be required, except one, to act as librarian.

14. The Secretary, by the law of Congress, is alone responsible to the Regents. He shall take charge of the building and property, keep a record of proceedings, discharge the duties of librarian and keeper of the museum, and may, with the consent of the Regents, employ assistants.

15. The Secretary and his assistants (during the session of Congress) will be required to illustrate new discoveries in science, and to exhibit new objects of art. Distinguished individuals should also be invited to give lectures on subjects of general interest."

In his "Explanations and illustrations of the programme" presented to the Regents at the same time with the foregoing, Henry remarked: "The plan of increasing and diffusing knowledge, presented in the first section of the programme, will be found in strict accordance with the several propositions deduced from the Will of Smithson, and given in the introduction. It embraces—as a leading feature, the design of interesting the greatest number of individuals in the operations of the Institution, and of spreading its influence as widely as possible. It forms an active organization, exciting all to make original researches who are gifted with the necessary power, and diffusing a kind of knowledge now only accessible to the few, among all those who are willing to receive it. In this country, though many excel in the application of science to the practical arts of life, few devote themselves to the continued labor and patient thought necessary to the discovery and development of new truths. - - - The second section of the programme

gives — so far as they have been made out, the details of the part
of the plan of organization directed by the act of Congress establishing the Institution. The two plans, namely that of publication
and original research, and that of collections of objects of nature
and art, are not incompatible, and may be carried on harmoniously
with each other. The only effect which they will have on one
another is that of limiting the operation of each, on account of the
funds given to the other." *

That the fundamental assumption of this plan as to the true and
just interpretation of Smithson's Will, was not however peculiar to
Henry, is abundantly shown by many utterances of the thoughtful
and judicious.

In an appreciative memoir on the scientific work of Smithson,
written by Professor Walter R. Johnson of Philadelphia, in 1844,
he speaks in his introductory remarks of the gratitude due to the
public benefactor, "whether with Franklin be found a library, with
Maclure endow an academy for researches in natural science, or
with Smithson seek to stimulate into activity the spirit of philosophical research, to 'increase' by deepening the sources, and 'diffuse' by multiplying the channels of knowledge." And after
recounting the various investigations of Smithson, the writer concludes his review by asking: "What would have been the purposes
of an institution founded by Smithson in his life-time? To this
his *life-time* is a sufficient answer. Researches to 'increase' positive
knowledge, and publications to 'diffuse' and make that knowledge
available to mankind, — such were the great objects of his own constant praiseworthy and laborious efforts." †

The first Chancellor of the Institution — George M. Dallas,
(Vice-President of the United States,) in his address on the occasion of laying the corner-stone of the building, May 1, 1847,
remarked that the foundation was designed by Smithson to be
"an institution not merely for disseminating, spreading, teaching
knowledge, but also and *foremost* — for creating, originating, 'increasing' it."

A committee of the American Academy of Arts and Sciences,
appointed to examine the "programme of organization" submitted
by Henry to that body for its consideration, in a very full report
presented to — and unanimously adopted by — the Academy at Boston, December 7, 1847, expressed an entire concurrence in the views

---

* Programme, and Explanations. Smithsonian Report for 1847, pp. 128-133, of Sen.
ed.— pp. 126-133, of H. R. ed. Also Smithsonian Report for 1853, pp. 7-11.

† *A Memoir on the Scientific Character and Researches of James Smithson. By
Professor Walter R. Johnson. Read before the National Institute, Washington,
April 6, 1844.*

indicated, and a warm approval of the establishment proposed. After a recapitulation and analysis of the several details, the committee pronounced the opinion that "The most novel and important feature of the plan, is that which proposes to insure the publication of memoirs and treatises on important subjects of investigation, and to offer pecuniary encouragement to men of talent and attainment to engage in scientific research. It is believed that no institution in the country effects either of these objects to any great extent. The nearest approach to it is the practice of the Academy and other Philosophical Societies, of publishing the memoirs accepted by them. These however can rarely be works of great compass. No systematic plan of compensation for the preparation of works of scientific research, is known by the committee to have been attempted in this or any other country. It can scarcely be doubted that an important impulse would be given by the Institution in this way to the cultivation of scientific pursuits: while the extensive and widely ramified system of distribution and exchange by which the publications are to be distributed throughout the United States and the world, would secure them a circulation which works of science could scarcely attain in any other way. It is an obvious characteristic of this mode of applying the funds of the Institution, that its influence would operate most widely throughout the country; that locality would be of comparatively little importance so far as this influence is concerned; and that the Union would become (so to say) in this respect a great school of mutual instruction." [*]

- - - -

Note I. (From p. 375.)

THE ELECTION OF THE FIRST "SECRETARY."

A special Committee of the Board of Regents appointed September 8th, 1846, "to digest a plan to carry out the provisions of the Act to establish the Smithsonian Institution," presented a somewhat elaborate report December 1st, 1846; in which they thus express themselves:

"Before concluding their report, your committee desire to add a few words touching the duty and qualifications of one of the officers of the Institution. Inasmuch as the Chancellor of the Smithsonian Institution being a regent, can receive no salary for his services, it results almost necessarily that the Secretary should become its chief

[*] This Report, dated Dec. 4, 1847, was signed by Edward Everett, Jared Sparks, Benjamin Pierce, Henry W. Longfellow, and Asa Gray. (Smithsonian Report for 1847, pp. 154, 155.—Mem. ed.)

executive officer. The charter seems to have intended that he should occupy a very responsible position. - - - Your committee will not withhold their opinion that upon the choice of this single officer more probably than on any one other act of the Board, will depend the future good name and success and usefulness of the Smithsonian Institution."

The Board of Regents two days later proceeded to the election of this officer; and the result was announced in the *National Intelligencer* of the following day — December 4th. In the *Intelligencer* for Saturday, December 5th, 1846, the following editorial notice of this important proceeding was given:

"In a brief paragraph yesterday we announced that the Regents of the Smithsonian Institution had fixed their choice of Secretary, on Joseph Henry, LL. D. of Princeton College, New Jersey. The appointment of this officer was one of their most important and responsible duties. There has perhaps never been an occasion in the literary history of our country when so much depended upon the decision of so small a number of men. The success of one of the most liberal institutions in the world, depends much on the personal influence of the Secretary to be chosen by the Regents. Men of the highest literary distinction as well as personal merit in the nation were numbered among the candidates. It is no disparagement to their attainments to point out some of the circumstances which sanction the decision just made; for the statement of which, and the reference which it embraces to Professor Henry, we are indebted to the pen of a scientific friend.

"Foremost among American savans stands the name of FRANKLIN; — a name which belongs to the science of the world, and can hardly be said to have a locality. Second perhaps to Franklin only, stands the name of the philosopher of Princeton. It is not now the time nor place to enter into an enumeration of the extensive advances made in physical science by his researches. The brilliant discovery of Franklin of the identity of lightning and the electrical fluid, might have been supposed hardly to have left room for a gleaner in the field. Yet we venture the opinion that if Franklin's favorite aspiration could have been realized — if he could have been permitted to revisit after a lapse of half a century, the busy scenes of human life, he would have found himself a novice in his favorite science. A whole science — that of galvanism, (voltaic electricity,) electro-magnetism, magneto-electricity, thermo-electricity, etc. has been created since the time of Franklin. If the discovery of Franklin enables us to make the lightning harmless, that of the recent school of philosophers enables us to turn it in various ways to practical account in the business purposes of life. If we ask who gave to the electro-magnet of soft iron, now used for the telegraph, its present form, and discovered the laws by which its effective power could be made active, the answer is Joseph Henry. The discovery was first published in the proceedings of the Albany Institute. This was the earliest contribution to the progress of discovery made by the individual whom the choice of the Regents has elevated to the first literary station in the United States. Soon after this discovery Henry was called to the Chair of Experimental Philosophy at Princeton, where for the last fifteen years or more, he has filled the duties of his office in such a manner as to win for him the general esteem of the literary community of that time-honored seat of learning.

"With the relations between Professor Henry and his pupils we have no concern at present. It is of other relations in which he has stood toward the general cultivators of physical science throughout the world, that we propose to speak. One of the most important discoveries of recent date, that of the identity of the laws which regulate electric and magnetic, and electro-magnetic induction, was among the early fruits of his researches at Princeton. If Franklin discovered the identity between lightning and electricity, Henry has gone further, and reduced electric and magnetic action to the same laws. It is impossible in a short compass to do justice to the beauty and simplicity of Henry's laws of the action of the imponderable agents. Whoever will read the progress of his discoveries as published in the Transactions of the American Philosophical Society, will learn something of the spirit of inductive reasoning of which Henry's researches furnish one of the happiest illustrations. These discoveries are not confined in their sphere of utility to the limited circulation of the volumes of that Society. The student of physical science may read the reprints of them and the encomiums pronounced upon them in every language of civilized man throughout the globe. It was doubtless a knowledge of the extensive reputation which these and other discoveries have conferred on so young a man, which influenced the Regents in their selection of a Secretary. It is the man that gives dignity to the office, and not the office to the man. In his new sphere, Professor Henry will have advantages for the personal cultivation and advancement of science which the limited means of the Princeton College too frequently circumscribed. Men of science throughout the Union will find a central point for correspondence, and will pay to the individual that tribute of respect which among freemen would never be given to men of less attainments. We doubt not that the members of the republic of letters throughout the United States will applaud the choice, and give to the Regents their cordial support. It is not our purpose to enumerate all the claims which the Secretary elect has on the literary community. We have said enough to show that in discharging the responsible duty of this appointment, the Regents have looked with a single eye to the purpose of the munificent testator, the advancement of knowledge among men." *

Note J. *(From p. 276.)*

HENRY'S PURPOSE OF ADMINISTRATION.

Perhaps no better inside view of Henry's primitive purpose can be obtained, than from the following private and unpublished letter to his personal friend President Nott, of Union College, Schenectady, N. Y. written during a visit to Princeton, very shortly after his election and removal to Washington:

"PRINCETON, December 26th, 1846.

"MY DEAR SIR: — Your favor of the 9th came to Princeton while I was at Washington, and I now answer it as soon as possible after my return. Please accept my thanks for your kind congratulations on my appointment to the office of Secretary of the Smithsonian Institution. I am not sure however that my appointment will prove a subject of congratulation. The office is one which I have by no means coveted, and which I have accepted at the earnest solicitation of some of the friends of science in our country, to prevent its falling into worse hands, and with the hope of saving the noble bequest of Smithson from being squandered on chimerical or unworthy projects. My first object is to urge on the Regents the adoption of a simple practical plan of carrying out the design of the Testator, viz: the "*increase and diffusion* of knowledge among men." For this purpose in my opinion the organization of the Institution should be such as to stimulate original research in all branches of knowledge, in every part of our country and throughout the world, and also to provide the means of diffusing at stated periods an account of the progress of general knowledge compiled from the Journals of all languages. To establish such an organization, I must endeavor to prevent expenditure of a large portion of the funds of the Smithsonian bequest on a pile of brick and mortar, filled with objects of curiosity, intended for the embellishment of Washington, and the amusement of those who visit that city. My object at present, is to prevent the adoption of plans

---

* *National Intelligencer*, Washington, Dec. 5, 1846, vol. XXXIV. no. 10,441.

which may tend to embarrass the future usefulness of the Institution, and for this purpose I do not intend to make any appointments unless expressly directed to do so by the Regents, until the organization is definitely settled.

"The income of the Institution is not sufficient to carry out a fourth part of the plans mentioned in the Act of Congress, and contemplated in the Report of the Regents. For example, to support the expense of the Museum of the Exploring Expedition presented by Government to the Smithsonian Institution, will require in interest on building and expense of attendance upward of 10,000 dollars annually. A corps of Professors with necessary assistants will amount to from 12,000 to 15,000 dollars. From these facts you will readily perceive that unless the Institution is started with great caution there is danger of absorbing all the income in a few objects, which in themselves may not be the best means of carrying out the design of the Testator. I have elaborated a simple plan of organization, which I intend to press with all my energy. If this is adopted, I am confident the name of Smithson will become familiar to every part of the civilized world. If I cannot succeed in carrying out my plans—at least in a considerable degree, I shall withdraw from the Institution.

"With much respect and esteem, I remain
"Your obedient servant,
"JOSEPH HENRY.

"Rev. Dr. ELIPHALET NOTT,
"President of Union College, &c. &c."

Note K. (From p. 281.)

STRUGGLE WITH THE LIBRARY SCHEME.

From the first organization of the Smithsonian Institution, or indeed from the still earlier times of its discussion on the floors of Congress, the great need of a general library of reference, on a scale comparable to that of the large European establishments, felt by every historical and literary student, naturally led such readers to look eagerly to the endowment of Smithson for the attainment of this desirable end. On December 15, 1843, the Hon. Rufus Choate—chairman of the Senate committee on the library, obtained the reference of the matter of Smithson's bequest to his own committee: and when on June 0, and again on December 12, 1844, Senator Benjamin Tappan, a member of the same committee introduced a bill establishing on the Smithson fund, an agricultural institution with a botanical garden, natural-history cabinet, library, laboratory, lecture-rooms and professorships, Mr. Choate in opposition to the plan, on January 8, 1845, contended that "we cannot do a safer, surer, more unexceptionable thing with the income, or with a portion of the income—(perhaps twenty thousand dollars a year for a few years,) than to expend it in accumulating a grand and noble public library; one which for variety, extent, and wealth, shall be confessed to be equal to any now in the world. Twenty thousand dollars a year for twenty-five years, are five hundred thousand dollars." And he offered as a substitute section, "that a sum not less than 20,000 dollars be annually expended of the interest of the fund aforesaid, in the purchase of books."* This proposition however was not adopted.

In the House of Representatives, the Hon. Robert Dale Owen—chairman of a special committee on the subject, presented a bill February 28, and April 22, 1846, establishing a normal educational institution; a feature strongly opposed by Hon. John Q. Adams, and on the 29th of April, 1846, stricken out. On the same day, Hon. Bradford R. Wood moved as an amendment "that the sum of 20,000 dollars of the interest of said fund be and is hereby appropriated annually for the purchase or publication of a library." A substitute bill presented by Hon. William J. Hough on the same day, provided among various specifications, for an appropriation from the interest of the fund—"not exceeding an average of 25,000 dollars annually for the gradual formation of a library." Which bill was adopted. † This act passed the Senate, and became a law, August 10, 1846.

This organic Act of Congress provided (in sect. 3) a directorship for the Institution, to consist of fifteen Regents,—six of whom should be members of Congress, selected equally from the two chambers; and (in sect. 9) authorized the said managers "to make such disposal as they shall deem best suited for the promotion of the purposes of the testator,"—of any income not appropriated or required by the provisions of the act.

The Board of Regents, after considerable discussion, by resolution adopted January 26, 1847, apportioned one-half of the annual income (exclusive of building expenses) to the purpose of forming a library and museum, and one-half for the publication of original researches and for the support of public lectures. This compromise between contending parties, by no means satisfied the judgment of the Secretary. In his first report to the Regents, presented Decem-

* *The Smithsonian Institution: Documents relative to its Origin and History.* Edited by William J. Rhees. (Smith. Mis. Coll. No. 329.) pp. 262, 212, and 330.

† *The Smithsonian Institution.* By W. J. Rhees. Pp. 355, 385, 462-'4, 469-472.

ber 8, 1847, Henry strongly urged that "In carrying out the spirit of the plan adopted, namely that of affecting men in general by the operations of the Institution, it is evident that the principal means of 'diffusing knowledge' must be the *Press*."[*] In his second report he sets forth that "The Institution is not for a day, but is designed to endure as long as our Government shall exist; and it is therefore peculiarly important that in the beginning we should proceed carefully and not attempt to produce immediate effects at the expense of permanent usefulness. The process of 'increasing knowledge' is an extremely slow one, and the value of the results of this part of the plan, cannot be properly realized until some years have elapsed."[†] In his fourth report he recapitulates: "To carry out the design of the testator, various plans were proposed; but most of these were founded on an imperfect apprehension of the terms of the will. The great majority of them contemplated merely the 'diffusion' of popular information, and neglected the first and the most prominent requisition of the bequest, namely the 'increase of knowledge.' The only plan in strict conformity with the terms of the will, and which especially commended itself to men of science, a class to which Smithson himself belonged, was that of an active living organization, intended principally to promote the discovery and diffusion of new truths. - - - It was with the hope of being able to assist in the practical development of this plan that I was induced to accept the appointment of principal executive officer of the Institution. Many unforeseen obstacles however presented themselves to its full adoption; and its advocates soon found in contending with opposing views and adverse interests, a wide difference between what in their opinion ought to be done, and what they could actually accomplish. - - - After much discussion it was finally concluded to divide the income (after deducting the general expenses) into two equal parts, and to devote one part to the active operations set forth in the plan just described, and the other to the formation of a library, a museum, and a gallery of art. It was evident however that the small income of the original bequest —though in itself sufficient to do much good in the way of active operations, was inadequate to carry out this more extended plan. - - - Though one-half of the annual interest is to be expended on the library and the museum, the portion of the income which can be thus devoted to the former, will in my opinion never be sufficient without extraneous aid to collect and support a miscellaneous library of the first class. Indeed, all the income would

---

[*] Smithsonian Report for 1847, p. 154 (Sen. ed.)—p. 120 (H. R. ed.)
[†] Smithsonian Report for 1848, p. 156 (Sen. ed.—p. 140 (H. R. ed.)

scarcely suffice for this purpose."* In his fifth annual report he maintains that "the idea ought never to be entertained that the portion of the limited income of the Smithsonian fund which can be devoted to the purchase of books, will ever be sufficient to meet the wants of the American scholar."† In his sixth annual report, exhibiting the valuable contributions to knowledge which the Institution had already effected in the few years of its existence, he remarks: "All the anticipations indulged with regard to it have been fully realized; and after an experience of six years, there can now be no doubt of the true policy of the Regents in regard to it. I am well aware however that the idea is entertained by some that the system of active operations though at present in a flourishing condition, cannot continue to be the prominent object of attention; and that under another set of directors other counsels will prevail and other measures be adopted, and what has been done in establishing this system will ultimately be undone." He presents however the inspiriting and consoling reflection: "But if notwithstanding all this, the Institution is destined to a change of policy, what has been well done in the line we are advocating, can never be undone. The new truths developed by the researches originated by the Institution and recorded in its publications, the effect of its exchanges with foreign countries, and the results of its cataloguing system, can never be obliterated: they will endure through all coming time. Should the Government of the United States be dissolved, and the Smithsonian fund dissipated to the winds, — the 'Smithsonian Contributions to Knowledge' will still be found in the principal libraries of the world, a perpetual monument of the wisdom and liberality of the founder of the Institution, and of the faithfulness of those who first directed its affairs. Whatever therefore may be the future condition of the Institution, the true policy for the present, is to devote its energies to the system of active operations. All other objects should be subordinate to this, and in no wise be suffered to diminish the good which it is capable of producing. It should be prosecuted with discretion, but with vigor: the results will be its vindication."‡ In his next annual report he reiterates: "A miscellaneous and general library, museum, and gallery of art, (though important in themselves,) have from the first been considered by those who have critically examined the Will of Smithson, to be too restricted in their operations and too local in their influence, to meet the comprehensive intentions of the testator; and the hope

* Smithsonian Report for 1850, pp. 146, 147, and 205 (Sen. ed.)—pp. 178, 179, and 197 (H. R. ed.)

† Smithsonian Report for 1851, p. 234 (Sen. ed.)—p. 238 (H. R. ed.)

‡ Smithsonian Report for 1852, pp. 213, 214 (Sen. ed.)—pp. 221, 222 (H. R. ed.)

has been cherished that other means may ultimately be provided for the support of those objects, and that the whole income of the Smithsonian fund may be devoted to the more legitimate objects of the noble bequest." *

At a meeting of the Board of Regents held March 12, 1853, a committee of seven was appointed to consider and report upon "the subject of the distribution of the income of the Institution, in the manner contemplated by the original plan of organization." Hon. R. Choate, a member of this committee, being unable to attend its meetings, (having returned to Boston at the end of his Senatorial term in 1846,) Hon. James Meacham (of the House of Representatives) was appointed to take his place, February 18, 1854. At a meeting of the Regents held May 20, 1854, Hon. James A. Pearce, chairman of the committee, submitted its report, presenting a very full discussion of the legal questions — as to the discretionary power of the Regents, and the true policy of the Institution. On the first point, after showing how faithfully the specific requirements of the organic Act had been executed, the committee in referring to the clause that the annual expenditure for the library should not exceed 25,000 dollars in the average, maintained that "this is nothing but a *limitation* upon the discretion of the Regents, and can by no rule of construction be considered as intimating the desire of Congress that such sum should be annually appropriated. The limitation while it prevented the Regents from exceeding that sum, left them full discretion as to any amount within that limit." On the second point, the committee say: "What then are the considerations which should govern them in rejecting the plan which proposes a great library as the best and chief — if not the only means of executing the trust created by the Will of Smithson, and fulfilling their own duty under the law? The 'increase and diffusion of knowledge among men,' are the great purposes of this munificent trust. To increase knowledge implies research, or new and active investigation in some one or more of the departments of learning. To diffuse knowledge among men, implies active measures for its distribution so far as may be, among mankind. Neither of these purposes could be accomplished or materially advanced by the accumulation of a great library at the city of Washington. - - - The application of 25,000 dollars annually (five-sixths of the whole income at the date of the Act) to the purchase of books, would be inconsistent with and subversive of the whole tenor of all that precedes the 8th section.† - - - The committee need not repeat in detail all the

---

* Smithsonian Report for 1853, pp. 10, 11 (new. ed.)

† The residue of the income would indeed have been wholly insufficient even for the necessary salaries and incidental expenses of the library itself, — to say nothing of the other interests specifically provided for by the 8th section of the act.

parts of the plan of organization, but may mention that it included
the exchange of the published transactions of the Institution with
those of literary and scientific societies and establishments, and provided for a museum, and library, to consist of a complete collection of the transactions and proceedings of all the learned societies
in the world, of the more important current periodical publications
and other works necessary to scientific investigations; thus employing the instrumentalities pointed out in the law, as means of increasing and diffusing knowledge, entirely consistent with and
necessary to the plan of research and publication. This plan is no
longer experimental; it has been tested by experience; its success is
acknowledged by all who are capable of forming a correct estimate
of its results; and the Institution has every encouragement to pursue steadily its system of stimulating, assisting, and publishing
research. - - - The committee submit to the Board the following resolutions: *Resolved*, That the seventh resolution passed by the
Board of Regents on the 26th of January, 1847, requiring an
equal division of the income between the active operations, and the
museum and library, (when the buildings are completed,) be and it
is hereby repealed. *Resolved*, That hereafter the annual appropriations shall be apportioned specifically among the different objects
and operations of the Institution in such manner as may in the
judgment of the Regents be necessary and proper for each, according to its intrinsic importance and a compliance in good faith with
the law."[*] This report was signed by six of the committee: Mr.
Meacham the last appointed member dissenting, and submitting an
elaborate minority report, which comprised a very able and ingenious argument in defence of the library plan.[†] The resolutions
offered by the committee were adopted by the Board of Regents
January 15, 1855.

As six of the fifteen Regents were by law selected from senators
and representatives, a very obvious resort for a member dissatisfied
with the action of a majority, was a motion in Congress for the
familiar "committee of inquiry." Accordingly Hon. James Meacham moved in the House, January 17, 1855, that a select committee of five be appointed, "and that said committee be directed to
inquire and report to the House whether the Smithsonian Institution has been managed, and its funds expended in accordance with
the law establishing the Institution; and whether any additional
legislation be necessary to carry out the designs of its founders:
and that said committee have power to send for persons and papers."
The resolution was adopted by a vote of 93 to 91.[‡]

---

[*] Smithsonian Report for 1855, pp. 61-67 (Sen. ed.)
[†] Smithsonian Report for 1855, (appendix to H. R. ed.) pp. 357-382.
[‡] The Smithsonian Institution. By W. J. Rhees, pp. 569-572.

On the 3d of March, 1855, Hon. Charles W. Upham, chairman of the select committee, submitted to the House what must be regarded as a minority report; declaring "No doubt we think can be entertained that the framers and enactors of the law expected that about 200,000 dollars would be expended 'for the formation of a library composed of valuable works pertaining to all departments of knowledge,' in eight years." After criticising the system approved by the Regents, of devoting a large portion of the Smithsonian income to the promotion of original research, the report states: "At the same time they do not cast blame or censure of any sort upon those who suggested and have labored to carry out that system. The design was in itself commendable and elevated. It has unquestionably been pursued with zeal, sincerity, integrity, and high motives and aims; but it is we think necessarily surrounded with very great difficulties. - - - But a few words are needed to do justice to the value of a great universal library at the metropolis of the Union;" &c. - - - The report concludes with the judgment that as a measure of mutual concession, "the compromise adopted at an early day by the Board of Regents, ought to be restored, and that all desirable ends may be ultimately secured by dividing the income equally between the library and museum on one part, and the active operations on the other." This report was signed by the chairman, Mr. Upham, alone;—two of the committee (Messrs. William H. Witte and Nathaniel G. Taylor) presenting a dissenting report, and the remaining two (Messrs. Richard C. Puryear and Daniel Wells) declining to sign either. The report submitted by Mr. Witte (no less elaborate than that by the chairman) concluded: "They believe that the Regents and the Secretary have managed the affairs of the Institution wisely, faithfully, and judiciously; that there is no necessity for further legislation on the subject; and that if the Institution be allowed to continue the plan which has been adopted and so far pursued with unquestionable success, it will satisfy all the requirements of the law, and the purposes of Smithson's Will, by 'increasing and diffusing knowledge among men.'"* Upon these conflicting and balanced reports no action was taken by the House.

Simultaneously in the Senate, Hon. John M. Clayton, January 17, 1855, introduced a resolution "that the Committee on the Judiciary inquire whether any, and if any—what action of the Senate is necessary and proper in regard to the Smithsonian Institution?" On the 6th of February, 1855, Hon. Andrew P. Butler, chairman of the Judiciary Committee, submitted to the Senate a report completely vindicating the course pursued by the Regents;

* The Smithsonian Institution. By W. J. Rhees, pp. 649-651.

in which it is maintained that "any increase of knowledge that might be acquired was not to be locked up in the Institution or preserved only for the citizens of Washington or persons who might visit the Institution. It was by the express terms of the trust, (which the United States was pledged to execute,) to be 'diffused among men.' This could be done in no other way than by publications at the expense of the Institution. Nor has Congress prescribed the sums which shall be appropriated to these different objects. It is left to the discretion and judgment of the Regents. - - - These operations appear to have been carried out by the Regents under the immediate superintendence of Professor Henry, with zeal, energy, and discretion, and with the strictest regard to economy in the expenditure of the funds. Nor does there seem to be any other mode which Congress could prescribe or the Regents adopt, which would better fulfill the high trust which the United States have undertaken to perform. - - - The committee see nothing therefore in their conduct which calls for any new legislation, or any change in the powers now exercised by the Regents." And the report concludes in "the language of the resolution, that 'no action of the Senate is necessary and proper in regard to the Smithsonian Institution;' and this is the unanimous opinion of the committee." *

And thus ended an earnest struggle of many years between Science and Literature for the possession of Smithson's endowment: and though the interest in the controversy has long since passed away in the permanent establishment of Henry's far-reaching policy, its history is suggestive and instructive. No better concluding summary can be presented, than by an extract from a quite recent judicious and dispassionate recapitulation of the discussion and its results, written for *The International Review*, by Mr. A. R. Spofford, the scholarly librarian of the Government Library at Washington:

"The net result of the protracted controversy was to leave the Regents to put their own interpretation upon the law, and every step since taken in the management of the Smithsonian bequest, has been in the direction of curtailing every expenditure for other objects than the procuring, publishing, and distributing of what were deemed valuable original contributions to human knowledge. In strict accordance with this theory, the library gathered by the purchases and exchanges of twenty years, was transferred to the Capitol in 1866, and became a part of the library of the Government. This large addition formed a most valuable complement to the collection already gathered at the Capitol. It embraced the largest assemblage of transactions and other publications of learned

---

* Smithsonian Report for 1855, pp. 10-11.—Rhees' Smithsonian Institution, pp. 512-513.

27

varieties in all parts of the globe and in nearly all the modern languages, which is to be found in the country. - - - The Smithsonian deposit, kept up as it is from year to year by additions of new contributions in every department of scientific literature, supplies — in connection with the extensive Library of Congress, a larger collection of scientific books for use and reference, than is to be found in any one body elsewhere in the United States. The waste of means incident to the duplication of two extensive libraries at the seat of Government is thus obviated, while the convenience and interests of scholars pursuing their researches, are in the highest degree promoted by the consolidation." *

Note L. (From p. 285.)

DISTRIBUTION OF SMITHSONIAN MATERIAL.

For the great organic purpose of furthering scientific research, not only have vast numbers of duplicate specimens been liberally distributed, but even reserved specimens of special interest or rarity have been loaned under proper conditions to original workers. Perhaps the review of a single year's application of such material, will best convey an idea of its general character:

"It has always been the policy of the Institution to furnish specimens for special study and investigation to naturalists of established reputation, either in this country or abroad. The use of these specimens is granted under the express condition that they are to form the subject of investigation, the results of which are to be published by the Institution or some other establishment, and that in all cases full credit is to be given to the Institution for the assistance it has rendered. Furthermore, in the case of the preparation of a monograph, a full set of the type specimens correctly labeled is to be put aside for the National Museum, and the remainder of the specimens made up into sets for distribution. The following list presents the more important cases of the loan or assignment of materials during the past year. Some of the specimens have already been returned, while the remainder are still in the hands of the parties to whom they were intrusted:

"Crania of the recent and fossil bison, musk-ox, &c. to Professor L. Agassiz, of Cambridge, Mass: — land shells of Central and South America to Thomas Bland, of New York: — land and fresh-water shells of North America to W. G. Binney, Burlington, N. J. — nests and eggs of North American birds to Dr. T. M. Brewer, Boston: —

* The International Review for November, 1878, vol. v. pp. 782-784.

birds of South America and Alaska to John Cassin, Philadelphia: — Alcidae of North America to Dr. Elliott Coues, U. S. Army: — collections of American and foreign reptiles to Professor E. D. Cope, Philadelphia: — fungi from the Indian Territory to the Rev. M. A. Curtis, Hillsborough, N. C. — unfigured species of North American birds to D. G. Elliott, New York: — diatomaceous earths and deep-sea soundings to Arthur M. Edwards, New York: — Lepidoptera from various North American localities to W. H. Edwards, Coalburg, Va. — seeds of Buchneria received from the Department of Agriculture, to Dr. Earl Flint, Nicaragua: — plants collected in Ecuador by the expedition under Professor Orton, to Dr. Asa Gray, Cambridge, Mass. — miscellaneous specimens of North American insects to Professor T. Glover, Department of Agriculture, Washington: — general collection of birds of Costa Rica and Yucatan to George N. Lawrence, New York: — American Unionidae to Isaac Lea, Philadelphia: — series of North American salamanders to St. George Mivart, London: — American Diptera to Baron R. Osten-Sacken, New York: — Lepidoptera of Ecuador and Yucatan to Tryon Reakirt, Philadelphia: — plants collected in Alaska by various expeditions to Dr. J. T. Rothrock, McVeytown, Pa. — birds of Buenos Ayres received from W. H. Hudson, and a series of small American owls, to Dr. P. L. Sclater and Osbert Salvin, London: — miscellaneous collections of American Orthoptera to S. H. Scudder, Boston: — collections of American Hemiptera to P. R. Uhler, Baltimore: — American myriapods and spiders to Dr. H. C. Wood, Philadelphia: — human crania from northwestern America and the ancient mounds of Kentucky, also collections from the ancient shell-heaps of Massachusetts and New Brunswick, to Dr. Jeffreys Wyman, Cambridge, Mass.

"Few persons are aware of the great extent to which this Smithsonian material has been used by American and foreign naturalists, or the number of new facts and new species which have been contributed to natural history through its means." [*].

Note M. (From p. 285.)

OVERFLOWING CONDITION OF THE MUSEUM.

"It is a question whether any museum in the world is in receipt of so great an amount of material as the National Museum at Washington; and were the rule of the British Museum to prevail, it would be crushed by the weight of its own riches.   The constant

---

[*] Smithsonian Report for 1864, pp. 36, 37.

effort however on the part of the Smithsonian Institution to utilize this material in the interest of science and education, tends to keep down the mass, though it is only at the expense of the incessant activity and constant labor of the Museum force that this object is in any measure accomplished. - - - It may be proper to state that for the exhibition of the full series of objects now in possession of the Institution, and not including any unnecessary duplicates, much ampler accommodations will be needed than can be had in the building; and if these are to be displayed as they should be, it will be necessary at no distant day to provide means for extending the space, either by a transfer of the entire collection to new buildings, or by making additions to that of the Smithsonian Institution. In illustration of this statement it may be remarked that of sixty-seven thousand specimens of birds entered in the catalogues of the museum, and of which more than forty thousand are on hand,—(the remainder having been distributed,) less than five thousand are mounted and on exhibition, these occupying fully two-fifths of the present hall: the rest are preserved as skins, in chests, drawers, and boxes, and of them fifteen thousand—or three times the number at present on exhibition, require to be displayed for the proper illustration of even American ornithology. The urgency for additional room is still greater for the mammals. Here, out of some five or six thousand specimens, less than so many hundred are exhibited, the remainder alone being almost sufficient to occupy half of the hall. Of many thousands of skeletons of mammals, birds, reptiles, and fishes, a very small percentage is shown to the public, while exhibition-room to the amount of thousands of square feet is required for specimens that now occupy drawers in side apartments. Of the very large collection of alcoholic specimens which constitute the most important material in every public museum, scarcely anything is on exhibition, although the selection of a single series for this purpose is very desirable." [*]

"The Museum portion of the Smithsonian edifice consists of two rooms of about 10,000 square feet area each, with a connecting range and gallery of about 5,000 square feet. The specimens in cases are at present very much crowded, while very many others are in boxes occupying the passages and intermediate spaces. The basement of the Institution, nearly 400 feet long, is a series of store-rooms for the reception of portions of the collection not yet exhibited in the upper halls, and thus without benefit to the general public. - - - An estimate of 25,000 square feet, or a space equal to that of the upper halls, is by no means extravagant for the proper display of the specimens thus excluded.

"Anticipating the necessity of increased accommodations for the Centennial collections and accessions, the Smithsonian Institution in 1875 made application to Congress for the use of the Armory building in the square between Sixth and Seventh streets,—an edifice 100 feet by 50, having four floors. This it was supposed would be adequate at the close of the Centennial, for the reception and exhibition of at least the fishery exhibit and that of economical mineralogy. So great however was the surplus of Centennial material to be provided for, that the building is now filled with boxed specimens, occupying for the most part the entire space from floor to ceiling of each room. The building is not fire-proof, and although the specimens in it represent some of the most valuable and important of the series, there is nothing to prevent their destruction by fire, or their injury from damp, vermin, or other causes;— a result which would constitute an irreparable loss. As the four floors of the Armory referred to, present 20,000 feet of area, an estimate of 50,000 feet for the proper display of the specimens now stored in them cannot be considered extravagant; thus making the entire additional space required,—75,000 square feet. Only one-fourth of the specimens in charge of the Institution are at present on exhibition, the remainder being entirely withdrawn from public inspection; so that the necessity for prompt effort to secure the proper accommodations will be readily understood. - - - In view of the fact that the collections for which provision is needed represent a bulk of at least three times the present capacity of the Smithsonian building, it is evident that to accommodate these, and to make reasonable provision for probable increase in the future, a building of great magnitude will be required." *

Note N. (From p. 309.)

INVESTIGATION OF ILLUMINANTS.

"At the commencement of the operations of the Light-House Board in 1852, sperm oil was generally employed for the purpose of illumination. This was an excellent illuminant; but as its price continued to advance from year to year, it was thought proper to attempt the introduction of some other material. The first attempt of this kind was that of the introduction of colza oil, which was generally used in the light-houses of Europe, and is extracted from the seed of a species of wild cabbage—known in this country as rape, and in France as colza. For this purpose a quantity of rape-

---

* Smithsonian Report for 1876, pp. 48, 88.

seed was imported from France and distributed through the agricultural department of the Patent Office to different parts of the country, with the hope that our farmers would be induced to attempt its cultivation. Although the climate of the country appeared favorable to its growth, and special instructions were prepared and distributed by the Light-House Board for its culture and the means of producing oil from it, yet the enterprise was not undertaken with any approximation to success, except in Wisconsin, where a manufactory of rape-seed oil was established by Colonel C. S. Hamilton, formerly of the United States Army. To this manufactory the Light-House Board gave special encouragement and purchased at a liberal price all the oil that could be supplied. The quantity however which could be procured was but a small part of the illuminating material required for the annual consumption of the Light-House Establishment."

After referring to some investigations made for the Board by Professor J. H. Alexander, of Baltimore, the Report quoted proceeds: "The chairman of the committee on experiments commenced himself to investigate the qualities of different kinds of oil, and was soon led to direct his attention to the comparative value of sperm and lard oils. The experiments made by Mr. Alexander were with small lamps, and the comparison in this case (as will be shown) was much against the lard oil. The first experiment of the new series, consisted in charging two small conical lamps of the capacity of about a half pint, one with pure sperm oil and the other with lard oil. These lamps were of single-rope wicks each containing the same number of strands: they were lighted at the same time, and the photometrical power ascertained by the method of shadows. At first the two were nearly equal in brilliancy, but after burning about three hours, the flame of the lard had declined in photometric power to about one-fifth of that of the flame of the sperm. The question then occurred as to the cause of this decline, and it was suggested that it might be due — first, to a greater specific gravity in the lard oil, which would retard the ascent of it in the wick after the level of the oil had been reduced by burning in the lamp; or second, to a want of a sufficient attraction between the oil and the wick to furnish the requisite supply as the oil descended in the lamp; or third, it might be due in part to the imperfect liquidity of the oil, which would also militate against its use in mechanical lamps.

"The lard oil was subjected to experiments in regard to each of these points. It was found by the usual method of weighing equal quantities of the two fluids, that the specific gravity of the lard was greater than that of the sperm; and also by dipping two portions of the same wick into the two liquids and noting the height to which each ascended in a given time, that the surface attraction of the sperm was greater than that of the lard, or in other words that the ascensional power of sperm was much greater than that of lard at ordinary temperatures. This method was also employed in obtaining the relative surface attraction of various other liquids; we say surface attraction instead of capillarity, because it was found in the course of these investigations that substances which had less capillarity (that is less elevating power in a fine tube) had greater power in ascending in the meshes of a wick. The relative fluidity of the different oils was obtained by filling in succession a pear-shaped vessel with a narrow neck, of about the capacity of a pint, having a hole in the lowest part of the bottom, of about a tenth of an inch in diameter. Such a vessel filled with any number of perfect liquids, would be emptied in the same time — whatever their specific gravity. As at any given horizon, inertia is directly proportional to gravity, the heavier the liquid the greater would be the power required to move it; but the motive power would be in proportion to the pressure, or in other words to the weight, and therefore all perfect liquids should issue from the same orifice with the same velocity. To test this proposition, eight fluid ounces of clean mercury and then the same bulk of distilled water, were allowed to run out of the vessel above mentioned: the time observed was the same within the nearest second. It was found in repeating this experiment with sperm and lard oils that the rapidity of the flow of the former exceeded considerably that of the latter; the ratio of time being 100 to 167.

"The results thus far in these investigations were apparently against the use of lard oil: it was observed however that in the experiments on the flow of the two oils, a variation in the time occurred, which could only be attributed to a variation in the temperature at which the experiments were made. In relation to this point, the effect of an increase of the temperature above that of the atmosphere, on the flowing of the two oils was observed. By this means the important fact was elicited that as the temperature was increased, the liquidity of the lard increased in a more rapid degree than that of the sperm, and that at the temperature of about 250° F. the liquidity of the former exceeded that of the latter. A similar series of experiments was made in regard to the rapidity of ascent of the oil in the wick, and with a similar result. At about the temperature of that before mentioned, the ascensional power of the lard was greater than that of the sperm. These results were recognized as having an important bearing on the question of the application of lard oil as a light-house illuminant. It only required to

be burned at a high temperature; and as this could be readily
obtained in the case of larger lamps, there appeared to be no
difficulty in its application.

"The previous trials had been with small lamps with single solid
wicks instead of the Fresnel lamp with hollow burners. After
these preliminary experiments, two light-houses of the first order,
at Cape Ann, Massachusetts, separated by a distance of only 900
feet, were selected as affording excellent facilities for trying in
actual burning, the correctness of the conclusions which had previously been arrived at. One of these light-houses was supplied
with sperm and the other with lard oil, each lamp being so trimmed
as to exhibit its greatest capacity. It was found by photometrical
trial that the lamp supplied with lard, exceeded in intensity of
light that of the one furnished with sperm. The experiment was
continued for several months, and the relative volume of the two
materials carefully observed. The quantity of sperm burned during the continuance of the experiment, was to that of the lard, as
100 is to 104." *

This remarkable success in elevating the disparaged lard oil to
the highest rank as an illuminant, was of course very damaging to
the new manufacture of colza oil; and no more characteristic tribute
to the energetic skill of Henry could be offered, than that contained
in the following frank and manly letter by Colonel C. S. Hamilton,
the manufacturer, (who by special invitation had been present at
several competitive photometric trials,) addressed to the Naval Secretary of the Light-House Board, Commodore Andrew A. Harwood:

"FOND DU LAC, WIS. May 16, 1868.

"DEAR COMMODORE: I must confess my great disappointment at
the result of the experiments at Staten Island. It is however not
really so much the failure of rape-seed oil, as the undeniable excellence of lard oil as a burner. I am satisfied now that for self-heat-
ing lamps there is no oil that will bear comparison with lard, but I
am equally satisfied that no colza oil will yield a better result than
ours, under exactly the same tests. We have but one more experiment to make with colza; it is its extraction by chemical displacement. If this fails we shall abandon the whole business.

"If all things are put together, I think the following statement
will be allowed, to wit: Our colza oil of this year is equal to any
foreign colza. It is better than any we have heretofore made. It
is better than sperm, or any other burner, excepting only lard oil.
Our failure then is owing to the superior excellence of lard oil,
which under the persistent investigation of the Board, has been

* Report of the Light-House Board for 1873, pp. 68-80.

shown to be the best and cheapest safe illuminator available. The Board are entitled to great credit in producing this result. It will be remembered that but a few years since, lard oil was pronounced unsuitable for light-house purposes; but the perseverance of the Board has brought out the fact that it is much the best and cheapest oil, and that the expenses of lighting the coast and harbors have been thereby greatly reduced. Surely the country at large should acknowledge this, and give due credit to the Board. We have endeavored to do with coke what the Board have effected with lard oil, and we have been unsuccessful both for ourselves and the light-house interest. - - -

"We are grateful to each member of the Board for the interest they have always shown in our undertaking, and for their uniform kindness and courtesy. Accept, my dear Commodore, for yourself and your associates in the Board, my warmest thanks for your many kind expressions of interest, and believe me

"Truly and gratefully, yours,

"C. S. HAMILTON."

OBITUARY MEMOIR*

PROF. JOSEPH LOVERING,

VICE-PRESIDENT OF THE AMERICAN ACADEMY OF ARTS AND SCIENCES.

JOSEPH HENRY, who was united with this Academy as an Associate Fellow on May 26, 1840, was born in Albany, N. Y. on December 17, 1799, and died in Washington, D. C. on May 13, 1878, in the plenitude of his years, his labors, and his honors. The child is always father to the man: but there was nothing in the childhood or youth of Henry to proclaim the advent of one whose life would be a blessing to mankind, and whose death would be felt as a nation's loss. Descended from Scotch ancestors, who had recently immigrated to this country, and losing his father at an early age, he passed a large part of his youth under the care of his maternal grandmother, at Galway, in Saratoga County. Here he attended the district school until he was ten years old. Then he was taken into a store, where he was treated kindly and allowed to be present at the afternoon session of the school. Obtaining access to the village library, at first by accident, afterwards by stealth, and finally by permission, he revelled in an ideal world of fiction, and perhaps cultivated, unconsciously, that faculty of imagination which served him as the interpreter of Nature.

At the age of about fifteen Henry returned to Albany and entered a watchmaker's shop as an apprentice. Whatever knowledge of mechanism and delicacy of touch were thus acquired were not thrown away upon one destined to plan and handle the nice appliances of physical research. And yet his heart was not in the new occupation. The stage, before the scenes and behind the scenes; private theatricals; a club of amateurs of which he was president,

[* Report of the Council of the Am. Academy of Arts and Sciences, May 27, 1879.]

and for which he wrote and acted tragedy and comedy, — absorbed his time and thoughts. All who have seen and admired the refined, intellectual face, and the erect, dignified form of the ripe philosopher, can easily imagine the success of the young aspirant for dramatic distinction when these charms of person and mind were decked in the beauty of youth: the self-possession, the repose, and the grace of this expounder of physical science alone remained to tell of his short-lived eccentricity. Those readers, who allow the mythical apple to divide with Newton the glory of a great discovery, will listen eagerly to the statement that the theatrical career of young Henry was suddenly arrested by his accidental encounter, during a brief illness, with Dr. Gregory's popular lectures. The literal truth of the story is not questioned; for Professor Henry himself believed it, and reverently cherished the precious volume to the last. Such however was the occasion, but not the cause, of his dedicating himself henceforth to science. Innumerable accidents of a similar kind happen to every one, but not with the same result. Man, especially such a man, is not the creation of any accident. The inspiration comes from within: it is the unbidden thought, and not the external events with which it is associated. Said a great divine, "If you say that man is the creature of circumstances, it must be with the understanding that the greatest and most effective of these circumstances is the man himself."

Bidding farewell to the stage and his theatrical companions, Henry went seriously to work to complete his education; at first in an evening school, then with an itinerant pedagogue, and finally in the Albany Academy, where he was successively pupil, and teacher. Next he was private tutor in the family of the patroon, devoting his leisure to the study of mathematics, and subjects which would fit him for the medical profession. In 1826 he made, in connection with Amos Eaton, the survey for a road across the State of New York. In this work he displayed so much energy and ability that his friends hoped to find, or to create for him, a permanent position as engineer. But the State failed to respond, and Henry returned to the Albany Academy as assistant teacher, and in 1828 as Professor of Mathematics.

Only a few years had elapsed since the science of electricity had taken a new departure under the name of electro-magnetism. Oersted, of Copenhagen, had kindled the flame, which passed rapidly from hand to hand among the scientific workers of Europe, until it culminated in the splendid generalization of Ampère. This western continent may have been tardy in welcoming the bright light in the east, but the response, when given, was not a fire, but a conflagration. Professor Henry led in the new line of physical research with a self-born enthusiasm which seven hours of daily teaching in mathematics could not extinguish or cool. The limits of this notice forbid a lengthened statement of his contributions to electro-magnetism. But the fertile principle which he deduced from his experiments must not be passed over in silence. His distinction between *quantity* and *intensity* magnets, and between *quantity* and *intensity* batteries, (though now differently expressed,) is all-important and of manifold applications. Every experiment with electro-magnetism, in the laboratory, in the lecture-room, and in the arts, is a success or a failure in proportion as this law is obeyed or ignored. If this discovery has linked Professor Henry's name with the telegraph especially, it is because that was the great problem of the hour, — unsolved, and as some supposed unsolvable. It is not easy to draw the dividing line between the merits of the discoverer and the inventor, when one follows closely upon the heels of the other. Professor Henry's contribution to the final triumph was large, and brilliant, and indispensable; but it was not all-sufficient. An alphabet was wanting; a sustaining battery must be invented; moreover, a man must appear with a capacity for business and a courage born of hope, with no original knowledge of the familiar laws of electricity but with an easy absorption of the science of other men, who, by a happy combination of experimental devices and the devotion of years, might finally achieve a grand commercial success. In view of Professor Henry's additional conquests in the realm of physical research, science will ever rejoice that he was not himself dazzled by the inviting prospect of riches and popular applause; that he renounced the fruits of invention when they were almost within his grasp; that he preferred to any short-lived, meteoric display the chance of shining for ever as a star in the upper heavens, with Agassiz, Cuvier, and Faraday.

Loyalty to the devotees of scientific research does not demand any disparagement of the usefulness or the genius of inventors. If the former enlarge the area of human knowledge, the latter contribute to the civilization of the race. If there are individuals in one class who think only of their pecuniary success, the other class is not without examples of those who meant to achieve, even if they do not deserve, a high scientific reputation. It is not incumbent on every scientific man to think, with Cuvier, that he must abandon a discovery the moment it enters the market,—that its practical application is of no concern to him. No one certainly has a better right to the fruits of this application than the discoverer himself. Inventors may sometimes stumble on good fortune; but the rich prizes are comparatively few, and, on the average, they are dearly earned by years of severe thought and anxious waiting. No graveyard holds so many buried hopes as the Patent Office at Washington. Since the first introduction of the telegraph, discovery and invention have advanced, hand in hand, over continents and through the ocean, leaving the world in doubt which to admire the most,— the conceptions of pure science, or the exquisite mechanism in which they are embodied. If on one occasion this harmony was disturbed by the repudiation of an indebtedness which had often before been freely acknowledged, the ingratitude was rebuked by the indignant voice of science, and the just claims of Mr. Henry were established on an impregnable foundation.

It does not detract from the merit or the originality of Professor Henry's early discoveries that the same ground had been covered by Fechner, in a work published in 1831, and that both had been anticipated by Ohm's experimental and mathematical analysis of the galvanic circuit, which dates back to 1827. For Ohm's little book of that date, which now shines as a foreland light for the guidance of all who explore in that direction, was known only to a few in Germany, and was unknown in France, England, and America at a time when, if known, it might have illuminated Professor Henry's researches. At a later period, Pouillet published the results of his own experiments, without knowing that he himself had been anticipated by Ohm. The father of Ohm had intended his son for a locksmith; but, unlike Henry, he did not

even begin his apprenticeship. He pursued his studies to the verge
of starvation; his heated brain worked while his body shivered
before a fireless stove, often covered with ice. His book, which
placed him before his death, in 1854, among the greatest of German physicists, was coldly received by his colleagues in the College
of Jesuits, at Cologne. On the contrary, Professor Henry's recognition was prompt and sympathetic, at home and abroad; at a single
bound he came to the front, and there he always remained.

In 1832, Professor Henry removed to Princeton to fill the chair
of Natural Philosophy in the College of New Jersey. Here he
found sympathizing associates, congenial duties, and the opportunity
for original research. One year earlier Faraday, already widely
known by his chemical discoveries, appeared upon the field of
experimental electricity, and immediately became the most conspicuous figure thereon, the cynosure of admiring eyes in every land.
His discovery of induced currents, and of the evolution of electricity from magnets, marked a new era in the science of electricity,
elucidating facts which had defied the ingenuity of Arago, Herschel,
and Babbage, creating the science of magneto-electricity as the cor-
relative of electro-magnetism, and justly claiming for its last-born
the splendors and wonders of the Ruhmkorff coil, the Gramme
machine, and the telephone. Henry supplemented the work of
Faraday by his own discoveries of the extra-current in the primitive circuit, and of induced currents of higher orders in as many
adjacent circuits. He also succeeded where Faraday had doubts
about his own experiments; viz: in obtaining unequivocal indications of similar induction in the momentary passage of electricity
of high tension; proving also the oscillating discharge of the Leyden jar. Numerous experiments were made on induction by thun-
der-clouds, and on atmospheric electricity in general, by means of
tandem-kites and lightning-rods.

Nobili and Melloni had widened and deepened the foundations
of thermotics, unveiling new and intimate analogies between radiant
light and heat, and enriching physical cabinets with many novelties,
especially the thermopile and the galvanometer. Henry took advantage of the new instruments for measuring the heat of different
parts of the sun. Secchi, the late astronomer and meteorologist of

the Collegio Romano, distinguished as the foster-brother of Victor Emmanuel, but more as the gifted expounder of solar physics, owed his first inspiration in science, in his youth, (for he died in 1878, at the age of fifty-nine,) to Henry, whom he assisted in these experiments. Doubtless, other young men, if they could be heard, would confess to an equal enthusiasm for science, caught from the same high example. But the multitudinous productions which issued in rapid succession from the prolific brain and pen of Secchi, without the adventitious reinforcement of imaginary cases, justify and demand the assertion that what Henry led others to do is second only in importance to what he did himself.

More than fifty years ago, a little book was published under the fascinating title of "Philosophy in Sport made Science in Earnest." Of the many ingenious, complex, and costly instruments of research, has any one been richer in its revelations to science than the child's soap-bubble? But where the child saw only an evanescent display of colors, Newton read with mathematical clearness his celebrated theory of fits of easy transmission and reflection, and Young measured the constants of the undulations of light. To-day, the microscopic molar or molecular motions of the telephone-plate are translated into visible speech by the colors of a sympathetic film of liquid in the phoneidoscope. In 1844, Henry experimented with this every ready minister to the delight and instruction of all ages, so beautiful but apparently so tender, and found that its cohesion and its contractile force were those of a giant if its own thinness were made the standard of measure. Thus was opened an avenue into the study of molecular action which Plateau has extended and embellished with the most varied and original experiments, not disheartened by the total loss of eyesight: finding by the way a beautiful experimental illustration of the cosmogony of La Place, and building architectural forms out of liquid films as if they had the cohesion of marble.

When, at the close of 1846, Professor Henry left the quiet walks of the Academy for a more public career in Washington, in obedience to the summons of the Regents of the Smithsonian Institution, though all applauded the wisdom of the choice, not a few regretted the sad interruption in his scientific life, already rich in performance and bright with the promise of more and perhaps greater discoveries. The sacrifice seemed to be too great to demand of science in a country where the taste and the mental qualifications, combined with the opportunity, for original research are rare. If Professor Henry had remained at Princeton, he would certainly have added other jewels to his crown: would it, however, have shone more brightly than it now shines? When posterity makes up its verdict on his claim to its gratitude and remembrance, his discoveries will not be counted, but weighed.

On the other hand, no friend of science can contemplate with complacency the possible alternatives if the Regents had come to a different choice, or if they had been defeated in their first selection. Literature or science; popular lectures or original research; the diffusion of old truth or the discovery of new truth; a national library, a national university, or a national museum,—each had warm and influential advocates. Professor Henry's plan of organization bears the date of December 8, 1847, and was adopted by the Regents on the 13th of December. It took its departure from the words of the founder, viz: *an establishment for the increase and diffusion of knowledge among men;* and it emphasized every word of the pregnant sentence. Not science in its restricted sense, but knowledge was to be first increased, then diffused world-wide,—by the endowment of research; by the publication and liberal distribution of contributions to knowledge, which may have little value in the market, but which are of transcendent importance to man's culture and civilization; by elaborate reports in special departments, in which the known would be separated from the unknown for the benefit of new explorers; by the translation of writings otherwise inaccessible to most students; by opening a highway along which the current literature and science of the day could easily pass from continent to continent, and reach their remotest corners. This sober and catholic scheme, in literal fulfillment of the will of Smithson, was less dazzling to the popular imagination, and enlisted a smaller numerical support, than rival propositions which were more on the level of the average understanding. Because these antagonistic plans narrowed the enjoyment of a benefaction, (itself absolutely unfettered,) to a small community, they secured a local influence which threatened to defeat the comprehensive views of the Secretary. These views, recommended by their reasonableness and indorsed by individuals, academies, and societies of science and learning, had a tower of strength in the high scientific reputation and the weight of character of the Secretary himself. Winning and persuasive in his manner, he was inflexible in his purpose.

Experience has proved the truth of that which was the contention at the time; viz: that universities, libraries, museums, lectures, because they confer local benefits, will never lack endowments, whereas the Christian world had waited eighteen centuries for a large-minded and large-hearted benefactor, whose bequest was all knowledge, existing or to be discovered, and whose recipients were all nations of men. Slowly but steadily time has revealed the wisdom and foresight of the Secretary; individuals and communities, in increasing numbers, have felt the benefits of his administration; the Government of the United States has known where to look for impartial advice on matters outside of its own knowledge, in times of prosperity and also in its darkest days; and now all opposition has died out; and, after a trial of thirty years, no one probably desires any thing better for the Smithsonian Institution than that the plan, so wisely conceived and so faithfully administered by the first Secretary, should continue the abiding rule for his successors.

Moreover, the plan of Professor Henry, cosmopolitan in its geographical embrace, did not sacrifice the interests of the unborn to those of the living. He would not allow the hopes of Smithson to be frustrated by lavishing upon a single generation what was intended for all time; or, what is worse, sacrificing both the present and the future upon the altar of an ambitious architecture. Examples abound, if experience is all which men need, of fatal shipwrecks on these alluring shores; of endowed churches, colleges, observatories, laboratories, libraries, which have nothing to show but a mass of masonry, lacking in the highest beauty of art, (fitness for its purpose,) however much it may please the eye, even if the merciless architect had left any thing for administration. The rigid rules of science, unqualified by good common sense, may work a disaster in matters of business. The consummate mathematician, La Place, omnipotent in the domain of physical astronomy, when appointed by Napoleon I. to a high office of state, attempted to carry the laws of the infinitesimal calculus into his administration, and failed.   Not a few men of brilliant intellect, masters of thought and of the pen, have prided themselves on a childlike simplicity in the ways of the world.   If Professor Henry had been one of these, much would have been forgiven to his honesty of purpose, to his love of truth, and to the success with which he had wooed her in her most secret recesses.   Therefore, it is not the least of his triumphs that he did not, in imitation of an old astronomer, walk into a pitfall on this lower earth while gazing into the depths of space.   He could roam with Emerson through the universe of thought, but the feet of both were firmly planted on the ground. Henry's judicious system of expenditures, so essential to the permanent prosperity of the Institution, put to shame the short-sightedness and the short-comings of many professed financiers; and exemplified, by anticipation, the magical products of the Holtz and Ladd induction machines, in which a trifling capital of well-invested electricity, the income of which is partly spent and partly saved, yields an ample return for the present, and by the law of compound interest secures still more brilliant results for the future.

When Professor Henry left Princeton, he knew, and his friends knew, that he must leave behind him the object of his highest ambition, viz: the undisturbed and the unostentatious study of the unfolding laws of the material universe.   But he did not, and he could not, renounce the spirit of independent research which had made him what he was.   As opportunity offered in the discharge of his official duties he manifested this spirit himself, and communicated it to others.   His second report to the Board of Regents, for 1848, exhibits the promptness with which he had conceived, and begun to execute, the project of covering the United States, and eventually the North American continent, with a net-work of meteorological stations, which, with the facilities of the telegraph, yet in its infancy, would prove a perennial blessing to commerce and agriculture ; and, by consolidating the scattered efforts of eminent meteorologists, (among whom Coffin, Espy, Loomis, and Guyot were conspicuous,) throw some light on the law of storms and meteorology in general.   In the Patent Office Report for 1857, he

gave his views of the relations between meteorology and agriculture. In this and other ways, the Smithsonian Institution has been
a hot-bed for starting and nursing new projects in their days of
infancy and weakness. After they have outgrown its accommodations and proved their usefulness, they have been adopted by the
general Government and transplanted to a richer soil.

For many years Professor Henry has been a conspicuous figure,
not merely in scientific circles, but in the full view of the public;
his name and his co-operation have been in constant demand. He
naturally gravitated to places of honor which were often places of
additional labor. Men of leisure have no time to give to occasional
calls upon their public spirit. The hard-workers must also do all
the extra work. Professor Henry was no exception to this rule.
To the day of his death, he filled positions of trust and responsibility, with duties sufficient to crush an effeminate man. But they
seemed to rest lightly upon shoulders which sustained, beside, the
weight of a great institution. His mind was ever in a state of
prolonged tension; but it kept its balance under these distractions,
as do the rings of Saturn amid the multitudinous disturbances of
its satellites. Often he waited for the leisure which never came to
him, when he might write out for publication scientific communications which he had made from a brief. He was President of the
American Association at its second meeting, in Cambridge, in 1849.
He gave the usual address of the retiring President at the fourth
meeting, in New Haven, but it was not printed. He was Vice-
President of the National Academy of Sciences in 1866, succeeded
Dr. Barbe as President in 1868, and died in office.

The most responsible and the most onerous of the gratuitous services which he gave to science and the country were rendered in his
capacity of member of the Light-House Board, of which he was
for seven years the chairman. The substitution of lenses for mirrors began the revolution in light-houses; but lens or mirror, without the light, is no better than a steam-engine without steam. To
conquer prejudice by experiment, and save millions to the country
by exchanging sperm oil for lard oil, is not so brilliant a service as
the discovery of a new law of nature. But, more than any discovery, it makes science respected in high places, and enlists the

sympathy of the unscientific community. There are times when
sextants, chronometers, tables of the moon, and even light-houses,
are of no avail, and an impenetrable veil of darkness shuts out the
mariner from the lights of heaven and earth. But what is opaque
to light may be pierced by sound. The experiments which have
been made by Henry in this country and by Tyndall in England, in
their official capacity, on the fog-penetrating power of the fog-horn,
the fog-bell, the siren, the steam-whistle, and cannonading, have
raised interesting questions in science, to which different answers
have been given; but the facts remain, above controversy, to instruct
governments in the best way of supplementing optical signals by
acoustic signals. These last investigations of Professor Henry, to
which it is feared he was a willing martyr, will always have a
pathetic interest for those who knew and loved him.

It has been the aim of this notice to place in strong relief a few
of the salient points in the intellectual life of Henry. Any statement in detail of the accumulations of his long life, in the way of
experiment or deduction, must be very voluminous or very meagre.
For he was not a concentrated specialist. His expanded thought
swept the whole vast horizon of the physical sciences; not to specu-
late, but to discover. The severe discipline of science did not
harden him against the fascinations of literature, poetry, and art.

It would be a delicate task, and premature, to attempt to assign
to Henry his exact rank among those who have legislated for science
in this and former centuries. There are laws of perspective in
time as well as in space, whereby a small eminence seems to out-
climb the distant Alps, and the present generation dwarfs apparently
all its predecessors. Foreign countries and posterity will pronounce
their irreversible verdict in this as in other cases. In his own
country, and among his contemporaries, Mr. Henry was long and
easily the acknowledged chief of experimental philosophers. If the
earlier science of the country is passed in review, only a few names
shine so brightly across the intervening years as to deserve any
comparison with him who has recently departed. Winthrop and
Rittenhouse in astronomy, Franklin in electricity, Rumford in
thermotics, and Bowditch in mathematics, exhaust the catalogue of
possible rivals. Of these, all but Winthrop were self-instructed,

as was Henry, at least in what relates to their higher education. Of these, Franklin and Rumford, no less than Henry, were as remarkable in administration as in science; Franklin and Rumford from taste, and Henry from a sense of duty. All three served their country well,—Franklin and Henry while living, and Rumford by his bequests. Winthrop, Rittenhouse, and Bowditch reached their exalted position by paths wholly untrodden by Henry. They cannot therefore be the standard for his measure. Rumford's mind was essentially practical, even in its science. He had more of the spirit of an inventor than a discoverer. In Henry's place he would have been more interested in pushing the telegraph to its final issue than in supplementing Faraday's laws of electro-dynamical induction. But in dealing with the heat of friction, Rumford displayed an experimental skill and a boldness of conception which have vindicated his claim to a high scientific position. The progress of recent discovery and the tendency of scientific speculation have promoted Rumford from the position which he long held, as leader of a forlorn hope, to the place of hero in the last act of the scientific drama. In this connection Henry's views on the correlation of the physical and organic forces may be recalled, which only lacked the fuller development and the wider publication which he finally gave to them, to have secured for him the first complete announcement of one of the grandest generalizations of modern science.

It might seem to be easy to institute a comparison between Franklin and Henry in reference to the value of their original scientific work, which was largely in the field of electricity. But a century has made great changes in the starting-point, the opportunities, and the resources of the discoverer. Franklin, with humble tools, had a virgin soil to cultivate. He had also the rare felicity, for which Newton also was envied, of living at a time when the scattered facts of a new science were waiting for a comprehensive generalization. If Franklin had made no experiments on the Leyden jar, or on the thunder-cloud, his theory of electricity, which has held its own to this day without any amendment, (though its final doom is written upon it,) would have secured for him a place second to no other among the worthies of science. Now the instruments of

physical research are numerous and delicate; but useless unless the
senses are educated to them. The literature of science is voluminous and in many languages. Success in scientific investigations
demands now original thought, disciplined senses, scientific culture,
and a well-chosen field, where the discoveries of other men will not
be repeated. Both Franklin and Henry burned brightly in their
allotted spheres, and in the future may differ only as one star differs
from another star in glory.

The funeral services on May 16, 1878, proclaimed to the world
that the republic had lost an illustrious citizen. There was no
hollow pageant of empty carriages of state, but the highest and
best in the land felt a personal bereavement. A patriotic and
devoted servant of the Government was dead; a bright light in
science had gone out; a noble man, born to attract and to sway, in
whom science was illuminated by faith, and faith was enlightened by
science, lived on earth no longer except by his example; a long life,
crowded with beneficent services to truth and to man, was closed.
Not less affecting were the memorial exercises of January 16, 1879,
in the hall of the House of Representatives, before the assembled
wisdom and grandeur of the nation. Science may be proud of this
spontaneous tribute to her favored child, if she only remembers
that it is character which makes intellect a blessing and not a scourge
to mankind, and awakens genuine sympathy and admiration. Mr.
Henry was not the favorite and ornament of a court, but the peer
of the greatest and wisest in a free republic. The monument of
Humboldt was not thought to be worthy of a place in sight of the
king's palace in Berlin. That was a spot consecrated to princes
of the blood and military heroes. Will any American think that
any ground in this country is too sacred to contain a monument to
HENRY?

BIOGRAPHICAL MEMOIR:[*]

BY

PROF. SIMON NEWCOMB.

In presenting to the Academy the following notice of its late lamented President the writer feels that an apology is due for the imperfect manner in which he has been obliged to perform the duty assigned him. The very richness of the material has been a source of embarrassment. Few have any conception of the breadth of the field occupied by Professor HENRY's researches, or of the number of scientific enterprises of which he was either the originator or the effective supporter. What, under the circumstances, could be said within a brief space to show what the world owes to him has already been so well said by others that it would be impracticable to make a really new presentation without writing a volume. The Philosophical Society of this city has issued two notices which together cover almost the whole ground that the writer feels competent to occupy. The one is a personal biography — the affectionate and eloquent tribute of an old and attached friend; the other an exhaustive analysis of his scientific labors by an honored member of the society well known for his philosophic acumen. The Regents of the Smithsonian Institution made known their indebtedness to his administration in the Memorial Services held in his honor in the Halls of Congress.

Under these circumstances the only practicable course has seemed to be to give a condensed resumé of Professor HENRY's life and works, by which any small occasional gaps in previous notices might be filled. That in doing this the writer may repeat much that has already been better said by others is a fault which he hopes the Academy will pardon in view of the difficulty of avoiding it.

* An Address read before the "National Academy of Sciences," April 21, 1880.

BIOGRAPHICAL NOTICE.

THE interest which, in the light of modern theories of heredity,
attaches to the ancestry of men possessing uncommon intellectual
powers would naturally lead us to desire a knowledge of Professor
HENRY's ancestors. We have, however, no sufficient historical data
for gratifying any desire of this kind. Little more can be said than
that his grand-parents were of Scottish origin, and landed in this
country about the beginning of the revolutionary war. Of his
father little is known, and that little does not enable us to explain
why he had such a son. His mother was a woman of great refinement, intelligence, and strength of character, but of a delicate
physical constitution. Like the mothers of many other great men
she was of deeply devotional character. She was a Presbyterian of
the old-fashioned Scottish stamp, and exacted from her children
the strictest performance of religious duties.

The son Joseph was born in Albany, on the 17th of December,
either 1797 or 1799.* The doubt respecting the year has not yet
been decisively settled. At the age of seven years he left his paternal home and went to live with his grandmother at Galway, where
he attended the district school for three years. At the age of ten
he was placed in a store kept by a Mr. Broderick, and spent part
of the day in business duties and part at school. This position he
kept until the age of fifteen. During these early years his intellectual qualities were fully displayed, but in a direction totally different from that which they ultimately took. He was slender in
person, not vigorous in health, with almost the delicate complexion
and features of a girl. His favorite reading was books of romance.
The lounging-place for the young villagers of an evening was
around the stove in Mr. Broderick's store. Here young Henry,
although the slenderest of the group, was the central figure, retail-
ing to those around him the stories which he had read, or which
his imagination suggested. He was of a highly imaginative turn
of mind, and seemed to live in the ideal world of the fairies.

---

*This uncertainty appears to have resulted from the difficulty of deciphering the
faded record of date in the old family Bible.

At the age of fifteen he returned to Albany, and, urged by his imaginative taste, joined a private dramatic company, of which he soon became the leading spirit. There was every prospect of his devoting himself to the stage when, at the age of sixteen, accident turned his mental activities into an entirely different direction. Being detained in-doors by a slight indisposition, a friend loaned him a copy of Dr. Gregory's lectures on Experimental Philosophy, Astronomy, and Chemistry. He became intensely interested in the field of thought which this work opened to him. Here in the domain of Nature were subjects of investigation far more worthy of attention than anything in the ideal world in which his imagination had hitherto roamed. He determined to make the knowledge of this newly opened domain the great object of his life, but did not confine himself to any narrow sphere. He devoted himself immediately, with great ardor, to study. During the three years following he was successively English teacher, pupil of various masters, and a student at the Albany Academy. At about eighteen years of age he was recommended by Dr. BECK to the position of private tutor in the family of the patroon. He found this situation to be a very pleasant one, and was treated with great consideration by the family of Mr. Van Rensselaer. His duties required only his morning hours, so that he could devote his entire afternoons to mathematical and physical studies. In the former he went so far as to read the *Mécanique Analytique* of La Grange.

His delicate constitution now suffered so much from confinement and study that at the age of twenty-two he accepted an invitation to go on a surveying expedition to the western part of the State. In this work his constitution was completely restored, and he returned home with a health and vigor which never failed him during the remainder of his long and arduous life. Soon after his return he was elected a professor at the Albany Academy. Here a new field was opened to him. It is one of the most curious features in the intellectual history of our country that after producing such a man as Franklin it found no successor to him in the field of science for half a century after his scientific work was done. There had been without doubt plenty of professors of eminent attainments who amused themselves and instructed their pupils and the public by physical experiments. But in the department of electricity, that in which Franklin took so prominent a position, it may be doubted whether they enunciated a single generalization which will enter into the history of the science. This interregnum closes with the researches now commenced by Professor Henry. His first published paper on the subject was read in 1827 before the Albany Institute, and is entitled, "On some modifications of the electro-magnetic apparatus." It consisted simply of a brief discussion of several forms of apparatus designed to exhibit the mutual action of the galvanic current and the magnet, but does not appear to comprise any discussions of new ideas. Two years later he published a topographical sketch of the State of New York, which also appeared in the Transactions of the Albany Institute. It comprises a brief sketch of the physical geography of the State with especial reference to the newly inaugurated canal system.

In 1831, he published in Silliman's Journal, a paper on the development of great magnetic power in soft iron with a small galvanic element. This paper is in some sort a continuation of his first paper, the fundamental object of both being to show how the greatest development of power could be obtained with the smallest battery. The ideas were suggested by the study of Schweigger's Galvanometer. He shows that in a piece of soft iron the magnetic power produced by the galvanic current may be greatly increased by increasing the number of coils. A still further improvement is made when, instead of passing a single coil between the two poles of the battery, a number of separate insulated wires are wound around the magnet, so that each shall form an independent connection. He was thus enabled with a battery of a single pair of small plates (4 by 6 inches) to form an electro-magnet which would lift a weight of 39 pounds. He also intimates that by winding a separate wire on each inch of the magnet a yet greater effect could be attained. This paper also contains the germ of the theory of electro-magnetic force, and of electrical resistance and quantity, though not developed in any generalized form. He explains that with one very long wire a combination of several plates must be used so as to obtain "projectile force," while when several larger wires are used the battery must consist of a single pair. A great number of experiments illustrative of the theory are described. With a battery having a single plate of zinc, of half a square foot of surface, he made a magnet lift a weight of 750 pounds,— more than thirty-five times the weight of the magnet.

In the same year, 1831, he describes a little machine for producing continuous mechanical motion by magnetic attraction and repulsion. He considered the apparatus to be merely a philosophical toy involving a principle which at some future time might be applied to a useful purpose.

In 1830, at the request of Professor Henwick, he commenced a series of observations to determine the magnetic intensity at Albany. This gave him occasion to investigate a subject of which the evidences had before been very conflicting, namely, the effect of the aurora upon the magnetism of the earth.

In 1831, April 19, at 6 P. M., a remarkable phenomenon was noticed, namely, an extraordinary increase in the number of vibrations of the needle, and in the consequent magnetic intensity of the earth. Every precaution was taken that no local influence should affect the magnet, but the result was the same. About 9 o'clock in the evening a brilliant aurora commenced. The idea now occurred to him that it might be connected with the magnetic disturbance, and another observation of the magnet was therefore made. The result was the opposite of what had been anticipated, for instead of showing a continuous increase the intensity was now far below the average. An extended discussion of other results of the same sort is given, followed by an inquiry into the origin of the aurora.

The next important investigation in which Professor Henry appears is that which led to his being an independent discoverer of magneto-electricity. In the early experiments in this direction we have an interesting example of how a discovery may be long retarded through the want of correct theoretical notions. The idea entertained by the early experimenters of the present century seems to have been that since a galvanic current passing around a core of soft iron renders it magnetic, it may be expected that a magnet placed inside of a coil of wire will cause a current of electricity to pass through it. Accordingly, endeavors were made to produce this current by using powerful magnets. But since a continuous galvanic current can be employed to produce both heat and mechanical force, it follows that if it could be produced and kept up by simply inserting a permanent magnet in a coil of wire we should have a machine working without any supply of power. Since it can hardly be supposed that these experimenters would have hoped to realize the perpetual motion, the direction in which their efforts were prosecuted could have been taken only through a failure to grasp the proper principles. These principles once apprehended, it would have been obvious that either the project of producing electricity from magnetism must be given up, or the production must be accompanied by motion or change in the magnet. The latter idea being grasped, success would at once have been assured. It happened, however, that the experiments pursued in a wrong direction necessitated this motion or change, because the magnet had to be moved to get inside the coil, or magnetism had to be produced in it in commencing the experiment.

In 1831, Faraday and Henry were independently working upon the problem. The former was entirely successful in showing how a momentary electric current could be produced by changes of magnetism in a soft iron body, or by other electrical currents, before Henry published anything of his work. No question, therefore, can attach to Faraday's claim to priority, and on the system sometimes adopted no other name than his would be mentioned in a history of the subject. But a more liberal principle now prevails, and the propriety of giving due credit to the independent investigator, though he may be behindhand in publishing, is very generally acknowledged. From Professor Henry's paper it would appear that he had actually reached a similar result before Faraday's work came to his knowledge. The magnet with which electricity was to be excited was the soft iron armature of his great galvanic magnet. A piece of copper wire thirty feet long was coiled around the middle of this armature and connected with a distant galvanometer. The great magnet being suddenly excited, the north end of the needle was deflected 30 degrees to the west, indicating a current of electricity in the helix surrounding the armature. The needle soon returned to its former position, and when the plates were withdrawn from the acid moved 20 degrees to the east. The conclusions of these experiments are now too familiar to need discussion. We can only regret that the American physicist did not immediately publish his first experiments.

In this same paper Professor Henry appears as the first observer of another previously unnoticed phenomenon, sometimes called the self-induction of the current. A vivid spark is seen when a current through a long wire of considerable resistance is suddenly broken by withdrawing the wire from the cup of mercury through which the connection is produced. The longer the conducting wire and the larger the plates of the battery, the more vivid the spark. He attributes it to the long wire becoming charged with electricity, which by its reaction on itself projects a spark when the connection is broken.[*] The same discovery was independently made two or three years later by Faraday, who does not appear to have noticed Henry's description of the phenomenon.

Shortly after this Professor Henry was called to the chair of natural philosophy in Princeton College. Although the duties of an American college professor seldom allow much time for original investigation, he soon resumed his electrical researches, and the first of a regular series was communicated to the American Philosophical Society in 1835. On February 6 of that year he continued the subject of the self-induction of the electric current with especial reference to the influence of a spiral conductor upon it. The series of experiments on this subject are very elaborate, but cannot be fully described without going into a series of minute details.

On November 2, 1838, he presented an extended paper on *Electro-Dynamic Induction*.[†] He states that since the discovery of magneto-electricity by Faraday in 1831 attention had been almost exclusively devoted to the induction of electricity from magnetism. He had therefore been engaged in reviewing and extending the purely electrical part of "Faraday's admirable discovery" in the direction indicated in the title.

Among the least known works of Professor Henry during this period are his researches upon solar radiation and the heat of the

[*] *American Journal of Science*, Series I, Volume XXII, 1832, page 403.

[†] *Transactions of the American Philosophical Society*, Volume VI, page 303.

solar spots. In connection with his relative, Professor Alexander, he may be said to have commenced a branch of modern solar physics which has since grown to large proportions, by comparing the temperature of the solar spots with that of other parts of the photosphere. The first experiments were made on January 4, 1845. A very large spot was then visible upon the sun, the image of which was formed by a four-inch telescope upon a screen in a dark room. A thermopile was placed in such a position that the image of the spot and of the neighboring parts of the solar disk could be thrown upon it in quick succession. The result of observations extending through several days was that decidedly less heat was received from the spot than from the brilliant part of the photosphere. It is believed that it was these experiments which started Secchi on the brilliant investigations in solar physics which he carried on in subsequent years.

Among Professor Henry's latest electrical researches was his analysis of the dynamic phenomena of the Leyden jar. The one of his discoveries which he most often referred to in later years was that the discharge of a Leyden jar did not consist of a single restoration of the equilibrium, but of a rapid succession of librations back and forth, gradually diminishing to zero. This was proved by passing the discharge through a coil of wire containing needles of different degrees of magnetic force. After the discharge these needles were found to be magnetized in different directions, according to their size and hardness.

In one of his numerous communications presented to the Philosophical Society he appears as one of the inventors of the electro-chronograph. On May 30, 1843, he presented and read a communication on a new method of determining the velocity of projectiles. It was in its essential parts identical with that now generally adopted. It consisted, he says, in applying the instantaneous transmission of the electrical action to determine the time of the passage of the ball between two screens placed at a short distance from each other on the path of the projectile. For this purpose the observer is provided with a revolving cylinder, moved by clock-work at the rate of at least ten turns in a second, and of which the convex surface is divided into a hundred equal parts, each part therefore indicating in the revolution the thousandth part of a second. Close to the surface of this cylinder, which revolves horizontally, are placed two galvanometers, one at each extremity of a diameter; the needles of these being furnished at one end with a pen for making a dot with printer's ink on the revolving surface. In the appendix to the paper he proposes to dispense with the galvanometer and produce the marks by direct electrical action, as is now done in the usual astronomical chronograph.

While at Princeton a number of researches on other branches of experimental physics were published. It is not however necessary to describe them at length, because they are most exhaustively discussed in the memoir of Mr. Taylor before referred to. Whether they pertain to the most familiar phenomena of every-day life or the most complex combinations in the laboratory, they are all marked by the qualities of the author's mind,—acuteness in cross-examining nature, a clear appreciation of the logic of science, and an enthusiasm for truth irrespective of its utilitarian results. Reserving for the future some general remarks on the scope of Professor Henry's scientific work, the qualities which it displays, and its relation to the progress of our country, we may pass at once to his connection with the Smithsonian Institution.

The origin of the Smithsonian Institution is so remarkable and many features of its early history so instructive that it must long continue to be a theme of interest to the historian of our intellectual development. The writer may therefore be excused for touching upon a threadbare subject by repeating the story of the origin and early difficulties of this establishment. He does so the more willingly because he believes some features connected with it have not been fully brought out.

James Smithson, a private English gentleman of fortune and scientific tastes, a chemist of sufficient note to be elected a Fellow of the Royal Society, led a comparatively retired life, and died, unmarried, in 1829. He does not seem to have left any near relatives except a nephew. On opening his will it was found to be short and simple. Except an annuity to his servant, he left the nephew, for his life, the whole income from his property, and the

29

property itself to the nephew's children should he leave any.   In case of the death of the nephew without leaving a child or children, the whole property was bequeathed "*to the United States of America, to found at Washington, under the name of the Smithsonian Institution, an establishment for the increase and diffusion of knowledge among men.*"

Probably few men have ever written a clause so well fitted as this to excite a curiosity which can never be gratified.   The views and motives of the writer in making this provision are involved in impenetrable obscurity.   The first idea to strike a reader would be that Smithson had some especially kindly feelings toward either the United States or its form of government.   But no evidence of this has ever been discovered.   He is not known to have had the personal acquaintance of an American, and his tastes were supposed to have been aristocratic rather than democratic.

It would also have been supposed that the organization of an institution which was to carry his name down to posterity would have been a subject of long and careful thought, and of conversation with friends, and would have been prescribed in more definite language than that used in the will.   Some note, some appended paper would certainly be found communicating his views.   But nothing of the sort has ever come to light.

The next explanation to suggest itself would be that the death of his nephew without children was a contingency so remote that very little thought was given to what might happen in that event.   But it is said that on the contrary Hungerford, the nephew, was unmarried and in infirm health, and that his death without children might naturally have been expected.

We thus have the curious spectacle of a retired English gentleman, probably unacquainted with a single American citizen, bequeathing the whole of his large fortune to our Government to found an establishment which was described in ten words, without a memorandum of any kind by which his intentions could be divined or the recipient of the gift guided in applying it.

Hungerford died in 1835.   An amicable suit in chancery was instituted by our Government, through the Honorable Richard Rush as its agent, the defendant being the Misses Drummond,

executors of Smithson. Although there was no contest at any
point, the suit occupied three years. On May 9th, 1838, the property was adjudged to the United States, and during the next few
months disposed of by Mr. Rush for about £105,000. The money
was deposited in the Treasury in the following autumn.

The problem now presented to Congress was to organize the Institution described by Smithson. The writer must confess that he does
not share the views of those who maintain that the intent of SMITH-
SON was too clear and definite to be mistaken, and that the difficulty
which our legislators found in deciding upon a plan shows their lack
of intellectual appreciation. It is very much easier to see the right
solution of a problem after it is obtained than before. It ought to
be a subject of gratitude rather than of criticism that it took the
country eight years to reach a conclusion. The plan at length
adopted was better than any of those previously proposed, and the
form into which the Institution grew was still in advance of the
plan which at length passed Congress.

Whatever view we may take of this point, the diversity of
projects considered by Congress shows that the meaning of the will
was not made clear to our legislators. First of all there was a
body of strict constructionists who maintained that our Government
had no power to accept a bequest of the kind, and that the money
should be returned to the English Court of Chancery. One
Fleischmann, an employé of the Patent Office, petitioned for the
establishment of an agricultural school, and his memorial seems to
have received much attention. Another memorialist prayed for the
establishment of an institution for prosecuting physical experiments,
and a third that the fund might be applied to the instruction of
females. A vigorous effort was made by the Columbian College
to obtain assistance from the fund. Mr. John Quincy Adams
desired to appropriate a considerable amount to the establishment
of a great astronomical observatory. Mr. F. A. Hassler, Superintendent of the Coast Survey, desired the establishment of an
astronomical school before the erection of Mr. Adams's observatory.
A strong move was made by Mr. Poinsett to place the whole fund
at the disposal of the National Institute for the Promotion of Literature and Science. Mr. James P. Espy, the meteorologist, proposed

that a portion of the fund should be devoted to meteorological observations all over the Union.   Mr. Franklin Knight wished the whole fund applied to the establishment of a farm school.

After a seven years' discussion of these and other projects and combinations, the act under which the Institution was at last organized became a law in August, 1846.   This law provided that the business of the Institution should be conducted by a Board of Regents, who should choose a suitable person as Secretary of the Institution. It also provided for the erection of a suitable building of plain and durable materials and structure, without unnecessary ornament, for the reception of objects of Natural History, a Chemical Laboratory, a Library and Gallery of Art, and the necessary lecture rooms. The Secretary had charge of the building and property of the Institution, and was also to discharge the duties of librarian and keeper of the museum, and, with the consent of the Board of Regents, to employ the necessary assistants.   All the officers were removable by the Board of Regents whenever in their judgment the interests of the Institution required them to be changed.

The Board of Regents created by the act immediately commenced active operations.   In December, 1846, a committee of the Board, consisting of Mr. Robert Dale Owen, Mr. Henry N. Hilliard, Professor A. D. Bache, Mr. Rufus Choate, and Mr. Pennybacker, made a report on the plan of organization.   Among the recommendations of this report the qualifications desired in the Secretary are of interest to us.   It was pointed out as an almost necessary condition that the Secretary should become the chief executive officer of the Institution.   After some general remarks respecting the qualifications of Secretary the report proceeds:

"Your committee think it would be an advantage if a competent Secretary could be found, combining also the qualifications of a professor of the highest standing in some branch of science.   If to these be added efficiency as an executive officer and a knowledge of the world, we may hope to see filling this distinguished post a man who, when brought into communication with distinguished men and societies in this and other countries, shall be capable, as representative of the Smithsonian Institution, to reflect honor on the office, not requiring to borrow distinction from it.

"Your committee will not withhold their opinion that upon the choice of this single officer, more probably than on any other act of the Board, will depend the future good name and success and usefulness of the Smithsonian Institution."

Previous to the election of Secretary the following resolution, from the same committee, was adopted by the Board:

"*Resolved*, That it is essential, for the advancement of the proper interests of the trust, that the Secretary of the Smithsonian Institution be a man possessing weight of character, and a high grade of talent; and that it is further desirable that he possess eminent scientific and general acquirements; that he be a man capable of advancing science and promoting letters by original research and effort, well qualified to act as a respected channel of communication between the Institution and scientific and literary individuals and societies in this and foreign countries; and, in a word, a man worthy to represent before the world of science and of letters the Institution over which this Board presides."

Although couched in general terms it may be supposed that these expressions had direct reference to the subject of our notice, and were meant to justify the Board in selecting a scientific investigator of so much eminence to take charge of the establishment. Professor Henry was elected on December 3, 1846, and signified his acceptance a few days later. It was a frequent remark of his in after years that he had never sought a position, and had never accepted one without fear and trembling. Of the few positions he ever accepted we might well suppose that this was the one on which he entered with most hesitation. His position at Princeton was in every respect most agreeable. His enthusiasm as a teacher could not fail to bring around him an appreciative body of pupils. He was not moved by any merely worldly ambition to seek a larger and more prominent field of activity, and was held in the highest esteem by the authorities of the college. He thus enjoyed what is almost the happiest lot of man, that of living in a community suited to his tastes and pursuits, and of being held in consideration by all with whom he came into contact. He was now to take a position around which had raged for eight years a conflict of opinion, which might at any time break out anew. That all parties could be satisfied was

out of the question, and his aversion to engaging in anything which
would lead to controversy was so great that he would hardly have
accepted had it not been for the urgent solicitation of Professor
Bache. The latter pointed out to him that the proper administration of Smithson's munificent bequest was at stake, and that
he, Henry, was the only man available to whom all parties could
turn with the assurance that the Institution would be carried
through its difficulties. This was an appeal which he could not
withstand; he therefore determined at least to make the attempt, and
entered upon his duties with the assurance from the college authorities that, should he fail, his position at Princeton would always be
open to him, and the college authorities ever ready to welcome him
back.

After two or three years the divergent views respecting the
proper direction to be given to the activities of the Smithsonian
Institution gradually began to aggregate themselves into two groups
and thus to assume a partisan aspect. Many of the projects which,
during the eight years of discussion, had found supporters, were
entirely given up, such, for instance, as the agricultural college, a
great observatory, the instruction of women, and the establishment
of a school of science. The act of Congress provided, as already
stated, for a library, a museum, a gallery of art, and courses of
lectures. Henry, while yielding to the necessity imposed upon the
Institution of complying with the law directing the establishment
of these accessories, was in the main opposed on principle to their
permanent support by the Institution. The position he took was
that as Smithson was a scientific investigator, the terms of his
endowment should be construed in accordance with the interpretation which he himself would have put upon his words. The
increase of knowledge would mean the discovery of new truths of
any sort, especially the truths of nature. The only way in which
an extended diffusion of increased knowledge among men at large
could be effected was by publication.

The departments of exploration, research, and publication were
therefore those to which Henry was most inclined to devote the
energies of the Institution. While he made no factious opposition
to the collection of a library, he did not consider it as increas-

ing knowledge or contributing to that wide diffusion of it which
Smithson provided for.   True, it might indirectly contribute to
such diffusion by giving authors the means of preparing books:
but this assistance was of too indirect a character to justify the
appropriation of a large proportion of the Smithson funds to it.
Nearly the same objections applied to the museum.   The objects
therein preserved were at first the property of the Government,
and the contributions to its increase would naturally come, for the
most part, from Government explorations.   The explorations undertaken on behalf of the Institution would naturally be only such
as, from their nature, would not be undertaken by the Government, or such as were necessary to supplement the governmental
collections.

That a gallery of art would neither increase nor diffuse knowledge
on the plan required by Smithson hardly needed argument.   It
does not seem that any serious attempt was ever made to carry out
this part of the project on any considerable scale.   The Indian
portraits which constituted the principal part of the collection of
paintings were, the writer believes, the private property of Mr.
Stanley, the artist.

Perhaps the project on which the Secretary looked with most dis-
favor was the building.   The system of operations which he would
have preferred required little more than a modest suite of office
rooms.   The expenditure of several hundred thousand dollars on
an architectural structure seemed to him an appropriation of the
funds to which he could give no active encouragement.   In later
years one of the warnings he often gave to incipient institutions of
learning was not to spend more money in bricks and mortar than
was absolutely necessary for the commencement of operations, and
it can hardly be doubted that his sentiments in this direction had
their origin in his dissatisfaction with the large expenditure upon
the Smithsonian building.

We must not be understood as saying that Henry antagonized
all these objects, considered them unworthy of any support from the
Smithsonian fund, or had any lack of appreciation of their intellectual value.   His own culture and mental activities had been of too
varied a character to admit of his forming any narrow view of the

proper administration of the establishment. The general tenor of his views may be summed up in two practical propositions:

(1.) The Institution should undertake nothing which could be done by other agencies. A paper or report which would naturally find its outlet in some other channel was never to be published by the Institution. A research made for a commercial object would find plenty to engage in it without his encouragement. It was the duty of the Government to provide room for its own collections and to make them accessible to investigators, rather than to draw upon the Smithson fund for this purpose. As a natural corollary of these views the Institution should not engage in competition with other organizations in any enterprise whatever.

(2.) Objects of merely local benefit, which no one could avail himself of except by a visit to Washington, were to be regarded as of subsidiary importance, as not well fitted to carry out the views of Smithson to the wide extent he would have desired, and as properly belonging to the local authorities.

Putting both these principles together, the library, the museum, the art gallery, the courses of lectures and the Smithsonian building were looked upon as things only temporarily undertaken by the Institution, to be turned over to other agencies whenever such could be found ready to assume the responsibility of the operations connected with them.

The affairs of the Institution went on for several years without any interruption. The general policy of the Secretary was to keep the expenditure upon those objects which he considered least germane down to the lowest limit consistent with the law and with the resolutions of the Board of Regents, hoping gradually to win the Board over to his views. Among the accessories on which he wished to retrench, the library was the only one which gave serious trouble. In the act organizing the establishment, the Regents were authorized to make an annual expenditure, not exceeding an average of $25,000, "for the gradual formation of a library composed of valuable works pertaining to all departments of human knowledge." This sum was two-thirds of the whole annual income, and had the provision been mandatory, would have left little for any active operations. At a meeting of the Board the day after the election of Professor Henry the sum of $20,000 had been appropriated for the purchase of books and the fitting up of the library. Amendments reducing the sum to $12,000 and $15,000 were successively voted down. At another meeting a more definite plan of operations was agreed upon, to take effect after the completion of the building. This was a compromise, under which one-half of the annual income should be devoted to the library, the museum and the gallery of art, and one-half to the transactions, reports, publications, lectures, and original researches. The library project thus commenced as the leading feature of the Institution. It was greatly strengthened by the character of the assistant whom Professor Henry called to its charge, Mr. C. C. Jewett, formerly librarian of Brown University, a gentleman whose high character and professional ability marked him as well fitted to undertake the work of collecting and arranging a great library. Mr. Jewett very naturally desired to expend the full admissible amount upon his department, and thus a difference gradually arose between him and his chief, which widened as the building approached completion. He began to assert his claims to an extent which met with the strong disapproval of the Secretary, and in 1854 the difference culminated in an appeal to the Board of Regents.

The question was first brought before the Board in the form of a resolution respecting the proper division of the fund. In April, 1854, the executive committee recommended an appropriation in which only $6,000 was devoted to the library, more than half of which was for the salary of librarian and assistants. The appropriation for the purchase of books was only $1,800. In presenting this recommendation the committee say that they have not recommended an equal distribution between the active operations on the one hand, and the library, museum, &c., on the other, because the compromise resolutions which required such equality of distribution do not go into effect until after the completion of the building.

This reduction was opposed by the other party on both legal and political grounds. Two members of the Board presented resolutions relative to the distribution of the income, which were referred to a sub-committee. This committee, through Hon. J. A. Pearce, its chairman, made a very elaborate report on May 25th following, reviewing the whole subject at great length, reciting what the Institution had done, and justifying the small appropriation for the library. The report closed with resolutions repealing the compromise arrangement, and leaving the apportionment among the different objects to the judgment of the Regents.

In the meantime the differences between the Secretary and the Librarian reached a stage at which the further co-operation of both in the affairs of the Institution was no longer practicable. The Secretary made known his intention of removing the Librarian, taking the ground that while the Board of Regents had power to remove either the Secretary or his assistants, the Secretary himself could remove the latter without reference to the Board. A resolution to this effect was introduced by Mr. James M. Mason, of Virginia. The question was, in principle, the same which has been raised from time to time since the foundation of our Government relative to the general power of superior officers over their subordinates in cases where the law makes no express provision. Under the terms of the organic act the Secretary and the Board of Regents, so far as the assistants were concerned, stood in nearly the same relation to each other than the President and Senate stand under the National Constitution. The Secretary, an executive, had the power of appointment, with the consent of the Board of Regents, but the law was silent on the subject of removal. Mr. Mason's resolution, after several amendments had been voted down, was adopted by a vote of 6 to 4, and the position of the Secretary as the responsible head of the Institution was thus fully defined.

It would however appear that Mr. Jewett continued his efforts to secure a larger appropriation for the library than the Secretary or the executive committee considered desirable, and carried his opposition to such a point that the Secretary removed him from office on the 12th of January following.

The resolution of the executive committee repealing the compromise and leaving future annual apportionments to the judgment of the Regents was then passed by a vote of 9 to 5. A further resolution to the effect that a compliance in good faith with the letter and spirit of the charter required a large proportion of the income of the Institution to be appropriated for a library was lost.

Mr. Rufus Choate, who had been the most active supporter of Mr. Jewett and the library scheme, now resigned his position as Regent, and accompanied his resignation with a letter addressed to the Senate and House of Representatives, stating his reasons for the course he had taken, and expressing the opinion that the Smithsonian fund was being managed on a system not in accordance with the provisions of the organic act. In the Senate the subject was referred to the Committee on the Judiciary, which made a unanimous report in favor of the majority of the Board of Regents. In the House there was a more serious contest. Mr. Choate's letter was referred to a select committee of five, appointed to inquire and report to the House whether the Smithsonian Institution had been managed and its funds expended in accordance with law, and whether any additional legislation was necessary. After a careful examination, extending through a period of six weeks, the committee seems to have been unable to agree upon a report. Two reports were, in fact, made. One, signed only by Mr. Upham, the chairman, took ground against the power of removal by the Secretary of the Institution, and against the restriction of the increase of the library as contemplated. Another very elaborate report, signed by two members, sustained the Secretary and the majority of the Board. The remaining two members of the committee signed neither report; nor did either report propose any action on the part of Congress except the payment of the clerk of the committee.

The contest which had been going on for a period of seventeen years thus ended in a complete vindication of Professor Henry and the position he had assumed. During the remainder of his life he had the great satisfaction of feeling that he was held in constantly increasing esteem both by the Regents and the public.[*]

In January, 1865, an event occurred which, though an almost irreparable calamity, tended materially toward the appropriation of the Smithsonian income toward those objects which the Secretary thought most proper. A considerable portion of the upper story

[*] As an expression of Professor Henry's views in his own language we append to this address an extract from his examination before the English Government Scientific Commission.

of the main building and a part of the lower story were burned.
The incipient art gallery, the chemical laboratory, and the lecture
room were all involved in the destruction. Happily the library
and the museum remained nearly intact. An opportunity thus
offered itself to have some of the trusts imposed upon the fund
undertaken by other agencies. The library of Congress was rapidly
growing into a great national institution, so that there was no longer
any sound reason for collecting a separate Smithsonian library.
An act was therefore passed by Congress providing for the deposit of
the Smithsonian books in the library of Congress, so that all could
be consolidated together and the Institution at the same time be
relieved from their care. The necessity for reconstructing the art
gallery was obviated by the prospective establishment of the Corcoran Art Gallery in a neighboring part of the city. The erection
of Lincoln Hall and the establishment of courses of lectures,
sometimes of a high intellectual character, by the Young Men's
Christian Association, did away with the necessity of reconstructing
the lecture room. The principal immediate drawback was that the
building had to be reconstructed at the expense of the Smithsonian
fund, although Professor Henry was not entirely satisfied that so
large a building was necessary for the Institution.

The only serious burden which remained upon the Institution
was the National Museum; but the expense of its support was now
undertaken by the Government, and it therefore ceased to be a
charge upon the Smithsonian fund except in this indirect way that
the building which housed it had been paid for out of that fund.
No advantage would therefore have been gained by removing the
museum unless the building was purchased by the Government.
The Secretary was therefore desirous of effecting such a sale, but
his views do not appear to have met with the entire concurrence of
the Board of Regents. The latter were not unnaturally averse to
seeing the Institution surrender its imposing habitation and the
associations which clustered around it. A very natural compromise
would have been for the Government to pay the Institution a suitable moderate rent for those portions of the building devoted to
the care of Government property, but it does not appear that this
measure was ever proposed.

The position of the Smithsonian building in the public grounds led Professor Henry to take an active interest in measures for the improvement of the city. Among his latest efforts in this direction were those made with the object of having the old canal which bounded the Mall filled up. Some of us may remember a witty argument with which he urged this measure upon the Board of Public Works. "The great inefficiency of the Smithsonian had been said by its opponents to be illustrated by the fact that, although formed to diffuse knowledge over the whole world, it had not diffused knowledge enough among the local authorities where it was situated to make them see the necessity of abating the pestilential nuisance of this obsolete canal." The work of filling up was immediately commenced by the board to which the argument was addressed.

The following extract from one of Professor HENRY's early journals will be of interest as showing the character of his early efforts for the improvement of the Smithsonian grounds:

"NOVEMBER 25, 1850.

"Occupied this morning examining the public grounds between the Capitol and the Monument. I have been impressed since my connection with the Smithsonian Institution with the importance of improving the public grounds on which the Smithsonian is placed in accordance with a general plan, and I have taken every opportunity of expatiating on the capacity of the Mall to be made one of the most beautiful drives in the world. My enthusiasm on this point was much dampened a few months ago, when it was proposed to place the Botanic Garden on the Mall near the Smithsonian. The site was chosen and, as I supposed, all things settled, when to my surprise some influence at once changed the location.

"My interest in the project was again awakened by a movement on the part of Mr. Corcoran. An appropriation was made to improve the grounds around the President's House. Mr. Corcoran was interested in the square opposite his residence. He requested me to go with him to the President to ask him to interfere. We called on the President, who manifested an interest in the subject but said he had no power to act, but if we would show him the authority he would do what he could to forward the object. On this assurance Mr. Corcoran and myself left the President, and I was requested to search for the law authorizing the action of the President. For this purpose I called upon Peter Force,

who, after a search of some time, found the law, gave me a copy,
which I afterwards presented to the President. The same evening
I called a meeting at the office of the mayor, of Mr. Mudd, the
commissioner of public buildings, and the mayor. After some
conversation it was at length concluded to send for some competent
landscape gardener to give a general plan of the improvements,
and, on the suggestion of the mayor, it was resolved to request the
President to direct that Mr. Downing, from Newburgh, be requested to examine the grounds and report a plan of improvement.
We (the mayor, Mr. Mudd, and myself) called next day on the
President, presented the matter, and received from him the sanction
for writing to Mr. Downing. A few days after this I started for
New Jersey and was absent several days, and when I returned I
found that nothing had been done,—Mr. Downing had not been
written to. I therefore drew up a form of a letter of invitation in
accordance with my views of the manner in which the invitation
should be worded, and sent this to the commissioner. This letter
was sent, and in conformity with this invitation Mr. Downing has
come on. I called with Mr. Downing on the President, who gave
us a very pleasant reception and entered with much interest into the
plans of Mr. Downing. This morning Mr. Mudd, Mr. Downing,
and myself have examined all the ground between the Capitol and
the river, and found it admirably adapted to the formation of a
landscape garden and a drive."

The administration of the Smithsonian Institution does not
appear to have been compatible with the continuance of the experimental researches in which our colleague was so eminently successful during the earlier years of his life. The fact is that the
general science of electricity was passing almost beyond the experimental and into the mathematical stage, so that little of real value
could be effected by mere experimentation without reference to
purely mathematical theories. But it would be altogether a mistake
to suppose that his scientific activity was diminished or that his
contributions to knowledge were confined to his earlier days. The
talent which had before been directed to investigations of a purely
scientific character, (understanding by this term such as were designed
only to improve the theories of natural phenomena,) was now turned
to practical application of scientific principles. Whether such applications are less worthy of the investigator than the advancement of
purely theoretical notions, we shall not attempt to discuss, but shall

only remark that our colleague brought into his new field that same unselfish devotion to the intellectual interests of mankind which marks the purely scientific investigator. Whatever utilitarian objects he may have aimed at, they had no personal reference to himself. He never engaged in an investigation or an enterprise which was to put a dollar into his own pocket, but aimed only at the general good of the world.

One of the earliest of his new enterprises was that of receiving notices of the weather by telegraph and exhibiting them upon a map, thus laying the foundation of our present meteorological system. In 1847 he called the attention of the Board of Regents to the facilities which lines of telegraph would afford for warning observers to be on the watch for the approach of a storm. As a part of the system of meteorology, the telegraph was to be employed in the investigation of atmospheric phenomena. The advantage to agriculture and commerce to be derived from a knowledge of the approach of a storm was recommended as a subject deserving the attention of Government. About 1850 the plan of mapping the weather was instituted. Many of us remember the large maps of the country suspended in the entrance to the Institution, on which the state of the weather in different regions was indicated by movable signs. This system continued until 1861, when the breaking out of the civil war prevented its further continuance.[*]

After the close of the war a renewal of the system was proposed and some efforts made for the attainment of this object. But with this as with every other enterprise, Professor Henry would never go on with it after any one else was found ready to take it up. In 1869 our colleague, Professor Abbe, commenced the issue of regular weather bulletins from the Cincinnati Observatory, showing the state of the weather at a number of telegraphic stations, followed by a brief forecast of the weather which would probably be experienced at Cincinnati during the next twenty-four hours. About the same time provision was made by Congress for the national system now so thoroughly organized by the Chief Signal Officer of the Army. This system received the cordial support of Professor Henry, who

[*] See Historical Notes on the System of Weather Telegraphy, by CLEVELAND ABBE, American Journal of Science and Arts, Volume 11, 1871, page 81.

gave every facility at the disposal of the Institution to General Myer for the completion of the organization, and indeed turned over the whole practical part of the subject to him.

Among the services of Professor Henry outside of the field of pure science and of the administration of the Smithsonian Institution the first place is due to those rendered in connection with the Light-House Board. This Board was organized by act of Congress in 1852 to discharge all administrative duties relating to the light-house establishment on the American coasts. The duties assigned to Professor Henry in this connection included experiments of all kinds pertaining to lights and signals. The illuminating power of various oils was made the subject of exact photometric experiments, and large sums were thus saved to the Government by the adoption of those illuminators which gave most light in proportion to cost. The necessity of fog-signals led to what are, for our present purpose, the most important researches in this connection, namely, his investigations into the phenomena of sound. Acoustics had always been one of his favorite subjects. As early as 1856 he published a carefully prepared paper on the acoustics of public buildings, and he frequently criticised the inattention of architects to this subject. His regular investigations of sound in connection with the Light-House Board were commenced in 1865. It had long been known that the audibility of sounds at considerable distances, and especially at sea, varies in a manner which has seemed quite unaccountable. There were numerous instances of a sound not becoming audible until the hearer was immediately in its neighborhood, and others of its being audible at extraordinary distances. Very often a sound was audible at a great distance and was lost as the hearer approached its source. The frequency of fogs on our eastern coasts and the important part played by sound signals in warning vessels of danger rendered it necessary to investigate the whole theory of the subject.

One of the first conclusions reached related to the influence of reflectors and of intervening obstacles. That a sound in the focus of a parabolic reflector is thrown forward and intensified in the manner of light has long been a well-known fact. The logical consequence of this is that the sound is cut off behind such a reflector, so that at short distances it is many times louder in front of the reflector than behind it. In the case of light, which moves in right lines, it is well known that such an increased volume of light thrown in one direction will go on indefinitely. But in the case of sound the law was found to be altogether different — the farther the observer went away from the source, the less the influence of the reflector, and at the distance of two or three miles the latter was without effect, — the sound being about equally audible in whatever direction the reflector might be turned. Another important discovery, made the following year, was that when a sound was moving against the wind it might be heard at an elevation when it was inaudible near the surface of the water.

These observations were continued from time to time during the summer season until 1877. They resulted in collecting an immense mass of facts, including many curious abnormal phenomena, descriptions of which are found in the annual Reports of the Light-House Board. Our president was extremely cautious in formulating theories of the subject, and had no ambition of associating his name with a generalization which future researches might disprove. The result of his observations however was to show that there were none of these curious phenomena which might not be accounted for by a species of refraction arising from varying atmospheric currents. The possible effects of this cause had been pointed out by Professor Stokes, of England, in 1857, and the views of the latter seem to have been adopted by Henry. One of the generalizations is very clearly explained on this theory: A current of air is more rapid at a short height above the water than at its immediate surface. If a sound-wave is moving with such a current its upper part will be carried forward more rapidly than its lower part; its front will thus be presented downward and it will tend to strike the water. If moving in an opposite direction against the wind, the greater velocity of the latter above the water will cause the upper part of the sound-wave to be retarded. The wave will thus be thrown upward, and the course of the sound will be a curved line convex to the water. Thus an observer at the surface may be in a region of comparative silence, when by ascending a few yards he will reach the region of sound vibration. A corresponding effect

30

would be produced by a difference in the motions of two contiguous bodies of air, whether the line of change was vertical or horizontal. As we know very well that the motion of the air is by no means uniform, and that eddies, gusts, and whiffs prevail nearly everywhere, it is to be expected that sound will not always move uniformly in a direct line, but will be turned from its direct course by the sort of refraction that we have described. It is however impossible to prove by observation that this is the only cause of the abnormal phenomena referred to, because the exact velocity of local currents within a space over which the sound extends cannot be a subject of observation. Professor Henry was however disposed to claim that, having a sufficiently general known cause to account for the phenomena, it was not philosophical to assume other causes in the absence of decisive proof.

It was at the light-house station in the month of December, 1877, that Professor Henry noticed the first symptom of the disease which terminated his life a few months later. After passing a restless and uncomfortable night, he arose in the morning, finding his hand partially paralyzed. A neighboring physician, being sent for, gave a prognosis of a very serious character. A more detailed subsequent examination by two members of our Academy led to the conclusion that he was affected with an incipient nephritis. Although no prospect of recovery could be held out, it was hoped that the progress of the disease would be so slow that, with his healthy constitution, he might still endure for a considerable period. This hope however rapidly failed. During the winter the disease assumed so decided a form as to show that his active work was done and that we could have him with us but a few months longer. But beyond a cessation of his active administrative duties there was no change in his daily life. He received his friends, discussed scientific matters, and took the most active interest in the affairs of the world so long as his strength held out. It was a source of great consolation to his family and friends that his intellect was not clouded nor his nervous system shattered by the disease. One of the impressive recollections of the writer's life is that of an interview with him the day before his death, when he was sustained only by the most powerful restoratives. He was at first in a state of slumber, but, on opening his eyes, among the first questions he asked was whether the transit of Mercury had been successfully observed and the appropriation for observing the coming total eclipse secured. He was then gradually sinking, and died at noon on May 13, 1878.

A mere sketch, like the foregoing, of the lines of activity followed out by our late President, gives no adequate idea either of his mental force or of his public services. The contributions to science of an American of the last few generations afford an entirely insufficient standard of judgment, though it is a standard which writers are prone to adopt as if it were the only one. We are apt to forget that science is a plant of cultivation which rarely or never flourishes in a state of isolation, and reaches full fruition only when it can absorb into its own growth the fertile ideas of many associated minds. Leaving out a few powerful intellects who started our modern system of investigating nature, a high development of the scientific spirit has been attained only by a communion of ideas through the medium of academies, institutions, and journals. We may pronounce it an entire illusion to suppose that a professor in one of our ordinary American colleges, without personal contact with men engaged in similar pursuits, and without access to the publications in which foreign investigators publish their researches, can permanently take a leading position in any branch of investigation. If it shall appear that Henry's contributions to electricity were less numerous and brilliant than those of Faraday, let us consider not simply the immensely wider field of Henry's intellectual and public activity, but the different situations of the two men. The one occupied the focus of the intellectual metropolis of the world, commanding at pleasure of every sort of apparatus which money could purchase or art produce, and was surrounded by an admiring crowd of the *élite* of society, eagerly hearing of his every discovery and listening attentively to all his utterances. The other was, during his early prime, an overworked instructor, almost out of the reach of the great treasures of foreign scientific literature, and with none of the advantages enjoyed by his great competitor.

Another circumstance not to be lost sight of is that Henry, in obedience to one of the great principles of his life, voluntarily .

relinquished to others each field of investigation at the very time
when he had it so far cultivated as to yield most fame and profit
to himself. It is an unfortunate fact that the world, in awarding
its laurels, is prone to overlook the sometimes long list of those
whose labors have rendered a result possible, and to remember only
the one who gave the finishing stroke, or applied previously known
principles to some useful result. There are few investigators to
whom the criterion in question would do less justice than to the
subject of our notice. In his unselfish devotion to knowledge
he sowed that others might reap on the broad humanitarian
ground that a valuable harvest would be sure to find a reaper
while the seed might wait in vain for a sower. Had this been
done solely in his individual character we should have looked
upon his course with admiration; but in bringing the principle into
the administration of the Smithsonian Institution he avoided a
danger and rendered a benefit for which we cannot be too grateful.
To this principle is due the fact that the Institution never appeared
as a competitor, seeking an advantage for itself, but always as the
active co-operator in every enterprise tending to carry out the object
prescribed by its founder.

Notwithstanding a uniform adherence to this course through his
whole life it would be difficult to find a physicist of our time whose
researches cover more ground than his do. Any adequate analysis
of his published papers and notices would have transcended the limits
of the present memoir. Besides his electrical researches, they include
meteorology in almost all its phases, the physical geography of his
native State, terrestrial magnetism, capillarity, molecular physics,
observations of meteors, phosphorescence, solar physics, protection
from lightning, observations of the aurora, the radiation of heat,
the strength of building materials, experiments on an alleged spontaneous separation of alcohol and water, aeronautics, the ventilation
of buildings, the phenomena of sound, and various other subjects
hardly admitting of classification.

Notwithstanding his literary productiveness, he rarely if ever
wrote a paper to yield him the honorarium of a magazine contributor. Nor did he ever seek a source of income beyond the modest
salary paid him for administering the Smithsonian Institution.

This sufficed, not only to satisfy the wants of a simple mode of life, but, with the aid of the accommodations allowed him in the building, to dispense a hospitality to a wide circle of friends and admirers as pleasant to the recipients as if it had won the title of princely. Although not drawing a salary from the Government, and entitled therefore to compensation for any services rendered, his numerous public services were entirely gratuitous. It must however be said to the credit of our Government that after his death Congress voted his family a small compensation for his twenty-five years of administrative service in the offices of member and president of the Light-House Board.

One of his interesting traits of character, and one which powerfully tended to make the Smithsonian Institution popular and useful, was a certain intellectual philanthropy which showed itself in ceaseless efforts to make others enjoy the same wide views of nature which he himself did. He was accessible to a fault, and ever ready to persuade any honest propounder of a new theory that he was wrong. The only subject on which the writer ever had to express to him strong dissent from his views was that of the practicability of convincing "universe-makers" of their errors. They always answered with opposing arguments, generally in a tone of arrogance or querulousness which deterred even the modest Henry from replying further; but he still considered it a duty to do what he could toward imbuing the next one of the class who addressed him, with correct notions of the objects of scientific theories.

It is hardly necessary to say that in Professor Henry's mental composition were included a breadth of intellect, clearness of philosophic insight, and strength of judgment, without which he could never have carried out the difficult task which his official position imposed upon him. His mental fiber was well seen in the stand which he took against the delusions of spiritualism. On no subject was he more decided than on that of the impossibility and absurdity of the pseudo-miracles of the mediums, who seemed to him to claim no less a power than that of overruling the laws of nature. An intellectual person yielding credence to their pretensions seemed to him to be in great danger of insanity. An old and respected friend, who had held a prominent position in the

Government service, in speaking to him on the subject, once described how he had actually seen a spiritual medium rise in the air and waft himself out of the window. "Judge," answered the Professor, "you never saw that, and, if you think you did, you are in a dangerous mental condition. If you do not give this delusion up you will be in the insane asylum before you know it. As a loving friend I beseech you to take warning of what I say, and to reflect that what you think you saw is a mental delusion which requires the most careful treatment."

He used frequently to relate a curious circumstance as an illustration of the character of this legerdemain. A noted spiritualist had visited Washington during Mr. Lincoln's administration, and held several seances with the President himself. The latter was extremely desirous that Professor Henry should see the medium, and give his opinion as to how he performed his wonderful feats. Although Henry generally avoided all contact with such men, he consented to receive him at the Smithsonian Institution. Among the acts proposed was that of making sounds in various quarters of the room. This was something which the keen senses and ready experimental faculty of the Professor were well qualified to investigate. He turned his head in various positions while the sounds were being emitted. He then turned toward the man with the utmost firmness and said, "I do not know how you make the sounds, but this I perceive very clearly: they do not come from the room but from your person." It was in vain that the operator protested that they did not, and that he had no knowledge how they were produced. The keen ear of his examiner could not be deceived.

Sometime afterward the Professor was traveling in the east, and took a seat in a railway car beside a young man who, finding who his companion was, entered into conversation with him, and informed him that he was a maker of telegraph instruments. His advances were received in so friendly a manner that he went further yet, and confided to him that his ingenuity had been called into requisition by spiritual mediums, to whom he furnished the apparatus necessary for the manifestations. Henry asked him by what mediums he had been thus engaged, and was interested to find that among them was the very man he had met at the Smithsonian. The sounds which the medium had emitted were then described to the young man, who in reply explained the structure of the apparatus by which they were produced, which apparatus had been constructed by himself. The apparatus was fastened around the muscular part of the upper arm, and was so arranged that the sounds would be produced by a simple contraction of the muscle, unaccompanied by any motion of the joints of the arm, and therefore entirely invisible to a bystander.

A trait of Professor Henry's character which contributed powerfully to his success and usefulness was the many-sidedness of both his intellect and his taste. The great development of the imaginative and æsthetic faculties which led to the precocious dramatic activity of his boyhood made itself felt throughout his life. Although he did not seek to beautify his public addresses or communications with ornaments drawn from foreign sources, he was always ready with an apt quotation to clothe a sentiment. Apart from all intellectual and scientific claims, American science could not have desired a more fitting representative and leader at the National Capital, or found one whose physical and mental constitution afforded so little ground for adverse criticism. His principles kept him outside of all competition, jealousies, and cross purposes, and all combined gave his recommendations a force, founded on the assurance of their entire disinterestedness, which they otherwise could not have commanded. If he had any eccentricities or prejudices they were those of the philosopher. The mental qualities so well fitted to secure the affection as well as the respect of all with whom he became intimately acquainted, were supplemented by a healthy constitution, a well-built person, and a commanding yet modest presence, finely calculated to win confidence.

In conclusion, we believe that we but feebly express the sentiment of every member of the Academy, in saying that our late President will be entitled to the gratitude of posterity as the leader of that intellectual band of the last generation, to whom is due the great advance in the national appreciation of scientific research which has been witnessed during the last thirty years; and the state of society of which he would not be an ornament is still beyond our intellectual vision.

SUPPLEMENTAL NOTE.

(From page 68.)

The following statement by Professor Henry was made at the request of the English Government Scientific Commission, June 28, 1870, during his visit to London. To the request that he would give the Commission a general idea of the character of the Smithsonian Institution, Professor Henry replied:

"There was at first a great diversity of opinion as to the manner in which the income should be applied to realize the design of the testator, as expressed in the brief but comprehensive terms of the bequest. The distinction at that time between an Institution for the advancement of knowledge by the discovery of new truths, and one for the teaching of the knowledge already in existence, was not so generally recognized as it is at present, and Congress, after several years of delay, placed the expenditures of the income under the care of a Board of Regents, and directed that they should make provision, by the erection of a building and otherwise, for the formation of a library, a museum, and a gallery. It also gave fifty acres of unimproved ground, surrounding the site for the building, with indications that it should be planted with trees. Afterward however, though not without much opposition, it was concluded by the directors that those objects, although very important in themselves, were too local in their influence to come up to the liberal spirit of the bequest, which was intended not merely to benefit the citizens of Washington, nor even exclusively those of the United States, but mankind in general; and that the efforts of the directors should be to induce Congress to make a separate appropriation, from the public treasury, for the support of the objects just mentioned, and to devote, as far as possible, the income of the Smithsonian fund to the direct increase and diffusion of knowledge, by promoting original researches, and by distributing accounts of the results of these to every part of the civilized world. In this the directors have been in a great measure successful, though time and much persevering labor have been required to produce a change in the policy originally contemplated. A large portion of the income of the funds has been expended on the building. A library, principally consisting of nearly a full series of the proceedings and transactions of the existing learned societies of the world, has been accumulated, the expense of the care of which has absorbed another portion of the income; a museum has been collected, consisting principally of specimens to illustrate the natural history and ethnology of America, and also a collection of engravings and plaster casts to meet the original requirements of Congress as to a gallery of art; but experience has abundantly proved that any one of the specified objects, if properly sustained, would soon absorb all the income of the bequest, and vindicated the policy of transferring the support of them to other funds. In accordance with this, Congress was first induced to take charge of the grounds and take the steps necessary for their improvement. It next took charge of the books which had been collected and incorporated them with the national library, giving the Institution and its collaborators the free use of the books of both collections. By this transfer the Institution is saved, in the expense of binding, cataloguing, and attendance, nearly $10,000 annually, while it has the same use of its books as before the arrangement was made. Again, the Agricultural Department has taken charge of the plants of the Institution, and the osteological specimens have been transferred to the Army Medical Museum. Furthermore, a wealthy citizen of Washington has made a large appropriation of money to establish and support a gallery of art, and it is proposed to transfer to this the articles which the Institution has accumulated in the line of art. The object of this policy is to establish at Washington a collection of objects of nature and art, without trenching on the Smithsonian fund, which shall be worthy the capital of the nation. As a step towards this desirable end, Congress, at its present session, has appropriated $10,000 towards the support of the museum, under the care of the Institution, and also $10,000 for the commencement of the fitting up of the upper story of the Smithson building for the better display of the collections. The $10,000 for the care of the museum will, for the present, be an annual appropriation."

Q. "What does the building itself represent?" A. "Externally a Norman castle, and it has cost a very large sum. Unfortunately, architecture is frequently in antagonism with science, and, too often, when an architect gets his hand into the purse of an establishment everything else must stand aside. Much trouble has resulted from this building; it has been a source of constant anxiety and expense,—the cost having greatly exceeded the original estimate."

Q. "What was the original object of the building?" A. "It was intended to accommodate a library, a museum, and a gallery of art; but, inasmuch as the Institution has turned over the library and the gallery of art to other establishments, the building will now be devoted entirely to the museum. The upper part of it was burnt, and it remains unfinished; and if Congress would accept the building as a gift, allowing one of the wings for the use of the Institution, and devoting the main portion to the museum, it would be a gain to the Institution."

HENRY AS A DISCOVERER.[*]

BY

ALFRED M. MAYER.

AT the meeting of this Association in 1878 a committee, composed of Professors Baird, Newcomb, and myself, was appointed to prepare a eulogy on our revered and lamented colleague and former President, Joseph Henry.

This, I will not say labor, but duty of affection, has devolved on me alone. I would that the other members of this committee had laid before you their tributes to his memory, because for years they had been closely associated with him in his social and professional life in Washington. Yet, while Professor Henry had been the friend of their manhood he was the friend of my boyhood; and during 25 years he ever regarded me—as was his wont to say—with "a paternal interest." To his disinterested kindness and wise counsels is due much, very much, of whatever usefulness there is in me. Hence, I have said that it is a duty of affection for me to speak to you about one who was my beloved friend.

I shall not however attempt a biography of Joseph Henry, nor will I speak of his administrative life as Director of the Smithsonian Institution, for this is known and valued by the whole world. His best eulogy is an account of his discoveries; for a man of science, as such, lives in what he has done, and not in what he has said; nor will he be remembered in what he proposed to do. I will therefore with your permission, confine myself chiefly to HENRY *as the Discoverer*; and I do this the more willingly because I am familiar with his researches, and also because Professor Henry, from time to time, took pleasure in giving me accounts of those mental conceptions which preceded his work, led him to it, and guided him in it.

[*] A Memorial Address read before the Meeting of the American Association at Boston, August 26, 1880.

(475)

To rightly appreciate a discoverer we should not look at his work from our time, but go back and regard it from his time; we should not judge his work in the fullness of the light of present knowledge, but in the dim twilight which alone illuminated him to then unknown—but now well known—facts and laws. I will therefore endeavor first to present you with a clear but necessarily very concise view of the state of our knowledge of electricity when Henry began his original researches in that branch of science, and then point out the value of his discoveries by showing what they added to knowledge and how they instigated and influenced the discoveries and inventions of other men.

Henry began his electrical researches at the age of 28, in the year 1827, while he was Professor of Mathematics and Natural Philosophy in the Albany Academy. At these he continuously worked till 1832, when, at the age of 33, he moved to the College of New Jersey (Princeton). After a year's break in his work, caused by the preparation of his course of lectures for the college, he is again at original research, and continues his contributions to electrical discoveries till 1842. Thus, during 14 years, while between the ages of 28 and 43, he was a constant and fertile worker. What he did in these years will be given after a review of what had been already discovered up to the time he began his original experiments.

Through the labors of Gilbert, Boyle, Otto von Guericke, Newton, Wall, Gray, Franklin, Æpinus, and Volta, it had been discovered that all matter could be electrically excited, and that bodies differed greatly in permitting the diffusion of electricity over their surfaces; the facts of electric attraction and repulsion, of electric induction, the action of points, and the identity of lightning and electricity had been discovered; and these facts had been explained and bound together in a body of doctrine by the hypothesis of Dufay or by that of Franklin; while Coulomb and Poisson, in a series of beautiful experimental and mathematical labors, had given us the knowledge of the laws of the actions at a distance of electric attraction and repulsion, and had shown in what manner electricity diffuses itself over conductors of various forms.

About 1820, men of science spoke of electrical knowledge as almost complete. The mathematical consequences of the laws discovered by Coulomb and others having been, they thought, fully developed; electricity was hardly to be regarded as an experimental science, but henceforth might be grouped with mechanics. Such opinion was so general that Faraday (in 1831), when he began his ever remarkable series of discoveries, was influenced by this prevailing feeling to style his papers "*Experimental Researches in Electricity.*"

It seemed almost impossible that any discovery could again give an impulse to electrical studies equal to that produced by the brilliant and most fertile researches of Volta; yet to the universal surprise of the scientific world this happened. In the winter of 1819 Oersted announced that he had at last discovered a correlation of actions between electricity and magnetism in his celebrated experiment of the deflection of a magnet athwart the conjunctive wire of a battery when the latter was laid parallel to the direction of the magnet.

During the month of July, 1820, the news of Oersted's discovery reached Paris. It at once excited profoundly the ever active and versatile mind of Ampère. This man, already celebrated as a mathematician, was now destined to show greater genius as an experimenter. He at once began a series of researches in the field opened by the discovery of Oersted; and with astonishing rapidity reached results of such importance that they gained him the title of the Newton of electro-dynamics; and justly, for he did for this branch of science even more than Coulomb had previously done for electro-statics.

On the 18th of September, 1820, Ampère read before the Academy of Sciences of Paris his first paper on electro-dynamics. In this he shows that the battery exerts an electro-magnetic action as well as its conjunctive wire, and he gives a rule by which one can readily predict the direction in which a magnet will be deflected by a voltaic current. He supposes a current to flow from the copper to the zinc plate of the battery; then, says he, if you imagine yourself at full length and facing the wire, the current entering your heels and passing out at your head, the north pole of the magnet is always

deflected toward your left hand. In the same paper, he says that
he will soon experiment with spirals and helices of wire which, he
predicts, will have the same properties as magnets as long as a current of electricity flows through them. He then gives his well-
known hypothesis of the nature of a magnet. He says that if
we assume a magnet to consist of an assemblage of minute currents
of electricity whirling all with the same direction of rotation around
the steel molecules and in planes at right angles to the axis of the
bar, we will have an hypothesis which will account for all the
known properties of a magnet. Ampère constructed his spirals
and helices, and to the astonishment of the scientific world made
magnets formed only of spools of copper wire traversed by electric
currents. We can readily imagine the intense interest awakened
by this discovery; a discovery which caused Arago to exclaim:
"What would Newton, Halley, Dufay, Æpinus, Franklin, and
Coulomb have said if one had told them that the day would come
when a navigator would be able to lay the course of his vessel
without a magnetic needle and solely by means of electric currents?"

"For several weeks physicists of France and from abroad crowded
Ampère's humble study in Rue Fossé Saint Victor, to see with astonishment a suspended loop of wire, in the circuit of a battery, take a
definite position through the directive magnetic action of the earth."

This hypothesis of Ampère had a powerful hold on Henry's mind,
and as I know that he used it as a guiding light in his researches, it
may here be well to give Arago's account of how Ampère was led to
its conception:

"Thanks to the profound researches of Ampère, the law which
governs celestial movements, the law, extended by Coulomb to the
phenomena of electricity at rest or in tension, and then, though with
less certainty, to magnetic phenomena, becomes one of the characteristic features of the powers exercised by electricity in motion. The
general formula which gives the value of the mutual actions of the
infinitely small elements of currents once understood, the determination of the combined actions of limited currents of different forms
becomes a simple problem of integral analysis. Ampère did not fail
to follow out these applications of his discoveries. He first tried to
discover how a rectilinear current acts on a system of circular closed

currents, contained in planes perpendicular to the rectilinear current. The result of the calculation, confirmed by experiment, was that the planes of the circular currents would, supposing them movable, arrange themselves parallel to the rectilinear current. If like transverse currents pass over the whole length of a magnetic needle, the cross direction which, in the experiment of Oersted, seemed an inexplicable anomaly, would become a natural and necessary fact. Is it not then evident to all how memorable would that discovery be that would rigorously establish the fact that to magnetize a needle is to excite, to put in motion around each molecule of the steel, a small circular, electrical vortex? Ampère fully realized the wide reach of the ingenious generalization that had taken possession of his mind; and he hastened to submit it to experimental proofs and numerical verifications, which, in our day, are the only processes considered entirely demonstrative."

About this time Arago found that the conjunctive wire of the battery had the property of causing iron filings to arrange themselves around it in concentric rings. Guided by Ampère's discovery that a helix conducting a voltaic current had properties similar to those of a magnet, Arago inferred that these properties could be given to iron and steel by placing wires or bars of these substances in the interior of one of Ampère's helices. Experiment showed that his inference was correct. The same effects he obtained by passing electrical discharges from an ordinary frictional electrical machine or from a Leyden jar through a helix inclosing a steel needle.

In subsequent memoirs, exhibiting great philosophic acumen and marked ability in the application of mathematical analysis to the elucidation of physical phenomena, Ampère developed the consequences of the general laws he had previously discovered.

In 1821, six years before Henry began his work, Faraday—then 30 years of age, and as yet an assistant of Davy—published his first paper on electrical research. In this he shows that a wire conveying an electrical current can be made to rotate around the pole of a magnet. He then reverses the action, and holding the wire at rest makes the magnetic pole rotate around the wire. These phenomena were shown by Ampère to be entirely conformable to his hypothesis of the electro-dynamic nature of a magnet.

While Ampère, in 1820, was pursuing his researches, Schweigger, of Halle, invented his galvanometer. This he formed by wrapping an insulated wire in several turns and layers around a suspended magnetic needle. This instrument excited a powerful influence in electrical researches, and the contemplation of its action led Henry to make his first trials as an original experimenter.

The history of another research is now in order as bearing directly on one of Henry's investigations—and one which he ever regarded with considerable pride. In 1827 Savary began experiments on the magnetizing actions of the discharge of the Leyden jar on steel needles. These needles, of various lengths, diameters, and degrees of hardness, were placed at right angles to the wire conveying the electric discharge. They were also put in the interior of Ampère's helices, after the manner of Arago's original experiments. The phenomena thus observed were found to be of the most complex characters. It was found that the direction of the polarity in the needle and the intensity of its magnetization depended on its distance from the wire, on the diameter of the needle, on the potentiality of the discharge, and on the resistance of the wire through which the discharge took place. Similar phenomena were observed when the needles were placed in one of Ampère's helices, through which the discharge was thrown. After a long and tedious research Savary concluded that these facts could only be explained by the supposition that the discharge of a Leyden jar was not continuous, but consisted of a series of rebounds or reflections to and from the two coatings of the jar. In 1842, Henry, apparently ignorant of this research of Savary, went over the same ground, and arrived independently at the same inference which Savary had formed fifteen years before—an inference directly confirmed by the experiments of Feddersen, who, in 1862, got the life history of the electric spark of the Leyden jar by photographing its image reflected from a concave mirror revolving 800 to 1,000 times in a second.

Two years previous to Savary's work, i. e. in 1825, William Sturgeon, of Woolwich, England, improved on Arago's experiment of magnetizing steel and iron with the voltaic current. Sturgeon's improvement consisted in bending the straight rods used by Arago into U-shaped pieces, and then, coating them with shellac varnish, he wound them with uncovered copper wire. The coils of the wire were separated, so that the current flowed through the wire around the surface of the iron. This magnet, in proportion to its weight, was the most powerful made up to this date. It certainly did not require great mental effort or acumen on the part of Sturgeon to bend a straight bar magnet into the then common U form of the permanent steel magnet known as the horse-shoe magnet; yet his experiments with this magnet mark an important point of departure in electric science, and evidently led Henry to his first and his most important scientific research.

I have now given as much of the history of electrical research as is requisite to the understanding of Henry's position as a discoverer in this branch of knowledge when, in 1827, he began to make original experiments in electricity.

As with many other men of originality, Henry's first essays were in the direction of improving the means of illustrating well-established scientific facts and principles. His first paper, of October, 1827, is interesting because it was his first. In it he improves on the usual apparatus which had been used by Ampère and others to show electro-dynamic actions, by employing several turns of insulated wire instead of one, as had previously been the practice. Thus, for example, to show the directive action of the earth's magnetism on a freely-moving closed circuit, Henry covered copper wire with silk and then made out of it a ring about 20 inches in diameter, formed of several turns of the wire. The extremities of this wire were soldered to zinc and copper plates. The coil was then suspended by silk filaments. On plunging the metal plates into a glass of dilute acid the ring rotated around its point of suspension till its plane took a permanent position at right angles to the magnetic meridian. By a similar arrangement of two concentric coils, one suspended within the other, he neatly showed the mutual actions of voltaic currents flowing in the same or in opposite directions; which facts are the foundations of Ampère's celebrated law.

We now reach a period when Henry appears as a discoverer, and truly one of no mean order. As I remember his narration to me in the year 1859, it was as follows: He said that one evening he was sitting in his study in Albany with a friend, when, after a few

31

moments of reverie, he arose and exclaimed, "To-morrow I shall make a famous experiment." For several months he had been brooding over Ampère's electro-dynamic theory of magnetism, and he was then deeply interested in the phenomena of the development of magnetism in soft iron as shown in the experiments of Arago and Sturgeon. At the moment he had arisen from his chair it had occurred to him that the requirements of the theory of Ampère were not fulfilled in the electro-magnets of Arago and of Sturgeon, but that he could get those conditions which the theory required by covering the enveloping wire with a non-conductor like silk, and then wrapping it closely around the soft iron bar in several layers; for the successive layers of wire coiling first in one direction and then in the other would tend to produce a resultant action of the current at right angles to the axis of the bar; and furthermore, the great number of convolutions thus obtained would act on a greater number of molecules of the bar and thereby exalt its magnetism. "When this conception," said Henry, "came into my brain I was so pleased with it that I could not help rising to my feet and giving it my hearty approbation."

Henry did go to work the next day, and to his great delight and encouragement discoveries of the highest interest and importance revealed themselves to him week after week. When he had finished his newly-conceived magnet he found that it supported several times more weight than did Sturgeon's magnet of equal size and weight. This was his first original discovery.

I will now give, as far as possible, Henry's own words in narrating his subsequent investigations of these very interesting phenomena:

"The maximum effect however with this arrangement and a single battery was not yet obtained. After a certain length of wire had been coiled upon the iron, the power diminished with a further increase of the number of turns. This was due to the increased resistance which the longer wire offered to the conduction of electricity. Two methods of improvement therefore suggested themselves. The first consisted, not in increasing the length of the coil, but in using a number of separate coils on the same piece of iron. By this arrangement the resistance to the conduction of the electricity was diminished and a greater quantity made to circulate around the

iron from the same battery. The second method of producing a
similar result consisted in increasing the number of elements of the
battery, or, in other words, the projectile force of the electricity,
which enabled it to pass through an increased number of turns of
wire, and thus, by increasing the length of the wire, to develop the
maximum power of the iron.

"To test these principles on a larger scale, an experimental magnet
was constructed. In this a number of compound helices were placed
on the same bar, their ends left projecting, and so numbered that
they could be all united into one long helix, or variously combined
in sets of lesser length.

"From a series of experiments with this and other magnets it was
proved that, in order to produce the greatest amount of magnetism
from a battery of a single cup, a number of helices is required; but
when a compound battery is used, then one long wire must be
employed, making many turns around the iron, the length of wire,
and consequently the number of turns, being commensurate with the
projectile power of the battery.

"In describing the results of my experiments the terms *intensity*
and *quantity* magnets were introduced to avoid circumlocution, and
were intended to be used merely in a technical sense. By the
intensity magnet I designated a piece of soft iron, so surrounded with
wire that its magnetic power could be called into operation by an
intensity battery; and by a *quantity* magnet a piece of iron so surrounded by a number of separate coils that its magnetism could be
fully developed by a *quantity* battery.

"I was," says Henry, "the first to point out this connection of
the two kinds of the battery with the two forms of the magnet, in
my paper in *Silliman's Journal*, January, 1831, and clearly to state
that when magnetism was to be developed by means of a compound
battery, one long coil was to be employed, and when the maximum
effect was to be produced by a single battery, a number of strands
were to be used."

Here is Henry's description of one of his quantity magnets: "A
bar of iron 21 inches long and 2 inches square with rounded corners
was bent into a U form, having legs about 9 inches long. This bar
weighed 21 pounds. Its armature was formed of a piece of a similar

bar and weighed 7 pounds. Nine coils of copper bell-wire, each 60 feet in length, were wrapped in sections on the iron. These coils were not continued around the whole length of the bar, but each strand of wire, according to the principle before mentioned, occupied about two inches, and was coiled several times backward and forward over itself; the several ends of the wire were left projecting and all numbered, so that the first and last end of each strand might be readily distinguished. In this manner was formed an experimental magnet on a larger scale, with which several combinations of wire could be made by merely uniting the different projecting ends. Thus, if the second end of the first wire be soldered to the first end of the second wire, and so on through all the series, the whole will form a continued coil of one long wire. By soldering different ends the whole may be formed into a double coil of half the length, or into a triple coil of one-third the length, etc. The horse-shoe was suspended in a rectangular wooden frame 3 feet 9 inches high and 20 inches wide.

"In order to ascertain the effect of a very small galvanic element on this large quantity of iron, a pair of plates exactly one square inch, was attached to all the wires: the weight lifted was 85 pounds. To find out the greatest supporting power of the magnet, with all of its 9 coils in circuit, a small battery formed of a plate of zinc 12 inches long and 6 inches wide, and surrounded by copper, was substituted for the galvanic element used in the former experiments: the weight lifted was 750 pounds."

The most powerful of Henry's magnets was constructed while he was at Princeton, and is thus described by his successor in the chair of Natural Philosophy, Professor Richard S. McCulloh: "It is formed of a bar of rounded iron nearly 4 inches in diameter, weighing about 100 pounds, and surrounded with 30 strands of copper bell-wire, each about 40 feet long. With a calorimotor on Dr. Hare's plan, consisting of 22 plates of zinc each 8 inches by 12, alternating with plates of copper of the same size, it supports 3,500 pounds, or more than a ton and a half.

"After the connection with the battery is broken, this magnet supports a thousand pounds for several minutes, and from year to year the lifter adheres with a force which is overcome only by a weight of several hundred pounds. When the lifter however is detached, nearly all the magnetism disappears."

On a recent visit to the College of New Jersey by the electrician Mr. Frank L. Pope, he examined this magnet. "There," he says in his admirable and justly appreciative eulogy on Henry, "there, too, was the reversing commutator or pole-changer, a device first invented by Professor Henry, with which he was accustomed to delight and astonish his pupils, by suddenly reversing the polarity of his large magnet, causing it to drop its armature and seize it again before it had passed beyond the sphere of attraction, a principle which we see exemplified in every stroke of the neutral relay of the quadruplex telegraph of to-day."

We will now return to Henry's study of the properties of his intensity magnet. This magnet was formed of a piece of iron one-fourth of an inch in diameter, bent into the U form and wound with 8 feet of insulated wire. His batteries were two,—one formed of a single element with a zinc plate 4 inches by 7, surrounded by copper and immersed in dilute acid; the other, a Cruikshank's battery, or *trough*, with 25 double plates. The plates of this battery were joined in series and altogether had exactly the same surface of zinc as that in the single-cell battery.

The magnet was now connected directly to the single cell. The magnet held up 72 ounces. Then 530 feet of number 18 copper wire led the current from the cell to the magnet; it now supported only *two* ounces. Five hundred and thirty feet more of the wire were introduced into the circuit and then the magnet held but *one* ounce. In these facts Henry faced the same results as confronted Barlow five years before, and caused Barlow then to say: "In a very early stage of electro-magnetic experiments, it had been suggested [by Laplace, Ampère, and others] that an instantaneous telegraph might be established by means of conducting-wires and compasses; - - - but I found such a sensible diminution with only 200 feet of wire, as at once to convince me of the impracticability of the scheme;" and such, at that day, seemed to be the common opinion of men of science. But this opinion is presently to be shown by Henry to be ill founded, by reason of the ignorance of the relations which have of necessity to exist between the kind of battery and the kind of magnet in order to produce electro-magnetic action at a distance; relations which Henry was the first to discover. This accomplishment justly entitles him to be regarded as a man of genius and a discoverer of no mean order. This discovery will always remain the one important fact that was to be known, to be understood, and to be applied, before it was possible to have constructed any form of electro-magnetic telegraph.

Let us see how Henry made this discovery. After ending the experiments with the one-cell battery and reaching results which seemed to confirm the opinion of Barlow as to "the impracticability of the scheme" of an electro-magnetic telegraph, Henry attached his magnet to the second battery formed of 25 cells, arranged in series. The current from this battery was sent to the magnet through 1,060 feet of the same wire as had been used in the experiments with the first battery of one cell. The magnet now lifted eight ounces. It had held up only one ounce when with the same length of interposed wire the battery of one cell was used.

He now attached his electro-magnet directly to the poles of the 25-cell battery, when, to his astonishment, it only held 7 ounces. The same magnet, it will be remembered, when attached to the one-cell battery supported 72 ounces.

Here were facts of the highest significance, and Henry was not slow to seize them in all their bearings. Referring to these experiments he says: "It is possible that the different states of the trough, with respect to dryness, may have exerted some influence on this remarkable result; but that the effect of a current from a *trough* (i. e. a series of cells) is at least not sensibly diminished by passing through a long wire, is directly applicable to Mr. Barlow's project of forming an electro-magnetic telegraph, and it is also of material consequence in the construction of the galvanic coil."

Henry speaking, in 1857, of these, his first gatherings into the garner of science, says: "These steps in the advance of electro-magnetism, though small, were such as to interest and astonish the scientific world. With the same battery used by Mr. Sturgeon, at least a hundred times more magnetism was produced than could have been obtained by his experiment. These developments were considered at the time of much importance in a scientific point of view, and they subsequently furnished the means by which magneto-electricity, the phenomena of dia-magnetism, and the magnetic effects in polarized light were discovered. They gave rise to the various forms of electro-magnetic machines which have exercised the ingenuity of inventors in every part of the world, and were of immediate applicability in the introduction of the magnet to telegraphic purposes. Neither the electro-magnet of Sturgeon nor any electro-magnet ever made previous to my investigations was applicable to transmitting power to a distance."

Henry however was not satisfied with the mere statement that his discovery was "directly applicable to Mr. Barlow's project of forming an electro-magnetic telegraph;" he actually constructed an electro-magnetic telegraph. Sometime during the year 1831, "I arranged," says he, "around one of the upper rooms of the Albany Academy a wire of more than a mile in length, through which I was enabled to make signals by sounding a bell. The mechanical arrangement for effecting this object was simply a steel bar, permanently magnetized, of about ten inches in length, supported on a pivot, and placed with its north end between the two arms of a horse-shoe magnet. When the latter was excited by the current, the end of the bar thus placed was attracted by one arm of the horse-shoe and repelled by the other, and was thus caused to move in a horizontal plane and its further end to strike a bell suitably adjusted."

This was the first electro-magnetic telegraph which had worked through so great a length of wire; it was the first electro-magnetic telegraph in which an electro-magnet had worked successfully; it was the first "sounding" electro-magnetic telegraph.

On this occasion we have not the time to enter into a discussion of the relative parts played by Henry and Morse in the invention of the electro-magnetic telegraph; nor do I think such a course necessary. Henry's own words as given in his "Statement in relation to the history of the electro-magnetic telegraph," and published by the Regents of the Smithsonian Institution in 1857, give all that is required to a just understanding of the relations of these two distinguished men to this invention.

"The principles," says Henry, (referring to his discoveries in electro-magnetism of which I have just given an account,) "I had

developed were applied by Dr. Gale to render Morse's machine
effective at a distance." This statement seems to me to be as direct,
as clear, as truthful, and as comprehensive as one can desire. They
are Henry's own words, and we all receive them as entirely satisfactory. "The principles I had developed were applied by Dr.
Gale to render Morse's machine effective at a distance." Observe,
Henry does not claim to have had any part in rendering Morse's
machine effective when near the battery; no, because that was the
condition of the machine before Morse called in the assistance of
Dr. Gale in the winter of 1836–'37; but Henry does claim this:
by his discoveries to have given Dr. Gale the *principles* which Dr.
Gale applied to Morse's machine and *rendered it effective at a distance;* nor does Henry claim Morse's ingenious marking machine—
a lever, one of whose ends is attracted by the electro-magnet against
an opposing spring, while the other end of the lever makes a mark
on a moving surface. Nor does Henry claim any of the other
ingenious mechanical combinations invented by Morse. Henry's
claim is the claim of a *discoverer* not of an *inventor;* for he says:
"The *principles* I had developed were applied by Dr. Gale to render
Morse's instrument effective at a distance."

Henry does not claim that his own telegraphic machine (which
was undoubtedly an original invention) had been appropriated by
Mr. Morse; certainly not, because it is an entirely different invention. And here let me call your attention to an important fact, viz:
Neither Henry nor Morse could lay claim to having originated the
idea of causing a voltaic current to produce electro-magnetic actions
at a distance; yet the majority of persons, who have not examined
into the history of telegraphy, think that this is the very point at
issue between Henry and Morse.

Finally, I will take the liberty of remarking that had Henry
taken out a patent in which he claimed as his invention an electro-
magnet *formed of two or more layers of insulated wire,* Morse's patent
would not have been so valuable. Remember, I speak not of the
merit of the invention, but of the merit of the patent; for the
invention, so far as Morse is concerned, would have remained the
same, because one essential part of a Morse telegraph is Henry's
intensity magnet, and certainly Morse never invented that.

Let us pause here awhile from following Henry in his career of
discoverer and examine a little more curiously into what he has just
done. I said, in the beginning of this discourse, that to judge
rightly of a discoverer's achievements we should view them in the
light of the knowledge of his time. What was that knowledge?
I have already sketched it sufficiently to show how much Henry
was indebted to knowledge then existing, at least in so far as he was
guided thereby in his work. In this light his achievements appear
indeed remarkable, and as admirable as those of any philosopher of
his time.

Simultaneously with Henry's first publication in 1827, on the
improvement of electro-magnetic apparatus by increasing the length
of the galvanic conductor and the number of its coils, Ohm published
at Berlin, his mathematical law of galvanic circuits, in a book entitled
Galvanische Kette, mathematisch bearbeitet. This publication was
not only received with indifference, but almost with contempt by his
countrymen. Professor H. W. Dove, of Berlin, says that "In the
Berlin *Jahrbücher für wissenschaftliche Kritik*, Ohm's theory was
named a web of naked fancies, which can never find the semblance of
support from even the most superficial observation of facts; 'he who
looks on the world,' proceeds the writer, 'with the eye of reverence
must turn aside from this book as the result of an incurable delusion,
whose sole effort is to detract from the dignity of nature.'"

Henry's researches were based avowedly on a thoughtful study
of the work and theory of Ampère in 1820–'21, and of the galvanometer of Schweigger, (of the same date,) as applicable to the electro-
magnet of Sturgeon in 1825; and his series of ingenious experiments during the years 1828–'30, were then completed by the full
announcement of his discoveries, January 1, 1831. At that time,
no writer or physicist appears to have had any just conception of
the consequences flowing from Ohm's announcement,—particularly
of that most important deduction, viz: that the interpolar resistance should equal the internal resistance of the battery, in order to
obtain the maxima of electro-magnetic effects. This theory or
law of Ohm,—utterly neglected at home,—unknown to Wheatstone, to Faraday, or to Roget,—could hardly make its way abroad
in the garb of a foreign tongue, and reach Henry in Albany. Henry

could not read German, and Ohm's papers were first published in English in *Taylor's Scientific Memoirs*, vol. ii, London, 1841. From the very manner in which Henry worked at his problems and viewed the results of his experimenting it is evident that, at that date, he had no knowledge of Ohm's law; otherwise, he would not have been so astonished at the results when his "intensity magnet" was connected with his "intensity battery."

Henry, now in possession of the powerful magnets of his own creation, turned his thoughts to the uses to which he might put these instruments as aids in making other discoveries. He began with work on a problem which had baffled many able men before him. He tried to do the reverse of what he had already done. He had made his great magnet by the action of the electric current, he now tried to obtain an electric current from the magnetism of his great magnet,—and he succeeded.

It is not generally known or appreciated that Henry and Faraday independently discovered the means of producing the electric current and the electric spark from a magnet. Tyndall, in speaking of this great discovery of Faraday's, says: "I cannot help thinking while I dwell upon them that this discovery of magneto-electricity is the greatest experimental result ever obtained by an investigator. It is the Mont Blanc of Faraday's own achievements. He always worked at great elevations, but higher than this he never subsequently attained."

The history of Henry's connection with this notable discovery is, I think, best given in Henry's own words, which I take from *Silliman's Journal* of July, 1832. Referring to Faraday's discovery, he says: "No detail is given of the experiments, and it is somewhat surprising that results so interesting, and which certainly form a new era in the history of electricity and magnetism, should not have been more fully described before this time in some of the English publications. The only mention I have found of them is the following short account from the *Annals of Philosophy* for April, under the head of Proceedings of the Royal Institution: 'Feb. 17. Mr. Faraday gave an account of the first two parts of his researches in electricity, namely, volta-electric induction and magneto-electric induction. - - - If a wire, connected at both extremities with a galvanometer, be coiled in the form of a helix around a magnet, no current of electricity takes place in it. This is an experiment which has been made by various persons hundreds of times, in the hope of evolving electricity from magnetism. But if the magnet be withdrawn from or introduced into such a helix, a current of electricity is produced *while the magnet is in motion*, and is rendered evident by the deflection of the galvanometer. If a single wire be passed by a magnetic pole a current of electricity is induced through it which can be rendered sensible.' [Henry continues:]

"Before having any knowledge of the method given in the above account, I had succeeded in producing electrical effects in the following manner, which differs from that developed by Mr. Faraday, and which appears to me to develop some new and interesting facts: A piece of copper wire about thirty feet long, and covered with elastic varnish, was closely coiled around the middle of the soft-iron armature of the galvanic magnet described in vol. six of the American Journal of Science, and which, when excited, will readily sustain between six hundred and seven hundred pounds. The wire was wound upon itself so as to occupy only about one inch of the length of the armature, which is seven inches in all. The armature thus furnished with the wire was placed in its proper position across the ends of the galvanic magnet, and there fastened so that no motion could take place. The two projecting ends of the helix were dipped into two cups of mercury, and these connected with a distant galvanometer by means of two copper wires each about forty feet long. This arrangement being completed, I stationed myself near the galvanometer, and directed an assistant at a given word to immerse suddenly in a vessel of dilute acid the galvanic battery attached to the magnet. At the instant of immersion the north end of the needle was deflected 30° to the west, indicating a current of electricity from the helix surrounding the armature. The effect however appeared only as a single impulse, for the needle, after a few oscillations, resumed its former undisturbed position in the magnetic meridian, although the galvanic action of the battery, and consequently the magnetic power, still continued. I was however much surprised to see the needle suddenly deflected from a state of rest to about 20° to the east, or in a contrary direction, when the battery

was withdrawn from the acid, and again deflected to the west when
it was re-immersed. This operation was repeated many times in succession, and uniformly with the same result, the armature the whole
time remaining immovably attached to the poles of the magnet, no
motion being required to produce the effect, as it appeared to take
place only in consequence of the instantaneous development of the
magnetic action in one and the sudden cessation of it in the other.
- - - From the foregoing facts it appears that a current of
electricity is produced for an instant in a helix of copper wire surrounding a piece of soft iron whenever magnetism is induced in the
iron; and a current in an opposite direction when the magnetic
action ceases; also that an instantaneous current in one or the other
direction accompanies every change in the magnetic intensity of the
iron."

I will now give Henry's account of the experiment by which he
obtained a spark from the magneto-electric current—certainly the
first flash of a magneto-electric current ever seen in this country:
"The poles of the magnet," says Henry, "were connected by a single
rod of iron bent into the form of a horse-shoe, and its extremities
filed perfectly flat so as to come in perfect contact with the faces of
the poles: around the middle of the arch of this horse-shoe two
strands of copper wire were tightly coiled, one over the other. A
current from one of these helices deflected the needle one hundred
degrees, and when both were used, the needle was deflected with such
force as to make a complete circuit. But the most surprising effect
was produced when instead of passing the current through the long
wires to the galvanometer, the opposite ends of the helices were held
nearly in contact with each other and the magnet suddenly excited:
in this case a small but vivid spark was seen to pass between the
ends of the wires, and this effect was repeated as often as the state
of intensity of the magnet was changed. - - - It appears
from the May number of the Annals of Philosophy, that I have
been anticipated in this experiment of drawing sparks from the
magnet by Mr. James D. Forbes, of Edinburgh, who obtained a
spark on the 30th of March, my experiments being made during the
last two weeks of June. A simple notification of his result is given,
without any account of the experiment, which is reserved for a

communication to the Royal Society of Edinburgh. My result is therefore entirely independent of his, and was undoubtedly obtained by a different process."

A few words now will place Henry in his proper and just relation to these important discoveries. We have seen that all the information he had received about Faraday's discovery was the account of Faraday's production of magneto-electricity by the sudden insertion of a magnet into a helix and by its sudden withdrawal therefrom. This is the experiment described in section No. 39 of Faraday's paper of November, 1831. Henry's experiment is entirely different, and certainly was entirely original with him, but it is essentially Faraday's experiment described in sections 27, 28, 29, 30 and 31 of the same paper, and is the first in the order of those which Faraday gives of his various methods of evolving electricity from magnetism. Of this experiment Henry had no knowledge when he obtained the electric current from the magnet, no more than he had of the other experiment in which Faraday moved a permanent steel magnet in a helix. Thus it clearly appears that though Henry cannot be placed on record as the *first* discoverer of the magneto-electric current, yet it can be claimed that he stands alone as its *second* independent discoverer.

As to the production of the electric spark from the magneto-electric current, both Henry and Forbes were anticipated by Faraday, who describes an experiment, which in all essentials is the same as Henry's, in section No. 32 of the same paper of November, 1831.

I may have been somewhat tedious in these long quotations and minute narrations of dates, but my object is to place Henry before you as a discoverer and make you appreciate him, and that justly;— not to ask too much for him, for that would injure his fair name.

Henry's next discovery was that of the induction of a current on itself, or of the "extra current," as it is sometimes called. Here he had the good luck to anticipate Faraday by nearly two years and a half in the observation of the fundamental facts of this discovery, Henry publishing his observations in July, 1832, while Faraday's first appear in the Philosophical Magazine for November, 1834. Therefore, to Henry should be given the honor of having made the first observations of these phenomena; but not in opposition to any claim set up for Faraday, because Faraday expressly states in his paper read before the Royal Society on January 29, 1835, that "The inquiry arose out of a fact communicated to me by Mr. Jenkin, which is as follows: If an ordinary wire of short length be used as the medium of communication between the two plates of an electromotor consisting of a single pair of metals, no management will enable the experimenter to obtain an electric shock from this wire; but if the wire which surrounds an electro-magnet be used, a shock is felt each time the contact with the electro-motor is broken, provided the ends of the wire be grasped one in each hand." Notwithstanding this explicit statement of Faraday's, neither to Henry nor to Jenkin is generally accorded the credit for the original observations, but it is given to Faraday. This is accounted for by the fact that although Henry had the good fortune to anticipate others in the observations, he had not the leisure to follow up these observations to their full explanation till after Faraday had completely unravelled their nature. This was owing to the removal of Henry to Princeton in November of 1832, shortly after he had made his few preliminary experiments; and he did not resume and finish this research till 1834; and in 1835 he gave the results of his work to the American Philosophical Society in a paper "On the Influence of a Spiral Conductor in Increasing the Intensity of Electricity from a Galvanic Arrangement of a Single Pair, etc."

In 1838, after Henry's return from his first visit to Europe, he discovered an entirely new class of phenomena in electrical induction; and as the field was entirely his own he entered into this work with great enthusiasm. In these researches he extends greatly our knowledge of electrical induction. He first showed that an induced current may excite a second induced current in a neighboring closed conductor, and this last may induce a third current in another neighboring closed circuit, and so on. These various induced currents Henry styled currents of the first, second, third, fourth, fifth, &c., orders. He shows that these currents alternate in their directions in the successive orders,—at least when these currents are induced by the discharge of a voltaic battery. He investigates the differences in the properties of these currents according as they flow through conductors formed of few convolutions of low resistance or

through many convolutions of high resistance. He shows that plates
of metal, when their surfaces are continuous, screen the inductive
action of a current of one order on the succeeding order, but that
when a sector is cut out of the metal plate the screening effect disappears.   The same phenomena of induced currents of different
orders he tracks through the inductive actions of the discharge of
the Leyden jar and of the ordinary frictional electrical machine in
the most skillful manner, and shows in what these phenomena differ
from those produced by the inductive actions of the discharge of
the voltaic battery.

In the time allotted us it is impossible to give even the most concise abstract of these beautiful investigations. They are however
known to you all. They form part of the doctrine of modern physics.
These researches into the nature and laws of the induced currents
of different orders are the most finished of Henry's works and will
ever be regarded as models of careful and thorough scientific work.

We here leave Henry's researches in electricity with the regret
that we have been able only to give but meagre and imperfect
accounts of them; and that the occasion does not permit me to
mention even by their titles several of his investigations in this
department of knowledge.

Henry had a versatile mind, and did not confine his attention to
the study of electricity. His genius has adorned all departments
of Physics. His researches in molecular physics, though not extensive, are remarkable. Here his fertile suggestions and original
methods of research have instigated others to follow out the paths
which he has pointed out.

In 1839 Henry made a very curious discovery as to the permea-
bility of lead to mercury. So permeable indeed is this metal to the
fluid that he found mercury would ascend a lead wire to the height of
a yard in a few days. He even made what might be called, so far
as their forms are concerned, syphons of lead which would nearly
empty a vessel of mercury by gradually drawing the fluid over its
sides. Subsequently, in 1845, with the assistance of Mr. Cornelius,
of Philadelphia, he succeeded in showing that copper when heated
to the melting point of silver would absorb the latter metal. This
he distinctly proved by subsequently dissolving off the surface of

the copper plate with zinc chloride, when the absorbed silver made its appearance, having penetrated to a slight distance into the copper.

In 1844 Henry is again at work in molecular physics, investigating the nature of the forces acting in liquid films. This Investigation was duly valued by Plateau, who has given us his beautiful researches into the conditions of equilibrium of polyhedra with surfaces formed of films of water, and Plateau chided Henry for having neglected to investigate further into phenomena which he was the first to discover. Of Henry's work in this direction there only remains the record of a scanty verbal communication which he he made to the American Philosophical Society in 1844. From this I make following abstract: "The passage of a body from a solid to a liquid state is generally attributed to the neutralization of the attraction of cohesion by the repulsion of the increased quantity of heat; the liquid being supposed to retain a small portion of its original attraction, which is shown by the force necessary to separate a surface of water from water,—in the well-known experiment of a plate suspended from a scale beam over a vessel of the liquid. It is however more in accordance with all the phenomena of cohesion to suppose, instead of the attraction of the liquid being neutralized by the heat, that the effect of this agent is merely to neutralize the polarity of the molecules so as to give them perfect freedom of motion around every imaginable axis. The small amount of cohesion, (52 grains to the square inch,) exhibited in the foregoing experiment, is due, according to the theory of capillarity of Young and Poisson, to the tension of the exterior film of the surface of water drawn up by the elevation of the plate. This film gives way first, and the strain is thrown on an inner film, which, in turn is ruptured; and so on until the plate is entirely separated; the whole effect being similar to tearing the water apart atom by atom.

"Reflecting on the subject, the author has thought that a more correct idea of the magnitude of the molecular attraction might be obtained by studying the tenacity of a more viscid liquid than water. For this purpose he had recourse to soap-water, and attempted to measure the tenacity of this liquid by means of weighing the quantity of water which adhered to a bubble of this substance just before it burst, and by determining the thickness of the film from an observation of the color it exhibited in comparison with Newton's scale of thin plates. Although experiments of this kind could only furnish approximate results, yet they show that the molecular attraction of water for water instead of being only about 52 grains to the square inch, is really several hundred pounds, and is probably equal to that of the attraction of ice for ice. The effect of dissolving the soap in the water is not, as might at first appear, to increase the molecular attraction, but to diminish the mobility of the molecules and thus render the liquid more viscid.

"According to the theory of Young and Poisson, many of the phenomena of liquid cohesion, and all those of capillarity, are due to a contractile force existing at the free surface of the liquid, and which tends in all cases to urge the liquid in the direction of the radius of curvature towards the centre, with a force inversely as the radius.

"According to this theory the spherical form of a dew-drop is not the effect of the attraction of each molecule of the water on any other, as in the action of gravitation in producing the globular form of the planets, (since the attraction of cohesion only extends to an inappreciable distance,) but is due to the contractile force which tends constantly to enclose the given quantity of water within the smallest surface, namely that of a sphere. The author finds a contractile force similar to that assumed by this theory, in the surface of the soap-bubble; indeed, the bubble may be considered a drop of water with the internal liquid removed and its place supplied by air. The spherical form in the two cases is produced by the operations of the same cause. The contractile force in the surface of the bubble is easily shown by blowing a large bubble on the end of a wide tube—say an inch in diameter; as soon as the mouth is removed the bubble will be seen to diminish rapidly, and at the same time quite a forcible current of air will be blown through the tube against the face. This effect is not due to the ascent of the heated air from the lungs with which the bubble was inflated, for the same effect is produced by inflating with cold air, and also when the bubble is held perpendicularly above the face, so that the current is downward.

"Many experiments were made to determine the amount of this force, by blowing a bubble on the larger end of a glass tube in the form of a letter U, and partially filled with water; the contractile force of the bubble, transmitted through the enclosed air, forced down the water in the larger leg of the tube and caused it to rise in the smaller. The difference of level observed by means of a microscope gave the force in grains per square inch, derived from the known pressure of a given height of water. The thickness of the film of soap-water which formed the envelope of the .bubble was estimated as before, by the color exhibited just before bursting. The results of these experiments agree with those of weighing the bubble, in giving a great intensity to the molecular attraction of the liquid; equal at least to several hundred pounds to the square inch. Several other methods were employed to measure the tenacity of the film, the general results of which were the same; the numerical detail of them are reserved however until the experiments can be repeated with a more delicate balance.

"The comparative cohesion of pure water and soap-water was determined by the weight necessary to detach the same plate from each; and in all cases the pure water was found to exhibit nearly double the tenacity of soap-water. The want of permanency in the bubble of pure water is therefore not due to feeble attraction, but to the perfect mobility of the molecules, which causes the equilibrium, as in the case of the arch, without friction of parts, to be destroyed by the slightest extraneous force."

Another of Henry's investigations in molecular physics, having important practical bearings, should be more generally known than it is. Among his other duties as chairman of the United States Light-House Board was the testing of the various physical properties of the oils submitted to the Government for purchase. Fluidity was one of these properties of which it seemed most difficult to get reliable comparative tests. Henry discarded all the crude instruments and methods which give results in which the different degrees of fluidity of the oils are masked by their various powers of adhesion to the surface over which they flow during the process of testing. Henry very ingeniously applied the theorem of Torricelli, which shows that equal quantities of all liquids—supposing them to be all

alike in fluidity—will in equal times flow out of an orifice in the
bottom of a vessel. Henry found that equal quantities of mercury
and water flowed out of the vessel in equal times; but with
different oils the times of flow of equal quantities were different.
Thus the rapidity of flow of sperm oil exceeded that of lard oil in
the ratio of 100 to 167. I think that this method of experimenting
suggested itself to Henry about fifteen years ago. I remember
when he was working with this apparatus, and of his telling me that
to his surprise he found that alcohol was less fluid than water.

Henry always took a deep interest in the study of acoustics. His
additions to this branch of knowledge were chiefly the results of his
experiments in connection with our system of coast fog-signals. He
made extensive experiments on various sound-producing instruments, such as bells, cannon, steam whistles, and steam reed and
syren fog-horns. He eventually decided in favor of the latter as
the most powerful and effective instrument yet invented. He
determined that these instruments send their sounds to the greatest
distances when they emit a note in the treble part of the musical
scale. They are, in fact, tuned very near to the treble C. Henry
also showed the uselessness of applying reflectors to these instruments. But his principal researches were in the direction of
determining the influence of various atmospheric conditions on the
audibility and manner of propagation of the sounds of the fog-horns
on our northern coasts. The results which he reached, though of
great importance, appear to bear a very small relation to the great
amount of time spent and fatigue and exposure endured in procuring
them.

During eleven years Henry did not cease to labor most devotedly
to do all he could to advance the efficiency of our fog-signals by
studying the action of these instruments in all kinds of weather.
Many facts were collected, and very puzzling were these to explain
by any known laws pertaining to the propagation of sound. Thus
it was observed that a sound coming to the mariner against the
direction of the wind would cease to be audible on the deck of his
vessel, while it continued to be heard to a listener on the mast-head.
An observation made at Block Island showed this fact in a marked
manner. The lens of this light is about 200 feet above the beach

at the base of the cliff on which stands the light-house. The wind was blowing seven miles an hour. The vessel sounding its steam whistle steamed away from the light, going in the direction towards which the wind was blowing. The listener on the top of the light-house heard the sound four times longer than the observer on the beach; but when the vessel ran away from the light-house against the wind, the sound disappeared first to the observer on the top of the light-house.

It was also observed that sometimes on approaching a fog-horn from a distance the intensity of its sound would gradually increase, then die down quite rapidly and become inaudible through a space of from three to four miles, and often would not reappear till the vessel was within a mile of the fog-horn. Often when the sound came to the listener against a moderate wind the fog-horn would become inaudible at a distance of three or four miles, while on other days, when the wind was going with the sound, the listener had to sail away 25 miles before the horn ceased to be heard. Observations made at Block Island and Point Judith showed this fact in the following manner: The distance between these fog-horns is seventeen miles, and the sound of one can be distinctly heard at the other when the air is quiet and homogeneous; but if the wind blows from one towards the other the listener at the station from which the wind blows is unable to hear the other horn.

The most remarkable series of Henry's observations was made at Whitehead Station, Maine, situate on a small island about one mile and a half off the coast. The vessel was approaching the station from the south and with the wind. "The belt of silence" was reached and traversed, and then the sound reappeared again. This happened whether the vessel was steaming towards or away from the station, the wind remaining all the while southerly. But during these observations on the vessel the sounds of the steamer's whistle were heard without interruption at the station. Now the steamer's course was directed to the other side of the station; and steaming away from the fog-horn and against the wind the whistle at the station was constantly heard by those on the vessel, but those at the station now perceived the steamer's whistle to go into and out of "the belt of silence."

These facts demanded explanation, and for a long time remained enigmas to Henry; till one day he met with a short paper by Professor Stokes, of Cambridge, England, in the Proceedings of the British Association for 1857, "In which the effect of an upper current in deflecting the wave-surface of sound so as to throw it down upon the ear of the auditor, or directing it upward far above his head, is fully explained." In the Report of the Light-House Board for 1874 Henry says: "The explanation, [of these phenomena,] as suggested by the hypothesis of Professor Stokes, is founded on the fact that in the case of a deep current of air the lower stratum, or that next the earth, is more retarded by friction than the one immediately above, and this again than the one above it, and so on. The effect of this diminution of velocity as we descend towards the earth is, in the case of sound moving with the current, to carry the upper part of the sound-waves more rapidly forward than the lower part, thus causing them to incline toward the earth, or in other words, to be thrown down upon the ear of the observer. When the sound is in a contrary direction to the current, an opposite effect is produced,—the upper portion of the sound-waves is more retarded than the lower, which advancing more rapidly in consequence, inclines the waves upward and directs them above the head of the observer. To render this more clear, let us recall the nature of a beam of sound, in still air, projected in a horizontal direction. It consists of a series of concentric waves perpendicular to the direction of the beam, like the palings of a fence. Now, if the upper part of the waves have a slightly greater velocity than the lower, the beam will be bent downward in a manner somewhat analogous to that of a ray of light in proceeding from a rarer to a denser medium. The effect of this deformation of the wave will be cumulative from the sound-centre outward, and hence, although the velocity of the wind may have no perceptible effect on the velocity of sound, yet this bending of the wave being continuous throughout its entire course, a marked effect must be produced. A precisely similar effect will be the result, but perhaps in a considerably greater degree, in case an upper current is moving in an opposite direction to the lower, when the latter is adverse to the sound, and in this we have a logical explanation of the phenomenon observed by General Duane, in which a fog-signal is only heard during the occurrence of a northeast snow-storm. Certainly this phenomenon cannot be explained by any peculiarity of the atmosphere as to variability of density, or of the amount of vapor which it may contain."

Henry's services to the Light-House Board were of great value to the country. The fact that his investigations showed that lard oil when heated to about 250° Fahrenheit is superior in fluidity and illuminating power to sperm oil, caused the substitution of the former for the latter; and thus was saved a dollar on each gallon of illuminating material purchased. This amounted to about one hundred thousand dollars a year in favor of the Government.

In light and heat Henry made several interesting investigations which, reluctantly, we are obliged to pass over. One however holds so important a place in the history of science that it cannot be omitted from any discourse which would treat of Henry as a discoverer. I refer to his application of the thermopile to the determination of the distribution of heat on the optical images of distant objects. It occurred to Henry that images in the foci of mirrors and lenses are formed not alone by converging pencils of light coming from corresponding points of the objects placed before these mirrors and lenses, but that images are also formed by the convergence of rays which have no effect on the optic nerve, such as the rays of heat. Indeed Henry looked upon the image as having, on a small scale, the same distribution of physical actions as exists on the surface of the large object, of which this image is the optical reproduction.

He applied this conception in a bold and wonderful experiment; which was no other than to study the distribution of heat on the surface of the sun. In 1845, in company with his brother-in-law, Professor Stephen Alexander, he formed an image of the sun by pointing a telescope to that body and then drawing out the eye-tube of the instrument till the solar image was clearly defined on a screen. In this screen was cut a small aperture, closed by the surface of a thermopile. By motion of the telescope any part of the solar image could be brought on to the surface of the pile. A solar spot of considerable magnitude being then present, he brought it on to the pile and noticed the amount of deflection produced in the needles of the galvanometer by the thermo-electric current. Then the parts of the sun's image adjacent to the spot were brought to the thermopile; and now he observed a greater deflection in the galvanometer than in the previous experiment; thus "clearly proving," as he says, "that the spot emitted less heat than the surrounding parts of the luminous disc."

This new method of research originated with Henry. It was shown to Secchi while he was in this country as Professor in the College of Georgetown. On his return to Europe Secchi obtained no inconsiderable repute by extending these observations—using the methods of Henry, but, I fear, not giving sufficient credit to the originator of them. But let that pass; for the bread which Henry cast upon the waters has returned to our own shores—thanks to the genius and perseverance of our colleague Langley.

Most reluctantly do I here desist from citing further the works of Henry. It is impossible to crowd into one brief hour the thoughts which were his occupation during more than half a century. I have at least endeavored to exhibit before you the more important of the labors of his life. What shall we think of them? Surely they are on as high a plane as those of any of his contemporaries, and show as much originality as theirs in their conception—as much skill in their execution. Yet it has been said that Henry was not a man of genius. As I have not been able to find that the philosophers, who have the special charge of giving from time to time definitions of genius, have been able to come to any satisfactory conclusion among themselves, I will leave their company, and, with your liberty, take my definition from a book which, if we accredit Thackeray, is one of the very best novels ever written in English. After listening to this, you may form your own opinions as to whether Henry did or did not possess genius: "By genius I would understand that power, or rather those powers of the mind which are capable of penetrating into all things within our reach and knowledge, and of distinguishing their essential differences. These are no other than invention and judgment: and they are both called by the collective name of genius, as they are of those gifts of nature which we bring with us into the world. Concerning each of which, many seem to have fallen into very great errors; for by invention, I believe, is generally understood a creative faculty, which would indeed prove most romance writers to have the highest pretensions to it; whereas by invention is meant no more (and so the word signifies) than discovery or finding out; or, to explain it at large, a quick and sagacious penetration into the true essence of all the objects of our contemplation. This, I think, can rarely exist without the concomitancy of judgment, for how we can be said to have discovered the true essence of two things, without discerning their difference, seems to me hard to conceive. Now this last is the undisputed province of judgment; and yet some few men of wit have agreed with all the dull fellows in the world, in representing these two to have been seldom or never the property of one and the same person."

My own judgment, if of any value, would rank the ability of Henry—I do not say his achievements—a little below that of Faraday. Indeed, their lives and their manners of working were strangely alike. Each born in humble condition, without any of the adventitious aids of position or influence, was destined apparently to mechanical occupation. Faraday was an apprentice to a bookbinder. Henry served in the same capacity under a silversmith. Each started in life with moral and benevolent habits, well developed and healthy bodies, quick and accurate perceptions, calm judgment and self-reliance tempered with modesty and good manners,—a good ground surely in which to plant the germs of the scientific life. Each by innate force of taste and intellect, was impelled to the pursuit of knowledge under obstacles which would have damped the ardor of ordinary youths. Each, endowed with a lively imagination, was in his younger days fond of romance and the drama; and, by a singular similarity of accidents, each had his attention turned to science by a book which chance threw in his way. This work in the case of Faraday was "Mrs. Marcet's Conversations on Chemistry;" and the book which influenced Henry's career was "Gregory's Lectures on Experimental Philosophy, Astronomy, and Chemistry." Of Mrs. Marcet's book Faraday thus writes: "My dear Friend,—Your subject interested me deeply every way; for Mrs. Marcet was a good friend to me, as she must have

hero to many of the human race. I entered the shop of a book-
seller and bookbinder at the age of 13, in the year 1804, remaining
there eight years, and during the chief part of the time bound books.
Now it was in those books, in the hours after work, that I found the
beginning of my philosophy. There were two that especially helped
me, the 'Encyclopædia Britannica,' from which I gained my first
notions of electricity, and Mrs. Marcet's 'Conversations on Chemistry,' which gave me my foundation in that science.

"Do not suppose that I was a very deep thinker, or was marked
as a precocious person. I was a lively, imaginative person, and
could believe in the 'Arabian Nights' as easily as in the 'Encyclopædia.' But facts were important to me and saved me. I
could trust a fact, and always cross-examined an assertion. So
when I questioned Mrs. Marcet's book by such little experiments
as I could find means to perform, and found it true to the facts
as I could understand them, I felt that I had got hold of an
anchor in chemical knowledge, and clung fast to it. Thence my
deep veneration for Mrs. Marcet — first, as one who had conferred
great personal good and pleasure on me; and then as one able
to convey the truth and principle of those boundless fields of
knowledge which concern natural things to the young, untaught,
and inquiring mind.

"You may imagine my delight when I came to know Mrs. Marcet
personally; how often I cast my thoughts backward, delighting to
connect the past and present; how often, when sending a paper to
her as a thank-offering, I thought of my first Instructress, and such
thoughts will remain with me."

Henry wrote on the inside of the cover of Gregory's work the
following words: "This book, although by no means a profound
work, has, under Providence, exerted a remarkable influence on my
life. It accidentally fell into my hands when I was about sixteen
years old, and was the first book I ever read with attention. It
opened to me a new world of thought and enjoyment; invested
things before almost unnoticed with the highest interest; fixed
my mind on the study of nature, and caused me to resolve at the
time of reading it that I would immediately commence to devote
my life to the acquisition of knowledge.   J. H."

Each of these philosophers worked with simple instruments mostly constructed by his own hands, and by methods so direct that he appeared to have an almost intuitive perception into the workings of nature; and each gave great care to the composition of his writings, sending his discoveries into the world clothed in simple and elegant English.

Finally, each loved science more than money, and his Creator more than either.

There was sympathy between these men; and Henry loved to dwell on the hours that he and Bache had spent in Faraday's society. I shall never forget Henry's account of his visit to King's College, London, where Faraday, Wheatstone, Daniell and he had met to try and evolve the electric spark from the thermopile. Each in turn attempted it and failed. Then came Henry's turn. He succeeded: calling in the aid of his discovery of the effect of a long interpolar wire wrapped around a piece of soft iron. Faraday became as wild as a boy, and, jumping up, shouted: "Hurrah for the Yankee experiment."

And Faraday and Wheatstone reciprocated the high estimation in which Henry held them. During a visit to England, not long before Wheatstone's death, he told me that Faraday and he had, after Henry's classical investigation of the induced currents of different orders, written a joint letter to the Council of the Royal Society, urging that the Copley medal, that laurel wreath of science, should be bestowed on Henry. On further consultation with members of the Council it was decided to defer the honor till it would come with greater éclat, when Henry had continued further his researches in electricity. Henry's removal to Washington interrupted those investigations. Wheatstone promised to give me this letter, to convey to Henry as an evidence of the high appreciation which Faraday and he had for his genius; but Wheatstone's untimely death prevented this.

Both Faraday and Henry gave much thought to the philosophy of education, and in the main their ideas agreed. I may, in this connection, be excused for reading abstracts from a letter from Henry soon after he had received the news that I had given my son his name. He says—what may be news to the most of you: "I did not object to Henry as a first name; although I have been sorry that my grandfather, in coming from Scotland to this country, substituted it for Hendric, a much less common, and therefore more distinctive name." He then proceeds: "I hope that both his body and his mind will be so developed by proper training and instruction that he may become an efficient, wise, and good man. I say efficient and wise, because these two characteristics are not always united in the same person. Indeed, most of the inefficiency of the world is due to their separation; wisdom may know what ought to be done, but it requires the aid of efficiency to accomplish the desired object. I hope that in the education of your son due attention may not only be given to the proper development of both these faculties, but also that they will be cultivated in the order of nature: that is, doing before thinking; art before science. By inverting this order much injury is frequently done to a child, especially in the case of the only son of a widowed mother, in which a precocious boy becomes an insignificant man. On examination, in such a case, it will be generally found that the boy has never been drilled into expertness in the art of language, of arithmetic, or of spelling, of attention, perseverance, and order, or in other words, of the habits of an active and efficient life."

Henry was a man of extensive reading, and often surprised his friends by the extent and accuracy of his information, and by the original manner in which he brought his knowledge before them. Not only was he well versed in those subjects in which one might naturally suppose him proficient, but in departments of knowledge entirely distinct from that in which he gained his reputation as an original thinker. Although without a musical ear, he had a nice feeling for the movement of a poem, and was fond of drawing from his retentive memory poetic quotations apt to the occasion. He was a diligent student of mental philosophy, and also took a lively interest in the progress of biological science, especially in following the recent generalizations of Darwin; while the astonishing development of modern research in tracking the history of prehistoric man had for him a peculiar fascination. Yet with all his learning, reputation, and influence, Henry was as modest as he was pure.

One day, on opening Henry's copy of Young's "Lectures on Natural Philosophy,"—a book which he had studied more than any other work of science,—I read on the fly-leaf, written by his own hand, these words:

"In Nature's infinite book of secrecy
        A little I can read.
                            Shakspeare."

And did he not read a little "in Nature's infinite book of secrecy"? and did he not read that little carefully and well?   May we all read our little in that book as modestly and as reverently as did JOSEPH HENRY.

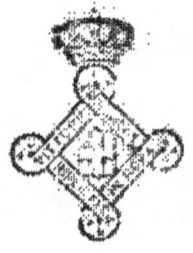

APPENDIX.

PROCEEDINGS IN CONGRESS

A MONUMENT TO JOSEPH HENRY.

IN THE SENATE OF THE UNITED STATES.

Monday, May 3, 1880.

Mr. MORRILL (Senator from Vermont) asked, and by unanimous consent obtained, leave to bring in the following bill;* which was read twice and referred to the Committee on Public Buildings and Grounds:

"A Bill for the erection of a monument, in the city of Washington, to the memory of JOSEPH HENRY, late Secretary of the Smithsonian Institution.

"*Be it enacted by the Senate and House of Representatives of the United States of America in Congress assembled,* That the Regents of the Smithsonian Institution be and are hereby authorized to contract with W. W. Story, sculptor, for a statue in bronze of JOSEPH HENRY, late Secretary of the Smithsonian Institution, to be erected upon the grounds of said Institution; and for this purpose, and for the entire expense of the foundation and pedestal of the monument, the sum of fifteen thousand dollars is hereby appropriated out of any moneys in the Treasury not otherwise appropriated."

Thursday, May 6, 1880.

Mr. MORRILL reported back to the Senate this bill, (S. No. 1702,) with the title amended so as to read: "A Bill for the erection of a bronze statue of JOSEPH HENRY, late Secretary of the Smithsonian Institution."

---

*Senate bill No. 1702, Forty-sixth Congress, Second Session.

IN THE SENATE.

Monday, May 24, 1880.

Mr. MORRILL. "I ask the Senator from Kentucky (Mr. Beck) to allow me to call up a bill that will receive (I have no doubt) the unanimous assent of the Senate. It will not take up five minutes; and as the bill the Senator proposes to take up will probably occupy all the morning, I ask him to allow me to get up the bill for a monument to JOSEPH HENRY, to be erected in the Smithsonian grounds."

Mr. BECK. "I hope I shall not lose my place by giving way."

The PRESIDENT pro tempore. (Senator ALLEN G. THURMAN, of Ohio.) "The Senator from Vermont asks that the Senate proceed to the consideration of the bill (Senate No. 1702,) for the erection of a monument, in the city of Washington, to the memory of Joseph Henry, late Secretary of the Smithsonian Institution. Is there objection?"

Mr. VOORHEES. (Senator from Indiana.) "Let the bill be read for information."

The Chief Clerk read the bill (Senate No. 1702) entitled "A Bill for the erection of a monument, in the city of Washington, to the memory of JOSEPH HENRY, late Secretary of the Smithsonian Institution."

The PRESIDENT pro tempore. "Is there objection to proceeding to the consideration of this bill?

"The question is on the motion to proceed to the consideration of the bill named by the Senator from Vermont," (Mr. MORRILL.)

The motion was agreed to; and the Senate (as in Committee of the Whole) proceeded to consider the bill (Senate No. 1702) for the erection of a monument, in the city of Washington, to the memory of JOSEPH HENRY, late Secretary of the Smithsonian Institution. It authorizes the Regents of the Smithsonian Institution to contract with W. W. Story, sculptor, for a statue in bronze of JOSEPH HENRY, late Secretary of the Smithsonian Institution, to be erected upon the grounds of that institution; and appropriates fifteen thousand dollars for this purpose, and for the entire expense of the foundation and pedestal of the monument.

Mr. VOORHEES. "Mr. President, I am opposed to legislating a contract into any one man's hands on a subject where competition ought to take place. I do not know how often it has been done heretofore, but in every instance where it has been done it is wrong. A work of this kind ought to be open to competition. Every artist ought to be allowed to compete for a work of this character. The Senator from Vermont very justly reminds me that Mr. Story is an eminent artist. I know that. There are other eminent artists in the country; and all of them think they are. Every one of them desires to put his skill on exhibition, and it is his right to do so. I think that the bill ought to be amended by making this work subject to competition, rather than a direct contract with Mr. Story."

Mr. MORRILL. "I hope my friend from Indiana will not move any amendment. Mr. Story is the son of the late Chief-Justice Story, and is one of the most eminent artists of this country or any other, and has never received an order from the Government. He is eminent in very many other respects than as a sculptor. I trust there will be no amendment offered. It is no more than justice to the very eminent men,—the living as well as the dead,—to both the philosopher to whom we propose to erect the monument, and the artist whom it is proposed to employ; and the sum offered is a very small one indeed."

Mr. VOORHEES. "It is difficult for me to withstand an appeal or request preferred by the Senator from Vermont, but I am satisfied that the bill ought to be amended so as to allow competition."

Mr. MORRILL. "I hope not."

The PRESIDENT pro tempore. "Does the Senator from Indiana move an amendment?"

Mr. VOORHEES. "I have not done so."

The bill was reported to the Senate without amendment, ordered to be engrossed for a third reading, read the third time, and passed.

The title was amended so as to read: "A Bill for the erection of a bronze statue of JOSEPH HENRY, late Secretary of the Smithsonian Institution."

33   ————————

In the House of Representatives.

Tuesday, May 25, 1880.

Mr. CLYMER. (Member from Pennsylvania.) "Mr. Speaker, I ask unanimous consent to take from the Speaker's table the bill (Senate No. 1702) and put the same upon its passage."

The SPEAKER *pro tempore.* (Mr. J. C. S. BLACKBURN.) "The Clerk will read the bill, after which the Chair will ask for objections."

The Clerk read the bill (Senate No. 1702) entitled "A bill for the erection of a bronze statue of JOSEPH HENRY, late Secretary of the Smithsonian Institution."

The SPEAKER *pro tempore.* "Is there objection to the present consideration of the bill?

"There being no objection, the question is on the passage of the bill—Senate No. 1702."

The bill was accordingly taken from the Speaker's table, read three several times, and passed.

The following is the Act as passed:

[Public Acts, No. 7L.]

AN ACT for the erection of a bronze statue of JOSEPH HENRY, late Secretary of the Smithsonian Institution.

Be it enacted by the Senate and House of Representatives of the United States of America in Congress assembled, That the Regents of the Smithsonian Institution be and are hereby authorized to contract with W. W. Story, sculptor, for a statue in bronze of JOSEPH HENRY, late Secretary of the Smithsonian Institution, to be erected upon the grounds of said Institution; and for this purpose, and for the entire expense of the foundation and pedestal of the monument, the sum of fifteen thousand dollars is hereby appropriated out of any moneys in the Treasury not otherwise appropriated.

APPROVED BY THE PRESIDENT, June 1, 1880.

INDEX.